DATE			

Also by Marilyn Harris

KING'S EX
IN THE MIDST OF EARTH
THE PEPPERSALT LAND
THE RUNAWAY'S DIARY
THE CONJURERS
HATTER FOX
BLEDDING SORROW
THIS OTHER EDEN
THE PRINCE OF EDEN
THE EDEN PASSION
THE WOMEN OF EDEN
THE PORTENT
THE LAST GREAT LOVE
EDEN RISING
THE DIVINER
WARRICK
NIGHT GAMES
AMERICAN EDEN

EDEN
and
HONOR

Marilyn Harris

EDEN and HONOR

DOUBLEDAY
New York London Toronto
Sydney Auckland

All of the characters in this book are fictitious,
and any resemblance to actual persons, living or dead,
is purely coincidental.

Published by Doubleday,
a division of Bantam Doubleday Dell Publishing Group, Inc.
666 Fifth Avenue, New York, New York 10103

DOUBLEDAY and the portrayal of an anchor with a dolphin are trademarks of
Doubleday, a division of Bantam Doubleday Dell Publishing Group, Inc.

Library of Congress Cataloging-in-Publication Data

Harris, Marilyn, 1931–
Eden and honor / by Marilyn Harris. — 1st ed.
p. cm.
ISBN 0-385-24196-8
I. Title.
PS3558.A648E27 1989
813′.54–dc19 88-25774
CIP

ISBN 0-385-24196-8

BOOK DESIGN BY PATRICE FODERO

February 1989
FIRST EDITION
BG

For
Katherine O'Neal Gunning—age two years
and
Justin Harris Springer—age seven months

may their world be a peaceful one.

If any question why we died,
Tell them, because our fathers lied.

RUDYARD KIPLING

EDEN and HONOR

Eden Castle
March 13, 1896

Eleanor, Lady Eden, went up to the parapet alone in the chill early morning drizzle to escape Eve's cries of labor and to catch the first sight of the sorrowful procession of carriages coming toward Eden Castle. She saw them in the distance slowly making their way across the moors through the cold mist of dawn. By her estimate they were over a mile away and at times did not seem to be moving at all. Now and then the carriages disappeared, devoured by the thick early morning fog, only to reappear too quickly, confirming the truth that had been relayed to her two days ago by a messenger: her son Geoffrey was coming home, ill, seriously wounded, from a foolish battle in a remote place called the Transvaal in South Africa.

She wrapped her shawl about her in scant protection against the chill rain and found the distant procession again amidst the gray monotony of the moors and fog. Impatiently she wondered why the carriages were traveling so slowly, and then she knew: Geoffrey was that ill, that wounded.

She lifted her face to the cold drizzle and focused on gray broiling clouds. Above her a seagull screeched, startling her, the bird's cry reminding her of the terrible screams coming from the east wing, where Eve was still in a prolonged and difficult childbirth. Eleanor had listened to her cries all night, as had everyone in the castle.

Eleanor could understand childbirth, even the tragedies and risks. She had suffered two miscarriages herself before giving birth to Geoffrey. The thought of her firstborn brought her cruel pleasure, for in the next moment she realized that her perfect son, the hope and future of Eden Castle, lay suffering inside one of those carriages, feverish, maimed, his left foot amputated.

She hurried to the opposite side of the parapet, unmindful of the puddles of cold rain water which saturated her slippers and soaked the hem of her skirts, unmindful of anything except the difficult hours and days which lay ahead. She must begin by going downstairs and joining Richard and the others. All of them must be on the Great Hall steps in a display of unity and courage to welcome Geoffrey home.

Though not given to revolution by nature, Eleanor felt a peculiar sense of betrayal burning in the center of her soul. Damn Queen and Empire, damn England if it meant sending off a whole and perfect son and welcoming home a pale and wasted invalid. Damn Queen and Empire for sacrificing the young sons of Britain in a damnable place called the Transvaal. South Africa, the British South Africa Company, the whole world should be damned for encouraging and fostering such madness.

These completely unacceptable thoughts were strictly contained within the forehead beneath the curly auburn hair. Her small revolt was powerful nonetheless and left Eleanor clinging to the side of the parapet and gazing out at the dull blue waters of the Bristol Channel.

"Eleanor? Are you alright?"

The voice startled her. She looked over her shoulder and saw Susan, John Murrey Eden's wife. A skilled nurse, she had passed the night at Eve's bedside.

Though grateful for her company, Eleanor turned back to face the safe void of the Bristol Channel and did not try to conceal her grief or her confusion.

Through tears she whispered to the strong woman standing close behind her, "I–don't understand–"

"What, my dear?"

"Everything. Why was Geoffrey in South Africa?"

Susan put her arm about Eleanor's shoulder. "He's a career man. He goes where his regiment goes."

"But why South Africa?"

"There are resources there that England wants."

"What resources? Who is the enemy?"

"I'm afraid I'm not certain, though Dutch farmers are the enemy, I think. They were there first."

"Who is right and who is wrong?"

Susan's supply of ready answers gave out. "I don't know," she confessed wearily.

Susan was quite knowledgeable, the arbiter of all disputes at Eden Castle. If she didn't understand why Geoffrey was being brought home, ill and wounded, how in the name of God were the rest of them expected to deal with it?

"You now join a select and noble society, did you know that?" Susan whispered.

Eyes burning, shaking with spasms of grief, Eleanor shook her head.

"Mothers from the beginning of time have sent their sons into battle and have been there with the strength of their love to welcome them home."

"I–do not feel strong–"

"No, but you will be when Geoffrey sees you and you sense Geoffrey's needs."

"What if he dies, Susan?"

"He won't die. Your love won't let him."

Eleanor studied Susan's face, a face she had come to love over the years, and tried to understand the source of her strength.

"Eve?" Eleanor inquired, realizing that she'd not heard the painful cries since coming out to wait for Geoffrey.

Susan shook her head. "There is an obstruction of some kind in the birth canal. It could end badly."

No more tragedy, Eleanor prayed, seeing Eve in memory. The beautiful young American singer was John Murrey Eden's niece, the daughter of John's half sister, Mary. Eve had been born in a faraway place called Mobile, Alabama.

Her thoughts were interrupted by Susan's voice. "Look Eleanor, the carriages are drawing near."

For a moment Eleanor felt obstinate and fully capable of refusing to go down. But she couldn't do that. There was an expectation of strength on Susan's face. Because she was strong, wasn't everyone?

As they stepped through the low wooden door into the stone corridor, the shrill wind and blowing rain was instantly replaced by a distant scream, one short punctuation of human agony. Eleanor shuddered as she closed and bolted the parapet door behind them. She turned to see new concern on Susan's face.

"There is a physician accompanying Geoffrey. Is that correct?"

Eleanor nodded. "A German, I believe, or at least a German-sounding name. Richard engaged him in London."

"A surgeon?"

"I have no idea, but it's possible."

"He may be needed in Eve's chamber."

"Of course, dear."

Deep inside, Eleanor suffered new disintegration. When had her placid rural world gone topsy-turvy? Their recent Christmas had been so calm: Geoffrey had been serving with honor in far-off South Africa; Lucy, her eldest daughter, had been concerned only with her studies and with pleasing her tutor, Mason Frye; Charlotte had been content to sit in front of her mirror and study her beauty as though puzzled by it and not quite certain what to do with it. Meanwhile, the old folks–John Murrey and Richard and Susan and herself–had sprawled before the fire satiated, wassail cups in hand, warming their toes and yawning at nine o'clock.

Such a sweet memory.

Again Eleanor heard screams. Quickly she hurried down the low-ceilinged corridor after Susan. Perhaps her dread was groundless; Geoffrey had been a strong child, plump, happy, racing through the corridors of Eden in endless pursuit of the other children, always the aggressor in their shrieking, imaginative games.

The memory was so sharp and clear that she felt transported.

"Coming, Eleanor?"

"Coming," she whispered, trying to imitate Susan's strength, hoping that when the carriages rattled to a stop at the bottom of the Great Hall steps, she would see beyond the mutilation, that she would see only the pink-cheeked son who had been always her pride and joy.

The stump of his left leg was still bleeding. Geoffrey could see it from where he lay on the makeshift pallet on the carriage seat. A fine sight with which to greet his family. He closed his eyes against the raw, unbearable pain and wondered when the carriage would stop its infernal rocking.

"Damn," he gasped as the carriage took a hard bounce, and through blurred eyes, he saw the German doctor stare back at him with his plump face and circumflex eyebrows.

"Not far, your lordship," he soothed, his German accent still discernible through his cultivated English speech.

Geoffrey pressed his head against the pillows and dwelt almost pleasurably on how much he hated the Germans, all Germans, even this overfed Dr. Reicher. Geoffrey's two trusted aides, Teddy and William, good lads from Mortemouth, should be riding in the lead coach with him. Instead, the German had placed them in the second coach and had settled himself opposite Geoffrey.

Without warning, above the rattle of the coach, he heard a voice in memory cry, "Boot and saddle!" With his eyes closed, he saw the dust as it swirled across the parade ground at Pitsani, saw his gray-suited, slouch-hatted fellow police as they paraded back and forth in the hollow square.

Dress by the left! Bugler!

Defiantly the bugle call echoed off the tin walls of the stores and drifted over the three miles of desolate white veld between Pitsani and the Transvaal frontier. Silence then except for the shuffling of the troopers' horses and the hum of the wind in the single telegraph wire.

The plan had been to make a three-day dash for Johannesburg before the Boer commandos could mobilize. The point of the aggression was to create a revolution at Johannesburg supported by this raid from Pitsani, led by Dr. Jameson. The spoils of victory in the Transvaal included a naval base on the sea route to India and the East and, as if that were not enough, gold and diamonds in undreamed of quantities.

Eyes front!

In the falling dusk the bugle sounded as Jameson mounted a black stallion. He took off his felt hat and there were three ringing cheers for Queen Victoria. They trotted out of Pitsani, followed by officer servants in mule carts. The moon had risen, reflecting an eerie light off the tin walls of the village. Then the column was engulfed in dust.

Four days later, on the morning of January 2, the column halted close to a small whitewashed farm south of Doornkop. Ahead was their goal, Johannesburg, the golden city, only a couple of hours' ride.

Then they were betrayed—that was the only word for it. Johannesburg had not revolted. Outlanders of the city, mainly Germans, had made their peace with President Kruger and his Boers. Not one armed volunteer had ridden out to join the column. They were alone.

For two days they had carried on a running fight with the commandos. The last night they had huddled together in a rough square formed by the ammunition carts, the ambulance wagons and the horses, firing into the darkness across their saddles.

Then the Boers came, in rows of fifty materializing out of the morning fog, and still Geoffrey had stood his ground until his own frightened horse had thrown him. He had tried to scramble up and grasp his sword, but the Boer bastard was bearing down on him and he thought he saw the man smile in the instant before he attacked. Geoffrey remembered the silver of the man's blade catching the light of the rising sun while all about them was smoke, fire and the inhumanity of battle.

They had been warned that the Boers went for their enemy's feet so they could not fight again. He had felt the weight of the giant man push against him, knocking him off balance with one tremendous effort. The sword descended in a murderous blow against Geoffrey's left leg. The pain and blood issued forth simultaneously. Geoffrey screamed pitifully, and yet the man chopped again and again, bracing himself against Geoffrey's hip for balance and a better angle.

Suddenly Geoffrey flailed his way to the surface of consciousness, fighting against restraints visible and invisible. Strong hands, he remembered strong hands, holding him down and the field surgeon's blade cutting deeper, taking up where the Boer bastard's sword had left off.

"No!" he howled.

"Your lordship, *please,* I beg you, rest easy. Driver, stop, stop, I say, immediately. His lordship needs–"

But the fever and the pain and the memory of defeat and humiliation could not be contained, and Geoffrey sank back into the black abyss, seeing at the center of his feverish brain only one image: the weeping Jameson as he was led away in a cart to the jail at Pretoria.

Eden Castle

John Murrey Eden, sixty and feeling every year of it in his aching bones, stood slightly apart from the rest of the family on the Great Hall steps in the cold drizzle; his was an emotional distance as well as an actual one. Intently he watched the two carriages as they made their way slowly toward the gatehouse of Eden Castle.

He wiped the cold rain from his face and wondered at the thousands of comings and goings that these worn steps had witnessed during the past centuries, moments of sharp tragedy and unrestrained joy, all commencing and departing here. Now they were witnessing another remarkable occasion–his nephew, Richard and Eleanor's eldest and the hope of Eden, returning home an invalid.

The accounts of the Jameson Raid in the Transvaal had been sketchy in the London papers, and John looked forward to hearing of the events firsthand. Less sketchy had been the painful specifics of British surrender and humiliation at the hands of the Dutch and Germans. The defeat had swept the entire country and left all Englishmen in a state of shock and disbelief.

He looked up as the carriages drew nearer. At the same time, he saw the knot of people at the bottom of the Great Hall steps lift shawls and hoods in meager protection against the increasing rain.

Behind him he heard the Great Hall door creak open and looked back to see seventeen-year-old Charlotte, Richard and Eleanor's perfect creation, a full-figured beauty with black hair and blue-violet eyes who never seemed to quite fit into any function at Eden Castle. John loved to watch his niece. She was so beautiful and so unmindful of her beauty.

"Are they near?" she called out softly, and John nodded and pointed toward the gate and the slow moving coaches just beyond.

He saw Charlotte look fearfully in that direction, saw her pretty face cloud, knew that she was dreading the ordeal of welcoming her brother home as much as any of them.

Quietly she disappeared into the Great Hall, and as the heavy door closed behind her, it was John's guess that she would take refuge in the library. She loved to settle there before the roaring fire and beneath the oil portrait of the Lady Marianne, the fisherman's daughter who in 1797 had become mistress of Eden Castle and to whom Charlotte bore a striking resemblance.

To be honest, John would have given anything to join her, but his place was here and he had lived longer than pretty Charlotte and understood that there were times when it served one better to carry through with the painful task than face the endless reverberations of censure and condemnation. As his wife Susan was fond of saying, "It's as easy to march in step as out of step."

Susan. At the thought of her he hastily scanned the group at the bottom of the stairs without success. Then he remembered that she was with Eve and poor distraught Stephen and that weirdest of all birds, the American Yorrick Harp, the theatrical manager who arranged for Eve's concert tours.

Shouting beyond the gate reached his ears, and he saw those waiting at the bottom of the steps start forward in alarm, Richard and Eleanor in the lead, followed by nineteen-year-old Lucy, their eldest daughter. Lucy was as shy and plain as Charlotte was beautiful. She would cause no mischief in this world, but she would make someone a splendid wife.

Others were moving toward the gate–his own daughter, Alice, aged twenty, a skilled nurse like her mother, home on leave from St. Martin's Hospital in London. And close beside Alice, he saw his son, Albert, seventeen, a weak young man who had requested permission to come home from Cambridge when he had learned of Geoffrey's wounds. What Albert thought he could accomplish by leaving school and coming home, John had no idea. Susan had reminded him that the two boys had grown up together and were very close. Unlike him, she had found it sweet of Albert to think his presence would make a difference to Geoffrey in his time of need.

This then was the welcoming committee, children who had grown up together in Eden Castle, as well as Lord Eden and Lady Eleanor and, of course, himself, all standing in what was now a driving rain awaiting the two carriages which seemed to have come to a complete halt about fifty yards the other side of the gatehouse.

He saw the door of the lead carriage swing open and a portly figure step out into the rain and motion toward the second coach. In an instant the doors of the second carriage flew open and out stumbled two men. For a moment there seemed to be complete confusion.

"Hurry, John, please, we need you–"

He looked up through the rain and saw his sister-in-law Eleanor calling back to him, frantically motioning him forward. At the same time, he saw an awkward procession, two men carrying a litter between them, the plump gentleman hovering on first one side, then the other, the entire grizzly parade seeming to slip precariously in the muddy approach to the gate.

As he hurried forward, he caught a glimpse of Geoffrey Eden, who appeared dead on his litter, his face drained of color, the rain plastering his sandy hair in jagged scars across his forehead, his mouth slack, his lips blue.

Most disturbing of all was Geoffrey's left leg, minus the foot, swathed in a bandage that was more red than white. Eleanor was weeping openly against Richard's shoulder.

"Here, let me give you a hand," John shouted to the lead litter bearer, who looked none too strong himself.

John stared briefly at Geoffrey's pale, lifeless face and suspected his nephew was gone forever, his soul abandoned in a remote place called Doornkop in the Transvaal.

Susan placed a cool cloth on Eve's forehead, grateful that the hot milk, honey and whisky had worked as a sedative, but she knew the relief was only temporary. The agony of labor would awaken her shortly.

"Poor Eve," she whispered, studying the beautiful young girl who possessed the voice of an angel and thought of Eve's mother, the Lady Mary, in far-off America and wished with all her heart that she was here. Several times in her agony Eve had called out, "Mama."

"They're coming," a weary male voice announced.

Susan looked up at Stephen, Eve's husband, who stood near the window drained and worried as they all were by a labor which was in its third day. Susan pulled the comforter up about Eve's shoulders and heard the shouts in the courtyard three stories below and knew that another crucible was ahead for all of them.

"The coaches have stopped. Look."

Susan went to the narrow window clouded with frost and cold, and took Stephen's arm in an affectionate gesture. She cleared the fog from one window and looked down on a bizarre sight, three men, one of them John, carrying Geoffrey forward on a litter, a group of people hovering close while beyond the gatehouse at the edge of the moors sat the two coaches, apparently stalled.

Following after them was a man dressed professionally in business black, carrying an impressive looking satchel.

"The doctor, Stephen, do you recall the name of the–"

"A German–Reicher, wasn't it? Something like that."

As Susan pointed at the man hovering close to Geoffrey's side, she saw a glimmer of hope cross Stephen's face. "Do you suppose the doctor could help us?"

"My very thought," she soothed. "But let's wait until he attends to Geoffrey. Then I'll go to John and–"

"No, I'll go now," Stephen said, newly alive with the realization that professional help was close at hand. He hurried to the door and out, stopping briefly on the other side to exchange a few words with his friend Yorrick Harp, the old man who managed Eve's singing career. Known throughout England and Europe as The Lark, possessing the most dazzling voice in memory, according to enthusiastic critics, Eve had passed the last few years in triumph, toasted by royalty, acclaimed by critics, worshipped for her beauty, her grace and her magnificent voice.

Susan remained by the window as the two men outside the door held a whispered conversation. She saw the procession below disappear into the Great Hall and her thoughts returned to Eve.

Susan did not hear Yorrick enter the room. Only as he drew near to Eve's bed did Susan see him, a giant of a man physically, quite tall, dressed in black–black trousers, black velvet smoking jacket and black silk shirtwaist, the only color a theatrical pale peach silk scarf knotted loosely about his neck. He resembled a venerable old Shakespearean actor. His gray hair was long and wavy, his beard a darker gray and neatly trimmed. He was a splendid figure of a man, endlessly fascinating with his tales of the American West, which he had enthralled them with nightly since his arrival at Eden last month.

Yorrick gently reached out to touch Eve and at the last minute changed his mind. Instead, he clasped his hands in prayer as he knelt at Eve's bedside.

Finding the moment too intimate to witness, Susan turned back to the window and offered up a quick prayer of her own.

"Mistress Susan?"

At the sound of his voice, Susan looked back.

"Yes, Mr. Harp," she said, returning to bedside, rubbing her arm against the chill of the window.

"Is she– I mean, will she– What I am trying and failing to say is–"

"That you are worried, Mr. Harp, as we all are."

"But you are a professional, and know the hazards of nature. Surely you–"

Even as he spoke Susan shook her head. "No, sir, I'm afraid not. In all my years as a nurse and midwife, I have lost track of the numbers of births I have assisted with–enough, I'm sure, to populate a fair-sized village. On too many occasions I've pronounced hopeless what later resulted in a robust baby. Conversely, I've turned away from a healthy delivery believing the job well done and looked back less than five minutes later to find the infant blue. So, I'm afraid, Mr. Harp, being at God's elbow doesn't mean very much. God dictates the results according to His own plan."

"Still, you must know something more. Please, my need for reassurance is great."

Susan saw tears in the old man's eyes and wished she could give him a simple answer. But she couldn't.

"Mr. Harp, all I can say is that Eve is young and strong and terribly determined. These characteristics will serve her better than any medical evaluation I might be tempted to give you."

"Then we all are held captive by the moment and the event?"

"I'm afraid so."

She watched as Yorrick gently caressed Eve's hand. "I have never been on the best of terms with my Creator. I must confess I find Him tedious at times, with His endless need for worship and adoration, not unlike some of the prima donnas I've encountered in the theatrical world," he said, his voice hoarse.

He went on studying Eve's hand as he spoke. "Somehow the Eastern gods have always seemed more reliable and appealing to me, with their love of silence, their wonderful sense of humor, their diversity and self-sufficiency."

Susan glanced through the door, wishing that Stephen would return. She felt a need to be down in the Great Hall with John and Eleanor and Richard.

Then she had an idea. "Mr. Harp, as you may know, Geoffrey is home."

The man nodded. "I saw the mournful procession while it was still on the moors. Wars must cease so that young men can remain whole and intact."

Susan blinked at the simplicity of this sentiment.

"I was wondering," Susan asked tentatively, "if you could–"

"Stay with Eve? Of course I will. There is not a spot on this green earth where I'd rather be. See to your duties elsewhere. If love and devotion are the twin needs to see Eve through her ordeal, then she is already safely on the other side. Go now, I beg you. And in your absence I'll search for a responding God, one that will agree that this episode must end happily."

At the door she looked back to see Yorrick bowed in prayer.

Quietly she closed the door behind her and hurried toward the distant hum of voices below, her eyes skipping ahead to the darkened corners of the long corridor, a corridor which at its end gave way to another corridor exactly like it, endless gray stone, gray masonry floors and cold–cold everywhere with no promise of warmth.

As she reached the bottom step she saw everyone just inside the door. Eleanor was bent over the litter, Richard at her side, John on the other side saying something to one of the attendants, two young men from Mortemouth, whom Susan recognized as Geoffrey's aides. To one side stood the children–young people really, though she still thought of them as children–Lucy and Alice and Albert hoping to be of service to Geoffrey. And there was Stephen looking as helpless as he had at Eve's bedside. On the fringes of the group stood Dr. Reicher.

This gathering included a group of servants who stood a respectful distance away, their faces reflecting the seriousness of the occasion. A few of the housemaids pressed the hem of their aprons against their mouths. Mrs. Calvin, the stern Scots nanny who had raised the children of the combined families, stood apart from the servants in her perennial black mourning clothes for a husband who had died a senseless death in a place called Balaclava in the Crimea nearly forty years before.

Susan had taken no more than a dozen steps across the Great Hall toward Geoffrey and the people around him when she heard a low grumble rising somewhere above the muddle of all the other voices. It grew into a clearly audible protest, "Leave me alone." Then, louder, more agonized, "Leave me alone, all of you! Get away, get away from me," the man's voice rising until he finally screamed. The sound caused the hairs on Susan's arms to stand. Geoffrey's was a prolonged howl of misery that seemed to echo endlessly about the Great Hall.

Susan closed her eyes as the voice dissolved into tears. Through the sobs, he repeated, "Leave me alone, please do not look, leave me alone."

There was no movement in the Great Hall until the German doctor stepped forward, a strange half-smile of apology on his face in an attempt to soothe the others. Still clasping his medical bag, he motioned for Geoffrey's two aides to lift the litter; then he held a brief whispered conversation with Eleanor, who motioned to Elsie, the head parlormaid. With Elsie leading the way, the aides carried the still weeping Geoffrey through the stunned group of people and up the stone steps. The German doctor followed, turning at the last moment to hold up a staying hand to Richard and Eleanor.

Predictably, poor Eleanor covered her face with her hands, and Richard led her into the small reception room near the far side, where she could recover in private and out of sight of the servants.

Next the servants turned away with suspect efficiency and moved in the directions of their various duties, some down to the kitchen court, others throughout the castle. She saw John in loving fashion gather the children, Albert, Alice and Lucy, and lead them toward the fire at the far end of the Great Hall, obviously to deliver to them a brief, comforting lecture on the ways of God.

Only Stephen stood adrift near the door of the Great Hall. Susan started to signal to him, but she didn't want to call attention to herself. Clearly her and Stephen's hopes for fetching the German physician had been dashed for the moment. Let him help poor Geoffrey, then, when the time was right, Susan would approach him with a new and perhaps more serious medical problem.

Her thoughts were interrupted by the sudden loud clanging of the gatehouse bell, always a signal that someone unexpected was approaching the castle from across the moors. She saw Stephen start toward the door, saw John follow after, passing Ghostly, the butler, who had appeared from out of nowhere. The shrill clanging had summoned the other servants as well. Heads covered with white lace caps appeared through doorways.

John drew open the heavy doors and received a drenching of cold, blowing rain from the increasing storm. Despite his discomfort, she saw him step all the way out of the door and thought, as she frequently had thought before, that John was the true lord of Eden Castle, not Richard, who had never wanted the title, had never understood it or its accompanying responsibilities.

But John understood all too well and reveled in being the caretaker of the Eden family. When the children had been young, he had drilled them on the succession of lords of Eden Castle, considerately dwelling equally on the bastards and the saints. There were quite naturally a bit of both in a line which stretched from 1100 to the present.

Just then, John returned, soaking wet and accompanied by a man, equally soaked and road-weary, a brown leather pouch slung over his shoulder.

"Messenger!" John called out. "Send for Richard."

Richard appeared as if on cue, timidly peering out of the reception room, where he had taken Eleanor.

"What is it, John?" he called out, clinging to the door and giving Susan the impression that he really couldn't deal with anything else.

"Messenger for you," John shouted, as though by sheer volume he might stir his half brother into some sort of action.

Bewildered, Richard approached the messenger, who carefully withdrew a brown envelope and gave it to Richard, who simply stared at it.

"Well, for God's sake, open it, man," John scolded gently. After a moment he took it from an unprotesting Richard, who seemed relieved to be rid of it.

John broke the seal and held the letter up to the nearest wall lamp. He read the entire message before handing it back to Richard.

"Another homecoming," he announced full-voiced for the benefit of everyone in the Great Hall. "Frederick, our churchman from India, will be arriving in the company of his new bride, one Marjorie Housman."

His words settled agreeably over the Great Hall. Frederick was Stephen's younger brother; their mother had been John's first wife, the beautiful Lady Lila Harrington, who died shortly after Frederick's birth. As boys, Stephen and Frederick had lived in Dublin with their maternal grandfather. Then Lord Harrington had died, and at ages seven and eight, the two boys had been returned to John and his new wife, Susan, who had raised them in the loving and child-filled atmosphere of Eden Castle.

Now Frederick was coming home. And with a bride. Susan smiled at Stephen and John, who were embracing one another and thought how pleased Stephen must be. It had been years since he had seen his brother, and the two had always been close. Stephen had gone off to America to find dear Eve, and Frederick had gone to Oxford and then into the Anglican ministry and had been sent to a mission in India.

Frederick home. The thought continued to please Susan as Lucy, Albert and Alice joined the happy group, all talking at once, all eagerly reading the message, which apparently had been sent from Liverpool.

A young housemaid led the messenger down the steps into the kitchen court, where a warm fire would greet him and a cup of Mrs. Partridge's mulled wine.

As for the others, the sadness of Geoffrey's condition had been relieved somewhat by Frederick's impending arrival.

The world moved on. How sad in a way. Yet, how safe and, ultimately, how sensible.

Slowly Susan started back up the stairs. She been gone longer than she intended. Pray God Eve was still asleep.

"Susan–"

At the sound of the familiar voice she looked back and saw John at the bottom of the stairs slightly breathless from his sprint across the Great Hall.

"Why didn't you join us?" he asked, climbing the stairs.

"I did, not physically but emotionally," she replied smiling.

"Did you hear Geoffrey's outcry?" he asked somberly.

"I did and I'm certain the dead heard as well. Still, he'll come around in time. Pray God there's no infection."

"I'm not sure. His leg is so mangled."

"Life doesn't stop for a one-footed man."

"He's proud."

"Then perhaps he will learn to be less so. He has a great deal to give to himself and others. He will find a way, I'm certain."

John leaned against the banister. Susan thought him, even at sixty, the most handsome man she had ever seen. "A world filled with women like you," he smiled. "What a Utopia that would be."

She laughed. "I doubt it."

"The news about Frederick is a balm for us all."

"I know. How pleased and excited you must be."

"Stephen's the one who's absolutely over the moon. You remember how close they were. How is Eve?"

"I was just telling myself that I'd better get back and see."

"Do you need help?"

"Not now. One thing, John, the German physician–"

"Dr. Reicher?"

"Does he have medical experience in female matters?"

"I don't know. I could ask."

"Is he a surgeon?"

"I don't know."

"See if you can talk to him. Tell him of Eve's prolonged labor. I'm sure I'll need him."

For a moment they exchanged the softest of glances, a shared certainty of their love, of their place in this unique Eden world.

"I'll get the others settled," John said quickly, "and then I'll come to you, Dr. Reicher in tow."

"I'm grateful. Mr. Harp is sitting with her now."

"O my God," John moaned, "that idiot. You had better get back."

"He's very concerned and quite harmless."

"He is an unpredictable fool."

Susan started to offer another defense but changed her mind. John was the only inhabitant of Eden Castle who had resisted Yorrick Harp's unique and theatrical charms–charms which could hold a large dinner party enthralled for hours. Susan suspected that was one reason John disliked him. Enthralling diners was usually John's domain.

"Are you well?"

"Yes, I'm merely fatigued, as we all are."

"Then you must get some rest. I'll send Alice up immediately to relieve you."

Susan started to object but changed her mind. She didn't want to be relieved, but she would welcome her eldest daughter's company. Alice was a special child–strong-willed, self-confident, bright. At times she seemed to be a female version of her father, lacking fortunately his most unappealing and troublesome characteristics and possessing all that made him great.

"Yes, send Alice up," Susan agreed and was just turning when they suddenly heard one sharp scream.

Eve.

"Fetch the doctor as soon as possible," Susan repeated, rushing up the steps. At the second outcry she lifted her skirt and ran down the chill stone corridor. She knew only one thing for certain: this could not go on much longer, for either mother or child.

Charlotte dared to unplug her ears just once and heard the distant screams of a woman and instantly returned the little round wooden plugs that her mother used in secret to obliterate her father's snores at night.

Thus safely insulated, she looked about at the comfortable library in which she had taken refuge this morning, vowing to stay out of sight until she was certain it was safe to resurface.

Truth was, she did feel guilty and awful. She should have been on the Great Hall steps with the others to welcome her brother home, but she couldn't. There was something in her that made such a spectacle impossible to endure.

Not that she didn't love Geoffrey. She loved him immensely. As children they had spun out fanciful theatrics for themselves; unable to engage Lucy in their fantasies, they had often played alone. Together they believed in the black monster with the purple eyes who lived at the bottom of the Bristol Channel. They draped themselves in Elsie's old lace window curtains and pretended to be swordsmen or highwaymen or evil spirits or good ones, depending upon the mood and the day.

Remembering her happy childhood, Charlotte sank into the chair in front of the library fire.

With her eyes half closed she only sensed movement, the quick passage of someone through the room. By the time Charlotte had straightened herself in her chair, all she saw was a suspect dark green velvet drape by the far bank of windows which protruded slightly as though someone were behind it.

Curious, she started slowly in that direction, drew back the drape and discovered her sister Lucy, two years older and the one person Charlotte respected without qualification.

"What in the world are you doing behind the drapes?"

For several moments, Charlotte saw Lucy's lips moving but heard no sound and only then remembered her mother's earplugs and hastily removed them.

"Mason Frye asked me to chart the tides of the Bristol Channel," Lucy said, without blinking. She lifted her notebook, pen in hand, and looked intensely at the swirling waters three stories below.

"Why?" Charlotte asked; it seemed a sensible question.

"Mason said you can tell everything by the movements of the tide," Lucy replied.

"What are *you* doing?" Lucy asked.

"Hiding," Charlotte said honestly and saw no need to add anything more. Someone would come and find her soon enough and undoubtedly scold her. In the meantime she was perfectly content to wait for them here.

"It was awful," Lucy said, settling more comfortably on the window seat cushion.

"Did you see Geoffrey?" Charlotte asked.

"I saw him; he looks awful, Charlotte. His leg is purple and bleeding. Did you hear his cries? He was like a crazy man, yelling for everyone to get away from him. He made Mama cry, and finally the German doctor ordered him upstairs."

"Where's Mama now?" Charlotte asked, thinking she might redeem herself if she went to her mother.

"She was with Papa, but then a messenger arrived."

"What messenger?"

Lucy looked up, mildly scolding, "Where *have* you been all morning?"

"What messenger?" Charlotte repeated.

"The one from London. Frederick is coming home."

Charlotte blinked at this news. "He's in India."

"Not anymore. He's in Liverpool, and what's more he has a new wife with him, a bride of less than a year."

Excitement rising, Charlotte hurried across the library for confirmation of this great news. "And he's coming to Eden Castle? When?"

Lucy shrugged, "Soon, I should imagine. Everyone is quite excited."

Charlotte adored her cousin Frederick, who had written long letters to her from India, describing in moving detail the unique beauty of the Indian people, his frank and confidential conviction that Christianity was not superior to their own quite beautiful religions, his description of olive brown skin, black eyes, gentle ways, kind manners. More than once Charlotte had lived for Frederick's letters, always sharing them with the rest of the family but exulting in the fact that they were addressed to her, in her name, to be opened by her hand alone.

Suddenly there was a knock at the library door. The two girls exchanged furtive glances. It wasn't family. Family wouldn't knock.

"Is someone looking for you?" Charlotte asked in a whisper.

Lucy shook her head. "It might be Mason."

Mason? Did she mean Mr. Frye? When had Lucy started calling their tutor by his first name?

The knock came again, louder this time, accompanied by Mr. Frye's deep voice. "My dearest Lucy, I was wondering if you have made note of the times of the tides?"

Charlotte saw Lucy's face light up as never before. "It's just Mason," she whispered.

Just Mason. There it was again, and yet Charlotte sympathized with Lucy for getting trapped by the tutor. All of the children of Eden Castle at one time or another had been trapped by Mason Frye's gentle insistence that whatever wisdom resided inside his head he would sooner or later transfer to theirs, whether they wished it or not. Despite his bookish ways and wavy dark hair now turning gray, everyone in Eden Castle had agreed with John Murrey Eden's oft-repeated comment that whatever Mason Frye didn't know probably wasn't worth knowing.

Charlotte liked him, despite a few epic battles she had waged with him.

"Good day, Mr. Frye," she said as her smile invited him to enter the library. "Good day," he said distractedly as he quickly located Lucy by the window. The moment his eyes found her he seemed to blush. Charlotte watched, fascinated. Why in the world would Mason Frye blush when he saw Lucy? He'd seen her every day of her life.

"There you are," Mason smiled, taking advantage of his passage close to the fire to warm first his hands, then his backside.

"I have them, Mason, the tides, the exact minutes."

He looked up and smiled. "I knew you would, my dearest."

My dearest? Charlotte watched with increasing interest. Suddenly these two people were viewing one another in a very different light.

Abruptly Mr. Frye's expression changed, growing more sober, more intimate. "Might I see them?"

"Of course, Mason. Did you hear about Frederick?"

"Good news indeed," Mason beamed. "A fine mind, Frederick, with a heart and a soul to match."

He paused.

"But poor Geoffrey," she heard him murmur now, more to the fire than anyone else.

"He's quite ill, you know," he said to his hands, alternately rubbing them, then staring at them. "Such a waste," he mourned, "such an unforgivable waste."

In the silent interim when only the driving rain could be heard on the window, Charlotte saw Lucy turn away as though she were suffering in similar fashion.

Suddenly Charlotte felt very much the intruder. "If you will excuse me," she murmured. "I should go find Mama and see if I can be of help."

She closed the library door behind her. The next time she and Lucy were alone she'd ask her precisely what was going on. She was dying to know. She had never seen Lucy or Mr. Frye behave in such a peculiar manner.

Charlotte walked rapidly down the corridor that led to the Great Hall. Several yards ahead she heard urgent voices. Someone was calling out, "Hurry, boiling water, hurry please."

Charlotte stopped suddenly. She wanted no part of it. Quickly she assessed her position in the corridor; ahead was the closet where guest linens were stored, lovely French lace-trimmed pillowcases smelling of her mother's heavenly summer potpourri.

She increased her step, drew open the linen closet door and took refuge inside the sweet-smelling darkness. Moments later she heard an urgent storm of footsteps outside the door. She recognized her Uncle John in the lead and thought she heard her cousin Stephen's voice.

It didn't matter. They were blessedly passing her by, and as the sound of footsteps receded, Charlotte felt her way to the back of the linen closet, found the low wooden stool on which the housemaids stood to reach the uppermost shelves, and sat down, wrapping her skirts about her legs to protect them against the chill. She scooped up a handful of rose potpourri from a bowl on a near shelf and held it to her face. In the darkness she re-created summer, the high emerald green headlands of Eden Point, Geoffrey running ahead, peering across the channel at Wales with his spyglass while she settled comfortably in the warm sun on the low white bench and lost herself in Frederick's last letter, beautifully poetic descriptive passages of endless warm sun, dazzling flowers and handsome, civilized brown people.

Dr. Rolf Reicher, age forty-six, originally of Hamburg, Germany, now of London, England, had some experience with the birthing process. He took one look at the suffering young woman with the heaving belly and knew immediately that the Eden family was about to suffer a second tragedy.

"Clear the chamber," he ordered and looked sternly back at the gallery of faces that hovered too close to the bed.

"You! You are . . ."

"Susan Eden, sir, a trained nurse."

"And you?" he asked, pointing at Alice.

"This is my daughter Alice, Dr. Reicher. She, too, is a–"

"You two, stay. The rest of you must clear the chamber immediately."

All appeared to be on the verge of obliging except one, a distraught-looking young man who, Dr. Reicher correctly assumed, was the husband.

"Please, sir," the weary-looking man began, "let me–"

"No, no, out of the question. You wait outside. As soon as there is news–"

"But I've been with her, sir, from the beginning. She will expect me to–"

"She will expect nothing of you except your obedience to me. Is that clear?"

There! He'd done it again. But it was just his manner. His wife, Sonia, had warned him repeatedly that it tended to put people off.

"Look," he began, wasting time he did not have in a softer approach. "Your wife is in extreme labor. Something is impeding the birth process. I must find out what it is."

"I won't be in the way. I'll sit over there. You won't know–"

"Please," Dr. Reicher shouted through clenched teeth. "Someone help me clear these chambers."

He did not suffer fools gladly, not even mournful and distraught ones. He turned back to the bed, washing his hands of the young man and leaving his removal to someone else. For the first time, he saw the face of the young woman on the bed. Her eyes were open now and filled with pain and fear; her mouth was struggling to draw in enough breath to accommodate the upheaval that was taking place inside her body.

"My child," Dr. Reicher murmured, bending close and grasping one of her outstretched hands, "my name is Dr. Reicher. I have just accompanied Geoffrey Eden home from London. Your family has asked for my professional assistance in your delivery. Are you opposed to this in any way? Shake your head once please."

She did so immediately. Dr. Reicher put his listening piece to her chest and heard an ominous rattling in her lungs. He knew that time was limited.

He looked around to see if the chamber had been cleared. The two nurses were already carrying kettles of steaming water to a near table and a young serving girl rushed in with yet a third. He saw, to his annoyance, that the young man was still standing, unmoving and as helpless as before.

Temper ignited, Dr. Reicher turned toward him, hand outstretched, ready to bodily remove him if necessary when, without warning, a giant of a man emerged from the deep shadows of the far side of the room. He was dressed all in black like a specter, with flowing gray hair and a neatly trimmed gray beard. His voice cut through the tension of the room like a surgical instrument.

"Do not touch him. I warn you, Hun. He is in a vulnerable state and will bruise easily. Your lack of gentleness normally would alarm me, but I know as well as you–better, I suspect–that the birth of anything is not a gentle process and therefore may not require gentleness in the attending physician."

Dr. Reicher, stunned by the appearance of this most unusual man could not respond. One word had lodged in his heart: "Hun."

Only last week a ruffian near Trafalgar Square had called him that. The climate was ugly because of South Africa and getting more so. The English had expected German assistance and had received none.

He was on the verge of issuing a tense apology when the large man placed his arm about the young man's shoulders in a protective fashion. "No need for words now, Doctor. I'll take charge of Stephen as he and his lovely wife have taken charge of my heart for the last eight years. But I warn you–"

He stopped at the door and pointed toward the young woman on the bed. "That child is not of this earth; she is a gift of God, and if anything goes amiss, you will answer first to God and then to me."

Dr. Reicher could not believe his ears. A threat was being leveled at him. Why him? He had traveled all this way to look after a rich young amputee. His agreement with Richard and John Murrey Eden had said nothing about difficult pregnancies and complicated labors. If Dr. Reicher so chose, he could walk out of this room and let the girl die along with her baby. They both might well die anyway. But whoever that mammoth fool was, he had no right, to threaten a man who was preparing to save two lives.

Dr. Reicher was on the verge of responding when he heard a terrible moan from his patient.

"Please, Mr. Harp," Susan said as she pushed the two men gently out the door. "Leave us for a while. I assure you we will do our best for Eve."

When the room had cleared, Dr. Reicher ordered Susan to close and bolt the door as he turned back to the bed.

"Her name?" Dr. Reicher asked, stripping off his coat and methodically rolling up his sleeves.

"Eve," Susan Eden replied.

"And who is she to this family?"

"Her mother is my husband's half sister. Eve's husband is my stepson."

"And where is her mother?"

"Lady Mary lives in America with her husband."

Hurriedly Dr. Reicher threw off the bedclothes. He stopped, appalled at what he saw. The girl was lying in a pool of her own blood; continuous hemorrhaging was soaking through the bedding.

"Help me turn her," Dr. Reicher ordered Susan. Pointing to Alice, he said, "In my bag there's a chloroform cup. Get it."

Instantly the girl responded like a good nurse and returned with the soft gauze cup and a small brown bottle of chloroform.

"Have you ever administered it before?"

"I have."

"Only a drop or two at first," he warned. And to Eve he advised, "Relax as much as you can. Take deep breaths. We are going to do our very best for you."

For several moments, Dr. Reicher stood back and watched the anesthetic take over and issued a silent prayer of thanks to Sir James Simpson and Justus von Liebig, who in their respective geniuses had discovered this blessed balm.

"She's asleep now, Doctor," Alice said, still holding the mesh cup over Eve's nose.

"Be on guard," he warned and reached into his black bag, which Alice had positioned on a nearby table, and withdrew a tincture of oil. He must examine the birth canal, though he knew what he'd find–an obstruction which could result in death for both mother and child. Even if it were surgically altered, the end result could be the same, for the young woman had lost dangerous amounts of blood.

He looked up straight into Susan Eden's experienced eyes. It was his professional guess that she knew the exact nature of his thought.

"Do the best you can, Dr. Reicher," she encouraged softly. "That's all anybody has a right to ask of anyone."

He was grateful for her words and wished, as he always wished at difficult times like these, that he'd followed in his father's footsteps and gone into the family brewery business.

"Lift her legs," he commanded the women. At that moment he saw a new convulsion: the baby was struggling to get out.

Hard work ahead. For all. There was nothing to do but get on with it and hope for the best.

Richard, Lord Eden, aged fifty-two, fifteenth baron and seventh earl of Eden Castle and Eden Point, walked off the Oriental runner which stretched the length of the corridor outside young Eve's bedroom and saw the mussed fringe at the end coming closer like a welcoming beacon. Few things brought him as much pleasure as bending over in chambers throughout his castle and combing with his fingers the mussed fringe of any and every Oriental.

At the far end of the corridor was a family group awaiting news from Eve's chamber. It had been a dreadful day in all respects; the quiet rural world of Eden Castle had been turned upside down.

Where Eleanor was he had no idea. He always felt adrift when they were apart. Usually they moved in tandem throughout every hour of the day. But this day was far from ordinary and was merely a harbinger, Richard feared, of chaos to come.

He paced the corridor again, moving back toward the silent group sunk deep in chairs outside Eve's door. Why in the name of God had young Stephen wanted to remain in there? When Eleanor had given birth to their children, Richard had managed to find something that needed doing as far away from the castle as possible.

Suddenly he heard footsteps running up the stone stairs. Richard stepped back and saw a chambermaid carrying a stack of fresh linens hurry by and knock at Eve's door. Someone unlocked it and she disappeared inside. The three in the alcove rose to their feet as the door opened, hopeful that some word would be received.

But no word was forthcoming, and he heard the heavy door slam shut and heard nothing else, though he saw the fringe on the Oriental had become hopelessly mussed again.

Slowly he started forward, eager to set the strands straight, when he again heard steps on the stairs, slower this time, accompanied by a familiar wheezing and an occasional groan of effort. It was Eleanor.

"You shouldn't have come up," Richard scolded lovingly, reaching for her hand to assist her up the last few steps.

"Had–to come," she gasped. "Has Eve–"

"No, not yet. Dr. Reicher just cleared the room."

"Poor darling," she soothed, her breath returning. "Why aren't you with them?" she asked, peering over his shoulder at the others.

"I . . . don't feel comfortable."

"No, of course not. I understand."

"Geoffrey . . ."

". . . is asleep, blessedly. Dr. Reicher gave him a sedative before coming to Eve's room." She bowed her head and straightened her handkerchief. "I saw him, Richard," she whispered. "Teddy and William let me see him. He was sleeping. He looked as he did when he was a little boy, ringlets on his forehead. He could have been any age except for . . ."

Her tears were controlled, and Richard was grateful for that. He would have hated for her to attract the attention of the others.

She drew free of his embrace and applied the handkerchief to her eyes. As she dabbed at them she asked, "What are we going to do, Richard? What will Geoffrey do?"

"He will heal, then resume his position as my heir."

"But he has a terrible impediment."

"He has lost a foot. I daresay no single aspect of his manhood was attached to his foot."

"How will he manage?"

"Dr. Reicher told me there are ingenious new walking sticks now to serve amputees. He will manage. We'll help him. At least we will do our best."

What was that?

At the peculiar sound, Richard glanced down the corridor. The others, John, Stephen and Yorrick Harp, were frozen like children playing a game of statues.

There it was again–a tiny cry, distinct and very angry.

The group surged across the hall, Stephen in the lead, followed fast by Yorrick Harp and Eleanor.

As the sharp and now continuous infant cry increased, so did the population in the corridor, as though everyone had been merely in hiding, waiting to see how the event would turn out.

As a group of servants rushed past him, Richard bided his time. When the traffic had eased, he moved along the opposite wall and came to a halt directly behind the chair in which John was sitting.

"So all's well that ends well, pray God," Richard murmured. The door to Eve's room remained closed, despite Stephen's insistent knocking and the congregation of servants now gathering in an excited knot.

Surprised, John looked over his shoulder but did not get up. "Ah, Richard, I saw you hanging about down there and envied you your isolation. Sometimes it gets to be too much, doesn't it?"

"Nearly always," Richard mused, catching Eleanor's eye and returning her excited smile. He slipped into the chair next to John, feeling at ease in his half brother's presence. Over the last few years they had grown as close as true brothers. Richard was fairly certain that John made fun of him behind his back on occasion, but everyone made fun of him behind his back from time to time. He'd grown accustomed to it.

Still the infant screams came from behind the bolted door. Hovering behind Stephen was Yorrick Harp, whose craggy features seemed fixed in the mask of the tragedian, even though the infant's screams clearly indicated the baby lived.

At last, when waiting no longer seemed possible, the door opened and Susan appeared, looking much the worse for wear. In her arms she carried a cloth cocoon from which the infant cries were increasing in a series of three shorts and two longs, like a cosmic code signaling the end of something, the beginning of something.

Susan handed the bundle to Stephen. Above the infant's protestations, she said, "Your son, as healthy a specimen as I have ever seen."

Following the news of the child's sex, a pleasurable murmur swept through the servants. Richard noticed a few of the older women dabbing at their eyes with the hems of their aprons. But then his attention was drawn back to Stephen, to that particular and memorable miracle when a man holds his future in his arms for the first time, so helpless now but containing the potential to move and secure worlds.

Clearly overcome, Stephen bowed his head into the blanket, and either the closeness of his father or the warmth of his breath soothed the baby boy, who instantly ceased his screaming and filled the air with the sweetest silence.

John drew himself forward in his chair, apparently entranced by this sweetest of scenes. "You have made me a grandfather," he said, smiling. "At least let me hold my grandson for a minute."

Though the American had been second in line for that privilege, he stepped back, apparently more than willing to sacrifice his place to John, who came up without a word and with impressive skill angled the baby into his arms. Carefully he drew back the blanket and held the baby for all to see.

During the inevitable chorus of oohs and aahs, the baby responded to the rough treatment by bellowing again, causing Susan to rescue him, while giving John her stern look.

As she started back into the chamber with the baby, Stephen reached for her, "May I come in? I want to see Eve–"

For a moment Richard thought he detected a look of consternation on Susan's normally contained face. "Shortly, Stephen," she smiled nervously. "Surely you understand. Give us a few minutes."

Reluctantly Stephen watched as Susan carried his son into the bedroom. Harp was quickly at his side and Richard saw him place an affectionate arm about Stephen's shoulder. Clearly John also saw the gesture and was not pleased by it.

"Come, Stephen," John commanded briskly in his best voice of authority. "We must lift a glass to this new Eden."

As he spoke, he deftly retrieved his son from beneath Yorrick Harp's arm and angled him toward the staircase a distance away. "Come, all of you," he called over his shoulder. "We've successfully completed our vigil here. The rest is women's work. Now the baby deserves our toasts and best wishes."

Twice Stephen tried to object to his hasty escort down the corridor. "I should wait here, Papa. Eve will . . ."

". . . will need her rest and is being well attended. She has done well. Now leave her be."

The American suddenly caught the spirit of the occasion.

"The man speaks the truth," he bellowed in a voice so theatrical that all else seemed like silence by comparison.

With the most graceful of movements, Richard observed a subtle choreography; the giant came up alongside Stephen and turned him in the opposite direction, all the while filling the corridor with a slightly splintered Shakespearean cadence.

" 'Now all the blessings of a glad father encompass thee about!' " he pronounced. " 'O, wonder!' " he proclaimed. " 'How many goodly creatures are there here! How beauteous mankind is! Oh brave new world that has such people in't!' "

The procession was almost at the end of the corridor now, the others, John, Eleanor and the servants, trailing behind the aberrant Pied Piper. Still Harp's theatrical voice filled the corridor.

" 'Look down, you gods!' " he proclaimed, " 'And on this young *father* drop a blessed crown; for it is you that have chalk'd forth the way which has brought us all hither.' "

Gone, the lot of them, though the Shakespearean voice continued to echo and bounce off the old stone walls like iambic volleys.

Richard was amazed at such powers of projection, and at the same time, he belatedly realized that he probably should have fallen in with the rest of the parade, for now he found himself quite alone in the alcove without the slightest idea of what he should do next.

Then he remembered the fringe of the Oriental runner, beautifully mussed now after the theatrics of Mr. Harp and the passages of all those eager feet on their way to a celebration.

As no one was around to see him and as his need to restore something to order was great, he fell to his knees and bent over the mussed fringe and began carefully, with the tips of his fingers to comb it out until each silken strand was perfectly aligned with the silken strand next to it, perfect order, safe, reliable, impeccable order.

Alice resented the arrogant German doctor, but for her mother's sake, she kept quiet and obeyed each order.

"There's blood on the floor. Wipe it up quickly, fetch a clean gown and linens; I must work with clean linens."

Alice moved rapidly to keep pace with the barrage of mundane commands. At St. Martin's in London, where she worked as a student nurse, orderlies would be called upon to do what she was now doing. She didn't mind these duties under such primitive circumstances, but the doctor's attitude annoyed her. His countless oblique references to the fact that he was surrounded by mediocrity, reminded Alice of every doctor at St. Martin's, all certain of their male superiority and their physicians' knowledge.

On her hands and knees, Alice scrubbed up the blood until the water in her pail was red. Eve had lost so much blood and was still losing it. Alice had witnessed the cuts the butcher had made, three times as large as necessary. She had protested twice and for her troubles had received stern orders. Her mother had looked at her pleadingly. Under these difficult circumstances she wanted submissive obedience.

But the fact remained, the bleeding would not stop and the man did not seem to know what to do. He was hovering nervously over Eve, whose face was as pale and ashen as the pillow cloth on which she was lying. She had not yet regained consciousness from the chloroform. Now was the time to act quickly, a series of small stitches in the torn area to aid healing and to control the bleeding.

"Sir, I beg you, may I–"

"There's more over here," Dr. Reicher interrupted.

"I know, sir, more blood," Alice said, rising from her knees. "And there will be more unless you–"

"My dear lady," Dr. Reicher said archly, "it is your job to scrub the floor. It is my job to tend the patient."

"Then you're not doing a very good job."

Alice heard the echo of her impudence, then heard the deadly silence that followed. Even the screams of the baby seemed to diminish, as though the infant, too, was aware of her heresy.

Alice knew full well what she had done. She had dared to challenge the built-in superiority of a male doctor. She'd done it before at St. Martin's. It had cost her a promotion. Here fortunately it would cost her nothing, although the man's ignorance could cost Eve her life.

"She needs stitching, sir," Alice said, pointing directly to the spreading red circle that only moments before had been clean white linens. "She must be stitched immediately or she will bleed to death."

The doctor stepped carefully away from the bed, moving steadily toward Alice.

"I will forgive you," he said, his voice cold. "I am aware of the strain of the last few hours on an inexperienced mind. I will forgive impudence out of deference to your mother."

"My mother has nothing to do with this," Alice snapped, weary of waiting a lifetime for the right to act and speak on her own best judgment.

"I didn't ask for your forgiveness, sir," she went on, approaching the bed on the opposite side. "I don't even ask for your approval. All I wish to point out is that you are allowing your patient to die, and I will testify to this at the inquiry that is certain to follow such a tragedy."

"Alice!"

This stern maternal voice came from across the room. Alice pondered the wisdom of proceeding without any allies, even a maternal one.

"Dr. Reicher," she began, changing her tone of voice. She had learned at St. Martin's that though she might feel belligerent, it accomplished little to reveal belligerence. The best method of dealing with the male ego was to stay calm–as calm as possible *and* as objective.

"I work at St. Martin's in London."

"Good. I know where to file my report of your insubordination. When I finish with you, young lady, I doubt seriously if you will be working for any reputable medical institution in the city of London."

"And my ward is the lying-in ward, second floor, west wing."

"Did you hear me? Did you hear what I said to you?"

"And I have seen countless such surgeries, a simple procedure whereby–"

"Alice!" Again her mother's voice.

"Please, Mama," she said, her voice low. "I know what I'm talking about."

"But Dr. Reicher is–"

"A good doctor, I'm sure, but in this case simply not as informed as he could be."

"Not as– I never in my life– What in God's name has gotten into this creature?"

"Dr. Reicher, please hear me out." Alice lifted her voice in an attempt to top the man's blustering inarticulation. In a way, she almost felt sorry for him. What a blow to discover that you fall short of perfection.

"I will not listen to you," Dr. Reicher said. "You are speaking from ignorance. Dangerous ignorance, I might add. Stitching is not performed in such an area."

"But it is, Doctor, and has been time and time again with great success."

"And if it is done, it would only result in infection and, ultimately, death."

"Death will result from loss of blood. Look at her, Doctor, does she resemble a recovering mother?"

The near-lifeless face on the pillow spoke for itself. Alice watched the rage on Dr. Reicher's face to see if good sense and reason could still perhaps intervene and win out.

Neither did. Instead, he grabbed a towel and rubbed his hands vigorously, all the time talking. "I've had the misfortune to know a few women of your ilk," he pronounced. "Rebellious, willful, God's own curses which He has sent down to plague mankind." He drew on his coat, his face as red and livid as his recently scrubbed hands. "It's women like you who make men beg for the return of public whippings; females who don't know their place can only learn it through a sound beating."

He was at the door, still adjusting his waistcoat, sputtering in anger—an anger which seemed to be growing by the minute. "Why I came to this godforsaken place I have no idea. I do know that I did not come to be abused and insulted or to attend pregnant women, nor did I journey all this way to be maligned by an inferior who is not fit by nature or training to clean my boots."

The door was open now and he stood pompously in the frame. Alice suddenly realized he probably was quite grateful for her insolence. It provided him with the excuse and opportunity to walk away from a dying patient.

"Mark you, girl, I shall remember your name. And if I ever have the chance to bring you down from your false perch, believe me, I will do so."

And with that pronouncement he was gone. Quickly Alice turned about, searching for the one object she needed far more than Dr. Reicher. And that was Dr. Reicher's black bag.

There it was. She hurried to it and pulled open the flaps. In its depths she immediately found what she was looking for: two small surgical needles and a spool of stitching.

"Alice, do you know what you're doing?"

"I do, Mama. I've seen it done repeatedly."

"You shouldn't have spoken as you did."

"I said nothing but the truth, a lesson that you taught me, remember?"

"Yes, but where some men are concerned, the truth–"

Alice moved quickly past her, not wanting to hear such nonsense, particularly from her mother. Surely in all her years of living, it must have occurred to her that women were capable of far more than what they were presently permitted to accomplish, which wasn't much. Men had systematically denied the world fully one half of its God-given resources. It was an intolerable situation and it must be changed.

"Do you want to stay, Mama?" she asked quietly. "Feel free to go if you wish. That way I'll be solely responsible."

The two women exchanged a brief glance. Grateful, Alice watched as her mother placed the baby in the cradle by the fire and returned to the bed.

As Alice drew back the bedsheet, her mother asked, clearly worried, "You *are* sure you've seen this done enough times to do it yourself?"

"Almost every other delivery in the city requires it."

"Then why didn't Dr. Reicher know about it?"

"Hard to say. Not his speciality. Not a woman." She looked up at her mother in a pointed glance. "Never given birth."

"Then to work," Susan said. "Tell me what to do?"

Alice handed her the surgical needles. "Dip these in the boiling kettle over the fire." As her mother left, Alice pushed the hair back from Eve's face and prayed that the effects of the chloroform would last for at least another few minutes.

Then they would be faced with another problem–trying to awaken her from her chloroform sleep. Only then would they know if they had truly succeeded or magnificently failed.

Exhausted and still worried, Stephen stood before the fire in the Great Hall. He kept his eyes on the steps leading down from Eve's room. Surely someone would come soon and tell him that she was awake.

With him were his father, Yorrick Harp and young Albert, his half brother, a rather timid, uncertain young man who bore not a trace of resemblance to his half brother or their shared father.

As he turned from the fire, he saw Albert at Yorrick Harp's side, listening to his endless and always exaggerated tales of the American West.

"And surrounded she was," Yorrick intoned in a hushed voice to the extreme pleasure of all; even Uncle Richard and Aunt Eleanor had drawn close, mouths agape, intently listening, along with his cousins Charlotte and Lucy.

In fact, the only one who was not a part of Yorrick's enthralled audience was Stephen's father, John, who sat slumped in his immense chair.

"Yes, surrounded she was," Yorrick repeated. "That same young lady up there who has just given birth to a perfect son, surrounded by at least one hundred and fifty of the fiercest red Indians in the American West. Comanches they were–bloodthirsty savages, to be sure–who had appeared on their ponies out of the dust. Young Eve had just hopped from the lead wagon and had gone in search of the wagons behind.

"Twice I tried to call her back, but she was headstrong. Well, when the wind ceased and the dust settled, there before us all was a sight out of my worst nightmare."

He paused to drain his glass, and Stephen, watching from the fire was sure that Albert had not drawn full breath in a good ten minutes.

"And then what happened, sir?" Charlotte ventured tentatively.

"Well, she was completely surrounded by Comanche braves, bows drawn, the arrows pointing directly at her fair breast."

Stephen smiled despite his worry and fatigue. Embellishment upon embellishment lightly worked to stretch the tale and heighten the tension.

Stephen had heard this particular story of Eve's adventure with the Comanches on the trail from Abilene to Dodge City countless times. However, if Stephen remembered correctly, Eve had told him there had been seven Indians, all half-starved. Eve had been scooped up by a horseman and her party had continued on their way unharmed.

Somehow Stephen had the feeling this would not be the tale told tonight. He turned from the too hot fire and joined the others. As always, Yorrick was diverting, if nothing else. But, of course, he was something else to Stephen, perhaps everything to Stephen, the best friend he had in this world, certainly the most trustworthy, more of a loving father to him and Eve than his own father. His depth of feeling for Yorrick was hard to conceal and thus, perhaps, one of the causes of his father's clear antagonism toward the American.

Stephen heard footsteps on the stairs and turned to see Dr. Reicher, his face contorted in anger, hurrying down the steps and proceeding past the room without a word.

"Dr. Reicher," he called out, "a word if I may, please–"

"I have no word to give you," the man snapped. "Your wife is being tended to by a–woman." The word came out like an obscenity. "Ask *them*, for no mere man can even approach their wisdom and expertise and experience. I will now return to Lord Geoffrey, a charge I was hired to do. Good night to you."

With that, he was gone, his boots leaving sharp measured echos on the stone stairs. The family was left gaping after him, Yorrick's tale in shambles.

John drew himself forward first. "What in the world?" he asked, clearly bewildered. He hurried after the doctor, confused but apparently pleased that Yorrick Harp had been upstaged.

On Stephen's right, he saw his Uncle Richard and Aunt Eleanor in a whispered conversation. A moment later, Eleanor patted Stephen on the arm and whispered, "I'll go and see if your wife can receive you now."

Stephen started to call after her, hoping he might accompany her, but she was already well out of earshot.

Now Stephen saw Yorrick eye his empty glass as though longing for more spirits. Albert saw the gesture as well and reached for the pitcher of brown ale and lifted it with an ease that indicated it had already been emptied.

"Uncle Richard?" Albert asked, apparently wanting more than anything in the world to satisfy Yorrick's thirst so that he might continue with his tale. "Could we have more ale?" He held up the pitcher.

For a moment Richard blinked at the request. "No, I think not, Albert. Temperance, you know is a valuable virtue."

His words lacked conviction. Even Uncle Richard's voice paled in comparison with Yorrick's deeply sonorous one, which, in a curious way, still could be heard in imagined echoes about the Great Hall walls.

The pointed denial registered only briefly on Yorrick's face. Then the light was back, the empty glass abandoned on the table, the tale resumed, though from experience Stephen knew that sooner or later, somehow or other, Yorrick would find his drink.

As the narrative about Eve continued, Stephen saw Richard disappear up the stairs leading toward Geoffrey's chamber, apparently in pursuit of John, who had gone after Dr. Reicher.

"And then we heard something, a most macabre something . . ."

The stage whisper was Yorrick's. The hushed audience had now gathered closely about him and was composed of Albert and Lucy and Charlotte with two footmen on the near wall listening intently as well and trying not to show it.

". . . rising ever so softly at first into the prairie wind, captivating the attention of the marauding Comanches as well . . ."

"Was what?"

"Well, at first we couldn't be certain. Then I recognized it: a voice—that angel voice that has moved millions to tears was engaged in the most raucous, most barbaric rendition of song it has ever been my misfortune to listen to."

"You mean—she was singing?" Albert asked, beside himself with interest.

"That's exactly what I mean. In the face of all those painted, red savages, that angel lifted her face and voice in song."

Charlotte giggled. "It sounds silly."

"It *was* silly," Yorrick agreed. "But I'm here to tell you that it totally disarmed the natives. Yes, it did. They allowed their arrows to go limp in their bows; they exchanged the most bewildering and puzzled glances. And at last they moved away, leaving Eve seated on the prairie floor, screeching her heart out."

Yorrick shook his long gray hair. "I want you all to know that as an unforgettable display of courage and ingenuity, it left nothing to be desired."

"What was the song?" Lucy asked, looking up from her book.

Yorrick clapped his hands in childish delight. "A most irresistible number entitled 'Jenny Crack Corn.' Do you know it here? Any of you?"

No one did.

"Then I shall teach you, and I shall do so in honor of Eve and her new son. I shall also teach you the square dance. Yes, what a splendid gift for Eve and her baby, echoes of 'Jenny Crack Corn,' helping her to recall another moment in her life when she was truly triumphant. Come, all of you. How many of us are there?"

Stephen watched, smiling, as Yorrick led Albert and Lucy and Charlotte out into the middle of the vast Great Hall, which had in the past seen balls with guest lists exceeding four hundred.

Now as these three young people took their places at the center of the hall Yorrick found something out of kilter. He frowned. "Four counting me. Still won't do. Need at least eight for a proper configuration." He looked about.

"You two fine male specimens," he shouted at the two young footmen against the far wall.

The lads looked surprised.

"Yes, you," Yorrick bellowed. "Do you by chance possess dancing feet? No matter, I'll make you a gift of some if you'll come and join us in song and dance. A simple melody, strong beat, good rhythm designed precisely to match the beat of your hearts. Come, don't dawdle."

Charlotte giggled. Lucy tried to hide a smile and failed. Albert looked up at Yorrick with unmistakable adoration. Poor boy. He'd probably never seen so much energy coming from one source in his entire life. Yorrick would be good for him.

At last the two young footmen approached, looking shy and ill at ease, caught in the conflict of their training. Having been told to always obey the commands of guests at Eden Castle, they now stood a safe distance apart until Yorrick flew to their sides, took his place between them, his mammoth arms around their shoulders, and propelled them forward.

At the same time, just coming up the steps from the kitchen court, he saw two young serving maids.

"Wait!" he bellowed, abandoning the two footmen close to the others and running across the room, his arms waving as though he were trying to catch a train. "Wait, my pretties." He caught up with them and stopped short before their alarmed glances.

"Your names," he gasped, patting his chest. "Not much to ask, not much to give, is it?"

"Lilly, sir," said one.

All at once Yorrick fell backward into a broad theatrical movement, one hand now clasping his forehead, another his heart. "I had a Lilly once," he stammered. "The fairest face and warmest heart in all of Christendom. Oh, my Lilly," he murmured and grasped the young girl's hand and kissed it warmly.

Still by the fire, Stephen settled on the arm of a near chair. As always, Yorrick was the best performer within a hundred country miles.

As introductions were taking place, Stephen glanced up the steps. Where was Eleanor? She should have returned by now.

Introductions over, Stephen looked back to see partners being chosen. Charlotte, naturally, was Yorrick's personal choice. Lucy was Albert's partner and the two footmen selected one each of the serving maids, and at last the square was formed, a remarkably egalitarian feat which perhaps only Yorrick could have pulled off. Centuries of hardened class distinction were dissolving before his loving insistence that *all* were needed for a proper square dance to take place.

"Now," he began, his old cheeks glowing pink like an out-of-season Father Christmas. "Hear me out. I shall do a full rendition of the ditty. It is a catchy tune and you'll adore it, I know."

As he launched into a splintered though enthusiastic version of the song, Stephen saw two tired-looking men slip down the steps from the direction of Geoffrey's bedchamber. Their coats were dusty and their low-brimmed hats almost covered their faces. He recognized them as Geoffrey's aides, the two men from Mortemouth who had accompanied him to the Transvaal and had helped to bring him home. Apparently they had remained in Geoffrey's chamber for most of the day and were now going home.

Yorrick saw them as well and immediately called out, "You two, we have need of as many voices as we can muster. May I have a kind word with both of you."

No, a voice inside Stephen's head advised. Clearly Yorrick did not understand. Those two men had nothing to celebrate. Indeed, the defeat in the Transvaal at the hands of the Boers was most likely a humiliation from which they would not soon recover.

As he watched, Yorrick danced his way across the Great Hall toward the two men who had yet to acknowledge him in any way.

"I say, perhaps you will allow me to persuade you to throw off the gloom of war and help us perfect the only endeavor in the world worth pursuing–the lifting of a song in celebration of birth. Come, allow me to–"

The two men stood listening with polite coldness, neither registering any emotion until Yorrick lightly touched one on the arm. Then the swarthy man turned with a fierceness that captured the attention of everyone in the Great Hall.

"Don't be touching me, you bastard. Leave me be. You're a ragman, that's what you are, nothing more or else you'd know the sorrow visiting this honorable castle and not be wasting your time on women's ditties and children's play."

Though his voice was low, its venomous tone carried every word to the farthest corner of the Great Hall.

Stephen saw the dancers divide nervously into their ancient class systems, servants on one side, Lucy, Charlotte and Albert on the other, all of Yorrick's good intentions reduced to nothing.

Yorrick didn't move; his great head remained cocked to one side as though he were trying to better understand what had been said.

In the interim, the two aides nodded briskly to the family and commenced walking toward the great doors.

Leave it be, Stephen prayed. But he didn't.

"Another word, kind sirs, I pray you," Yorrick called out, his voice softer. "I'm sorry," he apologized. "It was not my intention to intrude on your grief, though from what I saw of young Geoffrey, he is in large measure intact and needs only to rally a portion of his spirit in order to survive the lack of a foot."

He was even with them now, standing a short distance away, his hands behind his back, head down, pose thoughtful. The two men had stopped and were listening.

"Did I ever tell you of my friend, Gus by name, lord and master of twenty-three thousand of the most beautiful acres God ever created. Utah is Gus's kingdom; Utah is in America. Perhaps you've heard of it. Gus runs a tight kingdom there with over five hundred hands and a wife as lovely as the first spring morning in the history of the world. They have eleven children of mixed gender, all as fresh and newly minted as the dawn of creation. And Gus does all this from a chair with wheels, for both his legs were separated from his body in a wagon accident when he was but a boy. So you see Gus's accomplishments put young Geoffrey's accident into perspective."

"It wasn't an accident," the second aide said, his voice low.

"Oh, but you're wrong, sir. All war is an accident, a foolish, childish, preventable accident. Geoffrey needn't have gone, you know. He might have told whoever summoned him to participate in such foolishness, 'No sir, no thank you. I have a future I must attend to.' "

The two aides stared back at Yorrick, their faces smudged masks of incredulity. "That would have been cowardly," one quietly said.

"Oh no, oh my, no," Yorrick persisted. "It would have taken more courage to say no to the parade than it obviously did to join it."

Stephen closed his eyes and predicted what was coming next. And it came.

"Then you are calling *us* cowards as well?" one aide asked, stealthily drawing nearer to where Yorrick Harp stood.

"I'm calling you to join us in a dance, that is all," Yorrick smiled with unfailing charm. "My sentiments on war are my own and must be respected as such. For years, I have begged for someone to explain it to me, the benefit and wisdom that pits man against man in mortal combat until one or both dies. I live for a Utopia where war is outlawed, where men recognize and welcome the challenge of devising ways to live together, not die together."

The two aides were menacingly close to Harp, the bitterness on their faces twisted slightly into sneers of condemnation. Both had removed their hats and one wore a large, thickly padded head bandage. Clearly these two warriors were ready for laurel wreaths, not condemnation.

What now?

Stephen started forward, ready to intervene if necessary. Yorrick raised both hands in a conciliatory gesture. "No offense intended, gentlemen, I assure you. I sympathize with your grief, even though it might have been avoided. Come to me when you are rested and we will talk again of battle and war and song and peace. We'll see who pleads the most appealing case."

"Don't care ever to see you again, you bastard," one aide muttered, circling close enough to shove Yorrick with moderate strength and send him reeling directly into the path of the second aide, who shoved him back in the opposite direction, a mild sport which brought amusement and relief to the aides but which angered Albert and sent him hurrying to Yorrick's defense.

"Leave him alone. He did nothing to you except speak the truth. Now leave him–"

As the aides turned on Albert, their war-weary faces split into a wide grin. Sadly their spirits were being lifted by the promise of another conflict.

"Enough, gentlemen," Stephen said, approaching from the fireplace, hoping to bring a modest voice of authority with him. "I beg you all. Go your own ways. Mr. Harp meant no offense. Young Albert meant no offense. We are only grateful to both of you for accompanying Geoffrey home. I'm certain as soon as he is capable of speaking, he will tell us of your loyalty and courage under fire. Please now, return to your homes and families in Mortemouth. You've been away long enough. I'm sure you both have mothers who are waiting."

The tired faces softened even as Stephen spoke. "Aye, sir," one muttered and kneaded his hat into an unrecognizable lump.

"And we meant no offense either, sir," the other one nodded. "Just don't like the sound of his words. He's–different."

Stephen smiled at the epithet. Perhaps in large measure it was the cause of all wars since the beginning of time. "He is an American," Stephen shrugged apologetically.

"At your service," Yorrick bowed with a grand Elizabethan sweep.

"Home with you, now," Stephen urged, sensing renewed antagonism and literally coming between them and moving them toward the door. "It is my hope that as soon as we are able, Eden Castle will have a dual celebration, rejoicing in the safe return of Geoffrey and his two trusted aides from the field of battle, and a celebration in honor of the birth of my first son."

"Sir, we didn't know. When?"

"Today, only hours ago."

As both aides heartily shook Stephen's hand, he was pleased to see no trace of their earlier hostility.

Then they were gone, hurrying across the courtyard, running the last few yards to the gate, undoubtedly looking forward to a hero's welcome at The Hanging Man in Mortemouth.

As the two footmen scurried to secure the large doors, Stephen took Yorrick by the elbow and steered him back toward the waiting dancers. "You must realize, my friend, that large portions of the world's population are not yet ready for your dreams of Utopia."

"They should be. Why, if you had left me alone with them, I could have persuaded them to my point of view."

Stephen smiled. "They were prepared to knock your head off."

Albert stepped close. "I would have given him my full support," he said with youthful enthusiasm.

"Of course you would have," Yorrick confirmed, drawing the boy close under his arm. "And you're wrong, Stephen. All men of goodwill must consistently try to share the news that destruction begets destruction, hate fosters hate, and if violence is the law, then death is the end."

He walked a few steps ahead of Stephen, Albert still close under his arm. "What were their names?" he asked, turning back on a point of curiosity.

Stephen shrugged.

"Anyone?" Yorrick demanded of his would-be dancers.

One footman said, "The big one is Teddy, the other William."

"Brothers?"

"Aye, sir. Considered good men in Mortemouth. Their father's the smithy."

Yorrick scratched his head and repeated the names. "Teddy. And

William. Good names. Good men. I know with a certainty that alarms that we shall meet them again. Well, come, children, the interruption was long and damaging. We must now work doubly hard to recapture the spirit of festivity and rejoicing. Stephen, we need your good, strong, clear voice. I left you alone earlier, but won't you join us?"

Stephen begged off with a smile. "I'm going up to see Eve. Something has delayed Eleanor and I can't wait any longer."

"Of course you can't. Your son and your wife await you. Fly to their side while we sing and dance in their honor. Now, children, listen carefully . . ."

Stephen hurried across the Great Hall just as Yorrick erupted into a spirited version of Eve's song, repeating the simple melody line by line to the delight of his willing chorus.

Eve would be pleased. He would leave her door open so that she could hear Yorrick's unique tribute.

As for his son, how hungry he was to hold his son again in his arms, to study the miracle that he and Eve had created, to contemplate names, and to contemplate the child's dazzling future.

While impressed with her daughter's expertise with the surgical needle, Susan was worried about her recent ugly confrontation with Dr. Reicher. A truly professional nurse did not speak such words to an attending physician. A wise nurse did not speak such words to anyone.

But Alice had always been thus since childhood, blunt to a fault like her father when she felt she was right. Still, Susan wanted to speak to her, or else Alice's lack of tolerance and tact could lead her into serious trouble and she was far too good a nurse to risk what surely could be a brilliant career.

Now Susan ceased her maternal brooding and concentrated on the manner in which Alice was massaging Eve's feet with warm oil, strong, skillful gestures, clearly trying to force circulation back up toward the head.

The bleeding had stopped immediately following the suturing. They changed the bed linens again carefully; the clean white muslin remained clean and white this time.

Alice had discovered a hardness in Eve's abdomen that seemed unrelated to her pregnancy. Susan had watched her examine it for several minutes, a worried look on her face.

Then they had bathed Eve, and now Alice was systematically massaging her, the effort clear on her face in beads of perspiration.

In the quiet of the room, Susan glanced toward the cradle where the baby was sleeping peacefully. A false calm, she was certain. At any moment the baby would awaken, hungry, in search of a nipple.

"Can she nurse?" Susan asked.

"Of course," Alice replied. "Not right away though. She's far too weak."

"A wet nurse."

"Yes, do you know of one?"

Susan thought for a moment. She'd delivered Theresa Johnson only last week. A robust young woman, Theresa would have milk to spare.

"Yes, I know a girl."

"You'd better fetch her. The baby will be–" Alice's voice broke.

Susan looked down, startled, to see Eve opening her eyes.

"Hello," Alice said with a smile.

"Is the baby–"

"Fine," Alice reassured her.

"What is–"

"A boy. You have a fine son, Eve."

Susan and Alice watched as Eve closed her eyes in relief and gratitude. "May I see him?"

"Of course," Alice said as Susan immediately lifted the infant from his cradle. He was sleeping like a cherub, his perfectly shaped head turned to one side, his mouth opened like a pink rosebud. He had a soft covering of fine dark hair on his head, a gift from his father, though Susan was positive that the perfect features and wide-set eyes were Eve's gift to her son.

"Here he is," Susan said, placing the baby in Eve's arms and standing back. The two women watched Eve gently kiss her son on the forehead, study him for a moment, then enfold him in her arms.

A knock at the door sounded through the chamber.

"Stephen," Eve murmured, still clasping her son to her.

Susan hurried to the door to find Stephen and a very apologetic Eleanor on the other side. Eleanor had been waiting for some time in the alcove across the corridor, afraid of knocking after Dr. Reicher's angry appearance, for fear something had gone wrong.

Susan smiled reassuringly at both. "Nothing has gone wrong. In fact everything is perfect. Come and look for yourselves."

She saw the need in Stephen's face and stood back as both women allowed him free and easy access to the bed. Even Alice backed away, relinquishing all claim, at least momentarily, to her patient.

As for Stephen, he stopped first at the foot of the bed and merely spoke her name, a simple sounding "Eve" that Susan suspected contained all the love in his heart.

"We have a son," Eve whispered, smiling up at him. That was all the invitation he needed; in the next minute he was on his knees at her side, trying to enfold both Eve and the baby in his awkward, loving embrace.

"He's perfect. Have you seen him?"

"Yes, darling. Let me hold him again."

"Of course. Names, Stephen, we must think . . ."

"Oh, look at him, Eve. He has your eyes, most definitely. Don't you think?"

"Your nose, I should say."

"Come," Alice whispered to Eleanor and Susan. "I know for a fact that we are intruders here." She raised her voice. "Only a few moments, you two. Eve needs rest. And the baby needs food."

"I'll nurse, of course," Eve called out weakly.

"Of course you will," Alice nodded, "as soon as you are stronger."

"I know a wet nurse in Mortemouth," Susan offered. "I will go and fetch her."

As Alice closed the door behind them, Eleanor sank exhausted into a chair. "As I said, I was too afraid even to knock on the door. When Dr. Reicher stomped across the Great Hall, denying all responsibility, I was certain things had gone wrong."

"They had," Alice interrupted.

"I don't understand," Eleanor said.

"Dr. Reicher refused to administer the proper treatment."

At this harsh accusation, Susan stepped forward. "Perhaps 'refused' is not the wisest word, Alice."

"I'm not looking for wise words, Mother. I'm looking for true ones. He knew Eve was hemorrhaging badly enough on her own. After his surgical cuts he should have–"

"You mean, he is incompetent?" Eleanor gasped, sitting on the edge of the chair.

"No," Susan began.

"Yes," Alice said, topping her. "Most incompetent, Aunt Eleanor, at least in female matters."

"But Richard has hired him to attend Geoffrey. I certainly don't want my son in any danger."

Susan gave Alice a stern glance, then moved quickly to put out the blaze of doubt before it became a firestorm. "Dr. Reicher is not incompetent, Eleanor, I assure you. He said himself he had scant experience with female problems. He delivered a healthy baby. We should be thankful."

"That's not what he said in there," Alice protested. "In there you would have thought he was the final word in every aspect of medical expertise. Lord, but I'm tired of the fragile male ego. Bloody experts on any given subject. And you encounter them everywhere. The hospital is the worst because lives are at stake. But no matter where you turn, in the bookstall, in the greengrocer, in the trolley, the theater, everywhere, you find the insufferable male ego, which requires constant feeding whether it warrants it or not, constant soothing, constant worship. It's all an illusion, you know, their genetic superiority, a myth created by them to keep women subservient and in bondage. Well, it won't do, it simply won't do. The end is coming, I promise you both that, the end of female tolerance and long suffering and patience. There is too much we can accomplish in this world. If men are not strong enough to make it on their own, then let them sink to whatever natural levels their ability dictates. I'm going for a breath of air, then I must return to my patient."

Susan blinked after the angry voice that she scarcely recognized as belonging to her daughter. She watched along with a totally stunned Eleanor as Alice started off down the corridor. Susan knew she owed Eleanor an apology and had just turned to deliver it when suddenly her angry daughter was back.

"And another thing," she went on, pointing her finger at both of them as though they were misbehaving children. "I once thought that the problem was created solely by men. I don't think so anymore. Women like yourselves, intelligent, educated, capable women who continue to play *their* game, heaping them with false praise, perpetuating the myth of their superiority at every turn instead of confronting them with the hard truth, which might conceivably, though painfully, lead to a better world for all of us, you, too, cause and perpetuate the problem."

Stunned, Susan watched her daughter turn and walk off down the corridor for a second time.

Surprisingly, Eleanor rallied first, displaying amazing tolerance. "She's tired, that's all, Susan. No need for worry."

"That's more than fatigue speaking."

"You must remember Alice is a city girl now and susceptible to city influences."

"What does that mean?" Susan challenged, wondering where her sweet little Alice of five years ago had gone.

"It simply means that she is being exposed to new ideas."

"Such as?" Susan persisted, amazed at how tolerant and informed Eleanor was.

"Well I read about a quite young and talented group of ladies in the *Pall-Mall Gazette*. It's promising, oh so promising for the future. They call themselves 'feminists' and they suggest equality of the sexes."

"In what matters?"

"In all matters. I even read that a few support the vote for women."

Susan smiled despite her worry. If these were new ideas, they were also harmless ones–farfetched and dreamlike. Susan was not altogether opposed to them, but she knew that this was, and always would be, a male world. The truly clever female learned that lesson early and concentrated her energy on ways in which to circumvent the male ego without damaging it. The wise woman did not court direct confrontation. She would be a tragic loser and much the worse for wear.

She glanced down the corridor and heard her daughter's step returning. As she came into sight, Susan stood, ready for a word if given a chance.

But she wasn't.

"It's late, Mother. I'm certain you and Eleanor are hungry. I know we have a hungry baby in there and we're going to need that wet nurse for several days. Send her up when she arrives, please."

And with that she stepped into Eve's room and closed the door behind her, leaving both Susan and Eleanor to stare after the closed door.

It was Eleanor who broke the tense silence first. "She's very much like John, you know."

"Yes, and John has spent the larger portion of his life in extreme suffering for trying to impose his will on others."

"Oh, don't worry. Your Alice is far too sensible for that. I, for one, believe the world needs more women like her. She's not like us, and perhaps that's just as well."

Susan started to pursue this strange logic, but she knew Alice was right; the baby would need feeding and soon. "Eleanor, I'm going down the back way and into the village to find a wet nurse. Theresa Johnson probably."

"Oh, can't someone go for you, my dear?"

"No, Theresa is shy. She wouldn't return here with anyone else."

"Shall I have Ghostly fetch you a carriage?"

Susan laughed. "I can walk there and back by the time old Ghostly gets organized."

"Do be careful," Eleanor called after her. "And hurry back. I'll ask Mrs. Partridge to arrange a buffet in the library. That way people can come and go. What do you think?"

Susan smiled. "It sounds most sensible, Eleanor, and I will hurry, I promise." Susan walked rapidly to the narrow door which led in a steep, though direct, descent to the kitchen court in the basement.

She wanted to hurry so she'd have less time to think about her daughter's new convictions. When the time was right and cooler heads prevailed, Susan intended to sit Alice down and explain that there was an order to the world, a way of doing everything. This order had evolved over the centuries, and people of reasonable intelligence accepted it. To do otherwise would be folly and bring untold pain. With the world filled with unpreventable suffering, why create more?

At several points during her recent ordeal, Eve had been certain that she would not survive. But then, despite the haze of continuous pain, she had remembered past times when she'd felt the same thing, when she'd been abducted by the Knights of the White Camellia, when Jarmay Higgins had launched the brutal assault upon her, when she had disobeyed Yorrick and had left the wagon on the trail and had been surrounded by Comanches, just so many times in her life when she had thought calmly, I will not survive this.

But she always had, and it was that remembered certainty that had seen her through the final hours of her labor. And now, exhausted to the marrow of her bones and yet filled with thanksgiving, Eve clasped her baby in one arm and feasted on Stephen's face bent low over her own in love and concern.

"I was so worried–"

"Don't," she smiled. "I'm fine, and look at our son. He is perfect."

She touched his face and felt her arm like a deadweight, so heavy, and allowed it to fall back onto the bedclothes. "I feel as though someone has removed all of my bones."

"It will take time."

"Yorrick. Where's Yorrick?"

As she remembered her old friend, she tried to raise herself up, certain that Yorrick would not be far away on an occasion like this.

Stephen started to his feet when he saw the door open and Alice returning.

"Leave the door open, Alice," he called out, "for just a moment."

"There's a chill draft in the corridor."

"Just for a minute."

Puzzled though unable to hold her head erect, Eve fell back onto the pillow, her eyes closed against her fatigue and heard only the crackling of the fire–and something else.

Eve opened her eyes. Quite distant it was, the singing of several voices raised in a loud but splintered rendition of . . .

" 'Jenny Crack Corn,' " Eve smiled.

Stephen bent close. "You should see the chorus that old Yorrick has organized. Two footmen, two parlormaids, Lucy, Charlotte and Albert. They are attempting the dance as well, all in your honor."

Eve listened a moment longer. "Tell Yorrick I want to see him," she whispered.

Then Alice appeared on the opposite side of the bed. "Not now, Eve. You need rest badly."

Eve agreed, but was still eager to see Yorrick, to show him their son, to confer with Stephen on names, on the various communications that must be sent to America.

"Just a few more minutes, Alice," Eve begged.

"Just *one* minute," Alice countered sternly. "Say your say to each other and then to sleep–I mean it."

Grateful for the reprieve, Eve looked up at Stephen. "Name. Do you have a name for your son?"

"He's your son as well."

"The one we agreed upon?"

Stephen nodded. "Most certainly. And I think it suits him."

Eve drew back the blanket and kissed her son on his cheek. "Alexander Burke Eden," she whispered. "Such a large name for such a tiny baby."

"He'll grow into it."

"Tell Yorrick. Tell the others."

"I will."

"Stephen, I want Mama and Papa to know as soon as possible."

"Of course. I will have a courier deliver a message from the Cunard office in London."

Without warning, Eve felt a piercing pain in her lower abdomen. She closed her eyes and waited it out, though the intensity left her eyes watering.

"Alice, come quick," Stephen called, and Eve heard the fear in his voice and longed to reassure him; but the pain was still there, muted but spreading throughout her lower abdomen.

"She needs rest," Alice scolded. Eve was aware of the baby being taken from her arms, aware of Stephen backing quickly away from the bed. "And another thing," Alice suggested softly to Stephen alone, "as soon as she is able, I would suggest you take her into London for a thorough examination, not at all unusual after a difficult childbirth. I would feel much better if a really good doctor examined her thoroughly."

"Is anything–"

"I don't know, Stephen. I am simply suggesting with all of the professional expertise at my command that as soon as she is strong enough, the two of you travel to London and let a good doctor examine her."

For several moments no one spoke. The pain was receding and Eve saw the fear in Stephen's face and wished that Alice had not made the suggestion. He looked so worried. She needed to change his focus.

"Tell Yorrick, Stephen," she said softly, "that I want to see him as soon as possible."

"I will," Stephen promised again and threw her a kiss.

Then he was gone and her son was gone, and Eve saw Alice back at her side checking her bedclothes, checking for something beneath the coverlet.

"No blood. Good," she murmured. She readjusted the comforter about Eve's shoulder and stopped to smooth back her hair. "You've done a good day's work," Alice smiled brightly. "Close your eyes now. Let sleep come."

And Eve did as she was told and found the most welcoming sight inside her closed eyes, found her childhood home, Stanhope Hall, found a warm and sunny southern day, heard her brother David splashing in the ice pond, saw her father lounging in his favorite chair in the library, her mother doing her needlework in the opposite chair, a quiet, peaceful, safe, loving interval.

They all must have sat like that a thousand times in Eve's childhood, and each time the impatient and youthful Eve would lounge on the bottom step of the old veranda and long for the day when she could leave the confinement and restriction and rural simplicities of Stanhope Hall.

Now here she was, thousands of miles away, with a successful career, a loving husband, and a new son. And all she wanted most in this world was to sit at the bottom of those veranda steps again, listening to the rustle of her father's newspaper, the delicate click of her mother's knitting needles, the distant laughter coming from the ice pond, and the cicadas singing in the shade of the old live oaks.

John could hear the ruckus all the way up to Sir Geoffrey's chamber, a multivoiced and talentless chorus raised in the most god-awful screeching it had ever been John's misfortune to hear. That, combined with Dr. Reicher's angry accusation that Alice had insulted him, had plunged John into a foul mood.

"Geoffrey will come around," Dr. Reicher promised, "but it will take time and a quiet atmosphere would certainly speed the healing process, both of his body and his soul."

With that, John had left the corridor, Richard directly behind him, heading on a direct collision course with whatever idiots were causing such ungodly sounds.

On the second-floor landing, the noise increased, accompanied now by the sound of hysterical laughter, male and female, the voices raucous, like alehouse voices, inconsiderate of anyone else.

Then John was at the top of the first staircase that afforded him a clear view of the Great Hall, and the sight that greeted him only served to increase his anger.

He might have known. It was that damnable American, Yorrick Harp. Endeavoring to follow him was his band of mismatched youth, family and servants grasping hands in some bizarre configuration of a reel, skirts flying, even timid Lucy laughing outright at the stupid antics of a—footman.

The gasp came from Richard.

"They're dancing," he said, his eyes wide in disbelief.

Indeed they were, and all led by the rabble-rouser Harp. And as if this were not bad enough, he saw lining the far side of the Great Hall nearest to the kitchen court door at least a dozen other servants all grinning like jackasses and keeping time with the strident melody, the lyrics escaping John except for an occasional "Jenny" who did something or another.

Then enough!

"Stop it! Stop it this instant, all of you!"

As John Murrey Eden spoke in his strongest, most authoritative voice, he was shocked to see that no one was paying the slightest attention. Not until he stopped a scant ten feet from the heart of the merriment and again shouted, "Stop it!" did any of the revelers even look in his direction.

Then, finally, the voices fell silent.

As the last reveler slowed to a standstill, John looked past the children to his real adversary, the great classless, uncouth man who somehow had stolen the affection of John's son and daughter-in-law.

"You, sir," he called out, pointing an accusatory finger toward the giant, whose flushed face bore the expression of bewilderment.

Yorrick Harp slowly and carefully withdrew a large linen handkerchief from his vest pocket. With maddening deliberation, he held the fine linen by the hem and delicately shook it out, all the while breathing heavily from the exertion of the dance.

"You are addressing me, Mr. Eden?" Harp asked, not once looking at John but continuing to focus on his handkerchief.

"I am," John nodded, "though I scarcely know what to say to a gentleman who is a guest in a place where there is sickness and who yet persists in filling the air with the most raucous noises and corrupts the young people of the family in the bargain."

Before Harp could frame his own defense, young Albert stepped forward. "You're wrong, Father," he said with surprising courage. Usually the boy kept to the corner and scarcely spoke, even when spoken to.

Now he brushed Albert aside as one would a minor annoyance and stepped closer to Harp, who was meticulously refolding his linen handkerchief after delicately patting his brow.

"Did you hear me, Harp?"

"I heard," Yorrick said. "And I offer my sincere apologies. It was not my intention to offend anyone."

"You didn't, Mr. Harp," Albert declared angrily, and as John turned to confront his son's insolence, he saw the others, all standing about in a familiar closeness, their young faces as flushed as Harp's from the exertion of the dance.

"You're dismissed," John shouted at the servants, and to emphasize his point he waved his hand at them and watched with pleasure as they went flying back to their respective duties.

"Go along, the rest of you as well," John ordered, finding no more need for an audience.

But it was Charlotte who defied him.

"I promise you, Uncle John, Yorrick meant no harm. Nor did any of us. We were just having fun."

"And do you think Eden Castle is an appropriate place for having fun today?"

"Why not?" This challenge came from Harp himself, who came up alongside Charlotte and placed his arm about her waist with obscene familiarity.

"Why not?" Harp repeated, smiling. "There has been a successful birth, a young prince for my Eve and my Stephen–"

His Eve and *his* Stephen? Inwardly John fumed.

"And a young man has returned home, soul intact from the waste of war. Now if all that does not warrant a celebration, Mr. Eden, this old Yorrick doesn't know what does."

As he spoke, he cast about for an ale mug abandoned on the far table.

"Instead of investing your energy in a futile display of anger, which is always impotent when confronted with natural joy, why don't you find us a full tankard of this delicious elixir and come and join us. In my opinion, you bear the imprint of a dancing man."

John had seen and heard enough, and now looked forward to taking the floor and displaying a true voice of power.

"First of all," John began, taking his time. "There will be no more ale. Not for you. The cellar is closed."

He saw Albert turn and walk a few steps away in a combination of disgust and anger. John went on.

"Now, I suggest that you practice a degree of consideration for the inhabitants of this house, who wish that this day be concluded with a degree of propriety and solemnity and not made cheap by the foolish antics of a drunken clown. Have I made myself clear?"

At first John couldn't tell if Yorrick Harp had heard, but John heard his own words in echo and feared perhaps he'd gone too far. His voice sounded hard, without margin or inflection, and only at the last minute did he remember that Susan was fond of this old fool, and if news of his actions and words ever got back to—

He heard a step on the opposite stairs and looked hurriedly in that direction, fearful that Susan had come down from Eve's room in time to hear his verbal assault on Yorrick Harp.

Relieved, he saw only Eleanor, looking as timid as ever as she glanced into the Great Hall. Daintily she lifted her skirts and without a word hurried along the back wall and disappeared up the steps in the direction of Geoffrey's apartments. John was certain she'd not find much up there to cheer her.

But he waited until her steps had ceased, then turned back to Harp, only to find he'd taken the children, Lucy, Charlotte and Albert and had retreated quietly to the fire, leaving John feeling abandoned while the four of them chatted quietly, conspiratorially, seemingly unaware of John's existence in the Great Hall.

"You!" John shouted. At the sound of his voice the close little group looked up. "I wasn't finished with you!" He hurried to the fire, his anger increasing with each step.

But as he drew near Harp spoke, his voice peculiarly soft and repentant.

"Mr. Eden, I beg you, forgive us, forgive me, for the dance and the song were both my idea, unique tributes to that young woman upstairs who has just passed through three days of agony in order to bring forth a son who will delight and perhaps save the world. It did seem appropriate to me to honor an occasion as spectacular as that with a song and dance. But then, I am by nature given to song and dance—"

As a pleasant laugh was shared around, John lost his appetite for humiliating the old man. Harp had a knack of taking an insult and turning it into an expression of affection for the one who had insulted him. It was like throwing rocks at someone who returned flowers, no fun and ultimately boring.

"I beg your pardon, sir? Have I caused new offense? It is not my intention—"

As Harp continued, John moved toward the library and the promise of a fire and a glass of sherry. And hopefully an interval alone.

There was an uneven pad of footsteps behind him, and he knew without looking who it was. Richard. Not the best of company, poor simple Richard, but perhaps better than nothing.

He looked back to see Lucy and Charlotte drifting off toward the sewing room in the central wing and Yorrick Harp and Albert still by the fire, though both appeared subdued, neither speaking. The Great Hall was now silent, in somber contrast to the mood in which he'd found it.

A job well done. Then why didn't he feel better, why didn't he enjoy a greater sense of accomplishment?

He moved into the chill library, feeling like a man under sentence of death. The small fire was dying; a lazy servant had failed to bank it properly. The light of the stormy day was gone from beyond the windows. Dark. And cold. And Richard was behind him, grunting in gout-ridden misery, sinking into the first chair and then struggling to elevate his foot.

John walked straight to the darkened windows and gazed out at the cold landscape, which seemed now to resemble the landscape of his soul, a frozen state where nothing moved except regret and remorse.

When would he ever learn Susan's invaluable lessons–that it was far easier to open the human heart than to close it, far easier to extend a hand in friendship than in hate, easier still to laugh than to weep.

With a sigh of disappointment, he vowed that he would have to learn the lessons soon or it would be too late.

Albert was still adjusting his jacket halfway across the courtyard. He grinned with pleasure at the thought of going off on an adventure with a man like Yorrick Harp, a man as loving and giving as his father was cold and selfish.

"Step lively, young Albert," he heard Yorrick call, his spirits newly risen at Albert's quiet suggestion that they leave the inhospitable confines of Eden Castle and seek warmth and liquid solace down the cliff walk at The Hanging Man, Mortemouth's leading public house.

How Yorrick's face had shone when Albert had made the proposal, half certain that a man like Yorrick Harp would never wish to be seen in the company of someone as young and inferior as Albert.

But apparently it had made no difference to Yorrick, for within five minutes Yorrick and Albert were scurrying like conspirators across the frozen courtyard, having taken only a moment to retrieve jackets from the cloakroom. Yorrick had chosen a dark brown smoking jacket and had adorned it with a lengthy white silk scarf, which he had twisted about his throat three times, leaving the tag ends to fly in the breeze, giving him the appearance of a man about to become airborne.

"Young Albert, put wings on your heels," Yorrick shouted and placed the most loving arm about his shoulder and seemed to transfer a portion of his energy to Albert.

"Allow me, Mr. Harp," Albert said, taking the lead. "I know Mortemouth like the back of my hand."

Yorrick looked shocked. "Better than that, I hope. We all are such strangers that even the backs of our hands appear to be a foreign country. But I'll take your word if you'll lead me to good spirits and a warm fire. I felt a chill in Eden Castle that would have forewarned even Satan himself."

"It's not the castle; it's my father," Albert commented, the two men walking abreast now, Albert with his hands shoved deeply into his pockets, Yorrick Harp with his arm about Albert's shoulder.

"Ah, your father," Mr. Harp mourned. "A strange and sad man. I've known his kind before. Really to be pitied, and you must remember that, Albert. No sadder sight in this world or any other than the spectacle of a man incapable of giving or receiving love. He suffers a perpetual chill that no fire can warm and departs this vale of tears as he entered it–alone, always alone."

"Sometimes I hate him."

"No, you must never hate him, or any other man, even those who give you just reason. The expense of hating someone is too great."

"But he insulted you."

"Insults are always in the eyes of the beholder, Albert. No man can insult you if you try to understand a modicum of his inner pain, for insults grow out of pain, jealousy, a sense of abandonment and loneliness; all these things contribute to the soul's discomfort and precede insults. Now where are we? You are my beacon. Pray, do not lead me astray."

They had come to the inner courtyard gates. About thirty yards beyond, Albert saw the manned outer gates, full watchmen on duty around the clock, charting the identity and progress of anyone entering and departing the castle courtyard. It was Albert's intention to circumvent the outer gatehouse and cut along the castle wall to a spot he had discovered long ago as a child, as had every other child in Eden Castle, a place where there was a small narrow escape hatch, built into the original wall hundreds of years ago, to accommodate the pirating activity of an earlier lord of Eden Castle.

"This way, sir," Albert signaled and turned abruptly as they passed through the unattended inner gate and led the way down a slight incline, always following the line of the inner wall.

"A diversion?" Mr. Harp asked, keeping his voice down in the spirit of adventure.

"More or less," Albert nodded. "A small door in the castle wall, straight ahead."

"Imagine," Yorrick marveled. "Did pirates use it?"

"So I've been told."

"Imagine–"

The joy and excitement in Mr. Harp's voice washed over Albert like warm channel waters on an August morning. When he was ready, he reached out, despite the darkness, and found the door exactly where he had remembered it and felt it give, the hinges only mildly creaking, felt on the other side the first blast of chilling channel breeze and knew of the hazards yet ahead, the treacherous cliff walk which led down into Mortemouth, a stone descent made doubly dangerous without benefit of lantern.

No matter. As Albert stood back to hold the door for Mr. Harp, he felt his excitement yet increasing and vowed to be alert, recording everything, so that on those cold, lonely nights at school, secure in his cell, surrounded by books informing him of dead events, Albert might close his eyes and recall this miraculous evening in which he had the good fortune to be in the company of the most rare, most alive, most caring man that Albert had ever met.

Though exhausted beyond description, Eleanor sat late before the Great Hall fire, enjoying the relaxed company of Richard and John. Stephen was there as well, clearly delighted with his new son.

Alexander Burke Eden.

Quite a name, Eleanor thought, very distinguished. She had sensed John's disappointment that Eve and Stephen had given the baby the middle name of the maternal grandfather and had ignored John altogether.

She had promised Alice that she would wait in the Great Hall until Susan returned with the wet nurse and would bring both of them up immediately. Alice had managed to forestall young Alexander's hunger with sugar water for several hours, but he could not be forestalled for much longer.

"Richard, the time, please," Eleanor requested, amazed at how loud her voice sounded in the silence of the Great Hall, which was broken only by the crackling of wood.

"Ten past," Richard murmured, examining his pocket watch.

"Ten past what?"

"Midnight."

"So late," Eleanor worried. "What could be keeping her?"

John drew himself forward as though to better focus on a point of fascination deep in the fire well. "Where was she going?"

"To Mortemouth. I believe she said to young Theresa Johnson."

"You know Susan," John muttered. "She has undoubtedly found at least a dozen lost and injured souls along the way. She will return only after she tends to them."

"Where's Alice?" Eleanor asked in a clear attempt to change the subject. John Murrey was at heart a good man, but sometimes it taxed one's patience to the limit to be around him.

"Alice is upstairs with Eve," Stephen volunteered.

"And Eve? How is she doing?" John asked, reaching forward and patting Stephen's knee in an affectionate gesture.

"She's weak. Alice thinks we need to take her to London for a thorough examination."

"What does Alice know?" John demanded angrily, sitting upright with a ferocity that drew everyone's attention.

Stephen looked surprised. "Alice is tending to Eve. She's–"

"Has my daughter become a physician when I wasn't looking?" John asked of anyone who cared to answer his sarcasm. "No, of course not. She is a nurse practitioner, a young practitioner still hard at her studies. Dr. Reicher told me of her insolence, and I fully intend to deal with it."

Eleanor saw a new look of weariness pass over Stephen's face, as though he knew his father's moods as well as anyone and really didn't care to become involved with them.

"She was instrumental in saving Eve's life," Stephen pronounced slowly, as though this was all he was going to say on the subject and nothing more.

"Nonsense," John countered flatly.

Against her better judgment, Eleanor stepped closer to the fire with a contribution of her own. "It isn't nonsense, John. I was there. Outside the door. But Susan was in the very chamber and told me herself how Dr.

Reicher saw no need for sutures after he had performed the surgery that freed the birth canal."

"Eleanor, please, spare us the details," Richard said, looking quite pale about the gills.

She heard Stephen murmur, "Never again," and slowly he leaned forward to bury his face in his hands.

"Here, here," echoed Richard. "It is just . . . too unpredictable. And too difficult."

Eleanor listened. It was both sad and amusing to see this male gallery swearing off any future birth ordeals. She wondered with a faint smile if they remembered the necessity to swear off another favorite activity nine months before the birth. Poor men, Eleanor mused. At times they were pinnacles of strength, and at other times . . .

Suddenly there was a loud knock at the Great Hall door. They all looked up and then at each other.

"I imagine it's Susan," Eleanor said.

"Why would she knock?" John asked.

The knock came again, a bit louder, a bit more insistent.

"I'll go," John offered. "If it is Susan, why didn't she come in through the kitchen court?"

"Perhaps she has the girl with her," Eleanor offered.

"She's not going to bring her in here, is she?" Richard complained, clearly not looking forward to the sight of a buxom North Devon girl with full breasts dripping milk.

For several seconds there was no sound except the measured tread of John's boots as he walked the distance to the Great Hall doors. Halfway there, Eleanor saw two footmen, lamps in hand, coming from the small room to the left, where they'd apparently been dozing.

"Bring the light closer," John ordered.

One of the footmen drew back the heavy doors, and though Eleanor could not see who was standing on the other side, she did see John freeze in a welcoming position, saw Stephen hurry up behind him and stop, stunned. Richard was the last to arrive, and he, too, stared into the cold night with an expression of bewilderment on his face, equal to the others. Suddenly she heard Stephen's hushed, surprised voice.

"Frederick? Is it you?"

Eleanor increased her step, thinking, How grand–Frederick home safe from far-off India. New bride, he was bringing a new bride. Late March? This wasn't late March. They had arrived early.

As she hurried toward the happy confusion at the door, she saw that it was indeed Frederick, a very tall, lean, weary-looking Frederick, quite grown-up and dignified in his black coat and white clerical collar. Father Frederick, imagine! The Edens after all these centuries of scoundrels and pirates had at last managed to produce a priest for the Church of England.

She saw John embrace him, then Richard warmly shook his hand, while Stephen waited impatiently to be next. The two boys, always close, had not seen each other for years. Eleanor stopped a distance from the reunion as the two boys embraced, a prolonged intimacy that caused her eyes to blur.

The two boys said something to each other, so quietly no one could hear. Then Frederick withdrew a handkerchief and wiped his eyes. As Stephen did the same with the back of his hand, the boys grinned at one another.

Then it was Eleanor's turn. She'd waited long enough. After all, it was she who had spent countless hours reading the stories of the Bible to Frederick and felt that perhaps, just perhaps, she had set him on the path that had led him into God's work.

As she stepped forward, Frederick saw her, and she found the expression of affection on his face extremely gratifying and opened her arms to him and was not prepared for his warm embrace, a massive bear hug that literally swept her off her feet and left her gasping at this tall, handsome young man who once had sat on her lap and begged just one more time to hear the Parable of the Prodigal.

"The prodigal," she said at the end of the embrace.

"In a way," he smiled. "It's so good to see you, Aunt Eleanor, to see you all. I know we are early, but we arrived in Liverpool and saw no need to wait around."

We?

Eleanor looked beyond the gathering out onto the cold, wet Great Hall steps, hoping that they hadn't been so rude as to leave someone standing about unwelcomed on this horrible night.

"My wife," Frederick grinned. "I warned you in the message, remember?"

"Of course we remember," Stephen exclaimed. "Where is she? Surely you haven't abandoned her in the night?"

"No, she is waiting in the carriage. I thought it best—considering. May I call her forward?"

"Please do," John commanded. "You should have brought her to the door."

Frederick stepped out onto the Great Hall steps and hurried down to a very muddy and road-weary carriage. It was plain black and stolid-looking and bore the small insignia of the Church of England on the side of its door, obviously loaned to Frederick by the Church.

As they all craned to catch a glimpse of Frederick's bride, Eleanor wondered again with rising annoyance where Susan was. She should be here. After all, Frederick was her stepson and they were very fond of each other.

She looked down the steps to where Frederick was helping a young woman out of the carriage. Eleanor saw only the top of her head at first, a lovely reddish blond head of hair, her hood having fallen back.

She seemed to be moving out of the carriage with extreme difficulty. Frederick was very attentive and clearly concerned. Eleanor peered past John's shoulder and heard his muffled curse, saw Richard's shocked expression and then saw Stephen's face break into a wide grin.

"This is my wife, Marjorie," Frederick smiled up from the bottom of the steps and, carefully supporting her by the elbow, guided a very lovely, a very weary, a very apologetic, a very pregnant young wife up the stairs.

All the way down the steep cliff walk, Yorrick Harp sang "Jenny Crack Corn" at the top of his voice, exhibiting no fear of the treacherous old stones, wet now and polished smooth from years of traffic.

Amazed, Albert brought up the rear and wondered how long a man had to live, what he had to do, in order to reach such an inspiring level of bravery.

Yorrick stopped at midpoint where the stone face of the cliff had been chiseled away and a crude bench had been carved to accommodate weary climbers who had successfully reached this position of relative safety. Albert watched him staring out over the black, turbulent waters where the channel collided with the Atlantic Ocean. The sea was rough, covered with dancing whitecaps as far as the eye could see.

Quietly Albert came up alongside Yorrick Harp, feeling neither the chilling rain nor the cutting wind.

"The abyss is great," he heard the older man say quietly as he reached back and drew Albert forward until he was standing alongside him. He placed his arm around Albert's shoulder, a closeness that caused Albert to shiver in a way that had nothing to do with the cold night. He had never been touched thus by a man–by a woman either, for that matter. He had grown up with a busy nurse for a mother and a distant father. If it hadn't been for his cousins and his Aunt Eleanor, Albert would very likely have made it from birth until now never knowing the touch of a human hand at all.

"You're shivering," Mr. Harp exclaimed and, within the instant, unbuttoned his heavy jacket and drew it around Albert's shoulders, pulling him yet closer.

"I'm certain this is an old experience for you, my boy," Mr. Harp said quietly, "this spectacular night scene, but I've never seen anything quite like it. Look, light in the distance, the welcoming light of a far country and yet between you and its welcoming shores the deepest, blackest abyss imaginable. Look down if you dare. There is nothing there."

Politely Albert disagreed. "A sandy beach–"

"In summer perhaps, but not visible now."

"No."

"Nothing is visible except distant lights and vast empty places."

He paused and stood still, but caught in the folds of his jacket, Albert could feel his heart beating.

"My life has been like that," Yorrick Harp mused. "Distant lights and vast empty places. I had wanted so to make a difference."

"I'm sure you have."

"No, not in any significant way. I will be forgotten."

"I will never forget you."

Yorrick Harp laughed. "I'll tell you a secret," he confided, still staring over the blackness of distance and night. "Despite the faraway beacons of light, I am most curious about the vast empty places, the creases in the universe where no one has been, the voice that no one hears, the adventures that no one returns to tell us about. I am endlessly, painfully curious about all that. As much as I love this life, I have frequently thought that of late I have come to love death more."

Albert determined to ask this rare man one question, a very important question, because in all his life no one had satisfactorily answered it. "How, Mr. Harp, does anyone learn not to be afraid?"

For several seconds Albert wasn't certain his question had been heard.

"My dearest Albert, one–at least this one–has never learned not to be afraid. The best one can manage to learn is how costly fear is and how dreadfully expensive to the soul. So the only accommodation one makes to fear is to learn how to say, 'No, I'm sorry, but I can't afford you. My poor purse simply will not go the distance.' "

Albert listened carefully, not certain that he was understanding everything but recording it in his memory, to be brought out on a day when he needed it.

"You are meant for a great destiny, Albert," Mr. Harp said, "and don't ever doubt it. Keep your vision fixed on the future. I suspect that there is a desperate need somewhere that only you can fill."

"I will."

"Of course you will. You don't need old Yorrick to nag at you. Come, the chill is at last beginning to penetrate. We have a birth to toast and a warrior to welcome home. Come, lead the way to– What was the name of the pub?"

"The Hanging Man."

Yorrick Harp smiled. "Not very promising. Still, it's not names we're interested in, is it? Just a few pints, a warm fire, friendly faces, then back up these same steps to Eden Castle. Quite a grand place, isn't it? What memories you must have of growing up within those ancient walls? Will you tell me someday? Everything? I want to hear them all. Promise?"

Albert saw his wide grin in the dark and grinned back. "Come along, Mr. Harp," Albert said and led the way down the steep cliff walk. He felt more surefooted now, more capable of leading the way. Now it was Albert's turn to lift his face and smile at the moonless night and issue a soft, brief, but very heartfelt prayer to the generous God who had sent him Yorrick Harp.

"Please, always let me bask in the warmth of his company, Dear God. Let me follow him wherever he goes."

At the end of his prayer he called back in a voice surprising in its strength and purpose. "Not far, Mr. Harp, straight ahead as soon as we touch bottom."

And the miraculous voice came from behind him sailing over his head and into his heart, a raucous, full-throated Old Testament voice: "I am your servant, Albert, always your servant. Destiny awaits! Lead on!"

And Albert did. With remarkable speed, they traversed the lower half of the cliff walk, the dim lights of the sleepy little fishing village named Mortemouth drawing ever closer.

Mortemouth had nestled at the foot of Eden's cliffs for as long as anyone could remember. Albert's father had told all of the children, in one of his endless lectures on Eden history, that mention of a community at Death's Mouth had been found in the earliest writings on Eden Point in the eighth century. Apparently they had called it Death's Mouth because of the frequently stormy collision of the channel with the Atlantic Ocean.

Now it was called Mortemouth, the Latin influence clearly that of an early papist, though long since had the Roman Catholic Church fled. "A godless place," the last priest had pronounced as he had fled back up the cliff to the rest of England and civilization.

Now there was a small Anglican church there, though the bishop usually sent to Mortemouth a man who was dead or dying, and with a wife to match. There was little of soul saving, little of plate passing, and little of hymn singing. The locals were fond of saying that Mortemouth had won out over God.

And it was a rough, no-holds-barred, law-unto-itself sort of place, no one could deny that. None of the Eden children had ever been permitted to run the cliff walks alone. In fact, Albert wasn't too certain even now that his father would be pleased with what he was doing, but damn his father.

Albert halted at the bottom to catch his breath and get his bearings. It had been years since he had made the descent into Mortemouth, though once, as a boy, he had joined Stephen and Frederick and Geoffrey in a late-night adventure down the cliff walk. But once down, they had grown so frightened that they had raced all the way back up to the safety of Eden Point and the friendly sight of the burly watchmen at the gatehouse.

Albert looked about at the dark, narrow, fogbound streets straight ahead. The cobbles shown in the night with the reflected dull yellow eye of the shopwindow lanterns. Everywhere he heard the constant meowing of hungry cats.

"Where are the good citizens of Mortemouth?" Yorrick Harp asked, close by his elbow.

"Abed, I imagine, or in the pub."

"And where is this pub?" Yorrick Harp asked with simple politeness. Clearly his thirst was increasing.

"This way," Albert nodded and started down the rough cobbles toward the end of the street.

Their boots gave off an eerie clatter in the silence of the night. Once, Albert heard movement coming from a darkened doorway and warned himself not to turn on it. According to his father and Uncle Richard, the fishermen of Mortemouth were harmless when left alone, but they intensely disliked any intruder. The sea, the tides and the catches were whimsical and cruel enough. On land the fishermen craved certitude and no surprises.

"Turn here," Albert instructed as they reached the end of the street. To his right, exactly as he remembered it, was a narrow, cobbled alley. At the end of this alley, Albert saw the signboard squeaking in the cold wind which blew in off the Atlantic, a salt-faded hand-lettered sign announcing The Hanging Man. The town gallows had stood directly in front of the pub, a convenient location, because hanging a man apparently produced a powerful thirst.

Even several yards from the pub, Albert heard laughter, shouting and a flat violin screeching out a discordant melody. The small soot-covered front window was coated over with steam from the warm bodies inside.

"Is this the place?" Yorrick Harp asked.

"I'm afraid, sir, that it is all Mortemouth has to offer."

"It's perfect," Mr. Harp beamed and led the way toward the low front door. "Come, lad, let's join the locals in their merriment. I've coin enough in my pocket to buy a pint for all."

It was Yorrick who pushed the door open and was forced to stoop in order to clear the low doorframe. Albert followed and heard the violin slowly squeak to a halt, heard no sound at all coming from the once lively and crowded pub.

He peered about while Yorrick Harp was closing the door, and saw a low-beamed ceiling and several oil lamps on the walls burning too high, filling the room with the smell of dead fish. At the end of the narrow room he saw an open-pit fire, the carcass of a pig roasting on the spit, fat-flared flames shooting upward toward the browning meat.

He saw a haphazard arrangement of a dozen or so small tables made out of low-cut whisky barrels. On each barrel burned a candle, the combined half-light sending shadows skittering over the darkened walls and the weathered faces which stared back at them with expressionless eyes.

To the left was the bar and behind it a rotund barkeep with red hair and full, ruddy cheeks. He worked slowly, drying off a row of mugs with the hem of his soiled apron. There were at least fifty people crammed into the narrow, smelly, overwarm room, and their faces froze as they watched Albert and Yorrick Harp. Not one eye blinked, not one mouth opened in a smile of welcome, not one word was spoken, the entire pub was filled with suspicious, hostile citizens of Mortemouth.

Albert realized he had made a mistake in bringing Yorrick Harp here.

"Come, Mr. Harp," he murmured, but Yorrick had started off in a jagged direction, heading unerringly toward the bar and the barkeep, who in turn had leveled his gaze on the advancing stranger as though warning him to keep his distance.

"The best of evenings to you, my good friend," Yorrick Harp pronounced with unfailing politeness.

He waited a moment to see if any response would be forthcoming, and when it wasn't, he stepped closer to the bar all the while glancing about at the silent pub.

"Please correct me, sir, if I am wrong. My young friend and I were of the opinion that this is a public house."

"It is that," the barkeep said gruffly and went on wiping a mug on the hem of his apron.

"Well, then," Yorrick Harp said with a smile of relief, "if it isn't asking too much, would it be possible for us to purchase two pints of your best ale? We have a joyous celebration to get under way."

"No celebration here," the barkeep responded and turned his back, leaving Yorrick Harp to contemplate his backside and the deepening silence.

"I fail to understand," he said at last and glanced toward Albert, who continued to stand by the front door.

In the prolonged silence, Albert looked around the shadowy pub. He saw seated in the back of the room at a single table which sat on a small raised platform Geoffrey's two aides, the same men who had accompanied Geoffrey into battle and who had recently accompanied him back across the moors to Eden Castle and home.

Apparently the habitués of the pub, led by Teddy and William, had been trying to drown their embarrassment at England's defeat in South Africa. It was a mood, Albert feared, that stretched the length and breadth of England, for up until now the word "defeat" had been foreign to Englishmen.

Now, since no one had answered Yorrick Harp's soft admission that he failed to understand, Albert started forward out of the shadows, intent on pleading with his friend to leave with him at once.

"Ah, there you are, young Eden. Come, come greet these good people. I am certain they would appreciate a word from an Eden of Eden Castle and Eden Point."

Albert felt heat rising on his face. He considered turning and exiting the pub, confident that Yorrick Harp would follow. He was on the verge of doing this when he heard the barkeep speak his name in quite a different tone of voice.

"Mr. Eden. Begging your pardon, I–we–did not see you there by the door. Please come forward. It is an honor to welcome you."

By the time Albert reached the bar, there was a smile on the barkeep's face, an extended hand and two filled pints waiting side by side.

"Again, my apologies, Mr. Eden."

"No need, I assure you."

"It's him there we don't know, don't you see?"

"Then allow me to introduce all of you to Mr. Yorrick Harp, a very important man from America and an honored guest at Eden Castle."

Mr. Harp executed a low theatrical bow and extended his hand to the barkeep. "My most sincere pleasure, I assure you," he smiled. "Barkeeps are, in my opinion, among the world's greatest treasures. They provide us all with a ready means of escape from this web of reality in which we find ourselves ensnared. They lighten our hearts and make short our days and promise us peace at the end of the struggle, and for that we all should be eternally grateful."

As again Yorrick bowed low, Albert saw the expressions of bewilderment increase on the nearby faces. Clearly they had not understood a word Yorrick had said.

No matter. It was Albert's wish simply to down his ale as rapidly as possible and flee this dim, smoky place.

As he lifted his pint, he saw Yorrick Harp swallow thirstily, never stopping for air, while the barkeep and everyone else looked on.

When the mug was drained, Yorrick Harp placed it on the scarred bar and grinned.

"The best," he praised. "Just the best I have ever tasted. Is it local?"

"Comes from Exeter," the barkeep muttered and started to whisk the empty pint away.

But Yorrick Harp protested. "Oh, another, if you will," he said. "The first was for my thirst, the second will be for the cause of my celebration."

"No celebration," the barkeep repeated now with single-minded insistence. "I shouldn't have to tell you why, Mr. Eden, not when your cousin lies wounded and bleeding this very moment inside the walls of Eden Castle."

Suddenly from the back of the pub came a strong voice. "You've had your pint. Now get out, both of you."

As Albert turned toward the voice, so did Yorrick Harp. They squinted through the smoky interior of the pub, back toward the table from whence the voice had come.

For a moment, there was no recognition, then, "Ah, yes. Our two friends from the Great Hall. The reluctant dancers, you remember, don't you, Albert?"

Despite what he had said, Albert saw a warm smile on Yorrick's face as he began to make his way slowly through the crowded pub to where the two aides were seated.

Albert considered going after him, but he didn't particularly want to navigate that crowded canal by himself and now, after Yorrick Harp had passed, the crowd had filled in behind him as though to block his exit.

Albert glanced nervously toward the barkeep. But the man hurried toward the end of the bar, the better to hear and see.

Reluctantly Albert followed him and found it easy to see the raised platform at the far end of the pub where Yorrick Harp was greeting the two aides as though they were old friends instead of new enemies.

"My greetings again to both of you," he said in that grand theatrical manner which in Eden Castle had seemed courtly and appropriate but which in these mean surroundings seemed to mock the inhabitants of this simple community of fishermen.

There was no response from the two aides.

"May I sit with you?" he heard Yorrick ask, his voice clear, his motives less clear.

The request caught the two aides off guard. Albert saw them glance at one another, and while they were trying to agree upon a response, Yorrick sat in an empty chair to their left, his mug still in his hand.

"Now tell me of your exploits in South Africa. I want to hear every detail. Wars and warriors fascinate me. They are throwbacks to a lost age when men knew only one way to settle their differences and that was by selecting a sizable club and beating each other senseless." Yorrick held up both hands in mock amusement. "Two men dead, differences settled."

Albert closed his eyes and prayed that the two aides would not be able to understand precisely what Yorrick Harp was saying.

Apparently they didn't, and for that Albert offered up a brief prayer and heard the aide named Teddy begin to speak.

"We've told our story before–"

"Then I beg you, tell it again."

"You go to hell–"

As their voices dwindled off in a compression of hate, Albert pushed his mug aside. Enough. Fetch Yorrick Harp as quickly as possible and leave these people alone to mourn in their own way.

He was about to start forward when he saw Harp rise to his feet, mug lifted.

"I came up here for a toast and now I offer one. Please join me," he said, addressing the entire pub.

He waited a moment. When no mugs were lifted, he went on. "I toast new life on this night. I toast men who possess the courage to order their own destinies, to resist the hysteria of false patriotism, who on all occasions and in all matters are moral leaders rather than followers."

"Wait a minute," the aide named Teddy protested angrily.

"For the last three days," Harp went on, "a young woman in Eden Castle has labored to bring forth life. Tonight she was successful. A new Eden was born. Now my only prayer for this new life is that if the time comes when he is confronted with the false call of his greedy country that he possess the moral conviction to tell them he has no appetite and less inclination to help slaughter his fellow man."

"He will be a coward then," someone shouted from the back of the pub.

"No, my friend, he will be one of the bravest men who ever lived."

"He won't be no Eden then, for Eden men have answered the call of their country for centuries and always will."

"Even the Edens go through a period of evolution. They are not born perfect, just more blessed than most."

"Then you're saying that what we did was wrong?" William asked, slowly rising from his chair.

"Yes," Yorrick replied.

Albert listened, eyes down. When Yorrick Harp's voice fell silent, Albert tried to read the silence. Had he truly persuaded the aides to any point of view other than their own?

"There's a foul smell in here."

Albert looked up at the sound of this deep male voice but could not locate it. It wasn't the aides. They had not spoken.

Then there was another voice, "Aye, I've been smelling it for some time now."

"Can you name it?"

"I can. Cowardice. It's the yellow, putrid smell of cowardice."

Alarmed, Albert stood. Yorrick Harp had accomplished nothing except perhaps to anger them further.

"Mr. Harp–" As Albert lifted his voice above the rising voices of the others, he caught Yorrick Harp's eye and with one hand strongly motioned him to come forward quickly and join him at the door.

Relieved, Albert saw Yorrick step down from the platform and lift both hands in a staying gesture to the angry voices rising all about him.

In order to speed their exit, Albert placed more than sufficient coin on the bar to cover the cost of the ale, then hurried toward the door. Beyond the soot-stained window, he saw sleet, the storm increasing. The cliff walk would be even more difficult going up than it had been coming down. No matter. Anywhere would be better than this place, with voices rising all about, resentful voices that England's exploits in general, and Teddy and William's in particular, should be so cruelly criticized and belittled and–Albert suspected that this was the worst–by an American.

When he reached the door, he looked back to check on Yorrick's progress. Shocked, Albert observed that he had scarcely made it a quarter of the way out of the pub. Men were rising from their chairs to block his passage. A woman spat upon him. Yet another hurled the rind end of a piece of cheese and all the time the voices were rising yet higher, shouting insults.

He tried to make eye contact with Yorrick Harp, to speed him on his way, but the large man merely smiled with great tenderness on his persecutors, reaching out his hand in greeting to the woman who had spat upon him, saluting the man who had just given him a particularly brutal shove.

Suddenly there was a peculiar sound that seemed to cancel all other sounds, one of speed followed by a soft impact.

Following that there was silence falling rapidly upon the once shouting patrons of The Hanging Man.

As Albert was turning, he caught a glance at Yorrick Harp. The man stood as though suspended in the middle of the narrow passage that led to the front door. His face was curiously uplifted, mouth opened, his eyes fixed on the low-beamed ceiling. His lips were moving as though he were trying to speak but was for some reason unable to articulate a word.

"Mr. Harp," Albert called out, pleased that the unruly crowd seemed to have come to their senses and were now slowly withdrawing.

As Albert extended a hand, Yorrick took one step forward, then suddenly fell face downward.

"Mr. Harp," Albert called out, new alarm taking the place of old. What now? Was the man ill? How in the name of God could Albert carry him up the cliff walk?

But as he drew near to his friend, his thoughts stopped, as he saw, imbedded in the fabric of Mr. Harp's jacket, a knife, hurled with murderous speed and accuracy, and penetrating the ribcage in the vicinity of the heart.

Unable to move, unable to speak, unable to focus on anything except the knife and the rapidly spreading blood on Yorrick Harp's back, Albert stared down, aware of the growing silence about him as though at last, with this single barbaric act, the people had managed to shock themselves.

"Mr. Harp," Albert murmured. He dropped to his knees beside the sprawled man and noticed slight movement in one hand.

He saw Yorrick Harp's face, turned sideways, mouth opened. His lips were moving but Albert couldn't hear what he was saying and bent lower.

"Let me get you home, sir," he begged. "Back to Eden Castle. There's a doctor. He can–"

But as Albert spoke, he saw a new grimace on Yorrick Harp's face, saw fresh blood seeping down the side of his jacket in a continuous stream. Again he saw Yorrick Harp's lips moving and bent closer.

"Tell Eve . . . that the first statement I shall make upon meeting this . . . God is to thank him for . . . her, for her beauty, her soul, her song. Tell her . . ."

Albert listened, aware of new movement in the pub behind him.

As he looked up, he saw several men rising from their chairs as though a new alliance was being formed, saw the two aides, Teddy and William, gone, saw the few women present move together, strange hard smiles of satisfaction on their lined faces.

One of the men stood directly over Mr. Harp's legs. "Your friend has passed over," the man smiled.

"No, he was speaking to me–"

"He's dead, laddie," the man insisted, louder this time, his manner threatening.

Albert continued to kneel beside the lifeless body as he struggled to digest the truth of what had happened. What would he tell the others? What would he tell Eve and Stephen?

"Laddie, you'd best run off now. We got things to do here."

It was the male voice again, clearly threatening.

"No," Albert protested, wiping tears from his eyes, "I must take Mr. Harp–"

"You'll be taking him nowhere."

The voice turned low and menacing. The large man stepped closer, and behind him, Albert saw a half dozen others.

"Please," he begged, trying to back away, not wanting to leave his friend but wanting desperately to escape.

In the last moments before he collided with the door, he heard the raucous laughter of the men and saw one man bend over and pull the knife from Mr. Harp's back.

Then he felt the opened door behind him, felt the chill night air, and fleeing the scene, he turned and ran off into the night, racing in the opposite direction of the cliff walk that led back to Eden Castle, for Eden Castle was the last place he wanted to go now.

On down the cobbles he ran toward the end of Mortemouth and the beginning of the moors, in search of a dark, quiet place where he could no longer see the knife embedded in Yorrick Harp's back or hear the blood gurgling in his throat as he spoke his last words of Eve and souls and song.

Eden Castle

Frederick awakened early to a dazzling sun in his boyhood room on the third floor of Eden Castle, one he had shared with Stephen. Turning away from the narrow window that afforded a perfect view of the Bristol Channel, he closed his eyes, drew his dressing gown more tightly about him and gave heartfelt thanks for their safe arrival at Eden Castle. Their journey had seemed endless and full of hazards. It had been three full months ago that they had sailed from India, weathering two storms, poor Marjorie spending her days in bed in their cabin below deck.

At the thought of his wife, Frederick concluded his prayer and glanced back toward the four-poster and saw Marjorie still asleep. Her beauty, both inner and outer, filled his heart, as it never failed to do. Why God had been so generous as to allow him to share his life with Marjorie Housman, Frederick still wasn't certain.

She was the eldest daughter of the Anglican Bishop of Northern India, the Reverend Michael Housman. Frederick had first noticed young Marjorie six years earlier when he had gone out to India as scarcely more than a young man. A schoolgirl then, she had nonetheless captured his attention with her almost mesmerizing presence, a gentle spirit half English, half Indian, for she had been born and had spent her entire life in the simple white mission house outside Delhi. And at some point the little schoolgirl had blossomed into the rarest flower Frederick had ever seen, fair-haired, blue-eyed, with alabaster skin and a character that contained the best of both the Eastern and Western worlds.

Marjorie had worked alongside him in the classroom and clinics of Delhi, and her parents had even permitted her to go out into the country missions with him as though they had known from the beginning and had approved of his affections. It had been on one such mission that Frederick had watched her take an infant from a dying mother, had watched her hold the dark-skinned baby close, had seen her kiss it and cradle it and weep with it for its dead mother and walk with it a distance away into the high heat of the Indian sun. When she returned, her eyes red from weeping, she announced that the little girl would grow up in the mission of Delhi.

Thinking on these events, Frederick returned to the bed and sat on the edge, slowly drinking in his wife's beauty.

"Good morning."

The soft voice coming from the sleeping face startled Frederick. Pleased, he saw her eyes open, saw her stretch as much as her protruding belly would permit, saw her frown, then smile and reach for his hand and place it on her stomach.

"Your son is awake," she smiled, and beneath his hand he felt movement, a rippling effect at first, followed by a thump.

"Not long now," Marjorie said.

"How did you sleep?"

"Like the dead."

Suddenly she propped herself up on her elbows, a worried look on her face. "Is there a breakfast hour? We mustn't be late."

Frederick shook his head. "There's always just a buffet in the dining room and Stephen told me we should sleep until we are fully rested."

"He seems nice, Stephen. I look forward to knowing him better."

"He's a good brother. I've missed him. He's all that a man need ask for both as a brother and a friend."

"And a new father as well," Marjorie smiled. "Two little cousins born in the same month. Imagine . . ."

Frederick stretched out beside her, clasping her hand, and stared straight up at the low, cracked ceiling. "Stephen and I once shared this bed."

"I look forward to meeting his wife today."

"Eve–"

"Do you know her?"

"No, they met in America. Her mother is my father's half sister."

"There were so many names last night, so many faces," sighed Marjorie, "I'll never get them straight."

"Of course you will."

"I think we should go to London for the birth, Frederick."

"Why?"

"Your father and your uncle appeared less than happy with my . . . condition."

Frederick laughed. "They have just gone through a difficult time with Eve. Besides, Aunt Eleanor would insist that we stay."

"Still, I think we should offer."

"Then we will, of course. How are you feeling?" he asked, wondering if it was possible to love her any more than he did now.

"I'm feeling immense," Marjorie smiled. "And I'm ready for him to come, but I shall miss him."

"How do you know it's a boy?"

She shrugged and smiled, "A feeling, just a–"

There was a knock at the door. Like guilty children, they drew the coverlet up around their necks.

"Who is it?" Frederick called out.

"It's me, sir, name of Trudy, a lady's maid, sir. Lady Eleanor sent me to help Miss Marjorie with her morning affairs."

Puzzled, Frederick looked at Marjorie who returned his glance, equally puzzled. "My . . . affairs?" she whispered, then broke into irrepressible giggling and withdrew under the coverlet, hiding her head entirely.

"Did you hear, sir?" came the voice again. "And there's a gentleman in your dressing room, name of Henry, come to help you with your affairs."

Frederick closed his eyes and shook his head. "We are home," he murmured. The last time he'd had a gentleman's man was here at Eden Castle, and it was his guess that Marjorie had never in her life known the services of a lady's maid.

Then perhaps it was time. "Give us just a moment, Trudy, then you may enter."

Marjorie came up out of the cover, protesting, "No, Frederick, please. I have never–"

"Then it's time. You'll enjoy it. You deserve to be pampered."

"No, Frederick, I would feel embarrassed."

"She will help you dress, that's all, and help you fix your hair–"

"I've been dressing and fixing my hair since I was four."

"You are at Eden now. When in Rome, . . ."

As Frederick spoke, he eased out of bed, straightening his dressing gown, delighted at the new color freshly risen on Marjorie's face. She looked scarcely more than a little girl herself, despite her condition.

"Frederick, please," was her last plea before he opened the door to find a woman in black dress, white apron and lace cap with a small wicker basket of bottles in one hand and a stack of fresh white towels in the other.

"Hopin' I'm not disturbing, sir. As I say, my name is Trudy. Lady Eleanor said I was to come back if–"

"No, not at all, Trudy. I'm afraid I have no idea of the time."

"It's half past eleven, sir."

"Good Lord," he heard Marjorie gasp from the bed behind him.

The efficient Trudy waved behind her, and a second female appeared as if by magic, in her hands a delectable pot of steaming tea.

"Your gentleman's gentleman has yours, sir," Trudy smiled, seeing Frederick's look of longing. "Now be off with you," she added and took charge of the door. "It is good to have you home, Mr. Frederick. The entire family is looking forward to luncheon. The hour was so late last night–"

"I know," Frederick said, beginning to recall the feeling of Eden Castle, with its army of servants, all of whom seemed to dictate the order of every day, causing one at times to lose track of who was master, who the servant.

In his final glance through the bedroom door, he saw that Marjorie was having similar trouble. At the sight of the young serving girl carrying the heavy breakfast tray, Marjorie had left the bed as rapidly as her cumbersome size would permit, and, impervious to the shocked expression on Trudy's face, had taken the tray from the young girl and placed it on a near table.

"My lady, you mustn't," he heard Trudy scold.

"Of course I must," Marjorie countered, and at that, Frederick closed the door, coward that he was, and decided that the servants of Eden Castle were on their own as far as his wife was concerned. They would just have to find out for themselves that her one passionate dislike was the British class system. She felt one human being should perform services for another out of love and caring, not duty, an attitude that on occasion had confounded her own father, who was not opposed to her philosophies so long as they did not embarrass him.

Frederick walked thoughtfully down the corridor toward his dressing room and issued a brief prayer for the servants in Eden Castle, that they try to understand Marjorie's most heartfelt dream, the world united into one, no masters, no servants, only the whole fabric made strong by love and trust and mutual dependence.

It sounded so simple. Why was it so difficult to achieve?

Amazed as always by the strange ways in which God moved, Susan helped to settle Molly Jones in a chair near Eve's bed so that Eve might witness her son's first suckling. Susan had left Eden last night in search of Theresa Johnson, who was the wife of a Mortemouth fisherman and had given birth last week. But Susan had found Theresa gone to Ilfracombe to visit her mother.

Despairing, Susan had passed within a short distance of the waterfront and The Hanging Man pub when she had collided head-on with a very frightened Molly Jones. The last time Susan had seen the young woman, Molly had been quite pregnant. God alone knew who the father was. Now she wasn't pregnant at all, but in tearful fright, Molly told Susan that she had lost her baby three days before and had taken a job as barmaid at The Hanging Man and that there was a fearful ruckus going on there.

There was always a fearful ruckus going on at The Hanging Man, but Susan was more interested in Molly's condition.

"Are you all right?" she asked, drawing the girl to one side and feeling her shivering in the cold night.

"I'm . . . fine."

"Your milk, has it come down?"

"Oh, indeed, it's all over me all the time. No man wants nothin' to do with a cow like me."

Susan wished that she could keep it that way, for she suspected that poor Molly would go from one pregnancy straight into another as soon as possible.

"Will you come with me, Molly?" Susan asked kindly.

"Where, mum?"

"Up to Eden Castle."

The girl's eyes had grown wide. "I have no business at Eden Castle."

"Yes, you do. There is a very hungry newborn baby whose own

mother can't nurse him for a while. You will have a clean, warm room and all the food that you want if you'll come."

It had taken Molly about a half a second to nod eagerly and Susan had hurried her up the cliff walk, sharing her shawl, thanking God for the ruckus at The Hanging Man pub that had driven Molly out into the night and straight into Susan's arms.

Now she stood with Stephen and Alice and watched the hungry baby eagerly find the nipple, watched Molly grimace slightly as he drew down on her milk. But the discomfort lasted only a moment, then she had cuddled the baby close and announced in a whisper, "My dead 'un was a boy too."

Then all that was heard was the sound of suckling and the crackling of the fire.

Stephen moved back to Eve's bed and kissed her on the forehead. As the two talked lovingly, Susan was worried to see Eve still so pale.

She saw Alice sink wearily into a chair before the fire and doubted seriously if her daughter had slept or taken food for at least twenty-four hours. Now she came up quietly behind her and gently rubbed her neck. "You were marvelous, you know," she said softly. "I am so proud."

Alice reached for her hand in gratitude and pressed it against her cheek. "So little is known about women's medicine," she said. "Male physicians scarcely consider it a legitimate course of study."

"I know," Susan agreed.

"No, you don't," Alice replied without rancor, merely a statement of fact. "The numbers of women who die daily at St. Martin's is criminal. The really difficult cases are left to the nurses."

"You must do the best that you can and that's all you can do," Susan counseled quietly. As she spoke the words she realized how empty and hollow they sounded when countered by Alice's passion.

"Look," Susan went on, affectionately stroking Alice's hair. "I want you to go and rest, then change for luncheon. It's going to be quite a grand affair in the dining hall, according to Eleanor. You haven't greeted Frederick and his wife yet. By the way, she's very pregnant."

Alice groaned. Susan laughed and hugged her affectionately. "They said something about going to London for the birth."

"Has she time?"

"Who knows? You go along, now. I'll stay."

"Eve should sleep."

"She's been asking all morning for Yorrick Harp. Apparently he hasn't been in to see her yet. Would you know where–"

From the bed Susan heard Stephen ask the same question. "Susan, have you seen Yorrick? Eve wants very much to see him."

"I have no idea. I'm sure he's about someplace. I shall have John launch a search."

"Probably he's sleeping," Eve said. "He used to say that one of the greatest luxuries in the world was a morning sleep."

"Not a bad idea for you," Alice suggested.

Molly whispered, "Look, he's fast asleep."

All eyes turned to the baby, clearly well satisfied with Molly's milk.

Carefully the wet nurse leaned forward and placed the child in Eve's arms. She took him eagerly and snuggled deep beneath the coverlet.

She grew tired almost instantly. "Find Yorrick, Stephen please. I want to see him so badly. I want him to see Alexander. I want him . . ."

Stephen stood up carefully from the side of the bed and bent over to kiss her. "I will. You rest now, and when I return, we will all have tea–you, me, Alexander and Yorrick."

Eve nestled deeper into the pillow, and even as they watched, her breathing grew steady, her whole body settled into a healing, peaceful sleep.

Placing a finger on her lips, Alice motioned that Molly and Stephen were to come with her. To Susan she said, "I'll be back within the hour."

"No, take your time. Tell John where I am and he's not to come to me or worry. And tell him to find Yorrick."

Susan watched as her most efficient daughter cleared the room and turned back with a smile. Then she was gone, closing the door behind her, leaving Susan staring down on the sleeping Eve cradling her son and looking more beautiful than ever.

She would leave them alone, mother and son. Their closeness was good and was of God and the infant could feed on his mother's love as surely as he had fed on Molly's milk and grow strong on both and face an imperfect world from a base of perfect love.

Eleanor had not been so nervous over entertaining since two years ago when Lord Kitchener and his entourage had passed the weekend at Eden Castle. His Lordship had spoken of nothing but war, had spoken longingly–or so it had seemed to Eleanor–of war with the Africans, war with the Germans, war with the French. It *was* coming, he had assured one and all and what the British army needed most desperately were well-trained officers who regarded war as war and not like polo with intervals for afternoon tea.

Now, waiting alone in her Great Dining Hall, corseted in her best navy blue silk, her hair done up and secured with a small nosegay of silk violets, Eleanor studied the splendidly set table and realized that it had been Lord Kitchener's visit that had first fanned Geoffrey's interest in all matters military. Then damn Lord Kitchener, Eleanor thought angrily. She turned to inspecting the buffet which she and Mrs. Partridge had planned at dawn this morning.

She wondered now if it would be sufficient, this long sideboard on which rested lobster salad, chicken salad, oysters, roast pheasant, cold meat salad, a tureen of chowder, roasted potatoes, boiled potatoes, a dome of sprouts, a shrimp mayonnaise, three aspics (two tomato, one celery), five rashers of bacon, a tureen of shirred eggs, cinnamon rounds, kippers, creamed curled onions, a rack of lamb, and a basket of Mrs. Partridge's famous raisin muffins.

Eleanor knew that Marjorie and Frederick had had only breakfast tea, knew for a fact that Richard and John had eaten breakfast before dawn and then had ridden out to check on a tenant farm. One of the housemaids had brought word that it had been abandoned, the tenants having packed up and left for London.

Eleanor brooded quietly, constantly arranging and rearranging the silverware on the sideboard. It was so difficult to keep tenants nowadays to work the land. They all believed the end of the rainbow was Trafalgar Square, complete with a pot of gold and their names on it.

Three maids were applying finishing touches under the precise guidance of Ghostly.

"It all looks splendid, Ghostly," Eleanor praised and saw the rigid, slim old man snap to attention.

"All thanks, my lady," Ghostly said. "Truly it will be a happy meal. Both boys returned."

Eleanor knew that Ghostly had reference to Stephen and Frederick and felt mild hurt as she thought three boys had returned, mindful of her Geoffrey, who had ordered his chamber doors locked to all except Dr. Reicher.

"I'm sorry, my lady–" It was old Ghostly again who belatedly realized his error. "Of course, there are three lads returned."

"No, Ghostly, you were right the first time," Eleanor agreed sadly, shaking her head. "Geoffrey might as well be–"

"I pray, don't say it, my lady. These things take time. Lord Geoffrey has suffered a terrible loss. He will come around, I assure you."

Grateful, Eleanor gave him a smile. "What would we do without you, dear Ghostly."

She saw a half smile of embarrassment on the lean old face, then saw him turn about and gently correct a young maid on the placement of cutlery. She wondered indeed what she or any of them would do without her household staff. Most had been with her at Eden Castle for at least twenty years. Many she had brought with her from her parents' home in Sussex. A great house such as Eden Castle needed an army of loyal workers in order to run at maximum efficiency, and it *did* run at maximum efficiency, with all credit due to her skillful household staff.

"If you will excuse us, my lady, will it be champagne for lunch?"

"Yes, of course. And Ghostly, please see to it that the staff in the kitchen court gets a glass as well."

Behind the scarecrow figure of Ghostly, Eleanor saw the three young maids smiling broadly. Then the old man was ushering them out of the dining hall and down the corridor to the kitchen steps where undoubtedly the true authority at Eden Castle, the cook, Mrs. Partridge had additional jobs awaiting them all.

Well then, all was ready and Eleanor paused near the vast sideboard mirror with its massive Gibbons frame. She looked up to admire Gibbons's artistry and to regret the harsh hand that nature appeared to be dealing her. In the wavy mirror she looked old, well beyond her forty years.

"Aunt Eleanor, have you seen Yorrick Harp?"

She whirled on the voice, embarrassed to be caught preening in front of the mirror, and saw Stephen poised in the doorway, looking quite rumpled and fatigued. Obviously he had passed the night at Eve's bedside.

"Yorrick? No, oh dear, nothing wrong, is it? Eve, is Eve–"

Stephen smiled reassuringly and came all the way into the dining hall. "Eve is fine, splendid as a matter of fact, Aunt Eleanor."

"And the baby . . . ?"

". . . is fine as well. Susan fetched an admirable wet nurse."

"Molly Jones," Eleanor sniffed, unable to mask the contempt in her voice. "She is, I'm afraid, a very loose young woman."

"No matter," Stephen reassured her. "She has rich milk, and my son will thrive on it until–"

"Of course," Eleanor agreed, mildly embarrassed to be discussing such matters with a man.

"Have you seen Yorrick Harp?" Stephen asked again. "Eve wants to see him."

"Mr. Harp?" Eleanor repeated vaguely and tried to place the last time she had seen him. "Yes, I saw Mr. Harp–"

"When? Where?"

"Last evening, late it was, in the Great Hall. He appeared to be trying to teach the girls, Lucy and Charlotte and, I believe, Albert–oh dear, I can't remember. It was quite a noisy crowd, I do remember that, and I remember as well that John was furious, felt it was a sign of disrespect to Geoffrey."

She saw bewilderment on Stephen's face and realized she wasn't making much sense. "I am sorry, Stephen. I'm afraid I haven't seen your friend since last evening."

"Albert then. Could you tell me where–"

At that moment Lucy and Charlotte appeared in the dining hall door. A sense of pride filled Eleanor as she watched the girls inspect the buffet, and a sense of bewilderment that she and Richard, plain people both, should have produced such a rare and natural beauty as Charlotte.

Now Lucy, following close behind her younger, prettier sister, was clearly their offspring. Plain but good-hearted, shy but sweet, gifted but not exceptional, Lucy clearly was theirs, and while Eleanor adored them both, Charlotte fascinated her as someone from an alien race might fascinate her, someone foreign to her and very exotic.

"How splendid you look, Charlotte," Eleanor smiled.

"Thank you, Mama. I wanted to make a good impression on Frederick and his new wife. The last time Frederick saw me I was a fat little schoolgirl."

Not likely, Eleanor thought with a smile. But she was certain that Frederick's missionary eye would indeed be dazzled by this vision in larkspur blue, a tucked lace bodice that climbed in delicate progression all the way up to a slim white throat while the rest of the bodice clung to perfectly shaped breasts, then plunged to the smallest waistline Eleanor had ever seen and at last flowed out in a becoming flounce that moved gracefully as Charlotte inspected the buffet, sampling a bit of lobster here, a grape there.

"You'll spoil your appetite," Eleanor warned and glanced once at Lucy in a plain, shapeless navy blue dress, her bodice loose-fitting and comfortable, her reddish hair pulled plainly back in a knot in the same fashion as old Mrs. Calvin, the nanny. In her pocket Eleanor saw the spine of a book. The girl was never happier than when she was tucked away in some quiet place reading. She would make some plain young man who did not demand too much of a woman a splendid wife.

Behind her at the dining hall door Eleanor turned to see Richard and John, both their faces ruddy from their early morning ride. Eleanor saw their dirty boots as well, their trousers mud-splattered.

"Gentlemen, please," she begged, approaching rapidly, though trying to keep her voice down. "There is time yet for you to change if you hurry. You must not–"

"Perhaps there is time, my dear Eleanor," John said, in rare good spirits, "but there is absolutely no inclination on either of our parts. Now is there, Richard?"

As John headed unerringly for the buffet, he glanced back and waved as though to inform his hapless half brother that he was on his own where his wife was concerned.

"Richard," Eleanor scolded, still trying to keep her voice down, but furious that neither man had deigned to clean himself or change his apparel.

"According to John," Richard began weakly, clearly calling on John's courage as well as his words, "we are country men and must to our own selves be true."

Eleanor breathed an indulgent sigh and was just on her way to join the gathering crowd at the buffet when again she heard footsteps and thought, Good, Mr. Yorrick Harp at last has been found. But as she turned she saw Mrs. Calvin the nanny and Mason Frye, the Eden tutor, a mismatched twosome if ever there was one, Mr. Frye with his egalitarian, almost socialist philosophies and Mrs. Calvin with her strict and rigid Scottish background.

"Good afternoon," she smiled warmly, greeting the two who were always invited to participate in family meals and family celebrations.

"Did you see her?" Mrs. Calvin whispered as she passed Eleanor by.

"Of course I saw her. But she was quite weary as they both were."

"They arrived so very late," Mrs. Calvin commented critically.

"Indeed they did. Carriage problems near Exeter."

"And Frederick?" Mr. Frye asked pleasantly. "How is my once most capable student?"

"Well," Eleanor smiled. "I think the warm climes of India agreed with our Frederick."

"Will they be joining us?" Mrs. Calvin asked, looking suspiciously about as though to say if those two weren't here, she might as well return to her private apartments.

"Oh, of course, certainly," Eleanor reassured her. "As we know, they did arrive late and Marjorie required a full night's sleep, considering her condition."

Mrs. Calvin looked shocked. "What *is* her condition?"

"A term pregnancy, or close to it."

As Mrs. Calvin's eyebrows went gliding upward in condemnation, John, with a heaping platter, moved close. "Are you ready to go through another birthing, Eleanor? Why don't you suggest London as an alternate choice, with its vast medical establishment?"

"I'll do nothing of the sort," Eleanor snapped, already miffed with John. "Frederick's child will be born at Eden, just as Stephen's son was, just as Geoffrey's will be—if, of course, he decides to marry."

As Eleanor glanced about in search of a duty that she was certain she was neglecting, she saw Stephen still at the door, apparently still looking for his friend Yorrick Harp.

"Shall I send up a footman, Stephen?" she offered, touching him lightly on the elbow and distracting him from his interest in the empty corridor.

Abruptly he shook his head. "No, no, I'm certain he's sleeping. I'm equally certain that he found spirits somewhere last evening and, knowing Yorrick as I do, he consumed far too much."

His voice drifted vaguely off as again he searched the corridor in both directions.

In the hope of putting his worries at ease, Eleanor said, "Albert is among the missing as well."

Stephen looked back, surprised. "Is that unusual? Albert always strikes me as being very punctual."

"Oh he is, normally."

"Well—"

Eleanor shrugged. "The last few days have not been . . . normal, Stephen. You should know that better than anyone."

"Still, has anyone seen him?"

Baffled by Stephen's now ardent interest in Albert's whereabouts,

Eleanor cast about for someone who might shed some light on the twin mysteries.

"Charlotte?"

"Yes, Mama?"

"We're missing Albert it seems," Eleanor said, keeping her voice down.

"And Yorrick Harp," Stephen contributed. "We were wondering if–"

Charlotte smiled. "Mr. Harp was teaching us a dance last evening, something called a square dance, though it was very much like a reel. It was great fun. Albert was with us, as was Lucy."

"And what happened?" Stephen asked.

Charlotte shrugged. "Uncle John told us to stop. Forgive me for saying so, but he was very rude, said terrible things to Mr. Harp about having no respect for this house and the people in it."

Eleanor tried to shush her. The worry on Stephen's face now turned to despair.

"What happened then?" Stephen asked, looking back.

"Nothing," Charlotte concluded. "Lucy and I went to the sewing room. She needed to size the emerald green taffeta. Oh, Mama, it's so beautiful. You must see it."

"I shall," Eleanor smiled reassuringly and tried to keep this pretty daughter on track. "Did you see where Mr. Harp got to then?" she asked.

"No, both he and Albert were still in the Great Hall when we left. The dance was ever so much fun, really it was, quite spirited. I don't know why Uncle John–"

Eleanor was on the verge of hushing her when she heard footsteps in the corridor, as did Stephen, who turned toward the door.

"Frederick," she heard him exclaim, and a moment later Frederick appeared, his young wife on his arm, both looking rested from their morning sleep, Marjorie particularly radiant in a simple pearl gray taffeta morning dress cut full in an attempt to disguise her swollen figure.

At their appearance, everyone at table ceased eating, ceased talking. Eleanor thought she detected a look of apprehension in Marjorie's eyes, as though she imagined herself to be a Christian entering a lion's den.

But if she was truly apprehensive, it faded rapidly, as did all talk of missing persons, as did all other interests, for Frederick, with great affection, gently took Marjorie by the elbow and guided her to the end of the long dining table and with unfailing charm smiled, "It gives me the greatest pleasure to introduce to you all this rarest of women, Mrs. Marjorie Housman Eden, my wife."

Once, when Marjorie was five, her father had allowed her to go with him up to a remote mission in the hill country, a long day's journey away from the dust and heat of Delhi. When they were almost there, at dusk, on a path that was scarcely discernible, their bearers suddenly stopped. Ramophur, her father's lead bearer, indicated that no one was to move. In this frozen, frightened position, Marjorie the child watched with wide eyes and held breath as a large family of tigers strolled unhurriedly across their path. One, the old mother, looked suspiciously in their direction and a moment later ambled off into the dense forest. It was several long moments before anyone was permitted to move.

Marjorie remembered all of this, remembered the twin emotions she had felt at the time–fear, of course, and a touch of envy. The tiger family had been very impressive, each looking after the other.

Now she confronted this enormously long and ornate table filled with strange faces, old, young, servant, master, and *all* gazing up at her with the same suspicious interest of that old mother tiger. Could she ever become a part of this?

Even when Frederick took her elbow and guided her forward, Marjorie still felt awkward and lumpish and out of place. The baby in her womb was doing cartwheels. Surely the thumps were visible against the side of her morning dress. And while she knew that the Eden family was one of the oldest and most respected in England, she was in no way prepared for the size, the grandeur, the incredible scope of everything she had seen. Even the walk down from their apartments had seemed endless–endless corridors, endless turnings past an occasional chambermaid who had looked as lost as Marjorie had felt.

Must pay attention, Marjorie sternly scolded herself and looked down the long table at all those upturned and curious faces and tried to think of something to say and, to her complete mortification, found her mind blank and her tongue paralyzed. The best she could do was to smile inanely and pray feverishly that the floor would open up and swallow her whole.

Her endless silence could not go on, and just as Marjorie was in the process of summoning enough courage to say something, she felt a soft hand on her arm and turned to see the most beautiful young girl she had ever seen in her life.

"My name is Charlotte," she said sweetly. "I'm Frederick's cousin. Yours as well now and that gives me even greater pleasure."

So pleased was Marjorie by the young woman's compassionate daring that she turned at once and clasped her hand warmly. "I assure you it gives me equal pleasure, and although Frederick told me much about Eden, he failed to tell me that he had a cousin so beautiful."

Frederick came to his own defense. "I assure you when I left Eden, she was not so–what I mean to say is–clearly the duckling has changed into a swan in my seven-year absence."

Then he opened his arms wide, and Charlotte embraced him, standing on tiptoe to deliver a kiss. "Oh, Frederick, it's so good to have you home. I want you to tell me everything, will you, everything about India? Is it very romantic? The sun is warm and constant isn't it? Or at least you said so. And flowers, tell me of the flowers. And the people, I want to know–"

Frederick held up both hands in an attempt to stay her enthusiasm. "This should be your tutor," he said and Marjorie felt his hand on her elbow. "Marjorie was born there, grew up there. Ask her to talk. She will tell you more than I ever could."

All at once, a plump pretty woman came up between them, hushing Charlotte in a maternal way. Marjorie knew that this was Eleanor of Eden Castle, though in Marjorie's opinion she looked far too vulnerable to be mistress of such an imposing place.

She kissed Marjorie lightly and embraced Frederick. "You both look rested, and for that I am grateful. I must say, you looked dreadful last evening. I was very worried."

"Perhaps we should have stayed in London," Frederick said. "It was our plan to arrive earlier in the evening. Apparently carriages aren't what they used to be." He turned to the left and saw his brother as though for the first time. "Stephen."

As the two brothers drew close, Marjorie again looked the length of the table, where faces were still gaping toward her, where forks had yet to be picked up, the rhythm of hearty eating reestablished.

"Well, come," Eleanor sighed. "Let me do the honor of introductions."

Marjorie felt a gentle hand guiding her closer to the table. The irrepressible Charlotte was on her right, as though to claim a kinship the others had not yet established.

Thus flanked and feeling moderately secure, Marjorie stopped at the first chair and saw a young woman smiling up at her.

"This is our Lucy," Eleanor smiled proudly.

Marjorie took the young woman's moist hand. Obviously a nervous and shy girl and clearly lacking the beauty of the ravishing Charlotte. Strangely Marjorie felt an instant kinship with Lucy.

"She is an excellent student," Charlotte boasted, "better than Frederick." Charlotte looked on her older sister with obvious affection.

"Good," Marjorie smiled. "I love to read. Mr. Dickens is my favorite. And yours?"

She saw a blush on Lucy's face. "All. I love them all. Dickens, of course, and Ruskin and Shakespeare's plays, and particularly the Sonnets."

"And this, dear Marjorie, is Mason Frye. For almost twenty years he has served as tutor to this unruly brood of ours, and we are all forever in his debt."

Marjorie found herself facing a very tall, very thin, but very sincere-looking gentleman, in his forties. He had a full head of salt-and-pepper hair, quite wavy, and a trim beard fashioned after that of Edward, Prince of Wales.

"My pleasure, Mrs. Eden, I assure you," he said in a deep, well-cultivated voice, as he firmly took her hand. "Your husband was my most able student–most able, that is, until Lucy came along. But by fifteen he had read his way through the Eden library, through my personal library, and I was having to send to London for monthly book shipments."

As he spoke, Marjorie saw him look affectionately toward Stephen and Frederick and was pleased to see both men come forward and join the rituals of introduction. Frederick extended his hand in greeting to Mason Frye and then clasped him in an embrace.

"The warm climes clearly agree with you," Mason Frye smiled. "Most impressive," he added, indicating the cleric's collar.

"I prefer not to wear it," Frederick replied, embarrassed, "but the bishop, who met us at the ship, insisted that I wear it while in England, something about an identification tag for men of God."

"I should hope their actions would be identification enough."

"It *is* good to see you, Mason," Frederick said. "I owe you so much."

"Nonsense. Come, there are others waiting to meet your wife. We will talk at length later."

"And this," Eleanor went on, "is Mrs. Martha Calvin, *the* mainstay of

Eden Castle, the children's nanny, and a better one does not exist the length or breadth of England."

Marjorie smiled at the stern-faced plump little woman, as short and thick as Mason Frye was tall and lean. Her features were plain and her smile quick, and her eyes moved across Marjorie's face at lightning speed, yet Marjorie had the feeling that they had seen deeper and clearer than anyone she had met in this grand dining hall.

"My pleasure, Mrs. Calvin," Marjorie smiled. "I can only hope that you will be available to care for the next generation of Edens."

"I will be available as long as it pleases God for me to be."

"Of course," Marjorie smiled, and was guided past Mrs. Calvin toward the end of the table, where she saw Richard, Frederick's uncle, whom she had met briefly last evening. And next to him, the man about whom Frederick had spoken endlessly and with a wide variety of emotions, the man whose reputation had stretched all the way to India. Even as a young girl, Marjorie had heard of the exploits of John Murrey Eden during the Indian Mutiny of the fifties, over forty years before.

"And this, as you know, is my husband, Richard."

The shy, dark-haired gentleman rose instantly and took her hand. "Welcome to our home, Mrs. Eden. I trust you will be happy here."

Even as he spoke, she saw two red circles of embarrassment on his chalk-white English complexion. Clearly he was ill at ease speaking to strangers, perhaps ill at ease speaking to anyone.

"Thank you," she smiled, aching to put him at ease. "I can't tell you how often Frederick has spoken of his childhood here at Eden."

"Too often, I'm sure. The question is, What did he say?"

This bemused, softly spoken comment came from John Murrey Eden, who even as he spoke finished spreading a large square of butter on a piece of toast, a job he seemed to prolong until he was certain all eyes were on him.

Then, with deliberation, he carefully placed the toast on his plate, wiped his hands on a linen napkin and stood to confront her.

Marjorie smiled in greeting as well as recognition. She'd seen that harmless posturing before. Her father, the Anglican bishop, adored to put on his fine robes and posture his way through chapel. There was something about John Murrey Eden that reminded her of her father. They were both born actors who had missed their calling.

In answer to his challenge Marjorie stepped forward, pleased at last to meet this legend. "He speaks only with the greatest affection, Mr. Eden, I assure you. In fact he has told me so often of Eden Castle, I feel I know every nook and cranny. What I was not . . . prepared for is–"

"What?" Mr. Eden demanded.

"The size," Marjorie gestured, "the scope; it is beyond human proportion."

Mr. Eden smiled as though immensely pleased with her comment. "You know its history, of course. It was designed to house an army in the eleventh century. Even back then we couldn't trust our Welsh neighbors. They were forever crossing the Bristol Channel and taking our livestock and our women. Our women, of course, we could do without; our livestock was quite another matter."

"John!"

Eleanor tried to make her voice stern and commanding, but it merely came out comical and cracked.

Marjorie smiled at the interplay between the two. Obviously both families had become united in strong emotional bonds years ago. In a curious way the young people seemed interchangeable. Did pretty Charlotte belong to John and Susan? Or was she Eleanor's and Richard's? Marjorie wondered if she'd ever get them sorted out, particularly when they seemed to appear and disappear at will.

Now Marjorie found herself gazing up at Mr. John Murrey Eden, who was waiting patiently, as though certain she had a question for him. She did. "You left quite a reputation in India, Mr. Eden. Are you aware of that?"

She had meant to do nothing more harmful than instigate a luncheon conversation. Thus, she was not prepared for the sudden silence that had fallen over the large dining hall. Even Charlotte looked up from the end of the serving table.

"Since I was a very young girl," Marjorie went on, "I have heard of the exploits of the Englishman who broke into the treasury of the Red Palace and took what he wanted. And then, in a bit of further daring, took the emperor's granddaughter and great-grandson as well."

"Believe me, they needed rescuing, both of them," he said quietly.

From the end of the buffet, Marjorie heard a softly scolding voice, the beautiful Charlotte with a martyred look on her face. "You never once told me you were in India, Uncle John."

"You never asked."

"Did Stephen and Frederick know?"

"Of course we knew." They laughed. "We knew Dhari and Aslam as well. Aslam used to tell us stories of India."

Stirred to even greater interest, Charlotte placed her platter on the end of the buffet and walked directly toward the group by the table. "And who is Dhari?" she asked.

"Dhari was the emperor's granddaughter," Frederick volunteered.

"And where is she now?" Charlotte persisted, "this . . . Dhari?"

Everyone looked to John to answer. "Dhari became the wife of an associate of mine. I've not heard from them in years. Nor should I."

"And the little boy?" Charlotte asked in relentless pursuit. "Where is the little Indian boy, Uncle John."

John Murrey Eden looked at all of them. There was a new expression on his face, a blend of hate and something else. "How in the hell should I know," he muttered. "Last I heard he was in London."

"*In* London?" Stephen exclaimed, laughing. "Last I heard he owned London or at least a large portion of it."

Frederick came up alongside the ever curious Charlotte and placed an affectionate arm about her shoulder. "And the little boy, Charlotte, is now a middle-aged man and quite the eccentric, or so I hear, but of course eccentricity is always enhanced by the presence of millions and millions of pounds."

"Why doesn't he ever come to visit you, Uncle John?" Charlotte asked, clearly reluctant to let the subject drop.

"Because I have never invited him."

Briefly Marjorie regretted mentioning India at all. It seemed to be a chapter that was best forgotten.

"Come, Marjorie," Frederick suggested, "let us choose from this bountiful table."

As he was handing her the platter, he glanced toward the door and Marjorie saw a new light in his eyes. "Ah, Alice," he smiled. "Come and meet your new cousin-in-law."

Marjorie turned about to see a pleasant young woman just entering the dining hall. She was dressed in navy blue in the manner of a nurse and only as she approached in a direct line did Marjorie see the small insignia on her breast pocket. She *was* a nurse.

"My name is Alice. My mother sends her regards and regrets. She is sitting with Eve. When are you due?"

"I'm . . . due . . . I think mid-April. I'm not sure."

"No, it will be sooner than that," Alice pronounced and drew closer and placed a very professional hand on Marjorie's belly. Embarrassed,

Marjorie started to withdraw, then changed her mind. If Alice wasn't embarrassed, why should she be?

"Then when?" she asked, keeping her voice low, somehow trusting this woman she had just met.

"No later than the end of this month would be my guess. Perhaps sooner. The child is very low already."

Marjorie glanced at Frederick, who was the only one who had remained in close proximity to the quick and unofficial examination.

"Then perhaps we should leave for London within the week," Frederick proposed, clearly worried.

"Why?" Alice demanded, looking at him as though his proposal was the height of stupidity.

"We thought it best," Marjorie tried to explain. "What I mean is–"

"Do you think that because one baby has been born at Eden, we can't have a second birth in the same month?" Alice looked puzzled, as though she were surrounded by ignoramuses.

"No," Frederick said. "It's just that–"

"Then it's settled. And don't worry," she comforted Marjorie, "I am a maternity nurse. It is my speciality. I work at St. Martin's in London. If you wish, I will attend you."

"Of course I wish," murmured Marjorie, pleased with the new decision. It had been her desire for Frederick's son to be born at Eden. Not that they would ever fall into the direct lineage. Richard's offspring would have that pleasure. Still, Eden Castle was both Frederick's ancestral and his emotional home, so she felt it would please him to have his child born here. Of course, neither of them had known about Stephen and Eve; their presence had simply made the journey home all the sweeter.

As Frederick guided Marjorie down the lavish buffet, she heard Stephen ask Alice, "Have you seen Yorrick Harp?"

"Not a sign of him."

"He hasn't been up to see Eve?"

"No, I was surprised. I would have expected him."

Marjorie detected a worried silence and wondered who Yorrick Harp was. But her thoughts were soon occupied with the anticipation of what fun this large and varied family would be. Everything was so different here from her upbringing in Delhi, from the austere, low-ceilinged white-washed house in which she had passed her childhood and youth.

Platter filled, she followed Frederick to the far side of the table, to chairs opposite John Murrey Eden and Lord Richard and next to Charlotte.

She noticed Eleanor at the buffet giving instructions to the serving maids, some replenishing existing dishes, others bringing in new ones.

Marjorie thought of the dark-skinned Indian children, thin-legged, with swollen bellies and never enough food or medicines. Briefly the scope and excess of Eden Castle pinched her like a pair of ill-fitting shoes.

"And Albert too?" she heard Alice exclaim. "Then it would be my guess that the two truants are off together."

"Where?" Stephen asked.

Marjorie arranged her napkin on her shrinking lap and assumed that at least two of the family were missing. The name Albert she recognized. The youngest son of John Murrey Eden and his wife, Susan.

Apparently, Eleanor had now become worried. "Well, I've had enough. I'm going to send a footman up to their chambers. If they are merely sleeping, they need to be awakened; if they are ill, they need attending. If they are–"

Marjorie saw Eleanor lift a hand to a young uniformed boy standing near the door. He approached, received instructions from Lady Eleanor and immediately disappeared.

Now, in the manner of one who has solved a bothersome problem, Eleanor took a platter for herself and slowly made her way down the long buffet.

For several minutes the only sounds to be heard in the Grand Dining Hall were the clink of forks on china, the squeaking wheels of the trolleys bringing reinforcements to the buffet table and the whisper of servants' feet as they scurried to keep tea and coffee cups filled and whisk away soiled platters.

It was Eleanor who broke the silence. "Richard, should I prepare a tray for Dr. Reicher? Do you suppose he will be joining us? I don't quite know what to do with him."

It was John Murrey Eden who gave Eleanor a response. "I doubt if the good doctor will appear in any of Eden's public rooms until Alice issues a heartfelt and sincere apology to him."

From the end of the table came a spirited response. "Then yes, Aunt Eleanor, I most strongly advise that you prepare the man a tray or else he may starve to death."

John Murrey Eden leaned angrily forward and peered down the table.

"How would it hurt you? It would be the courteous and ladylike thing to do."

"It would be the false and insincere thing to do," Alice said, apparently having no fear of her father, unlike most of the others. "I have nothing to apologize for."

"You insulted the man."

"He was permitting Eve to die."

"I doubt if that is true. It sounds a bit melodramatic."

"Ask Mother. She was there."

"I shall. For now, however, I think you should apologize to Dr. Reicher."

"I won't do that, Father," Alice said, quite calm and without rancor. "But I would be most happy to take my meals in my room if Aunt Eleanor will make all the arrangements. That way Dr. Reicher will be free to come to table."

Eleanor looked newly distressed. "Oh, no, no, dear Alice, that won't be necessary, not what I meant at all. John, shame on you, shame on you for–"

As new tension enveloped the table, everyone continued to eat silently, except for Alice, who took her platter back to the buffet, refilled it and without a word left the table and dining hall.

For several moments all that could be heard was the determined tread of her step as she moved down the corridor, leaving the dining hall a shambles of tension and regret.

"Stubborn," muttered John. "Always too damn stubborn for her own good. It will be her downfall one day, mark my words."

"What should I do now?" pleaded Eleanor, who looked like the captain of a sinking ship.

Frederick stood and gently escorted her back to her place at the table. "Come, Aunt Eleanor, we all should know by now that Alice is quite resilient, as well as stubborn. She will survive. As will we all."

"But should I–"

John stood then and snapped, "Oh, for God's sake, send the doctor a platter when you send Geoffrey's. Frankly I hope they all stay away."

His angry voice trailed behind like the wake of a ship as he headed toward the dining hall door without a word of excuse or farewell.

Marjorie had never witnessed a disagreement at the dining table and was mildly shocked by it. At home, family meals were gentle prayerful affairs, presided over by her mother, who kept the appetites in check and the wits sharp by asking challenging biblical questions that required complete identification.

Now this squabbling, quarrelsome family into which she had married both offended and fascinated her. She had never heard people speaking so honestly, so bluntly with each other, had never been exposed to such freedom of thought and objection. Apparently no one hesitated to speak his or her own mind, regardless of the social occasion or the consequences and, that was a freedom that intrigued, fascinated and frightened her.

The young footman who had been sent to fetch Albert and Yorrick Harp reappeared at the door.

Eleanor left the table and met him for a whispered conversation.

While this was going on, Frederick made an inquiry of Richard. "Might it be possible later for me to visit Geoffrey, Uncle Richard? I promise I won't stay long, but I long to see him and perhaps I could be of some service to him. I know he is ill, both in body and in spirit, and–"

Richard looked directly at him with those wide-set and noncommittal eyes. He appeared to be on the verge of speaking, then apparently lost his train of thought and murmured, "I . . . don't . . . doubt . . . he has refused to see any of us. According to the doctor, he wants his chamber doors locked at all times."

"This can't go on," Frederick said compassionately. "He must deal with it as soon as possible."

"We don't . . . know what to do?"

"Then may I try? How would it hurt?"

"Of course, feel free," Richard said, draining his coffee and placing his napkin on the table. He quietly left the dining hall.

Again the large room was plunged into a brooding silence. How easily this large and complex family went from joy to sadness, for as Marjorie looked about the table, she thought she detected an air of sorrow on every face, young and old alike. Even those who were not family members, like Mrs. Calvin and Mr. Frye, seemed to have caught the family mood like a dreaded contagion.

Marjorie considered stepping into the awful breach, but at that moment the young footman reappeared at the dining hall door and cast a quick glance about for Lady Eleanor, who spied him immediately and hurried to receive his message.

A moment later she exclaimed, full-voiced, "Neither? Are you certain?"

The young man nodded with renewed conviction.

Then Lady Eleanor turned back to the table and all those waiting faces. "The boy tells me their chambers are empty, both Albert and Mr. Harp. Neither slept in their beds."

Stephen pushed out of his chair and hurled his napkin onto the table. "I think I know what's happened," he muttered and looked genuinely angry. "Yorrick wanted drink and talked Albert into taking him down to Mortemouth. God alone knows where they are now. But I had better go look for them."

Frederick offered his services. "I'll come with you. Two can–"

"No, please, you stay here," Stephen urged. "Go and see if Geoffrey will let you in. He needs someone."

Reluctantly Frederick agreed. Stephen straightened his jacket.

"Then I'm off. Aunt Eleanor, if Susan or Alice asks for me, tell them where I've gone. But please say nothing to Eve. She would only worry about Yorrick. I just hope they both can walk," he smiled. "If not, I'll have to come back for the horse cart."

Eleanor patted Stephen on the back and told him to take care. She mentioned something about ruffians and hoodlums, and all the while, Stephen proceeded on down the corridor until it was no longer feasible for her to call after him.

Slowly she returned to the dining hall and all those gaping faces, and she looked so uneasy that Marjorie took pity on her and left her chair and hurried to her side.

"Come, Eleanor," she invited as though she were mistress of Eden. "I spied a lovely small fire not far from here."

"Yes, the library–"

"And two of the most comfortable-looking chairs I've ever seen," Marjorie went on. "Let's go toast our toes and talk the afternoon away."

Apparently the proposition held great appeal for Charlotte, as well as Eleanor, who asked if she might be included in the afternoon tête-à-tête.

"Of course." Marjorie smiled.

"When we settle by the fire, Marjorie," Charlotte asked, "will you tell us of India, all about it, everything you remember, please, will you?"

Marjorie laughed and put her arm about Charlotte as she felt her baby kick inside her womb. Eleanor came up close on the other side and took her arm in sweet intimacy, and with a smile of happiness and a prayer of thanksgiving, Marjorie wondered if at last perhaps she had become a part of this large and dangerous and beautiful tiger family she'd always dreamed about, always wanted.

Stephen felt a slight warming on his back from the dull afternoon sun. But the wind was chill and the sky gray over the Bristol Channel, an early spring sky promising more of winter.

He shoved his hands into his pockets as he approached the top of the cliff walk, a route he used to race mindlessly as a boy but now approached with caution.

He would have to speak to Yorrick, of course, inform him that there were certain places on this remote point of England that could be dangerous for a free-spirited American.

Hopefully, in a few weeks, by late spring, Eve would be stronger and they could all book passage back to America. Though born and bred an Englishman, Stephen wanted nothing more than to return to America, to her spirit, her openness, her generosity, her freedom. And, more important, he wanted his son to grow up an American.

His son!

Those two words seemed more miracle than reality. Yet Stephen had held him, had carefully examined each tiny fist and finger, each eye, each ear, and along with Eve had pronounced him perfect in all respects.

A sudden gust of channel wind brushed against him as though reminding him of his task.

"Damn you, Yorrick," Stephen cursed, not really meaning it beyond the inconvenience of this stupid search itself, for Yorrick Harp had been a good friend, a man who once had literally saved Eve's life; thus, he was the sole architect of Stephen's happiness now.

Thinking such thoughts softened Stephen's attitude and somehow made this laborious descent easier. At the halfway point he paused and looked out over the channel at far-off Wales and remembered the time as a boy that his father had loaded all of the Eden children into a fishing boat and ordered the fisherman to head straight across to the Welsh coast on the opposite side of the channel. Once there he had instructed the children to get out of the boat and gaze back across the channel at the grand parapets and flying banners and imposing stone walls of Eden Castle.

It had been a memorable sight. Memorable also was his father's sermon concerning viewpoint and the clear vision of what one was, the nature and history of his blood, his origins, the gifts given to him by a generous

Divinity who fully expected every Eden to live up to his name, strong, yet compassionate, wise, yet not arrogant, just, yet not weak.

Stephen fixed his eye on that distant beach where they first had seen themselves as others saw them. It had been one of his father's most memorable lessons.

As Stephen started off again, he lifted his face to the ever-blowing wind and called aloud, "Yorrick," knowing full well his voice would carry only as far as the seagulls over the channel. Still, there was no harm in trying to raise an early alarm, for Stephen hadn't the faintest idea where to start his search.

The fishing boats would be out at midday. Mortemouth would be filled with women and elderly men. Nothing to do but to start at The Hanging Man and make inquiry of anyone who was willing to talk with him.

As he turned the last corner around the curve of Eden Point, he caught a clear view of Mortemouth beach. In July and August people came from miles around, for the waves here were high and cool at this convergence of the Atlantic Ocean and the Bristol Channel.

Now, in March, the beach was empty except for a small gray knot of people who stood at water's edge—women, for he saw their long skirts lifted by the wind. They appeared to be bent over something, some curiosity washed in from the sea no doubt.

Stephen dismissed the distant group and started down the uneven cobblestones and thought the town strangely deserted, even for the middle of a cold March day.

He had taken no more than a dozen steps when he realized that something was wrong. To his right, inside the butcher's window, he saw a hand quickly draw down the blind. Across the way at the hardware shop, he saw the door locked and bolted. And it was the same up and down the street, the shops either closed or closing, no one in sight of whom he might make inquiry.

Alarm increasing, Stephen started off in one direction, then abruptly stopped and reversed himself. He began running back in the direction from which he had come, approaching the beach at a good speed and feeling his shoes bog down in the wet sand.

He looked up and saw the group still there, women, four of them, all hovering over something at water's edge, a dark rolled something, flattened, no discernible shape as yet, just a form resembling—

At that moment the huddled circle of women moved back, although he was still at least thirty yards away. He saw a clearer shape to the rolled form, saw legs sprawled, saw a torso, saw arms, saw too much, saw a gray wet beard and hair, and as he drew closer, the women moved away as though to disassociate themselves from the form on the beach. The man had one lifeless arm curled across his face as though to obscure the truth for as long as possible.

Stephen knew, while he was yet twenty feet away. He approached more slowly now, recording all aspects of the grim tableau, the old women now flanking the body, two on one side, two on the other, like unorthodox guardian angels.

"Yorrick?" he whispered as though the corpse were capable of identifying itself.

"He ain't one of us," came the hoarse whisper from behind, and Stephen looked over his shoulder to see the four old hags closing in.

"He was supposed to go out with the tide, like garbage–"

"But he's stronger than the tide and come back, he did. It's an omen."

Slowly Stephen dropped to his knees beside the body and closed his eyes for a moment's prayer, asking for strength if nothing else. Then he gently lifted the arm that obscured the face and instantly regretted it, for he saw the face, unblemished except for a white pallor, saw the piercing eyes yet open, the mouth opened as though at any moment he might launch into a spirited and inspired Prospero or Lear or his favorite, Prince Hamlet.

"Yorrick," he mourned, and lifted Yorrick into his arms, held him, rocked him and let the tears come.

The four old hags squatted a distance away, clearly baffled by Stephen's expression of grief.

Then a terrifying thought occurred. Albert. Where was Albert?

In his rising fear he turned to confront the squatting hags.

"There was another–"

"A young 'un–"

"Yes."

"He run off."

"Where?"

No response except for the in-sucking of toothless gums. Stephen stared at their curiously matching faces, all ruddy and weathered, wiry gray hair protruding from beneath faded kerchiefs.

"Do you know . . . how did this . . . what happened? Could you tell me?"

"It was at The Hanging Man," one began. "They was there drinking together."

"Who?"

"The young 'un and him. He was saying bad things."

"About what?"

"About our brave lads."

Stephen gazed down on Yorrick's face. He passed his hands over the eyelids, closing them. Then he placed Yorrick on the wet sand, eased his body inward, away from the receding tide, and stood and stripped off his jacket and placed it over Yorrick's face.

" 'Twas a knife," cackled one old hag, "one well thrown, that's what got him."

Stephen closed his eyes and wished he might close his ears as well. Albert. Where was Albert? Would his body, too, wash ashore on some distant beach? And Eve. He was the one who would have to tell Eve. There would have to be an investigation, with accusations leveled in all directions and a good chance that the true murderer or murderers would never be found.

"Was he your friend, lad?"

The question brought him back to the present, and he looked up to see one old harridan's face moving closer.

"He was my friend," he whispered. "A good man. Your men were very wrong to harm him."

"He was harmin' us."

"How?"

"By tellin' us we was foolish to obey our old queen."

"He was American and did not understand blind obedience."

"He's dead now."

"Yes." Again Stephen's grief washed over him and in an attempt to check it, he turned to the old woman nearest to him and appealed for her help.

"Do you know Eden Castle?" he asked.

"I'd be a fool not to," the old woman grinned. "I've served my penance up there, as have all my sisters. We cleaned out chamber pots for the old lord and lady, and got our bread and cheese free for doin' it."

"Then would you be so kind as to climb the cliff walk and go to the gates and tell the guards that Mr. Eden needs them. Then bring them back here. Could you do that?"

"What's in it for me?"

Stephen saw the scheming look in the watery old eyes that somehow suggested that bread and cheese would no longer be sufficient compensation. "Coin," he said.

"How many?" she asked, wily to the last.

"I'll give you five. Now hurry."

For the first time he saw light in the old face as she stood and did a little jig around Yorrick's body.

"We'll all go and do your errand for that, your lordship," she grinned toothlessly. "We'll go and come with the wind. Won't we, sisters?"

And with that they were gone. Stephen watched them as they lifted their long skirts. One stumbled and three came to her aid, and then all were hurrying toward the cliff walk.

Alone, Stephen stared back down on the man at his feet.

Where was Albert?

As the worry burned anew, he knelt beside Yorrick Harp, then sat flat on the wet sand and lifted a cold, stilled hand and studied it and saw encrusted blood where apparently Yorrick had grasped the wound caused by the knife. Soon he saw not the dead, cold, sea-washed body but saw the man himself, onstage, treating one and all to his artistry, his voice the deepest male voice Stephen had ever heard, capable of penetrating the highest balcony in the largest theater in San Francisco.

What right did anyone have to extinguish this rare flame? Quickly anger joined the grief, and he sat next to Yorrick Harp and pressed the blood-encrusted hand to his lips.

Where was Albert? He looked in both directions and saw only emptiness.

His greatest fear was for Eve, weakened and ill, missing her parents, finding solace always in Yorrick's nearness, Yorrick's strength.

What would this news do to her? Clasping Yorrick's hand, he prayed quickly, quietly, for wisdom and guidance in the difficult tasks which lay ahead of him.

Feeling stronger with every passing hour, Eve sat up in bed and closed her eyes as Susan brushed her hair.

She wanted to look her best, her prettiest, for Yorrick, who always had proclaimed that Eve Stanhope Eden was the most beautiful woman God had ever created.

"You'd better let me have the mirror, Susan," she sighed playfully. "The truth must be faced sooner or later."

Susan shrugged and gave it to her. Slowly Eve surveyed her face framed in an ornate silver circle, a face she scarcely recognized. Pale, so thin, the eyes staring back at her from deep hollows. She looked haggard, and the slight surge of strength she had felt earlier ebbed under this new disappointment.

Gently she felt the mirror being taken from her. And in its place she saw Susan's good, strong face, her eyes filled with compassionate understanding.

"It will take time," she said. "Please be patient with yourself."

There was a knock at the door.

"Yorrick," Eve gasped and felt a rising excitement at seeing her old friend again. He had never even had a chance to hold Alex.

"Are you ready?" Susan whispered from the door. Frantically Eve adjusted the lace collar on her pale pink bed jacket and tried to fluff her hair, which Susan had just brushed. Then she whispered, "Yes, let them in."

As Susan swung open the door, Eve strained forward for her first glimpse of Yorrick. But she saw Aunt Eleanor, fluttery as always, followed by a tall, very attractive and very pregnant woman.

"I'm sorry, Susan," Eleanor murmured nervously, "if this isn't a good time– What I mean is, Marjorie here was so anxious to meet Eve that I simply– Is it alright?"

Despite her curiosity over who the woman was, Eve continued to search the open door, hoping that Stephen and Yorrick were with them and merely waiting their turn.

But the door remained empty.

"No, it's quite alright," Susan smiled reassuringly.

"You are Marjorie, I'm sure," Susan said and took both her hands, then lightly embraced her. "I'm sorry I missed your arrival last night."

"No, please think nothing of it," the woman replied warmly. "I'm afraid we upset the entire household. We would have arrived earlier except for–"

"A broken carriage axle," Susan nodded sympathetically. "Yes, I heard. What a terrible mishap, particularly for you. Are you feeling–"

"Quite heavy," the woman laughed and patted her protruding belly, and Eve sympathized immediately.

"It does get better," she contributed from her bed, swallowing her disappointment over Stephen and Yorrick's failure to appear. Surely they would be along soon.

Susan took the woman by the arm and led her close to Eve's bed. "This is Marjorie Eden, Eve, Frederick's wife. Unless I miss my guess, you two will have a lifetime in common for your firstborns will be mere weeks apart."

The woman extended a hand to Eve and bestowed upon her a warm smile, and Eve indicated that Marjorie was to sit on the side of the bed.

"Tell me all," Eve began, "when did you leave India? Was the passage rough? And where's Frederick? I'm so anxious to meet my brother-in-law."

Marjorie laughed. "One at a time, then it's my turn."

At that moment, young Alexander gave a hearty burp after his full meal of Molly's milk, and all at once questions of India and sea passages and London faded in importance.

Susan retrieved the baby and brought him to bedside. "Now there's only one problem–who gets him?" she smiled.

Marjorie looked hopeful. "Might I . . . hold him, Eve? Just for a moment?"

With a nod, Eve watched carefully as the transfer was made from Susan's arms to Marjorie's, saw the clear love in her eyes as she drew back the blanket and bent over and lightly kissed Alexander on the forehead.

"He's so pink," Marjorie marveled, daring to draw the blanket back even further.

"And yours?" Eve asked, "when–"

"According to our best calculations, in about a month, though Alice claims it will be much sooner."

Susan spoke from the opposite side of the bed. "Then I would listen to Alice if I were you."

"Oh, I will."

"Will you be staying on at Eden?" Eve asked hopefully.

Marjorie nodded. "We had thought to return to London, but all have convinced us to remain here."

"You'll be in good hands," Eve smiled. "Take it from one who knows."

"He is so beautiful, Eve," Marjorie sighed. "I only hope I can do half as well."

"I'm sure you will," Eve said, remembering her own fears immediately before delivery.

She lay back into her pillows and closed her eyes and felt that awful fatigue again, that sudden cessation of energy as though a major power source had suddenly abandoned her.

"Eve–"

An alarmed Susan hurried forward.

"I'm fine," Eve murmured, "just . . ."

"I'm afraid we've stayed too long," Eleanor fretted. "Come, Marjorie, we'll run along for now and return later."

"Of course," Marjorie agreed quickly, though first she leaned forward and kissed Eve lightly on the forehead, and when Eve opened her eyes, she saw that kind face suspended directly before her vision.

"I'm so glad we are sisters, and what fun we will have raising our children together. Please rest now."

"Come back, will you?" Eve pleaded. "We have so much to talk about."

She was only vaguely aware of footsteps departing the room, of Molly taking Alexander from her arms. The terrible fatigue was increasing, invading every part of her mind and body.

"Susan . . ."

She called out, hoping they wouldn't all go away and leave her alone.

A moment later, Susan stood at her bedside, a bottle of elixir in her hand, spoon at the ready.

Eve had no idea what it was, but when Susan promised that it would help get her strength back, Eve opened her mouth eagerly and swallowed the sweetish red syrup.

"Try to sleep now," Susan advised. "You are not quite ready for a full social calendar."

"Yorrick . . ."

"Stephen has gone to search for him."

Alarmed, Eve opened her eyes. "Where is he?"

Susan smiled. "If we knew that, Stephen wouldn't have gone in search."

"I don't . . . understand," Eve worried.

"Please," Susan begged, "just relax. There is nothing to worry about. It seems that late last night, Yorrick and my Albert left the castle in search of spirits."

Eve closed her eyes and breathed a sigh of relief and recognition. Of course, Yorrick would have to have his spirits. There was much to celebrate. What she couldn't understand was why he had to leave the castle in the company of a boy? The Eden wine cellars were vast and well stocked. They might have had all the spirits they wanted right here. She longed to ask Susan this question, but her energy was gone now. She had no choice but to lie helplessly upon the pillow and watch as Susan drew the comforter up around her shoulders.

"Sleep," Susan smiled, "it is the best medicine in the world."

"Yorrick . . . ," Eve whispered.

"Soon," Susan soothed.

Still dazed and grieving, Stephen looked back from the Great Hall steps and marveled at how quickly the alarm had been raised. There seemed to be guardsmen scurrying in all directions.

Apparently the four old hags had conveyed his message, for in a remarkably short time he had seen five Eden guardsmen hurrying toward him across the beach. As they had lifted Yorrick's body, he had paid off the hags and had led the way back up the cliff walk.

As they had approached the gatehouse, he had seen a new contingent of men hurrying to meet them, and in the lead, he had seen his father and his Uncle Richard with sober faces.

Both men had hastily examined the body. Richard had issued instructions that it be washed and laid out for burial in the Eden graveyard. Both his father and his uncle had expressed their sincere regrets that such a barbaric act had taken place within the shadow of Eden Castle.

His father had enlisted the aid of half a dozen guardsmen and had led them off down the cliff walk, where it was his avowed intention to launch an investigation before the trail grew cold and memories dim.

His Uncle Richard had agreed with Stephen that most likely Albert was unharmed but merely frightened and in hiding. Richard had ordered a large contingent of guardsmen to go in search of the poor boy, in the hope that perhaps he could tell them precisely what had happened and who had hurled the knife that had brought Yorrick's life to an end.

Now, as the last horseman cleared the gate, all that was left in the cold, windy courtyard were the curious scullery maids who had climbed up out of the basement kitchen court.

Stephen felt momentarily weak with grief. Conflicting instincts told him, "Go at once and inform Eve. Get it over with– No, wait, until she is stronger. Don't confront her with news of this tragedy now."

He closed his eyes against the voices inside his head and pushed open the Great Hall door and hoped to find someone passing by on whom he might place at least a portion of this burden.

But the Great Hall was empty.

Then do it. He broke into a run, trying desperately to arrive at Eve's door before courage deserted him.

There was no movement outside the door.

As despair caught up with him, he leaned against the near wall and pressed his forehead against its rough surface.

"Stephen?"

Startled by the sound of a voice, he looked up to see Susan, only her head visible around the edge of the door to Eve's room.

"Thank God," she said and stepped all the way out, leaving the door ajar. "Where is Mr. Harp? Eve has been so anxious. She has–"

Then it was time. At least here was someone with whom he could share his horrible news, doubly horrible for poor Susan, for he must tell her that her son is missing and perhaps dead.

"Stephen, what is it?"

She met him halfway in the corridor, and he took her arm and led her to the small alcove across the way from Eve's chambers.

Twice he insisted that she sit down and twice she refused, leaving him no choice but to commence his story staring her straight in the eye, a story he condensed as much as possible, wishing with all his heart that he could condense it out of existence.

Not until he reached the point of discovering Yorrick's body did Susan's face reflect the tragic bewilderment of such a senseless and mysterious death.

"Who?" she murmured.

"We have no idea. Uncle Richard and Papa have launched a search."

"Then where's Albert?" she insisted. "Ask Albert. If he was present he would know."

"Albert is missing," he said simply.

"Missing?" she repeated. "I thought you said he was with Yorrick."

"He was, but I was told that he ran from the pub after Yorrick was–"

"Who told you this?" Susan demanded.

"Four old women."

"Were they at The Hanging Man?"

"They claimed to be."

"And they saw Albert?"

Stephen nodded. "They said they saw him run out, frightened no doubt."

"Has anyone thought to look in his rooms?"

"Yes."

"These women, they were certain that he–"

Her voice broke, as did her aggressive line of questioning. "They were certain, Susan," Stephen comforted. "I'm confident that he is merely frightened and disoriented. Uncle Richard has sent out several horsemen."

"I know his favorite places."

"It might be helpful to tell one of the guardsmen–"

Susan had taken no more than three steps down the corridor when she stopped and looked back. "Eve," she whispered, her face contorted with new pain.

Stephen looked into Eve's bedchambers and saw her propped up on her elbows, watching them carefully, listening.

"Stephen? Is that you?"

As the weak voice reached his ears, he knew Eve had seen enough to suspect something.

"What should I–" Stephen began, but Susan merely shook her head and proceeded down the corridor. "I must go and help them find Albert," she called back. "Eve has been waiting for you. You will have to tell her."

Something about the speed with which she was moving down the corridor suggested to Stephen that there was no force on earth capable of luring her back.

"Stephen, is that you?"

It was Eve again.

"God help me," Stephen prayed quickly, and lifted his head for one good long breath, then started across the corridor and into Eve's room.

"Where is Yorrick?" she asked. "Why is he staying away? Have I displeased him? Will he be here soon?"

The time had come. "No, you have not displeased him. He left the castle last night with Albert."

"Where did they–"

"They wanted spirits." And so he began the dreaded account, and did not stop once, and when he announced Yorrick's death, he heard only one outcry and that was not from Eve, but from Molly, who apparently had been listening to his story by the fire.

Now that there was nothing more to tell, he prepared himself for the onslaught of grief and questions.

But there was nothing, no sound coming from Eve who gazed up at him as though his words were still echoing inside her head. Then he saw her eyes close, saw her sink back into the pillows, heard only two whispered words, "Yorrick, please," then heard nothing else, for she had turned her head away and lay absolutely still, as though she had nothing left with which to fight.

Stephen leaned over her, searching for a way to help her so that they might share, and thus lessen, each other's burden of grief. But there was no way in. She had sealed herself beneath the bedclothes, by the angle of her body and inside her closed eyes.

Helpless, Stephen looked up to see Molly staring back at him. At that moment his son cried out in his sleep. As there was nothing he could do for Eve, he went to the cradle and looked down on his fretful son and gently lifted him into his arms and walked steadily about the chamber, so grateful that at least here was someone he could soothe.

Late that evening, wrapped in a shawl for protection against the cold drizzle which had commenced at dusk, Susan waited in the gatehouse for John and the search party to return.

Richard was with her, looking timid and out of place as usual. Poor man. He was so ill equipped by nature for the responsibilities and duties of lordship of this vast castle. Still, he tried, and for that she was fond of him.

Outside the gatehouse, warming their hands by a small wood fire, were the half dozen guards who had remained behind. Now and then they glanced toward their gatehouse, which had been taken over by the lord of the castle. All of the guards were men from Mortemouth, and Susan wondered if perhaps they didn't know of the murder, know even of the murderer. The town was a close-knit community. Susan knew most of them by name, having treated them or members of their family at her clinic on Eden Rising.

"Excuse me, Richard," she murmured. "I'm going to step outside for a moment."

As she approached the men, she saw them move away from the fire as though more than willing to share with her their warmth as well as their gatehouse.

"No, please," she protested, motioning for them all to return, searching their weathered faces to see if she knew any on a first-name basis.

She did. "Jonathan, good to see you," she smiled at a tall young man near her.

He touched his hand to his cap. "Mrs. Eden," he smiled. And that was all he said, though Susan well remembered his garrulous gratitude on that cold December day only a few months ago when she had sat with his infant daughter until a fever had broken.

"And Henry," she went on, spying another recognizable face. She had seen Henry and his wife and brood of four through measles last spring.

"And Dennis," she added, "and Billy," and she realized she knew them all, had served them all, cared for all their families. Now would they return the favor and share any information they might have with her?

"One man is dead, a man who was a guest in this house, and my son is missing. If any of you have the smallest piece of information that would help us, I would be forever in your debt."

For several minutes all six men studied the fire with unnatural concentration. One glanced over his shoulder into the dark as though he had heard something.

Finally Dennis said, "Your boy is alright, ma'am. He will return safely to you."

"How do you know this, Dennis?"

"Because the quarrel weren't with him."

"Was there a quarrel?"

Another guard spoke up. "He weren't one of us."

"Yorrick Harp?"

"Don't know his name, don't care. He was speaking insults is what he was doing."

"About whom?" Susan asked.

"He said we was fools, was what he said," one added and spit into the fire. "He was the bigger fool."

"Why did he call you fools?" Susan persisted.

"Because we obeyed the old queen and the call of the colors," a voice from the back spoke up. "Said only fools do that without knowin'—"

"Knowing what?"

"What they're getting themselves into. Imagine. Fine kettle this country would be in if every bloke took it upon himself to call the order of the day."

"There's a master even on the smallest fishing boat, someone who calls the orders for all the rest."

Susan heard a rumble of approval all around and feared they were straying far afield of her inquiry.

Suddenly she posed a painfully direct question. "Were any of you at The Hanging Man last evening? Did any of you by chance happen to witness Mr. Harp's death?"

"Saw nothing. I swear it. I was home with my Florence all evening."

"And I with my Betty."

"I was visiting my old grandparents. They was the ones who worked for his lordship's father."

"No, ma'am, not I. I was nowhere near The Hanging Man. I promised Sarah that I–"

As the protests and denials came from all angles of the circle, Susan was on the verge of asking a slightly different question when out of the darkness she heard horses. The guardsmen moved instantly forward, relieved to be called by duty and away from her line of questioning.

From the dim light cast by the fire she saw the lead horse, recognized John's black stallion and then caught a shadowed glimpse of his face.

"John?" she called out and saw him glance down in her direction, saw him quickly dismount and give the men orders to see to all the horses.

"And I want a full watch on the gates tonight, understand?"

"Albert? Did you learn anything about Albert?" Susan murmured, trying to keep her voice low.

"Nothing," he said. "You would be amazed. Everyone in the town of Mortemouth has gone deaf and mute, and if they aren't deaf and mute, they were visiting kin. By my best judgment Yorrick Harp and Albert were the only two customers at The Hanging Man last night."

They were turning back into the courtyard when again the sound of distant horses shattered the quiet chill night air; they heard a voice, a triumphant and distant cry, "We found him."

Then evolving out of the darkness were a dozen horsemen, who all reined in sharply before John, their horses shying and whinnying at the sudden stop.

Keeping back a safe distance, Susan searched each horse until she found Albert, looking much the worse for wear, clinging to the back of a guardsman.

"Help him down," John shouted, and Susan heard a harshness in his voice that he always seemed to reserve for this son. At the same time, she saw him reach a hand up to Albert, who looked frightened and tired. His hair was disheveled, bits and pieces of straw clinging here and there, testimony as to where he'd passed the last day and night.

She saw him accept John's extended hand, and John pulled him off the horse with such force that Albert lost his balance and ended up flat on his backside in the mud.

Lifting her skirts, she moved through the horses and caught Albert's eye and tried to convey love and compassion. Now she, too, offered him a hand up.

"Come," she whispered and took his arm, aware of all those superior gaping male eyes, but for the moment she was heedless of them.

As they were turning back toward the gatehouse and the castle gate, she heard John call after them, "Wait! There are questions that must be asked of the boy."

"Later," Susan called back.

"Not later! Now!"

She wasn't alarmed or intimidated by his tone of voice, merely curious, for she had detected anger and couldn't imagine why he was angry at his son's return.

"Yes?" she asked with suspect calm and sensed embarrassment among the surrounding guardsmen, as though all knew they were witnessing a private matter.

Now John ignored her completely and approached Albert.

"Of course, you know I must ask where you were?" John's voice sounded accusatory, even in a simple question.

"In the barn," Albert replied.

"Which barn?"

"Our barn."

John looked puzzled. "You mean the one on Eden Rising?"

"Yes."

John scratched his head and glanced toward Susan, then toward the guardsmen, who all ducked their heads in an attempt to hide their amusement.

"May I ask why?" John continued.

"I was afraid."

"Of what?"

"It was terrible. At The Hanging Man. Mr. Harp did nothing. He just–" Albert's voice broke, and Susan was surprised by the depth of his grief.

"He just what?" John demanded, either not seeing his son's despair or not caring to see it.

What was the point, Susan brooded. She began to doubt that Albert had any information at all that he could share. She doubted as well if he had even seen who had hurled the knife. If John truly wanted that piece of information, he should turn about and question the grinning guardsmen still on their horses.

"Come, Albert," she said, taking his arm and turning him about. "I'm glad you're safe," she whispered.

"I'm sorry I disappointed you," Albert said despondently.

"You didn't disappoint me," she protested.

"It was so terrible, Mama."

"We'll talk later," she soothed, seeing a gathering on the Great Hall steps. "You have a welcoming committee."

She felt his grip tighten on her hand as they approached the bottom of the stairs and looked up to see Charlotte first, shivering despite her shawl, her face taut with concern. "Albert, are you alright? We were so worried."

With surprising ease, Susan made it to the top of the steps, only to find a second greeting committee of house servants.

Susan spied Elsie, the head parlormaid, near the door. "Elsie, would you ask Mrs. Partridge to fix a tray for Albert and bring it to his rooms. Hot soup would be nice and a good meat platter."

Then Susan led Albert through the door and into the Great Hall. Her destination was Albert's chambers on the third floor, where they might sit and talk in private, and perhaps then he could help her to understand what had happened. In turn, she might help him to understand the presence of death and the strange paths of life. What worried Susan most was that hope and faith seemed capable of being toppled at the slightest provocation.

As far as John Murrey Eden was concerned, good riddance.

Yorrick Harp had been the sort of man one must always be on guard against. Clearly he had taken possession of Stephen and Eve. So perhaps in a way his untimely death was just as well, Providence's way of rearranging history.

Well, no matter now. From the looks of all those grim faces gathering in the Great Hall for the funeral procession, it promised to be a soggy hour at best. Thank God, nature had seen fit to send a glorious March day, with a high, early spring sun to cut through the maudlin sentiment of the occasion.

Frederick would officiate, at Stephen and Eve's request. John's two sons had spent the better part of the night discussing Yorrick Harp and, in the process, had elevated the old theatrical manager to sainthood. Then John was forced to bid his sons good-night and seek saner refuge in his own warm bed with Susan close beside him.

Now where was she? He didn't like to lose sight of her for long. She was quite simply his compass. When he lost track of her, he lost track of himself.

There she was, tending pale Eve, who was reclining on a makeshift chaise which four footmen were assigned to lift and put down on cue, Cleopatra-fashion. But sadly there was nothing robust or sensuous about that poor child. Clad in a heavy wool dressing gown, she resembled a very pale, very ill old woman who never lifted her eyes to the people gathering in the Great Hall.

Well, what was holding up the parade?

Beginning to feel the bleak mood of the occasion invade his thinking, John saw the reception door open at last, saw Frederick resplendent in purple brocade robes, cleric's collar visible, an enormous gilt Book of Common Prayer in one hand.

The four footmen carefully lifted the chaise and carried Eve in. No one spoke and the only sound was the soft drone of Frederick's voice reading from the service of burial. As Frederick led the way out of the door, John saw eight guardsmen lift a freshly milled coffin fashioned from virgin timber, the smell of rosin still pungent, all men struggling with the weight of the coffin as they angled it about and aligned it with the Great Hall doors.

Within a few minutes the entire procession had cleared the Great Hall doors and had made its way down the steps to the inner courtyard and had moved across the gravel into the high, deep shadows cast by the castle itself.

Looking ahead, John saw that Frederick was leading them toward the black iron fence which surrounded the graveyard where Edens had been buried since the eleventh century.

They entered through the narrow gates and formed a rough circle around the grave. The guardsmen, clearly straining under the weight of the coffin, placed it to one side of the grave.

Eve sat up straight, her eyes fixed on Yorrick's coffin, her expression one of complete desolation.

As Frederick's voice fell silent, all John heard was birdsong in the tops of trees and the peculiar singing wind as it whipped between the marble tombstones.

What now? he wondered and felt the same lack of direction move across the gathering as all focused nervously on Eve and the coffin.

Get him in the ground quickly, John prayed and was baffled by Frederick's hesitancy when all at once he saw Eve push back the coverlet, despite Alice's protest.

What now?

John saw a brief discussion taking place over old Yorrick's coffin. Then he saw Frederick motion the guardsmen to step forward, saw one take a piece of metal from the pocket of his heavy coat and slip it beneath the coffin lid, to pry it open.

He heard the sound of splintering wood and saw two guardsmen lift the lid. He saw Eve pull away from the support of other arms and reach out for the edge of the coffin, where she clung, head bowed, eyes closed.

Suddenly there was movement beyond the coffin. It was Albert, looking not much better than when the guardsmen had brought him in from the barn on Eden Rising. He was clad only in dark trousers and a loose-fitting shirtwaist; his hair was disheveled and, from the look on his face, he had passed yet another sleepless night.

He stepped forward until only the coffin was between them. "Yorrick spoke of you at the moment of his death," he said in a voice so soft that it seemed little more than part of the wind. "He said tell Eve that the first words I shall speak upon meeting God will be to thank Him for her—"

He turned away and left all to focus on Eve, who lifted her face to the sun and seemed to be deriving strength from some hidden source, for John saw a smile on her face as she reached one hand into the coffin as though to touch the face there, then slowly she leaned forward and kissed him and whispered something too softly for anyone but Yorrick to hear.

She turned away from the coffin, and took one step forward and collapsed. Stephen got there first and lifted her into his arms and, ignoring the offer of the chaise, carried her quickly from the graveyard.

The procession followed after them, leaving Frederick alone to speak the final words.

John waited at the gate for Frederick to join him, and was pleased with his son who seemed so at home with the mysteries.

"Was Eve alright?" Frederick asked.

"I don't know."

"Poor woman. Obviously she felt deep affection for Mr. Harp."

John said nothing and walked beside Frederick with his head down, seeing the hem of his son's robes and the toes of his highly polished shoes. "Do you enjoy it?" he asked.

"What?"

"Presiding over the rituals."

Frederick smiled. "I'm not certain enjoyment is the proper word."

"What then?"

Frederick shrugged. "I feel honored and blessed to be a part of all that is important to humankind."

"Do you believe?"

"What?"

"The words you speak."

"Of course."

"Can you explain?"

"No, it is not our task to explain."

"What then?"

"To help to ease the passage, to teach faith in God and acceptance of God's will, to help the believers grow stronger in their belief and to try to bring the nonbelievers to a state of grace."

There was something rehearsed and pat about his response, like one of the litanies memorized and trotted out upon demand.

They were nearing the end of the high north wall now. The wind was chill here, the shadows dark and damp, and yet just beyond, the sun was high and bright and promised warmth.

Frederick stopped abruptly and smiled. "Here is my job," he grinned, "to lead all who ask for my help out of the shadows of doubt and into the warmth of God's everlasting sun."

John smiled, though he felt full of doubt himself. "My father," he began, "was possibly the most loving and giving man I've ever known."

"I know," Frederick agreed. "Some of the schools Grandfather established in London still function as schools for deprived children. Did you know that?"

John didn't. He had little contact with London now. It seemed a faraway and irrelevant place.

"Did you know," John went on, "that my father was a doubter, saw only charlatans who paraded as men of God, saw the great cathedrals of

England and thought how far the gilt and gold would go in feeding the poor–"

Frederick walked quietly beside him with downcast eyes. John had hoped to shock him. Obviously he had failed, for he saw now a smile on his son's face.

"Papa," Frederick began softly, "I would never confess this to anyone but you. My own doubt on occasion is monstrous."

He lifted his eyes heavenward as though already feeling the need to seek Divine Forgiveness.

John was shocked. "Then all of this is charade, a mockery?"

"Oh no. I said my doubt on occasion is monstrous. At other times I am so absolutely convinced of the viable existence of my Savior and my Maker that the conviction leaves me breathless."

"Why have you never told this to anyone but me?" John asked, confounded and intrigued by Frederick's duplicity.

Frederick laughed. "Because no one ever asked. Yet I am convinced that in this early stage of my journey through this difficult world that there can be no true faith without equally true doubt, that the greatest prophets and teachers were fired in the furnace of doubt, that life everlasting is possible only after life limited."

Together they moved from the shadows of the north façade of Eden Castle out into full sun. The warmth instantly felt good. John experienced a peculiar peace. He couldn't account for it, but it was such a rare good feeling that he really didn't want to examine it too closely.

Ahead he saw the last of the mourners making their way into the Great Hall. Frederick saw them too and changed the subject. "You must excuse me now, Papa," he said. "I promised Geoffrey I would return today."

John looked up, surprised. "He unlocked the door for you?"

"No," Frederick said, picking up his robes as he walked backward. "We spoke through the locked door, but nonetheless I told him I would return and I shall."

He turned about for a wave and straightened his robes. "I'll join you later, Papa; we'll have a sherry before dinner."

Then he was gone, ducking through the low door to avoid striking his head.

John glanced up toward the Great Hall. Empty. Closed, everyone no doubt tending to poor Eve. He shut his eyes, feeling every day of his sixty years. He stood quite still, enjoying the sun on his head until he heard the

Great Hall door creak open and looked up to see Charlotte's face, visible around the heavy oak frame.

"Uncle John, are you busy?" she called down.

"No, I don't think so," John quipped, always pleased with Charlotte's appearance. The world would ask little of her except that she stand still and allow all to drink of her beauty.

"I need a bridge partner," she smiled, very much the coquette now. "Are you up to it?"

"And who are to be our opponents?"

"Lucy and Mason Frye."

The game was stupid, though quite the rage, and the opponents were both unskilled. So why not? Better than standing alone in the middle of the inner courtyard. "Be right up," he called out and was rewarded instantly with Charlotte's smile.

As he climbed the Great Hall steps, he wondered what had happened to the funereal mood he had felt in the graveyard. Gone and good riddance.

"I would love to beat them today, Uncle John," Charlotte whispered conspiratorially.

He put his arm about her shoulder and drew her close and cursed his sixty years and envied the man who would one day intimately know her beauty. "Then we *shall* beat them," he promised.

"Mason Frye is very clever and he has been practicing," she warned.

"But he is not as clever as we are," John smiled as he led her through the Great Hall doors and successfully put death and doubt and grief and age behind him.

Stanhope Hall
Outside Mobile, Alabama
April 12, 1896

After a too heavy noon meal, Mary retrieved her sewing basket and went out onto the front gallery to wait for David's return from Mobile with the post and hopefully news of Eve. She lifted her face to take in the spring air, to enjoy the burgeoning azaleas which lined the front gallery in a blaze of pink and white and to put the finishing lace trim on the blue satin infant's blanket. It always calmed her to work on the baby's clothes, helped to banish the fear and apprehension that her daughter was pregnant and so far away, established for the term of her pregnancy in Eden Castle, that bleak, cold pile of masonry in which Mary had spent that living nightmare which had passed for her childhood.

Carefully now she lifted one of the dainty satin rosettes from her sewing basket, steadily aligned it on the lace hem of the blue satin blanket, aimed her needle downward and attached it with one tiny stitch. Hundreds to go, yet it did help to fill the hours, waiting for the news of Eve's delivery.

There! Listen! She heard a horse. Quickly she looked up, and saw a rising dust cloud in the distance, approaching Stanhope land at a fast rate of speed.

Horse and rider turned into the avenue of live oaks, lost momentarily in their own dust cloud, a voice shouting something, and Mary felt the hair on her arms stand up despite the heat.

Behind her at the door she heard Nettie, "What is it, Miss Mary?" the old servant asked in hushed tones.

"Nettie, would you go and fetch Mr. Stanhope, please. He is in his study. If he is napping, awaken him gently."

"Yes, ma'am."

Mary turned immediately back toward the live oaks and saw David, something clutched in his hand, a piece of paper upraised. And he was still shouting.

"Mama, it's come. It's here. A boy. Eve has a baby boy."

How she was able to hear those words so clearly, she had no idea, for he was still at least seventy-five yards away. But she had heard, and now she closed her eyes in thanksgiving and would have given anything to open her eyes at Eve's bedside, to hold the infant.

"It's called a marconigram, Mama, look! It's a telegraphic message that Stephen sent through Cunard of the White Star Line. It was picked up at sea and then radioed–"

But Mary really could not have cared less about how the message had arrived. Here it was, in her hand, and signed by Stephen Eden, and addressed to Stanhope Hall.

> On March 13, after a prolonged labor, Eve was successfully delivered of a healthy baby boy. He will be christened Alexander Burke Eden.
>
> We are anxious to return home and will book passage as soon as Eve is capable of travel.
>
> Yours lovingly,
> Stephen Eden

Despite the excited throng gathering around her, Mary read it twice, her sharp maternal eyes snagging on certain key phrases—*after a prolonged labor*—how prolonged? *As soon as Eve is capable of travel*—

She heard Burke's step behind her and turned to see him grinning down. Apparently word had reached him.

"So," he smiled and put his arm about her and drew her close. "We have both reached the ultimate–grandparents."

She looked up at the sound of his voice, amazed at the size of the gathering. Almost all of the house servants had abandoned their duties as the word had spread.

"Well?" Burke prompted softly. "Shall I read the message to them or do you want to?"

Mary handed over the marconigram. "You do it," she urged and wished with all her heart that she could get past the worrisome nature of certain words in the message.

As Burke's strong voice rang out over the uplifted and expectant faces, Mary listened closely to see if the words sounded less worrisome when read aloud.

"We are anxious to return home," he concluded, "and will book passage as soon as Eve is capable of travel."

Is capable of travel—

"Why the long face?" Burke murmured, drawing near again.

"I'm worried."

"Why?"

"You read the message."

"Stephen would have told us if all was not well."

"Would he?"

"Oh, come, Mary, don't be a worrier. Let's lift a glass to our new grandson. Alexander Burke Eden." He thought for a moment. "It has a strong ring to it."

Then he led the way up the porch stairs, followed by a grinning David, who in turn was followed by an equally grinning corps of house servants, and at last Mary was alone on the portico, standing beside the rocker, staring down at the blue satin baby blanket.

Blue. Her instinct for color had been right, as were most of her instincts. That was why it was difficult for her to ignore them, particularly when they were as strong and persistent as this one, informing her that all was not well with her daughter, that there was more to a successful birth than producing a healthy child, that there was the health of the mother to be considered, and was anyone in that cold, distant castle paying the slightest attention to Eve's welfare?

The progression of her thoughts led her steadily forward into doubt and anxiety. She turned quickly in all directions, as though searching for the right path that would take her to England, to the North Devon Coast, to Eden Castle, to Eve.

Eden Castle
April 13, 1896

Around midnight John Murrey Eden heard that Marjorie had gone into labor, so he retrieved Richard from the hopelessness of a chess game with Mason Frye and the three men took refuge around the Great Hall fire, well fortified with several bottles of champagne.

"When?" Richard asked, clearly relieved at not having to face defeat at the hands of Mason Frye again.

"Who knows?" John shrugged, settling in close to the fire, his slippered feet resting on a hassock. "We must endure the screams first. Have you forgotten so soon?"

Mason Frye sat farthest from the fire. Mason always set himself apart with the unerring instinct of a superior man. Generally John objected to such arrogance. But in Mason's case, it was quite justified. He was far and away superior to most men.

"Come, Mason," John urged. "Closer. We desire your company and your conversation this evening. Perhaps you can enlighten us."

"On what subject?" Mason smiled and eased his chair possibly ten inches closer.

"On all subjects," John sighed. "For example, why has Eden Castle suddenly become the nursery of the world?"

"You have two sons of reproductive age. They both have gone forth and–reproduced."

John glanced over at the pat and extremely accurate answer. "Well spoken, Mason."

Suddenly the door leading down into the kitchen court opened and John saw two maids hurry past, their arms filled with linens. It had started.

"It's second floor, third door on the right," John called out with weary authority.

The two maids stopped, bewildered. "Oh no, sir, begging your pardon, this here ain't for Miss Marjorie. This is for poor Miss Eve. She's awful sick."

With that they were gone, leaving John and the other two gaping after them.

Mason offered, "Shall I go and see what–"

But John shook his head. "Stephen is there and Susan said she would divide her time–"

Listen! He looked up and glanced at the other two to see if they had heard it as well. A distant scream. Lord. It was starting all over again. He leaned forward, close to the fire, and put his hands over his ears and went blessedly deaf and wondered how long he could sit in this ridiculous position without someone making comment.

A few moments later he opened his eyes, not because he had heard something but because he sniffed something, a lovely rose fragrance which generally accompanied Charlotte wherever she went.

"Uncle John," Charlotte said. "May I . . . sit with you? I don't like it when they start to scream. Why do babies always have to come at night, when the gates are bolted and the sun is gone and everyone is forbidden to leave the castle?"

Quickly John moved his chair to one side and angled the hassock into position before the fire and with a pat indicated that Charlotte was to sit.

"No studies, Charlotte?" Mason Frye asked.

"All done," Charlotte said and reached out toward the fire in a graceful manner as though she meant to gather the warmth to her.

"Uncle John," she asked dreamily, studying the fire, "please tell me about India."

John groaned and leaned back in his chair. Why the child was constantly interested in that hot, dusty, insect-ridden hellhole he had no idea. Of course, Frederick had fanned the fires by writing to her during his six years in Delhi.

Before he had a chance to answer, Charlotte turned and looked up at him with a radiance that briefly rendered him speechless. "Frederick and Marjorie told me that you knew the last emperor of India? Is that true? And Marjorie told me that you rescued the emperor's granddaughter and great-grandson from the mutineers who were trying to kill them. Is that true, Uncle John?"

Confronted with such beauty yet recalling such tragic occurrences, John floundered. Her urgent questions had done nothing but stir a dusty chamber of his mind which he had closed off and sealed years ago. Now, with these innocent questions, the chamber doors had swung open and a good portion of his imagination was filled unexpectedly with the sights, sounds and smells of that day long ago when, in terror for his life as well as for the lives of Dhari and Aslam, he had confronted the Guard, had demanded Dhari's release as well as the release of her son, Aslam.

He tried to shake off the past, but it didn't shake so easily. Who would have thought it still resided so close to the surface of his consciousness?

"Aslam," he murmured, staring into the fire, seeing the dark-skinned, dark-eyed little boy who had maintained a vise-like grip around John's waist in that life-or-death horseback ride as they had fled from the insanity that was Delhi during the Indian Mutiny.

"What did you say, Uncle John?" Charlotte asked, moving her hassock closer, clearly not wanting to miss a word.

As John was slow to answer, Richard answered for him. " 'Aslam' was what he said. The name of the boy, the great-grandson of the old emperor."

John could sense the girl's increasing interest and knew that he could do better in describing that rich and varied world than Richard's flat account.

"I brought Aslam to London when he was a lad of seven, along with his mother."

"Did they cut out her tongue?" Charlotte asked, dwelling on the grotesque.

John hesitated before answering. Somehow such barbarism seemed out of place in the presence of Charlotte's pristine and innocent sweetness. Still, he answered truthfully. "Yes."

"How awful," Charlotte whispered compassionately and placed her hand to her lips. "Did she die?"

"Oh no," John said briskly, only too happy to change the subject. "Actually she married a good friend of mine and they emigrated to Canada. Last I heard there were several children, even a few grandchildren."

"And the little boy?" Charlotte asked.

John laughed. "Now he is one of the richest men in London, I dare say."

"And one of the most eccentric," Richard added beneath his breath.

"And he still lives in London?"

John nodded.

"Do you write to him?" Charlotte asked.

"No, I haven't corresponded with Aslam in ever so long."

"Do you see him when you go to London?"

"As you very well know Charlotte, I do not go up to London."

"You did once, several years ago."

John refilled his glass. He was more than ready to dismiss the subject.

"He took your name, didn't he?" Mason asked. "He is known as Aslam Eden, isn't he?"

John shrugged. "He was called Aslam Eden years ago at Cambridge."

Charlotte sat up, newly interested. "He went to Cambridge?"

"A good student, too," John said. "I think he's more English than Indian. In fact, I sometimes had the feeling that he resented his dark coloring."

"I think it's beautiful," Charlotte sighed. Then she looked at John with an expression that he had learned over the years meant trouble.

"Uncle John, I have an idea," she smiled.

"You generally do," John replied.

"Why don't you write to Aslam and invite him to come to Eden Castle?"

"Why?"

"Why not?" Charlotte countered. "You said yourself you hadn't seen him for years. If at one time you meant a great deal to one another, I should think you would be interested in seeing him. After all you saved his life. Why did you abandon him?"

"I didn't abandon him," John protested. "He no longer needed or wanted me."

"Nonsense. We always need and want the people we love and who love us in return."

John heard Mason Frye move his chair closer. "I think it is a splendid idea," he said. "I've heard that the man is reported to be a genius."

"You have heard of him?" Charlotte asked, rearranging her hassock, this time to include Mason Frye in the conversation.

"Of course I've heard of him. He is a stock market genius and truly, as John says, one of the richest men in England, if not the richest."

John sat back and let Mason Frye take the conversational floor, as he listened with interest to the opinion of an objective outsider. The last time he had seen Aslam Eden, circumstances had been far from happy. They had parted with bitter words.

He looked up out of his thoughts to hear Mason Frye still holding forth on the virtues of Aslam Eden: ". . . just off Knightsbridge, in Belgravia, or so I'm told, a palace in itself and one that rivals Buckingham."

"What is this?" John asked.

Charlotte glanced at him. "His palace, Aslam's palace, or at least Mr. Frye says it's a palace."

John found this of interest and was on the verge of pursuing it when suddenly he heard footsteps.

"Frederick?" John called out, recognizing the walk, the slant of the head.

Then he saw his son at the top of the steps, a broad grin on his face and a small lightly wrapped bundle cradled in his arms.

For several moments there was neither sound nor movement in the Great Hall. Was this Frederick's child? So soon? Was it dead? Why was it so still? And why had they heard none of the earsplitting screams of last week?

But then there was no need for further questions, for the smile of love and pride on Frederick's face said clearly that this was his child.

"Aren't you going to come and welcome your grandson, Papa? His name is Christopher Edward Eden, named for your father, Papa, a good man."

John was vaguely aware of the collective sighs of relief around him. But he was more aware of the extreme pleasure he felt as Frederick came forward and placed the baby in his arms. "Christopher, this is your grandfather, a most remarkable gentleman."

John stared down at a wide-eyed baby who was returning his gaze with matching intensity.

Two sons having two sons.

Alexander Burke Eden.

Christopher Edward Eden.

The best of John, the best of his father, the best of every Eden that had preceded him back to the eleventh century.

"May I see, Uncle John?"

It was Charlotte, and behind her Richard and Mason Frye, all inching carefully forward as though they were approaching a holy place, which in a way they were, for in his arms he held the continuity of the Eden line, the same blood that had coursed through a long, unbroken succession, and in this age of transient values and transient beliefs, when the nature and face of everything was changing so rapidly, this small bundle encompassing the past, the present and the future *was* holy.

Reluctantly, he passed the infant to Charlotte's waiting arms. She took him wonderingly and lightly kissed his forehead.

"He's perfect, Frederick, truly perfect," she marveled, and for just an instant John saw through her great physical beauty to an inner beauty that he had seldom glimpsed before with such clarity. She would be capable of giving great love one day.

"Look, Papa," she whispered, and carried the infant to where Richard and Mason Frye were waiting. Both men seemed awkward, made a cursory examination of the small face framed by the blanket, then stepped back as though wanting no responsibility.

"You, Mason," John called out good-naturedly, still amazed at the speed and ease with which this grandchild had arrived, "I hope you are up to educating a whole new generation of Edens." He smiled and motioned for Charlotte to return the baby to him.

"Marjorie . . . ?" he asked of Frederick who was standing close beside him.

". . . is well," Frederick smiled. "She asked me to send her love to all of you and said she would join us for breakfast. Alice said it was the easiest birth she had ever attended."

John was pleased with all the news. Frederick stepped closer. "Eve is ill again."

The announcement sat heavy on the air, curiously juxtaposed with the good tidings. Then Charlotte was before him, transferring the baby from her arms to John's. John grasped him, carried him to the fire, sat in his comfortable chair, drew back the blanket and studied the perfection before him.

Though less than one hour old, he was perfect in all ways. Plump, pink, with steady dark blue eyes which seemed to survey his world with great understanding. John placed his index finger in the tiny hand and felt a firm grasp.

"A marvel," John murmured more to himself than anyone else, moved anew by the potential of this child. His cousin, too. Two little boys ready to race into the new century, mint-perfect and full of promise.

Suddenly the perfect features contorted in anger. John lifted him instantly, trying to ease the squeal that clearly was imminent.

"He's hungry," Frederick laughed. "Marjorie is waiting," and quickly he scooped up his son, rewrapped the blanket and promised John, "You may have him anytime you wish, except at feedings. And though you are capable of many things, I doubt if–"

"Thank you for bringing him to us," John said, following after him to the stairs. "Tell Marjorie that she has labored well."

At the top of the steps Frederick looked down. "Pray for Eve and Stephen," he added, and John recognized the priestly voice taking the place of the new father's voice.

"Is she very ill?" Charlotte asked, the one question that was on everyone's mind.

But Frederick shook his head. "According to Dr. Reicher, the fever is the result of a lingering infection. He's trying to take steps now. Susan is with him."

"Alice?" John asked warily.

"She is with Marjorie," Frederick said.

"Keep her away from Dr. Reicher," John added with a sigh. "I would like to remain in his good graces for a while."

Again Frederick agreed. Then he was gone, carrying his new son down the darkened corridor toward Marjorie's room. John heard him talking to the baby, nonsense sounds of pure love, soothing the child's hunger with promises of food.

John waited, staring into the darkened corridor until he could hear nothing else. Then he turned back to the fire, smiling, feeling strangely weary and exhilarated at the same time. Out of the corner of his eye, he caught Mason Frye resettling in his chair.

"I meant it, Mason," he said with sudden force. "Are you up to taking on these two boys?"

"And I meant it as well," Mason nodded. "I will do my best for as long as I can do my best. I think perhaps, however, it is wise if they grow for a few years first."

"Mustn't wait too long," John said, ignoring the humor in Mason's voice. "I want them to be inferior to no man, do you hear? And I think, Richard, that we should hire physical instructors as well, teach them athletics, the Greek model. I have often thought that is where I failed with Albert. I don't want to fail with these two. They will be the best in all respects, I swear it. The very best."

"But," Charlotte said, "what if Stephen and Eve wish to take Alexander back to America? It is her home."

John glared at her. "Unthinkable," he said curtly. "Stephen would not permit it."

Richard made an unwanted contribution. "I have heard Stephen say he is very fond of America."

"He is an Englishman through and through," John replied.

"Still, there is that possibility."

"Nonsense," John snapped and wished they would all go to bed and leave him alone. He had plans to make, and he could do it best alone.

Then, as though they had heard his wish, all three shifted out of their toasted lethargy before the fire and bid John good night.

Charlotte kissed him sweetly on the top of his head, and he reached for her hand and clasped it tightly. "It will be your turn one day," he smiled, "and how beautiful your children will be."

She lightly shook her head. "I wish one didn't have to swell up like a melon. Surely God could have thought of a better way."

John laughed and thought her the most entrancing creature.

"My congratulations, John," Richard smiled. "I shall awaken Eleanor and give her the joyous news," he promised. "She will be very put out, hates to miss anything, as you know."

John waved good night and saw Mason Frye, books in hand, moving slowly toward the staircase that would lead him to his chambers in the east wing. Unfinished business there.

"Mason, I need your word on it. I mean about the two new Edens."

"And you have my word on it as far as it is in my power to give it. But you know some things are out of my hands."

"I don't understand."

"I'm forty-two, not in the best of health. Another plan for my life might present itself. I might want to marry."

John sat up, shocked. "Marry? Who? And are you ill? And if so why didn't you–"

Mason Frye lifted restraining hands. "Do not worry, please. I have no specific complaint and no mate on the horizon, and yet I don't climb those stairs with the agility and speed I once did and at times I suffer a loneliness that books can't cure."

"Why haven't you spoken of this before?"

"Please don't worry, John. The two little boys will need my services in about three years at the earliest, and that I feel confident I can fulfill. Beyond that, I suggest we wait and see."

It was not the arrangement John had sought, but he smiled and nodded, thinking that one thing Mason Frye had said was true, and that was how lonely the man must be, educating other people's children, living in other people's homes, well paid, but nonetheless confined and limited–and lonely.

John had just turned back to the fire after Mason's departure when he heard someone speak his name.

"John?"

At the sound of the beloved familiar voice coming from the opposite side of the Great Hall, he looked up and saw Susan, a very tired Susan, whose white nurse's apron had become twisted, whose face was fringed by locks of loose hair and whose stance suggested that if she did not sit down soon, she would fall down.

"My dearest," he smiled, so pleased to see her.

"Sit," he ordered and reached back for a bottle of champagne on the table, poured a glass and handed it to her.

She looked at it briefly as though debating whether or not to take it; finally she did, drank several sips and leaned back in her chair.

Slowly she shook her head. "So different those two," she mused. "Alice said they could serve as textbook cases."

"I don't understand."

"Eve and Marjorie," she replied.

"Is Eve in danger?" he asked.

"Dr. Reicher says no. Alice says yes."

"And whom do you believe?"

Susan shrugged. "We should go to the cottage, early clinic tomorrow," she murmured, her eyes already half closed.

John wished she weren't so tired. He wanted to make love to her. But he knew she was exhausted.

He sat up carefully on the edge of his chair and watched her, watched the champagne glass begin to tilt to one side under the effects of her relaxation. As her head fell heavily to one side he caught the glass before it could fall. Carefully he placed it on the table and stood over his now sleeping wife and tenderly lifted her into his arms, then cradled her close, enjoying the feel of her head against his shoulder, a soft moan of comfort as she nestled yet closer.

"John?" she murmured sleepily. "Where are you . . . ?"

"To bed."

"Will you make love to me?"

He kissed her forehead and thanked God for His gift of this remarkable woman and promised her with firm conviction, "Yes!"

Eden Castle
May 3, 1896

The day dawned with a bright sun and a chill wind, one of those indecisive North Devon days when winter and spring seemed locked in a fierce battle for possession of the elements.

Dressed in real clothes for the first time in three months, Eve felt uncomfortable in the confinement of hooks and buttons and tried to take her mind off her discomfort by watching the distant whitecaps in the channel. Behind her, close to the fire, she heard Alexander suckling contentedly at Marjorie's breast. Marjorie had already nursed Christopher, who was sleeping peacefully in the double crib which John had ordered, handmade by craftsmen in Exeter. Now there was one in Eve's chambers and one in Marjorie's, interchangeable beds for two little boys who were themselves fast becoming interchangeable.

Eve glanced back toward the fire. The envy she once had felt was gone. It had been determined that her milk was neither rich nor plentiful enough. Marjorie it seemed, had more than enough for both infants.

"They're both hungry today," Marjorie said, glancing up.

"They know they are going to be christened," Eve replied, returning Marjorie's smile. She was growing close to Marjorie, a sisterly bond that seemed to please them both.

"Are you feeling stronger today, Eve?" Marjorie asked. "We all want you in the chapel with us. Stephen and Frederick–"

"I'll be there," Eve smiled, and as though by way of demonstrating her new strength, she walked in a steady gait back toward the fire. She received Marjorie's smile of praise and sat opposite her and extended her bare feet toward the fire.

"No shoes?" Marjorie laughed. "Good heavens, Eve, you are tempting fate. Please, where are your warm slippers?"

Eve didn't know and said as much. "As for tempting fate," she added, staring into the fire, "I used to care a great deal about fate and destiny, all of those empty words which Yorrick mouthed with such frequency."

"You don't believe in them now?" Marjorie asked.

Eve hesitated before answering. She didn't want to hurt Marjorie, who after all was the wife of an Anglican priest and who obviously believed terribly in almost everything.

"It's not important whether I believe or disbelieve," Eve replied. She leaned back against the chair, feeling tired at midmorning. Sweet Lord, she had been out of bed for less than four hours and she was tired.

Now aware of Marjorie's close scrutiny, Eve completed her explanation, sorry that the subject had even come up. "It is good," she said softly, "like putting down heavy luggage. For so long I worried about so much, mostly subjects pertaining to vanity. Now I suspect that nothing I was worrying about truly mattered anyhow."

"What does matter to you now?" Marjorie asked, shifting Alexander from her breast to her shoulder.

"Him," Eve smiled, looking at her son, growing plump on Marjorie's milk.

"Anything else?"

"Stephen, of course. And you."

As Eve confided her feelings of friendship for Marjorie, the two women exchanged a good silence. Then Marjorie stood and deposited Alexander in Eve's arm, lifted Christopher from his cradle and drew her chair close to Eve.

In the spirit of two little girls playing with their dolls, they rested their babies in their laps and studied their unique beauty.

"What do you think?" Marjorie mused. "Would you call that the Eden jawline?"

"Without a doubt," Eve said. "Look at Alexander. Same jaw, same angle."

"I want them to be close," Marjorie said.

"They will be," Eve said. "As soon as Christopher is old enough, perhaps he will come and spend some time with Alexander in America. You and Frederick as well. How I would love to show you Stanhope Hall. It's so beautiful. And it's just the right place for little boys, complete with a pond for bathing and the Mobile River for fishing. These two will love it, I know, and I'm certain–"

She looked up from her memories to see a new expression on Marjorie's face, one of mild shock. "You are . . . not– What I mean is, you aren't going to stay here, in England?"

Eve laughed, "Good heavens, no."

"Does Stephen agree?"

"But of course. At least I think he does. We have never really discussed–"

There was a knock at the door. "Come in," Eve called out and lifted Alex to her shoulder. Of course they would go home. Alex was going to be an American, as she was.

As the door pushed open, she saw first Susan and then the smiling, mildly self-conscious faces of Frederick and Stephen. They looked quite elegant in their dress blacks.

It wasn't until the two men had come all the way into the room that Eve saw the small nosegays of violets, Frederick clutching one, Stephen the other. The formal way in which they clasped the flowers made them look like young schoolboys who had come courting.

"Eleven o'clock," Frederick said somewhat witlessly, for no one had asked for the time.

"Of course," Marjorie murmured, and drew up her shirtwaist and disappeared behind the screen to the left of the fireplace.

The christening was set for half past eleven in the family chapel. Was it time? So soon?

This was Eve's first voyage out into the world since her confinement, and she wasn't looking forward to it. Her knees felt weak. Perhaps it was too soon.

"Eve?" The voice was Stephen's, who apparently saw the lack of spirit and went to her side. "Here," he smiled, "for you. I'm afraid it was Aunt Eleanor's idea. Still–"

Eve took the violets and buried her nose in the soft purple fragrance. "They smell like spring," she said.

"How are you feeling?"

"Well," she lied.

From the door Susan called back, "We are gathering in the chapel. As soon as you are ready–"

Quickly she closed the door as though sensitive to their needs at this remarkable moment. Two brothers, two wives, two sons.

"Well, what do you think?" she heard Stephen ask of anyone who cared to answer. He had removed the blanket from Alex and held him up for inspection.

"Near perfection," Frederick replied, a light tone to his voice as though both men knew they were playing a game. "Now, this," Frederick said and held Christopher up in a similar fashion, "*is* perfection. Just look."

"Who will lead and who will follow?" asked Stephen.

"They will keep pace," Frederick replied.

Marjorie stirred. "One I fear will grow up in America, so they will have to be long-range friends."

All at once both Stephen and Frederick turned on her, the wonder of their expressions gone, replaced by shock.

"What do you mean?"

As Stephen began a disjointed question, Eve wished that Marjorie had not chosen this moment to bring up this subject.

"Later," Eve said.

"No," Stephen insisted, "what did Marjorie mean?"

"You said so yourself," Eve apologized, aware of Marjorie and Frederick's growing embarrassment.

"Said what?" Stephen asked.

"That we could go home," Eve murmured.

"But not to stay, not to live."

Eve looked up at her husband. "Why not? You said you felt comfortable there. At home."

Stephen laughed. "Of course I feel comfortable. But my life is here, my past as well as my future. Eve, I thought you knew that. But to visit, of course, and soon and as often as you wish."

Eve turned back to the window. Of course this was his home. But America was hers.

Stephen put his arms about her. "We needn't solve this problem now. There will be time, I assure you. And besides, I have booked passage for America for the last of June. A short seven weeks from now. And all you must do is to regain your strength."

For several moments there was no movement in the room except for the soft nonsense sounds made by Alexander. At some point they became quite comical, like a small, slightly inebriated bird, and despite her weakness, Eve laughed. "I'm ready," she said, and to prove her new strength, she led the way to the door and looked back on the others, all of whom were watching her as though she were a bomb on the verge of exploding.

Eleanor was certain that this drafty old castle had never seen such a celebration as the baptism of Christopher and Alexander.

She stood near the rear of the chapel, hoping to appear in charge. The setting was lovely, a late morning sun striking the stained glass windows. One window in particular caught Eleanor's eye as being appropriate, Christ surrounded by the children.

"Suffer the little children to come unto me . . ."

As Frederick commenced the ritual of baptism, Eleanor looked about. Everyone was present and accounted for.

She smiled at Mrs. Partridge, who was just leading in a small parade of favored servants. It was perfectly alright with Eleanor. In fact, she had told Mrs. Partridge to fill the chapel if she wished. Normally baptisms were rituals of great celebration, with fetes before, during and after and frequently concluding with a formal ball. She had only mentioned her ideas for a grand celebration to Richard, and he had been adamantly opposed.

Now, however, seated at the rear of the chapel, studying the back of Richard's head, she thought again that it was time they all sat down and planned a grand celebration, let all of England come and see how well the Edens were doing. It had been years. Actually she couldn't even remember the last time that formal invitations had gone out under the Eden seal.

In her excitement she must have made a sound, for Lucy and Molly turned around and stared at her as though she had spoken to them.

Eleanor gave them a reassuring smile and crossed herself. The two little boys were beautiful, and for that reason and of course several others, the Midsummer Eve's ball had now become a fixed and unalterable certainty in her mind. And Eleanor knew herself well enough to know that when that happened–

"Blessed be God the Father, Son and Holy Spirit–"

Eleanor heard a rush for the Book of Common Prayer as the audience realized Frederick was waiting for the response.

"And blessed be his kingdom now and forever."

Frederick and Marjorie were Alexander's godparents and Stephen and Eve were Christopher's, so the dialogue in the small chapel involved no one but the four at the altar, all bathed now in the rosiest hue of noon sunlight coming from the high rose window.

From the front, she heard, "Do you renounce Satan and all spiritual forces of wickedness that rebel against God?"

And the answer, "I renounce them."

There were other questions, other responses, softly spoken, softly answered.

So the two little boys were now welcomed into the Kingdom of God. Surely little boys everywhere were welcomed by God, even without this ritual. Still, it had been good and Eleanor settled back to wait out the Eucharist, so pleased with the new life that had been recognized today, pleased that Geoffrey was home, perhaps not yet fully intact, but he would be soon, of that she was certain.

Now in the passivity of all religious ritual, she allowed her mind free play: *Lord and Lady Eden cordially request the very great honor of your presence at their Midsummer Eve Fete to take place—*

When?

Stymied, Eleanor looked up just as everyone else was looking down and kneeling in prayer. Hurriedly she followed suit, and as she went down on one knee, she caught a clear view of the back of John Murrey Eden's head.

There was her one and only obstacle. She could handle Richard, could persuade him to anything if she so desired. The staff would not present a problem. Certainly the children would not block her, nor would Susan, nor would anyone on this earth—except John Murrey Eden.

Her eyes leveled in determination while everyone else's closed in prayer. Belatedly she closed her eyes and prayed briefly for the souls of Alexander Burke Eden and Christopher Edward Eden, then prayed that she might, just this once, outfox, outmaneuver and outwit John Murrey Eden.

Frederick's praying voice soared, "In the name of the Father and the Son, and of the Holy Spirit, Amen."

"Amen," Eleanor smiled and felt strong and determined and successful.

Dr. Reicher was putting the last items from the bureau into his satchel, making certain that he was forgetting nothing. He was already dreading his departure from this idyllic castle, yet he sensed the time had come. Geoffrey had made all the improvement he was going to make physically, and his mental and spiritual condition was beyond the expertise of Dr. Reicher.

He paused, lovingly caressing the two sterling silver picture frames which closed upon each other like a book, on one side his Sonia, and on the other his miracle son, Rolf.

He had met Sonia in Munich as a medical student. The fact of their love had never been a matter for debate, and one year to the day after their meeting, they had married.

Dr. Reicher hurried to complete his schooling, confident their first child would be along soon. But it was not to be.

A colleague had sent them to a Dr. Smyth-Trent on Harley Street in London. They had visited Dr. Smyth-Trent for three months of treatment, and in the fourth, Sonia was pronounced with child and their joy had known no bounds. Because Dr. Smyth-Trent had wanted to see her to term, they had moved to London, where Dr. Reicher had established a small private practice. Nine months later a baby boy had been born. They named him Rolf.

He studied the two faces a moment longer, snapped the frame together and packed it carefully into the valise.

Back to London then. Little more he could do here. While he had not counted on playing midwife to the two Eden women, he was happy to have been of what little service he could, though the confrontation with Mr. Eden's young daughter had been distasteful. Dr. Reicher had seen her type before, aggressive, more male than female, hating all masculine authority, given to the delusion of feminine superiority.

Still, that one confrontation had been the only blight on an otherwise pleasant, as well as profitable, stay, and for that Dr. Reicher was grateful.

Now it was time to go back to London, and with the exception of his anticipation at seeing Sonia and Rolf again, he dreaded it.

He had read in the newspapers that anti-German feeling was running high in London. Since the British defeat in the Transvaal, German shopkeepers had had their windows broken.

Still seated on the edge of his bed, Dr. Reicher stared glumly at the Oriental patterns beneath his feet. Perhaps he should just return to London and gather up Sonia and Rolf and return to the Fatherland. It would be a simple matter to relocate in Munich, for both had distant relatives there and distant friends, but German politics were unstable now. In fact, all the major European powers were playing dangerous games of advance and retreat, accusation, counteraccusation, taunt and run.

Suddenly weary, Dr. Reicher leaned over and cradled his head in his hands. Where to go?

All at once there was a rap on the door. He looked up from his confusion.

"Who is it?" he called out.

"It's John Murrey Eden, Dr. Reicher. A word if I may, please."

Dr. Reicher stared at the door, curious as to why Mr. Eden had come all the way up to say farewell.

"Just a moment," Dr. Reicher called out, adjusting his tie and jacket, which had become twisted. After a brief glance in the mirror, he drew open the door to find Mr. Eden on the opposite side.

"Mr. Eden," Dr. Reicher smiled cordially.

"May I come in?"

"Of course," Reicher apologized, standing back to make room for the man's passage, still bewildered as to his presence. Dr. Reicher had understood that a family christening was to take place about noon. He had assumed that the entire family would be occupied for some time.

"The christening–" Reicher began.

"It is completed," Mr. Eden said, strolling at leisure through the apartment.

He disappeared into the sitting room, then reemerged in the bedroom.

Finally he came to a halt near the bed and glanced down on Dr. Reicher's valise. "I see you are packed."

"Yes, I had hoped to leave earlier."

"You must be eager to return to London and your family."

"It has been a long time."

"You have a child, don't you?"

"Yes, a little boy. Almost a year."

"Name?"

"Rolf."

"Rolf Reicher," John repeated and once again started pacing throughout the apartment. "You realize, of course," he called out from what sounded like the farthest quarter of the apartment, "that London might be hazardous just now."

"Yes, I am aware of that."

"Have you considered returning to Germany?"

"Not seriously."

"Why not?"

"Because Germany, too, is now a hazardous place."

Eden nodded as though he knew the answers all along and was just testing him.

For several moments neither man spoke, though Dr. Reicher felt a new tension in the room. Then Eden sat in a nearby chair, crossed his legs, rested his arms on the curved back and without hesitating pronounced, "Dr. Reicher, I have a proposition for you. Now hear me out before you speak. Even then, I would advise that you ponder carefully before you reply, for I *have* thought it over and believe that I may have found a solution to our mutual problems."

"Go ahead, Mr. Eden, I'm listening," Dr. Reicher urged and stood curiously at attention.

"Well then, it's simple," Eden pronounced. "In my opinion, and Lord Eden agrees, that for now and for a considerable time in the future, Eden will be requiring the full-time services of a skilled medical man."

Dr. Reicher thought as much and thought at the same time, no thank you.

"And not only will Geoffrey require care from time to time; Eve, as you know is not faring well. We are quite frankly very worried."

As well you should be, thought Dr. Reicher.

"And then, even if these two invalids recuperate, we have the joyous task ahead of raising two little boys."

Mr. Eden shook his head in the manner of an authority. "I have raised boys, Dr. Reicher. Every day seems to bring a new crisis of splinters, cuts, falls, bruises, childhood ailments, too much sun, too little sun. They seem in constant need of medical attention."

"Your wife is a trained nurse," Dr. Reicher reminded him.

"My wife is slightly beyond middle age. She has worked hard all her life. I would like to see her granted some time off."

"I can understand that, and I agree that the presence of a medical man within the walls of Eden Castle would be most beneficial for the next several years." He paused before delivering his final response. "But I'm afraid it can't and won't be me."

"Why not?"

"As you well know, Mr. Eden, I have a family in London."

"I know that."

"Well, what am I to do with them?"

"Bring them, man, are you out of your mind? Of course bring your wife and your son. He has two playmates now, a full contingent for Mason

Frye, who by the way can provide your son with a caliber of education that he will get nowhere else."

Dr. Reicher was momentarily stunned. He had no idea, had not dreamed that Eden was willing to let him bring his family.

"For how long?"

"That is entirely up to you. Mason Frye arrived at Eden and announced that he would stay for only three years." Eden paused for effect. "That was over twenty years ago."

For the first time in several minutes the room was quiet. Somewhere in the distance, Dr. Reicher heard the neighing of impatient horses.

"Your salary will stay the same," Mr. Eden said as though with an additional enticement. "However, all of the current living expenses for your family in London would quite naturally be eliminated."

Dr. Reicher looked up. "This apartment?"

"If you wish. However, I had a larger, more spacious one in mind directly beneath this one on the second floor. Our goal is to make you and your family comfortable. Your goal will be to make the burgeoning Eden family as healthy as possible." Another pause. "Do you have an early opinion, Dr. Reicher?"

"I have a request," Reicher said.

"Anything."

"My one bone of contention with Eden."

"Name it and it shall be removed."

"Your daughter, sir, the one they call Alice, the one who fancies herself superior to all men."

For a moment it was difficult to tell what Mr. Eden's reaction would be to this harsh criticism of a member of his family.

"Done," he muttered. "She returns to London anyway at the end of this week, to her duties at St. Martin's."

"How do you intend to keep her out of my affairs?"

"By telling her to stay out of them."

Now Reicher heard the ringing of the departure bell in the courtyard, the signal that a carriage was ready and waiting.

"My thanks, Mr. Eden, for all your consideration. I shall give the matter serious thought."

"I don't want your thanks," Eden smiled. "Send me word soon that you will be joining us in the delightful task of raising two small boys—three really, counting yours."

"Goodbye then. I can find my way out."

With that Dr. Reicher closed the door, shifted his satchel to the other hand and for the first time smiled, pleased with the offer.

It literally was an answer to all their prayers. A place of safety outside London.

They are German, you know.

And Sonia would flourish in the North Devon air and, in his opinion, would fit in nicely with Lady Eleanor, who seemed a devoted wife and mother. As for Mr. Eden's wife, well, that was another matter.

Still, so long as he didn't have to encounter that Alice creature, he could foresee a pleasant tenure at Eden Castle and only hoped that Sonia would agree.

Why shouldn't she? She was a good wife, submissive, the best. Perhaps she could give a lesson or two in womanhood to the headstrong and willful women of Eden.

Eden Castle
June 15, 1896

Charlotte looked about at the cluttered dining room table. On one end sat three sizable stacks of velvet-smooth ecru envelopes. Invitations. Hundreds of them. The entire world, or so it seemed, would be invited to come to Eden Castle.

By mid-June, plans for the Midsummer Eve ball, scheduled to commence on July 13, had reached fever pitch. Of course they were celebrating Midsummer Eve later than the calendar date, but the time was needed for preparation. The small library off the Great Hall had been designated as the battle room, and Charlotte made it a point to be at her position all day, every day, and sometimes well into the night. The servants had been forbidden to tidy the room for fear of disrupting a logic which made sense only to Eleanor.

Now, though it was scarcely half past six, Charlotte was already up, dressed, and ready for another exciting day. The early morning half-light cast eerie shadows on the various chalkboards which her mother had asked Mason Frye to bring down from the schoolrooms. Four of them stood like an orderly Stonehenge about the shadowy room, their surfaces smudged from repeated erasings as plans were made, then unmade, and minds were changed and changed back again.

Almost reverently Charlotte approached the master guest list on the largest chalkboard, each name written in her father's tiny, precise handwriting, row upon row of names, hundreds of names, all bearing a connection with one member of the Eden family or the other. There were her father's guests, aristocrats all, thin-lipped, ruddy-cheeked blue bloods who were coming only for the fox hunt and, or at least so her mother hoped, bringing their thin-lipped, ruddy-cheeked marriageable sons.

Charlotte allowed her eyes to run over the list of Lord So-and-so and Lady This-and-that. She wasn't interested. There was only one name she really wanted to see on that enormous chalkboard, and thus far she had not seen it.

Aslam Eden, the great-grandson of the last emperor of India. Aslam Eden, the little boy her Uncle John had rescued from mutineers before the fall of Delhi.

"You're up early, my lady. Tea?"

"Trudy, I didn't hear you come in." For some reason Charlotte felt embarrassed and moved quickly away from her thoughts of exotic strangers.

"Tea, my lady?" Trudy repeated, and Charlotte sniffed the delicious elixir of morning tea and toast squares.

"Thank you, Trudy," she smiled and took the cup being offered.

"Some doings, my lady," Trudy murmured, turning her attention to the chalkboards covered over with names. "They've already started down in the kitchen court, you know. Mrs. Partridge has filled the smokehouse three days in a row, and today she's hiring extras from Exeter and anyplace else she can find them."

Charlotte drank her tea and said nothing as Trudy launched into a close inspection of the chalkboards. "What is all this, my lady, if I may?"

"This," Charlotte said, pointing to the first board on which her father had meticulously pinned a master guest list, "is a list of everyone who will be in attendance at the Midsummer Eve fete."

"Gawd!"

Charlotte looked back at Trudy's shocked voice. "Is this here really what I see?" she whispered and pointed to a certain name at the top of the list.

Edward, Prince of Wales.

"Will he come?" Trudy asked, her eyes still wide with disbelief.

"Of course he will. Oh, I don't know. But then why not? It will be the grandest occasion of the season."

Just as Charlotte was returning her teacup to the serving tray, she heard steps outside in the corridor, the steps she had been waiting to hear.

"Papa," she smiled, and ran to the door to greet him. She kissed him lightly on the cheek and saw a look of sleep still in his eyes. Good. Catch him now in a half-asleep moment before he has time to think and object.

"You are up early," Richard said, embracing Charlotte and looking longingly at the tea tray.

Charlotte saw the look.

"Trudy, would you ask Mrs. Partridge to serve breakfast tea and muffins here in the library. Please . . ."

Her father appeared to freeze until Trudy had closed the door behind her. Now he stretched lightly and at last came to a stop before the triple mountains of carefully addressed invitations, which would all go out today. He stared fixedly down upon them.

"Dear God," he prayed.

"Oh, Papa," she scolded. "It isn't going to be the end of the world."

She permitted a touch of disappointment to enter her voice, having learned long ago that her father could never resist that tone of disappointment.

Ultimately, and true to form, he shook his head and put his arm about Charlotte's shoulders and walked slowly to the far end of the library, to the window that looked out over the channel.

"No, it won't be so bad. Anything can be endured for a limited period of time. And your mother is right on one score: you must be brought out properly for your sake as well as the family's."

Charlotte didn't quite understand this last comment but quickly dismissed it. She walked easily beside him and realized anew how much she loved him, despite the fact that he was shy and limited and provincial.

"Papa . . ."

Charlotte let her voice drift off, always an effective device for getting her father's attention.

"Yes, my dearest," he answered, standing directly before the window now, hands laced behind his back.

"I want to ask a favor of you."

"Anything, my dearest, you know that."

She hurried back to the library table and lifted an unaddressed invitation from the small stack next to the addressed ones and carried it back to the window where her father stood.

"Address this," she said bluntly.

He looked puzzled, first at the invitation and then at her.

"You mean we have forgotten someone?"

"We have," she said.

"Then you address it. Your penmanship is far better than–"

"No, Papa, this one must come from you."

Again he looked bewildered. "Why? I don't understand–"

"It must have your seal on it, Papa. Papa, please don't say no."

"To what, Charlotte? You are not making sense."

She knew she wasn't and closed her eyes in an effort at self-composure. "It must be a surprise for Uncle John."

"What must?"

"This invitation."

"To whom?"

"Aslam Eden."

Her father blinked, started to speak, then shook his head and moved past her back toward the fire. "Out of the question," he said flatly.

"Papa, wait, please," she begged and hurried after him.

"Now, first of all," she began, still holding the invitation in her hand, "we all agreed that there would be a certain Auld Lang Syne feeling to the Midsummer festivities, friends gone out of our lives but not forgotten.

"Aslam Eden once threatened to kill John Murrey Eden."

She blinked at the announcement.

"Uncle John has a way," she said, "of infuriating people and causing them to say and do things."

"Do things!" her father repeated incredulously. "The two men despise each other."

"Uncle John did not give that impression the last time he spoke of Aslam. He sounded almost nostalgic."

"He was recalling Aslam the boy, not Aslam the man."

"Papa, I think we should give Uncle John the chance to renew his friendship with a man who was once so important to him."

"If he wants that chance, he knows how to contact Aslam."

"But he won't. You know Uncle John. He is stubborn to a fault. Stephen has told me how he alienated Eve's mother, *his own sister*, and now he would give anything to be back in her good graces."

Her father looked doubting from the window. "Stephen told you that?"

"He did indeed–and more. He said Uncle John confided that he was a fool as a young man, headstrong and willful and arrogant. He said that he had driven away everyone that he loved and who loved him."

Her father looked down at her. "What is your interest in all this?"

She shook her head and looked up innocently. "Reconciliation," she said sweetly. "No more drifts and chasms between Eden Castle and the world. How would it hurt, Papa, this one invitation? Aren't we taught to forgive? You know as well as I that Uncle John is not an evil man, just a–"

"I know what your Uncle John is far better than you," her father snapped and walked farther away, as though needing to put distance between himself and her considerable persuasive abilities.

"Oh please, Papa," she concluded, still pursuing. "All you have to do is address it and put your seal on it. That way we can be sure that it will be brought to the attention of Mr. Aslam Eden. After that, he can do with it as he likes and we at least will have followed our religious teachings, everything that we have been taught since we were children, love thine enemies, do good to–"

Defeated, he raised a restraining hand like a white flag. "Oh, spare me the sermon, Charlotte. I loathe them even from the qualified. From you they are intolerable."

"Will you sign it and seal it, Papa?"

He looked at her over his shoulder as though newly aware that he could deny her nothing. "Hand it to me," he said, seeming exhausted at eight-thirty in the morning. "If trouble results, however, I swear I will disclaim all knowledge of this act."

Quickly she handed over the invitation, and then assumed his position by the window, seeing not seagulls or fishing packets but, instead, the dark-skinned great-grandson of the last emperor of India. Suddenly she shivered in a direct ray of sun and listened carefully to her father's quill as it scratched its way across the linen parchment.

She looked back and saw him affix the Eden seal in red wax, the all-important signal to any servant that this particular parchment was from a lord of the Realm and must be placed directly in the hands of the addressee.

"Thank you, Papa," she whispered and came up behind him where he sat at the table, the invitation now addressed before him, his hands limp in his lap.

"I have done the deed," he pronounced with what she thought was undue melodrama. "Shall you tell John?" he asked, clearly looking to her for advice now in this matter.

"Oh no," she gasped. "We mustn't do that because . . . Uncle John's heart might not be in a receiving and forgiving mood until he glimpses this man whose life he saved. I suspect that only then will forgiveness come and healing and . . . all those other things."

As she exhausted her storehouse of biblical "things," she looked closely to see if she had a reliable ally in her father. She did. Of course she did. It had always been so easy to manipulate him, a fact that both pleased and saddened her.

"Don't worry, Papa; it will be a glorious moment, I assure you, and you can take full credit. I want none."

"Nor do I," he said firmly and slowly rose from the chair and looked toward the library door. "Where is that blasted girl with my breakfast?"

"I'll go and see, Papa."

"No, I don't–"

"No trouble, not for my father." She stood on tiptoe and kissed him lightly on the cheek and saw the love in his eyes and was grateful for it.

"I'll be right back," she smiled and quickly lifted the most important invitation and slipped it safely into the center of the stacks on one end of the table. A special messenger would take them at noon today to London for immediate personal delivery. Then it was done. She smiled and closed the door.

"May I ask what you're doing?" The close familiar voice stirred depths of panic, and she looked directly up into the face of John Murrey Eden.

"I . . . am– I . . . was going to– What I mean is–"

"Good Lord, girl," Uncle John laughed, "you sound witless. Is your father in there?"

She immediately stepped to one side and felt her heart beating so fast that it felt as though it were on the verge of bursting through her breast.

Would Papa say anything? Should she think up some pretext for reentering the room?

No! She had accomplished her goal. She trusted her father, and now she had much to do. She had set wheels in motion that might conceivably change her life, and she wanted more than anything in the world to be ready when destiny arrived.

London
June 17, 1896

Aslam Eden, forty-four, sat alone in the dining hall of his mansion in Belgravia, off Knightsbridge in London, sipping his breakfast tea, idly catching the rays of the morning sun in the large ruby he wore on the little finger of his left hand, wondering what God meant for him to do in this lonely world except make money.

He had already made a great deal of it. He controlled a large section of the London stock market, a power he had not sought and did not cherish, for over the years, he had learned the hard way that his money could buy him everything in the world but the one thing he ached for: desirable, trustworthy human companionship.

Gently he replaced the cup in its saucer and stared fixedly at it for a moment. Somewhere in the dark, shimmering tea he caught a glimpse of a long-gone but never quite forgotten world of hot days and nights, of red dust blowing across copper turrets, of a green oasis inside a high palace gate, of dusty, heart-wrenching poverty beyond those gates, of cows roaming free through the streets which in turn were cluttered with the half-starved, the maimed, the deformed.

But inside the gates, in his great-grandfather's red fortress castle, in the green oasis, there was nothing but plenty: dark faces and white turbans and black eyes, the most colorful butterflies in the world, peacocks, flowers of every hue and fragrance and stern-faced guards whose sole task was never to let the ugly outside world creep close to the beautiful, plentiful, green inside world.

Aslam blinked and felt his heart accelerate. The memories were so close to the surface, as though that world of the past was the real one, and this world of bustling London, the bogus one.

"Your breakfast, sir."

At the sound of the voice, he looked up to see Sind, his young Indian houseboy, place before him his customary breakfast of one poached egg and one piece of dry toast.

A good lad, Sind, picked off the docks at Southampton to come and live at Aslam's mansion.

"Thank you, Sind," Aslam said. "Morning post yet?"

"No, sir, not yet."

"Bring it to me immediately."

"Yes, sir, of course, sir," and with that Sind was gone and he was alone.

He was suffering from a soul-deep loneliness, and it was getting worse.

He was busy during the day, working in his office on the third floor, a parade of business associates filing in and out, secretaries taking dictation, countless charts to read, the sport of making a good, clean profit, watching the stocks soar, knowing precisely when to move and when not to move.

There was a thrill to be sure. But at six o'clock the parade up to the third-floor offices ceased, and the only sound that he heard was the servants beating the dust of the day out of the Orientals. Aslam would walk down to the dining hall, to this enormous table where he was seated now, and he would, without appetite, consume a piece of mutton or lean chicken, perhaps a boiled potato. Then he would climb the steps to his bedchamber on the fourth floor, and prepare himself for bed.

Half a life, that's what it was, and on a morning as glorious as this, with the roses in full bloom outside in his courtyard, the birds singing in the copper beeches, the sun casting dappled shadows on the mosaic tiles of his courtyard, it seemed like nothing less than a sin to be so unhappy.

His breakfast tea was getting cold, and his food along with it. Had he lost his appetite along with everything else?

The answer was too near. Abruptly he stood and strolled to the French doors which gave a view of his serene courtyard. Through the black wrought iron work of his front gate he saw the traffic of London off busy Knightsbridge, already clogged with carriages, cabbies and cumbersome trams with their incessant clatter on raised rails.

The wrought iron fence which he had erected some time ago successfully kept out all trespassers. Now if he could only devise a way to keep out the sounds of the city as well.

Feeling reflective and lonelier than usual, Aslam allowed his customary military stance to weaken, leaned lightly against the French door and pressed his brow against the cool window glass.

Had the boy Aslam ever existed? Of course he had, running free, yet protected, in his great-grandfather's palace in Delhi. What a heaven it had been—the loving arms of his mother always open and waiting for him, countless playmates and cousins and children of the guards, strong Indian tea, endless sugarcakes, almond cookies, laughter and companionship . . .

For a moment the memories almost overwhelmed him. He closed his eyes, painfully aware of his need to weep, and pressed his forehead harder against the glass, childishly wishing that he might pass through it and reemerge in that other world of his youth.

Of course, it wasn't possible. He wiped briskly at his eyes, then settled in a nearby chair, knowing his breakfast was now cold and beyond eating. It would have to be wasted, and generally he abhorred waste, was seldom guilty of it himself and was severe with those who were.

But the morning, the mood, his growing sense of lostness allowed him to set different rules, as though the game had changed when he wasn't looking.

Then waste the breakfast. Suddenly, without warning, when he was least expecting it and was ill prepared for it, he caught one clear mental picture of John Murrey Eden, a face as familiar to him as his own, yet one which he had not thought of for years.

Now Aslam stared fixedly at one perfect pink summer rose bobbing gently in the early-morning air.

John Murrey Eden. My God. Was he still alive?

Abruptly he leaned forward and covered his face with his hands. He had so deeply loved the man once. He had so fervently worshipped the man once. In the darkness of his hands he felt dangerous emotions again. But emotions served no one and solved nothing. Then why, in the name of God, was he behaving in so childish a manner?

He opened his eyes and removed the barrier of his hands and stared once more at the perfect pink summer rose.

Abruptly he pushed open the French doors, stepped out onto the balcony, withdrew his pocketknife and cut the pink summer rose, lifted it to his nose and sniffed deeply.

Caressing it gently, he withdrew back into the dining hall, placed the rose in his water goblet and leaned back in his chair to focus on its perfection, in the hope that he could abandon all the memories of his imperfect past.

There was a knock at the door. "The morning post, sir," Sind called out.

"Come in," Aslam called, pleased for diversion.

As the young boy entered, he placed the mail on Aslam's right and at the same time seemed to notice at a glance the pink rose and the uneaten breakfast.

"Would you like a fresh pot of tea, sir?" Sind asked.

Aslam shook his head. "Not now."

As Sind bowed his way out of the dining hall, Aslam drew a deep breath as though he had forgotten to breathe for several moments. Then the mail was before him. He proceeded to sort and restack, business envelopes on one pile, solicitations on another, general mail to be immediately discarded in yet another and–

His fingers, moving rapidly through the envelopes, stopped suddenly on one oversized parchment envelope. For a moment he studied the penmanship, the addressee's name and number. In the past he had received social invitations intended for Admiral Theodore, retired, his nearest neighbor on the next estate.

Beyond the annoyance of misdelivered post, he had never thought anything about it. Now the first thing he did was to check the name and address.

It was for him.

He sat up, the rest of the post temporarily abandoned. He stared at the handsome envelope, clearly an invitation, and slowly he turned it over in his hand.

A crimson seal, imprinted with a coat of arms and one solitary name–Eden.

John Murrey Eden.

All at once Aslam placed it on the table, face up, as though the envelope had become hot.

Eden. Who at Eden would send him an invitation? And on what occasion?

Eden Point and Eden Castle were never mentioned anymore in either the Tattlers or the legitimate press. It had been years since Aslam had heard anyone speak of Eden Castle. It was as though a curtain had fallen about that great pile of masonry that sat on the edge of the Bristol Channel and kept a pointless watch on Wales.

Aslam had visited there many times as a boy. Dhari, his mother, had been quite fond of the Eden women, the Lady Mary and sweet Elizabeth. He remembered happy times, racing through the darkened corridors of Eden with no one in pursuit except the phantoms of his imagination. But he remembered as well that it was a cold place, always a cold place, even at the height of summer.

Now who would be inviting him to Eden? And for what purpose? Slowly, carefully, he lifted the large envelope, split the seal with his finger and withdrew an invitation that was a veritable book. Immediately he turned to the first page and read the signature–Richard, Lord Eden–John's brother, half brother really, a weak though harmless man.

Now how mysterious, he thought, that after a morning of thinking of Eden, here should come in the morning post the first word he had had from Eden in over twenty years. Truly destiny was afoot.

He turned to the next page. A Midsummer Eve fete, it seemed, written in elegant script, at midpoint of July, including a hunt, a formal banquet, numerous teas, all culminating in a Midsummer ball to be held in the Great Hall of Eden Castle.

The cause for the occasion, or so it seemed, had to do with children. In the intervening years, Eden had been fruitful, if nothing else. Lord and Lady Eden were announcing the coming of age of their daughter Charlotte, and Stephen Eden and Frederick Eden, John Murrey Eden's sons, were announcing sons of their own. One named Alexander Burke Eden, aged four months, and Christopher Edward Eden, aged three months.

Aslam read to the end and felt weary: endless crowds, endless chatter, endless vanity, endless boasting, endless displays of wealth, both near and great.

No thank you. He had yet to attend a country house party, and he had no intention of starting now.

He returned the invitation to the envelope, placed it to one side of the table and drew forward the business correspondence.

Quite large, this stack, easily requiring his attention for the better part of the morning. He would take these to his office.

Then that was it, an early morning which netted him only one major satisfaction, a single perfect pink summer rose.

As for Lord Eden and his invitation, he must have grown senile in his old age to think that Aslam would make the journey from London to North Devon over bad roads to spend four days listening to ladies gossip and men complain, with John Murrey Eden presiding over the entire circus.

At the door Aslam looked back toward the table at the invitation.

A Midsummer fete. How dull.

The rose. He wanted to take the rose with him to his office, so he returned to the table, lifted it from his water goblet and stopped once again to gaze down on the large ecru envelope from Eden.

It *was* pleasant not to have to send a servant around to Admiral Theodore's with a misplaced invitation.

This one was clearly his, and though he had no intention of attending any of the festivities, he didn't want it burned, not yet, not for a while.

So he lifted the invitation along with the rose, abandoned the dining hall and started to climb three flights upstairs, thinking never, never, never would he attend such a function.

Still . . .

Eden Castle
June 25, 1896

Eve sat in the sunniest corner of her sitting room, listening to Marjorie talk excitedly of the coming festivities and wished that her own feelings of excitement would spring to life so that she might share this joyous occasion with everyone in the castle.

But so far, despite the rising spirits about her, she felt only dread. Hundreds were coming, or so it seemed. Everyone in the castle had come to sit with her of late and share their private guest lists. Even Alice had written from London to say that she was bringing her best chum, one Christabel Pankhurst.

"And Lord and Lady Chatsworth will be here, or so I'm told," Marjorie went on, "even though Eleanor stole their pastry chef for the occasion. Isn't that marvelous?"

Eve tried to share Marjorie's good humor. And failed. If the truth were known, the only source of Eve's happiness these days slept there, in the corner of the crib, next to his cousin Chris, two dimpled, perfect little boys.

Eve leaned forward, the better to study her son and in the process crushed the recent letter from Stanhope Hall, from her parents, who were growing impatient to see their grandson. She had hoped to be home by now. But twice the bookings had had to be canceled because on the brink of each departure Eve had fallen ill with recurring fever.

But she had been remarkably well throughout June, and Stephen had again promised that immediately following the festivities in July, they would at last sail for America. That hope alone sustained her and gave her the strength to go on.

"Look," she whispered, seeing Alex reach out one tiny fist and place it on Chris's cheek, both babies still fast asleep.

At last Marjorie ceased her nonstop chatter about the party and focused her attention on the babies. "They're more like brothers than cousins, aren't they?"

"Do you ever wonder," Eve asked, "what their futures hold?"

Marjorie stood, stretching out a stiffness. "At the rate that both of them eat, I would say they are headed straight for the circus, strongmen or perhaps fat men."

Eve laughed. "They are a far cry from that now. They look so helpless–"

"Helpless!" Marjorie echoed in mock disbelief. "They have enslaved every adult within a country mile."

"Still, what will they be?"

"Anything they wish."

"Do you have desires for them?"

Marjorie thought for a minute. "Only broad ones," she replied, encircling the crib, looking down, "that they both be happy and productive and compassionate. Beyond that they are on their own."

A tall order, Eve thought. Happy, productive, compassionate, and yet somehow the three wishes were bound together as one.

"Not to change the subject," Marjorie said, "but Stephen has told me a secret."

"What?"

"That you are going to sing for the guests at the Midsummer ball."

Eve drew away.

"I said I would try. It's been so long. Yorrick always helped me train. I miss him so much."

"I know you do," Marjorie sympathized.

For several moments, neither woman spoke.

Finally Marjorie moved close. "I know I am not Mr. Harp, but if I'm not being too presumptuous, may I help you train? Nothing would give me greater pleasure."

Everything in Eve resisted the offer.

"What do you do when you train?"

"Vocalize," Eve said and moved to the opposite side of the crib.

"You mean you do the scales?"

"I need a pianoforte."

"I know where there is one."

Eve looked up, surprised. "Where?"

Marjorie looked mischievous. "Before I show you, you must promise to let me help you. Oh please, Eve, I have no talents for doing anything. I can't sing; I can only play a little. Musical tutors were in short supply in the mission at Delhi. But I love music. Please let this be my contribution. Let me help you to dazzle the guests next month. I assure you, nothing would give me greater pleasure. Please . . ."

Eve looked up at the heartfelt plea. It really wasn't a matter of her promise to Marjorie. Of greater importance had been her promise to Stephen. She had promised him that she would use the occasion of the ball to make her first reappearance as The Lark.

Now the mere thought seemed to plunge her deeper into melancholy. She knew that Stephen equated her return to singing with her return to life and good health. And she did not want to disappoint him, did not want to disappoint herself. She must regain her strength in all ways for the voyage home. Then, once she was safe at home in Stanhope Hall, Mama would make her truly well, the warm southern sun would chase away this endless chill and fever, and she could try to put Yorrick's senseless death behind her.

"Eve? Are you alright?"

"I'm fine," she replied with renewed conviction, hopeful that if she assumed the position, the genuine feelings would soon follow. "Now, where is this pianoforte? Are you sure you're not making it up?"

Marjorie smiled, reached forward and drew Eve into a quick embrace. Then she scooped the still-sleeping Christopher into her arms.

"Well?" she said, seeing that Eve had yet to follow suit. "I'm sure you don't plan to leave him, do you; hurry before someone comes."

Eve did as she was told, gently lifting Alexander into her arms.

"Grab their blankets," Marjorie whispered. "It might be chilly where we are going."

"Where are we going?" Eve asked.

"Near the top of the castle," Marjorie whispered as though suddenly the chamber were filled with listening ears. "Frederick took me there. I had left something in one of my trunks and the stewards had already carried them up to storage."

"The attic?" Eve questioned.

"No, not the attic. There is a storage room directly above us."

As both women stood at the door, their sons cradled securely in their arms, Marjorie looked up and down the hall. "All clear," she whispered, her eyes sparkling with enjoyment.

And Eve was happy to admit that she, too, was enjoying herself. Apparently Marjorie saw the new light in her eyes.

"Let's never be separated, Eve," Marjorie whispered. "I'm sure our sons won't be separated, and we must follow suit and live as sisters as our husbands are brothers. Promise."

Eve started to speak of her need to go home, but for now she changed her mind. The moment was too good. When the time came to depart for America, she was certain that Marjorie would understand.

So, for now, all Eve did was to nod to Marjorie's heartfelt plea and be grateful for this new surge of life, hoping that it lasted long enough to get her through the performance at the Midsummer Eve party and all the way across the Atlantic Ocean. For once back at Stanhope Hall, she was certain that her world would be put to rights again.

Eden Castle
July 13, 1896

Eleanor stood on her balcony in the warm summer evening, relishing this last moment of privacy before the storm of the party commenced.

Before her was her perfectly tended private garden, which still had some wild corners in it to fire the imagination.

Curious, how quiet it was here, considering that the population of Eden Castle had on this day swelled to over ninety-five inhabitants.

She looked back into her bedchamber, thinking she had heard Richard's step. She was awaiting his presence before she dressed. It was one of the few intimacies that he requested of her anymore, just the honor of sitting on the overstuffed chintz chaise and watching Trudy dress her. He said it gave him pleasure, and she was only too happy to indulge him.

Now as she looked back into her bedchamber, she saw only Trudy, fussing over her ball gown for this first-night banquet.

"Trudy?"

"Yes, my lady."

"Please come and get me the moment that Lord Eden arrives."

"I will, my lady."

Carefully Eleanor made her way along the small, narrow staircase leading down to the garden, lifting the hem of her dressing gown so there would be no damp and clinging earth to offend Trudy.

Dr. Reicher. Her mind caught on the image of the man. How pleased they all were that he had accepted John's offer to become the resident physician. Geoffrey seemed to be in constant need of medication, not always the wisest course, but if it soothed his spirits, why not? It was also good to have the babies attended to daily, as well as Eve, who continued to have medical problems.

As a bonus, his wife, Sonia, and young son, Rolf, had proved themselves to be delightful company. They both had contributed to this renewed sense of life that had very pleasantly invaded Eden Castle.

As her foot touched grass, she closed her eyes and breathed deeply of the rose-scented air. A prime Red Splendor in full bloom greeted her at the head of the path.

She touched it, bent low, sniffed the fragrance, then raised up and glanced the length of the rose garden, admiring the various floral explosions of pink, rose, red and yellow.

The garden *was* good for her. It had been a full three minutes since she had worried about the busy days ahead.

In the past two months, over eighty rooms within the castle had been cleaned and refurbished. Her buyers in London had provided them with an endless supply of linens. Also lamps and lampshades, looking glasses, fire screens and occasional tables. Each chamber had been outfitted with a good clock; it was so important that the company stay on schedule.

Then there had been the endless meetings with Mrs. Partridge, her enlarged kitchen staff and the caterers from London, headed by Mr. Portman. There had been tension at first between the two kitchen groups, but ultimately she had made a heartfelt plea for their mutual cooperation on this very auspicious occasion and they all had kindly given it to her. The menu lists still ran through her head like some wild opera—for tonight eight different soups ranging from celery to chowder, fillets of sole and haddock, whiting curled with the tail through the head, whitebait, shrimp, lobster and scallops.

The meat courses would have something roasted as well as carved, cutlets in various guises, steaks and casseroles, also grouse, partridges and pheasants always to appear at dinners rather than luncheons. Also there would be perennial arrangements of Scotch woodcock, chicken livers, oysters wrapped in bacon, cheese soufflés and sardines on toast squares. All of the menus were written out on white china slates and each would be posted daily.

For afters there would be endless varieties of gateaux and fruit pies, custards of every variety, lemon, cheese and jam tartlets, pancakes and fruit fritters, to say nothing of thousands of continental chocolates and mousses and cordial fruits and tiers of scones and sweet biscuits and—

Suddenly she shook her head, one good, hard shake as though to put an end to the lists in her head.

Now it had all been done, thousands of silver pieces polished, port and sherry glasses glistening and set out by the hundreds, everything cleaned, cleared, polished, purchased, prepared, arranged, watered, fed, made up, made down, hung, fluffed up, smoothed out, whipped, beaten, chilled, warmed–

Abruptly she smiled, then laughed aloud at the antics of her mind. Anything that she had left undone would have to stay undone; but despite the work and anxiety, she was forced to admit that it had been a long time since she had felt so alive, so excited. For the next few days her one goal was to make the various comings and goings of her guests as enjoyable and as memorable as she possibly could. A tall order, and while she wasn't absolutely certain that she would succeed, she intended to have a very good time trying.

"My dearest, I'm sorry I am late."

At the sound of Richard's voice, she looked up to see him on her balcony in his dress blacks, looking terribly uncomfortable but rather handsome in his own way.

"I'm coming," she called and lifted the hem of her dressing gown and hurried up the steps, dreading the torture of her corset, hoping she had not tasted too many dishes these past weeks to undo the artistry of her London dressmaker.

Lord Eden had been delayed by the arrival of the musicians in the Great Hall–that and a failure of nerve, for he had something of monumental importance to tell Eleanor. Now, as though to compensate for the news, he had a small gift for her in honor of the occasion tucked away in his pocket in a black velvet case.

"I had no idea they would have so much luggage," he said, referring to the musicians, settling himself comfortably on the chintz chaise, carefully crossing his legs to avoid crushing the crease of his dress blacks.

He looked up to see Eleanor seated before her dressing table mirror, Trudy gently removing her dressing gown, revealing bare shoulders, a thin pink silk chemise and nothing else. In the reflection of the glass he saw the fullness of her breasts press against her bare arms. The sight pleased him, and Trudy moved away from the mirror as though she knew the sight had pleased him.

When he had looked his fill, he nodded once and Trudy returned with the mother-of-pearl hairbrush. In one skillful gesture, she swept Eleanor's hair up atop her head and pinned it, thus revealing her snow-white neck and throat and the broad plump field of her shoulders and back.

Their eyes met in the reflection of the mirror. Hers were patient and loving. In fact, at times she seemed to be flirting with him, as she'd once flirted with him when he had visited her parents' estate in Kent. She'd been slim and shy then and he had been plump and shy, and their wedding night had been a series of disasters; but the following night they both had got the hang of it, though they both had agreed later that it was a most uncomfortable act. Still they must have done something correct, for they had brought forth three unique children.

"Hold tight, my lady, and don't breathe," Trudy now instructed, leading Eleanor to one of the large bedposts. Then she encased her in a heavy white corset and commenced pulling the cords tightly through the hooks as Eleanor grasped the bedpost.

He saw Eleanor take a deep breath and hold it as though it might be her last. Perhaps this would be the time to tell her his news, while she was being laced up and therefore speechless.

But he was certain she would take the news poorly and Trudy would be forced to withdraw until she settled down, and she really did need to dress and take her position downstairs in the receiving line with all the others who were already gathering.

"Richard, darling, are you well? You look dreadful."

"I'm . . . fine. Did I tell you? Guests are starting to arrive."

"Who?"

At that moment Trudy finished lacing the corset and stood back to view her handiwork.

"Are you well, my lady?" she asked.

"Not comfortable, but well."

"I'm afraid it's necessary if you want to wear that," and she pointed toward the pearl-encrusted, orchid-colored silk gown.

After Trudy led her back to the dressing table, she sat stiffly. Again their eyes met in the mirror.

"You said you had news."

"Later."

"The children, are they–"

"Lucy is with Mason Frye in the library. Charlotte not yet down."

"Charlotte will be dazzling this evening," Eleanor promised the mirror. "You wait, Richard. Her gown is absolutely splendid."

"I'm sure."

"And Alice?"

"Alice is in the library with Lucy and Mason Frye."

"And her friend?"

"With her, of course. A most peculiar young lady. What is her name?"

"Pankhurst. Christabel Pankhurst."

"Yes, that's it."

"Do we know the family?"

"No, I don't think so."

"She looks very young."

"Sixteen, according to Alice, but a very dedicated student. They share a flat in Bloomsbury."

Again their eyes met over the blur of Trudy's hairbrush. There were key words that signaled danger. "Bloomsbury" was such a word, London's bohemia.

For a moment there was silence as Trudy heated a curling iron to a rosy red and curled Eleanor's bangs about it and held it tight for several moments.

As the odor of singed hair filled the room, Richard tried to imagine whom she would inquire after next.

"Neither Stephen nor Frederick has come down as yet. Marjorie is helping Eve to dress and the boys are being looked after by Molly and Mrs. Godwin. Now that's the family."

As Trudy combed out the bangs on Eleanor's forehead, she leaned forward to make her own adjustments, then sat back and looked critically at the face that stared back at her.

"I would give anything to be twenty years younger," she mourned.

"Why? You wouldn't be as lovely as you are at this moment."

"Oh nonsense, Richard. At least then my forehead and cheeks would be smooth."

"As well as your brain."

Eleanor laughed and held still as Trudy affixed a small diamond tiara in front of the French knot, a sparkling background for the curls on her forehead.

"There, my lady. His lordship is correct as always. You have never looked lovelier."

Normally Richard would not approve of this intimacy coming from a servant, but Trudy had fit into their private lives for over fifteen years. Some servants did. And some didn't. It was wise to treasure those who did.

Eleanor closed her eyes as Trudy dusted a light coating of rice powder on her face with special emphasis on her forehead, nose and cheekbones.

At last Trudy lifted the gown and briefly Eleanor disappeared into a soft, rich cloud of orchid-colored silk.

The gown *was* very pretty, albeit a bit snug.

"Breathe in, my lady."

"I can't breathe at all, Trudy."

But once buttoned, the gown did manage to make her waist appear quite small, her hips and bosom quite large and full, almost a perfect figure of a woman.

There were final touches of fluffing and arranging and smoothing. Richard patted his upper vest pocket beneath his jacket. Yes, the black velvet case was still there.

"Well?"

At the sound of the gentle voice, he looked up to see Eleanor, gowned and coiffed standing before the chair.

"You are beautiful," he said simply, and nodded his head to Trudy in wordless indication that they were now to be left alone for a few minutes.

"We mustn't linger too long," Eleanor reminded him. "I'm sure that poor old Ghostly is going quite mad downstairs."

"I know," Richard agreed. "But first, I have something for you." As he reached into his pocket, he decided to give her the bauble first and then the bad news. Perhaps the former would act as a softener to the latter.

He found the black velvet case and brought it forward.

"In honor of the occasion and of you," he said and drew back the lid to reveal one enormous perfect pink pearl, suspended in elegant simplicity from a single gold chain.

Now he draped the jewel about her neck and turned her about. It was perfect, her breasts forming a perfect setting for the pink pearl.

As she hurried to the mirror to see for herself, he found himself smiling at her pleasure. For some reason he wanted her terribly now, without a moment's delay. He knew that if he took her to bed now, he would not disappoint her, would not disappoint himself.

But, of course, it was out of the question. So he sent away his strange feelings of passion and regretted the dismissal because he enjoyed them so seldom, and watched as Eleanor preened first this way and that.

"Oh, Richard, it is splendid." She turned and approached him slowly. Her arms went about his neck, she drew him close and gave him a most unwifely kiss. The degree of her passion surprised him. "If only . . . ," she murmured, her eyes filled with regret.

"I know."

"Perhaps later."

With a degree of frustration, Richard closed the black velvet case and tossed it onto the table as he made his way back out to her balcony overlooking the private garden.

She followed, as he knew she would. "Are you ready, my dearest? I'm sure the company has gathered. We mustn't–"

"Our company includes one person not listed in the book of guests." He spoke bluntly, tired of carrying the burden of his news.

"I don't understand."

"It's a simple matter, really Charlotte's fault. She's the one who wheedled me into doing it."

Eleanor stood beside him as though summoning patience as well as understanding. "Tell me everything, Richard. Who is this guest?"

"Charlotte asked me to sign and put the Eden seal on an invitation to . . ."–he hesitated–". . . to Aslam Eden."

"I don't understand why you are so worried? I think it is a splendid idea. I can't imagine why John didn't think of it himself and include the man on his own guest list."

"Because he loathes him," Richard said quietly, hoping the true depths of John's feelings would penetrate.

Eleanor glanced up at him, obviously thinking of a rebuttal. "The man is here as your guest. I don't quite see where John has anything to do with it."

He watched her as she walked the length of the bedroom, annoyed at her naïveté. Didn't she know by now that John Murrey Eden had everything to do with everything?

"Come along, Richard," she called back to him. "I hear the musicians tuning their instruments. I'm sure our guests are waiting."

As he trudged across the bedchamber with his head down, he prayed that John would meet, and accept, Aslam Eden in the spirit of the occasion, one of reunion and reconciliation, and forget his violent claim that he would kill the man if he ever laid eyes on him again.

Eve requested a few moments alone prior to joining the company gathering in the Great Hall. Stephen had obliged, returning to his dressing room, leaving her in the silence that she feared would annihilate her.

"Yorrick," she prayed and sat at the center table, her hands folded before her, head bowed.

She felt chilled in her blue gown, felt how loosely it fit. She had no idea that she had lost so much weight.

She stood abruptly and clung to the edge of the table, waiting for the dizziness to pass, for the persistent though dull pain in her abdomen to pass as well.

Finally she ventured away from the table toward the fireplace, now filled with bunches of fresh flowers. In a way she missed the friendly warmth of a fire. It had sustained her during the difficult birth and the illness that followed. Many a day she had been too weak to focus on much of anything but the fire.

She stood on the hearth and felt a chill, always a chill, in this drafty ancient place. She remembered her mother speaking of the endless chill in Eden Castle. Then it had sounded romantic. Now she wanted nothing in the world quite so much as to feel the blistering heat of an Alabama summer sun on her face, to hear Mama's voice, to hear Papa's loving one, the servants rustling about in the kitchen, old Florence humming the gospel songs that she loved so well.

Quickly she closed her eyes, briefly overcome by new weakness. What had happened to her? What was happening to her? She had survived and endured so much. Why should she feel so weak and helpless and doomed now?

"Eve?"

She didn't look up at the sound of the voice coming from the door. It was as familiar and as constant as the beating of her heart.

With the opening of the door she had heard an increase of voices, hundreds of voices, or so it seemed. She would never be able to face them, let alone sing for them.

"Stephen, I can't," she pleaded and turned to meet him, to try and convince him that it was too soon, far too soon.

"Of course you can," he smiled in what was clearly a false confidence designed to bolster her.

"No, I can't, I swear it," she begged.

"Why?"

"I'm not ready."

"Of course you're ready. Marjorie says–"

"Marjorie loves me as you do. Love blinds."

He frowned down on her for a moment as though to dispute this claim.

"Look at me, Stephen."

"You look lovely."

"No!" she cried, newly desperate. "I've lost so much weight, my hair is–I can't– Oh, please, look at me just once without loving me."

As she felt the beginning of tears, she was tempted to turn away. But the stakes were too high. She had to convince him; then he in turn could set about to convince the others. She was aware of how important her performance was tonight to everyone, particularly to John Murrey Eden. But she couldn't.

She sat in the chair, feeling quite drained, her hands folded in her lap.

"Come, Eve, sing tonight for Yorrick. Let your song be a message to him. And don't think for a minute that he won't be within hearing distance."

Despite her bleak mood, Eve smiled.

"Will you come now? There are those in the Great Hall downstairs who, Eleanor swears, traveled a great distance just to hear The Lark."

She looked up, flattered. No one had told her that before.

"I love you so much."

She welcomed the warm support of his embrace and in a curious way did begin to feel stronger. Through the door she heard the voices growing louder. She'd heard this same noise before hundreds of times, immediately preceding every curtain.

"When am I supposed to–"

"Directly after the banquet," Stephen said.

"Then may I wait here until–"

"I'm afraid not. Eleanor is most insistent that we join the family in greeting the company. There are those who–"

Eve signaled no more flattery. She'd had enough of it and knew better than anyone that after the flattery was over, the job still remained to be done.

"You look lovely," Stephen murmured.

She started to reply, but Frederick and Marjorie appeared in the doorway, a baby in each arm.

"Are we ready?" Marjorie called out and handed Alex to Eve.

At four months Alex was pink and plump and rosy and beautiful. He smiled at everyone and was wholly irresistible.

As she cuddled him she saw Christopher in Frederick's arms. The two babies resembled twins.

"What exactly does John intend to do?" Eve asked of anyone who cared to answer.

"As far as I know," Stephen said, "my father wants to present the boys to the world."

Marjorie laughed. "Is that the world I hear down there?"

"A large part of the English world," Frederick said, brooding. "Speaking for myself, I could have done without this."

Eve looked up at her brother-in-law, a clear ally.

"But," he went on, "it does seem to be giving many people such a great deal of pleasure. I'm certain that we will all do the best we can when we are called upon."

Did his eyes rest on Eve a bit longer than anyone else or was it her imagination?

"Well then, are we ready?" Stephen asked.

Eve nodded and hoped that it would suffice. She knew she was fortunate. She knew she had a husband who adored her, a new son who was perfection itself. She knew she had been blessed beyond the wildest dreams of most people.

She knew all these things, but what she didn't know as the four of them walked in silence down the brightly lit corridor toward the maelstrom of noise coming from the Great Hall was why her hands were shaking, why her heart was beating too fast, why her brow was covered with perspiration, and why she was suffering a degree of terror unlike any she had ever experienced in her life.

Fully dressed in his formal blacks, his two manservants having already withdrawn, Aslam Eden stood before the full-length peer glass in a guest apartment of Eden Castle and wondered what had possessed him to make this god-awful journey to attend this god-awful and provincial function in this hostile and remote castle?

For several moments he stared unblinking at the face in the mirror. He was certain that his judgment of hostile was correct. Only one, Lord Eden, had been on the Great Hall steps to greet him, and even then the poor man had been so flustered as to appear apoplectic.

On recalling the strange welcome, Aslam turned away from the mirror. Of one thing he was certain–he should not have come.

With melting self-anger he strolled about the sitting room as though he had a destination when in fact he had none, had no purpose in mind whatsoever except to devise a way out of this place as soon as possible.

He stopped before the brandy decanter and poured himself a swallow, only a swallow. Generally he hated and avoided spirits. They robbed a man of his good judgment. But now he felt such an agitation coming on, as though he were a boy again and wholly dependent upon the strength and discipline of others.

Like John Murrey Eden.

As the brandy burned a pleasant path down his throat, he felt his earlier apprehensions receding, and for one unaccountable moment he was almost glad he had made the wretched journey out to Eden. Whatever John Murrey Eden was or had become, the truth was that Aslam had once loved him with a depth and degree of love that man seldom felt for man. And now much to his surprise, regardless of what had happened to either of them in the intervening years, he was amazed to discover a degree of that passion intact and as potent as it had ever been.

Then straighten your tie and go down to the Great Hall and search the man out and take his hand and tell him so, he thought.

As he turned toward the door, he noticed a lovely arrangement of summer flowers, a vase of perfect white roses. He lifted one from the vase, shook the water off, withdrew his penknife and snipped the stem beneath the bud and carefully attached it to his lapel.

Perfect. White on black. Well, then, he was ready for whatever fate had in store for him. He had taken the first step. If it was his destiny to be reunited with John Murrey Eden, then it would happen within the hour. If not, then he would return to London this very night.

Aslam had learned a long time ago that no one—*no one*—was indispensable in this life.

In the small reception room off the Great Hall, Lucy scolded Charlotte. "Hold still!" She tried again to reattach the delicate clasp on Charlotte's diamond necklace.

At last Lucy felt the strands connect. She scrutinized them again, then slowly turned Charlotte about for a final inspection.

The vision was almost too much. Lucy shook her head, smiling.

"You look splendid," Lucy smiled, taking great pride in this beautiful younger sister.

"The gown, Lucy," Charlotte worried anew. "Is the gown–"

"Perfect," Lucy smiled with all due immodesty, the dress having been Lucy's handiwork. While the other women in Eden Castle had summoned London dressmakers, Charlotte had requested that Lucy make her gown for the opening festivities of the Midsummer Eve fete, and what a dress it was. Pure white silk taffeta cut low on the bosom with gently draped sleeves, a nipped waist, flared slightly over the hips and down the back with a small bustle, the rest of the splendid fabric falling into a straight, narrow line to the floor. Then Lucy had finished it with a strand of diamonds and had done Charlotte's hair into a silky French rosette atop her head, had singed her neckcurls into tight ringlets, a matching band of ringlets gracing her forehead.

She was a vision, and Lucy took enormous pride in her creation.

"Soon I shall release you onto the unsuspecting company and then stand back and watch all the young men suffer broken hearts."

"I don't care about the young men," Charlotte said as she held perfectly still, arms extended for Lucy's final inspection.

"Well, Mama and Papa hope you at least learn to care for one. That's what this whole madness is all about."

"It is not," Charlotte protested. "It's to show off the babies."

"That too."

"And what about you?" Charlotte asked. "You're the oldest and you're not yet married."

Lucy passed behind her, blessedly out of sight, for she was certain the blush on her face was visible. So far, she and Mason Frye had been successful in keeping their growing attachment to each other a secret from everyone in Eden Castle. At this point it was only a growing attachment, though Lucy had known since she was a little girl that the slim bright man who tested her Latin grammar and made her conjugate verbs was a most remarkable man. Still, it was far too early to alert anyone else.

"Lucy? What are you doing back there?" Charlotte asked, puzzled by Lucy's prolonged silence.

"Checking the hooks."

As Charlotte turned back around, she caught Lucy's eye. "You didn't answer my question."

"I wasn't aware that you had asked one."

"Are you looking for a young man tonight?"

"Of course not."

"Aren't you ever going to marry?"

"Not until I am ready."

Charlotte hesitated. "Sometimes men frighten me. Do they frighten you, Lucy?"

"Sometimes, but Mama says that when you fall in love, everything else follows quite naturally."

"But how do you know if you're in love?"

"Mama says–"

"Oh, Lucy, I don't care what Mama says. Sometimes I don't believe even she knows."

"She loves Papa."

"I know. It's just that sometimes they seem so . . . ordinary."

Lucy smiled. "You don't have to be extraordinary to love someone."

Lucy watched her beautiful younger sister preen and thought of Mason Frye. He gave her peace and a wonderful sense of security and sometimes when they were walking on the headlands, he would rest his arm on her shoulders and study the grass as he talked of breathtaking things.

Beyond the reception room door, she heard the musicians start a Strauss waltz. Her mother had asked for both girls to be ready for the reception line at eight-thirty.

The Dresden clock on the mantel chimed half past eight. At the same time, she heard a knock on the door and knew who it was.

"Mason?"

The door opened only a crack and she saw him, such a good face, wise with deeply held convictions, yet so compassionate.

Briefly she forgot that they were not alone and returned his warm smile, hurried to the door and allowed their fingers to touch ever so lightly.

"Your mother sent me," Mason said.

"We're ready."

"You look so beautiful."

"Thank you," she blushed. Then remembered they were not alone. "Charlotte," she gasped and looked back to see her sister smiling.

"What is going on between you two?"

"Nothing, I swear it," Lucy protested.

"Your mother sent me to summon you," Mason Frye said, suddenly his voice firm, all business.

For a moment the grinning Charlotte continued to look back and forth between the two.

"Does anyone else know?" she teased.

"Know what?" Lucy murmured, embarrassed.

"Never mind. Your secret is safe," Charlotte smiled and passed by them and out the door.

Lucy started to follow her, but Mason took her hand.

"I hope I didn't embarrass you."

For several moments he seemed to hold her with his eyes alone, deep brown eyes that filled the silence with a most-pleasing message.

She *did* love him. "Mason, I–"

"I know. We'll talk later. We must. They must know."

"What?"

"What we . . . feel."

"And what–"

"I . . . care very deeply for you."

"And I you."

"I'm so much older."

"It doesn't matter."

"I love you."

Lucy closed her eyes and heard the miraculous words in echo as she would surely hear them every day for the rest of her life.

"Come," he whispered, "we must behave ourselves for the next few days as though nothing had changed. And after all this foolishness has receded into history, where it belongs, we shall talk at length, and if you wish, I shall request a private audience with your father."

As Mason took her hand and led her out into the Great Hall, she saw Charlotte only a few feet ahead, standing perfectly still, her eyes fixed on the opposite staircase, on a man just descending those stairs.

Quite tall and slim, with dark complexion, the man was very handsome and carried himself erect, with the regal bearing of nobility. Halfway down the staircase, he stopped and seemed to scan the crowd below for a familiar face. There was something about him, a magnetism that seemed to capture and hold everyone's attention.

"Who is he?" Charlotte whispered almost fearfully as Lucy and Mason drew even with her.

"I'm sure I don't know," Lucy murmured. "He's–"

From her right, she heard a curse of amazement coming from Mason Frye. "Well, I'll be damned," he said, a faint smile on his face as he, too, focused on the dark and elegant stranger still poised on the staircase.

"Do you know him, Mason?" Lucy asked.

"Me? No, of course not," Mason laughed. "Not personally. I don't move in such rarefied circles. But I daresay if you ask anyone in the London financial district they will know the man's name."

All at once, Charlotte looked back at Mason. "Is that– Do you know– Can you tell, Mason, that isn't–"

As her stammering increased, Mason began to nod slowly. "Aslam Eden," he said, "without a doubt the richest man in London, quite possibly the richest man in all of England. What I don't understand is who invited him here? He is John Murrey Eden's sworn enemy."

Then to their amazement, Charlotte boasted, "I invited him, Mason. I sent the invitation. Now I must go and greet him."

As Charlotte walked toward the staircase, Lucy saw people withdraw and make a generous passage for her. A few appeared to speak to her. But as far as Lucy could tell, Charlotte had yet to look to the right or to the left, taking a straight, unalterable route leading directly to the staircase and the man waiting.

Then suddenly Mason whispered, "If you are feeling particularly close to God at this moment, you might utter a prayer."

"Why?"

"Look–"

And Lucy did, toward the library on the opposite side of the Great Hall, where a figure was just starting toward the light and activity of the Great Hall.

John Murrey Eden.

"Has he seen . . . ," Lucy whispered, then saw no need to complete the question. Of course he had seen and was moving with the same directness of focus as was Charlotte, both approaching the man on the staircase, both due to arrive within seconds of each other.

Lucy looked at Mason and saw an expression of concerned excitement on his face.

Aslam Eden had clearly seen both the beautiful young girl in white as well as John Murrey Eden. Even the large, varied and laughing company seemed to sense the moment. Voices fell silent, laughs were aborted. Two clearly discernible paths were cleared to the staircase.

Charlotte and John stopped short of the stairs, each out of courtesy for the other, leaving Aslam Eden to select who was to greet him first.

Lucy held her breath, along with several hundred others, waiting for the man on the stairs to make this very difficult decision.

It was clear from the sudden tension in the Great Hall that most of the guests knew of the estrangement between John Murrey Eden and his adopted son, Aslam Eden.

Following a few steps behind John, Susan wished their company would carry on with their repartee.

Fortunately Richard had seen fit to make his confession several minutes earlier, so Susan had at least had time to adjust to the bizarre fact that Aslam Eden was a guest in residence in Eden Castle.

After Richard had shyly and tentatively made his revelation, John had turned about immediately, depositing his untouched sherry on the table and had departed the library as though to suggest that another moment must not pass before he located Aslam Eden.

Though Susan knew John well after twenty-five years of marriage, she still had been unable to identify the expression on his face. She had no idea what he was going to do.

He stopped abruptly at the grand staircase. Susan saw his head lift, saw him focus on a tall, slim, darkly handsome middle-aged man.

Susan saw Charlotte coming from the opposite direction, looking indescribably beautiful, and she, too, broke free of the crowd, which had grown silent in the face of the impending confrontation. Unhappily Susan heard the orchestra and the Strauss waltz fade into a discord of violins and cellos, and fall silent. Nothing was heard in that vast, overcrowded Great Hall save the pounding of Susan's heart, which she was certain was audible to all.

She considered joining John at the bottom of the stairs, but changed her mind and held her position a safe distance back and watched along with the others. John had one foot on the first step and Aslam seemed to be standing more erect, looking first at John, then catching a glimpse of white out of the corner of his eye and looking down on Charlotte, his focus remaining there for ever so long, then finally turning back to John.

Just when it seemed that no one in the Great Hall would ever move again, Charlotte stepped forward and took John's hand. She whispered something to him and led him, quite docilely, up the stairs, stopping short of Aslam by one step.

Susan felt herself mesmerized by Charlotte's graceful movements, and her beauty alone seemed to add to the confusion and tension of the silent and watchful company.

Quickly Susan moved to the bottom of the stairs, close enough to hear Charlotte, who was performing with all the artistry of an experienced hostess.

"Uncle John," she said softly, "you remember this man, I know. I know further that there is, unhappily a degree of bad blood between you. I must confess that my father and I schemed to bring about this reunion. It seemed the season for forgiveness. Please," she begged, "love each other as you once did."

Moved by Charlotte's innocent and yet profound entreaty, Susan felt a new tension in the company and prayed silently that John's heart would respond as she knew it wanted to respond.

Then it happened. Aslam merely lifted his right hand, and in the next minute, John embraced him, a good reunion, both men clinging to each other, while Charlotte looked on, a breathtakingly radiant and triumphant smile on her face.

Susan felt compelled to look away, somehow the moment seemed so intimate, not at all designed to be played out before hundreds of gaping eyes.

But gape they did, and continued to do so until someone, probably Eleanor, started the musicians to playing again and the strains of another Strauss waltz seemed to remind the guests of other interests, the reception line forming on the far side of the room, the delicious odors coming from the massive buffet set up in the Grand Dining Hall.

Susan looked back at the staircase and the two men who were at last releasing their embrace on each other, each now searching through the pockets of his dress blacks for a handkerchief.

"Here." It was the gentle voice of Charlotte, who extended her lace handkerchief to Aslam. He hesitated a moment, glancing at John as though for direction.

"Take it," John smiled. "There are hundreds of men in this room who would sell their souls for a similar offer from that fair hand."

Aslam took the handkerchief, his eyes settling on Charlotte's face, where they remained until John, restored, pocketed his handkerchief and moved closer with formal introductions.

"Aslam, this is my niece, Charlotte, the youngest daughter of your host and hostess, Lord and Lady Eden."

He glanced at Charlotte, then continued speaking to Aslam. "Obviously she knows who you are and I have her to thank for your appearance."

"It has been too long," Aslam smiled. Susan considered joining them, but decided to bide her time. It was going very well, and she was grateful.

"In Belgravia, in Knightsbridge," she heard Aslam saying now, "I'm sure you know the place."

"I know it well indeed. You used to admire it as a boy."

"I have made alterations."

"I'm sure you have."

"You must come for a visit."

"I seldom journey to London anymore. There seems to be no cause."

Charlotte smiled. "But now you have a reason, Uncle John."

John laughed and put his arm about Charlotte's shoulders. "Beware this temptress, Aslam," he warned with mock ferocity. "She is like no other woman you know or will ever meet."

"That I can clearly see," and again Aslam Eden's eyes rested ever so long on Charlotte's face. She returned his gaze with a steadfastness that somehow seemed out of place.

At that moment, Susan heard Trudy close behind her, whispering, "Mrs. Eden, if you please, Lady Eden is becoming quite upset. The receiving line must form because the cooks say the buffet is–"

"Very well," Susan said. "John–"

At the sound of her voice, he turned. "Ah, Susan, come. I was just–"

He never finished saying what he was about to do. Instead, he reached for her hand as though he were reaching for a lifeline.

"Aslam, may I present my wife, Susan, who twenty-five years ago took a rudderless ship and set it on a clear course toward a precise destination."

Susan smiled. "My pleasure, Mr. Eden. I have heard so much about you."

He took her hand with courtly, old-fashioned grace and kissed it, his lips lightly brushing the back of her hand, "I assure you it is my pleasure. What great good fortune John has had. And how I envy him."

Susan smiled. Then to John, she whispered, "Eleanor wants us in the line."

"Of course," John said with suspect enthusiasm. "Now, if you will excuse us," he said, backing down the stairs. "Charlotte, I entrust our guest to you. Please see that his every wish is accommodated."

Susan saw Charlotte smile.

"Until dinner," John said, still backing down the stairs, taking Susan with him. At the bottom of the steps, he turned about and took her arm and began to steer her through the company at a fast pace, his grip tighter than she might have wished.

"John, what is it?" she whispered, seeing the warm smile of hospitality change to one of grim soberness.

"How dare they?" he muttered through clenched teeth. "Without telling me. Has Richard lost his mind? I shall speak to him, I can promise you that."

Stunned, Susan struggled to keep up. "I thought you were pleased," she whispered, amazed at her inability after all these years to understand this man.

"Pleased? What choice did I have? The man was standing there directly before me. What else could I have done?"

"Then you are not pleased–"

"Pleased! He is a bastard. I could tell you things about that man that would shock you. He is not to be trusted. I knew that years ago and I know it now. He is here for a purpose, I can tell you that. What that purpose is I don't know. But I don't trust him. I don't."

To this absurd outburst, Susan smiled. "John, don't be melodramatic."

"You don't believe me? Then wait and see. A chapter in our lives which will end tragically has been commenced here today."

As he strode ahead of her, she slowed her pace, tired of dodging her way through the laughing company. As John moved ahead, Susan looked back toward the two striking people chatting quietly, Aslam so slim and tall, Charlotte breathtaking in her white ball gown, her fair skin in stunning contrast to Aslam's dark skin.

"Are you coming?"

At the sound of John's impatient voice, she joined the others in the receiving line.

"Where's Charlotte?" Eleanor whispered nervously.

"She is with Aslam Eden," Susan replied.

For a moment Eleanor looked even more flustered than usual.

"I'm sure it will be alright to start the line without her."

Eleanor nodded, though she continued to glance about as though she had lost something. Finally the orchestra fell silent, as Ghostly and the head steward, both resplendent in ceremonial garb with red and gold braid, announced that Lord and Lady Eden would receive the company.

With amazing docility, the guests ceased their private pursuits and began to form an orderly line that snaked its way about the perimeter of the Great Hall and then doubled back on itself.

"Dear God," Susan muttered, "all those hands to shake. John, are you–"

As she turned toward John, she saw his attention fixed on something at the far side of the Great Hall. Aslam and Charlotte were strolling away from the company, Charlotte's arm linked in his, moving toward the corridor that led to the library, a pleasant, wood-paneled room, always one of Charlotte's favorites.

"Where in the hell are they going?" John murmured, his eyes leveled.

"You asked Charlotte to serve as hostess," Susan reminded him.

Abruptly he broke off as the two disappeared down the corridor. She saw such a look of worry on his face that she was fearful he, too, would bolt the line and go in pursuit of the truants.

But he didn't. The steward's announcement of Lord and Lady Chatsworth drew his attention back to the task at hand, and as the overrouged Lady Chatsworth extended her hand, John took it.

"Madame, you are a vision," he smiled, and Susan marveled at his rare and dangerous ability to hide his feelings.

As the line continued, as name after name and face after face passed before her, she kept one eye trained on the library door at the far side of the Great Hall.

About two hours later, as the line was at last dwindling, the company hurrying off toward the Great Dining Hall and its tempting odors, Susan still had not seen the library door open. She presumed that Aslam and Charlotte were still inside and wondered what in heaven's name a forty-year-old foreign-born financier and a seventeen-year-old sheltered aristocratic country girl would have to talk about for such a very long time.

Stephen tried to stay close to Eve all evening, but people kept dragging him off, old friends, new acquaintances, all eager to hear his account of the American West.

On several occasions he tried to involve Eve in the conversations. But she seemed so withdrawn, so lacking in energy, so shy.

Thus had it gone all evening, provoking a mood of constant worry, reminding him that he must stay close to her, for time was drawing near for her performance and he wanted to lend her as much support as he could or as she required.

Now, shortly after ten-thirty, after all had eaten and drunk themselves into a pleasant mood of satiation, Stephen sat close beside Eve on the comfortable settee on which she had spent the better part of the evening, frequently alone, sometimes in the company of Alice and her close friend from London, Christabel Pankhurst. Eve seemed to enjoy their company the most. The only times that Stephen had seen her laugh had been at something that Miss Pankhurst had said.

He took Eve's hand. "Where is Alice and her friend?" he asked.

"I'm not sure," Eve said, looking about her. "She's very nice and so funny."

Stephen made a mental note to pass this information on to Alice with a plea that she arrange for Miss Pankhurst to spend some time with Eve during the next few days.

"Would you like to walk around for a while? There are so many here who would be honored to meet you but have been timid about approaching."

"No, please, Stephen, just let me stay here. I need to go through the lyrics in my head. I would hate to–"

At that moment Marjorie approached.

"John says we are to get the boys and join him on the staircase. Mrs. Godwin is watching over them in the large reception room. Come, we must hurry."

But even as she spoke, Stephen saw Eve withdrawing from both the invitation as well as the suggestion. "No, I can't. I really should wait here."

Helpless he exchanged a glance with Marjorie.

"It's alright," Marjorie soothed, her arm around Eve's trembling shoulders. "After all, this is your debut in a way, isn't it? You must conserve your strength. How thoughtless of me to suggest otherwise."

For a few moments Stephen and Marjorie stared down on her, a world of unspoken worry passing back and forth between them. At last Marjorie rallied.

"Stephen, please go and find Frederick. Tell him that his father wants him to fetch Christopher and meet him on the Great Hall stairs as soon as possible. And would you do the same? I'll stay with Eve."

Reluctantly Stephen nodded and bent low and kissed the top of Eve's head and would have given anything to be able to bring back the old Eve, laughing, joyous, the bright light in everyone's life. Where that beautiful and lively creature had gone, Stephen had no idea, but in the back of his mind an urgent plan was taking shape. He must send word to her parents at Stanhope Hall. It was clear that this pale young woman would not survive the rigors of an ocean voyage. And it was also clear that she needed something that she was not getting here, perhaps a mother's love or a father's support.

Then he spied Frederick a short distance away, cornered by two ladies who were quizzing him on the dangers of living in India.

"Would you please excuse us, ladies," Stephen said with a charm and a politeness that he did not feel. "I have been sent on an urgent errand to fetch my brother. You will shortly understand why. For now, if you will excuse us–"

"What's going on?" Frederick asked, clearly relieved to be out from under the burden of the two ladies.

"Father wants us."

"Where?"

"In the reception room."

"Why?"

"We are to join him in presenting our sons."

As they walked Stephen could sense Frederick's bewilderment. In a way it matched his own.

"Where's Marjorie?"

"With Eve. She isn't feeling well."

"She's understandably nervous, Stephen. One of her important sources of strength is now gone."

"Yorrick."

"Yes. It may take a while, and she may never totally resume her career. Sometimes we happen into a course of action because there was a guide to lead us. And when that guide is gone, we lose both our enthusiasm as well as our direction."

As they approached the reception hall, John Murrey Eden was pacing outside the door. "Where have you been? And where are–"

"They won't be coming," Stephen said, his voice topping his father's as though to signify he was not in a mood to be bullied.

At that moment the door opened and Mrs. Godwin appeared, her arms filled with babies. Stephen had not realized how much the boys had grown until he saw them in someone else's arms. They resembled twins, despite the month's difference in their age. Even their color was beginning to take on similar hues–blue eyes, and hair between dark blond and light brown. Both babies now smiled at anyone, and their greatest treat was to be taken for a walk on the headlands in the double pram which John had had built for them.

Now, as his son drew near in the arms of Mrs. Godwin, Stephen felt all worry, all fear, mysteriously eased in the beauty of his son.

"Here you are, gentlemen," Mrs. Godwin grinned and carefully held Alex to Stephen, Christopher to Frederick.

"What now, Father?" Frederick asked. "Please lead on. I'm afraid I'm rather new at presenting children to the world."

Stephen smiled in quick agreement, and John frowned at both of them as he used to do when they were misbehaving youngsters. "This way," he ordered in good military fashion and led them around the periphery of the crowd toward the Great Hall staircase.

About halfway up the stairs, John motioned for Stephen and Frederick to stand, one on one side, one on the other. The orchestra ceased playing and the crowd grew quiet.

Unprepared for such a terrifying focus of attention, Stephen felt an instantaneous heat on his face.

Frederick seemed to be faring better, but then he was accustomed to communal focus in the pulpit.

But for Stephen it was pure hell. He glanced over the heads of the company to the far side where he had left Marjorie and Eve and was pleased to see them both on their feet, a smile on Eve's face, which he could detect in spite of the distance.

"Ladies and gentlemen," John Murrey Eden called across the crowded Great Hall, "may I have your attention, please."

John waited until the Great Hall was silent and the attention was his. Then he spoke. "For several years Eden has slept. Time and circumstance dictated seclusion and contemplation, one of those restorative intervals that Fate foists on all human organisms from time to time, an interval of introspection and withdrawal, not necessarily an interval of unhappiness or discontentment, you must understand that, but merely a time of quiet, of healing, of gaining a second wind for the next race."

His voice seemed to have a hypnotic effect on the crowd. Stephen saw the faces near the front upturned, mouths agape, eyes fixed and unblinking.

"Now it is time for a most joyous celebration, for out of the silence of Eden have come two young princes, twin gifts from the Eden family to the British Empire and the new century."

Stephen was prepared to lift Alexander upward for purposes of display, but was surprised when his father took the child and positioned him in his right arm. John then turned to Frederick for Christopher and at last faced the company, both arms filled with babies who from time to time lifted a tiny fist to his face.

At first there was the loud collective "Ahhh." Then applause commenced in one quarter and was instantly picked up by the others until at last the ancient Great Hall of Eden Castle thundered with vibrations of several hundred enthusiastic guests.

When the applause started to diminish, his father lifted Alexander higher for his introduction.

"May I present to you, ladies and gentlemen, Alexander Burke Eden, born March 13, 1896, to my eldest son, Stephen, and his celebrated wife, whom we shall have the pleasure of hearing in concert in a short while."

Stephen was in no way prepared for the thunderous applause which erupted from all quarters of the company, a sound of adoration which he had heard many times before whenever Eve had performed.

Gradually the company contained their enthusiasm, though it was slow to die completely, but at last his father could speak over it.

"And this," he went on, "is Christopher Edward Eden, the son of my youngest son, Frederick, and his wife Marjorie, daughter of the Anglican bishop from northern India."

Again applause erupted, though somehow it seemed pale in comparison to what they had given to Eve.

"With these two new human beings, the Eden family is saying welcome to the new century, to a grand new age, to the continuity that is necessary for a civilized society."

The presentation was almost over now, his father growing sentimental and ineffective, speaking almost embarrassingly of angels and human endeavor and the richness of the Eden character as it had been passed on to his two grandsons.

Enough! Apparently his father's inner voice spoke at the same time, for now he was inviting one and all to gather as close as possible around the pianoforte at the north end of the Great Hall, where shortly his gifted daughter-in-law would entertain them accompanied by her sister-in-law, Marjorie Housman Eden.

This announcement caused a stir as part of the company turned to proceed toward the pianoforte and the other part witlessly blocked their progress, apparently believing the pianoforte to be in the opposite direction.

Stephen watched, helpless and mildly amused along with his father and Frederick. His father, having introduced his armload of infants to the world, apparently didn't have the slightest notion what to do with them now.

Stephen rescued Alex just as help arrived in the form of Mrs. Godwin.

Both Stephen and Frederick watched as their sons were carried off.

"I'd say they were something of a hit, wouldn't you?" Frederick beamed.

At the same time, Frederick pointed toward the pianoforte, and Stephen heard the crowd grow instantaneously quiet. Stephen saw Marjorie and Eve emerge from the crowd and walk unescorted toward the pianoforte. Marjorie had her hand on Eve's elbow in clear support.

"Please God," Stephen prayed, "let her regain her powers and thus reclaim her soul–for her sake."

Stephen completed his prayer at the sound of the first chord from the pianoforte. Then he looked up, along with the hundreds of others in the Great Hall, though he alone was holding his breath.

Marjorie felt Eve's trembling through the sleeve of her gown and her first thought was, Too soon, it's too soon to demand a public performance of her.

Then Eve stood alone in the curve of the pianoforte, and Marjorie had never heard such a silence. She thought she had seen Eve nod to her, their prearranged signal to start. Thus Marjorie had struck the first chord of "Greensleeves," one of three English folk songs which Eve had planned to sing for the company. If there were encores, then she would do a medley of American songs, primarily those of Stephen Foster, songs she had grown up with, songs which had been Yorrick's favorites.

Now, as the opening chord echoed over the quiet Great Hall, Marjorie kept her eyes fixed on Eve, who gazed down at the floor, an ominous focus, and Marjorie saw her rate of breathing increase, saw her reach out with one hand for the pianoforte.

Quickly Marjorie struck the chord a second time, louder in an attempt to remind Eve to focus on the task at hand.

The ploy worked. Eve looked up like a startled animal, her vision alternating between Marjorie and the vast audience. Marjorie started a brief musical introduction, playing the melody through once, then pausing on the opening bar, where Eve took over.

And she did, striking one crystal clear note and holding it, then leading into the first verse. Her voice was splendid, a bit low at first, as though she wasn't quite certain what would come out.

Then the refrain, and it was beautifully sung, Eve's eyes closed as though she had commenced seeing another world, another vision.

The audience appeared to be in a state of bliss. They seemed to sense the tentative nature of the singer, to share with her all grief, past, present and future. As Marjorie played, she knew that she had never been a part of such a remarkable experience before and quite probably never would again.

It was on the second stanza that the difficulty began. Eve lost the lyrics and tried to repeat the previous line, but the disrupted rhythm threw her completely off and she brought the song to a standstill.

Marjorie continued to play, feeling embarrassment for Eve, who stood trembling before the pianoforte, looking first at Marjorie for help, then out over the stilled company.

"Come on, Eve," Marjorie prayed. "Start back at the beginning with me. It will come the second time. Please, Eve, sing."

But Eve couldn't. She had known all along that she couldn't, though she had tried. At least no one could accuse her of not trying. But her voice was changed, weaker, without substance or body. She felt as hollow and piping as a child.

But more important, something was the matter with her spirit. She lacked point and purpose. This pampered, overfed company had no use for her or her voice. What was her voice to them? Merely an evening's diversion. These people were so unlike the lonely and isolated ranchers and farmers she had sung for in the American West.

As she looked out over the crowd, seeing not one familiar face, not even Stephen's, her mind had faltered, and though she heard poor Marjorie try to draw her back to the beginning, she could not find the will or the energy to start again.

As she turned in an attempt to convey this to Marjorie, the heat of her face rushed too rapidly up to the top of her head. The Great Hall and all those gaping faces began to spin hopelessly before her vision. She reached out for the edge of the pianoforte for support, and the last thing she saw before her legs buckled was poor Marjorie on her feet, her face contorted with alarm as she reached out for Eve and missed.

Someplace below the pianoforte was a safe, warm, silent blackness. As she saw the floor rise up to greet her, she felt only relief that it was over. She was at last freed from the expectations of others. She could now leave this place in search of a new identity, a new soul, a new world, a new peace.

Then the soft darkness was there before her, though now it wasn't an altogether silent one, for she heard the sound of women screaming and heard a rush of footsteps, terrible sounds of fear and confusion all about her.

Susan had been chatting with Alice and Christabel Pankhurst when Eve had commenced to sing. Of course, they had immediately ceased their conversation and had turned to listen along with everyone else in the crowded Great Hall.

For some reason Susan knew moments before the poor girl collapsed that trouble was inevitable. She motioned for Alice and Christabel to follow after her, made her way around the periphery of the crowd and was the first to arrive after Eve had fainted.

"Turn her gently," she warned Alice, who had arrived only a step behind her. As the two women knelt over Eve, Susan heard Christabel Pankhurst order the company to move back, a remarkable tone of authority in her voice that efficiently soothed even as it commanded.

"You, sir, please, I must ask you–"

"It's alright, Christabel. It's her husband."

As Stephen pushed his way to the pianoforte, Susan saw fear in his eyes. "She's just fainted, Stephen. No real cause for alarm. Am I correct, Alice?"

Stephen dropped to his knees beside Eve. He reached for her hand and Susan saw breaking emotion.

"Fainted is all," Alice said at last, releasing her hand where she had just monitored her pulse. "We must get her out of this place–"

Even before she had finished speaking, Stephen lifted Eve into his arms, and with Frederick and Marjorie clearing a path before them, they made their way toward the Great Hall steps.

Somewhere behind her, Susan thought she heard John calling her name, but she couldn't stop now. She would make a full report as soon as they got Eve to bed and made a careful examination.

Her one and only prayer as she climbed the Great Hall steps behind the others was that John did not send Dr. Reicher to Eve's bedroom.

At the top of the stairs, she looked back, almost fearful that Dr. Reicher was in fast pursuit. But he wasn't. In fact, mass confusion seemed to be the order of the day in the Great Hall. Susan saw poor Eleanor trying to start the orchestra again, and at the same time, John was trying to offer an explanation.

As Susan turned to catch up with the procession heading toward Eve's rooms, she glimpsed Charlotte and Aslam Eden.

Apparently the sound of Eve's voice had drawn them out of their seclusion. Now that the performance was over, they turned to go back into the library; though Charlotte looked back, clearly concerned. Then the tall, dark Indian took her arm in an intimate fashion.

Transfixed, Susan watched until the library door was closed.

Trouble there, she was certain.

Well, perhaps, she had a solution. Albert was due home tomorrow. Additional duties at school had detained him. He and Charlotte had been close as children. Susan would ask Albert to stay close to her, be her guide for whatever function was taking place, an unofficial chaperon, as it were.

Yes, speak to Albert, she reminded herself, then she hurried after the others and prayed quickly that Eve's collapse had been merely a case of nerves and nothing more.

What Mason Frye wanted more than anything in this world was a little privacy in this castle teeming with people. Was it asking too much? Apparently it was, for as he and Lucy broke free of the confused company following Eve's collapse and headed toward the small library, they saw Charlotte and Aslam Eden precede them into the intimate and comfortable room.

"Damn," Mason cursed beneath his breath, and he immediately apologized to Lucy.

"I know another place," she whispered, and he found her smile so radiant that he grasped her hand, indicating that she was to lead on.

Now, as he followed after her, he wondered how long he had been in love with her. He had always considered it significant that he had arrived at Eden Castle nineteen years ago on the precise day of her birth. Then he had been a young scholar fresh out of Cambridge, eager to do well for this noble family with its burgeoning offspring. He had looked forward to a future at a university perhaps or in public school, headmaster ultimately, certainly an academic environment, for that was where he felt most at home.

Eden Castle was to have been a stopgap measure, an opportunity to refill his coffers with the generous salary to be paid by John Murrey Eden.

On that day nineteen years ago, dusty and hot from his August ride across the moors, he had arrived at the Eden gatehouse to find the guardsmen toasting Lucy, new, firstborn daughter of Lord and Lady Eden.

Remembering the beginning caused Mason to move ahead of Lucy and then turn to see if his good fortune was still there. She was, and he saw in her eyes the same look of helpless bewilderment which Mason had at last decided was what the great writers meant when they spoke of love.

"Let's go to the headlands," Lucy whispered and looked furtively about as though all were watching them when in truth the company was still abuzz about the dramatic collapse of poor Eve.

A few minutes later they rounded the north side of the castle, and Mason was pleased to see that they had left all of the other strollers behind within the safety of the inner courtyard.

Then the headlands belonged to them, and there, straight ahead, running the length of the headlands, was a row of heavy stone benches situated about thirty yards apart from each other.

The third one was theirs, a place that provided a free and unbroken view of the dramatic north wall of Eden Castle and an unspoiled vista of the coastline of Wales across the channel.

When they reached the bench, Mason withdrew his handkerchief and carefully dusted the stone surface. Lucy sat and looked up nervously, as though eager for Mason to sit beside her.

He did, and for several moments neither spoke but seemed content to stare out across the dark waters of the channel.

"It's chilly. Are you chilled?" Lucy asked.

"No, I'm not, but–" Mason slid closer on the bench. "May I put my arm around you? For . . . warmth."

At that exact moment the moon slipped behind a bank of clouds, obscuring her expression. All Mason heard was a soft, "Yes, of course."

He slid forward and put his arm about her and applied no pressure at first, then drew her yet closer until it was quite the natural thing for her to rest her head on his shoulder.

"Are you warmer?" he asked and received one gentle nod, and for several moments neither seemed inclined to speak.

"Things are different now, aren't they?" Lucy asked with surprising directness.

"Yes," he replied. "I find that things are very different, at least for me and I hope for you as well."

"Yes."

"There are . . . questions and problems."

"Such as?"

"The difference in our ages."

"It means nothing."

"Others may not think so."

"I don't think we should concern ourselves with what others think."

"Perhaps not. Still . . ."

"I think I have always known—that I care for you."

Mason closed his eyes and drew her closer. He had long ago resigned himself to bachelorhood. Who would he ever find, he had asked himself time and time again, in this remote rural outpost of England? The answer had always been there, attending his tutorials, racing ahead of him on nature walks through dappled woods, curled cozily on his lap while he amused them both with selections from the Sonnets.

"Lucy."

As she turned toward him, he gathered his courage about him and bent low and found her lips waiting and eager and as lonely as his own and then felt her arm around his neck, and as the kiss intensified, he held her close and prayed only that this miraculous and glorious moment might never end.

"I have always loved you," she whispered.

"And I have always loved you," he confessed and clung to her, amazed at how naturally, how easily this confession had come, as though it had been rehearsed and waiting in the wings of his heart for many years.

At the end of the embrace, the clouds slipped past the moon, and he saw her face, saw the tenderness and the wealth of love waiting to be given.

Suddenly he felt inadequate. "Poor Lucy, you could do so much better, you know that, don't you? One of those young aristocrats dancing in the Great Hall–"

"I don't want a young aristocrat."

"Are you certain?"

"More certain than I have ever been of anything in my life."

He held her gaze for several long moments, more than content to study her beauty. He knew that there were those in Eden Castle who called Charlotte the great beauty of this family.

In his opinion, it wasn't so. Lucy's beauty was simpler, kinder, and spoke volumes of love and thoughtful giving.

"What is it?" she whispered, apparently alarmed by something she saw on his face.

He shook his head. "I am having difficulty," he confessed.

"In what way?" she asked.

"You. I cannot believe that I am here with you in this manner."

"It seems so right to me."

"It does indeed."

Gently he touched her face. "I will speak to your father," he said, dreading it even as he mentioned it.

"I will go with you."

"No, I think you should–"

"Don't be so old-fashioned, Mason. Of course I'll go with you. I think Mama will be pleased. I hope so. In the event that they are pleased, I want to see the pleasure on their faces."

"What about John?" he asked.

"Uncle John?" Lucy asked as though surprised. "What business is it of his? It's our concern and my mother's and my father's. No one else's."

She said this with such certainty that for a moment he almost believed her. When she stood and held her hand out to him, he took it and drew her under his arm, warning her again of the hazards of their union.

"I will be an old man long before you are an old woman."

"You will never be an old man."

"Oh, my darling, love is making fools of both of us."

"Not true," she protested in mock agitation and pulled free of his arm. "At least not for me. Speak for yourself. As for me, I look at you and see my husband. I look at you and see the father of my children. I look at you and see the face that I want to see on the day that I die."

Quickly he gathered her to him, needing to cancel the nature of her grim declaration.

"Dearest," he whispered, and with remarkable ease they kissed and at the height of passion, with all of his senses fully occupied, there still was one small, dark corner of his mind that dwelt on what the reaction of others would be.

Still, hadn't John Murrey Eden personally invited him to remain at Eden indefinitely and tutor the two young infants?

And hadn't Mason Frye accepted? Then nothing would change except that Lucy would share his private quarters with him as his wife.

Why would anyone object to that?

In the mounting heat of the kiss, he did not dwell on the question long enough to receive a clear answer.

In all ways, Charlotte felt as though she should date the true beginning of her life as being the remarkable evening she had just spent with Aslam Eden.

Now they sat on opposite ends of the sofa and listened to the clock strike midnight. Before them on the table were two half-empty platters fetched from the buffet by an obliging steward. Aslam's instructions had been brief.

"Bring us one of everything," he had laughed, and at the same time, he had lifted a bottle of champagne and two glasses from a wine steward. With the exception of the interval during which they had left the library to hear poor Eve sing, they had occupied these identical places and had, each in turn, opened the floodgates of their hearts and souls to each other in a marathon talk session that now clearly had left them both drained.

If only she could focus on something besides his dark beauty, his full head of wavy hair, his darker eyes, his satin-smooth olive complexion. She was absolutely certain that she had never seen a more beautiful man in her life.

As he had talked of his boyhood in India, hesitantly at first, then quite volubly as though his loneliness was years deep, she had noticed other aspects of his beauty as well; his long, tapered hands, moving like birds in flight as he spoke, and his prolonged soberness, punctuated by a most unexpected smile. Then there was something else, his modesty, his concern for others, the obvious love in his face and voice and manner as he spoke of Uncle John, the one who had rescued him from certain death during the Indian Mutiny.

She knew she could sit like this for the rest of her life and listen to him talk and watch his face, his most courtly and civilized manner.

"Charlotte?"

She looked up as he spoke her name, certain that she had never heard her name spoken so beautifully.

"If you had other preferences for this important first night of your family's fete, then I beg you, please do forgive me."

"No, Aslam, I promise you. This is where I wanted to be more than anything. Don't you remember? I was the one who issued the invitation. My father merely affixed his seal."

"Why?" Aslam asked, settling anew on the sofa as though freshly interested. "Surely you knew what I am to John, what our relationship is and was."

A hard question, that, particularly when his hand had just covered hers on the center cushion of the sofa, a subtle gesture, like that of a dear and intimate friend.

"India," she said flatly. "I have always felt a strong fascination for India. I suppose it started with Frederick's letters. Frederick has a way with words, and he had just fallen in love with India. I think he made all the rest of us fall in love with it as well."

"And what did John say?" Aslam asked.

"Oh, I can't remember what Uncle John said," she murmured. The conversation had been much more enjoyable when Aslam had been speaking of himself and his India. Now that the conversational tables had been turned on Charlotte, she was already bored. Nothing had happened to her in her life that could possibly be of interest to Aslam Eden.

"Tell me more of the Red Fort, please, Aslam. Tell me about the Peacock Throne and the Golden Tower and the copper-domed mosques and the Moghul emperors all clad in decorations of gold and silver and precious stones. Why did they call it the Red Fort?"

In response to her enthusiasm, Aslam threw up his hands in surrender. At the same time, he drew closer to her on the sofa and again took her hand and appeared to study it very closely.

"What a lovely hand," he murmured. "As white and delicate as fine carved marble. Now I am going to tell you something that I have never told anyone."

She tried not to let her joy show too much. His hands were warm.

"Oh, tell me, Aslam. I promise I will never tell anyone—on my honor."

Almost breathlessly, as though he had run a great distance, he leaned close and whispered, "You are so beautiful."

She blushed. "You were about to tell me a secret."

"Yes. On that day when John rescued me and my mother from old Bahadir Shah Zafir's guard, I begged my mother to let me return to my room. At first she was opposed, claiming we must be where John had told us to be at the appointed time."

He stopped talking as though he had resurrected a memory that he should have left alone.

"I was seven at the time, a very young and spoiled seven. I ran back up to my rooms and found my treasure chest, found the dragon's eye that my great-grandfather had given me only the week before on the promise that I never lose it."

"Dragon's eye?" she repeated.

"It was a ruby, flawless. It was to have been the beginning of my treasure trove."

"And your mother?"

"I went to the appointed place near the back wall of the castle. John wasn't there, but the guards were, as was my mother."

His voice broke. He cleared his throat. "They had . . . abused her. So that she could not identify them, they had cut out her tongue."

For too long, the brutal words sat unmoving on the air. Charlotte tried to think of something to say. But such an atrocity was beyond her ability to comprehend. In her world of gentle beauty and indulgent parents and loving servants, those words had no place, no point of reference.

But what she could, and did, respond to was the look of devastation in Aslam's face. "I'm . . . so sorry, Aslam," she whispered and reached forward and touched his hand, a gesture that immediately summoned his attention back from the tragic past to the new present.

"She survived," Aslam said, "with John's help. We both survived with John's help. He ultimately became very important to both of us."

"Then why did you become estranged from him?"

Aslam looked up at the ceiling, mouth open, ready to speak as soon as the heart and mind found an answer. "People change. People grow apart. People seek different visions," he said finally.

Charlotte heard nothing at the door until a moment later when it burst open with a suddenness that startled. She looked in that direction, saw Aslam on his feet as quick as a reflex, his face mirroring her alarm.

It was John Murrey Eden, a glowering John who seemed to stare forward, unmoving as though to give his anger a chance to recede.

"John," Aslam began cordially, and stepped to one side, easily indicating that Uncle John was invited, indeed welcome, into their fellowship as well as their conversation.

"This relentless young woman," Aslam went on, his voice soothing, "has been questioning me all evening on the mysterious charm of India. As I still, after all these years tend to homesickness, I can't tell you how much I have enjoyed myself. How very honored we would both be if you would join us."

Charlotte found herself smiling at his charming civility and wondered why Uncle John continued to stand in the open door, brooding.

"Is anything–" Charlotte began and was not given a chance to finish.

"Your mother is quite distraught and is searching for you." When at last he spoke, his voice was without inflection.

"Why?" Charlotte asked in perfect innocence.

"Because you have thoughtlessly abandoned her on this most important night when she was counting heavily upon your assistance in all matters."

Slowly Charlotte stood. "Abandoned her? I didn't know she–"

"No, you didn't know," John interrupted angrily. "Well, you should have. This evening was planned specifically for you, and yet you spoil it in a state of isolation, not even courteous enough to take part in the reception line or the opening waltz, people inquiring after you, and your poor parents–"

Aslam stepped forward. "Please, John, all that Lord and Lady Eden had to do was to send a steward. I would have delivered Charlotte to them immediately."

Abruptly John gave Aslam a most condescending look. "This is none of your concern," he said.

"Oh, but it is. I am afraid I am the one who has monopolized the lady."

"And she is not a lady. She is a child, a mere child."

Charlotte felt tears of embarrassment and protested while there was still time. "That is not true, Uncle John. I am almost eighteen, and that is far from being a–"

"I think that you had better go now and find your parents, Charlotte, apologize to them and beg their forgiveness."

"For what?" Charlotte asked, her sense of embarrassment rapidly escalating to anger.

But just as she was about to protest a second time, she felt Aslam at her side. "It might be wise," he suggested. "I am afraid that we both have been quite selfish."

"No," she protested weakly.

"Go as John says, please," Aslam murmured. "We will have time to talk again, I promise you, in the next few days."

For several moments she was held in his gaze. He seemed to be trying to tell her something else without words. Then Uncle John was there again at his bullying worst.

"Charlotte! Now! Go and find your parents!"

But she had heard enough, had been mortified enough, and without another word to either, she ran from the room. About ten steps down the corridor it occurred to her to stop and listen to the words that the two men would exchange after she left.

But as she moved back toward the library door, she heard nothing, as though the room had been mysteriously emptied, though she knew perfectly well that both Aslam and Uncle John were still inside, apparently facing each other, each waiting for the other to speak.

She waited for what seemed like an eternity, alarm rising. What were they doing? Why did neither speak? Did this mean that Aslam would be leaving Eden Castle to return to London?

"Dear God, please, no!" And with that furtive prayer, she turned about and ran down the corridor.

All she wanted was to find a place of privacy so that she might sit uninterrupted and close her eyes and think on this evening and commit it all to memory, for surely it had been the most important evening of her entire life.

Three days after Eve's collapse in the Great Hall, Alice stood beside her bed, Christabel Pankhurst at her side, both staring down at the young woman, who had not left her chambers since that embarrassing evening and who now appeared too weak to lift her head.

Beyond Eve's door, Alice could hear the Midsummer fete going strong, the guests scattering at midday, some riding out across the moors, some off on a fox hunt with her Uncle John and her father in the lead, others strolling through the gardens, and still others napping in preparation for the evening's festivities.

The entire fete had taken on all of the aspects of a marathon, for hosts and guests alike. Her mother was at this moment tending to a few ills in one of the reception rooms off the Great Hall. The quack–Dr. Reicher–had been called in to examine the sprained ankle of Lord Raventon. And there were other assorted upset stomachs and insect bites and scratches, enough to keep her mother busy well into the night.

But enough worrying about her mother's work. *Hers* was just there, a pale and near-lifeless form huddled beneath the covers on this hot late-July day, her hands grasping the hem of the blanket as though fearful someone would drag it from her.

Eve had had a serious recurrence of her fever. But the fever had broken and passed two days ago, and since then, everyone who might conceivably mean something to her had traipsed into the room, trying in every way they knew how to revive her spirits.

Stephen had told Alice that Eve particularly enjoyed Christabel's company, and though her friend was packing to leave, she was more than eager to stop in and see Eve. Christabel was the most intelligent woman Alice had ever met. Their paths had first crossed in nursing classes at St. Martin's in London. Christabel's mother was a firm believer in the independence of women, claiming, as Alice had heard her do on many occasions, that the worst fate that could befall any female was to find herself wholly dependent on the whim and generosity of a male.

Thus, Christabel was learning the nursing trade, and after that she said she had plans to enter law school, but for now she and Alice had become the best of friends and Alice was a frequent visitor to the Pankhurst home. She loved the ease of discourse, the informality and lack of pretense.

Now Alice saw Christabel, her pert traveling hat perched on the very top of her head, step close to the side of Eve's bed.

"Eve?"

There was no reaction.

"Eve? I've come to say goodbye. I'm going back to London today to meet my mother. I, too, will be entertaining, though on a much smaller scale than you Edens, mind you. I just wanted to say goodbye and to thank you for inviting me."

Eve did not move.

"Listen, Eve," Christabel went on, climbing up on the edge of the bed, pushing her traveling cloak aside. "There is absolutely no reason why you should be behaving in this manner. Did you know that? Look at me. I want to see your face."

Christabel reached for Eve's face and turned it toward her, a gesture that apparently startled Eve into opening her eyes.

"There," Christabel smiled and rearranged herself primly on the edge of the bed, "isn't that better?" There was something about her tone, her manner of absolute self-confidence that reminded Alice of Emmeline Pankhurst, Christabel's mother, the strongest woman Alice had ever known. Alice had on many occasions heard her debate men to the ground on any current issue, from trade unionism to the Irish problem. She stepped back for no man and firmly believed with all her heart and soul that women were equal to men in all ways and superior to them in most.

Now Alice looked down to see Christabel chatting quite easily with Eve, who appeared to be listening.

"And so I told her, the superior, I mean, that if I couldn't stay in the room with him while he did his dying, then I really didn't fully understand the philosophy of nursing. But it was the rule, don't you see? The rule!"

She repeated the word with all the emphasis of an obscenity. "God, but I hate rules, don't you? Oh, I suppose some serve a purpose, but my mother always taught us to examine them very carefully for the suspect things that they generally were. Do you agree, Eve?"

She waited only a moment, not nearly enough time for Eve to frame an answer.

"Do you know what else my mother taught us early on, possibly the very first lesson I ever remember. She told us that we must never waste these precious lives of ours in the futile and foolish pursuit of trying to please others. She said there is only one will, one conscience that must walk in harmony with you, and that is your own. Nothing else matters, no one else matters. Do you understand? Do you agree?"

"You sound like Sis Liz," Eve whispered.

Christabel smiled. "What a marvelous name," she exclaimed. "And just who is this insightful person who owns such a marvelous name?"

"My aunt."

"You are fortunate."

"She is dead."

"No, she's not," Christabel countered aggressively and without hesitation. "You just resurrected her, didn't you? You remembered something she said, and at the moment of remembering, didn't you see her?"

"Yes," she agreed.

"What did you see?" Christabel urged. "Please tell me all about her."

"She was my father's sister, and considered mad by most."

"And therefore the most sane of the lot, I imagine."

Eve laughed, a glorious sound, and struggled to an upright position. "Yes, oh yes, she was so sane, so wise. She lived in a cabin in the woods that once had been slave quarters, lived there with her dearest friend, a woman named White Doll, who was a mulatto."

"How fascinating," Christabel exclaimed and settled herself more comfortably on the bed and, in the process, shook free of her traveling cloak and gave every indication of a woman who would not be going anyplace for a while.

As Eve talked on of her childhood and the regal woman named Sis Liz, Alice looked back and saw Stephen at the door, a grin on his face where earlier there had been worry.

Quietly Alice left the bed, took Stephen by the elbow and led him out into the corridor.

"Christabel has worked her magic again," she smiled. "I watch her do it with the patients at St. Martin's. It's quite a gift, to draw them out and help them to remember those people from their past who loved them and shaped them and made them what they are."

"Eve misses home," Stephen said. "I have written to her parents, a discreet letter, trying not to alarm them. But perhaps I should alarm them. I'm sure they can't get away in the cotton season. And the North Atlantic passages aren't safe during the winter months. Therefore it will be next spring at least–"

"Don't worry," Alice soothed. "She may not need them to come at all. You may be escorting her home before you know. Listen–"

At that moment Eve laughed again and Christabel joined in.

"Let's leave them," Alice suggested. "I'll stay close by."

"Christabel is remarkable," Stephen murmured, peering back into the room.

"She is indeed. You should meet her mother. She's quite capable of remarkable action."

"Such as?" Stephen asked, walking easily beside Alice toward the end of the corridor.

"You wouldn't believe me even if I told you."

"Try me."

"Equal rights for women. The vote for women. Equal opportunities for women. Have I said enough?"

"No, I would like to hear more."

"You are a rare breed, Stephen. Sometimes I have difficulty believing that you are our father's son." She walked ahead a few steps and turned back, pleased with his sympathetic ear. She loved to test what they laughingly called the Pankhurst philosophy on the air, but in most quarters the air wasn't safe.

"Do you know what Mrs. Pankhurst would get for her radical proposals?"

"More attention than she wants I would imagine," Stephen said.

"More likely a prison term. Even now she stays one step ahead of the investigators by changing her lodgings from time to time. Most of the time she lives in Manchester, where she has done marvelous things in the workhouses. In fact, she serves on the board of the Poor Law Guardian."

"Obviously a woman of considerable conviction."

"Oh yes," Alice agreed. "But she hasn't even started yet. I could sit forever and listen to her speak of the future. Such a promising dawn it will be for women everywhere."

Alice talked on, aware of her own degree of enthusiasm and passion for the Pankhursts and their cause, but equally aware that others either found it alarming and threatening or uninteresting. Now poor Stephen looked the latter.

"I'm sorry, Stephen," she said. "I'll return to Eve's room and keep an eye on things. Don't worry. I think Eve will be fine. Instead of writing a letter of alarm to her parents, why don't you send an invitation? It will do John good to face his half sister again. From what Mother has said, the estrangement has gone on long enough. Yes, invite them for next spring, for the old queen's Diamond Jubilee. The whole country will be on its best behavior then, all spit and polish. Why not?"

Stephen agreed and she saw him wave a hand, as he disappeared from sight. She stood quietly for a moment outside Eve's room listening. She couldn't hear what they were saying.

It didn't matter. If anyone could revive Eve's flagging spirits, it would be Christabel, beautiful, brilliant Christabel.

Eden Castle
July 27, 1896

Susan stood on the Great Hall stairs, Stephen close beside her, both watching with a combination of curiosity and relief as the guests departed from Eden Castle. There seemed to be a definite feeling of auld lang syne on the warm summer air and the melancholy sense of a grand party now over.

"Thank God," Stephen muttered. Susan looked at him, pleased to see a smile on his face. Under Alice and Christabel's unique nursing, Eve appeared to be flourishing in all ways. Daily the girls took her for a walk—a forced march, Christabel jokingly called it—to the headlands, and the combination of sea air and summer sun had restored color to her cheeks. That, combined with the knowledge that her parents had been invited to Eden Castle next spring, seemed to have worked wonders in her recuperation.

Now Stephen was waiting for the three girls to appear so that he could join them. When the departures had commenced, he had joined Susan for a spectacle which was even more exciting than their arrivals.

"How do you think it went?" Stephen asked, leaning back against the railing.

"Splendidly I would say. I think Richard and Eleanor are pleased, and that's all that really matters."

"*That* surprises me."

As she followed the direction of his focus, she knew what he meant even before she looked. She had seen them leave the Great Hall by a lower door about fifteen minutes earlier, had seen Aslam's splendid carriage enter the courtyard, bypass the congestion at the bottom of the Great Hall steps and pull into a discreet position outside the kitchen court stairs. Now that was where Aslam and Charlotte stood talking.

"A girlhood infatuation, I suspect," Susan said, not particularly alarmed. John had rather deviously spied on the two for the better of the entire fete, convinced that Aslam meant Charlotte no good and, if that were so, they would all have a major scandal on their hands. Her scheme to have Albert serve as chaperon had failed on the second day of the fete. Albert had quarreled with John and left with his school chums.

Susan knew, however, that Aslam was a gentleman and Charlotte a rather silly and romantically inclined young girl. Quite naturally she had been attracted to this exotic foreigner. But the flirtation would end with the conclusion of the fete; Aslam would return to London, and Charlotte, to her studies, and that hopefully would be that.

"Look," Stephen invited beneath his breath, and Susan leaned forward to see a very scandalous kiss taking place.

Despite her shock, Susan found the scene rather moving, though she quickly looked about to see if anyone on the Great Hall stairs was bearing witness to this illegal kiss which could possibly feed the scandalmongers for weeks.

She saw no one watching, and fortunately when Susan looked back, the kiss had ended, though they continued to hold hands, Aslam making absolutely no move to board his carriage.

Again Susan looked nervously around. She had no idea where John was. She had left him sleeping peacefully in the cottage on Eden Rising, after too many late-night balls and banquets and too many early rides and hunts.

"Lucy seems to be taking her lessons seriously," Stephen commented now. And Susan followed his gaze to the stone walk which encircled the castle and led out onto the headlands.

Surprised, Susan looked more closely. "Is that–"

"It is. Mason Frye."

"Are they–"

"Holding hands, yes."

"I'm sure it's nothing," she said weakly.

"Don't count on it," Stephen whispered. "I saw them yesterday at the far end of the third-floor corridor, outside Lucy's room. They were kissing."

Surprised, Susan looked directly up at Stephen. "Surely you are mistaken."

Stephen laughed heartily. "I know what a kiss is, Susan. Believe me, they were kissing."

Still shocked, Susan could only shake her head.

"Look."

At Stephen's soft insistence, she gladly abandoned her worries and followed his gaze to the top of the Great Hall steps, where a most attractive threesome had just appeared. It was Alice and Christabel flanking a very pale Eve. Still, compared to past days, Eve looked radiant in a blue gingham dress, her hair pulled up in a blue satin ribbon.

As the three stopped briefly to greet Richard and Eleanor, Stephen kissed Susan on the cheek. "I'll leave you now to watch this passing parade of monkeys alone. Cupid seems to have slipped in with the rest of the guests. Look carefully, and be sure that he slips out again."

She watched as he bounded up the steps and took charge of Eve, putting his arm about her shoulder and drawing her close.

Susan watched until they were out of sight, down the same stone walkway along which Lucy and Mason Frye had just disappeared.

Cupid seems to have slipped in with the rest of the guests . . . Be sure that he slips out again.

Quickly Susan glanced toward the spot where Aslam and Charlotte had stood beside his parked carriage. The carriage was still there, the footman waiting patiently with the horses, and just at that moment she saw the hem of Charlotte's dress disappearing inside the carriage. Then the door was shut.

For several moments she stared at the parked carriage and wondered what they were doing. Suddenly she felt a warm blush creep up the side of her neck.

Enough standing and gawking and speculating. She was certain that Marjorie and Sonia Reicher could use a hand in the nursery. Marjorie had virtually taken over the care of both infants, more than a full-time job. But Sonia Reicher had proved to be good company, and little Rolf was a dream child with irresistible dimples.

Yes, tending the future would be a much more productive way to pass the time than watching these overfed, overpampered guests take their leave.

As Susan started back up the stairs, she thought to herself, good riddance. It would be nice to get the old castle back to normal. She hadn't been able to hold a free clinic for over three weeks. She was certain the tenants missed and needed her. Perhaps now, with the end of the festivities, everyone would regain a portion of their good sense and put a halt to these difficult, if not impossible, alliances. She wondered, What would John say to all of it?

Well, this much could be said for the Midsummer fete: it had put Eden back on the social map of England. The enormous guest list had read like a Who's Who, from politicians to financiers like Aslam, from even one or two minor literary lions to an endless array of lords and ladies, dukes and duchesses, of every size and description. Now they all would be returning to their various seats of power with, she hoped, glowing reports on the renaissance that had taken place at Eden Castle in North Devon and of the two little boys who had been introduced as Eden's gifts to the Empire and the new century.

Stanhope Hall
August 30, 1896

For too many nights, Mary had suffered dreadful nightmares, none of them specific, all vague and all terrifying. Someone was in pursuit, not of her but of someone she loved, and no matter how hard she tried to overtake them and warn them, she couldn't succeed.

Now at midmorning on this hot August 30, she sat in her rocker on the veranda, feeling spent, gazing down the avenue of live oaks in search of one of the few sights that brought her pleasure, her son David, grown slim and tall at seventeen, riding hell-bent for leather up the avenue of live oaks from his trip into Mobile for the post.

There he was, and she was on her feet in a burst of energy that felt good. Quickly and with conscious effort she put the nightmares out of her mind.

"Mother! Post from Eden!"

Despite her rising excitement, Mary found a stray maternal wisp that enabled her to scold lovingly, "Your father told you not to race Snowball."

"I didn't race Snowball," David smiled, breathless from exertion. "He raced himself. How was I to stop him?"

She focused on the news of a letter and prayed that Eve and Stephen and the baby had sailed for America and would dock in New York within the week. It was her plan to ask Burke if they might travel to New York to meet them. She had waited long enough to see Eve and her grandson. A holiday in New York would be pleasant for them all.

"Hurry, David," she begged as he tethered Snowball to the hitching post and with maddening deliberation drew a large stack of letters and periodicals from his pouch.

"Here it is," David said at last, still grinning as though he knew all too well that he was testing her patience. "Here's your letter. Not Eve's handwriting though."

With that muted warning, she took the brown envelope and studied the penmanship and decided that it was Stephen who had written to her. No matter. Eve undoubtedly was kept busy by young Alexander.

She ran her finger beneath the envelope flap and carefully broke the seal, all the while settling comfortably back into her rocker.

With a degree of disappointment, she observed that the letter was not a long, chatty one but rather was less than a page. It was Stephen's handwriting all right, commencing,

> Dearest Mary and Burke,
>
> It grieves me to tell you that our plans have changed. We will not be sailing for America this fall as we had anticipated. While Eve has regained her health for the most part, she has not as yet fully regained her strength. She tires very easily and Dr. Reicher has informed me that a prolonged voyage could be dangerous for her.

For a moment, Mary's eyes and heart stopped on those last few words.

A prolonged voyage could be dangerous for her.

If she had regained her health, how dangerous?

"Mother? Bad news?"

She looked up at David, standing at the bottom of the stairs, carefully watching her.

"I . . . don't know," she said vaguely and read hurriedly on:

> But I do wish to issue to all the inhabitants of Stanhope Hall a most sincere invitation to come to England next summer for the celebration of Victoria's Diamond Jubilee and then to come for a glorious reunion at Eden Castle, where I assure you Eve and Alexander and I will be eagerly awaiting your arrival. Please respond as quickly as possible,
>
> Your loving son-in-law, Stephen

Your loving son-in-law, Stephen.

Curiously she reread the last line several times, seeing not those words but the all-important words above it.

A most sincere invitation to come to England.

John Murrey Eden was at Eden Castle.

"Mother, what is it? Is Eve–?"

Aware of David's concern and unable to answer his question, she handed the letter over for his inspection and leaned back in her rocker in an attempt to deal with her deep disappointment and to digest the muddle of news.

From inside the house, she heard Burke at the end of the hall. He had worked most of the night on a piece for the *Atlantic*, an assessment of the last two decades of the nineteenth century on the eve of the twentieth century.

She knew he was tired, but she had long since given up trying to suggest moderation in anything.

"I don't understand," David said, and held up the letter as though in proof of his bewilderment.

"Nor do I," Mary confessed.

"Are we going? Next spring, I mean? To England?"

Mary heard the hope in his voice and knew that such a journey would mean a great deal to him and to her as well. She would like David to see the place where she had grown up, and of course, Victoria's Diamond Jubilee would be a glorious time to be in London.

"Yes, I think we shall go," Mary smiled. "Apparently it is the only way that I will ever get to see my grandson, to say nothing of my daughter."

"What about John Murrey Eden?"

She was on the verge of dismissing the question for the irrelevant thing that it was when suddenly she heard Burke's voice behind the screen door.

"What about John Murrey Eden?" he demanded and headed straight toward the stack of post which David had placed on the top step of the veranda.

He scooped up everything and was heading back toward the door when apparently he realized that neither David nor Mary had answered him.

"What about Eden?" he asked Mary directly, pausing at the door.

"We have received a letter."

"From whom?"

"From Stephen."

"And?"

"You can read it for yourself." Mary motioned for David to pass the letter over, which he did. Burke took it and held it out to accommodate his weakening eyesight.

"What exactly is this supposed to mean? She has regained her health, but not her strength?"

"I don't know."

"Sounds suspicious to me."

"In what way?"

"If you ask me, John Murrey Eden will not let them leave."

"Oh, Burke, don't be absurd. How could he hold them against their will?"

Mary shook her head in ancient despair at the animosity which existed between Burke and John Murrey Eden.

"This doesn't make sense," Burke concluded and tossed the letter onto the table and pulled open the door, ready to retreat back into his study, quite possibly for the rest of the day.

"Burke?" Mary called after him. "We must talk."

"About what?"

"The letter."

"I said it doesn't make any sense. If Eve wanted to come home, she would come home. I would say that obviously she has found more of what she wants in England than here. So let it be. Life will go on."

"Burke, please," Mary interrupted and wished that David would find something to do elsewhere. When he was younger, she could have sent him on errands. Now that he was a young man, it was more difficult. He would be leaving for school at William and Mary in two weeks. She would miss him so much that she did not have the heart to dismiss him from her company. Besides, perhaps he was old enough to hear his parents speak as people, as well as parents.

"Burke, please come and sit down," Mary invited, wanting to reach a decision of some sort so that she could send a message back to Eden before the week was out.

"I can't sit, Mary. I have hours of work."

"All I want is a few moments. Please grant me at least that much."

Apparently he heard something in her voice. Reluctantly he allowed the screen door to fall shut, placed his unopened post on the table and sat slowly in a near rocker.

"Papa, can we go to England? We've been invited."

"No, we are going nowhere."

"Burke–"

She closed her eyes briefly, prayed for the ability to say the right words in the right tone of voice and didn't wait to see if her prayers had been answered, turning back with an ultimatum of her own.

"We will be going to England in the late spring."

"Speak for yourself."

"I'm speaking for all of us. I feel very strongly that Eve needs us."

"Then let her come home where she belongs."

"She can't."

"Why?"

"I don't know, Burke," she pleaded.

Abruptly he stood. She saw on his face a look of resolution. "I said I would not be going to England next year."

"Papa, it will be Queen Victoria's Diamond Jubilee."

"To hell with Queen Victoria," Burke replied with alarming venom. "To hell with Eden and all of its inhabitants. I can't seriously believe that you are actually considering a journey to–"

"I don't feel as though we have a choice in the matter."

"We always have a choice."

"Not if we want to see our daughter and grandson."

"Why can't they come as planned?"

"Eve apparently is . . ."

"Is what? Healthy but not strong? Fully recovered though still weak?"

As he spoke, his voice rose, and she heard beyond the sarcasm to his genuine bewilderment and something else–hurt. He adored Eve and somehow felt that if she wanted to see them, she would come home.

"Burke," Mary began as gently as possible, her tone and attitude tempered with new understanding. "I think we must put everything aside except our need to see Eve for ourselves, to judge her condition for ourselves. I am so weary of long-distance reports with months in between. I want to embrace her, to look into her eyes, to hear her speak, and I want to see Alexander. Now apparently if we want to do all of these things, then we must travel to England."

"Please, Papa, it could be a good trip. You have always said how much you would like to show me London."

For several seconds, no one spoke. Mary sat on the edge of her rocker, waiting for Burke's response, hoping, praying it would be a reasonable one.

Slowly he stood. There was an encouraging air of defeat about him now. He did not look directly at Mary but seemed instead to be speaking to the mail in his hands.

"I will go to England," he said simply. "To London," he added with emphasis. "I will not journey on to Eden. You can tell Eve for me that if she wishes to see her father, she will have to come to London."

Then he was gone, the screen door falling closed behind him.

Mary exchanged a glance with David, both seeming to ask the other without words, was this victory or defeat?

"Then we're going?" David asked, his face alive with excitement and hope.

"We are going," Mary said.

"Why does Papa hate John Murrey Eden so?"

She looked up at the complicated question so innocently asked. Should she tell him all? Or should she tell him nothing?

"It was years ago," she said simply. "John was my guardian, and he disapproved of my affection for your father."

"Why?"

"John never needs a reason. He sets the rules for the world and demands that everyone else play by them."

"But what did he do?" David asked, settling in with youthful enthusiasm for a good story.

At last Mary decided to give him one, a brief one. He was old enough. Perhaps it would help him to understand his father.

"Your father and I had a secret place in a remote corner of Hyde Park, a sunken garden where no one went. I would leave John's house, where I was living, on the pretense of going riding in Rotten Row. But at some point on each outing, I abandoned my horse and went to our private place, where your father was always waiting for me."

David smiled. "Sounds very romantic."

"It was," Mary said, "until one day John had me followed and discovered the sunken garden and discovered who I was meeting and decided upon a unique punishment for my disobedience."

She stood up, feeling a sudden need for movement, a need to move away from her own story.

"Go on, Mother, what happened?"

She drew a deep breath and plunged headlong into the pain of the past.

"He very cleverly forged a note to Burke, informing him that I wouldn't be able to meet him on this particular evening. Then he hired ruffians who came to–"

As she spoke the words, the faces of the men appeared before her, as real as they had been on that evening years ago, armed with sharp shears and instructions to frighten her and cut her long hair. But these were not ordinary men. They were half men, half animals, and they arrived that evening in a carnival atmosphere and allowed themselves to be carried away in their enthusiasm for their cruel task, and helpless against their strength, she had submitted to their attacks as they had raped her, a brutal assault that had left her physically and emotionally damaged.

Now why was she crying? Had she finished recounting the tale to David? She must have, for he had his arms around her with as much tenderness and protection as Burke had done in the past.

"Mother, don't," he pleaded and drew her closer, and she relished the tenderness for just a moment and then pulled free.

"I'm so sorry," David said and followed after her. "I'm so sorry. No wonder Papa hates him so."

Mary drew a deep breath and studied the lace hem of her handkerchief and finished her tale.

"John sent me away then, to a place in the Midlands called Miss Veal's School for Young Ladies. Of course Burke followed after me, and with the help of a sympathetic teacher he literally rescued me and took me to his mother's house in London."

"Did Papa ever seen John Murrey Eden again?" he asked.

"Once. We were married at Eden Castle a few months later, and John journeyed out from London, interrupted the ceremony and challenged Burke to a bout of fisticuffs in the courtyard. No holds barred."

"Who won?" David asked with youthful eagerness.

"Neither, though they almost killed each other in the process of proving nothing."

Somewhat disappointed, David sat back, his eye fixed on a patch of sun-dappled shadow, clearly seeing neither sun nor shadow but his imagined recreation of the fistfight between his father and John Murrey Eden.

"And that was the last time Papa saw him?"

"The last."

"John Murrey Eden must be as old as Papa now. They are just two old men. You would think they would decide that it was time to forgive and forget."

Mary was amused by David's concept of old. Still, there was some truth in what he had said. Surely time had tempered John Murrey Eden in some respects. The invitation had been issued by John's son Stephen.

Surely John had given his blessing and was now ready to apologize for his part in the grievous past, though he had always claimed that his only intention in hiring the ruffians that night had been to frighten Mary and that the men had admittedly gone too far. Later he had assured one and all that the men had paid a dear price for their excess. The rumor was that John had had them murdered.

Mary crushed the handkerchief into a ball. What barbaric thoughts and acts seemed to be irrevocably connected with John Murrey Eden. Now Eve resided in close proximity to this man who had tried his best to ruin Mary's life and all that she loved.

All that she loved—

Abruptly she sat up in the chair, her mind fixed on a horrid possibility. Was John harassing Eve, undermining her recuperation in ways known only to John?

The thought was devastating.

"Mother? What is it?"

"We must go to Eden."

"We will, although I'm not so certain now that I care to meet John Murrey Eden."

Belatedly Mary realized that she was faced with yet another impossible task, that of trying to explain to David the unique power of a man like John Murrey Eden, personal power combined with great wealth and powers of persuasion beyond the ability of ordinary men to understand. He resembled a singular and unique force of nature and, like nature, could blow both good and evil winds.

"Mother? Surely you don't plan to see him next spring? I hope not, because I swear if I ever set eyes on him, I sincerely hope that you won't hold me accountable for my actions."

With that he was gone, striding down the veranda steps with the same purposeful gait as Burke, clearly two like minds, at least on the subject of John Murrey Eden.

Eden Castle
October 1, 1896

With the coming of fall and a chill in the old castle that could not be dissipated, John found himself gravitating to the third-floor nursery.

In addition to Mrs. Godwin's plain and uncomplicated company, there was always a roaring fire in the nursery and, of course, the two babies themselves, changing every day, growing, both sitting up now, the joy and purpose of John's life.

Now on this chill Thursday afternoon, instead of joining the others for tea downstairs in the Great Hall, he quietly slipped away, climbed the stairs, knocked on the door and peered in only to find everyone dozing. The boys were fast asleep in their crib, and Mrs. Godwin was nodding off before the fire.

It was a scene of pure peace. Quietly he slipped in and assumed his customary stance, looking at first one boy, then the other.

How beautiful they were, and each time John saw them, he offered up a silent prayer that God might see fit to allow him a hand in their upbringing. He could hardly wait for them to escape their babyhood, to evolve into strong and sturdy little boys with boundless energies and limitless dreams. O dear God, how he longed for the time when he could run their first race with them, sit them astride their first pony, race with the surf off Eden Point, cast their first fishing line in the channel, explore this old castle and see everything new and fresh through their eyes.

"Might as well move a cot in here for you, Mr. Eden."

At the sound of Mrs. Godwin's sleepy voice, John did not even turn about. "Not a bad idea," he whispered, keeping his voice down. "I hope I did not awaken you."

"I wasn't asleep," the old woman lied. "Just resting my eyes. Have the mothers come in?"

John looked back. "I just got here. Are they due?"

Godwin nodded and stood slowly, carefully testing her old joints before one strong movement. "Nursing time," she said.

John looked back at the babies. Damn. He had hoped to spend some time alone with them. Now if as Godwin said, the mothers were due–

At that moment the nursery door opened, and Marjorie appeared first. "John, what a surprise. They're too young to go drinking. But wait a while. They'll catch up with you."

As she pushed open the door, John saw Eve directly behind Marjorie, rail-thin and as white as a shroud. Still, she was fully dressed and upright, which was an improvement over the last few months since she had humiliated the entire family during the Midsummer fete with her embarrassing failure of nerve. There was a congenital weakness there, passed on to her by her mother, Mary, and the scoundrel Burke Stanhope. John prayed that it had not been passed yet again to young Alexander.

"Ladies," he murmured and relinquished his position at the crib and carefully observed Eve as she gave him a wide berth, passing on the far side of the nursery in order to reach the crib.

As she approached her son, John watched carefully and saw elements of beauty, faded now and dissipated by her repeated bouts of fever.

"How are you feeling today?" John asked, forcing thoughtfulness when he felt none.

She looked up at him like a frightened animal. John had never felt comfortable around her. She always reminded him of Mary and of Mary's betrayal of him with the American Burke Stanhope.

"I'm feeling better, thank you," she said, bending over the side of the crib to lift her son, who, upon being roused out of sleep, greeted his mother with a lusty howl of protest. This seemed to upset Eve, who looked pathetically about as though asking for help.

John was only too willing to give it to her. "Here, let me walk him to the window," he said, purposefully inserting a tone of command in his voice, knowing full well that Eve would not dare to challenge him.

She didn't. She allowed him to take Alexander to the window, to lift him up for a seagull's view of the channel, to see his attention suddenly engaged by the distant water and dancing whitecaps.

Behind him in the nursery, John heard a silence of condemnation. Obviously no one had liked what he had done, but what did it matter? The baby was quiet, wasn't he? Was John to blame if Eve did not know how to handle her own son?

As he pointed out various sights to young Alex, he heard life slowly resuming in the nursery behind him, Marjorie conferring with Mrs. Godwin on feeding schedules and bath times, Godwin responding with admirable competence while Eve said nothing.

In a way John felt bad. Perhaps he shouldn't have taken the child from his mother's arms. But he really seriously doubted Eve's ability to perform as a mother. She seemed so preoccupied with death, visiting that old fool Yorrick Harp's grave as often as the weather and her strength permitted, keeping to her chambers, only occasionally joining the family for meals. Not once had she apologized to Richard or Eleanor for the shambles she had made of the opening-night festivities of the Midsummer fete. Not once had she apologized to *him.* For the most part, all that could be said of her was that she kept to herself and saw only Stephen and occasionally Alice and Alice's mannish friend from London when they were in residence at Eden and, of course, Marjorie. Eve seemed to adore Marjorie, who in turn treated her as though she were the third child in the nursery, which perhaps she was.

During this barrage of judgmental thoughts, John kept his eye on the channel and on young Alex's fascination with everything that moved on land and sea, when all at once he was aware of a tense silence coming from the room behind.

He turned about only to find all three women staring at him, Marjorie seated in the rocker, the top buttons of her shirtwaist undone, young Christopher in her arms.

"Ladies," he smiled. "If I had known . . ."

Mrs. Godwin stepped forward and took Alex from him, "Feeding time, Mr. Eden, I'm sure you understand. Best done in private, don't you know?"

As she took Alex from his arms, he felt a surge of anger that these three women were dictating to him. Marjorie gave him the sweetest smile of reconciliation. "I'm sorry, John. Please do return. In about an hour, I would say, wouldn't you, Eve? The boys enjoy your company so much. For now, however, unless I miss my guess, your presence and your wisdom are sorely needed down in the Great Hall."

John appreciated her kindness but resented her riddle. How needed? Or was this simply a female ploy to ease his exit?

"Haven't you heard, John?" Marjorie called after him.

"Heard what?"

"Of the meeting taking place in the Great Hall?"

"I've heard nothing."

"Then you are in for a surprise. Lucy has just made a stunning announcement."

"What sort of announcement?" John asked, hand on the doorknob.

"She is engaged to be married," Marjorie declared.

Certain that he had misunderstood, John held his position by the door. "Lucy?" he smiled, "To be married? To whom? She's seen no one in her entire life except–"

"Mason Frye," Marjorie interrupted.

"Are you telling me that Lucy and–"

"Mason Frye, yes," Marjorie smiled. "Poor Eleanor and Richard are, I'm afraid, in a state of shock. I really think perhaps that you should go to them."

Quickly John stepped out of the door and closed it behind him. For several moments he stared at the closed door, certain that he had misunderstood some key point of her account. Lucy, plain simple Lucy, and Mason Frye, one of the most brilliant men he had ever known.

How could he betray John in this fashion? Hadn't John just extracted a promise from Mason that he would remain in service at Eden Castle until Alex and Christopher were ready for him?

And Lucy? What in the name of God was there to Lucy's plain face and form and empty head to attract a man like Mason Frye?

No, surely Marjorie was mistaken or perhaps exaggerating just in an effort to clear the nursery.

As he started slowly away from the door, one thought nagged: Marjorie was not given to exaggeration or pretense.

Then perhaps he was needed in the Great Hall. For if someone were to ask him to create the greatest insanity of the decade, he would say without hesitation the union of brilliant Mason Frye with the empty-headed, plain-faced Lucy Eden.

Marjorie must have dispensed faulty information.

But what if she had not? Then it was John's intention to move with whatever power he had at his disposal, to put an immediate end to such a union. Perhaps it was time that Lucy be sent away. He knew of a place, in the Midlands, a Miss Veal's School for Young Ladies, a convenient place to stash family stubbornness and family embarrassment.

Would it be necessary? He increased his speed, eager to find out.

Eleanor sat at the head of the tea table, presiding over a clutter of soiled cups and saucers, and was pleased to feel her initial sense of shock subsiding.

Why not Lucy and Mason? Look at them there on the far bench, Lucy seated, Mason standing protectively at her side, one hand on her shoulder, the other tenderly holding her hand.

Their announcement had sent shock waves running through the entire family. They had gathered for a quiet afternoon tea. Then Mason had approached poor Richard with moving dignity to ask for his daughter's hand in marriage and Richard had initially thought Mason meant Charlotte, but the schoolmaster had quickly set everyone to rights on that score.

Then Mason had drawn Lucy forward, claiming that he had been in love with her since she was a little girl.

Eleanor smiled down on the biscuit jar and adjusted its lid. How romantic, that. And, of course, there was the vast difference in their ages, Lucy not yet twenty and Mason . . . why the good Lord only knew how old Mason was–midforties was Eleanor's conservative guess.

Then immediately after the announcement how peculiarly everyone had behaved; some had left the Great Hall, like Marjorie, who claimed she had to go to the nursery as it was time to feed the boys. Susan, usually a master at these delicate matters, had withdrawn to a chair near the fire and busied herself with her mending box. Poor Richard sat opposite her, gazing into the flames. He had complained of being cold earlier. Now he looked frozen into a position of stunned bewilderment. Yet Eleanor was fairly certain he had no real objection. Richard never did–to anything. She was certain he shared her bewilderment. When, in the name of God, had the romance developed? Both parties in question had lived under their noses forever, and there had been no indication of a close alliance or a developing romance, great or otherwise.

Still, if it was what they wanted, . . . Eleanor discovered now with a degree of pleasure that she had no real objection. Why not? They could go on residing right here at Eden Castle.

Suddenly she smiled and realized this was an occasion for rejoicing and celebration, that her plain daughter Lucy had perhaps made a good match of it after all.

"Come, everyone," Eleanor announced, "enough brooding. In my opinion, we owe Lucy and her fiancé our very best wishes. Come," she repeated, a tone of mock sternness in her voice as she rallied first Susan and then Richard.

"My darling," Eleanor murmured and bent low over him where he sat in the chair. "Do you suppose you might summon the wine steward? I really think that the occasion demands champagne."

"Of course, if you wish," Richard murmured and rose from his chair. "So there is to be a wedding," he smiled.

"Yes," Eleanor beamed. "Come, you two. First of all, let us kiss you both and bless your new happiness. Then I think we all would enjoy hearing how your love developed. I know I would."

Apparently the romantic suggestion fell on receptive ears, for soon the entire company had gathered around, Stephen and Frederick, Susan, even old Mrs. Calvin, the nanny who generally kept to the periphery of all family occasions.

Within minutes Richard returned with the wine steward and a trail of understewards, each carrying a silver cooler and a bottle of champagne, the last man carrying a tray filled with champagne glasses.

As Richard presided over the pouring, Eleanor saw Lucy beam as she tried to answer everyone's excited questions. Charlotte seemed almost beside herself with joy. Her questions predominated: When did Lucy and Mason know they were in love? Did they plan a honeymoon? Could she be Lucy's maid of honor?

Eleanor laughed and interrupted. "Charlotte, please," she protested lightly. "We all want to hear the answers to those questions, but first let's all lift a glass."

As the stewards passed the filled glasses around, Eleanor noticed a gathering of servants near the kitchen court door. Word had a way of traveling fast within Eden Castle.

With a wave of her hand, Eleanor invited them to come closer and share a toast. Then quickly she kissed Lucy and gave Mason a smile and saw that the entire company was waiting, glasses poised. Eleanor started to speak, but realized that it was Richard's place to do so and indicated as much with a bob of her head, seeing a crimson blush creep up his face.

For several moments, she was afraid he would say nothing at all. But at last he lifted his glass and looked directly at Lucy and Mason.

"To my daughter, Lucy on the occasion of her engagement to Mr. Mason Frye. We wish them–"

"Stop!"

The sudden command shot through the company like a command from God. For several moments, no one moved, all glasses raised, as yet untouched. And now that he clearly had captured their attention, John seemed more than content to hold his position on the step.

When he seemed disinclined to move or speak further, Susan slowly separated herself from the others and started across the Great Hall, sending her voice ahead in a sweet and musical invitation. "John, just in time," she said. "The family has received the happiest of news, Lucy and Mason are–"

"Are what?"

"Are engaged to be married."

"They are not."

"Yes, they just–"

"No, I forbid it. I will not have it."

On that somber note, he started down the steps. Out of the corner of her eye, Eleanor saw Mason Frye hand his glass of champagne to Lucy and start forward, making his way through the company until he stood alone, with only Susan between himself and the steadily approaching John Murrey Eden.

"John, I wanted to talk with you," Mason began.

But obviously John was not in a listening mood. He gazed at Mason Frye with an expression of contempt; then he looked beyond Mason to where Eleanor and Richard were standing, their champagne glasses still in hand.

"Did you know about this?" John demanded.

"No, John, of course not, until–"

"And you approve? You give your blessing?"

Eleanor saw Richard glance her way as though for an answer. John saw it too and put a stop to it. "Forget about the women," he commanded. "They have no sense in these matters."

"John!"

It was Susan, approaching from behind. Only two small, brick-red fever spots on her cheeks revealed the depth and intensity of her anger.

But still John was paying no attention to anyone but Richard, who slowly seemed to be wilting under the heat of that relentless gaze.

"So you only learned about it a few moments ago?" John asked.

"Yes, along with everyone. We . . . I . . . yes, I was shocked."

"Of course, such a union must not be permitted."

Now it was Lucy's turn to step forward, the happiness on her face quickly fading, replaced by anger and fear. "Uncle John, I must–"

"Get her out of here," John commanded of anyone who wanted to obey. Apparently no one did, for no one moved except Mason Frye.

"John–"

"I'm speaking with Richard."

"I need to know the cause of your objection."

"You are a bright man, Mason. Why are you so dense on this matter?"

Apparently Mason had no ready answer, and this silence was promptly filled by Susan, who tried to take John by the elbow and turn him away.

"John, please," she murmured, keeping her voice down. "Come with me. This is really none of your–"

"If you will excuse me," John replied, his voice like ice as he shook free of Susan's hand. "Aren't you due somewhere? Some pressing charitable business?"

There was in his tone now such a definite desire to inflict pain. Clearly Susan heard it as well and retreated as far as the fireplace, where she came to a halt, her back to the rest of the company. Torn, Eleanor did not know whom to aid, Susan or Lucy.

Now Stephen spoke up with a directness that startled. "Papa, I'm afraid you're out of step with the times," he smiled. "Cupid's bow has struck and there is absolutely nothing you can do about it."

"Like you?" John said sarcastically to Stephen. "Apparently there was nothing I could do to help you when Cupid's bow struck and left you with a weak and pampered girl-wife who now lacks the strength to nurse your son."

For several moments Eleanor could not move. She was stunned. As was everyone else in the company. Poor Stephen. She couldn't even bring herself to look at him. All she heard was Frederick's soft and moderating voice.

"Please, we tend to say and do things that we regret in moments of extreme–"

"My very point," John interrupted. "Someone must keep this family on the straight and narrow, must remind one and all of certain responsibilities to our predecessors who kept the line pure and uncorrupted. Now we have an actress. What next? A schoolmaster? No, no," he repeated, and again turned to Richard as though he knew instinctively, as do most bullies, where the weakest was located.

"Richard, I implore you," he said, changing his tone to one of caring and loving concern. "Tell me, what do you know of Mason Frye, his parentage, his background, his birthplace?"

"Happily will I answer all those questions," Mason said and stepped forward as though to demonstrate his claim.

But John wasn't interested in Mason Frye. His sole approach was to dissuade Richard, for that was the voice that carried the greatest weight of denial. If he could get Richard to withdraw his blessing and his permission, then he would have achieved his goal. But why, Eleanor grieved, would a union between Mason and Lucy upset John Murrey Eden so?

"Richard, you must listen to me," John pleaded and walked over to his half brother, took the champagne glass from his hand and set it on the table, and then led him away, almost to the Great Hall door, where despite the distance, their voices drifted back with crystal clarity, as though John wanted them all to hear.

"You must say no to this madness."

"Why, I don't understand–"

"He is twice Lucy's age, old enough to be her father."

"That shouldn't–"

"We know nothing about him."

"He's been in residence for over twenty years."

"That's not what I mean and you know it. His bloodline, for God's sake. Richard, try not to be so dense. His bloodline . . ."

Only Mason Frye seemed capable of movement. Slowly he came forward until he was standing directly in front of John, a look of understanding and forbearance on his face. "Ask anything you like, John, of me, of my parents. I have nothing to hide."

"And you have nothing to bring to this family except humiliation and disgrace. Can't you just hear the scandalmongers now? Lord Richard Eden's eldest daughter marries her tutor? Good Lord, have all of you lost your minds?"

Still Mason Frye persisted. "Then state what is on your mind, John?"

"You are on my mind."

"And what else?"

"Betrayal."

"How betrayal?"

"Whatever has transpired here happened behind my back, in corners, a secretive and tawdry affair. No, it must not be permitted. Don't you agree, Richard?"

"Perhaps we all need more time–"

"Papa!"

This anguished cry came from Lucy, who ran to Mason's side. He placed a protective arm about her shoulders and made a defiant claim that perhaps he should not have made.

"We will marry, John, with your permission or without it, I swear it."

"Yes," Lucy agreed, clinging to him as though to a life raft.

Triumphant, John beamed. "See, Richard, you see how much they respect the weight of your authority?"

Eleanor, sensing what was about to happen, stepped forward. "Please, everybody," she begged. "Say nothing more, not a word, please, let us all–"

"No, Eleanor," John insisted, "I think we have a right to glimpse this gentleman's true colors. We all know so well that blood tells, as I have tried to point out. Anyone who sanctions this union will be wholly responsible for bringing shame down on the Eden family, making it a laughingstock the length and breadth of England."

As he thundered on, sounding more and more like a madman, Eleanor turned to comfort Lucy, who was crying uncontrollably now, and poor Mason looked torn, trying to respond to all of John's outrageous accusations while being painfully aware of Lucy's grief.

As for the others, they all retreated to safe points of shelter, well out of the range of John's madness, as though all were intimately acquainted with the unstable nature of the man's personality and knew that the best course of action was simply to wait out the storm.

Eleanor considered doing that herself, but she changed her mind. Someone had to stand up to John Murrey Eden. He had played the bully long enough. Eleanor had tried very hard over the years to create a civilized household at Eden, and in civilized households men did not rage thus or make such preposterous accusations and charges.

"John, enough," she ordered, though how weak and ineffective her voice sounded in the thundering echo of John's voice.

At first he merely looked at her as though she were an annoying insect that had buzzed too close and now must be swatted down.

But just as she was on the verge of speaking again, John did a wholly unpredictable thing. He retreated. He held up both hands in a gesture of surrender, as though he could deal with anyone except Eleanor.

"I . . . ask your forgiveness," he said in a completely subdued tone of voice that summoned the attention of everyone back to the arena before the fire.

"I do apologize," he repeated to Eleanor. "Clearly I have overstepped my bounds. In my devotion and love for this family and what is right for it, I have made a spectacle of myself and hurt you, my dearest Eleanor. Forgive me."

Eleanor blinked, astounded, moved by his new gentleness and sweet tone of voice. She saw him start off toward the Great Hall door.

About twenty steps away he stopped and looked pitifully back from his position of outcast. So moved was she that Eleanor hurried to his side. She mustn't be too harsh in her judgment of John. He had done much for Eden Castle and for the Eden family name. She at least owed him the right of a platform.

"Speak, John, please," Eleanor invited and led him back toward the fireplace, close enough so that even Lucy could hear.

"All I wanted to suggest, however awkwardly, was caution on the part of everyone. Lucy is young."

"I'm nineteen–"

"And Mason Frye has waited this long."

"You've no right, John."

"Then let them separate for a period of time."

"No!" It was Lucy again, weeping out her protest.

"One year," John said with the gentlest of smiles. "If at the end of one year . . ."

He shrugged. Eleanor listened closely, despite Lucy's tears. It wasn't a bad idea. A year of separation to see if the flames would still be burning twelve months from now.

She looked to Richard for help in making this difficult and unpopular decision. But from the angle at which he sat slumped in his chair, she knew he had no intention of getting involved. So then it was up to her.

For several moments the only sound in the Great Hall was the cozy crackling of the fire. It had been an early and chilly fall, a portent of a hard winter to come. Eleanor looked at Lucy, seated a distance away, her face buried in her hands. Mason stood behind her, eyes down, looking angry and sad. He appeared so old in the half-light of the fire. Surely Lucy would be happier with someone closer to her own age.

Then Eleanor was speaking, sharing her agreement with John. But no one seemed interested. Lucy ran off across the Great Hall, trailing her sobs behind her. Mason stayed a moment longer, his attention focused only on John. He looked as if he might speak, but said nothing and finally departed in hasty pursuit of Lucy.

Even Stephen and Frederick exited quickly, Frederick moving toward the east wing in his daily attempts to draw Geoffrey out of what was rapidly appearing to be a permanent seclusion. And Stephen headed in the opposite direction, most likely in search of Eve.

Within moments, only Eleanor, Susan, John and Richard remained in the Great Hall. Good, Eleanor thought. Here was the core of Eden Castle. Perhaps these three would speak frankly on what had just taken place, ruining everyone's tea.

But no. Richard pushed painfully up out of his chair. With the coming of the damp rain, his gout had become active again. And no sooner had he hobbled out, heading toward the library, than Susan murmured about her clinic and moved toward the steps that led down into the kitchen court, where she would shortcut through the farmyard to the cottage on Eden Rising.

Eleanor looked up. Only John remained, a humble-appearing John who bowed his head and started slowly toward her through the clutter of chairs. "Thank you, Eleanor," he said, his voice sounding very tired. "I knew I could count on your rare good sense."

"I do believe they are very much in love, John," Eleanor said, in mild defense of her heartbroken daughter.

"Of course they are," John concurred readily. "But the state of their hearts is not what is at issue here. Rather, it is the state of their heads that concerns me." He stepped closer and took her hand in a warm and loving gesture. "All that we have asked is that they separate for a year and give their powers of reasoning time to catch up with the numbing effects brought on by Cupid's arrow. If at the end of that time they feel the same, well . . ."

Eleanor saw him shrug, something in his expression that suggested acceptance of whatever the future might bring.

"Yes, you are right, John," she agreed, and for that agreement received a dazzling smile and a light kiss on her cheek.

Then John backed off and bowed, something courtly now in his attitude. "I feel the need of sea air," he announced. "I'm going down the cliff walk."

"Dinner at nine," she called after him.

"It might be unpleasant tonight," he waved back at her. "But I'll be at table. You can count on it."

Then he was gone, the Great Hall door slamming behind him with a thunderous echo.

Wearily she turned back and saw two parlormaids appear to collect the tea things. Eleanor watched them for a few moments and could only guess at the rumors that were spreading down in the kitchen court.

Well, she'd have to set them straight before too long, but for now she was exhausted and in sore need of an hour's nap so that she might arise refreshed to face whatever crisis this evening might provide.

Of course there would be something. There was always something. But with John's continuing help and support and good judgment, perhaps they all stood a chance of surviving.

As rapidly as possible, Susan made her way through the kitchen court, knowing full well that as soon as she exited the castle, all tongues would start to wag again.

More angry than she cared to admit, she passed through the narrow passage that led to the farmyard beyond. On a long row of hooks hung a variety of outdoor garments. She lifted a heavy gray mackintosh and swung it over her shoulders in protection against the cold early-evening drizzle that had just started.

With only the steady rain to keep her company, she felt the impulse to review John's recent insanity. He had made a fool of himself, that much was certain, and he had caused both Mason and Lucy great and unnecessary pain, for which he would have to apologize later. It was as if the old, selfish, arrogant and aggressive John had newly surfaced. She had wrongly thought that John had reformed. But the man whom she had just witnessed shouting and parading about the Great Hall was the same man who years ago had in one way or another driven off everyone he had loved and who had loved him. Now here was the monster again, doing the same things again, and Susan wasn't certain she had either the energy or the ability to help him to see the error of his ways.

The rain was increasing, so she hurried her step, soon spying the roof of her cottage on Eden Rising. Of course, she understood John's anger to a certain extent. Clearly he had felt betrayed by Mason. Frye was John's property, hired by John, paid by John, enjoyed by John. How dare his loyalty and attention be usurped by Lucy.

Still, how childish, how unnecessarily childish. How much damage had John done today in the Great Hall? And could the two lovers abide by the decision he had forced on weak Eleanor?

Hurry! Rain was increasing. Despite her mackintosh and hood, she was getting soaked through. Perhaps she should have stayed inside the castle.

She knew that would have been impossible. She would surely have said something sharp and hurtful to John. He needed time, and then he needed someone with a quiet voice of reason to help him to see and assess what he had done.

She had no doubt that John was in pain, but for now she doubted seriously her ability to bring him relief. And even if she could, the relief would be short-lived, for there was another betrayal waiting for John in the wings.

The post messenger arrived weekly at the gates of Eden Castle, promptly every Friday afternoon at four o'clock. Susan had seen him as she was coming back from her visitations down in Mortemouth. Almost every Friday since the Midsummer fete, Susan had seen Charlotte stroll out of the Great Hall at about three forty-five and meet the post messenger several yards beyond the gatehouse, where letters were exchanged, one handed down to Charlotte while Charlotte in turn handed one up to the post messenger.

Of course, Susan had no way of knowing, but she would willingly gamble all her earthly goods on the possibility that Charlotte's London letters came from a Belgravia address, written on expensive parchment and in the flowery scrawl of Aslam Eden.

Lucy and Mason's announcement had been quite a surprise, had caught everyone off guard. But if John's reaction to Lucy and Mason had been this ugly, this unpredictable, then what in the name of God would he say and do when he learned of the affection between Aslam Eden and Charlotte?

She would have to speak with him, have to remind him of the lessons which he had learned in a very hard way, that he could not take control of all lives, that his wishes were important only to a very few and that everyone around him had the right to make their own mistakes.

It seemed so simple. Why could John not grasp it, this simplest of all lessons?

She heard the crackle of lightning, followed by thunder, and ran the rest of the way to the cottage, although she knew full well that while she might escape the ravages of this storm, there was a greater one coming.

Eden Castle
October 15, 1896

Mason Frye sat on the edge of his bed. John Murrey Eden had given him a fortnight in which to pack his belongings and leave Eden Castle. Beyond those orders no further words had been exchanged between them.

Now, as Mason stacked the last of his books into an already overloaded trunk, he looked up, overcome by a burgeoning sense of unreality.

How could this have happened?

That question had been central to every breath that he had drawn for the past two weeks. Susan had very kindly spoken to him of John's sense of betrayal, John's need to control, John's desire to arrange everyone's life to his own liking.

To hell with John!

On that revolutionary and extremely satisfying thought, he carefully stored the last of his books, closed the trunk lid and drew the heavy straps into place.

Hurriedly he looked at his watch. One forty-five. They were to meet at Susan's cottage on Eden Rising at half past two. Again Mason ceased his hurried packing and stared straight ahead at a circle of sun on the carpet where a million dust particles swirled in cosmic confusion.

Were they doing the right thing? Lucy had made it clear to him that she had no desire to remain at Eden Castle. When he had suggested that they be obedient to Eleanor and John's wish that they wait one full year, she had threatened to go to London and live with Alice.

No, Mason would not let her go like that. Besides, he quite simply could not conceive of life without her. So plans had been made, hasty plans. Mason had journeyed to Exeter last week, had confirmed the offer that had been made repeatedly to him over the years, the position of headmaster at Greenfield, a small but prestigious public school for boys on the outskirts of Exeter. In the past he had always rejected their annual offer out of loyalty and respect to John Murrey Eden.

To hell with John Murrey Eden.

Lucy would be waiting for him shortly with her few belongings. They would journey to Exeter, be married early tomorrow morning in the chapel at Greenfield and retire immediately to the small cottage provided for the headmaster and his wife by the school.

Somewhat astonished, he looked up at how suddenly perfect the future sounded, as though it had been waiting there for him all along in just this combination.

His life here was finished, a life he now realized had been one long preparation for his real life, for the one that he would spend with Lucy.

He smiled at nothing except at how right the name sounded on his lips and in his heart.

Hurry—the carriage would be waiting, the driver not aware of the need to detour down the path that led to Eden Rising off the moors.

There would be no need to stop and say goodbye to anyone. He had said his goodbyes to everyone, including poor Geoffrey, who had kept his door firmly locked. He was fond of Geoffrey, admired his intellect, but could not yet understand why the man was behaving thus. Surely his self-imposed exile would end one day. The man had a great deal to give to the world.

Farewell to this silent room, farewell, and on with the future.

With that rousing battle cry, and laden with baggage, Mason made his way through the chamber door and started off down the long corridor at a good pace and never once looked back.

Lucy sat on the front step of Susan's free clinic and stared down the dirt road which led off the central turnpike, heading across the moors to Exeter and points east.

Blessedly Susan was busy with a little boy suffering a cut finger from playing with his father's fishing knife. The child's little sister sat obediently on the bottom step of the clinic, and now and then she would look upward at Lucy, then shyly turn away. Lucy guessed her age to be about five. The girl was small in stature, with long, straight fair hair and frightened blue eyes. The front of her dress was spotted with blood where her brother's wound had stained it.

Like John. Lucy felt as though John's words had stained her.

The thought captured her attention and held it fast. How often she had heard tales of John's past, abandoned first by his mother, then by his father, raised by a common prostitute named Elizabeth, whom his father had met in the pit at Newgate Prison. "A childhood without love," Lucy had heard her mother sigh, and perhaps it was true. If it was, Lucy was very sorry for John, but whatever the nature of his past, it did not give him the right to inflict equal misery on anyone unfortunate enough to cross his path.

"Are you hurt?"

At the near and sweet voice, Lucy looked down on the little girl who apparently had just mustered the courage to speak.

"No," Lucy smiled, relieved in a way that the child's question had dragged her back into the present.

Behind her, coming from the clinic, was the sound of the little boy crying. She heard both Susan and the boy's mother try to ease his pain as well as his fear.

Lucy had no idea what she and Mason would have done without Susan these last difficult days. As though she had intuitively known of their plans to run away, she had offered them her clinic on Eden Rising as a safe meeting place, well away from family eyes.

Lucy had successfully slipped out of the Great Hall over an hour ago, taking with her only one small satchel, as Mason had suggested. Of course, she would send for her things later. It was not fitting for the wife of a headmaster to indulge in a new wardrobe.

Wife of a headmaster—

The description pleased her immensely, as though at last she had found her true role in this mystifying and bewildering world.

The boy's sobs had ceased, though the look of alarm on the little girl's face persisted.

"It's all right," Lucy soothed. "I promise you he will be fine."

The little girl drew her knees close on the bottom steps and rocked back and forth in a self-comforting fashion.

Lucy watched her a moment longer and hoped that there would be a child within the first year. What a marvelous father Mason would be. How fortunate and blessed the child who would sit at his knees.

"Someone's coming!"

At the sound of the child's voice, Lucy looked up and saw a carriage just turning into the road off the turnpike.

Mason—

Suddenly she stood up and adjusted her bonnet and smoothed her skirts and tried to quiet her heart, which was racing far too fast.

At the same time, she heard a step behind her and looked back to see Susan in her nurse's apron, now blood-splattered, still clutching a red gauze in her fingers.

"Then you're off," she smiled.

"I will miss you."

"And I you."

"When I have my baby, will you come?"

"Try and keep me away."

"Will you be able to handle every–"

"Don't worry."

"Uncle John . . ."

". . . will be furious. But he will calm down."

"Are you going to tell them?"

"Nothing until you are safely married."

Lucy nodded. "Then try to explain to Mama and Papa."

"They will understand, I promise."

For several moments they studied each other, volumes of love being spoken in the silence. "Take care now, and don't keep Mason waiting. You are the perfect wife for him."

Grateful, Lucy embraced Susan, then turned and ran down the steps to Mason, who had already loaded her satchel aboard and was now waiting beside the open carriage door.

She took his hand and saw him lean forward for a kiss and was aware of their audience, Susan and the little girl. Lucy kissed him anyway, figuring Susan would understand and the little girl would remember this moment when *she* received her first kiss, hopefully from a man she loved as much as Lucy loved Mason.

Then Mason assisted her into the carriage, and both waved a final goodbye as the horses drew sharply to the right and headed back down the road toward the turnpike and Exeter.

Eden Castle
October 16, 1896

Impatiently Charlotte bided her time, waiting for the furor over Lucy and Mason's elopement to subside.

It had been the upper-house parlormaid who had found Mr. Frye's chambers empty and later had found Lucy's chambers equally empty and had immediately reported the situation to Eleanor, who had taken it surprisingly well, with only a kind of resigned grace, as had Richard, who shrugged and blinked and reached for another luncheon kipper.

Uncle John was the only one who had taken it badly. He had pushed away from the luncheon table with such force that when he stood, his chair had fallen backward and he had demanded that guards be sent after them immediately, had shouted and carried on until Aunt Susan had led him from the dining hall into the Great Hall where she had tried to quiet him.

"He won't do that, will he, Mama?" Charlotte asked, rather enjoying both her strawberry tart and Uncle John's anger.

"Do what, my dear?" her mother asked.

"Send the guards for Lucy and Mason."

Her mother looked up, shocked. "No, of course he won't."

A strong expression of doubt crossed her face. She turned toward Charlotte's father. "He won't, will he, dear? It would be too embarrassing, for poor Lucy, for all of us."

Charlotte's father, enjoying his kipper, shook his head. "No," he said between bites. "I for one am pleased. I don't think we could have married her off to anyone else."

"Richard!"

This shocked voice belonged to Charlotte's mother, who scowled him back into silence and continued to stir her tea well beyond the point of necessity.

Charlotte finished her tart, still biding her time, her last precious letter from Aslam tucked securely into the pocket of her dress. Lightly she shook her head and caressed Aslam's letter. She wondered when she should confide in her parents and ask their permission on this most important matter. Of one thing she was certain, she wanted Uncle John to have nothing to do with it, preferred that he not even hear of it. Not that there was anything so terrible in it. Certainly nothing like Lucy and Mason. All that Aslam had done had been to kindly invite her to spend a few days with him in his London house, wholly chaperoned of course. He had invited Alice and her chum Christabel as well.

According to his letter, the "three ladies" would be assigned an entire floor to themselves in Aslam's London mansion, and in addition to that, he had planned to hire a church matron to be with them on all outings, all occasions. "It is just"–and this was the part that caused goose flesh to rise on Charlotte's arm each time she read it–"it is just because life has lost its savor without your beauty, your nearness, your sweet manner, and your loving heart."

Of course, she had memorized the words, could speak them backward if she chose–"your nearness, your sweet manner, your loving heart."

No one in her entire life had spoken to her like that, and each time she thought on him, on their friendship which had commenced that first night of the Midsummer fete, she felt as though she were a major participant in a divine miracle, for she had never known anyone quite like Aslam Eden.

"Charlotte? Are you ill?" It was her mother, apparently observing the weakness that washed over her each and every time she thought of Aslam Eden.

"No, Mama, but I long to speak with both you and Papa in private."

"Then speak," her father invited, pushing his luncheon platter aside.

Nervously Charlotte glanced over her shoulder in the direction of the Great Hall. "Where is Uncle John?"

Eleanor appeared to listen. At the moment, the air was blessedly silent. "Susan has quieted him, I imagine. He's a good man, just highly strung. And he *was* fond of Mason Frye. He will miss him."

For several moments, Charlotte continued to listen to the suspect silence coming from the Great Hall. A few moments earlier, Mrs. Godwin had left the table. Stephen had taken luncheon in Eve's chambers, and

Frederick and Marjorie were down in Mortemouth, visiting with the old rector there.

So the luncheon company had been small to start with, and now the only two who remained were her mother and father, the only two who really mattered.

"Well, for heaven's sake, do go on, Charlotte," her mother urged. "If it is something of importance, speak quickly."

"I don't know whether either of you are aware or not," she began, feeling suddenly nervous. "But for the past several weeks, since the Midsummer party I have enjoyed a weekly correspondence with–"

"Oh, who, my dear?" her mother exclaimed, clearly pleased.

"With Aslam Eden," Charlotte replied and hoped that her mother's expression of pleasure would hold fast and perhaps even increase.

Unfortunately it didn't. A puzzled look took the place of the pleased one, and her father suddenly leaned forward, his hand cupped about his ear, as though he hadn't heard correctly.

"Who?" he demanded, looking first at Charlotte, then at her mother and then back at Charlotte.

"Aslam Eden," Charlotte repeated.

For a moment nothing was heard but the echo of that one name, and while Charlotte tried to speak, something about the shocked expressions on her parents' faces advised against it, at least for the moment.

At last her mother rallied. "A proper correspondence, I would hope," she said.

"Indeed, Mama, quite proper. He writes to me of India. I write to him of life in North Devon. If you care to read them, Papa–Aslam's letters, I mean–you're more than welcome. I'm sure you would find them most interesting. He writes with compelling conviction of what India was and what he feels it must become in the future."

Prudence intervened and advised her to lower her voice as well as her enthusiasm. She must make this appear perfectly harmless and quite ordinary.

"I received a letter from him in the last post," she said matter-of-factly and, reaching into her pocket, withdrew the precious parchment.

Her mother sat up, still curious. "I didn't see such a letter. I've never seen a London letter in the weekly post addressed to you. Charlotte, how–"

Quickly she explained, hoping to douse the fuse before it was ignited. "I sometimes meet the post messenger when I'm out riding or just coming through the gatehouse after a walk. On occasion Aslam will send a letter by special courier."

Charlotte saw her mother's eyebrows lift and stay elevated. "The gentleman sends a letter to a seventeen-year-old girl on the future of India by special courier all the way from London?"

Charlotte heard the absurdity for herself and quickly offered an excuse. "Perhaps he doesn't trust the Royal Post."

"Nonsense," her father scoffed. "The man simply has more money than he knows what to do with."

Quickly Charlotte moved to get the subject back on track. "I have a recent letter," she said.

"Well, go on, Charlotte," her mother urged. "What does Mr. Eden have on his mind that warrants a special courier?"

Charlotte drew a deep breath and plunged in. "He has invited Alice and Christabel Pankhurst and myself to spend a few days in London at his home. He has hired a church matron to be in attendance at all our meetings. He has invited me to take a tour of London with him, as well as to see a performance of *Tristan und Isolde* at Covent Garden. He has quite carefully thought everything out. He would send his carriage for me one week from today. If, of course, you . . ."

She ran out of words and felt she had said it all anyway. Aslam's invitation was propriety itself. Surely they could see that, merely the generosity of a friend of the family to entertain a young country cousin. What harm in that? Now why didn't either of them speak?

Then her mother did, though it was little more than a whispered prayer. "Sweet Lord, I . . . had no idea . . ."

Her father reached out his hand. "The letter, please."

She had counted on her father's passivity and indifference.

"No, Papa, I've changed my mind. It's a private letter."

"Does your Uncle John know?"

As her father asked this most painful question, Charlotte heard a step at the dining room door. Too frightened to look, she breathed a quick silent prayer, "Dear God, don't let it be—"

"Does her Uncle John know what?"

At the sound of the familiar voice, the same one recently raised in shouted outrage at Lucy's happiness, Charlotte closed her eyes.

"Does her Uncle John know what?" came the question again. Behind him Charlotte heard Susan, gently herding him forward, apologizing, "It was a shock, you see," she said lamely to anyone at table who cared to listen.

"Disobedience and betrayal." John spoke the words in two sharp, staccato bursts like gunfire, then sat wearily. "Oh, God, I'm sorry," he sighed. "Well, I have now apologized, and that is that," John concluded and sat sharply up out of his position of remorse. "Of course, I am warning one and all that the union between Mason Frye and Lucy will be a disaster, a complete disaster. In the meantime, I must send word to my agent in London. Eden is now in search of a new tutor."

Charlotte's mother laughed. "For whom, John? Albert is away at school and Charlotte can conclude her own lessons."

"I was thinking of Christopher and Alexander."

Everyone at table laughed. Richard said, "They are busy with their nappies, John. They have a few years left before we plunge them into the mysteries and convolutions of Latin grammar."

"Time passes," John warned. "And I see no reason why we can't start their education sooner. They are both bright, eager to learn."

"John, they are not yet six months old," Eleanor protested, still laughing.

"Stephen said something about taking Alexander to America," Susan said, as though she were still punishing John for something.

"Nonsense," John exploded. "Never, never, you hear? I won't have Alexander coming under the dubious influence of that American cotton farmer."

"You mean Mary's husband, Burke?" Susan asked.

"You know damn well who I mean. No, the boy will stay here at Eden Castle where he belongs. He is a son of the Empire and deserves the best and I can give it to him and I personally shall see that he gets the best, both of them, I swear it on my life."

Wilma, the serving maid, appeared at the far end of the hall with a large tray in hand, two under-parlormaids behind her, ready to clear the table. At the sound all looked up. Charlotte's mother called out politely, "We need a few more minutes, please."

Wilma curtsied and offered her apology and quickly shooed her helpers back out of the door and closed it behind her.

Susan said, "I must excuse myself. There were several people waiting at the clinic before I came to lunch."

John interrupted by addressing Charlotte. "Now, my pretty, I believe I heard your father ask you a question: 'Does Uncle John know?' Well, does Uncle John know what?"

"It's nothing, Uncle John," Charlotte said quickly and pushed back her chair and tried to stand.

"Charlotte, please tell him what you have just told us," her mother said. "He knows the man. If he gives his blessing, then–"

"Does your Uncle John know what?" John repeated, and at the same time, he reached out with the speed of lightning and grabbed Aslam's letter from her hand and, in the manner of a mischievous schoolboy, fled to the far end of the dining table before she had even recovered enough from her shock to give chase.

"Uncle John, please," Charlotte gasped.

Quickly Susan came to her defense. "John, you have no right. Please give her back her letter. Let her speak directly if she wishes. If not–"

Susan's voice fell. She kept her eyes fixed on John as he carefully studied the envelope.

"There is no Royal Post mark on this letter," John puzzled.

Eleanor spoke. "No, Charlotte claims it arrived by special courier."

"From whom?"

When no one answered, Charlotte saw John lift the flap and start to remove the letter within.

"John, please," Susan begged, clearly sensing Charlotte's distress.

"No, go ahead," Charlotte's father insisted. "She offered it to me, then withdrew the offer. It's from the Indian chap, that acquaintance of yours, John. You remember. Perhaps you can shed some light on this new entanglement, though I for one have had enough of entanglements, new or otherwise."

As her father prattled on, Charlotte kept her eyes on Uncle John's face, which seemed quietly terrifying in the depth and degree of change that was taking place there.

While he read, there was not a sound in the Great Hall. Charlotte carefully studied her intertwined fingers and, despite the bleak nature of the moment, began to plot with hope and excitement.

Lucy had passed through this same crucible recently, had experienced this dreadful sense of doors closing, of a life finished before it began. As Lucy had found a way out, Charlotte would find a way as well. There was a limit to the degree of control that one person could exert over another.

"How long has this been going on?" The voice cut through the silence like a falling icicle.

"Answer me!" he demanded and strode the length of the table with such speed and force that Charlotte was certain he intended to run her to ground.

"If you are referring to my correspondence with Aslam Eden, I first wrote to him on the night I met him. That would be July 14, 1896, at precisely 10:44 p.m. I have since thereafter written him a letter every day, and he has written daily to me, or rather nightly. He claims his head is clearer at night."

John looked at her, then looked back down at the letter. "Do you have any idea what this implies?" he asked, and from where she stood, Charlotte could see a large vein throbbing in his right temple.

"It implies friendship."

Then John changed tactics. Instead of addressing her directly, he held up her letter as though for the inspection and censure of all. "Have any of you read this–drivel?"

He did not wait for a response. "No, of course not, I didn't think so. Well, allow me to read it aloud to you."

Suddenly Charlotte started forward. "No, you have no right. The letter belongs to me."

As she protested, she pulled at the arm that held the letter suspended in the air, and apparently the arm lost patience with her and, lifted as though of its own volition, fell with the speed of lightning and delivered a sharp slap to the side of her face.

As she fell backward, she heard screams all about her, Susan first, then her mother, and some place in the vague distance she even heard her father's muddled protests.

"I say, John, enough, you have no right–"

"I have every right," John persisted. "Now, you are to listen to me, Charlotte, as closely as you have ever listened to anyone in your entire life. Is that clear?"

Her neck and head still throbbed from his blow, as she fought back tears.

"This," he began and thrust the letter down until it was only inches from her face, "is the last you will ever hear from Aslam Eden in your life."

"No . . ."

"Yes!" The thunderous voice topped hers.

"You fool," John said now, his voice lower and somehow more cruel. "Do you fancy yourself the paramour of Aslam Eden? Do you? Answer me!"

"He is a gentleman," Charlotte murmured.

"He is twice your age," John shouted down on her. "Do you hear?"

Somewhere behind her someone was weeping.

"You will never write to this man again, is that clear, Charlotte?"

"Why?" she demanded at last. "He was your friend once."

"And he betrayed me. As he betrays everyone foolish enough to put their trust in him. He is immoral and unethical and is now trying to get to me through you."

"He never mentioned you."

"No, but I know what he is doing. His motive is revenge. Pure and simple revenge against me. Is that clear? Do you understand? Now I will write to him myself and–"

"No!"

"And tell him he has been found out and that there is no further need to send special couriers from London to North Devon as they will not be received at the gatehouse."

"No, please, you have no right. Mama, make him stop it," she pleaded. "Someone . . . please help me–"

"Go to your room, Charlotte," John commanded, and she saw him tear her letter in half and stuff it into his pocket.

Then she was aware of Susan on one side, her mother on the other. Behind, she heard John still ranting, trying to explain to her father, making those dreadful accusations over and over again about Aslam.

"Are you alright?" Susan whispered, and Charlotte heard the remorse in her sweet voice and wondered how she had stood being married to the monster all these years.

Charlotte continued to lean on both women and assured both of them that she was alright. In a curious way she was, for as they began to climb the steps to the second floor, she was working out specific details of her future, hers and Aslam's, for unwittingly John had mysteriously caused her love for this unique man to deepen, and though she was unable at this point to say how, she was certain that in some capacity she would spend the rest of her life in the company of Aslam Eden.

Now as she approached her bedchamber, she hoped the women did not fuss over her for too long. She had a letter to write, two letters really, a long one to Aslam, a shorter one of explanation to Alice, giving her complete instructions on the location of Aslam's house and telling her to put the letter directly into his hands. Charlotte would have to tell him that couriers no longer would be permitted to approach Eden. They would have to make other plans. He would have ideas, of that she was certain.

London
November 1, 1896

Aslam read the letter very carefully. The two young ladies who had brought it were closely studying his Grand Reception Hall. He had taken their heavy cloaks, then had turned immediately to the letter.

Though Charlotte's letter had contained unhappy news, it was not wholly unexpected. Aslam could have predicted John's reaction, though he would never forgive him for striking Charlotte.

"When did you say that you received this?" he asked Miss Eden.

"Only yesterday afternoon. It came in the post to my flat. As you can see, Charlotte asked me to deliver it immediately, but I was attending lectures until this morning and–"

"Of course, and I'm grateful," Aslam smiled and strode to one of the high windows overlooking his withered garden. Aslam's eyes seemed mesmerized by the sight.

The bastard.

"Mr. Eden, do you want to send a reply? If you do, let me take it and put it in one of my envelopes with my name on the cover. Uncle John will think nothing of my writing to the family."

The other young woman shook her head sadly. "What subterfuge. Truth is dealt another blow."

She seemed genuinely saddened by this slight tear in the moral fabric around her. "And your name?" Aslam asked politely, having missed it when introductions were made the first time.

"Miss Pankhurst. Christabel Pankhurst."

"Oh yes," he smiled. "I remember meeting you at the Eden Midsummer fete."

"Yes, I was there. What a circus," Miss Pankhurst smiled.

Aslam laughed, liking her honesty immediately. Now to Alice he said, "I would very much like to send a reply. Will you wait?"

"Of course."

"And while you're waiting, would you take tea with me? Ramophur will fetch it. I have a splendid Indian cook who is an artist at honey and almond cakes and date tarts."

He saw the girls exchange a longing glance and suspected that their nurses' fees did not always include such luxuries as high tea.

"Of course you shall stay," Aslam smiled, deciding for them and waved at Ramophur, who waited by the door.

"Mr. Eden, may I ask you a question?"

It was Alice, who still looked torn between the question and the surroundings.

"Of course, ask what you like."

"My cousin Charlotte spoke of unpleasantness, of Uncle John striking her when he learned of your correspondence with her."

"I am sorry for that," Aslam murmured and discovered the news was even more painful when he had heard the words spoken aloud.

"What, if I may ask was the nature of this provocation? Forgive my denseness, but . . ."

Aslam shrugged and turned back to the winter view beyond the window. "The fact of our correspondence, I assume. What else?"

Alice shook her head. "I don't know. That's why I asked you."

Slowly Aslam returned to the center of the Grand Reception Hall and tried to sort through his tumbling emotions. What made it so difficult was that he had disciplined himself over the years to feel as little as possible. As was always the case with disciplinarians, there was a curious sense of self-betrayal when the discipline failed.

"I first met your cousin Charlotte last summer at the Eden 'circus,' as Miss Pankhurst appropriately describes it. I went against my better judgment and for the first few hours of the visit saw no reason to stay and was on the verge of summoning my porters and returning to London that very night. Then I met Charlotte."

Miss Pankhurst smiled as though she completely understood. Alice Eden's face unfortunately remained a blank.

Aslam went on. "I have never met anyone quite like her in my life. Young, beautiful beyond any man's ability to describe, so quick and so curious about my world, India. She asked questions of me that night that forced me to open doors of memory that had been closed for years."

He paused, recalling those extremely pleasant hours and days he had spent with Charlotte. "Needless to say, I remained at Eden until the very last day. Charlotte showed me her world, all aspects of it. And when I left, it seemed as if I had left all light and warmth back at Eden Castle. For several days I was so incapacitated that I could scarcely address my business affairs. I felt lost inside my house, inside my own skin."

At that moment he heard a polite knock at the door, and a moment later Ramophur entered. Following behind him were two young houseboys, both carrying heavy silver trays.

Aslam saw the young ladies gazing in stunned disbelief at the ladened tea table, every inch covered with platters of silver and gold, some filled with delicate sandwiches, others piled high with almond and honey cakes, date tarts, glazed biscuits, fruit scones, pots of strawberry jam and, at the center a glistening silver tea service, good, strong Indian tea already steeping.

"Miss Pankhurst, would you do the honors?" Aslam asked with a slight bow. He saw the two young ladies exchange a glance, then saw Miss Pankhurst assume the ritualistic position behind the tea service.

As Miss Pankhurst poured with natural expertise, he urged Miss Eden to help herself.

"Please," he insisted, "as much as you like, and what remains I shall have Ramophur pack away into a hamper for you."

As tea commenced, Aslam strode back to the window overlooking the garden, wishing with all his heart that when he looked back, those two charming females would be gone, replaced by the beautiful Charlotte, with her deep blue eyes, her ready smile and her generous and compassionate heart.

"Mr. Eden, how do you take your tea?" Miss Pankhurst called out.

"Lemon only," he replied and tried to recapture Charlotte's image. But it was gone. As he returned to the tea table, he saw both young ladies thoroughly enjoying themselves, eating heartily.

For several minutes the bounty of the table occupied their attention. Pleased, tea in hand, Aslam asked a favor of them in return. "Would you excuse me while I pen a brief message to Charlotte? I'll try not to keep you waiting long."

"Of course."

"Please do post it for me in your stationery. I hate the deception, but . . ."

Then Miss Eden came up with a splendid plan. "Perhaps we can invite

Charlotte to London to stay with us for a few days." She broke off. "I doubt if we could allow her to be a houseguest under your roof, but I see no reason why we couldn't have an accidental meeting or two."

"Yes, of course, that would be ideal. In fact, I'll mention it to Charlotte in my letter. Before Christmas, please invite her before Christmas. I must see her again."

Quickly he excused himself, inviting them to partake again of the tea delicacies, to explore his house to their hearts' content, to do anything at all that brought them pleasure.

Then he was gone, closing the door behind him. As he walked down the corridor that led to his first-floor study, he thought on Charlotte and what she must have suffered because of him at John's hand.

Inside his study he quickly found his way to his desk, withdrew a sheet of his parchment stationery, took pen in hand and stared down at the blankness of the page.

What were these feelings that continued to plague him whenever he thought on Charlotte Eden? Why did the thought of her suffering in any way cause him to feel the sharpest pain he had ever experienced? Why did he miss her to a degree that made him no longer capable of working with competence or diligence?

What did it mean? And would the world agree with John Murrey Eden that a liaison between a seventeen-year-old girl and a middle-aged Indian would be unorthodox at best and wholly unacceptable at worst?

Aslam buried his face in his hands, beset by a torrent of anxieties and unanswerable questions. His despair was compounded by the realization that deep in his heart, no matter what happened, no matter anyone's opinions or convictions, no matter public censure and private gossip, his need to see Charlotte Eden again was as strong as any instinct he had ever experienced.

He *would* see her again, and on that note of certainty, he lifted his pen to parchment and commenced writing, "My dearest darling Charlotte . . ."

Eden Castle
March 27, 1897

Despite the pain, Eve sat on the bottom step of the Great Hall staircase and watched a small army of servants decorate the Great Hall for the late afternoon birthday festivities.

This party had been John's idea, always John's ideas. Since Alex had been born on March 13 and Chris on April 13, a midpoint had been selected as the day of celebration.

Close by was Sonia Reicher, watching over two-year-old Rolf. Eve had grown quite fond of the little German woman.

"No, no, Rolf," Sonia called out as the beautiful blond little boy toddled too close to where a steward was perched atop a stepladder hanging blue streamers from a low beam.

Her son in hand, she walked back to where Eve sat on the steps. "Do you really think the boys will notice all of this fuss?"

Eve smiled. "What do you think?"

"I think it is absurd. They're babies. Even Rolf–"

At the sound of his name he was off again, and Eve watched, smiling as Sonia hurried after him. He headed this time toward two parlormaids who were arranging cornucopias of sweets and paper hats around the table, which had been enlarged by the addition of two extra reception tables.

Eve closed her eyes to all the feverish activity and realized she should be helping, should be doing something, but her energy was so limited. A climb up one flight of stairs left her winded and gasping for breath.

She had said little to the others of this unending feeling of illness, nor had she mentioned to anyone the severe pains in her abdomen, pains such as she had never felt before. They were not persistent, thank God, or she would never have been able to disguise them.

They worried her, the fact that they were not getting any better. Still, she had her eyes fixed on one date of the calendar. June 20, a mere three months away, the date of her parents' arrival in London. She would go up a day early with Stephen and Alex, and be there waiting for them at the hotel; she would present them with their first grandchild and bask in their love and strength.

"Eve, you look to be a million miles away."

It was Sonia, red-cheeked and puffing with young Rolf in tow, tucked beneath her arm like an adorable sack of potatoes.

"I was," Eve confessed. "I was on my way home."

The words seemed to have a compelling effect on Sonia, who sat slowly beside her on the steps and cuddled Rolf in her arms.

"Sometimes I think that you are as homesick as I am," she said, keeping her voice down, as though not wanting the servants to hear. "Has it ever occurred to you," she went on, "that you and I are the only ones in Eden Castle who are not truly at home?"

Eve smiled. Of course it had occurred to her. She shook her head as though put out with herself. "I'm tired. Here it is midafternoon and I feel as though I have–"

"No need to apologize," Sonia said, standing, effortlessly taking Rolf with her. Eve watched, newly worried. As Alex grew, where would she find the strength to chase after him?

"Come along. I'll walk you to your chambers. Rolf is in need of a quiet time before dinner."

Eve ruffled the child's pretty blond curls. "Rolf, you and I should share the same crib. We're both babies, did you know that?"

The little boy grinned up at her. "Alex?" he said in his piping clear voice.

"Alex will be down shortly," Eve promised, "as well as Christopher."

"Chrisfer," Rolf repeated, stumbling on the name. He spoke very well for a two-year-old, not a trace of his parents' German accent. As the women walked slowly up the steps, heading toward the second-floor corridor, Eve asked softly, "When are you going home, Sonia?"

Sonia shrugged and shifted Rolf to the other arm. "Every time I ask, I am told soon, soon, Sonia, we go soon." She shook her head and put Rolf down and let him walk beside her. "Soon never comes. He says John Murrey Eden needs him."

"John? Why John?"

"For young Geoffrey. John doesn't want the family to be bothered with him. They want him out of sight, you know?"

Shocked, Eve stood still. "They want what?"

"Well, it's Geoffrey's idea too." Sonia hastened to add. "His stump embarrasses him. But if my husband were to leave, someone else would have to tend to him, dress his wound, try to bolster his faltering spirits."

Still shocked, Eve shook her head. "I thought that Geoffrey was a recluse by choice."

"Oh, he is," Sonia nodded. "It's just that . . . he has had help in making that choice."

For several moments both women gazed at each other. Eve was certain she had misunderstood and was on the verge of asking additional questions when, without warning, the pain, the knife-sharp pain, cut down through her stomach.

"Eve, what is it?" Sonia asked and stepped forward and gave Eve the support of her hand.

Eve took it and closed her eyes against the pain, bowed her head and prayed for relief and felt the waves of pain slowly subsiding, though she continued to grasp Sonia's hand until she could breathe again, her eyes filled with water, her mouth panting and dry.

"Eve, what in the world . . ."

"Nothing," Eve whispered, still not quite able to speak.

"Nothing?" Sonia exclaimed. "Come, I'll take you to your room. Then I'll call Susan. She will–"

"No," Eve begged. "I'm fine, Sonia, really. Please–"

"You don't look fine."

"I'm going to lie down now."

"Good."

"There's no need for you and Rolf to come all the way to–"

"It's no trouble."

"No, please, get Rolf down for his nap so he will be ready for the big party."

"Party," Rolf repeated, grinning.

"I'm fine now, it's just–"

"What is it?"

Eve laughed softly. "Sonia, you're worse than Stephen. Run along now. I'll see you in about an hour."

She walked backward down the corridor, waving, calling back at Rolf, who thought it was all very funny.

Sonia apparently failed to share her son's amusement and continued to stare after Eve with a worried expression.

Fortunately the end of the corridor was only a few more steps. She gave a final cheery wave to both and called out, "I'll see you shortly."

Then she was out of sight, her own apartments straight ahead, a welcoming refuge, for it had been her experience that one seizure was usually prelude to another. And then they would stop altogether for several hours, sometimes several days, and she would be pain-free.

But for now she knew that more were coming, and no sooner had she reached her door than the second seizure descended. Inside her room she fell to her knees and doubled over as the pain increased. And the only image that helped to distract her from the pain was the remembered vision of her mother and father and how she would see them shortly and how they would take her home, where surely she would regain her good health.

"Mama," she whispered and hoped that time moved along at a swift rate of speed, that the pain would ease, then disappear altogether, please God.

Marjorie hurried across the courtyard, her cloak drawn around her as protection against the cold drizzle that had just started. She looked forward to the welcoming warmth of the Great Hall and her son's first birthday party. She looked forward to a hot cup of tea and a good cucumber sandwich, perhaps a fruit scone and a pleasant interval with the family.

Lately it seemed that she and Frederick were spending more time down in Mortemouth at the little parish church than they were at Eden Castle. Old Father Thorndike and his wife, Agnes, were both in their late seventies, both in poor health and no longer capable of administering to the needs of the Mortemouth community. Frederick had offered his assistance first after clearing it with the local bishop. Then, inevitably, as was always the case with a minister's wife, she had been drawn into service.

Not that Marjorie minded. It was really all that she knew how to do, and there was a method in her madness, for she was hoping that upon the formal retirement of Father Thorndike the Church would see fit to appoint Frederick as his replacement. That way she and Frederick could be of service and yet maintain close ties to Eden Castle. She knew it was important to Frederick to stay close to his father and brother. Their separations had been long and frequent. In addition, she wanted Chris and Alex to grow up together and be lifelong friends.

She would miss India, of course, and her parents. But she had learned one very important thing about herself: she was never more an Englishwoman than when she had come to England for the first time. She loved it here, reveled in it–the coolness, the rain, the flowers, this large and unruly family whose members so often and so mindlessly seemed to inflict pain on one another.

"Marjorie, there you are."

She looked up from her thoughts through the gray late-afternoon drizzle to see Sonia Reicher waiting outside the Great Hall door. She had no cloak, no cape, no wrap of any kind.

"What is it, Sonia?" Marjorie asked and led the woman back toward the door in a position out of the chill drizzle, which was rapidly approaching a full-fledged rain.

"No, don't go inside just yet, please," Sonia begged and held her position in front of the door. "It's Eve, Marjorie. I must talk to you about Eve."

"What about her?"

"She's ill."

"Nonsense. She's getting better every day."

"No, not better. Worse. And she refuses to let my husband examine her."

Baffled and newly worried, Marjorie looked at Sonia, puzzled.

"This afternoon. We were in the Great Hall watching the stewards decorate for the party tonight. She said she was tired. Rolf and I walked her to her apartments, and on the way, she suffered some kind of seizure, acute pain. She could hardly stand erect."

Worried, Marjorie listened carefully. "What did she say?"

"She said it was nothing. But she's concealing something."

"Why?"

Sonia shrugged. "I don't know. But I think my husband should look at her."

"Well, of course. Certainly. As soon as possible."

It grieved Marjorie to hear this. Eve had suffered enough. But she had seemed content of late and relatively at ease. Hence, Sonia's news was doubly surprising.

"Come on, I'm chilled," Marjorie urged and led Sonia through the Great Hall door.

Once inside, Marjorie spotted the festivities going on at the far end of the Great Hall, a roaring fire, the good smell of India tea and cinnamon cakes coming from somewhere and most of the family already assembled.

Notable by her absence was Eve.

Then she saw her, just coming down the Great Hall steps in the company of Susan and Mrs. Godwin, each carrying one of the boys, adorable even from this distance in their sailor suits, while young Rolf had hold of Eve's hand.

Amidst the clamor over the boys, everyone smiling and making ridiculous faces, Marjorie saw Stephen hurry to Eve's side, where he hoisted Rolf into his arms effortlessly and drew Eve close.

Suddenly Marjorie saw Eve dart back up the stairs, tripping once as she forgot to lift her skirts, hesitating at the top of the steps and clinging to the banister as though she were going to faint. She looked trapped, in pain, a terrible look of distrust in her eyes, as though the entire world had now become her enemy.

Then she was gone, leaving Stephen standing alone at the top of the steps, clearly torn between his husbandly duties, which lay in one direction, and his paternal duties, which lay in another.

John was calling for everyone to gather around the birthday boys. He had placed them side by side in their high chairs confronting an enormous fruitcake, courtesy of Mrs. Partridge and her helpers in the kitchen court.

"Go after her," Sonia urged Marjorie, keeping her voice down. "Help her."

Marjorie moved rapidly through the company. She caught up with Stephen midstep. "You go on down and be with your son," she urged. "I'll go."

"She's not herself," Stephen said, shaking his head. "Yet she claims she's fine."

Again Marjorie urged, "Please go, Stephen, and keep John away, I beg you."

Then, without waiting to see the results of her plea, Marjorie hurried up the steps and down the corridor and did not look back until she was standing before Eve's door.

The door was ajar, and she heard a noise coming from inside the chamber, a soft noise like moaning. Quietly she pushed open the door and saw Eve lying upon the carpet, her knees drawn up tight to her chest, her arms wrapped around her body, rocking back and forth in a self-comforting gesture.

"Oh, my darling," Marjorie whispered and hurried to her side. "What is it, please tell me. Something is–"

But Eve was beyond speech, beyond anything except the task of dealing with her pain. Marjorie had no choice but to hold her and caress her as one might an ill child.

A short time later, the pain seemed to subside, though Marjorie continued to hold her for Eve obviously was spent and weak.

Marjorie was about to ask a question when Eve murmured, "You know what's wrong, don't you?"

Marjorie leaned close. "No, what? Please tell me. What is it that–"

"God has in the past given me too much of everything. He gave me His gift of a voice, the love and adoration of thousands, He has given me riches, and love–" She looked up at the ceiling as though she were addressing a Deity there. "Now He must take something away, must send grief instead of joy."

Marjorie started to contradict her concept of a God at once generous and mean-spirited, but she changed her mind. The first priority was to get her to bed and call Dr. Reicher up here immediately.

She was on the verge of saying as much when slowly but steadily Eve pulled up to her knees, then using the support of a near footstool stood erect, wavering slightly and at last steadying herself.

"Come on, our sons are having their first birthday party."

"Eve? Please let Dr. Reicher examine you."

"No!" The refusal was clear and sharp.

Quickly she moved out into the corridor as though to leave Marjorie behind. "I think Mrs. Partridge's cream must have been off this morning. I've had stomach cramps all day."

"That was more than a cramp."

"No, I'm fine. Hurry along now, or John will send the guards for us. You know John. And besides, first-birthday wishes are very important. We must help our sons make the right ones."

Then she was gone, leaving a very worried Marjorie alone in the room.

"Stomach cramps," Marjorie muttered as she started down the corridor after Eve.

Eden Castle
May 25, 1897

Though the clinic was due to open in a quarter of an hour, Susan had no choice but to wait until poor, hysterical Sonia calmed down so that she could hear her "confession" and thus try to understand Dr. Reicher's anger.

Only a few moments ago he had half-dragged Sonia into Susan's small kitchen, had positioned her in a chair, then had announced that his wife had a confession to make.

"What confession?" Susan asked.

"I only discovered it last evening myself," he began. "I would have informed Mr. Eden then, but it was late. And now this morning I cannot find him."

"He's gone riding with Lord Eden. They were going down the coastal route beyond Mortemouth."

"Then I view you as next in command, madame. Hence, I brought my wife here to you, so that you might hear–"

"Hear what, Dr. Reicher? Please, be direct."

"For a period of time now, weeks, months, I'm not certain–she'll have to tell you that–my wife, whom I trusted, has been stealing morphine from my medical supplies."

She found the blunt accusation difficult to believe. She had seen many morphine addicts. They were always slovenly and indifferent, possessed of a soft, dreamy demeanor. Sonia Reicher was a perpetual whirlwind of energy and activity. Sonia a morphine user? No, it was not possible. Susan was on the verge of saying all of this when apparently Dr. Reicher read her thoughts and began slowly to wag his head.

"No, the thievery was not committed to supply herself. Better that it were," he added mysteriously.

"Then who?"

Dr. Reicher paused. "Eve. The morphine was stolen to give to Eve, who–"

Again Susan began to shake her head.

"Yes, Eve," he now repeated in answer to the look of incredulity on her face. "Sonia," he commanded, "Tell all."

"It's t–true, Susan," Sonia stammered. "It was my intention to help her. She was in such pain, still is, but she said, 'Sonia, if only I could dull the pain when it occurs.' The rest of the time, she said she felt fine."

Susan listened closely and tried to match the image of what she was hearing to the reality. In truth, she had seen little of Eve lately. She generally kept to her chambers or walked the headlands in the company of Stephen. She adored Alice, but it had been several months since Alice had come home from her nursing studies in London. Marjorie usually was in close contact with Eve, but Marjorie had been spending most of every day down in the parsonage in Mortemouth.

So who had been spending time with Eve? The answer was standing before her. Sonia.

"What pain?" Susan managed.

"It's in her stomach. She begged me not to tell anyone, but I told Marjorie."

"And?"

Sonia wiped at her eyes with a well-dampened handkerchief. "She said we must watch her. But Marjorie is gone so much of the time, everyone is gone, even Stephen, who–"

"When did you start to give her the morphine? Think now, Sonia, please."

"About two months ago, the last of March, first of April, I don't remember. What she had asked for was a sleeping potion. But then she said the sleeping potion didn't help because the pain kept her awake, and what she really needed was something for the pain."

This burst of information seemed to take a toll, and briefly she sank back into the chair and closed her eyes. "She has suffered so. I begged her to let my husband look at her. But every time I would make the suggestion, she would get almost hysterical and finally made me promise to tell no one."

Susan looked up at Dr. Reicher. "Then how did you–"

"My morphine supply. I keep it under lock and key in the cupboard outside Sir Geoffrey's room. I keep a fairly large supply on hand so I won't have to journey to Exeter so often." He paused and looked sharply down on his suffering wife. "My supply is now sadly diminished. I must confess that initially I shared your anxiety, that it was Sonia herself who–"

He broke off, apparently unable even to voice that potential horror. A few minutes later, he resumed. "But the truth of the matter is, I caught her red-handed lifting the syringe and morphine from the cabinet. She had found the key in my vest pocket while I was sleeping."

"Is she ill, Dr. Reicher?" Susan asked now. "Eve, I mean? Why is she suffering pain so severe that she requires morphine?"

"How am I to know, my dear lady?" Dr. Reicher protested, lifting both hands as though wanting only to be rid of this troublesome subject. "As you so well know, the young lady has not allowed me to go near her since the birth of her child."

"Come, Doctor," she commanded now with dispatch.

"What, I don't–"

"We are going to see Eve."

Sonia quickly objected. "No, please, I beg you, she'll know that I told. And I promised."

"Sonia, listen to me," Susan said, exercising great patience. "Eve's family, her mother and father and brother, will arrive in London in less than three weeks. If she is ill, we must try to get her well. Surely you can understand that."

Whether she understood or not, it was difficult to tell. She seemed more concerned with the loss of Eve's friendship, and again Susan was astonished. She had no idea that the two had become so close. Of course, it made sense. They were the only two in the castle at all times except for Eleanor, and most of whose time Richard managed to occupy.

"I want you to do something for me," Susan said, speaking carefully. "First, I want you to carefully compose yourself. There is fresh water in the next room. Cleanse your face. Then, I want you to go into the surgery and out onto the porch. Invite the patients inside to wait. Tell them that I have been called away by illness in the family and that I will return as soon as possible. You might fix them a cup of tea and have one for yourself. I will appreciate it, Sonia, if you will do this for me."

For several moments after Susan had finished speaking, Sonia continued to sit unmoving in her chair. But at last her head bobbed slowly up and down, and she took a final wipe at her eyes.

"Thank you," Susan said and gave Dr. Reicher a pointed look which conveyed without words the message "Follow me."

He did, though not without first stopping to look back on Sonia, a sad, betrayed look.

A short time later, after a brisk walk back to Eden Castle, Susan and Dr. Reicher started down the long corridor that led to Eve's chambers.

During the long walk her fears had vaulted. What if Eve had concealed from everyone except poor Sonia the true and serious nature of her illness and what if her parents arrived in a few weeks to find their daughter ill—or worse?

The thought was intolerable, and she quickly dismissed it and knocked sharply on the door.

"Eve?"

She raised her hand to knock again and decided instead to push against the door to see if it was open.

It was. Slowly she leaned forward, peered around and saw Eve collapsed on the floor, less than two feet from her bed.

"Hurry, Doctor," Susan ordered and pushed the door wide open. Dr. Reicher bent over and felt for a pulse. Thank God, he found one.

With a degree of effort, he lifted her in his arms, and for the first time Susan saw Eve's face and was shocked.

The girl looked like a corpse. Her skin was bloodless and dark purple circled her eyes, and though it didn't seem possible, she had lost even more weight.

Quickly she assisted Dr. Reicher in placing Eve on the mussed bed and tried to straighten the bedclothes at the same time.

"Leave them," Dr. Reicher commanded. "Help me here."

Now she saw his intention to strip the nightdress over Eve's head, and she hurried to the other side of the bed and lifted the girl's hips. She had not yet dressed from the night's sleep.

"Oh, dear God," Susan murmured, looking down. Eve's abdomen was painfully distended, causing her to resemble a child in the last deadly stages of malnutrition.

She looked up at Dr. Reicher, seeing even a degree of shock on that stern German face. "I was afraid so," he muttered. "When Sonia told me the truth of the morphine and described the pain, I . . . was afraid so."

"What is it?"

"A tumor I would say, quite developed and very possibly malignant."

Susan closed her eyes as though to block out the steady march of his words. "Is there anything that you–"

But he commenced to shake his head. "It quite likely was why her pregnancy was so difficult. It is my professional opinion now that major organs are involved, most probably the liver."

He broke off speaking for a moment and bent low over Eve's neck. His hands probed gently, professionally on either side of her throat. Slowly he rose. "I'm afraid there are nodules everywhere. I don't know how she has endured."

As Susan heard the tinge of admiring pity in the normally stern voice, she felt her eyes fill quickly with tears. "She survived with the help of your wife's morphine, Doctor."

"But if she had told us, told someone, perhaps after the birth of the child, we could have taken her to London. There are specialists there."

Susan turned away from the bed. Alice had made the same suggestion. Why hadn't it been done? Because Eve had kept her secret from everyone, including Stephen. And Alice had not been home for months. Her studies were intense and becoming more so. Everyone was guilty of this tragic neglect.

Susan looked back to see Dr. Reicher draw the blanket up over Eve, who still lay unconscious upon the bed.

"Is she–"

"I would say a coma, and a blessed one at that."

"How long?"

Dr. Reicher hesitated before answering. "Hard to say. I would have to do a more thorough examination."

"Then do one, please, and quickly. I must tell–"

Susan broke off, withdrew to the window seat and, with apologies to no one, wept freely.

Generally she felt hardened to death and the ravages of pain. Not insensitive to it, just keenly aware of the natural progression of things.

Still this seemed unnecessarily cruel. Did it amuse the Deity to behave in this capricious manner? Or was there a Deity at all? Perhaps John was right when he said religious folks amused him because they were like children, convinced that a loving father looked after everyone when in truth there was no father, loving or otherwise, just a void filled with biological accidents and governed by the random selection of an impersonal and imperious nature.

Strangely enough, the cold, hard thoughts soothed her, relieved God of all accountability and left her facing a vacuum too great even to be questioned.

So Eve was dying. Her parents would arrive within three weeks to find a grave, not the daughter they had loved and missed for so long.

"She's . . . very ill," Dr. Reicher pronounced after his examination. "Her heartbeat is quite weak. At most, I would say a week, perhaps ten days."

Susan looked up at the bleak sentence of death. She stared dully out of the window down on the channel glittering blue and white under a dazzling late-May sun. Her eye caught a single white gull sailing through the bright, clear air. The bird swooped and dipped, then lifted his wings and soared upward again with enviable grace.

Susan watched it for several minutes and took peculiar solace in it.

At last she turned back to see Dr. Reicher struggling to replace the nightdress on Eve. She hurried to the bed. "Here, let me help."

"She's chilled. We must keep her warm and comfortable. That's all we can do," Dr. Reicher said. He hesitated and looked down at the palms of his hands. "Poor Sonia will not have to steal morphine anymore. I'll see that Eve has what she needs."

For several moments both stared down on Eve, who appeared to be merely sleeping. Her long hair was scattered across the pillow. One small hand lay beside her head, the other hidden beneath the blanket.

"I'll arrange a schedule."

"And the others will have to be told."

He had saved the hardest command for the last. Suddenly angry, Susan started toward the door, feeling strangely as though Eve had offended them all in some way. She had come to live among them, had shown them all how easy she was to love, and now she was in the process of leaving them.

"Doctor, if you will remain here while I make arrangements, I would appreciate it," Susan said from the door. "I will fetch Eleanor. She will relieve you as soon as possible. And then would you please tend to the patients at the clinic. I have no way of knowing when I will be finished here."

"Of course," the doctor agreed, a new tone of kindness and understanding in his voice. "I welcome the opportunity to return to the clinic. If my wife is still there, I owe her an apology."

Susan looked back, amazed at the softening effect of death. So it would be of everyone with whom she shared this tragic news. Everyone would be softened and morose and stilled, everyone except Stephen. Stephen would be inconsolable.

New York Harbor
June 8, 1897

It was completely baffling to Mary that they were sailing to England for this all-important and greatly anticipated reunion on the German liner *Kaiser Wilhelm.*

"I thought the Cunarders were the finest oceangoing vessels in the world," she said, standing railside, watching the valiant little tugs push and pull the gigantic liner out from its berth.

"They were–once." Burke smiled. "I think North German Lloyd's did it on purpose."

"What?"

Burke's smile broadened. "What better way to wound the British in the year of Queen Victoria's Diamond Jubilee than for Germany to bring forth not only the largest but also the fastest ship in the world."

Burke laughed openly and Mary was so pleased, not with what he said but the lighthearted manner in which he had said it.

During these last weeks of hectic preparation, Mary had noticed alternating moods in her husband. Some days, he would be buoyant, desperately looking forward to seeing Eve again; on other days, he would seem to fixate on his ancient hate for John Murrey Eden, and twice he had confessed to Mary that he really doubted seriously if he could go through with it, could shake the man's hand and pretend that nothing had ever happened.

"Are you cold?" Burke inquired.

Mary shook her head. "Just excited and so impatient. How long did you say this fastest ship in the world would take us to get to England?"

"If we're lucky, ten days."

"Ten days," Mary mourned. Ten days before she could see Eve. "I'm not certain I can wait that long."

"I'm afraid you must. Come," Burke invited, offering her his arm. "Let's tour this magnificent ship and find all those countless ways that we can divert ourselves for ten days."

"Where is David?"

Burke laughed. "Don't worry about David. He will be giving the captain advice before we reach England. Come, they are serving tea in the Grand Salon. A cup will warm us and help us plot the next ten days."

Mary took his arm as they strolled down the crowded deck. Beyond the railing, she saw the New York skyline slipping past. Off in the distance a series of deafening ship horns bellowed out farewell. Somewhere on the deck below, a band was playing "The Merry Widow Waltz." All about, elegantly dressed people were laughing and waving as stewards hurried by, carrying enormous bouquets of flowers and bon voyage baskets of fruit.

Mary tried to look in all directions at once and at last grasped Burke's arm and hugged him close. "I cannot tell you how happy I am. Thank you, my darling."

Something in her tone apparently caught his attention. He led her to one side of the crowded deck and looked soberly down upon her. "I owe you so much," he whispered, "but most of all I owe you my apology for the grief I have caused you."

Suddenly her love for him vaulted. She wanted to be close to him, to show him to the fullest the depth and intensity of her love.

"Our stateroom," she began, hoping his desire matched hers. "Do you remember when we sailed from England, years ago as newlyweds? Do you remember what we did as the ship was sailing out of Southampton Harbor?"

She watched his face closely for signs of remembrance. And then she saw it, the light of a brilliant smile. "I do remember," he murmured as his tone of voice changed.

"Eve was conceived on that voyage," she smiled.

He moved closer, his hand moving up to the fullness of her breast. "We both may well be beyond the age of conception, but I for one would like very much to continue our tradition aboard ship."

He bent low and kissed her, a kiss promising more passion to come.

"This way," he said, standing back and allowing her to pass before him.

All the way back down the crowded deck, she was indifferent to the crowds, to the passing New York skyline, to Lady Liberty herself. All she could think of was her coming glorious reunion with Eve and more immediately the pleasurable sensations her husband's body always aroused in her, sensations which over a quarter of a century had not paled, but had, if anything, grown more intense, more delicious.

Eden Castle
June 16, 1897

The morning brought little hope. Eve awoke after the worst night that Stephen had ever witnessed. What Dr. Reicher feared would happen had happened. Apparently she had developed a tolerance for the safe dosages of morphine, and during the night, despite repeated injection, her pain had run rampant and unchecked.

Now Stephen remained at bedside for a few moments as Susan prepared to bathe her.

"Poor . . . Stephen . . ."

At the sound of Eve's voice, Stephen tried to bring himself back to the moment, to the faint smile he saw on her face as she reached weakly out for his hand.

Susan ceased arranging things for the bath and looked up at the sound of Eve's voice. Stephen was certain that she shared his amazement at seeing Eve awake and conscious after the brutal night. At one point during the early morning hours, Dr. Reicher had informed them that death probably was near.

But now here she was, smiling, weakly to be sure, but awake all the same and capable of recognizing him. There had been days during the last few grim weeks when her pain had produced a kind of delirium and she had called out repeatedly for Stephen, for Yorrick Harp, sometimes for her mother, sometimes her father, once for her Sis Liz and once for her beloved younger sister, Christine, who had died years ago at Stanhope Hall.

"Yes, my darling," Stephen said, bending low over her, still unable to believe or to accept this tragedy that was consuming them.

"Promise me," she whispered with effort.

"Anything," Stephen replied and sat on the edge of her bed, aware of Susan retreating, the morning bath temporarily postponed. At the door, he heard voices, Susan and Dr. Reicher most likely. They had been constant and loyal companions throughout this ordeal, unlike some in the castle, like his father, John Murrey Eden, like Eleanor and Richard, who, according to Susan, had no tolerance for illness.

Frederick and Marjorie had been his mainstay of support, walking with him, trying hard and with loving patience to help him to understand God's ways.

Though he didn't understand. Any of it. All he knew was that the light and joy of his existence was slowly, agonizingly being snuffed out before his very eyes in the most cruel manner possible. Why was that? Why couldn't anyone give him an answer? At times in the past, she had seemed so well. Those few moments of weakness that he had witnessed, Eve had dismissed as "women's problems." He did not know, and never suspected that–

"Stephen–"

"Yes, my dear, I'm here."

"Promise–"

"What?"

"That you will go to London and meet Mama and Papa."

"Of course. I have said that I would."

"And David–"

"And David, yes."

"Bring them out to Eden."

"I will."

"And take care of Alexander."

"I will."

"Let Mama and Papa see him some of the time."

"Of course."

"Take him to America."

"We will take him–"

"No, you take him."

"Eve–"

"And when you are there, promise me that you will visit Christine's grave and put white lilacs on it."

"Eve, please–"

"She visits me every night. Did I tell you? She comes to me when I can no longer endure the pain, and she takes some of it into herself."

Stephen tried to think of a suitable response. But he couldn't. His eyes, already burning from lack of sleep, were filled with tears. He had wept at least once every day since Susan had given him this tragic news over three weeks ago. As for the dead Christine visiting Eve, how was he to know it wasn't so?

As he looked down on Eve, her eyes closed. Her breath was coming with increasing difficulty. She looked so tired, so exhausted.

"Eve?"

There was no response.

"Eve–please–"

At last her eyes opened briefly. She drew a long and shuddering breath. Her head pressed backward against the pillow as though the process of breathing had caused her pain.

"Don't leave me," she asked, her hand growing limp in his.

He let the tears come and wondered what had happened to that gloriously strong and beautiful young girl he had married only a few years ago.

"Tell Mama and Papa and David I love them and tell them that Christine is with me now."

"No, Eve–please–"

"Kiss Alex for me. Don't let him forget me."

"Eve–"

He knew she was dying. Something in her manner, her face, her voice, let him know. She knew it as well, such a sweet and private knowledge that passed between them, a final sharing of a great and short love.

"Stephen, look at me–"

With effort he obeyed. "Don't be sad for me," she whispered. "I've already found Christine. And I'm sure Yorrick is here. What a reunion we shall have. And please always remember how much I love you, will always love you, and I'll be waiting for you. We shall be together again. I promise–"

As he watched, he saw her press her head backward, saw her mouth open for a breath that wasn't there. For less than a second her hand lifted into the air as though in protest, then fell back at her side, her neck and head relaxed, eyes closed, the struggle for life and breath at last dissolving into sweet acceptance and sweeter peace.

"Eve–"

Though he knew she was gone, he called her name twice. "Eve–"

But he received no answer and braced himself for the torrents of grief that he knew were still unspent within him.

But instead of grief, he felt something quite unexpected, both in its nature and in the fury with which he could feel it building inside him.

Rage, unchecked and uncontrollable, commenced to build within him, rage that a mindless God had taken her from him, rage that he had now been consigned to a lifetime of loneliness, rage that his son would be forced to grow up without ever having even known his mother, rage that from now on he would be the object of condescending pity on the part of all the inhabitants of Eden Castle, rage that Burke and Mary Stanhope would arrive in London in less than four days, would fully expect to be met by Stephen and led out to a joyful reunion with their daughter and grandson at Eden–

Rage that–

But then the emotion itself swept upward and canceled all thought, canceled reason and common sense and good judgment as well, and left him gasping for breath.

He pushed up from the side of her bed, took a final look at this woman with whom he had fallen in love at first glance, on that hot, dusty summer morning eight years ago in a place called Stanhope Hall, outside Mobile, Alabama. He had seen her on an upper balcony, beautiful beyond description, her long golden hair loosed and tumbling down her back, wearing only her chemise in an attempt to stay cool in the August heat.

Remembering the beginning did nothing to check the rage but rather fired it and caused it to increase until at last he struggled to his feet, his hands outreaching as though rage was a thing of substance that he could fight his way through and be done with.

But he couldn't. It merely accompanied him with every step as he ran down the corridor away from the Great Hall.

He knew the castle well, knew of a hidden passage at the end of the third-floor corridor, a narrow cobwebbed imprisonment that led straight down into the bowels of Eden Castle and excreted the traveler of the moment into the dark, overgrown garden just this side of the graveyard.

Everything suited him, the passage, the untended garden, the graveyard. After that, his destination was less clear. It didn't matter. All that really mattered was the sure and certain knowledge that there was nothing left for him here at Eden, that and the equally certain knowledge that he refused to be the messenger who greeted Burke and Mary Stanhope in London with the news of Eve's death.

No! He wouldn't do that, couldn't do it. Another messenger would have to be found.

Still he ran as though some new threat were pursuing him, trying not to think on her as he ran, trying not to hear her screams as he ran, trying not to see her face as she pushed back in search of her last breath.

"Eve–"

He cried out her name at the top of his voice, welcomed madness, let it overtake him as he spied the low door with rusty hinges at the end of the corridor, pulled it open and looked down into an abyss of total blackness.

He took the narrow steps running, stumbling once, falling a distance, then pulling himself up, only to stumble and fall again.

No matter. There was nothing he could do about the rage that still accompanied him. He knew now that it would be with him always, as would the memory of Eve, torturing him until he too cried out for a mercy that wasn't there.

As was her habit when events became too much for her and circumstances threatened to overwhelm her, Eleanor took refuge high upon the parapets. She stepped out into the balmy June air in time to see the guardsmen ride away from the front gate and fan out in all directions in search of poor Stephen.

Quickly she closed the door behind her in an attempt to shut out the chaos and the confusion coming from Eve's corridor. Susan had found her dead about an hour ago, and quickly word had spread. A steward had been sent for Frederick, who was in Mortemouth. Dr. Reicher was doing a final examination in preparation for the death certificate. Richard and John had taken refuge with a full bottle of Scotch in the small library. And while Eleanor was certain there was something she should be doing, she couldn't for the life of her think what it was and decided that a small bit of fresh air couldn't hurt and thus was now in hiding on the parapet.

After the guardsmen disappeared across the moors, she moved slowly back from the edge and looked out from the top of Eden at the dazzling beauty of the landscape below. Here and there she saw neat farms surrounded by immaculate patches of cultivated fields. Beyond and to the east she saw the great undisciplined moors, stretching as far as the eye could see in a pale gray and lavender blanket.

Baffled, she leaned back against the rough crenellation and wondered why up here everything seemed so well ordered and beautiful while down below, the world had suddenly turned black and tragic and nonsensical.

No answer to her questions, but it did seem terribly willful of God to do this awful thing to them. To what purpose? Why couldn't young Eve have been granted a long life in which to raise Alex, to produce other children, to enjoy the fruits of her talent and labor?

Stunned anew by the grim nature of her thoughts, Eleanor walked slowly around the parapets, allowing fear to overtake her, then grief.

What had become of Stephen?

Frederick had been able to give the guardsmen a list of their boyhood haunts, though for some reason, Eleanor doubted if he would return to those places. They must find him and soon, for he was to leave day after tomorrow for London and his reunion with his parents-in-law.

Poor Stephen. What tragic news with which to greet them.

"Eleanor? Are you up here?"

Richard's beloved voice preceded him by only a moment and Eleanor smiled.

As he appeared around the door, the wind caught his thinning hair and caused it to stand up straight, giving him the comical expression of a clown.

She was glad to see him and called out, "Here, my dear, over here." As he turned about in the direction of her voice, she thought how much she still loved him and what a good marriage they had made. Nothing flamboyant, nothing very dramatic, just the plain son of Lord Eden falling in love with the plain daughter of Lord and Lady Forbes of Forbes Hall, Kent, a sensible union which had produced poor Geoffrey and plain Lucy and pretty Charlotte. They had shared and survived everything for over thirty years. Thus, it was inconceivable that they should not share and survive this.

"How did you know where to find me?" she asked as he came up alongside and tried to coax his thinning hair to lie down.

"You've been coming up to this chill and windy place for as long as I can remember when things downstairs don't quite suit you."

Don't suit me! It seemed a strange way to put it.

"Where's John?" she asked, remembering that the last she had seen of the brothers, they had been drinking heavily in the library.

Richard shrugged. "He felt compelled to ride off with the guardsmen in search of Stephen. He's worried."

"Understandably."

For several moments both stood gazing out at the vast and beautiful land that bore their name.

"Oh, I remember," Richard said, turning toward her. "Dr. Reicher and Susan were asking me questions I could not answer."

"Such as?"

"The burial, Eve's burial."

Sweet Lord, she hadn't thought of that.

"I would say as close as possible to her good friend, Yorrick Harp. I think Eve would like that."

"Do you think that Stephen would approve?"

"Yes."

"Then I'll tell Ghostly to instruct the gravediggers as near to Yorrick Harp's grave as possible."

For several moments both Richard and Eleanor let the seagulls and the wind do all the talking. She was aware of him moving closer to her, saying nothing, though she suspected tension and grief.

"Eleanor, what would I do without you? Poor Stephen, I feel so sorry for Stephen."

His voice was so sweet, his manner so entreating, that she looked back at him. When she did, she saw tears in his eyes, and the sight so moved her that she reached out for him, drew him close and felt his arms about her. They clung together, both weeping for Eve, for everyone who had known and loved her–for her parents, who would shortly be confronted with the tragic news, for Stephen, for young Alexander, who would grow up never knowing his mother, for themselves, for everyone who must deal with unexpected and tragic loss, for the entire world.

Eden Castle
June 19, 1897

Susan sat to one side of the family council that was taking place in the Great Hall. She had already formed an opinion. All she had yet to do was to voice it.

She held Alexander in her lap, seeing Eve's eyes in his eyes, Eve's smile in his smile, thinking this probably was the meaning of resurrection.

"No, I beg you, one and all, I can't, I simply can't. I–"

At the sound of this frightened voice, Susan looked up to see poor Richard rising awkwardly from his chair, his head wagging in pitiful terror, all the while backing away from his family as though they were a pack of wild animals. Which in a way they were.

For the question now under consideration was who was to go to London to meet Burke and Mary Stanhope? Eleanor had pointed out this morning that in the face of Stephen's continuing absence, someone must leave late tonight or at first light in the morning for London. Burke and Mary Stanhope were due at their hotel by early evening. They must be informed as soon as possible and brought out to Eden if they chose to come.

"Then I shall go."

Susan looked up at the sound of this strong voice. It was Frederick. He stood close beside Marjorie, who was holding Christopher.

Now Frederick's offer seemed to be held in suspension while everyone looked at everyone else, clearly considering its merits and liabilities.

She saw John with his back to the group, staring intently into a dead fire. He had behaved strangely the last few days since Eve's death. Deep emotion? Guilt? Where John was concerned, one could never be quite sure what he was feeling or thinking but he was obviously worried about Stephen.

Strangely Susan was not. Her instincts, generally reliable, had informed her that the grief-stricken young man would not kill himself, as that was the worry now running rampant through Eden Castle. She felt that he merely needed some time to himself and would return shortly, perhaps even in time to make this all-important trip to London.

And if he didn't, then in Susan's opinion, it should be–"John." To her mild surprise, she realized now that she had spoken his name aloud and had not only his attention but the full attention of everyone else as well.

"Forgive my interruption," she began and lifted Alex in her arms. He was getting heavy at fifteen months, an armful of wriggling little boy.

She walked around the table and placed Alex on the floor with Chris and Rolf amid squeals of joy, then slowly turned to face them all.

"It is my opinion that in the event Stephen does not return in time, John should go. First of all, his reunion with Mary is long overdue. And with Burke. I think they have come in good faith and need first to be greeted by John."

She saw Eleanor nod in agreement, saw Richard nod as well. The only two expressions of doubt seemed to reside on Frederick's face and, of course, on John's.

Frederick voiced his doubts. "If there is lingering animosity–"

"There isn't," Susan smiled. "I would swear to it. Mary has a forgiving heart. Eve told me how often her mother spoke of Eden and all its inhabitants. She said that Eleanor and Richard's letters were the high point of each month."

Frederick, she noticed, had retreated. All that remained was for John to voice his opinion and the matter would be closed, one way or another.

Slowly he turned his back on the dead fire. He looked strangely pliant, as though something had recently defeated him.

"I'm not certain I agree with Susan," he began, his voice low and weary. "I hope Mary has a forgiving heart. True, I grievously wronged her. But whatever wrong I have dealt her pales in comparison with her new loss."

Susan now felt as if the entire Great Hall and everyone in it was waiting with held breath for John's final reply.

"Very well, yes," he agreed at last, with a long-suffering air, as though he were making a monumental sacrifice.

"Then it's settled," Susan concluded with dispatch and moved toward the bell cord. A carriage must be made ready in the event that the Stanhopes wished to come out to Eden immediately. Susan suspected that they would. After all, there was not only a grave to visit but a beautiful grandson to welcome, kiss and hold. Then there was the matter of John's wardrobe, a small trunk to be prepared.

Now she gave John a grateful smile and knew that the impending journey would undoubtedly be one of the most difficult he would ever make and thus was doubly grateful for his decision. In fact, as she saw him now chatting with Eleanor and Richard, she wondered if he had fully grasped the arduous task that was yet ahead of him—a late-night ride to London, there to establish a vigil at the Hotel Kenilworth awaiting the arrival of Burke Stanhope, who hated him; his half sister, Mary, who possessed a generous heart despite John's ancient crimes against her—and if this imagined scene were not bad enough, John had to inform them that their firstborn daughter was dead.

For a moment Susan reeled under the impact of what was ahead. In a coward's way she was glad it would be happening in far-off London.

Shortly before seven o'clock, John stood at the top of the Great Hall stairs, watching the feverish activity below. The carriage had been brought around about twenty minutes before, and now the stewards were busy polishing it inside and out. To John it looked like a dinosaur, a huge, cumbersome relic.

He had read in a London periodical about the new motorcar. The article said they already clogged the narrow London streets.

Now he wished longingly that he had a brand-new motorcar in which to travel to London. That would certainly make a decent impression on the cotton farmer from America.

"Do you have any misgivings?" Susan asked, taking his arm.

"About what?" he asked, playing dumb.

She gave him a mock-stern look; then something going on beside the carriage caught her efficient eye, and she abandoned him, hurrying down the stairs, calling ahead, "No, don't put that there. It goes inside with Mr. Eden. That's right."

John watched her with love. She was his foundation and his inspiration. If only he could live up to her expectations of him.

Behind him now he heard the others beginning to gather to bid him farewell. He heard Richard's voice, Eleanor's and at last the one he had been waiting for all evening.

"Frederick," he called out, "may I speak with you in private?"

Frederick was quickly at his side.

"I beg you," John began, expressing his worry again for Stephen, "please go out in the morning–"

"I will, Papa, first thing come light. Don't worry, Papa," Frederick said lovingly and placed his arm about John's shoulders. Suddenly John felt childlike and very vulnerable, their roles reversed again, Frederick counseling like the father, John listening like the son.

"Papa, if I may–"

"What?"

"This . . . will not be easy, for any of you, this meeting in London."

"I'm aware of that."

"It has been my experience that when dealing with matters of death and grieving, the direct approach is best. People generally know when you have come with tragic news. I don't know how they know, but they do. So my advice to you would be to be direct and compassionate. And let me remind you that there is a possibility that Burke and Mary Stanhope will confuse the messenger with the message."

John listened carefully, both amused and amazed by this sober and gifted son of his. Wasn't it only yesterday that his nanny was wiping his nose? Now he spoke of "his experience." Ah, youth . . .

"Well, then," he said, grasping Frederick's hand, seeing the concern there and trying to ease it. "I'll take your words to heart," he smiled, "if you will promise me to continue the search for Stephen. I really don't understand all this mad dashing about for Eve. She's dead. We should be organizing our forces for Stephen now. And I pray God that he is still alive."

"He is, Papa. I would stake my life on it."

Then Richard and Eleanor were there with kisses, and at the top of the stairs he saw his favorite sight, Mrs. Godwin, carrying a child on each hip.

Quickly John climbed the steps two at a time for a final kiss, and stayed a moment to admire their ever-changing beauty. The boys were growing plump, with dazzling smiles and capable of a few nonsense sounds, pure joyful baby babbling.

"They're saying goodbye to you, sir," Mrs. Godwin grinned.

"Of course they are," John smiled back at her and nuzzled each baby for a final time. "This time next year these two will be running races on the headlands as Richard and I once did. Then we will see who is the strongest, the fleetest–"

"John."

The gentle voice was Susan's, coming from the bottom of the stairs. "It's time to go."

John nodded, eager to get this torturous journey under way. "They'll think Bertie, Prince of Wales, has arrived," he muttered, climbing up into the high carriage.

"Nonsense," Susan smiled. "It will accommodate all of you on the return trip."

A trip that will never happen, John thought and looked about at the rose velvet interior and wondered how in the hell he could survive the long trip to London in rose velvet.

"Safe journey," Susan called out over the rumble of the great wheels as the two drivers brought the whip down across the horses' backs.

John waved through the tassled windows and braced himself for the turn heading toward the gatehouse. My God, he *would* be the laughing-stock of every London street in this rolling salon. No, he couldn't do it. He would have to concoct a new plan when he was safely beyond eye and earshot of Eden Castle.

Then beneath the carriage he heard the thunderous rattling of the wheels as they passed over the grate beyond the gatehouse, and he looked back and saw the small, distant knot of people huddled together on the Great Hall stairs.

Alone at last, with only the clatter and rhythm of the carriage to keep him company, John tried to relax.

Tumbling about in his mind was the echo of every voice that had bade him farewell. Dominant among them was Frederick's.

Burke and Mary Stanhope will confuse the messenger with the message.

Newly sobered, John stared out of the window at the monotony of the moors, suddenly apprehensive. Why in the name of God had he allowed himself to be talked into making this ridiculous and dangerous journey? What if Burke and Mary still bore him ill feelings? What if they did indeed blame him for the death of their daughter? What if–

As his fears and anxieties mounted, somehow they all became focused on the dreadful and pretentious carriage. How could the drivers manipulate this monstrosity through London's narrow streets?

The answer was simple. They couldn't. Then what would he do? Now outside the carriage window he saw the turnpike road sign pointing to Exeter. He should be there by midnight at least. Exeter. Lucy and Mason.

As he stared out of the window, his eyes glazed with thought and memory. True, he had treated them badly, both of them. Perhaps he'd had no right to treat them so poorly; perhaps he'd had no right to send them away as he had done. He continued to stare outward, bobbing in rhythm with the cumbersome carriage.

He was not a man to hold a lasting grudge, particularly when it suited his purposes. He was certain his drivers could locate the school named Greenfield beyond the town a few miles on this very turnpike road to London. It would be a late-evening call, informing both Lucy and Mason of recent tragedies which had occurred at Eden. After all, they were *both* members of the family now. A cordial, healing half-hour visit, nothing more and perhaps at the conclusion of such a visit, he might be given permission to lodge this awful carriage in their carriage house along with the horses. The drivers were free to go and have a brief holiday for themselves. John's only stipulation would be that they not return to Eden for at least one week.

Then he would take the lead horse, a familiar one to him named Lightning, and he would see if he could live up to his name, and with one light satchel slung over the saddle, he could make for London, certain that he could see the dome of St. Paul's by midmorning.

He leaned forward and drew open the small door that gave him access to the high driver's seat.

"I say, change of plans," John shouted. "At Exeter, make for Greenfield. It's on the other side of the London turnpike, the headmaster's house. One brief stop," he concluded, at this point not wanting to reveal all to them.

The relief driver nodded immediately, indicating that he had understood. Quickly John slid the door shut to close out the ungodly racket.

He was pleased that his decision felt right. It was time that Lucy and Mason gave up this foolish schoolteacher life and returned to Eden, where they both belonged.

Briefly he closed his eyes as he tallied up the length of time they had been estranged from Eden. Almost nine months. As soon as John settled this unpleasant affair in London with the Stanhopes, he would take steps to refurbish one of the large, comfortable apartments at Eden and warmly invite Lucy and Mason back into the fold. How happy they would be. How happy they all would be.

Thus pleased with himself, relieved that once again he had schemed his way through a very difficult situation, he settled back and closed his eyes. A brief nap would stand him in good stead.

With his eyes closed, his head bobbing in rhythm to the carriage, he tried to make of his mind a calm, safe blank, though fears still plagued him. Stephen. Dear God, please keep him safe. Please let Frederick find him. Let both his sons be waiting his return from London.

And please let Burke and Mary Stanhope be forgiving and understanding. He had had nothing to do with Eve's death, nothing at all. And please let Susan–

It was in the middle of his prayers that sleep came, a safe black world where nothing moved, not even his conscience.

Greenfield School
June 19, 1897

Eight and a half months pregnant and unable to sleep, Lucy left the bed before her restlessness awakened Mason and sat on the window seat, a favorite perch where she could lift her legs, stretch them out, gaze over the peaceful calm of Greenfield and think on how happy she was. She wanted nothing to change, except of course, the shape of her swollen belly.

The doctor had told her only that morning that the birth was a good five weeks away. No one at Eden even knew she was expecting and Mason had suggested that they wait until after the birth, and perhaps Mason was right. He generally was.

She shivered, not from cold but from happiness, looked up, found a star in the blue-black night and made a wish as old Mrs. Calvin had taught her to do. "Star light, star bright–"

Curiously, when she was ready to make her wish, she found herself not to be in a wishing mood but rather in a mood of thanksgiving.

"Thank you, God," she breathed softly, "for all your many blessings to me." She closed her eyes and again felt the curious reflexive spasm of pure happiness. Then she heard something.

She opened her eyes and looked first toward the bed to see if Mason had heard it as well. But from the sound of his gentle snores, he still was deep in sleep.

There! She heard it again, a distant rumbling, something breaking the deep night's silence. About seventy yards away, across the green common, she saw the bobbling lantern of the nightwatchman. That would be Mr. Finn. He was a standard and loving joke at Greenfield, their nightwatchman, seventy if he was a day, walking with a cane, veteran of the Crimea.

Then she heard it clearly, a large carriage, many horses, coming fast off the turnpike road and heading straight toward old Finn and the gates of Greenfield.

No carriage passed in or out of Greenfield's grounds after ten at night. She was certain it was well past ten.

Then who–

All at once she caught a glimpse of the enormous carriage, the moonlight catching on every polished surface, six horses at least and all traveling at top speed toward–

Suddenly the driver saw old Finn and yanked back on the reins. The horses reared, the carriage shimmied and shuddered under the duress of the abrupt stop. Now she heard angry shouting.

A sleepy voice behind her caused her to look back and see Mason in his voluminous nightshirt, trying to rub the sleep out of his eyes, trying to focus through the window on the disturbance at the gate.

"Who–" Mason began, ducking his head in an attempt to see out of the window.

"I don't know," Lucy said. "I didn't want to awaken you."

He kissed her on the forehead and stepped yet closer to the window. The obscene shouting was still going on, someone outraged by the old man's stance and the near accident.

At some point as Mason was pulling on his robe, she heard a familiar tone in that shouting male voice, some cadence of arrogance, some inflection of superiority that she had grown up with and lived with all her life.

"John," she gasped, "it's John Murrey Eden."

Mason held the knotted cord of his robe in both hands, listening.

"It is, I'm afraid," he agreed and took a final look out of the window. Apparently old Finn was still managing somehow to hold the enormous carriage and the cursing man at bay.

Then they both saw a shadowy young figure, fleet of foot, running across the green common, heading straight for their house.

"It's Peter," Lucy said, recognizing the young boy from Exeter who did odd jobs around the school in return for a lesson now and then and food for his family. She always thought he went straight home at night. Apparently tonight he had been staying with old Finn in the gatehouse.

"Master Frye, Master Frye," he called now.

Mason stepped forward quickly, kneeling now on the window seat and stuck his head out.

"Here, Peter. What is it?"

"A gentleman, sir, mad as hell he is. Says he come to see you and your lady."

"Wait here, please, Lucy. Let me go and see. I know John. He means us no harm. And the hour is significant, I think. Something has happened. Let me go and find out. Then I'll call for you."

She sat on the edge of the bed and listened as Mason called out to Peter.

"Tell the gentleman to drive to our door, Peter. Tell Finn to let him pass. Then get home to your bed."

Lucy smiled as the headmaster in Mason surfaced, despite the hour. He was a brilliant headmaster. The boys adored and respected him, the other tutors admired him, and the staff was more than willing to work very hard for him. How many times Lucy had felt a pang of guilt for all those years that the Eden family had kept Mason Frye for their own.

"Stay here," Mason said pointedly yet lovingly and kissed her again and left the room, drawing on his slippers even as he walked.

She listened to his footsteps on the stairs and at the same time heard the rumbling of the carriage coming closer. She moved back to the window seat and saw clearly for the first time the source of the noise that had disturbed Greenfield's night calm–Eden's largest carriage, capable of seating eight comfortably with rose velvet interior. My Lord, she couldn't even remember the last time it had been hauled out for use.

By leaning farther out, she saw other wide-eyed witnesses, each house festooned with small boys in white nightcaps, all peering out of their windows, amazed at such a spectacle. Poor things. Obviously they thought someone important had arrived.

Then she saw Mason inform one and all that everything was well under control and that they were to return to their beds immediately.

As the carriage rolled to a rattling halt before their front door, she saw John step out.

She couldn't hear what was being said. Mason appeared to speak first, then John, who even from this distance looked repentant.

Slowly she saw Mason extend his hand, which John took immediately, and in the next moment and to her surprise, she saw the two men embrace, a spontaneous expression of genuine affection. As she watched, she felt a wave of relief, for the embrace was much more than just an embrace. It meant quite simply that now she could take her child back to Eden to see the place of her growing up.

Mason waved at her, a beckoning gesture. John looked up at the window and saluted, grinning broadly as she smiled down and drew on her robe.

When she reached the bottom of the steps, the two men were already in the parlor. Lucy made one last attempt to smooth her hair and gently patted her belly as though in an attempt to reduce its size; then she started through the parlor door and was instantly greeted by a warm John Murrey Eden.

"Lucy, my dearest," he smiled, reaching for both her hands. "Your generous husband has already forgiven me. All I lack is your forgiveness. Will you be so kind?"

"Forgive you for what, John?" she asked, seeing Mason's grin over John's shoulder and seeing a look of relief on his face as well.

"For what?" parroted John in a mood of good humor. "For making such an ass of myself when you announced your plans to marry. For behaving in such a despicable fashion, for–oh, my God, I don't know, for hurting you at the moment of your greatest happiness."

She wasn't certain that this was John Murrey Eden standing before her, not the brooding, sullen, self-centered, arrogant man of her childhood. This man seemed halfway human.

"Of course I forgive you, John," she said and was instantly rewarded with a warm embrace that concluded with John's awareness of her protruding belly.

"When?" he beamed and stepped back as though to put distance between himself and the mysterious birth process.

Mason answered for her. "In about five weeks, though the child is now quite active. We're not so certain that she won't make her entrance very soon."

"Her?" John smiled.

"I feel that it is a girl," Lucy said. "I remember Eve used to tell us that she felt she was carrying a boy before Alexander was born. I didn't know what she was talking about. I do now."

The reunion had been going very well therefore Lucy was surprised to see John's mood change abruptly. He turned and stood with his back to them.

"John?" Mason said, clearly as baffled as Lucy. "Is something–"

At last he turned back into the lamplight. "I am on a mission," he said at last, slowly coming out of the shadows, "a mission of great sadness."

"Mama," Lucy gasped, "is anything the matter with–"

"No, your mother is quite well. And your father too."

"Won't you sit down, John?"

But he declined to sit and instead commenced pacing in a limited circle between the couch and the corner bookcases.

"We have suffered a recent tragedy at Eden," he began and again Lucy held her breath.

"Eve," John said flatly, "died on June 16 after a painful and prolonged illness."

For several minutes the blunt words seemed to hang suspended in the air. Weakened by the news, Lucy sat on the edge of the couch and cried.

Mason knelt beside her, offering her the reliable support of his love.

"And that's not the end of it," John went on. "Stephen has disappeared."

"Disappeared?" Mason repeated. "I don't–"

"He was at her bedside when she died. Susan left them alone, and when she returned, Stephen was gone."

"You have searched of course," Mason began.

"Of course, night and day," John said. "We've had guardsmen out every day. They've gone as far as Clovelly in one direction, Taunton in the other–"

He broke off, and his manner changed, softened. "According to Frederick, he will be found when he's ready to be found. My most fervent prayer is that he refrains from harming himself."

Lucy looked up, stunned by this last possibility. Mason quickly interjected a note of hope. "Oh no, you can take my word for it. Stephen is incapable of such an act. I know him too well. He will return stronger than ever, mark my word. Yes."

John seemed to be listening carefully. When for several moments no further words were exchanged, Lucy issued a logical invitation.

"You will stay the night, of course, John. You are most welcome. We'll learn more about Eve in the morning."

"No," he said abruptly. "I cannot stay. And there is nothing more to say of Eve. She suffered widespread malignancies, according to Dr. Reicher. Her pregnancy disguised the largest, a tumor in her abdomen and a possible tumor in her uterus and that accounted for her difficult delivery.

As I said, I am on a mission. I must be in London. To meet Eve's parents. To tell them."

"Poor John," Lucy murmured.

"A horse, Mason, that's all I need. You understand, don't you? I'll be the laughingstock of London in that . . . contraption."

She saw Mason hide a smile. "I'm not sure we have a carriage house large enough at Greenfield, John," he offered in bemused protest.

"Then let the damn thing sit out in the rain and rot for all I care. I'll take just one fleet-footed horse."

"There's a morning train to London."

"No, no train. I can go faster than the train. The carriage was Susan's idea and Eleanor's. They believe that the Stanhopes will want to come back to Eden in spite of Eve's–"

He broke off. Lucy joined the conversation at the door. "Of course they will want to come out to Eden, John, to visit her grave, to see their grandson."

"Then they can bloody well provide their own transport. I'll be damned if I'll be forced to share the same compartment with Burke Stanhope."

"What about the drivers?"

"I'll give them their pay and a week's holiday. They'll take it in a minute."

Now he stood looking from Mason to Lucy with a most peculiar expression on his face, a small boy begging for permission to be naughty.

"It's fine with me," Lucy said. Strange how the peace of Greenfield had been so thoroughly shattered, not just the nighttime peace but the deep inner peace as well.

At last it was decided. The carriage would be stored in the school barn, and the horses, in Mason's stable, except for the lead horse named Lightning, who had been chosen to make the night ride with John.

"You'll have to change horses at Salisbury," Mason warned. "You can't run him into the ground. Blackmoor's stable is just off the turnpike–"

John was already moving toward the front door. Once there, he looked back. "Lucy," he smiled. "Thank you for receiving me. And thank you for your forgiveness. We look forward to seeing you, babe in arms, at Eden Castle soon. Your mother and father will be delirious with happiness." He turned and was out the door, Mason following him.

She stood in the narrow hall, eyes closed and listened to the activity in the night. She heard the carriage being led away. The young boys of Greenfield would love it as a plaything.

Then she heard Mason shout something into the night, heard a male response, both lighthearted and full of joy. Apparently they were delighted to have forgiven each other.

The echo of all this resounded for several minutes; then the night was silent again, as though nothing important had happened.

She heard Mason's step on the stair and looked up as he came through the door. "Can you believe it?" he asked softly, shaking his head.

"Where John is concerned, one is safe to believe anything."

"Why he wouldn't wait until morning and take the train, I have no idea."

"That idea made sense. John generally rejects ideas of common sense."

"Are you . . . was this alright with you? I haven't acted prematurely, have I? I thought that reconciliation was–"

She hurried to his side in an attempt to soothe the self-doubt. "No, of course, reconciliation."

"Then what?"

She shook her head and slid beneath his arm. "It's just John," she said, with amazing simplicity. "I have never trusted him, not since I was a little girl. I can't tell you why."

She walked easily beside him to the stairs. "Come, my darling," she whispered, "back to a warm bed for what is left of this night."

He hugged her lightly. "You go on. Let me lock up, extinguish the lamps. I'll be there in a minute."

Halfway up, she looked back and saw Mason standing in the parlor with his head down, as though contemplating the events of the evening.

Suddenly he lifted his head and she saw a dazzling smile on his face, a look of such extreme pleasure that she was momentarily taken aback.

Had John's friendship meant that much to him? If so, then she was doubly glad for the reconciliation.

At the top of the stairs, she stopped for breath and thought again on the tragic news concerning Eve. Poor, gifted, beautiful Eve.

She remembered the echoing screams of the crucible of her childbirth. Malignancies, tumors, awful things growing alongside the babe.

Suddenly she felt such an overpowering wave of fear for what was ahead of her that she hurried into the bedroom, sat on the edge of the bed, kicked off her slippers, lay back and drew the summer comforter up over her head.

There, safe in darkness, she prayed for strength in the difficult ordeal ahead and prayed further for the deliverance of Eve's soul to a place of no pain and perfect peace.

London
June 21, 1897

Shortly after three in the blaze of a hot afternoon sun, a very weary John Murrey Eden fought his way through the crowds of Euston Station and at last made his way to the pavement outside only to find the mob scene relatively unchanged.

For a while during the long ride of the night, John had actually thought how enjoyable to be in London again. It had been years since he had spent any time in the world's greatest city.

But Mason's words had proven prophetic and Lightning had given out in the early morning hours near Salisbury. John had gone to the stables looking for a replacement only to be told they were fresh out of horses, all of them having been either bought or hired out for Queen Victoria's Diamond Jubilee procession on June 22.

How fortunate it had been, at dawn, just as the sun was creeping up the spire of Salisbury Cathedral, to hear the beckoning steamwhistle of the early morning train. He had left Lightning at Blackmoor's stable and had made a run for the station, catching the last coach as the train had chugged its way out of Salisbury.

But even the train had been jammed with people eager to reach the city in time for the Jubilee festivities. As he had heard countless times, there was to be a large parade today and an even larger one in the morning, the latter to be graced by Victoria herself. Entire families, from old grannies to newborns, occupied the seats, complete with filled picnic hampers and jugs of ale.

John was exhausted, in dire need of food and drink and surrounded by pushing throngs of people. His head was splitting and his stomach growling, and he could still taste soot and grit from the train. Furthermore, he was quite certain that he looked as bad as he felt.

Then, of course, it was out of the question that he make his way directly to the Kenilworth in this condition. For that difficult meeting, he had to look and feel his best. All that remained was to find a suitable hotel, one not too posh, or he might be recognized by an old acquaintance. He was enjoying his anonymity if nothing else, something he could never have achieved in that awful coach.

It was his intention to head toward the old Morley's Hotel, large enough to be comfortable but old enough to eliminate all who might conceivably know and recognize him.

Morley's had been a favorite of his father's, a stucco Georgian building, circa 1825. John had spent many a happy hour as a boy listening closely as his father had tried to put the touch on Lord This and Lady That, in constant need of funds to feed his hundreds of orphans and to run his ragged schools.

Enough of the past. On with the present, a refreshing bath, a good meal and a soft feather bed in the safe anonymity of a hotel room.

The cotton farmer and his family from America could wait. No one would begrudge him a few hours sleep in order to better perform the difficult task ahead.

He quickened his pace on the crowded street and tried to lose his thoughts in the steady onslaught of faces.

Tomorrow would come soon enough. For now, he was still caught in the safety of today.

Kenilworth Hotel
June 22, 1897

Still exhausted from the long voyage, though excited over the impending reunion with Eve, Mary stood beside one of the broad windows in the elegant Kenilworth lobby, pushed aside the heavy red velour drape and peered out at the incredible London street scene.

There were banners everywhere; flags, pennants, coats of arms and the high-flying colors of every English regiment that had arrived in London from the four corners of the Empire. It had been rumored that shortly Queen Victoria's carriage would pass along this very route, and already guests were lining up on the steps, spilling over onto the pavement, eager to catch a glimpse of this beloved and tenacious old monarch.

It was true, as Burke had said only last evening at supper, that there had never been such an empire since history began and it was very unlikely that there would ever be one again. All the powers of the world, envious of its splendor, respectfully if reluctantly acknowledged its supremacy.

For a moment Mary clung to the red velvet drape and closed her eyes, which were still burning from lack of sleep. She had been so worried last night. It had been her understanding that Stephen was to meet them here on the afternoon of the twenty-first and that they were to leave London that very evening for Eden in order to escape the throngs of Jubilee Day.

She had waited at this very window, ignoring the repeated pleas of Burke and David, who had begged her to come with them as they poked about the old city. Burke delighted in showing David his old haunts—his office on Fleet Street where he had worked for the London *Times*, old Sim's Song and Supper Club, where he had seen Mary for the first time and had fallen in love with her.

Now Mary opened her eyes as a large brass band blared past, resplendent in black-and-silver uniforms, followed by another horse regiment, all riders astride dazzling snow white horses.

As she craned her neck first in one direction, then in the other, she heard the near chimes of the clock perched high atop the marble mantel of the Kenilworth.

Twelve. Noon. What if he doesn't come today?

Oh, but he would. Of course he would. And she could have been wrong about the date, June 21. Both Burke and David said the letter had read June 22. One more day. What matter? She had waited this long. Just to see Stephen would be a treat. And he could inform her firsthand about Eve and this "persistent weakness" that had prohibited her from coming to London with him. Stephen could tell them all about young Alexander, who would be returning to Stanhope Hall with them.

"There she is–"

She heard Burke's familiar voice, and as she turned, she saw Burke and David and a third man, wreathed in clouds of white hair, looking quite elegant in a dazzling white summer linen suit.

Though disappointed that it wasn't Stephen, she still managed a smile and went forward, recognition complete now, hand extended.

"Mr. Clemens," she said and warmly took his hand and remembered the night so long ago when he had been the honored guest at Stanhope Hall. He was a writer, Sam Clemens was, his pen name Mark Twain, and on that occasion years ago he had expressed interest in meeting Mr. Booker T. Washington, a close friend of Burke's.

"My dearest Mrs. Stanhope," Mr. Clemens smiled in return and in courtly fashion kissed her hand.

"Whatever are you doing on English soil?" Mary asked.

With a broad theatrical gesture, Mr. Clemens pointed toward the street and the increasing festivities. "Come to cover the grand moment in history," he said expansively.

He stepped closer to the window and peered out, closely surveying the many-colored pageant of imperial troops. "It is all sort of a suggestion of how it will be on the Last Day, isn't it?"

Burke laughed heartily. "Do you mean to suggest that Victoria is God?"

"Not God," Mr. Clemens said, mock stern. "Perhaps God's wife," he added. "After all, she has single-handedly changed the face of continents with new cities, new railways, new churches, myriad cantonments, and in the process, she has changed the manners and lives of entire peoples, placing her own values upon civilization from Lagos to Christchurch." He shook his head as though impressed by his own words. "I assure you that such a woman is not to be taken lightly."

He looked back at Burke and Mary. "Have you entered the wager?"

"What wager?" Burke asked.

"The hotel wager. Will Victoria choose an open or closed carriage?"

For a moment the dilemma seemed to rest lightly on the air between them. Mary thought it a silly thing to bet on and quite a transparent one.

"An open carriage, of course," she said at last, cutting through the male confusion.

"How can you be so sure, Mrs. Stanhope?" Mr. Clemens asked, a twinkle in his eye.

"Because *I* am a woman," Mary smiled. "And because Victoria, for all her power and age and authority, is also a woman. And I'm quite certain she has planned her appearance down to the last hairpin, and whether you choose to believe it or not, women do still dress largely to please men. And how, pray tell, can men enjoy her if she is hopelessly enclosed in a covered carriage. No, no doubt about it, and how foolish a wager on so apparent a subject. Take my word for it, Mr. Clemens, the queen will shortly appear in an open carriage, I promise you."

Burke applauded lightly. David whistled softly in admiration, and Mr. Clemens bowed from the waist.

"I know now the source of your daughter's charm. And yes, I do remember her."

At the mention of Eve, Mary looked back to the window. She must let nothing divert her from her vigil. It was not altogether impossible that Stephen might get swept right past the hotel by the marching regiments. Or he may not know the location of the hotel. He might at this very moment be trying just as hard to find them as—

Now as she looked out of the window, her eyes skimming the crowds lining both sides of the pavement, her attention caught for just a moment by what appeared to be a familiar face, not Stephen, but still a face from the past.

It hung there for a moment in her vision, and then it was swept away by the hordes following the marchers. She blinked once, then twice, wondering if she had imagined it. How could one single face stand out in that mob?

"Mrs. Stanhope? Are you well?"

It was again Mr. Clemens, who, standing close to her, had apparently seen something on her face. Now the alarm in his voice brought Burke immediately to her side.

"Mary? What is it? Did you see–"

"Nothing. I thought I– No, nothing."

Mildly embarrassed and certain now that she had mistaken a total stranger for someone she once had known, Mary felt obliged to ease the tension for all.

"Mr. Clemens, may I invite you to sit with us? It would be a simple matter to draw the drapes fully open, then push out the windows and arrange our chairs spectator fashion, then we would possess the best seats in London."

David warmed immediately to the idea, and even as Mr. Clemens nodded in agreement, David and Burke were busily drawing forward a semicircle of the Kenilworth's plush red velvet chairs. Mary drew the drapes, revealing a large expanse of French window, and Mr. Clemens released the window latch and pushed open the doors, letting in the deafening flood of shouts and cries and martial music.

Mr. Clemens held the center chair for Mary. Burke sat on her left, David on Burke's left and Mr. Clemens on her right.

"Your daughter, madame," Mr. Clemens asked, raising his voice above the blare of the regimental marchers, "is she–"

"That is why we are in London, Mr. Clemens, to see her."

"She is here?"

"No, not here. In North Devon at Eden Castle, my ancestral home."

From the look of confusion on Mr. Clemens face, Mary knew she had a brief tale to tell, of Eve's falling in love with Stephen Eden, the hideous year of kidnapping and pursuit when Eve at first was feared dead and at last the triumphant marriage, homecoming and subsequent departure for England.

Throughout her narrative, Mr. Clemens never took his eyes from her. At the end of her account, Mr. Clemens continued to gaze at her as if mesmerized.

Finally he spoke. "I have seldom heard a more compelling tale," he murmured.

"We have had to live it, Mr. Clemens. You cannot believe–"

"Oh, but I can, madame. I know as well as anyone the value of our children to us, what their victories mean, what their tragedies mean."

"How pleased Eve will be," Mary said, "when I tell her that we had the good fortune of encountering you in our London hotel."

"Please give her my very best and my warmest congratulations on the birth of her son," Mr. Clemens said graciously. "Alexander is a noble name," he mused and at last turned his attention back to the crowds and the endless parade.

Mary did likewise and felt more relaxed now, more at ease than she'd felt in days. Perhaps the chance encounter had been good for her, helped to blunt her anticipation, to calm her down.

Now, to her right, she saw someone else in need of calming down. David was out of his chair and hanging precariously over the window ledge.

"David, either take your seat or go down onto the pavement," Mary said, and she saw her son make an instantaneous decision. Obviously he had been waiting for permission to leave the party and join the mobs below. As he darted pell-mell back through the hotel, Mary caught Burke's eye. "It is all right, isn't it?" she asked.

"Fine" Burke soothed. "Now look–"

He summoned her attention to the right where there appeared to be a break in the regiments, though beyond the break she saw the beginning of the Royal Horse Guards, resplendent in their glistening helmets, their coal-black horses polished and shining in the high noon sun like burnished satin.

And beyond the Horse Guards she caught her first glimpse of the royal carriage, still too far away for a good close look at the old monarch. But now she contented herself with listening to the peculiar change in the roar of the crowd.

The mindless and exuberant cheering seemed to have diminished. The crowds, as though they were a single organism with but one mind and one set of responses, now fell almost silent as the Horse Guards marched past in regal tempo.

Then as the royal carriage drew nearer, the cheering started again, though this time they were crying out one name, "Victoria, Victoria, long live Queen Victoria."

Mary felt gooseflesh on her arms and stood as all the other spectators were doing and watched closely as the lovely gilt coach drew yet nearer.

"Take careful note, Mr. Clemens. It is an open carriage."

"My sincere congratulations," he beamed, "to your woman's intuition."

Then there was far too much to see for further talk, the carriage almost directly in front of them now, affording Mary a perfect view of the extremely plump though diminutive queen.

She sat alone in the open carriage, wearing a dress of black moiré with panels of pigeon gray embroidered all over with silver roses and shamrocks and thistles. Now and then she waved a small white gloved hand at her throngs of subjects, who seemed determined to shout out their love for her.

Mary watched it all, deeply moved, and was aware of the historical significance of the occasion, the importance to England and the world of this small grandmotherly woman whose imprint and personality had been powerful enough to stamp an entire age with her name.

At the exact moment the royal carriage passed in front of the hotel, the management unfurled an enormous banner from out of one of the upper floors, depicting the royal coat of arms. The gesture seemed to please Victoria, and she smiled broadly and looked on with the wonder of a child. Mary waved and was certain the old queen had caught her eye and waved back.

"Most impressive," Mr. Clemens murmured, watching the carriage pass further down the street. "Even for a member in good standing of that incorrigible republic of rebels, still, most impressive."

Mary laughed, strangely buoyed by the sight of Queen Victoria, as though that one glimpse of the monarch had awakened everything English within her.

"I've not met that many rebellious Americans, Mr. Clemens. They seem quite docile and steady to me. Just different philosophies of government."

Now she settled back into her chair and tried to concentrate on the crowds. But still her mind and her heart kept going out to Eve.

Where was Stephen? Why didn't he come? How much longer would God ask her to wait?

London
June 22, 1897

Well rested from a comfortable night at Morley's, John had awakened, eaten a hearty "Diamond Jubilee" breakfast, and even lifted several glasses of "Diamond Jubilee" champagne with his fellow guests in Morley's dining room.

Quite reluctantly, he had set out from the hotel for the brief walk to the Kenilworth, though he had been stopped at least a half a dozen times in as many blocks by the hordes of revelers. He had never seen old London town in such a jolly mood. Twice he had been forced to take refuge in pubs, only to find that free drinks were the order of the day.

Thus, shortly before noon, he had arrived at the Kenilworth, feeling little pain and no anxiety, though he had the good sense to keep his distance until his head had cleared. He had looked up and, to his surprise, had seen Mary at one of the hotel lobby windows.

Of course, he had recognized her. He had worshipped her once, before the American Stanhope had stolen her away from John's protective wing.

For a moment he had been terribly afraid that she had seen him as their eyes had met. But he had had the presence of mind to duck behind a convenient lamppost and hold his position of concealment, though he had noticed from his hiding place the face of Burke Stanhope.

For several minutes John had fixed on the man's face, and in those moments all the hatred, the resentment, the envy had welled forth as though there had been no passage of time at all.

Stunned by the depth and freshness of this hate, John had withdrawn a safe distance into the shadows of the storefronts. There, well out of the turmoil of the crowds, he had tried to deal with this hate and had watched Burke and Mary from a safe distance. They seemed quite unchanged by the years, though he could see gray in Burke's hair and a becoming fullness to Mary's flawless figure. There was a young man with them who bore a striking resemblance to Burke.

With them was an older man, white-haired, paying close attention to Mary and scant attention to the pageantry of the street. These four had settled comfortably in one of the broad ground-floor windows for a morning's watch.

Just a few moments later, the young boy had left the party and darted down the hotel stairs and had disappeared into the crowd. Then a short time after that, the old queen had driven past in stately procession, and deafening cheers had gone up. John's view of the hotel window had been momentarily blocked by the surging crowds, so he had taken advantage of the lull to walk a few steps down a shadowy alleyway and compose himself and to curse whoever it was who had talked him into this dreadful mission.

Now the roar of the crowds seemed to be diminishing; the royal carriage was well beyond the hotel. He looked back and saw a mammoth royal crest just unfurled from one of the upper floors of the Kenilworth, saw the trio still in the window.

Well, then–

He lifted his head and, starting out through the throng, experienced a surge of unbearable excitement. He felt like Destiny made manifest, moving steadily toward the three who as yet were unaware.

Curiously enough, it was the old white-haired gentleman who turned first, as though he had sensed Destiny approaching. Those squinting eyes with the bushy brows were the one that first engaged John, a strange look, almost one of recognition, though John was certain he had never seen the man before in his life.

Mary turned to see what had engaged the attention of her white-haired friend and her eyes came to rest on John.

John saw her start to her feet, mouth open. What was her expression? Pleasure? Fear? Burke Stanhope saw her alarm and followed her line of vision. He frowned and reflexively wrapped a protective arm about Mary's shoulders, which she instantly threw off, and with one brief, slightly girlish wave of her hand backed away from the window and briefly disappeared into the lobby, only to reappear at the top of the hotel steps just as John moved onto the sidewalk.

To his amazement he saw a most dazzling smile of pleasure and forgiveness, as she moved down the steps even as he moved up them.

Theirs was a joyous embrace, he lifting her off her feet, a private reunion in the midst of the grander pageant of Victoria's Diamond Jubilee.

"Oh, John," she gasped at the end of the mad and twirling embrace. "I've dreamed so often of this moment."

"And I as well," he grinned as he returned her to the safety of the top step.

"Here, let me look at you," he commanded lovingly, and held her at arm's length and saw her blush becomingly.

"And you," she murmured. "You look well. Something or someone has been agreeing with you."

"Life in general," he smiled and ached to take her in his arms again and hold her close, but dared not, for now at the top of the stairs he saw Burke Stanhope and behind him the white-haired gentleman, who seemed to be viewing the proceedings with special interest.

Apparently Mary sensed that they were no longer alone and turned. She smiled warily and invited, "Look, Burke, at last someone has come to fetch us. And look–"

As she indicated John, she stepped to one side with such an expression of dread on her face that John's heart went out to her. What a nightmare for her, bringing together on the steps of the old Kenilworth two men who once had come close to beating each other to death.

He took one step upward. Burke took one step down. By a broad extension of their arms, their hands barely touched in the briefest of handshakes.

"Mr. Eden," Burke muttered, and John knew all too well that this man had forgiven him nothing, would never forgive him anything.

"Mr. Stanhope," John repeated. "Welcome to London. You have selected an auspicious occasion for your arrival."

"We came to see our daughter," Burke Stanhope said brusquely.

"Yes," John said looking back toward Mary and suffering a severe failure of nerve.

"John, I want you to meet–"

He looked up at the sound of Mary's voice. She had the old gentleman in tow now, the sun reflecting off his immaculate white linen suit.

"Mr. Eden, I believe," he was saying. "My name is Sam Clemens."

John took his hand, felt a firm handshake and saw something in the man's face that he found most appealing, a wisdom, a private knowledge tempered by a soul-deep sadness.

"And they tell me you bring word of young Eve Stanhope," the old gentleman was saying now. "You know, I once had the honor of being her companion for dinner. Though thrice her age, I would have made off with her in an instant if her parents had only looked the other way."

John smiled and kept one eye on Burke Stanhope, while Mary stood next to the old gentleman, explaining that he was an author, America's finest.

"Mary, I must speak with you," John said at last.

"Of course you must," Mary smiled. "I'm quite certain that you and I could talk for days."

"No, I must speak now."

"Of course you must and you shall. At lunch. Mr. Clemens, you will join us, of course. Burke, would you ask the maître d' to arrange a very private table for us? And champagne—we must have champagne."

As Mary exulted on, John's despair deepened until at last he saw an encouraging sign from a most unlikely quarter.

Burke Stanhope was reading his expression accurately. "No, Mary, I think that Mr. Eden has something to—"

"Yes, yes," John muttered.

And at last the old gentleman caught the new tone as well and began graciously to withdraw. "I'm afraid I must decline your luncheon invitation, my dearest Mary. My London publisher is due momentarily, a dreaded meeting in which crass money and empty contracts will be discussed. But perhaps later."

As he backed up the stairs, John saw a bewildered look on Mary's face. What had happened to her glorious party so newly planned?

"Where is Stephen?" Burke demanded. "Stephen was to have met us here."

"He was indeed, but plans have changed."

"Why?"

"Not here, Stanhope, please, I beg you, find us a private room."

"Why private? Whatever news you have for us can be divulged here. I'm certain that no one else is interested."

"No, please—"

Then Mary caught his ominous tone. "John, what is it? Is it Eve? Is she sick?"

Caught between the rising despair in her eyes and Burke Stanhope's stance of defense, and against his better judgment but wanting only to be rid of the awful weight of the news itself, John spoke the dreaded words.

"Mary, you must listen closely," he began softly, reaching for her hand and missing. "Eve is dead."

At first he wasn't certain that Mary had heard, that anyone had heard. A party laughed raucously several windows down, and there seemed to be a constant parade of guests into and out of the hotel.

With some concern, John looked more closely. Had she heard? Why wasn't she speaking, weeping, asking further questions? Why was Burke Stanhope studying him now with this new intensity, his eyes leveled?

Suddenly Mary stepped back. "No, no, no, I don't believe you. See to him, Burke, he has been drinking, I can smell it."

John protested strongly. "No, Mary, you must listen. It happened only a few days ago. You were at sea."

Now he looked at the two of them. Nothing moved on either of their faces, as though all was held suspended in a state of desperate disbelief. As John watched them, trying to take his next cue from them, he saw the young man join them, the one he had seen earlier from across the street.

He sidestepped John and went instantly to his parents. "Papa, what is it? Mama–"

But Burke pushed his son to one side, moved in a straight line to John and without warning reached out and grabbed the lapels of his jacket. John responded reflexively by attempting to dislodge the hand that had grabbed him, all the while trying to take into consideration their shock, their grief.

"No, Stanhope, no violence, not now, I beg you. It is not necessary."

"It is always necessary where you are concerned."

"Please listen. I'm sorry to be the messenger. But you must understand that Eve is dead."

"Don't–say–that!" Burke shouted, his raised voice now attracting the attention of the entire hotel lobby.

John glanced toward Mary for help, for understanding. "Mary, please, I beg you. You cannot believe this is easy for me. Now listen. She was suffering from tumors, several large ones. She told no one about them. There was a good physician in attendance, plus my wife, who is a professional nurse. I assure you, everything was done that could be done. Of course, Alexander is well and healthy, a beautiful child in all respects. Please, God, try to understand, I beg you, please–"

But Mary was weeping, her head moving back and forth in wordless denial. Her son was close at her side, looking bewildered and confused.

John had just turned back in an attempt to deal with Burke when suddenly he felt his hands on his shoulders, bodily turning him about as though he were a misbehaving schoolboy.

"Where is Stephen?" Burke demanded.

"After Eve's death, he . . . disappeared. We are worried about him. He was going to come to London. I came in his place."

"You've been drinking."

"Yes, I had champagne."

"Why should we believe you?"

Stunned, John did well to shake his head. "Why would I make up such a hideous lie?"

"You have your reasons. You have always had your selfish and barbaric reasons. Why would you hire ruffians to attack your own sister?"

Burke's voice was rising in confusion and hysteria. John was aware of the concierge moving out from behind his desk.

He'd had no idea that Burke would dredge up such ancient and deadly history. It was as John had suspected from the beginning: Burke had forgiven him nothing.

"You bastard," Burke muttered, "you goddamn bastard."

John turned in time to see Burke step back with peculiar deliberation.

When the blow came, it sent John reeling backward in an explosion of pain, the side of his face first on fire, then throbbing. He heard a woman's scream, heard a youthful shocked voice protesting, "Papa, don't–"

The last thing he saw was Mary collapsed on the floor, the young boy trying to lift her, tears running down his face.

Then blessed blackness, where nothing moved, spoke, wept or protested.

Eden Castle
June 22, 1897

Stephen sat at the dining hall table, more than satiated by Mrs. Partridge's chicken pie. He was acutely aware of the faces all about him, each one eager for an accounting of his last few days.

Now he wished with all his heart that he could give them one. But the truth of the matter was that he remembered nothing except fatigue, hunger, cold, wet, sleeplessness and grief.

He must have wandered far afield, for it was a farmer in Clovelly who found him and fed him and gave him a ride to the edge of the moors in the back of his hay wagon.

"Poor Stephen," Eleanor murmured across the table. "You look exhausted."

"No, I'm alright," he said and tried very hard to keep his mind free of the past. Clearly Fate had seen fit to return him to the living. Then he must assume that he had responsibilities here, those who needed him.

"Alexander–" he said quickly and looked up into any face who could give him word of his son.

"He is with Mrs. Godwin," Frederick said, laying a gentle hand on Stephen's arm, "though mind you, he has been concerned about his papa."

Suddenly Stephen felt an embarrassment of tears and quickly checked them.

At that moment the dining room door opened and he looked up to see Sonia Reicher entering, head bowed. He knew that she and Eve had become quite close, knew also that it had been Sonia who had supplied Eve with the morphine when her pain had become unbearable.

Now he watched the plump little woman along with everyone else as she quietly took a seat at the far end of the table and allowed one of the serving maids to ladle a serving of Mrs. Partridge's tomato soup into her bowl. At first she seemed unaware of the focus of the family, and when at last she did look up, Stephen was appalled by the redness of her eyes. They were swollen almost shut, suggesting that the woman had done little but weep for the last several days.

"I am so sorry, Stephen," she murmured. "Repeatedly I have asked God for forgiveness, and as yet He has not responded."

Baffled, Stephen looked to Susan for clarification. "She feels that she is responsible for Eve's death. I have tried to speak with her, but–"

Now, wearily, Stephen pushed away from the table and walked slowly to where Sonia Reicher was weeping, sat opposite her and reached for her hand.

"You mustn't blame yourself," he said gently. "We all should have paid closer attention."

"I loved her so," Sonia cried, unashamed.

"As did we all."

"And her poor parents, what must they–"

Suddenly Stephen looked up. Dear God. Her parents. Burke and Mary due to arrive in London on–

"What is the date?" he asked frantically, on his feet now, fearing the worst.

Susan replied, "June 22. Why–"

"O my God. Burke and Mary. They were due to arrive yesterday in London."

"I know," Susan said.

"And no one was there to–"

"Yes, John is there," Susan smiled as though pleased with her words. "When you didn't return, we knew that someone had to go. Frederick offered, as did Richard. But in the final analysis, we all believed that John was the one who–"

"No!" Stephen shouted as though by the sheer volume of his voice to halt her words. "No, please tell me that you didn't send–"

Surprised, Susan said, "Yes."

"When?" he demanded of anyone at the table who cared to respond.

"Day before yesterday, wasn't it Eleanor?" Richard asked. "He was due to arrive on the morning of the twenty-first."

"And when were they to return to Eden?"

"Immediately. Unless something went–"

"Wrong," Stephen concluded. "It would be my guess that something has gone terribly wrong. I must leave right away," he said and hurried toward the door.

"No," Susan protested. "They are due to arrive shortly. We need you here."

"If John met them yesterday and gave them the news, then why aren't they here now?"

Susan stared at him across the length of the dining hall. "They will be soon–"

"No, they have had plenty of time," Stephen said. "Believe me, Susan, I know all too well the depth of antagonism that exists between my father and Burke Stanhope. I know you did what you thought was right. But my father is the last man on earth who should have been sent to London."

For several moments no one moved or spoke in the dining hall. "How will you travel?" Richard asked, just as Stephen pushed open the door.

"By horse to Exeter, where I'll see if I can catch the London train without too long a wait. If not, I'll ride on."

Despite the muddle of voices coming now from the dining hall, Stephen took the steps heading up toward his rooms three at a time.

Hurry! A quick wash, a fresh change of garments, then out through the kitchen court to the stables for a horse. No time to visit Eve's grave.

Later he would spend hours there, talking to her, trying his best to resurrect her, asking her advice on every matter. For the question still remained, precisely how was he to live out the rest of his days without her?

The Kenilworth Hotel
June 22, 1897

Burke paced in the corridor outside Mary's room and kept his eye on her closed door and wondered how long the hotel doctor would be in there.

Burke lifted his head and looked directly into David's worried eyes.

"Papa, was what that man said true? About Eve, I mean?"

"No, of course not. That man is a maniac. You are not to believe anything he says on any given subject. I should have killed him. Twenty-five years ago, I should have killed him."

"No, Papa, please. It makes Mama feel bad."

Burke looked up at the voice, more Mary's son than his at the moment. It was Mary who had always preached forgiveness of John Murrey Eden. Well, look what her forgiveness has wrought. A cruel practical joke by a drunken and deranged man.

"I thought Stephen was coming," David persisted with youthful indignation.

"I know," Burke nodded sympathetically and sat beside him.

At that moment the bedroom door across the hall opened and the old hotel physician appeared. He had introduced himself, but worried about Mary, Burke had missed the name.

"Doctor," he called out, on his feet, hurrying toward the old man, who seemed even more decrepit coming out than he had going in.

"Ah, there you are," the old man said, squinting at Burke over the rims of his glasses. "I was just about to go looking for you."

"My wife, sir, could you give me a report on my–"

"Fine, she's fine," the old man pronounced.

"But she–"

"Is overwrought is all," the old man said further, still fussing with the clasp on his black bag. "It was the day, you know, sir, quite an auspicious occasion. Ladies of refinement tend not to be prepared for such goings-on. Too much excitement. Delicate constitutions, I'm sure you understand."

"What do you suggest, doctor?" Burke asked.

"What do I suggest?" the old man repeated with maddeningly precise articulation. "Well, my good man, first, I suggest a cup of hot tea, then a square of plain toast, and a good night's rest. And I can promise you, she will be like new come morning. I have given your wife something to help her sleep. I will, of course, check back later to see how she is faring."

And with that he was gone, leaving Burke and David gaping after him. Burke had never felt so helpless in his life. John Murrey Eden had a way of doing that to people, hopelessly destroying the foundations on which they had created their lives.

"Papa, can I see Mama now?"

"Just for a moment," Burke agreed against his better judgment. Together they pushed open the hotel room door, only to find Mary sleeping.

"Is she–" David asked, still worried.

"Fine," Burke said. "Sleep is precisely what she needs. If you wish, why don't you run along and explore. Not too far. Three blocks in either direction of the hotel. Buy yourself some fish and chips."

"Where will you be, Papa?"

"Right here."

For a few moments Burke saw the doubt and fear still running rampant across David's face. "What are we going to–"

"I don't know, David," Burke confessed softly. "Let me think. I need time. Go along with you now."

David hesitated a moment longer; then, with clear reluctance, he began to back down the corridor.

For several moments Burke stood in the hallway, then he quietly pushed open the door, hoping to see Mary awake. But she still was sleeping, her face toward the door. Burke drew up one of the chairs and positioned it near to her bed and sat wearily, wondering what in the name of God they were to do now?

He closed his eyes and rested his head against the back of the chair and regretted the day that Stephen Eden had appeared at the end of the avenue of live oaks leading up to Stanhope Hall. True, he had proved himself to be a most honorable young man and Eve had more than convinced them of her love for him. But the hard truth remained. With the entrance of

Stephen Eden into their lives had come John Murrey Eden as well, and while they had been relatively safe in far-off America, they were wholly vulnerable to his tactics here.

With his eyes closed, Burke tried to clear his head and organize his thoughts. He knew that both Mary and David would look to him for guidance.

All right, then what? Wait for Stephen here? What if Stephen never came? Hire a conveyance and travel to Eden on their own? What if they were not welcomed? Stay here and send a message to Eve alone? What if Eve was really–

But the thought could not be tolerated, and Burke prayed now only that Mary stay asleep long enough for him to compose himself.

Still rubbing the side of his face where the madman Burke Stanhope had physically assaulted him without provocation, John stepped into King's Cross Road, heard the dramatic blaring of a horn, moved quickly back, and thus narrowly avoided being run over by one of the new motorcars which went whizzing past in a blur of polished black enamel, dazzling high white-walled tires and silver trim.

John watched, awestruck. He had never seen anything so beautiful in his life. The speed, the line, the perfectly tuned machine, all these things spoke of a dazzling future of speed, style and class. John would have given anything at that moment to sit behind the wheel of such a motorcar, guide it skillfully through London traffic and be aware of people waving, as they were now doing at the motorcar just disappearing at the end of the street.

Now John moved farther back on the curb. God, but he was tired. He looked about. Behind him was a small church, and to one side, he spied a secluded churchyard, two benches placed invitingly under the welcoming shade of a spreading yew.

Why not? A sit-down suited him. Of course he had handled things badly at the Kenilworth. He would be the first to admit that. But he had tried. He had done his best. It was Burke Stanhope. Stanhope was as unreliable and prone to violence now as he had been twenty-five years ago. The man hadn't changed. Mary hadn't changed. No Christian forgiveness on their part, and John fully intended to point that out to Susan when he returned to Eden.

At the thought of Susan and how disappointed she would be, John felt new fatigue and made his way slowly into the churchyard. In the cool shade, with the street noises just beyond the high hedge, John could still see the turrets and pennants of the old Kenilworth and was again reminded of how poorly events had gone on this day.

So it had gone badly. Now what? Should he retrace his steps and try again? Never! He was not a fool. Then should he return immediately to Eden Castle and report the bleak news to the inhabitants there? No, not right away. He was not a demon for punishment.

Then what?

As he leaned back, legs stretched out, arms raised on either side of the bench, he looked straight up into the full June greenness of the yew tree.

A brief stay in London might be advisable. Out of sight, out of mind. That way he would anger no one, would disappoint no one.

Slowly he shook his head from side to side, lifted it once and saw a young man staring at him from the gate that led into the street. He looked again, straightened himself on the bench and looked back only to see the young man gone.

Peculiar. He kept his eye trained on the gate a moment longer, thinking the man would reappear. He didn't, and John scowled as he tried to place him. He had the feeling that he had seen him before. But where?

He stretched again, beginning at last to relax in the cool shade and quiet peace of the churchyard. He wondered vaguely if he should pray and realized belatedly that he was trying to please Susan, even though Susan was miles away.

"I beg your pardon, sir."

The voice, so near and unexpected, caught him off guard. He sat up with a start and saw the same young man who had recently peered at him from the gate; then he recognized the possibility of more trouble.

"You are–"

"David Stanhope, sir. I hope I'm not intruding on your privacy, and I further hope that my father did not inflict serious pain."

The young man seemed so sincerely concerned that John straightened up on the bench.

"No, no, I assure you," John said in response to his thoughtful inquiry. "Oh, it still throbs now and then, to be sure, but–"

"I am sorry," the young man said.

A damnably awkward moment, John brooded, and wondered why of all the churchyards in England did young Stanhope have to wander into this one. Had the young man been sent in pursuit of him? Or was this strictly a highly embarrassing chance encounter?

When the young man continued to stand there staring at John with an unsettling intensity, John grew weary of the encounter. "Now if you will excuse me," he muttered, searching for another way out of the churchyard.

"I beg your pardon, sir, only a moment of your time if you will."

There was something civil in the young man's tone, unlike his father's. Clearly this was Mary's son.

"Of course," John called back, unable to find anything about the lad that was disagreeable, except, of course, the sadness in his eyes.

"My sister, sir," the young man began, moving to the cause of his pain with admirable courage. "Is she– What I mean to ask you, you said she was– Now I don't know whether to believe you or not. My father says no, says that this is only a cruel trick you are playing on us."

John groaned. Dear God, did Burke Stanhope really think he was capable of such cruelty? He turned and faced the young man directly.

"I want you to listen carefully. Eve died on June 16 of several malignancies which had grown unchecked in her abdomen and which the attending physician claimed had spread to other parts of her body. I'm . . . we're all so sorry."

David stood slowly as though he were an old man. He walked several paces away toward the churchyard wall, his head bowed.

John knew the boy was weeping and he ached to offer comfort, but he hadn't the slightest idea how to do it.

In the interim the traffic noise from the street beyond seemed to soften, as though out of respect for human loss.

Finally David turned back. "My parents don't believe you," he said as though merely to inform John of a tragic problem.

"I know," John said. "Their distrust is not without foundation," he confessed further, and immediately saw the grief on David's face replaced by something else.

"Damn," he said between clenched teeth. Anger had quickly replaced his grief. "Damn you all," David repeated. "How long do you plan to nurse this mutual hate and distrust? How long has it gone on now? A quarter of a century? What are you going to do? Try for a half a century?"

"David, please–"

"If you will excuse me, sir," David said now, his anger diminishing, replaced by what appeared to be soul-deep grief. "I must mourn in private for Eve. I loved her so." His voice broke, and John felt as though the lad were stretching him on the rack. He had never experienced such anguish, such remorse. If only he could think of something to say that would alter the pain in the boy's eyes. But he couldn't.

"Then I must return to the hotel and try to convince my parents that you spoke the truth. I'm not certain they will believe me."

"David, please–"

"Then it would be my guess that Mama will want to travel to Eden Castle to say goodbye to Eve and to fetch her grandson."

"David, please, stay, let me–"

"I can't, sir, I'm not feeling very manly at this moment. I need privacy. If you will excuse me–"

With that he was gone back down the path that led to the side door of the small Anglican church, where he disappeared inside the cool darkness.

John stared after him. Should he follow? No.

Fetch her grandson.

Those three words clung to the rim of his consciousness long after everything else slid off. Surely Mary wouldn't be so foolish as to pull a stunt such as that. Alexander belonged here in England. What earthly good could be accomplished by uprooting him from his natural home?

No, if Mary thought that she was going to get Alexander, just let her try. John would give her a fight she had not expected.

Slowly he left the churchyard, keeping a close eye on the side door. Birds were commencing an afternoon chorale in the treetops, and the clatter of horses' hooves on the cobbles of the street increased.

Then he heard it again, that most miraculous of sounds, the incredibly beautiful whir of a motorcar signaling the most advanced technology man was capable of creating.

Through the churchyard gate John hurried after the vehicle, mesmerized by the mechanical beauty.

At the end of the street, John saw the driver signal for a left turn and wait patiently for a slow-moving carriage to clear his side of the intersection.

Then John caught up and saw the car head toward the end of the block, toward a showroom:

The Lacree Motor Car Company, Ltd.
107 Palmerston Street

He came to a halt in front of the showroom, where he saw the most beautiful sight in the world, an immense motorcar, silver gray in color, with propped glass windshield, four silver spoked tires and a running board broad enough to support half a dozen men.

It was the future and it was so beautiful.

Inside the plate glass he saw the salesman, hands relaxed behind his back. He was smiling at John, the devil's own smile.

Why not?

He felt better than he'd felt for hours. David Stanhope's grief, as well as that of Burke and Mary, was behind him now. Man was not designed by nature to mope and grieve forever. It was now time to look ahead. He had two grandsons to raise and how they would love hurtling across the moors in that silver beauty.

"Sir? Won't you come in? Take a closer look if you will. It is our finest, our pride."

And he did.

London
June 23, 1897

Stephen stepped out of Euston Station about noon and signaled a cab while offering up the same silent prayer that he had prayed repeatedly since he had left Eden Castle yesterday: "Pray God that Father had not yet reached the Kenilworth. Pray God that Burke and Mary still did not know of Eve's–"

When would he be able to think it, let alone say it? As he climbed into the cab and gave the driver his destination, he tried to organize both himself and his thoughts. Such a mad dash. At Exeter he had called briefly on Lucy and Mason, only to learn that John had abandoned the large carriage in Greenfield's barn and had proceeded to London on horseback. Good. Undoubtedly his horse had given out and perhaps his father was at this moment bedded down in some comfortable country inn between London and Salisbury.

Lucy, very pregnant, had told him that John had seemed reluctant to make this journey. Another good sign. His father seldom did anything he didn't want to do.

The cab veered sharply to the left to accommodate a large motorcar which was hurtling directly down the center of the street.

"Damn fool," the driver shouted after the motor, and Stephen agreed, distracted by the inevitable collisions between the past and the present.

But the distraction was short-lived as he tried to think of the precise words he would speak to Burke and Mary, and for the duration of the ride to the Kenilworth he tried to imagine how it would go.

As he saw the turrets of the Kenilworth come into view, he realized bleakly that he still had no clear thought in his head and was now secretly praying that his father *had* arrived there first.

Suddenly he leaned forward and instructed the cabbie to let him out.

As Stephen dug through his pockets for the proper coin, he kept a close eye on the front of the hotel. He would much prefer to see them first than to be seen.

"Thank you, sir," the cabbie called down.

Stephen acknowledged the man, all the while keeping a close watch on the front of the crowded Kenilworth. Dozens of people were seated about in the large open windows taking tea. Others formed a constant stream into and out of the hotel.

He held his position on the far curb for a few moments, trying to make out individual faces. Were the Stanhopes still here? Or had his father–

"Stephen."

He looked up and saw a young man near the front entrance waving at him.

Stephen squinted forward, some element of recognition dawning, reminding him of Stanhope Hall, early morning swims in the ice pond, endless horseback rides through hot humid countrysides and a bright young lad who dogged his steps and begged him for tales of adventure.

"David," he called back, waving, amazed at how good it was to see him, this face from a distant and happier past, this brother-in-law.

They met at the bottom of the steps, and Stephen was amazed at the physical changes that had taken place. David was a very tall and handsome young man, who had Eve's eyes and ready smile.

"David," Stephen repeated at the end of the handshake and saw a telltale redness about David's eyes and knew that his father had been here and knew further that David knew. Without warning, the handshake no longer seemed adequate to express his feelings, and he embraced David and felt the young man clinging as though for life while all around them swirled the comings and goings of others, unaware.

"Stephen, it's good to see you," David murmured at the end of the embrace.

Stephen took David by the arm and led him up the steps through the congestion until they reached a far corner of the lobby.

"It *is* true, isn't it?" David asked softly, tears in his eyes. Before Stephen could reply, David answered his own question. "Of course it's true. I encountered your father just down the street in a small churchyard. He was quite bruised from my father's assault–"

Stephen looked up, horrified.

"Dear God," Stephen muttered. "Mary—where is your mother?" he asked suddenly.

"Upstairs in her room. She collapsed yesterday, and while the doctor says there is nothing wrong, she refuses to eat or drink and just lies there."

"And your father?"

"Not much better. I think he had clung to the hope that your father was lying. But when I returned from the churchyard and told him it was the truth, he became withdrawn. He stands by the window all day, looking down on the rooftops. He says nothing."

Stephen listened to the grim account and knew he had to go up to them immediately. "David, will you take me to your mother and father? I have come to take you all back to Eden Castle. My aunt and uncle are waiting eagerly for your arrival. And Alexander is waiting as well, our son, your nephew."

David listened carefully, softening at the mention of Alexander. "Perhaps you can help them," he murmured and led the way around the palms and across the central lobby, heading toward the grand staircase.

Stephen followed close behind, trying to organize his thoughts, trying to get a firm hold on his emotions, and long before he was ready for it, David stopped halfway down a corridor before a closed door.

"Here it is," he said and stood back.

"Are you coming?" Stephen asked.

At first David didn't respond. Then, "I'll wait out here. It might be for the best. They still tend to behave as parents when I am about."

As he turned and walked slowly away, Stephen started to protest, then changed his mind. How wise David was for someone his age.

He waited a moment longer, bowed his head in brief but heartfelt prayer for God to be with him, to grant him strength for this most difficult moment. Then he lifted his head, drew a deep breath, knocked but once, and pushed open the door.

Mary could not keep her mind off memories of Eve. Lying there in the hotel bed, she purposefully inflicted upon herself an entire progression of Eve's young life from the moment of her birth. She saw her in every posture, at every angle, saw her laughing, weeping, singing, speaking, smiling, but could not, would not and did not see her dead.

She heard the soft knock on the door and averted her face. From her bed she saw Burke turn back from his constant and unspeaking vigil at the window.

All she heard was his soft call of "Stephen." As Burke shook his hand, Mary quickly sat up and drew on her dressing gown.

"Stephen," she whispered and went to greet him and knew by the way he held her, by the way he spoke her name, that Eve was dead. Such a gentle transmission of such a harsh message.

"Mary," he soothed and walked with her back to the bed.

For several moments no one spoke. Then Mary uttered the first thought that entered her mind. "John was here."

"I was afraid–"

Burke turned back from the window. "We were expecting you."

"Where is my father now?"

"Who gives a damn," Burke muttered. "Stephen, you should have come."

"I know, and I apologize."

"Your apologies are not necessary, Stephen," Mary added kindly. "Please tell us everything. Speak carefully so that we might try to understand. It is so important."

She saw Stephen straighten in his chair, saw him sit erect and heard the first words, terrible words. "Eve had been ill for some time . . ."

Throughout the narrative Mary listened carefully without interruption. About a quarter of an hour later, it was over.

"I . . . was with her at the end," Stephen said, his voice low, his head down. "She spoke of both of you. She said–" His voice broke. Mary viewed him through a blur.

Stephen leaned forward in the chair, his face buried in his hands. At the window Burke turned away, maneuvered himself into a position where he was almost out of sight between the velvet drapes.

Only Mary wept openly, tears running down her face. Eve was dead.

The three words resounded in merciless repetition throughout her head and heart.

She lost track of time. At some point she laid back against her pillow and closed her eyes and was amazed to feel a kind of peace, an honest conclusion. The rich blessing that had been Eve Stanhope had graced their lives. Mary had had the pleasure of giving birth to her, of holding her as an infant and watching her develop into a child. Her greatest pleasure had been watching that child evolve into a dazzling and gifted young woman.

Slowly Mary sat up and glanced toward Stephen who stared back at her, hollow-eyed, looking like an old man.

She wiped away the last of her tears and beckoned for him to come and sit on the edge of the bed. At the same time, she saw Burke at the window wiping his face with a handkerchief, then wiping again as though the tears could not be staunched.

"Burke, will you join us?" she invited and held out her hand to him and was so pleased when he came forward and took it. "We three loved Eve more than anyone else. She will never be truly gone. We know that. She lives in our hearts and our memories and will do so forever. And more important she lives in her son."

She paused, amazed at her sense of growing strength. Someone had His hand on her. Of that she was certain, for she had moved from mindless, hopeless grief to a sense of steadfast love and purpose within a very short time.

"Stephen, may we journey out to Eden Castle? It is most important that we do so."

"Of course."

"When?"

"Tonight. This afternoon. There is a four o'clock train. If we hurry, we can make it."

"Good. Burke, are you–"

"I agree. We must go to Eden for Alexander's sake."

"Give me one hour, Stephen," she said, and lightly kissed him.

Burke stepped away. "I will see to the hotel clerk, tell him that we will be leaving. We will store our trunks here and only take portmanteaus."

Then they were gone, plans under way, a journey back to Eden Castle, to that place of her growing-up, which once she had pledged never to lay eyes on again for as long as she lived. She'd had no idea that while it was the place of her birth, it would also be the place of her daughter's death.

None of that, she scolded herself. Her grandson was waiting, little Alexander. How he would love America and Stanhope Hall! And what fun it would be having a baby in the house again.

That was better. Focus on life, not death. On that note of conviction, she left her bed and hurried into the dressing room, ready to do whatever was necessary to stake all claims to her grandson, even if it meant going back to Eden Castle.

London
June 23, 1897

It was the horn that fascinated John. It sounded exactly like an angry goose, and he applied it frequently at every intersection as he wheeled his way through London's narrow streets in his brand-new silver motorcar, a more advanced model of technology the world had yet to see according to the manager, a very knowledgeable man who had instructed John in the skill of driving, and now, a scant two hours later, John was handling the motorcar as though he had been born to it.

By God, it was just the finest motorcar in the whole world and it handled like a charm, the sleek, slim steering wheel turning first one way and then the other at John's gentlest prodding.

The black leather top was folded back like an accordion against the dickey, the better to see and be seen.

Now seated in the driver's seat, one arm resting lightly at just a certain cavalier angle, the other effortlessly holding the wheel steady, John moved down toward Buckingham Palace with all of the ease and grace and speed of a dolphin cutting through calm water. The softest of June breezes caressed his face, blowing away all cares, all memories of dead young women and angry, grief-stricken parents, cleansing his head and heart of all worries.

Susan would be proud of him. He had not returned the fisticuffs, had instead picked himself up in considerable embarrassment from the floor of the Kenilworth lobby and had walked away without a response of any kind.

Now his mind began to cast about for a specific destination. Something local, an acquaintance whom he could duly impress, someone he could take for a ride, someone who—

The name approached very stealthily at first. Aslam. John had treated him badly during the Midsummer fete, leaving him entirely to young Charlotte and her empty-headed prattle.

John drew a deep breath and relaxed against the seat while waiting for a bus to clear the road, waiting for a line of carriages to clear it as well, and during this brief interim he made a decision.

Knightsbridge. Belgravia. The neighborhood of Aslam's grand mansion not far from here. He felt certain that Aslam would be impressed with his new motorcar; also, it would give John a chance to apologize for his behavior at the Midsummer fete. Another bridge mended.

How proud Susan would be of him when he returned to Eden, how pleased with his earnest efforts to develop a "forgiving heart."

Having decided upon a destination and grateful that he had postponed the long trip out to Eden Castle, he applied his foot firmly to the pedal, felt the shiny gray wonder shoot out ahead of all other traffic, leaving horses to complain on both sides, their riders to complain as well.

No matter. He smiled waving a hand backward in friendly apology. One day soon, everyone would be driving one of these miracles, all horses put out to pasture where they belonged, the roads filled with drivers of unfailing courtesy and charm, speed and destination a certitude.

What a marvelous day that would be.

London
June 23, 1897

Seated in the window of his Grand Drawing Room, listening closely as Charlotte masterfully played a Chopin étude, Aslam knew beyond a shadow of a doubt that he had never in his entire life been as happy as he had been these last few months.

In the beginning, Charlotte had come down once a week, but lately she had spent the entire month with her cousin Alice, who always sent a message to Aslam, informing him that if he desired Charlotte's company, he could call for her at such-and-such a time.

Now he watched closely, lovingly, as her slim white neck bent in time with her music, her graceful hands moving across the keys like white birds in flight.

Suddenly, outside his window he heard the disagreeable rumble of one of the newfangled motorcars. How he loathed them, all glitter, polish, speed and noxious fumes, so foreign to his past and so threatening to the peace of his present.

Then the noise fell silent, and the air was filled only with the closing strains of Chopin. Charlotte's hands lifted a final time and settled on the closing notes like a benediction.

Silently Aslam offered up a prayer of thanksgiving for this perfect marriage of beauty and grace.

"Did you like it?" she asked shyly.

"My dear Charlotte," he said. "You play as though you had studied with Chopin himself. I had no idea. You never told me."

At last she looked at him, and though he had been with her a portion of every day for the last two months, he never failed to be surprised by her beauty.

"Thank you, Aslam," she replied softly, and he saw the palest blush creep up the side of her face and join the color in her cheeks. He was on the verge of asking her to play again when he heard the front bell ring, a very distant ring but one that indicated a damnable interruption.

No matter. He had given the new butler strict instructions that he was not to be interrupted. The new man, a staunch old professional named Forbes, whom Aslam had pirated away from Lord Chesterfield, would follow his instructions to the letter.

Apparently the intensity of his thoughts registered on his face, for Charlotte looked up, concerned. "Are you alright, Aslam?" she asked. "You look so–"

"I'm fine. Please play another selection, would you? Another Chopin preferably."

Clearly pleased, she bestowed upon him a dazzling smile, then commenced playing Chopin's "Fantaisie-Impromptu," the opening section crisp and melodious, and ultimately leading to the mournful and romantic central melody.

He thought he heard voices outside in the hall, but quickly dismissed them in favor of the increasing beauty before him. Despite the idyllic nature of time and setting, he was still bothered by so many unanswered questions.

How did she view him? As an old friend of her uncle's? He was twice her age and twice that in life experience. And yet she did not seem young in his presence. She seemed quite mature and worldly, aware of all the nuances of conversation, and she was conversant in all art forms, from music to theater, to literature. She had been splendidly schooled and polished and educated by someone. Still, did she even dream of how much he loved her, how much he looked forward to being in her presence, how much he dreaded the time when he was away from her, how deeply indebted he was to Alice for accommodating him in this manner and making it possible for them to–

There it was again, a loud, demanding, offensive voice splintering Chopin's music, and there was a second voice equally insistent.

He saw Charlotte look up from her music and glance toward the door. Then he saw apprehension on her face.

Just then the door to the Grand Drawing Room burst open and a man, quite disheveled appearing, his clothes mussed and soiled, his hair in need of grooming entered the room backwards, trying to fend off Forbes, who was now approaching him with a raised walking stick, obviously an impromptu weapon which he had grabbed from the front hall.

"Forbes, what is–"

But then the man turned and faced Aslam, and he saw a painfully familiar face, a face he had seen first as a boy of seven in India, a rescuer's face then, later a father's face, a brother's face, then a friend's face, now an enemy's face.

What a progression of relationships. And what was this new one to be? The question was unanswerable. Still Aslam went forward, quieting his fear, puzzled by the man's ungodly appearance, extending his hand and calling out as warmly as possible, "John–what a surprise. John Murrey Eden."

Charlotte held her position at the keyboard, with her head down. She had caught only a fleeting glimpse of the intruder and that was enough.

She held still, her back to the door, and heard Aslam greet John, a strained, surprised greeting, for she was certain that Aslam was as shocked as she was.

"What am I doing here?" she now heard John repeat in high good humor. "I'm visiting an old friend, a very dear and sorely missed friend. That's what I'm doing."

"It's alright, Forbes," Aslam said further.

"I am sorry, sir. I tried to–"

"I know. I said it's alright."

Charlotte heard John laugh.

"Quite a watchdog you have there, Aslam, in that old man. Believe me, I had to talk hard and fast just to–"

Abruptly he broke off. Charlotte could sense a change in focus, an awkward silence.

"I am so sorry, Aslam," John murmured. "I had no idea you were entertaining."

Charlotte held her breath. Clearly he had not recognized her yet. With her face averted all he could see was her back. Was there a chance? Perhaps Aslam would usher him out before–

"I *am* sorry. I would offer to come back, but I'm on my way to Eden, and I had the strongest sort of compulsion to pay you a visit."

"I am deeply honored."

"No honor about it. Would it be possible to ask the lady to depart and grant us an hour or so alone?"

"No, I could not do that, John."

"Of course," John said at last, "I fully understand. After all I did stop by unannounced."

"Quite."

"I say, Aslam, might I have the honor of being introduced to your–"

Slowly Charlotte shifted on the hard bench. Then to her shock she heard Aslam say, "Of course, John, though I assure you the pleasure will be all mine. I suspect you're well acquainted with the lady, for she–"

Why Aslam ceased speaking, Charlotte could not imagine, except perhaps at last he had come to his senses and realized that to reveal Charlotte's presence in his house would be madness.

As he came around to the side of the pianoforte, she looked up. Nightmare confirmed. It was John Murrey Eden glaring down on her, making no attempt for civility's sake to disguise the volcano that was threatening to erupt inside him.

"As I'm sure you know," Aslam said, in a voice as pleasant and civil as though he were dealing with a paragon of reason, "we met last summer at your splendid house party. She is dear to me beyond my ability to speak of it. Since she has been in London, visiting her cousin Alice, we have spent many happy hours together."

Then all at once Aslam's voice fell silent, and Charlotte looked up directly into John's face.

When for several minutes he still refused to speak, she started up from the piano bench. "Uncle John, I–"

Slowly he started to shake his head, the fury in his face replaced by an expression of stunned bewilderment. "I can't– I don't believe– Have both of you lost your– Goddamn you both!"

He was moving now in small erratic circles, once striding to the end of the pianoforte and looking back at her as though he could scarcely stand the sight of her.

"Uncle John–"

"Do not speak," he shouted and raised his arm, pointing it directly at her. "Do you have any conception, any ability in that feather-headed schoolgirl brain of yours to know precisely what it is that you have done, are doing?"

"John, please, there is no–"

As Aslam tried to intervene, John turned on him with only a portion of the fury he was aiming at her. "You stay out of this. I shall tend to you later."

Surprisingly Aslam retreated and stood a distance away, his arms crossed in quiet indulgence of this raving, ranting man at the pianoforte.

"I cannot believe it," John repeated over and over again in maniacal repetition, pacing faster now. "I cannot believe that you would do this to me, to the family." To Aslam, he shouted, "I cannot believe that you would encourage it. I swear to God, I thought you had more sense. What a grand display of disloyalty and ingratitude on the part of both of you."

As assault followed assault, as his mood grew uglier, more abusive, Charlotte closed her eyes and decided to wait out the storm and recalled the many times at Eden when she'd heard the same tone, the same bullying tactics.

Now, as his pacing began to range far and wide throughout the drawing room, Charlotte glanced once again at Aslam, who still was maintaining his position at the windows, a slightly bemused stance, or so it seemed to her, his arms crossed as he watched John, almost as an indulgent father watches a spoiled child.

Then Charlotte stood and confronted him with what she felt was a most reasonable request. "May I speak?"

"I can't imagine what on earth you would have to say," he sneered. "I'm quite certain that your mother and father will give you ample opportunity to speak in your defense when we return to Eden."

Surprised, Charlotte looked up, "But I am not returning to Eden."

For several moments these simple words rested on the already charged air like undetonated explosives.

"Did you hear me, Uncle John? I will not be returning to Eden for some time. I'm quite enjoying myself in London. Alice and Christabel are delightful roommates, and Aslam has been ever so thoughtful in taking me to concerts and lectures and the theater. I never tire of the theater. We are going tonight, *As You Like It* at the Drury Lane, isn't that right, Aslam?"

"Indeed. I probably could obtain a ticket for you as well, John, if you care to stay over."

She smiled at his cordial invitation and at last understood his ploy. He was trying to unsettle John with thoughtfulness.

So busy was she in her admiration of Aslam that she did not see John move close, too close, did not at first see him reach out and grab her shoulder and saw too late as he spun her about free of the piano bench. He delivered a stinging slap to her face, a blow of such strength that it caused her to fall with a single outcry.

Throughout her painful incapacity, she heard a scuffle, heard men breathing with difficulty, heard John utter a curse, heard nothing else until she looked up and saw Aslam leaning with all his weight against John, whom he had pinned against the side of the pianoforte. Aslam's hands were about his throat, strangely quiet hands that quivered now and then from applying deadly force. John appeared helpless, his hands flailing uselessly against the assault. At last Charlotte fully realized what was happening and came struggling up out of her pain and shock with one shrill cry, "No, Aslam, please, let him go!"

She saw Aslam look toward her, an expression of sadness in his eyes, and finally, almost reluctantly, he released John, who slumped immediately to his knees, gasping for breath, his shoulders heaving, his head limp.

Weak and weeping, Charlotte covered her face with her hands, wiped blood from the corner of her mouth and heard Aslam's voice as she had never heard it before, low, threatening. "Get out of here and never return. And if you ever so much as contemplate striking Charlotte Eden again, I will finish what I should have finished a minute ago. Do you understand me?"

For several moments Aslam continued to stand over him, his hands ready at his sides. Then slowly he backed away and went instantly to Charlotte. Gently he extended his hand, and she took it, looked into his eyes and, to her amazement, saw tears.

"My dearest," he whispered, and lightly touched her cheek and walked with her to the bell cord. He seated her on a near chair, pulled the cord and met Forbes at the door.

Charlotte could not hear what was said, but a few moments later two large stewards came into the drawing room. Effortlessly they lifted John to his feet and gave him an unceremonious escort out of the room.

After the first few steps John walked on his own, though one hand continuously massaged his throat while the other tried to straighten his apparel. He looked neither to the right nor to the left as he departed. Charlotte almost felt sorry for him and wondered if he had ever suffered such a humiliation in his life.

As the door closed behind them, Aslam bent over and whispered a command, "Wait right here. Do not follow. I beg you."

She shuddered and rested her head against the back of the chair while trying to conceive of the story that John Murrey Eden would take back with him to Eden Castle. She would have to speak with Alice, tell her exactly what had happened, then seek and follow her advice on the matter.

Alice was the only one of the cousins to whom everyone else seemed to listen. She had such good sense and would know exactly what to do.

And yet–and Charlotte frowned upward at the high paneled ceiling. What, in the name of God, had she done to warrant explanation and apology?

Nothing. She had done exactly nothing. True, she had spent hours in Aslam's presence, had looked forward to every new meeting and every appointment and had seen him at least once every day that she had spent in London.

Charlotte quickly shut her eyes in an attempt to shut out the truth as she knew it, for while Aslam had never touched her in anything but respect and honor, there had been times when she literally had ached for his closeness, had prayed that he take her in his arms.

Now she moved to the window and looked out on a bizarre sight, John, half in, half out of a huge gray motorcar, one arm resting on the side of the car while Aslam stood quite close, talking earnestly.

Apparently the battle was still raging, and suddenly she felt her knees grow weak, a delayed reaction to John's assault on her. She heard the door of the motorcar slam and saw Aslam just barely step back as the enormous machine rumbled forward.

Then her eyes lovingly returned to Aslam, who turned about and stared straight ahead at the facade of his elegant mansion. From where she stood, he looked sad and disappointed. Then he was walking slowly toward the door, and she heard voices coming from the front reception hall, Forbes again trying to explain his lapse in obedience and Aslam's voice continuously soothing, informing the old man that the interruption could not have been avoided.

The door opened. He was there.

"Are you well?" he asked.

"No."

A new look of alarm clouded his face. "Did he– Are you injured?"

"No," she replied.

For a moment he looked puzzled. Then, at last, he smiled, a tender expression of understanding. As he started toward her, she saw a new intensity in his eyes.

"When I saw him strike you–" Aslam murmured.

"Don't," she whispered.

"If he had harmed you–"

"He didn't."

"I would have killed him."

"I know, then I, too, would have had to commit a murder."

He looked puzzled.

"Because I could not have endured this world without you."

He drew her forward, a gentle gesture, his arms about her, holding her close, still more affection than passion, yet the closeness was stimulating, and as she lifted her face, she felt his embrace growing stronger, one hand flattened against her back, the other caressing her neck and shoulders. When at last their lips met, she closed her eyes and relaxed into his arms and felt a hunger such as she had never felt before.

As the kiss persisted, she felt the warmth of his tongue, clearly his needs were keeping pace with hers and a few moments later she heard him whisper, "Will you come and be with me?"

She strained upward as his lips moved down her throat to her breasts.

"We will seal our fate," he added in a kind of beloved warning.

"No," she whispered, beginning to resent the confinement of clothes and corsets. "We will create a new beginning, a new life. The other one is over. For both of us."

Without warning he lifted her into his arms and carried her out of the drawing room, out into the foyer and up the staircase, where they encountered only one parlormaid, who discreetly turned her face to the wall as they passed.

Inside his bedchamber, he put her down, and standing less than three feet from each other, they removed the obstacles of garments, came together in simplicity and passion. The only words spoken were Aslam's pledge, "I will love you beyond the grave."

At the exact moment of union Charlotte gasped, smiled and issued up a brief prayer of thanksgiving to John Murrey Eden, for it had been his blow to the side of her face that had destroyed their last lines of defense and brought them together in this moment of rapture.

She would have to thank him one day.

Eden Castle
June 25, 1897

"A baptism by fire," Frederick had called it.

"A descent into hell," Marjorie called it and tried to sit erect, the better to address herself to the awful scene going on before her, Mary Stanhope, red-eyed and still weeping, seated to her right, Burke Stanhope brooding before a dead fire, Frederick and Stephen smiling down on their two sons, who were romping the length of a large Oriental rug which had been spread so that the Stanhopes could watch their grandson, though in truth neither seemed to be doing much watching. Their son, David, had gone with them to visit Eve's grave, and the last Marjorie had seen of him, he was sitting on a bench overlooking the channel, clearly weeping.

"Oh, look!" Mrs. Godwin exclaimed now, trying to focus Mary's attention on the future. "Look at young Alexander. He's ever so strong, but then, of course, both of them are."

Marjorie smiled and saw the two little boys stumbling over each other, both just beginning to walk. At the exact center of the rug sat blond Rolf, age three and a half, busily engaged with the boys in a set of building blocks.

Again Marjorie tried to think of something appropriate and soothing to say to Mary and could think of nothing. The sight of Eve's grave had been her undoing. They had arrived late the night before from London, where apparently things had gone badly for them in their meeting with John Murrey Eden, who still had not arrived.

Also among the missing were Susan and Eleanor. A few days ago they had learned of Lucy's pregnancy. An excited messenger had come early yesterday morning from Greenfield School in Exeter, bringing a note from Mason Frye stating that Lucy had gone into labor.

Immediately Susan had fetched her bag and Eleanor had packed a small portmanteau, and they had left within an hour of the messenger's arrival, claiming that they would return as soon as possible, that Marjorie was now to act in the capacity of mistress and hostess of Eden Castle and try her best to explain to the Stanhopes the nature and cause of their absence.

This she had tried to do, though she was positive that she had failed miserably.

Suddenly young Alex squealed, a high-pitched siren of pure delight. Both boys were at the age when they were discovering the miracles of self, including a voice box and the ability to make wild and unpredictable noises.

The unexpected sound clearly startled Mary, who looked up, then started to weep again as though the sight and sound of her grandson had only added to her grief.

Stephen came forward and gently placed his arm about Mary's shoulder. "Would you rather go to your rooms?"

"No, I'm fine," the still-weeping woman claimed. "You said something about the doctor's wife, the one who befriended Eve? Might I–"

"Of course, I'll see if I can–"

"She's in her chambers, sir," Mrs. Godwin contributed.

There was a moment of indecision, and finally Mary shook her head and tried to wipe her eyes. "Later," she murmured, "perhaps later."

At that Marjorie saw Mr. Stanhope turn from his vigil at the dead fire. There was a look of impatience about him, as though he felt it was past time for leaving.

"Mary, we must go," Mr. Stanhope said, walking directly to his wife's side. "We need to be on our way home. There is nothing for us here. There is nothing more we can do. I pray, let us depart before–"

He broke off, though all present knew full well what he was about to say–"before John Murrey Eden returned"–and sadly enough no one objected to this hasty departure. It was as though none of them could rise up out of their various states of grief until these two, who had suffered and lost the most, had departed.

Burke Stanhope turned to Mrs. Godwin with a direct order. "Prepare Alexander for travel, please. He will need warm garments for the voyage. No need to pack everything. We will supply him with a new wardrobe when we reach America. Please see to it."

Marjorie started slowly up out of her chair. Stephen turned quickly and faced Burke Stanhope. Poor Mrs. Godwin's face went pale.

"No," Stephen said gently though firmly, canceling the command that had been issued only moments before.

"What do you mean, no?" Stanhope demanded, shocked. "I thought that was what we had journeyed out to this godforsaken place for."

"You came to see Eve's grave."

"And to fetch our grandson."

"No," Stephen repeated, new pain breaking on his face, clearly aware of the risks of what he was doing. "I can't come with you now," he said patiently, "and I will not allow my son to go without me."

"He is Eve's son too," Burke Stanhope said angrily.

"I know, and I will be grateful for that fact the rest of my life."

"Then come with us," Burke Stanhope urged. "You don't belong here. This is a rotting and decaying society. I don't want my grandson–"

"We both will come in time, I promise you," Stephen pledged.

"Why not now?"

"I must wait."

"Why?"

"My father is missing. And Alex is too young."

"You may be right."

At some point during this unhappy exchange, Mary had started to weep again.

Then they heard a soft voice, saw Alex toddling toward his father's leg, saw the look of alarm on his face, for clearly the voices raised in anger had disturbed him.

Stephen scooped him up and the child buried his face in his father's shoulder, one plump pink arm wrapped tightly about his neck.

Marjorie took a close look at Stephen's face and felt that emotionally the man was being torn in half.

"Mr. Stanhope," Marjorie began, trying valiantly to be of service to someone. "Please don't leave so hastily. I promised both Lady Eleanor and Susan I would keep you here so that they might greet you and make you feel welcome."

For a moment he appeared to study Marjorie as though not completely certain who she was to him or to this family.

"Madame, I would remain under this roof for only one reason, and that would be, if at the end of my stay, I might be assured of leaving with my grandson. I will not stay for any other reason."

He turned back to Stephen, who still was holding Alex. "For the last time, Stephen, will you and the boy come with us? We plan to sail at week's end. As you know a large cotton plantation does not run itself. I have been gone long enough, and Mary needs to be at home. So will you come? For the sake of Eve?"

Stephen bowed his head into his son's soft curly hair. He walked a few steps away. At that moment Christopher spied them both and let out a hearty squeal of recognition, toddled over as fast as his chubby legs would allow and raised both arms high in the air, clearly wanting to fill Stephen's other arm.

Stephen shifted Alex's weight as Chris scrambled up into his arms, two little boys, both looking extremely pleased with themselves, grinning with unfailing charm out over the entire company, completely impervious to the tragedy of the occasion and the increasing tensions.

"I cannot leave now, Burke," Stephen said. "Please understand."

"I understand nothing," the man replied coldly and waved forward a waiting steward near the staircase. "Fetch our luggage," he commanded, "and send someone out to the headlands for my son."

The man started off at a good pace, and Stephen, looking quite lost, continued to hold the two little boys.

He turned to Mary who had grown silent during the decision-making ordeal. "Please try to understand," he begged her. "I cannot–"

"I know, Stephen," she said with surprising sweetness and understanding. "I knew you couldn't. But you must promise."

"Anything, Mary."

"You must let us have Alex for at least a small portion of the time. Our only link to our daughter, buried in that small grave out there, is through that child. You will not deny us that, will you?"

"No, Mary, I wouldn't, and you have my word that in a short time, Alex and I both will come to you."

Now two stewards filed down the stairs carrying three portmanteaus and a hatbox. Stephen looked up. "Mary, please don't go so soon."

"We must."

"Why?"

"It is far too painful. For all of us. I'm sure you understand."

Marjorie came forward and took Chris from Stephen, thus leaving the focus on Alex, who now stood somewhat shyly at Mary's knee while Mary caressed the side of his face, smoothed back his curly hair and at last enclosed his hand in hers.

"Can you say 'Grandmama'?" she smiled. "No, of course not. Such a big word for such a little boy. But I am your grandmama and promise you will remember me and come and see me very soon. I'll show you all the things your mother loved to do, oh, so many things, and I'm sure–"

Alex moved yet closer and sweetly lifted his arms to Mary, clearly indicating he wanted her to hold him. With remarkable speed, Mary drew him close, wrapped her arms about him and hid her face in his hair.

From the Great Hall doors, Burke Stanhope issued a stern command. "Come, Mary, we must make the evening train back to London. No more time."

In a crushing embrace Stephen kissed Mary goodbye and walked with her to the door. Marjorie and Frederick trailed behind, not quite sure how insistent they should be on formal farewells.

There was something Marjorie wanted to say. "Mary, I am so sorry for Eve's passing. She was the most loving person I have ever known, and she occupies a permanent part of my heart. I will never forget her."

"Thank you. I can't tell you how much that means to me."

"Please come back to Eden under happier circumstances."

Mary nodded, although Marjorie saw the truth in those eyes. She would never again set foot on Eden soil. She was in a sense bidding both her daughter and her childhood home goodbye forever.

The time for departure had come. As the carriage arrived, Marjorie saw Frederick and Stephen shaking hands with David. She saw Stephen extend a hand to Burke, who took it; then, all at once, the emotions of the two men demanded more than a handshake, and there was one quick embrace.

Then all were aboard, Mary peering out of the window, waving up toward the top of the Great Hall steps. Marjorie looked back to see Mrs. Godwin holding Alex, instructing him to wave, and it was this important farewell to which Mary was responding.

All watched the carriage on its slow turn around the inner courtyard and across the gatehouse grate as the guardsmen on duty stood at attention.

Then they were gone, the carriage conveying its unhappy cargo back to London, then to America, where, pray God, the pain of grief would be gradually replaced by gratitude for God's brief gift of Eve Stanhope.

This was Marjorie's heartfelt prayer. As the rattle of the carriage was swallowed up in the moors, she turned back to the Great Hall steps and whispered aloud, "Amen."

Greenfield School
June 28, 1897

Though Lucy's labor had been long, the birth itself had been relatively easy, and now Susan lifted the baby girl dripping from her first bath, quickly wrapped her in swaddling and handed her to her father, who looked as if she had just handed him a creature from a distant planet.

He approached Lucy's bed, smiling, and said, "You take her. I have had absolutely no practice."

"Neither have I, my dearest. Come and we will learn together."

Eleanor, the proud grandma, had left the room at the height of Lucy's labor, but had returned at the sound of the baby's first cry and was now trying to appear efficient.

"How beautiful she is," Eleanor murmured. "I wish that your father–"

As the baby's cries increased, Susan instructed, "Give her your breast, Lucy, at an angle, that's right. Introduce the nipple. She'll know what to do after that."

She did, and within the instant, the room was filled with the contented sounds of the baby suckling. Lucy relaxed into the pillow and smiled up at all. Susan thought her quite beautiful, this plain woman. Motherhood was capable of doing that.

Another baby. Clearly Eden Castle was doing its part in producing the next generation for England. She hoped that the British Empire appreciated all these new Edens, for they assured the world a dazzling future.

She raised up from fetching the last soiled towel and looked toward the bed at a memorable tableau. All three, Lucy, Mason and Eleanor, beaming like Cheshire cats while the contented baby suckled.

"Have you thought of a name?" Susan called out.

Without hesitation, Lucy replied, "Anne Eleanor Frye. Anne for Mason's mother, who died when he was only three, and for you, of course, Mama."

Eleanor started to sniffle, as did Mason, for whom the name in honor of his mother was clearly a surprise.

For several moments all seemed more than content to stare down on the new Anne, quite delicate-appearing compared to the boisterous boys Susan had left behind at Eden. Alex and Chris were almost a year and a half now, both quite pudgy and both very noisy.

Remembering Eden, Susan interrupted the idyllic mood. "I really think that one of us should be getting back, Eleanor. I will go ahead, and you can stay here for as long as you wish. John–"

"Oh dear, I had quite forgotten about–everything," Eleanor exclaimed.

Lucy and Mason looked up. Briefly Susan tried to explain. "John went to London to fetch the Stanhopes."

Mason nodded, "Yes, he stopped off here. But that was days ago."

"Well, he has not yet returned. Stephen brought the Stanhopes back to Eden day before yesterday, on the same day your messenger arrived."

Lucy smiled sympathetically. "Poor Susan–"

"No, I'm certain everything is all right. We left all in Marjorie's capable hands. Still I think that I should–"

"How do you account for John's absence?"

"I don't, except Stephen said the Stanhopes spoke of trouble in the lobby of their London hotel."

"How serious?"

"Mr. Stanhope is reported to have struck John."

Mason's frown deepened, and he walked a few steps away to the window.

"So as you can see, I think it is important that I leave."

"May I stay?" Eleanor asked. "Just for a day or two."

"Of course, Eleanor. I'll tell Richard the good news."

Mason turned from the window. "I'll fetch your driver and tell him to prepare the carriage."

"Thank you, Mason."

As Mason left the room, Susan took his place beside the bed and gazed down on Lucy, who was in radiant good health, with color in her cheeks and a healthy baby at her breast.

"She's beautiful, Lucy. She'll break a heart or two before she's through."

Lucy smiled with new maternal pride. "Thank you so much for coming, Susan. There are several local midwives, of course. But I wanted you."

"You probably could have delivered her yourself," Susan smiled.

"Safe journey, dear Susan," Eleanor said, walking with her to the door. "Tell Richard I'll be home in a day or two."

Susan kissed her and received her warm embrace, then quietly closed the door.

She found the carriage and her driver waiting at the front steps with Mason, who was speaking quite soberly to a group of little boys. "Go on with you now and no more excuses. A proper young gentleman always takes time to straighten his tie."

Susan smiled. "You are a born headmaster, Mason."

"So I've been told."

"Still we miss you so much at Eden."

"Where do you suppose John–"

"I have no idea. He has few friends in London now. No one there to visit that I can think of. I really am quite baffled and a little worried."

"Should authorities be notified?"

"No, I'm certain he is alright," Susan said and lightly kissed Mason on the cheek. "Congratulations on your new daughter. How lucky she is to have you for a papa."

Mason looked pleased but skeptical.

"Time will tell. Safe journey. Let us hear from you as soon as possible."

She waved goodbye to Mason and called out for the driver to get under way.

Daring to relax, Susan placed her satchel on the floor at her feet, brushed back the hair from her eyes and gazed steadily out the window at the blur of passing green. She was exhausted. Perhaps it would be wise of her to take a brief nap during the two hour run across the moors back to Eden.

Eden. Bleakly she wondered what had transpired today in that unhappy place. The Stanhopes, upon their arrival had looked dreadful, poor Mary pale and red-eyed from weeping. Pray God all had gone well. In a curious way she now hoped that John had not as yet returned from–

Where was he? Why was he doing this to them? More like the John of old than–

All at once she heard a close rumbling, felt the carriage lurch dangerously to one side, grabbed the armrest for support as the driver struggled to bring the horses under control. Out of the window, she saw the cause, one of the newfangled motorcars speeding past the intersection.

Slowly her driver urged the horses forward onto the turnpike, and again Susan settled back into the seat, her heart beating too rapidly after the near miss. Still, it seemed to her less the motorcar's fault than the maniac who was driving it.

At last she relaxed against the comfortable cushions, her head bobbing gently in time to the rhythm of the carriage. It was amazingly good to sit alone even for a short time and plan ahead. She would invite Mary Stanhope to take charge of selecting the headstone for Eve. Perhaps that would help distract her, and she would encourage her to visit Mrs. Godwin's nursery whenever she saw fit, to feed young Alexander all his meals every day if she wished, to bathe him, to do anything she wanted that would help ease the pain of loss and focus her vision on the future.

Entering the moors she caught the sweet spicy fragrance of heather, a rare perfume.

Between the rhythmical bobbing of the carriage and the smell of the heather, Susan closed her eyes only a moment to rest them but fell instantly, soundly, into a deep sleep.

About two hours later she awakened at the driver's first cry of "Eden ahead," and sat up. Her neck was cramped and stiff, her hair in quite a state of disarray. And yet there was little she could do, for the carriage was now rattling across the grate, the jostling ride and impromptu nap at an end.

As the driver swung wide for the turn which led up to the Great Hall steps, she caught a glimpse of something out of the corner of her eye, an incredible sight, a monstrous gray motorcar bearing a remarkable resemblance to the one–

As the driver brought the carriage to a stop a distance from the Great Hall steps, she saw that the motorcar was parked exactly where carriages had always stopped to allow guests to disembark.

She thanked the driver for a safe journey, and as the carriage rattled off around the side of the castle, she took a moment to inspect the motorcar. Its condition suggested that it had made a long journey, for the sides were speckled with mud, the windshield a blur of dead insects.

All at once she saw the Great Hall doors open, saw one of the young stewards step out, followed by three others. The four young men quietly closed the Great Hall doors behind them and then, grinning, started down the steps toward the motorcar. At last the welcoming committee.

Susan stepped forward. She saw the grin on their faces fade into somber duty.

"Madame," one gasped, "we did not– You were not expected. No one told us–"

So much for the welcoming committee. "I returned unexpectedly," she explained, amused that she had nipped their pleasure in the bud. Clearly they had looked forward to a private interval of ogling the grand motorcar.

"Could you tell me," she began, "the name of the person who arrived in this?"

"Himself," one steward replied, "bought it in London."

Susan considered questioning them further but decided it would be a lost cause. Clearly all the answers to her questions lay straight through the Great Hall doors.

"The doctor's with him now, madame," one of the stewards called after her. "His throat looks awful. I caught a glimpse for myself."

On the bottom step, Susan frowned at this disturbing announcement. "Who? Who are you talking about?"

"Himself. Mr. Eden, Mr. John Murrey Eden."

Susan blinked but once, and then she was running to the top of the steps and pushing open the heavy door.

She looked straight down the length of the Great Hall and at last saw a small knot of people.

A few of the parlormaids hovering about the back of the circle saw her first and moved respectfully back. Then she saw Richard, his pale, transparent face bent over in examination of something, and Frederick was there, as was Stephen and Marjorie and Dr. Reicher. In the eye of this hurricane sat John, slouched on a chair, his head resting against the back, Dr. Reicher probing at his neck and throat.

Marjorie rushed to her side. "Susan, we didn't expect you, but I'm so glad that you are here. Something terrible–"

"Just in time," Frederick said wearily. "We seem to have developed a great talent of moving nonstop from one crisis to the next."

"What happened?" Susan asked, now close enough to see a pronounced purple swelling about John's neck.

"Susan–"

This pathetic and hoarse whisper came from John, who *did* look much the worse for wear. She remembered the dapper gentleman she had seen off to London about a week ago. No trace of him now. His clothes were filthy beyond description, and his hair, unkempt; clearly he had not shaved in several days. But by far the worst was his bruised and swollen throat.

"John, what happened?" she asked, drawing near enough to take his hand where it lay limp on the arm of the chair.

"A madman," he whispered with a grimace, as though it pained him to speak.

Of Dr. Reicher she asked, "What has happened?"

Reicher shrugged and continued to massage a smooth, clear salve into the flesh of John's neck and throat. "He says only that he was attacked by a madman."

"Is he seriously injured?"

"Murdered, that's what I could have been."

"Hold still!" Dr. Reicher ordered in a voice that left no margin for discussion. As Reicher commenced to wrap John's throat in soft gauze, Susan looked toward Stephen, who stood to one side.

"Do you know anything about this?"

But Stephen shook his head. "Nothing, only that he drove into the courtyard in that motorcar that you saw parked out there."

"*That* belongs to John?"

"Indeed it does," replied John, who was now sitting on the edge of the chair, just barely indulging Dr. Reicher. Then he ran out of patience and clearly wanted to speak for himself.

"Enough," he said gruffly, and holding his head at a stiff angle, he stood and appeared to waver for a moment, as though at some point he had lost his center of balance.

"I'm hungry," he said weakly, and Susan turned immediately to one of the maids. "Has the family had dinner?"

"Yes, ma'am."

"Would you ask Mrs. Partridge to prepare a platter of sandwiches?"

"Yes, ma'am."

"And the rest of you, I'm sure you have duties waiting elsewhere."

As the servants scattered, Susan looked back to see John speaking in a low voice to Richard, who was listening closely and apparently not understanding a word that was being said.

Marjorie, Frederick and Stephen stood to one side, looking lost and slightly guilty. Then Susan realized that a few others were missing.

"The Stanhopes," she said on a surge of anxiety. "Where are they?"

"They left, Susan, early this morning," Marjorie said.

"This morning? They only just arrived."

"It was their wish," Stephen confirmed. "Mary was suffering so much."

"But why did they leave? We were hoping they would stay a good long while." Angrily she turned to John. "Did you–"

"I only just arrived myself," he said, with matching anger. "I've had nothing to do with any of it."

Bewildered, Susan asked anyone who cared to answer, "What happened?"

"Nothing happened," Frederick explained gently. "It was just that it was very difficult for them to be here."

"Did they visit Eve's–"

"Yes," Stephen said. "I don't think that Mary has fully come to terms with it. They wanted to take Alex back with them."

"I hope you set them straight on that score," John said, still rubbing his throat. "And as soon as we are through worrying about the cotton farmer from America, would anyone care to hear of the tragic news that I bring to this family?"

Weary and worried, Susan sat down before the dead fire and heard the others settling in around her.

"Charlotte has been kidnapped," he announced in one terse statement and immediately captured the attention of all.

Richard was on his feet. "What are you saying?"

"You heard correctly. Charlotte has been kidnapped, and as I tried to bring about her rescue, I was assaulted myself and almost killed as you can see."

Richard continued to gasp out his disbelief. "I don't– I can't believe– You must have notified the authorities. The criminals must be found and brought to justice. Where, John? Can you identify– How could this happen?"

"You should never have allowed her to go to London alone."

Susan, less shocked than the others, said quietly, "She wasn't alone. She was living with Alice."

"Well, she may be residing with Alice, but that was not where I encountered her."

"Where did you encounter her?"

"At the well-known sodomite's residence, name of Aslam Eden."

This last pronouncement was made with increasing anger, though in a curious way it seemed to bring everyone else a degree of ease.

Richard, still pale and shaken, sat slowly in his chair. "Then she isn't–kidnapped? Why in God's name did you–"

"Well, she appeared kidnapped to me. No lady would stay for one minute in that man's company unless under certain duress."

"You once loved him," Susan reminded him quietly, retreating to the fire, fully understanding now exactly what had happened. John had made an impromptu visit to Aslam Eden, had found Charlotte in his company, had made a foolish gesture of chivalry and, for his trouble, had almost had the life strangled out of him.

"I have never been so shocked in my life," John was saying, still rubbing his throat as though to call attention to his wound. "At first the old butler would not let me in. Can you imagine? But at last I pushed my way into the drawing room, in an attempt to greet an old friend, nothing more, and I noticed a lady seated at the pianoforte. I did not recognize her at first because her back was to me, and I thought it rude that Aslam did not introduce me. Then I moved closer and understood all. She behaved as though she didn't know me. That's when it occurred to me that she might be drugged, rendered helpless by some Eastern elixir."

"Dear God, no," poor Richard groaned. Then quite helplessly he looked at Susan. "Where is Eleanor? I need Eleanor."

Quickly Susan went to pacify him. "She is with Lucy, you know that, Richard," she soothed, patting him on the shoulder. "I haven't told you the good news. You have a granddaughter. Lucy and Mason have a little girl. They have named her Anne Eleanor, and she is beautiful."

At first Susan wasn't certain that he had understood the message, but then Frederick, Stephen and Marjorie offered their congratulations. Only John made a thoughtless comment. "I cannot conceive of Mason as a father."

"Why not?" Susan countered. "He has spent more time with all of the Eden children than you or anybody else."

"We paid him. It was his job."

Weakly John addressed Dr. Reicher, who was restoring the bottle of salve and roll of bandage to his black bag. "Do you have something, Doctor, to soothe the pain? I am hurting."

"Brandy," Reicher suggested. "A snifter will put you to rights again. The damage is not serious, I assure you."

"Not serious!" John echoed. "He might have killed me."

Stephen stepped close. "I'm afraid I still don't understand, Papa. Why did Aslam attack you?"

"Because I tried to rescue Charlotte," John bellowed, looking about with a long-suffering air as though he were surrounded by idiots. "I tried to remove her from that infamous place and–"

"She didn't want to go," Susan said softly.

John glared at her, a clear warning for her to stop stealing his spotlight. "He is a madman, Aslam is," John said to the others. "He really doesn't need a reason to kill a man. All I know for certain is that he wrongfully attacked me and that a man of that temperament is quite capable of anything."

For several moments this last pronouncement sat heavily on the air, as though waiting for a response from someone. To Susan, it seemed that the far worse offense had been committed against the Stanhopes. She must write to them immediately, the letter to be waiting for them upon their arrival in Mobile. She must explain her absence to them and must try to help them understand–everything.

"Susan, where are you going?" John demanded.

"To bed."

"To bed? After what I've just told you?"

"There's little I can do about that now, John. Or you for that matter."

"But you don't even seem upset? Don't you care about Charlotte?"

"Of course I care about Charlotte, enough to let her manage her own life."

"She's a child."

"She's a woman, a young one, but a woman all the same."

Then Richard joined John. "She needs our help clearly."

"Why? I find it difficult to believe that Aslam intends her harm."

"He is evil."

"He is not."

She was aware of the others looking back and forth between John and herself, as though they were witnessing a slow-moving tennis match. Finally she suggested, "Let's send a member of the family to London to conduct a friendly investigation. If they feel that Charlotte is in danger, then–"

John turned in his chair, clearly rejecting her suggestion. But the others seemed to warm to it.

"Who?" Richard asked and rapidly answered his own question. "Not me. I don't . . . do well in London."

Susan looked at Frederick and Marjorie.

"You two," she smiled. "Why not? Marjorie has been confined to the castle since Christopher's birth. A few days in London would be beneficial to her. And I assure you the boys will be lovingly cared for."

Susan felt that Frederick was on the verge of protesting, but Marjorie warmed to the idea instantly. "It has been so long since I shopped."

Frederick still looked baffled. "What precisely are we to do?"

"Visit Alice first. See if you can speak with Charlotte in private. Then call on Aslam."

"He will never permit it," John grumbled. "I tell you, she is drugged and held prisoner."

"Then bring your opinions back to us please."

Frederick finally agreed. "I do need to see the bishop on the matter of the Mortemouth parish. He's in London now."

"Then it is settled," Susan concluded and took a few hopeful steps toward the door that led down toward the kitchen court.

"Eleanor will be with Lucy for a few days. No need to bother her with this until we know something for certain."

Everyone agreed. "Are you coming, John?" she called back, and receiving no answer, she shrugged. As she left, she saw Frederick and Marjorie hurrying up to their chambers, clearly to prepare for their trip, while Richard and Stephen drew chairs close to John, a comfortable male alliance. Then let them be.

As for herself, she felt certain that she knew the outcome of Frederick and Marjorie's investigation even before they left Eden. Charlotte was precisely where she wanted to be, as was Alice, as were all of the Eden children, including her beloved Albert.

She missed him so much.

Slowly she started down the narrow stone steps, following the good cooking odors coming from the kitchen court.

A good hot meal, a cup of tea and then to bed, a simple recipe that, if given half a chance, might cure the ills of the world.

Eden Castle
July 5, 1897

Seated atop the Great Hall steps, John called down, "Be very careful. No water on that leather upholstery, or I'll replace that hide with your own."

As John issued the threat to the young stewards who were polishing his motorcar, his throat still ached, as did his pride, and worst of all, no one was paying the slightest attention to him. Susan had adopted an absolutely callous attitude toward him, as though she blamed him for everything that had gone wrong. Richard had not come out of his private sitting room for four days, and poor Eleanor wept incessantly over her "lost baby." Frederick and Marjorie had not yet returned from London, though they were due sometime today.

Seated atop the Great Hall steps, he closed his eyes under the burgeoning sun and felt the discomfort of a mild headache, the harsher discomfort of bruised flesh about his throat.

"Carriage approaching!"

The cry came from the top of the southern turret.

Stirred to excitement, John stood up to prepare at last for vindication. He knew he could count on Frederick to tell a straight story. He could further count on Frederick to be morally appalled by what he had found in London. At last the family would hear the truth from a "reliable" source, from a priest of the Church of England.

Now the inner courtyard of Eden Castle seemed alive with activity, old Ghostly fussing at the stewards to move the motorcar because it was parked directly in the place where the carriage must stop and allow its passengers to alight.

"Leave it be," John called down, eager to settle the argument with the skeletal old man once and for all. He had done nothing but complain about the motorcar since John had brought it home from London.

"Very good, sir, as you say, sir."

"You're damn right as I say," John muttered. He might have to endure insolence from the family. He most certainly did not have to endure it from the staff.

"Is it them?" Richard asked, as though afraid he knew the answer.

"It's them," John confirmed.

"I had better get Eleanor. She will want to hear everything."

"And bring Susan while you're about it," John requested. For some reason it was most important to him that Susan hear this "reliable" repetition of his original tale. Perhaps then she would never doubt his word again.

As Richard disappeared into the Great Hall, John started down the steps, scarcely able to contain his eagerness. "Keep polishing," he ordered the stewards as he passed by his motorcar.

Then the carriage appeared, rumbling toward the gatehouse arch at a goodly speed. Only at the last minute did the driver choose to rein in the horses, who registered their objection with a sudden whinny, and at last the entire cumbersome contraption rattled across the grate, and through one of the carriage windows he could see Marjorie waving.

John waved back and at the same time waved the dust away, shutting his eyes briefly and hurrying back to the Great Hall steps, where he saw the company gathering.

As the carriage came to a halt, he saw the door open, saw Frederick step down, reach back for Marjorie and carefully assist her down to the gravel of the courtyard.

"Papa," he smiled and took John's hand. Then Marjorie was there with a kiss. The others came down the stairs, and for several minutes all was a babble of greetings.

John took Frederick by the arm and tried to lead him to one side. "May I ask what you found in London?"

Frederick looked ill at ease. He said quietly, "Not here. Give us a few moments to brush the dust off our clothes and to greet our son. In about an hour, I would welcome a cup of tea. At that time Marjorie and I will share with you all that we found in London."

"Of course," Susan said, taking Frederick and Marjorie by the arm and leading them up the stairs, with Richard and Eleanor close by.

John could feel the anger building, fury of the old sort that had plagued him years ago and that he thought he had conquered. "Damn," he whispered beneath his breath and turned about to face his motorcar, the most appealing sight within his entire range of vision.

He had the keys in his vest pocket. He had promised the young stewards a ride. Why not? To feel the tremendous power of the motorcar beneath his hands would be good for him. To know that he was in control of something would be very good for him.

"Come, lads," he shouted in rising enthusiasm, "Come on, climb aboard and take a seat. Let me show you the future."

For a moment the young boys looked at each other, uncertain whether they should accept his invitation or not. It was obvious they wanted to in the worst way, and at last, one tossed his polish cloth up in the air and climbed carefully into the dickey. Immediately the other four followed. John took his position in the driver's seat and looked back at his audience with a final warning.

"Don't stand up, do you hear? We will be traveling at a speed faster than any that you have traveled before."

The look of daring and excitement on their young faces pleased John enormously and helped to diffuse the building fury.

One hour, Frederick had said. Then he would return in one hour because he did not want to miss the satisfaction of hearing everything confirmed.

Once he was clear of all the castle encumbrances, only the straight, flat road that led in a pencil-sharp line across the moors stretched ahead of them. It was a perfect road for speed, for impressing the young boys in the back. He stepped on the accelerator, threw caution to the wind and saw the speedometer climb upward to thirty miles per hour, a speed that was capable of transporting a man straight into the future.

With the punctuality that had marked his entire life, Frederick reentered the Great Hall exactly one hour later. Susan could have predicted his arrival to the minute. She took her position with the others for this grim family gathering.

Now, as Frederick drew near, Susan looked about and realized that there was one person missing.

John.

"Where is Papa?" Frederick asked.

Stephen glanced up from rubbing a stiffness out of his shoulder, still sweaty from his work in the fields with the tenants. "One of the gatemen said they saw him riding out in his motorcar. The stewards were in the backseat."

Then Marjorie appeared, hurrying across the Great Hall, a smile of apology on her face. "Those two," she smiled, "They are acting like parrots up there, repeating everything they hear."

"Well then," Frederick began, all business. "Please let us tell you what we found in London."

Susan heard the roar first, like an approaching thunderstorm, accompanied now by a remarkably comic sound, like an excited duck, a noise she assumed to be the horn of John's motorcar.

Everyone else heard the commotion as well. Frederick looked relieved that he might only have to tell his narrative once.

A few moments later the awful mechanical commotion came to an end, and soon John appeared, looking red-faced, sweating, his hair windblown about his face.

"Am I late?" he bellowed as he pushed open the Great Hall door. "I am sorry; I tried hard to time it all properly. One never knows with motorcars."

He talked all the way across the Great Hall. Susan thought she recognized a forced good humor.

"Well, I'm here now," he concluded, and patted Stephen affectionately on the back. He sat in the first available chair and immediately withdrew a large white linen handkerchief and commenced to wipe at his face and neck. "Damn hot," he muttered. Then all was quiet.

Frederick continued to wait for a few minutes and watched his father as though he were a rare and unpredictable breed of animal who must be humored. Then at last–

"Marjorie and I went first to Alice's flat, as we didn't really know the direction to Mr. Aslam Eden's residence, but as it turned out," Frederick went on, "we had no need of the direction, for we found them all at Alice's flat, quite a lively gathering–"

"Even Albert was there," Marjorie smiled. "Susan, did you know he was in London now?"

This was something of a surprise. "No," she said.

"He said that Alice had invited him to stay with her. It seems that she has put him to work for the cause."

"What cause?" Susan asked, her bewilderment increasing, a little embarrassed that she had to find out about the activities of her son in this manner.

Marjorie and Frederick exchanged a glance, as though they were trying to decide who now would do the speaking.

Frederick started out, a worried look on his face. "It appears to be a hodgepodge of every radical cause. The Pankhurst girl lives with her now, and she preaches constantly of something called a suffragette movement."

"A what?" Eleanor asked.

"The rights of women to vote," Marjorie explained, a growing excitement betraying her.

"And there were others," Frederick went on. "Though the flat is spacious, it seemed filled with dozens of people, some preaching socialism, some writing labor union pamphlets and of course the Pankhurst girl lecturing to a group of young ladies on the . . . sisterhood."

"And Charlotte?" Richard asked at last. "Where was—"

Marjorie smiled. "Right in the middle of it. I have never seen her so—"

She caught herself in time, as though she were on the verge of praising this madness.

Susan looked up now, amazed. She had been expecting gentle condemnation. Instead, what she was getting was a kind of tacit approval. "Frederick, I still don't understand," she said, glancing once toward John, who throughout it all was being ominously quiet.

"Nor did we, Susan," Frederick conceded. "They are very young people, all of them, student-aged, a few slightly older, and Albert was not the only male. There were three others, though the group was predominantly female. The flat bore all the appearance of a combination of classroom, lecture hall and workshop. They were experimenting with new ideas, not all of them bad, just new and untried. I made it a point to speak with Alice in private. She told me that she was continuing her nursing studies, but that the ills of the world as she saw it were too numerous to confine them to a study of the physical body. She said the soul and the spirit were sick as well and that they were seeking a cure to those two important entities as well as to the physical body."

Then John at last came roaring up out of his suspect silence.

"Frederick!" he said, pacing about the group. "We sent you to London to investigate Charlotte's circumstances. You bring us back a full account of Alice and her radical friends. This is not news. I have known of her questionable activities for some time. She is, of course, headed for serious trouble. But nothing compared to Charlotte, who is—"

"We saw Charlotte," Frederick interrupted. "She is quite settled into Alice's flat. When we questioned her about Mr. Aslam Eden, she claimed that she sees him only occasionally and then under the strictest of chaperons. Alice and Miss Pankhurst confirmed all of this."

"They both are lying," John accused flatly.

Then Marjorie confronted John with her gentle voice. "We went to London expecting to find all sorts of horrors. But we are very pleased to relate that we found only a group of young people testing their wings and their considerable intelligences. Look, Charlotte gave me one of the suffragette tracts. Listen–"

Marjorie held the pamphlet toward the available light. " 'The suffragettes signal the discovery of woman by herself, the realization of her own powers, the overthrow by herself of traditions and–' "

"No!"

This bellowing command came from John, who had paced himself into center stage and who at last had released all those dragons of fury that had been lurking just beneath the surface. "I want you all to listen. These two innocents here have been royally lied to by your own daughter, and if any of you dare to think that all is well in London, then you are bigger fools than even I thought."

Susan tried to calm him. "John, please, let us–"

"Will you stay out of this?" he shouted with a fierceness that caused her eyes to burn. Public humiliation was an old trick of John's.

"Now you all must put aside these quaint tales of young people experimenting with new ideas and spreading their wings. I said before that Alice's causes are lost causes. As for Albert, I can't imagine what purpose he is serving these radicals except as court jester and clown."

Susan closed her eyes and prayed that the attack would be over soon and thanked God only that neither of her children were here to witness it.

"Which now brings us to Charlotte, who is in the process of ruining not only her reputation but the reputation of this entire family."

"What if they are speaking the truth, John," Susan said. "What if it is your account that is inaccurate?"

Slowly he turned. "I am afraid I don't understand."

"I just suggested the possibility that perhaps Aslam Eden's anger was turned upon you alone and had nothing to do with Charlotte."

"You are idiots!" bellowed John. "My God, what do I have to do? Someone must believe me. Charlotte is in danger."

"I don't believe so, Father," Frederick said. "She did not appear to be in danger. Said she enjoyed Mr. Eden's company and saw him only on a limited basis."

"Then I tell you she is lying."

Richard stepped forward. "I wish you would not say that again," he pronounced with curious formality. "After all, she is my daughter."

"You might not be so eager to make that claim when her reputation is gone."

Susan watched everybody leaving, moving about John as though he were not there.

"So it has come to this," he muttered. "My word means nothing, my warnings mean nothing, my concerns for this family mean nothing. Then why do I remain here where I am not wanted?"

Stephen appeared to study him as though debating whether or not to dignify the cry with a response. Then finally, "Poor Papa. You are a good father. But what you have never quite been able to understand, is that God did not send you all of these people as a personal gift to play with as you like or to control. We all have the right to walk off the first cliff we come to if we so desire, and neither you nor anyone else has a right to stop us."

"But I don't want control."

"Yes, you do, Papa. At least be honest."

"Why do I have to listen to you?" John shouted. "You are a mere boy. What right have you–"

"Correct, Papa." Stephen smiled, lifting his hands in a restraining gesture. "And now this boy is off again to the fields. Do you know why I like the fields, Papa? There is an honesty to the fields and to the tenants who work them. You must come with me sometime, meet these rare men who labor so hard on your behalf."

Then he was gone down the steps that led to the kitchen court and out into the barnyard.

Only Frederick remained. "I did not mean to anger you, Papa," he began. "Marjorie reported only what we thought to be true."

"Another lecture? Coming from another boy? Dear God, what would I do without these moral giants?"

The sarcasm was back stronger than ever, and Susan hated it and knew that if she stayed a moment longer, she would say words to him that ought not to be said.

Heading toward the same steps down which Stephen had recently disappeared, Susan approached the door and looked back in time to see Frederick just stepping out of the Great Hall. John was abandoned now.

Good! Let him think on things for a while. Let him remember his own past, those dreadful times when he had either chased away or destroyed everyone he loved.

The last thing she saw before closing the door to the kitchen court was John, bearing a frightening resemblance to the madman she had found in Eden Castle over a quarter of a century ago.

"Dear God, please, no–"

She could not go through it again, nor could he. This time there would be no resurrection, only the seeds of his own destruction, which he had so successfully sown today.

Fools. All of them.

Idiots, children, fools!

John stood alone in the Great Hall, still smarting from the rebuffs which he had been dealt.

Lectures! Moral lectures from his own sons!

His one satisfaction was in the realization that by ignoring him, this family ultimately would be dealt pain and tragedy beyond their wildest comprehensions. It would come to no good. The scandal attendant upon the sordid relationship that he had seen in the Belgravia estate of Aslam Eden would undoubtedly toll the death knell of the Eden family in respectable British circles everywhere on the face of the earth.

He turned once again, searching desperately for a way out of his misery. His children were dead to him; his treasured association with Mason Frye was dead. Mason had a wife now. Everyone else was gone as well, Richard's loyalty, Eleanor's worship, Alice, Albert–poor weak Albert apparently doing the bidding of his sister, like a well-trained spaniel–all gone, everyone gone, nothing for him here.

Except–

He heard it first, a familiar sound, the faint squeak of the heavy wire wheels, coming from the direction of the second-floor nursery.

He looked toward the sound, as a man drowning fixates on a lifeline. Not everyone in Eden Castle had rejected him, not everyone questioned his word, doubted his motives and rejected his authority.

"Mrs. Godwin, how are you?" he called out with warm familiarity as the old nursemaid came into sight at the top of the stairs behind the double pram.

Without waiting for her reply and ignoring the look of surprise on her plump old face, he hurried over to assist her with the pram, finally lifting it, boys and all, and setting it safely down onto the Great Hall floor.

"May I ask your direction, madame?"

"Just on my way, sir, to get the boys some air. They do enjoy a brief turn around the inner courtyard. Helps their appetites, helps their sleep."

"I'm sure it does, Mrs. Godwin, and how wise of you to think of it."

Now he walked easily beside her as she pushed the pram toward the Great Hall doors. The boys grinned up at him.

"Do you think they know me, Mrs. Godwin?" John asked, grinning stupidly down at both of them and waving like an idiot.

"Oh, I'm sure they do, Mr. Eden. You are a very important person to them both. You are their grandpapa."

Then there was his salvation, those two smiling perfect little boys. Let Frederick save the world, let Susan heal it, let Marjorie and Eleanor gossip about it. All John wanted was to watch these two grow to manhood, to have an influential hand in their thinking, their feeling, their philosophies, their convictions.

It was as though he had two clean slates. All he asked of Providence was a chance to make his own very significant marks on those slates. Since all of the other Eden children were now lost to him–and good riddance–then pray let God grant his access to these two new ones. Oh, if only He would do that.

"Mrs. Godwin, may I make a request?"

"Of course, Mr. Eden."

"May I suggest that you rest yourself and allow me to take the boys on their daily constitutional."

"Well, I don't– Of course, I'm sure you wouldn't mind that I took the air on the Great Hall steps and kept a close eye out."

"Not at all, Mrs. Godwin. In fact, your practical eye shall give me courage and confidence."

Once outside the Great Hall doors, John lifted the pram and carried it effortlessly to the bottom of the steps. There was his motorcar, less handsome now after the dust of the moors. Well, no matter. The stewards would polish it as soon as they finished their household duties.

Then he pushed the pram past the motorcar, keeping to the walkway that led around the perimeter of the inner courtyard.

He could scarcely keep his eyes off the little boys. They were beautiful, alert to every noise, every breeze, Christopher now staring straight up at the cloudless blue sky. They spoke nonsense syllables to each other with perfect assurance that they were being understood and looked at John as though wondering why he did not join in their unique conversation.

John felt all of the considerable unpleasantness of the day fall away. It was as though he, too, was made new again by his closeness to the boys in their pristine state.

Now all he had to do was to wait and watch them grow up. What a privilege that would be, what a joy, like clinging to the coattails of tomorrow and being lifted out of the past, over the present and into the future.

Eden Castle
December 31, 1899

Eleanor saw the stewards trimming the gas lamps mounted on the walls of the Great Hall. At the same time, she saw four other stewards bring in enormous candelabras and arrange them in a semicircle at the center of the hall, thus defining the "stagehouse." Next came two stewards carrying a large rolled Oriental carpet, which they unfurled to mark off the proscenium and the performance area.

The greatly anticipated event was about to commence, Eden Castle's own theatrical, entitled "Welcoming the New Century," written by Jeremy Neville, the brilliant young tutor sent to Eden by Mason Frye. The theatrical was to be performed by John Murrey Eden, Christopher Eden, Alexander Eden and Rolf Reicher.

The rest of the "audience" was beginning to drift out of the dining hall. John and the boys had already disappeared into the reception hall to put on their costumes and makeup for the theatrical, which they had been rehearsing for weeks.

Eleanor looked at Richard close beside her, his toes almost touching the flames of the roaring Great Hall fire, his eyes beginning to grow heavy-lidded.

"Richard, please," she whispered. "I beg you. Try to stay awake. It will so offend the boys if you–"

"I *am,*" he snapped, looking sheepishly about.

The rest of the family was gathering as well. Marjorie looked fully recovered from her recent miscarriage, a sad event, a little brother for Christopher. But it was not to be.

Dr. Reicher had gone to check on Geoffrey, but he had requested that the "actors" wait until he had returned.

Now, as the hum of voices increased, Eleanor sat in her big overstuffed chair and wondered how it was possible, with this circus going on about her, that she could be lonely.

But there was the truth of it. It had been three years since she had seen Charlotte.

"Consider her dead," Richard had advised, for John's warning had come true. The ugly gossip had filled every column in *Punch*, as well as the *Tattler*, cartoons and caricatures of Lord Eden's daughter living in sin with an Indian.

In a letter received by Susan only a few months ago, Alice had admitted that Charlotte had moved out of her flat and into Aslam Eden's mansion. Alice had reminded her mother that it *was* Charlotte's life and no one had a right to interfere.

"Are *you* napping, Eleanor?" Richard teased, leaning close.

She shook her head. "I miss Charlotte," she confessed.

Within the instant she saw his expression grow hard. "Charlotte is dead."

"Oh, Richard, don't say that; she is not dead."

"To us she is."

"Still, I miss her."

The quick exchange died and left both of them staring bleakly into the fire.

Then she heard a sweet voice. "Mama, would you watch after Anne for me?"

It was Lucy, her plain Lucy, who had married a plain man, Mason Frye, and had provided her with a beautiful granddaughter, sweet Anne. It was as though having taken Charlotte from her, God had returned Lucy to her and had given her Anne as a bonus.

Now, as Eleanor opened her arms to the dimpled, curly-headed little girl, Lucy bent low and whispered, "Mason tells me that Father Time needs help with his beard and that Baby New Year is losing courage. I'd better get down to the Reception Room."

Eleanor smiled, "Anne and I will have a walkabout while the others are settling into their places."

Pleased, Anne walked easily beside Eleanor. The little girl was so pretty, so dainty, a fringe of light curly hair framing her face, and a sweet disposition to match. At two, she resembled a doll.

"Come, my darling," Eleanor whispered to Anne. "Let's see if the actors are ready. Soon you will be taking your place in the New Year's theatrical. Would you like that?"

"Alex, where is–"

"We'll see Alex very soon. Come, let's hurry and see if Uncle Richard has saved us a ringside seat."

She heard Marjorie just striking an attention-getting chord on the old pianoforte. "Hurry," Eleanor whispered and lifted Anne the last few steps, then sat in the chair next to Richard, while Stephen and Frederick sat to one side. Behind her, near the kitchen court door, the servants were beginning to gather. They were always invited to family theatricals and seemed to enjoy them more than anyone, a chance to see the masters make fools of themselves, according to John.

To her left sat Mrs. Godwin, Mrs. Calvin and Mrs. Partridge. Beyond them sat Sonia and Dr. Reicher.

Now young Rolf, age five, strolled assuredly out of the Reception Room. He wore a smartly tailored suit and walked the length of the Great Hall with perfect self-assurance.

According to the tutor, Jeremy Neville, he was bright, bilingual at age five, capable of speaking flawless German as well as flawless English, and had a sweet manner with the younger children, Chris, Alex and little Anne when she came visiting.

"Rolf–" Anne squealed, recognizing him immediately and struggled to get free of Eleanor's grasp.

"No, no," Eleanor whispered and held the child tight amidst surrounding giggles. "Rolf is going to perform. Now we must sit and listen."

Reluctantly Anne agreed, though now she sat erect in Eleanor's lap, fascinated by the appearance of her friend Rolf, who was dressed in such funny clothes.

Rolf drew near to where his audience was seated. He seemed to survey the "theater" and apparently found something not to his liking.

"Lord Eden," he called out in a clear voice, "with your permission, might I ask those people to come closer and fill in the empty places?"

In surprise, Eleanor swiveled about to see who he was talking about. The servants. There was a sizable congregation of about fifteen servants bunched in the shadows about the door which led down to the kitchen court. Now young Rolf wanted them to come close and fill in around the family.

Eleanor spoke with a smile. "Rolf, what a splendid idea. Lord Eden agrees, don't you, Richard?"

Poor Richard did well to nod.

Rolf was delighted. "Thank you." Then he quickly assumed his position at center stage, straightened his tuxedo and his white tie, stood erect and lifted his face to the audience.

"Lord and Lady Eden, ladies and gentlemen, Mama and Papa, we have gathered this evening to say farewell to the old century and to welcome the new one."

Anne shifted restlessly on Eleanor's lap, her fascination with this serious Rolf fading. Clearly she preferred the Rolf she found in the playroom, the one who crawled about on all fours and let her ride piggyback.

"Now we must ask of ourselves a difficult question," Rolf went on, moving from his own irresistible spontaneity to what was clearly a memorized text, written and prepared by Jeremy Neville.

"What will the future make of the present?" Rolf asked, then paused for a few moments as though to give his audience a chance to absorb the question and frame an answer.

In this interim of waiting, Eleanor saw Mr. Neville creep silently forward from the Reception Room, his arms filled with props. Behind him trailed Alex and Chris, Alex completely encased in a sky-blue satin cape, Chris in angel wings, a silver cape and a slightly crooked halo attached to a stiff though bent wire at the back of his neck.

Eleanor saw Marjorie turn eagerly from her position where she sat at the pianoforte. Stephen and Frederick did likewise, both men beaming like fools.

Now it was Rolf's turn again, though clearly he was aware of the distractions behind him, did not like them and lifted his voice in an attempt to win back the undivided attention of the audience.

"Comes the dawn of the new century," he intoned and suddenly Alex appeared in his sky blue cape, carrying before him an enormous yellow cardboard ball, obviously the sun. He started from stage right and walked slowly across the Oriental rug.

"And we must ask ourselves, have we done well? Have we pleased God and the Heavenly Host with our accomplishments, with our visions, with our–"

Then Chris, in his wings and silver cape, clearly representing God and the Heavenly Host started off too fast from stage left and, concentrating as he was on the wobbly halo attached to the back of his head, failed to see "Dawn," who was equally preoccupied with peering over the cardboard sphere of the sun at the audience.

There was the inevitable collision. Dawn went tumbling in one direction while the Heavenly Host went tumbling in the other.

"Why don't you watch out?" Dawn shouted to the Heavenly Host.

"I was watching," the Heavenly Host argued. "Jeremy and Susan said you were already supposed to be across."

"Well, I wasn't."

Eleanor glanced to her right and saw Stephen and Frederick practically flattened on the floor with laughter. Unfortunately their sons did not find it so amusing. Struggling upward with his round cardboard sun, Alex lifted it high in the air and delivered a stunning blow to the top of the Heavenly Host's head, breaking his halo altogether in the process and provoking a squeal of outrage. Then the Heavenly Host came out swinging, as everyone knew he would, and before the mayhem got totally out of hand, Mr. Neville appeared, quite red-faced, accompanied by Susan, who had come running from the Reception Room. Mr. Neville took Dawn in hand while Susan grabbed the Heavenly Host, turned him quickly about and led him offstage, leaving poor Rolf to cover his own embarrassment.

"Our sincere apologies, ladies and gentlemen. If you will excuse—"

He fled behind the candelabras, where Jeremy and Susan were working frantically to repair the damage done to both boys.

For a moment there was only the whispered buzz of incipient chaos. Finally Dawn reemerged on the right side of the stage, and the Heavenly Host on the left, and on a cue from Mr. Neville, both boys started toward the center, this time with plenty of margin to avoid a collision though Eleanor noticed as Dawn approached the Heavenly Host that he stuck out his tongue and the Heavenly Host reciprocated, then both grinned maniacally at each other.

Rolf took center stage, trying valiantly to pick up his train of thought. So engrossed was Eleanor in these theatrics that she allowed a very wiggly Anne to slip from her lap to the floor only to reappear at Dawn's side, her favorite, who frowned at her and informed her full voice that she was too young to participate and she was to go immediately back to Grandmama.

As Eleanor was on her feet, moving to retrieve the little girl, Anne spied her mother standing in the Reception Hall door and started in that direction at a dead run. Apparently Lucy saw her coming, waved her approval and a few moments later scooped up her daughter, depositing her out of sight in the Reception Room.

In the meantime, Rolf was waxing eloquent about the promise of the new century. He spoke of flying machines and ships that could go underwater and motorcars and no more hunger and no more illness and no more disease, and as he spoke, everyone was focused on the two little boys who were being painfully transformed under Mr. Neville and Susan's guidance from Dawn and the Heavenly Host to–what?

Eleanor tried to make sense of these new costumes. To her left, the servants were giggling at the protestations taking place behind the candelabras.

Then all at once, Rolf spoke of peace everlasting, a utopia of the twentieth century, defined by God and practiced by man, where enemies both new and old, past and present, would live in peace and lie down together like the biblical lion and lamb.

The Lion and the Lamb. Of course. The boys reappeared in their makeshift costumes, Alex clad in rather moldy white fur, clearly someone's discarded fur piece, a comical lamb's head of papier-mâché which somehow gave him the appearance of a rabbit instead of a lamb. Meantime, Chris was losing patience with the nonsense of his lion's outfit, a rather mangy-appearing piece of yellow fur–God alone knew where Susan had found it–another crudely made papier-mâché headpiece, which made Chris look more like a sheep than a lion.

Stephen and Frederick could not contain their amusement any longer and laughed out loud. Eleanor shot them a withering look.

Now, as the Lion and the Lamb approached each other, Rolf stepped back to allow free and easy passage, thus avoiding a collision similar to the one suffered by Dawn and the Heavenly Host.

But Eleanor knew it was going to happen; something about the look on the Lamb's face. It was only a mild shove at first, but that was all that the Lion needed to force a retaliation. There was a shove, and the Lamb's head went flying, revealing an angry little boy, who countered by grabbing the mangy yellow fur mantle of the Lion and ripping it down the back. Ultimately both boys fell to the rug, turning over and over in mortal combat.

Eleanor started to her feet, as did Stephen, Frederick, Richard and everyone who felt it was their duty to break up the melee.

Rolf, older, wiser and more sophisticated, looked stricken as the Lion and the Lamb pummeled and pulled, kicked, grunted and groaned.

Just as Stephen was reaching into the broiling stew of squabbling little boys, a voice that resembled God's thundered out over the Great Hall.

"Leave them be" was what the voice said, and everyone, including

Eleanor, glanced up and saw a towering figure emerge from the Reception Room, a figure clad in long gray robes and ragged gray beard and bearing in his hand a long, rusty, ominous scythe.

Father Time? Eleanor thought he more accurately resembled Father Death.

Apparently the Lion and the Lamb saw him coming as well, and quickly the wrestling match was brought to an end, their recent hostilities now rapidly becoming a new alliance as they clasped hands and tried to move to the far side of the stage and away from the angry giant approaching them.

But then John was upon them, passing by Rolf, stopping to pay him a sincere compliment, "Well done, my boy," he said, loud enough for all to hear, even the two ruffians. "I commend your professionalism, unlike some I could mention."

As he said this, he glanced in the direction of Chris and Alex where they stood huddled together as though for protection on the far side of the stage.

"Come, both of you!" John commanded, and slowly the boys obeyed, holding hands, still looking sheepishly first at each other, then at the audience, which had grown breathlessly quiet.

Father Time stood midstage, his arms crossed, the scythe caught in the press of his arms against his body. He watched carefully as the two little boys, both much the worse for wear, dragged their feet in a shuffling approach.

When they stopped about ten feet from where John stood, he said, "Closer! Come closer the both of you."

They obeyed instantly, both standing about two feet in front of John, staring up at him with worried eyes, holding their lion and lamb heads limp at their sides.

"Now," Father Time pronounced. "Explain yourselves, if you can before this company. I believe that you owe them an apology."

The awkward silence stretched on, and Eleanor saw the boys bow their heads as though to soften the painful effects of all those staring eyes.

"Well?" John demanded. "We are waiting. You seemed possessed of sufficient energy only a few moments ago. Surely you can give us all just a brief word of explanation as well as apology."

Then all at once, Chris stepped forward in a manly fashion. He dropped his papier-mâché lion's head and admitted full-voiced, with a degree of pride, "I bumped into him. I didn't mean to."

"No, you didn't," Alex countered.

"Yes I did."

"Did not."

"Did so."

Had it not been for Father Time's immediate intervention, there would have been a second wrestling match. But he simply reached down and grabbed the boys by the backs of their collars and held them at arm's length and smiled at the company and with unfailing charm said, "These two young thespians will return to you as soon as they are capable of conducting themselves in a gentlemanly fashion. For now, Rolf will sing for you as Father Time and Baby New Year prepare for their march of time."

"Grandpapa," Chris objected, "we were supposed to sing too."

"No, absolutely not. Ruffians are not permitted to take part in the New Year's theatrical. Do go on, Rolf. The stage is yours."

Tentatively, with a degree of hesitation and a deep degree of regret, Rolf came downstage, looking lovingly at the two exiles, who had been placed on the floor just off the Oriental rug, a clear indication that they had been banished from the stage.

Marjorie struck a chord, struck it again and at last launched into the first line of "God Save the Queen," and apparently hoped that Rolf would follow.

He did, in a voice remarkable for its clarity and purity of tone. Eleanor was astounded, as was the rest of the company, as Rolf effortlessly raised the anthem a note on the scale and Marjorie ceased her piano accompaniment in order to listen to the little boy's beautiful voice fill every corner of the Great Hall.

Eleanor saw Sonia and Dr. Reicher beaming with parental pride, as well they should have. In her opinion the boy needed formal training and discipline. He was far too good to be ignored.

As Rolf brought the anthem to a close, Eleanor was certain she had never heard it sung so beautifully. Even the truants Alex and Chris seemed impressed and sat cross-legged where they had been placed by John, their mouths agape.

Then Eleanor saw little Anne toddling across the Great Hall clad only in her nappies with a broad white satin banner that read "1900" tied across her tiny chest. Grasping her hand in a stooped manner was Father Time, bending low to encourage her every few steps.

Alex and Chris started to giggle hysterically, falling about each other's necks and rolling on the floor, reminding Eleanor more than ever of bear cubs.

As Father Time approached them, clasping the New Year by her hand, he shot the two boys a withering look, and immediately they straightened up, though both still appeared to be on the verge of exploding with merriment.

Then Eleanor heard Ghostly's majestic voice announce from the library door, "Ladies and gentlemen, the century is passing. The new century is approaching."

In the sudden stillness of the Great Hall, Eleanor listened along with all the others as the massive clock in the library struck the hour of midnight. *Two—three—four—*

Alex and Chris stopped giggling.

—five—six—

Frederick left Stephen's side and moved quickly to where Marjorie was sitting at the pianoforte.

—seven—

Susan joined Father Time on the far side of the stage, where he opened his arms to her. At the same time, Lucy and Mason clasped hands.

—eight—nine—

Sonia and Dr. Reicher smiled at each other and motioned for Rolf to come and join them. He did.

—ten—

Eleanor felt Richard's hand as he clasped hers and drew her close.

—eleven—

Stephen went to where Alex was sitting and scooped him up in his arms. Chris ran to Marjorie and Frederick by the piano.

—twelve. Midnight. The new year. A brand new century.

For an instant, the moment and its meaning seemed to plunge the entire company into a respectful silence. So much was behind them. So much was ahead.

Very softly Marjorie started to play "Auld Lang Syne," and one by one the voices joined in and all gathered around the pianoforte, Stephen now holding both Alex and Chris, both little boys appearing to be quite content to be close to one another and at peace.

Behind her, Eleanor saw the servants bringing in the enormous lighted New Year's fruitcake, saw the stewards roll forth the carts of sandwiches and sweets, saw Ghostly supervising the champagne bottles. Soon there would be feasting and drinking for all.

But for this one moment in time, Eleanor felt as though she were standing on a brink.

A new century. How privileged she was to live to see it. How perfect was her world in all respects save two—Geoffrey and Charlotte.

How she missed Charlotte, her beauty, her sweet smile.

And Geoffrey. He was as lost to her in his remote seclusion as he would have been if he had died on the field of battle in the Transvaal. In a way, Geoffrey's exile was a living death, inconclusive, each day tortured by false hope, splintered by Dr. Reicher's daily bulletins, which he delivered in a monotone: "No change. No change at all. And he wishes to see no one."

Now Eleanor had but one prayer for the new year, for the new century. "Dear God, no more wars, ever, for any reason. No more untimely deaths of thousands of young Englishmen, no more wounded to be sent home to grieving families."

Was it asking too much?

She hoped not. She prayed not.

She looked up from her prayer to see Alex and Chris staring directly at her.

She waved at them and saw the sweetest of smiles on their young faces. Nothing would happen to them. She would personally see to it.

Then she joined in the last stanza of "Auld Lang Syne" and lifted her voice in song and looked about at the beloved faces surrounding the pianoforte and decided quite firmly that despite everything, life was good, so good.

London
January 18, 1901

Charlotte read Lucy's letter twice to herself before glancing up to see if the time was right to read it to Aslam.

It wasn't. He was still involved with his morning post and papers. She took the letter to the broad dining hall windows and looked out on a surprisingly mild January morning. The snows of last week had melted completely under an unseasonably warm January sun, the garden she had planted last spring clearly visible in all of its brown, stubbly ugliness.

Her garden, Aslam had called it.

She looked back at this man whom she had come to love more than life itself. She recalled the advice, the warnings and worst of all the dreadful silence coming from Eden Castle when she had written of her plans to share Aslam's life and home.

Now she kissed Lucy's letter and pressed her forehead against the cold windowpane and listened to the fire crackling in the fireplace, listened to the beating of her own heart and wondered why she did not view her own actions as scandalously as everyone else did.

Yet what was so scandalous in sharing your life with the one you loved? Would they ever marry? Perhaps. When they were ready.

Neither she nor Aslam could account for the glorious ease and joy of their relationship; the delight each took in the other, the serene and communal silences, followed by an almost giddy chatter of conversation, the passion of each evening or the peace of each morning. Once, Aslam had said that it was altogether within the realm of possibility that they had known and loved each other in another life.

For now, that remarkable explanation seemed to suffice for both of them.

"The old queen is ailing," she heard Aslam say over the crackle of the fire and the rustle of the newsprint.

She looked back. "Is it serious?"

"Well, she's ancient, isn't she? Anything for a woman that age could be serious. Bertie at last had better dust off his crown."

"Do you know him, Aslam?"

Aslam laughed. "Oh, indeed I do," and he continued to turn the pages of the London *Times.* "He's first-rate, very angry, of course, at having been denied the throne for so long."

Abruptly he put the paper down. "If he is around and if the old queen survives, we will invite them here. He has been here several times for cards and dinner. He loves a good card game better than anything."

Charlotte gaped. "The Prince of Wales? Here?"

"The new king. And why not?" Aslam smiled. "My only worry would be that he would most likely try to flirt with you. Still, we will keep such a date in the backs of our minds, and if it pleases you, then we'll do it."

He pushed the papers and his morning post aside, swallowed the last of his breakfast tea, then stood.

"What have you there?" he asked, seeing Lucy's letter in her hand as he slowly approached her.

For some reason, what Charlotte had in her hand was not nearly so important as the look in Aslam's eye as he drew near, a hungry look that only seemed to intensify as he put his arms around her and drew her close, a sheltering cocoon from which she never wanted to escape.

"Oh, my darling," he murmured, finding her lips ready and open.

She closed her eyes and gasped for breath at the end of the kiss.

"My dearest," Aslam whispered. "Tell me of your letter. And then we shall–"

She knew precisely what they would do and thought once that Lucy's letter would keep. But no. She wanted him to hear it, wanted to hear his opinion.

"It's from Lucy," Charlotte said.

"Still in Exeter?" Aslam asked, settling back quite relaxed in his chair.

"Still at Greenfield. She loves it; she claims that she was born to be the wife of a headmaster."

"She is suited for it. And the child?"

"She is about three. Talking quite voluably now, to Mason's delight. Lucy says he has started instructing her in French. At three, can you imagine?"

"The best time, I would imagine."

She watched him as he spoke and wondered if they would ever have a child. She hoped so.

"But the main body of the letter," she went on, "has to do with something else."

"What, my dearest?"

Charlotte unfolded the letter and read to him Lucy's own words:

> I beg you, dearest Charlotte, to consider a visit home. Mama and Papa miss you so much. I know because both have told me so. Further they have told me that while they do not approve of how you are living, that you are their daughter and your estrangement has left a painful emptiness in their hearts.
>
> I would not write to you thus except to remind you that I, too, was banished at one time, as was Mason. But we have since been welcomed back into the fold, and I feel certain that you and Aslam would be as welcome if you would but appear.
>
> Pray consider, Charlotte. Our family seems so splintered at times. Alice and Albert have vowed never to cross the moors as long as Uncle John is in residence at Eden. I pray that you have not taken the same vow.
>
> You must plan an evening with us if you come. Your niece takes after you in almost all ways. She is so beautiful. Thank God for His good sense in not making her after my plain likeness.
>
> And dearest Charlotte, please think on all of the above. And remember how much I love you.
>
> Your loving sister, Lucy

For several moments after reading the letter, Charlotte stared down on it, seeing only Lucy's good, sweet face and missing her terribly.

"What do you think?" she asked at last, looking up to see a worried expression on Aslam's face.

"I think it is a good and thoughtful letter," he began as though exercising a degree of caution, "written by a very good and decent woman. But I'm afraid . . ."

"What?"

". . . that she does not speak for John Murrey Eden."

"Why must we concern ourselves with him?" Charlotte asked. "We would be going to see my mother and father, not—"

"Come, Charlotte, you know, probably better than I who is the true authority at Eden Castle."

"But he has no right to meddle in our lives. He has done that for as long as I can remember, and everyone has let him."

"And he will continue to do so until he is in his grave. It is, I'm afraid, John's nature."

"Then what am I supposed to do?"

"I say, if you want to go, I will accompany you. Perhaps Lucy is right. Perhaps you do owe it to yourself, to your parents."

As if by magic, the worry lifted, as did the grief of separation.

"Oh, Aslam," she smiled. "When shall we leave?"

"Tomorrow. The weather is good. It may not be as good next week. We shall stop and visit Lucy and her headmaster on January 20, then journey on to Eden the next day."

He held her at arm's length and gave her an ominous smile. "From there, I suggest we wait and see what happens."

"How shall we go?"

"How do you want to go?" he asked, only too happy to indulge her in all matters.

She thought for a moment. The train would be quicker, but his carriage would be more comfortable and more romantic and afford them greater freedom. They could stop when they wished and as often as they wished. They could make it a true holiday of cozy inns and unscheduled meals at welcoming pubs.

Growing more excited by the minute, she gazed up at him, amazed at his consideration. "Are you certain, Aslam?"

"That we should go? No."

She frowned, bewildered. "I don't understand."

"I have no way of knowing how we will be received. All I know for certain is that if John Murrey Eden tries to inflict pain of any kind on you again, I shall–"

Quickly she hushed him by placing a finger upon his lips. "Don't," she whispered. "If we see that Lucy is wrong in her advice, we shall simply leave and never look back. You are my world now. The absence of Eden and everyone in it will cause only momentary sorrow whereas to lose you"–she shivered–"would cost me my life."

He stared at her for ever so long. "Then write a message to your parents. Tell them the prodigal is coming home. I'll have it sent within the hour by special messenger."

His eyes were dark and shimmering above her. Suddenly he embraced her with a strength that left her breathless. And in the next minute she felt herself being carried out of the dining hall into the foyer, past servants who stopped and looked the other way, up the grand staircase, on up to the bedchamber, where she knew very well what awaited her.

Paradise awaited her. And what was Eden compared to paradise?

Eden Castle
January 20, 1901

"Now, hang on, both of you. We're going to push it all the way up to thirty. Are you ready?"

John gripped the wheel of his motorcar, then looked back at Chris and Alex, flattened against the backseat, their cheeks flushed with excitement.

They never seemed to tire of John's motorcar, and the promise of an afternoon ride across the moors generally could persuade them to accomplish almost any task of the morning, no matter how distasteful.

"Grandpapa, let me hold the wheel," Alex shouted. "You let Chris hold it yesterday."

Oh, what careful books these two ruffians kept. "All right," John nodded and slowed down while Alex crawled over the seat and into his lap, his eyes shining with excitement.

Then Chris was leaning forward with a request for his ear. "You let Alex ride up front yesterday while I held the wheel."

"Come on," John laughed and reached back and grabbed Chris by the seat of his pants and dragged him over and settled him into the passenger's seat. He winked at him and laughed harder as Chris tried to wink back, both eyes opening and closing at once like a nearsighted little animal.

Dear God, how John loved these two. Sometimes late at night, with Susan sleeping beside him, he thought how dull and colorless his life would be now without the boys.

"Go faster, Grandpapa. We are just sitting still."

"Sitting still, are we? You just wait. All right, Alex, grab the wheel, firm grip now and here–we–go."

The speedometer climbed to twenty, then to twenty-five, then to thirty, then to thirty-five, then to forty–

"Do you like it?" John shouted, above the roar of the wind.

"Oh yes, Grandpapa. And one day we will go even faster."

"How do you know that?"

"Because it feels good, going fast does. Someone will figure out a way to go faster and make it feel even better."

John smiled. Not bad for a five-year-old mind.

It feels good. Someone will figure out a way to go faster.

"Look!" Chris shouted and pointed to the right of the motorcar, where a seagull appeared to be racing with them.

Alex saw it. "Let's go faster, Grandpapa. We can't let an old seagull beat us."

Against his better judgment, John stepped on the accelerator and saw the speedometer shoot up past forty, then forty-five. The engine seemed to be screaming in his ear, but at least they were leaving the seagull behind.

"We won," Chris shouted as the gull veered to the right, clearly choosing the sensible sea over this noisy man-made contraption.

John looked back to make certain that they had been victorious in their race. At the same time, Alex shouted, "Grandpapa, watch out!"

Quickly John looked back at the road to see a horse and rider less than thirty yards ahead. Reflexively he slammed on the brakes and felt the weight of his body push Alex into the steering wheel, saw Chris careen forward into the dash, saw a blur of passing moors on either side. He felt the motorcar shimmying and shuddering against the reduced speed, saw now the frightened horse and rider rear back and bolt the road, thus avoiding a direct collision at the last minute.

He brought the car to a screeching halt about forty yards beyond the horse and rider, the motorcar resting half on the road, half off. For several seconds, John slumped against Alex, who in turn slumped against the steering wheel, unmoving.

"Dear God–" John breathed a quick prayer, then hurriedly reached for the door handle and slid out from beneath Alex's slight weight which still seemed not to be moving.

"Alex," John shouted.

On the floor of the car, he saw Chris just pulling himself up, his eyes pinched shut as he rubbed the side of his head where clearly he had made painful contact with the dash.

"Are you all right?" John shouted, experiencing a degree of fear unlike any he had ever known in his life. "Answer me!"

"Yes, Grandpapa, I just hit my head."

"Sit still in the seat while I–"

Now he carefully turned Alex over and saw his eyes closed, body limp. Dear God, no.

"Alex! Alex, can you hear me?"

As he shouted, he rubbed the boy's hands, then his stomach and chest, trying to massage movement and life into them.

It worked. With a sharp gasp which indicated that the breath had been knocked out of him, Alex came to with a start, coughed and spluttered, his face turning bright red as the air flowed once again into his lungs.

"It's alright, you're alright," John soothed and ultimately pulled the boy close to him and hugged him, his hands shaking in delayed reaction to a tragedy narrowly avoided.

"Come, Chris, you too. Come." He welcomed Chris into his embrace and for several minutes hugged and caressed the boys, who in turn hugged him back, all three clinging together, all aware of how very lucky they were.

"It was the horse, Grandpapa," Chris said at last. "We didn't see–"

The horse. The damnable horse. And rider. Now where in the hell were they?

In belated anger, John pushed away from the motorcar and saw the horse and rider poised about twenty yards away. The man appeared to be a special courier of some sort, a grayish uniform with a leather pouch slung over the side of his saddle.

"You!" John pointed at the rider.

"Me, sir?" he called back in a voice breaking with adolescence.

"Didn't you see me?" John demanded as soon as the young man reined in his mount.

"No, sir."

"But it is a straight road."

"I'm begging your pardon, sir, but did you see me?"

John thought a moment. No, he hadn't.

"There's a sizable incline, sir, back there. In the hollow, it is impossible to see anything."

John studied the terrain for a moment. Funny, he had never noticed the dip in the road before. Then, too, he had been traveling far too fast, though he would have cut out his tongue before he would admit that to anyone.

Now there was no real need to blame the young rider. He could have been killed along with his horse as easily as any of them.

"Are they all right? The young lads, I mean?" the man asked now.

"Fine, a little shaken, but then we all are."

"My apologies, sir."

John shook his head. "And mine. Most incompatible, your mode of transportation and mine. Are you a courier?"

"Aye, sir, on my way to Eden Castle if I don't run out of road and fall into the ocean first."

John laughed. "First you'll reach the castle, then you will fall into the ocean."

"I've never been this far from London before."

"Who sent you?"

"A lady, sir, with a message for her mother, Lady Eden by name."

John blinked up at the announcement. A lady? In London? With a letter for her mother? That could only be–

"You're in luck, sir," John now called out expansively. "My name is John Murrey Eden. I, too, am in residence at Eden Castle. Hand over your message to me, and I shall deliver it personally for you and you can spare yourself another hour or so on these godforsaken moors."

John had tried to make his voice light and appealing. Why then the frown on the man's face?

"It's sorry I am, sir, but I am supposed to deliver it myself."

"Well, I'm offering to do it for you. My God, we're going to the same place. I was only out taking my grandsons for a ride in the motorcar. They are due back for tea within the hour. Come on now, hand it over. I promise the letter will be safely delivered to the lady by the name of Eleanor Eden within the hour. You have my word on it."

The man grinned. Clearly John's words and offer held great appeal. "Very well," the man sighed and reached into his pouch and withdrew a letter. John instantly recognized the handwriting. It was from Charlotte. Apparently she had removed herself from Aslam Eden's bed long enough to pen a letter to her mother.

"I shall see it delivered," John said, strangely sobered by the mere sight of the neat penmanship.

The horse and rider turned about. The man gave a salute. John acknowledged it. Then they were gone.

For several moments, John stood head bowed, studying the clearly expensive blue parchment.

"Grandpapa, are we going home?"

"In a minute," John called out. "I want both of you boys to get out of the motorcar and walk around it half a dozen times, check and see that everything on you works as it should, nothing bruised or broken. And Alex, take a deep breath with every other step. Out, now, the both of you."

John watched them from a distance for a moment, saw them marching around and around the car until predictably they lost interest and started their endless poking at one another, endless giggling, endless joy.

"Don't go too far," he shouted as he saw them break the circle and run out into the moors. It wouldn't hurt, and he needed a moment to persuade his conscience that to read this letter would not be a moral outrage, would indeed be merely fulfilling his obligation to the Eden family, to keep a close and vigilant eye on all things that might cause it harm.

Was his conscience convinced? Of course it was, and with one clean tear, John lifted the envelope flap and slid out a single piece of parchment and read the hastily scribbled message.

> Dearest Mama,
>
> I long to see you. I long to speak with you, to try and help you to see how important it is that you and Papa share in my new happiness. Aslam and I are journeying out to see Lucy and Mason and little Anne on January 21. We shall arrive at Eden Castle on the morning of January 22. Please, I beg you with all my heart, be on the Great Hall steps to receive a most loving embrace from your most loving daughter, Charlotte

John blinked at the letter. The spidery script seemed to dance under the rays of a cold January sun.

January 22.

The whore and her paramour were to arrive tomorrow.

No! John would not have it, would not have those two bring their scandalous and obscene lives into the castle.

How to stop them?

The two boys raced to his side, clearly as hale and hearty as ever.

"Come," John urged. "I am in sore need of a cup of tea and one of Mrs. Partridge's blueberry muffins. And you?"

"Grandpapa, Alex went to the bathroom over there," Chris announced in a suddenly sobered voice.

"So did you," Alex retaliated.

"We both had to go," Chris confessed. "Is that alright?"

John burst into laughter at these sober cherubs standing on either side of him.

"Well, so do I," he announced and herded them back into the motorcar and secured them inside, then walked off into the moors a few yards and unbuttoned his trousers.

Behind him in the motorcar he could hear Alex and Chris giggling. "What are you two laughing about?" he shouted in mock anger.

"You look silly."

"I'm sure you looked silly as well."

"Mrs. Godwin said only animals go to the bathroom outside."

"What Mrs. Godwin doesn't know is that we are all animals."

He shivered with pleasure and thought how fortunate he was to have apprehended the courier. Now all he had to do was to devise a plan to stop them dead in their tracks.

He would do it and would tell no one. As he started back to the motorcar, he saw Chris and Alex, on their knees, peering at him over the folded top. For just a moment their innocence almost took his breath away.

"What are you looking at, Grandpapa?" the boys called out.

"You! I'm looking at you."

"Why?"

"Because I love you so."

The boys dissolved into new giggling and disappeared behind the seat as John increased his step, then slid behind the wheel, turned about and summoned the two gigglers' strict attention.

"Listen! Now both of you, listen to me very closely."

Soberly, recognizing the tone of voice, they unfolded themselves from their impromptu tumbling and sat somberly at attention in the seat.

"I want you both to promise me–several things actually."

"What, Grandpapa?"

"First, there will be no more races. Is that clear?"

"But we won."

"It makes no difference who won," John corrected. "In the process of winning, we could all have been killed."

Both boys nodded soberly.

"Second, we will tell no one what happened today. Is that clear?"

"Why, Grandpapa?"

"Because–" John hesitated, struggling for a lie that these two would believe. "Well, if we were to tell anyone–Susan, your mother, Aunt Marjorie–they are only women, and they would be so frightened by our near mishap that I am quite certain neither of you would be allowed to go riding with me in the motorcar again. I don't think we want that to happen, do we?"

From the wide-eyed, shocked expression on both faces, John was certain that he had struck a live and responsive nerve.

"No, Grandpapa, then we won't tell."

"Of course you won't, and it is a harmless deception, for nothing really happened, did it? So you can recite your prayers each night as always and rest assured that our consciences are clean."

"Yes, Grandpapa."

"Now why don't both of you crawl up here and sit close beside me, and I'll keep you warm for the safe trip home."

All at once the motorcar was a jumble of upside-down little boys, all elbows and knees and giggles and smudged faces and silken hair and impish grins.

Once settled, they grew still, clearly wanting to please him.

"Are you ready, men?" John smiled, lifting his voice above the wind.

"Ready, Grandpapa."

Carefully he backed the motorcar out of the ditch, angled it about and headed it slowly toward Eden, traveling at a sedate pace which enabled him to plot his actions of the next few hours so that when the whore and her lover appeared at the Eden gatehouse, they would be soundly turned back, hopefully never to return.

January 22, 1901

Since Charlotte and Aslam had left Lucy and Mason's cozy cottage at Greenfield in Exeter, the wind had turned bitter cold and Charlotte noticed specks of snow outside the carriage window.

No matter. They would soon be warm before an Eden fire in the Great Hall, and she was certain that she had never known such happiness.

Now she pressed her leg against Aslam's beneath the warm fur carriage blanket and found his hand as well and grasped it and felt a returning pressure.

"Did you enjoy yourself at Lucy and Mason's?"

"I did, very much," he smiled. "Mason is a remarkable man, a brilliant man. You were fortunate to have had him as your tutor all those years."

"It was John who sent them away."

"You're shivering," Aslam noticed, alarmed.

"Not from the cold, my darling. I must confess, I'm frightened."

"Of what?"

"Of what we will encounter at Eden."

"If we encounter anything other than the hospitality we deserve, we shall leave immediately and seek lodgings elsewhere. I know a comfortable country inn in Ilfracombe, with feather beds and roaring fires. I promise I will not stand by and watch you suffer."

His manner was so intense, his words so kind, she leaned closer and kissed him. Briefly she considered the wisdom of simply giving their drivers the command to make straight for Ilfracombe and the country inn with the soft feather beds.

No, they had come this far and Lucy had assured them that in the end

John would come around. She knew for a fact that her Mama and Papa missed her.

Charlotte smiled and closed her eyes. What she wanted, plain and simple, was to go home. She drew a deep breath and prayed that the weather would hold for just a few more hours.

Then, once safely returned to the bosom of her family and with Aslam at her side, the storms of the world could break all around her. She wouldn't care then.

Aslam saw the parapets and turrets from a distance, despite the increasing snow. He remembered journeying out to Eden with John many times in younger, better days.

Despite everything that had happened, he had a small storehouse of treasured memories connected with this old castle—evenings in his mother's chambers with John reading aloud to both of them, running races on the headlands with Mary and Richard, then returning to the warmth of the Great Hall fire for cinnamon cakes and hot tea. He remembered slipping out early in the morning to go riding with John across the tenant farms, good camaraderie, the best of times.

Now he looked down on Charlotte. For a moment he thought she was asleep. But she wasn't. She was simply sitting quietly beside him, her eyes wide and fixed on the whirling snow.

"Ten minutes at most," he predicted and wondered if the special courier he had dispatched from London two days ago had successfully delivered their arrival notice.

Now he saw Charlotte sit up in the seat, throw back the lap rug and reach down for her small traveling case. She tried to prop the mirror on her lap, but the rattle and rumble of the carriage continually dislodged it until at last with a laugh Aslam held it steady for her.

"You look lovely," he smiled and wondered if the time would ever come when he would grow weary of gazing on her beauty.

"It's the best I can do," she sighed at last and restored the mirror to her traveling case with a laugh. "Mama has seen me in all conditions," she said. "I'm sure she'll forgive the disarray caused by the road."

They were on the last approach now, up a slight incline, down to the gatehouse, across the rattling grate and into the inner courtyard.

As Aslam traced the route in his mind, he suddenly felt the horses break speed, felt the carriage shimmy as the drivers attempted to stop.

The sudden reversal tossed them about, left Aslam clinging to the door handle and Charlotte clinging to Aslam.

"What happened?" she gasped, still struggling against the erratic movement of the carriage, which was at last beginning to slow.

Quickly Aslam looked out of his window. "What is it?" he shouted.

"The gates, sir," one of his drivers called back.

"What about the gates?" As he spoke, Aslam indicated to Charlotte she was to stay where she was. Quickly he swung down from the carriage and within the moment saw the cause for the sudden stop.

The massive filigree black wrought iron gates were closed, the connection wrapped about with heavy chain and a lock securing the chain.

Slowly Aslam walked down the incline past his drivers, who both called down their apology for the rough stop. He waved away their apologies and turned up the collar of his jacket against the cold wind.

As he approached the closed gate, he looked beyond to the gatehouse and concentrated all his attention on the shadow that he thought he had seen moving about in the dingy interior.

Quickly he moved forward, keeping an eye on the small room. The shadow was gone. Just inside the gate he saw the alarm bell, the twin standards recently uprooted, the bell itself lying uselessly on its side, as though at the last minute someone had withdrawn it from a position outside the gate to a position inside.

"Aslam? Why is the gate locked?" Charlotte asked, coming hurriedly down the incline.

"I don't know."

For several moments he watched her with breaking heart as she surveyed the closed gates, the empty gatehouse, the deserted courtyard and the uprooted alarm bell.

As for Aslam, his attention was still focused on the small rectangular window of the old gatehouse. He was certain that there was someone inside.

"Hello," he called out and scooped up a handful of pebbles and commenced pelting them one by one against the window. "Is anybody there?" he called out.

"Aslam, I don't–understand."

"Come along," he said, gently and tried to take her elbow, but quickly she pulled away.

"No, not yet. Please," she begged. "There is something wrong. I know it. The gate is never closed and bolted. And the bell. Why has the bell been–"

As her voice rose, she seemed to become more agitated, pacing back and forth now in front of the gate, peering in like a lost child and once calling out, "Mama."

Aslam bowed his head and felt the wind increase. Behind him the horses stomped impatiently at the earth, clearly ready and eager to find refuge and food.

Taking a lesson from the horses, Aslam realized that they too must take refuge and soon.

"Charlotte, come, please, we must–"

Aslam tried to turn her back toward the carriage. But she would not be moved. Her heart was breaking, of that he was certain.

He looked again through the narrow gatehouse window. The shadow was visible, the faint outline of a man.

John Murrey Eden.

Aslam would swear to it, would swear further that the closed and bolted gates, the empty courtyard, the uprooted alarm bell was John's handiwork as well.

Damn him, he cursed and kept his eyes fixed on the shadow even as he moved forward once again in a gentle attempt to dislodge Charlotte from the gates.

"Come, my dearest," he begged. But she held fast, her eyes lifted to the cold sleet, her face a pitiful contortion of grief and loneliness.

John had hoped to be out of the gatehouse and safely back inside the castle when the whore and her paramour arrived for their grand entrance.

Only at the last minute had he remembered the alarm bell. He had already paid off the guardsmen and urged them to treat themselves to a full day at The Hanging Man down in Mortemouth. The family was sequestered in the upstairs sitting room, listening to Richard's latest gramophone records played at top volume. The servants were staying toasty and dry around the kitchen court fire on such a miserable day, and as no messenger had arrived announcing the coming of anyone, then John was certain he could lock and bolt the gates, leaving the intruders to stand on the outside in this storm, which was worsening by the minute.

As he was closing the Great Hall doors behind him he remembered the alarm bell and thus had to run back to the gates, unlock them and literally wrestle the heavy bell and its standards out of the earth.

Then he had heard a carriage.

No choice but to take refuge in the gatehouse.

They had arrived, the two infidels, and clearly the locked gates had been a surprise to the horses and drivers. John had never seen such veering and neighing.

But the skillful drivers had brought the animals under control, and then he had seen Aslam get out, looking quite confident. He had surveyed the locked gates, and John had seen his confidence falter. He had seen Charlotte leave the carriage. The two of them had talked easily for a few moments, though John couldn't hear what was being said, but then he had heard pebbles strike the gatehouse window, had seen Charlotte peer closely through the locked gates, alternately clinging to them, then foolishly trying to shake them.

John was fairly certain that Aslam suspected the presence of someone in the gatehouse, and for one macabre moment, he even considered stepping out and confronting them both, allowing them to see the face of the one who had arranged this rejection.

Fortunately better judgment intervened. Wiser to let them go through the agony of wondering.

Well, now look at them, frozen with sleet, deep and permanent expressions of abandonment etched on their pitiable faces. For one weak moment, John almost felt sorry for them. My God, how long did they intend to stand in this dreadful weather and push against the gates that they knew would never be opened to them?

All at once John saw Charlotte collapse softly against the gates. One of the drivers hopped down to assist his master, and after they had placed poor, wet Charlotte back inside the carriage, Aslam suddenly stopped. With one hand raised to the hand support, one foot lifted to the step, he clung there for a peculiar moment of indecision, staring back toward the gatehouse. Abruptly he dropped back down to earth and started toward the incline at a slow pace.

John pushed further back into his limited corner, the one position in the narrow room that afforded him complete protection.

What in the hell was the man—

Aslam came to a halt in close proximity to the gatehouse, grabbed the bars as though he were in prison, lifted his face to the sleet and seemed to focus on the exact corner where John was hiding.

"John Murrey Eden!" he called out.

John held his breath, closed his eyes, flattened himself against the intersecting walls and wondered if Aslam was bluffing. How could he possibly know?

"You can hear me, and I want you to listen carefully," Aslam called further. "What you have done here today is unforgivable. You will pay, of course. You know it as well as I. Charlotte will recover. I shall see to it. But you are destined for tragedy and heartache beyond your ability to comprehend. Our friendship might have been rekindled on this day. I was looking forward to it. Instead, it was your choice to condemn it. Then I shall abide by your decision. I'm sorry for it. I'm sorry for you."

With that, he slowly turned about with his head down and walked back up the incline. John dared to peer out and saw Aslam approach the carriage a second time, draw himself up and close the door. A moment later the drivers turned wide and headed the horses back down the moor road toward Ilfracombe.

For several minutes, John held his position wedged tightly in the corner of the gatehouse.

What nonsense! What ridiculous melodrama! But then, even as a boy Aslam had been given to broad theatrics and unnecessary histrionics. Clearly age had not changed him.

You are destined for tragedy and heartache beyond your ability to comprehend.

What rubbish!

Well, he had certainly accomplished his goal. The infamous two had been turned back. Eden had been spared the ordeal of accommodating them. Eleanor would recover. She had much to occupy her attention now in the boys and in her granddaughter. Her life was full. Charlotte was dead to her now. So be it.

You are destined for tragedy and heartache beyond—

What foolishness!

"Grandpapa!"

He looked toward the Great Hall, where Chris and Alex were waving to him from the steps. What a glorious sight, though neither were dressed properly and the wind was yet increasing.

Damn! Where were the blasted women in the castle? Why had no one thought to dress the boys in their heaviest mackintoshes? Did John have to do everything, think of everything?

"Go on back," he called out as he hurried across the inner courtyard.

"Grandpapa, tea is ready."

"And I'm coming. Go on, get inside."

"Where were you?"

"Busy."

"Grandmama told us to come and find you. She said we could find you when no one else could."

"And right she is," John smiled and hurried up the Great Hall steps. Quickly he closed the doors behind him and considered locking and bolting them as well. "Race you to the sitting room," he grinned, challenging the boys to their favorite sport.

Then they were off, running at breakneck speed across the Great Hall, taking the steps two at a time while John huffed behind them and recalled the days when he had had to let them win.

No more. They were fleet of foot now and capable of outracing anyone and anything.

John prayed quickly that it would always be so. Then he struggled after them, knowing full well he would not win, but hoping at least to outrace the memory of Aslam's face, wet with sleet as he had clung to the gate and made those most absurd pronouncements.

Ilfracombe
January 23, 1901

It was almost dawn before the drivers brought the carriage to a halt before the Lion's Head Inn. Half-frozen, Charlotte peered out of the window through swollen and burning eyes and saw the friendly, beckoning glow of firelight through frosted mullioned windows.

"Come," Aslam invited softly. "We need warmth and food. Then, I promise you, the world will look better."

She accepted his hand and was grateful for his love and patience. During the long, bleak ride across the moors, he had held her until the tears had stopped.

Now, as her foot touched snow, she felt her knees buckle and would have collapsed if it had not been for his ready arms.

"Open the inn door," he called to one of the drivers. As Aslam and Charlotte entered the low-ceilinged inn, they were met by a most curious sight.

Near the fire, she saw a small gathering, partly guests, partly servants, and all were weeping.

The landlord, a ruddy-faced and quite fleshy gentleman named Mr. Hanover slowly separated himself from the others and tried to shove his wadded linen handkerchief back into his pocket. "Good evening to ye," he said and seemed to be making a desperate attempt to keep his emotions in check.

Clearly Aslam was puzzled. "We are in need of a room, sir, with a fire and a hot meal. Would that be–"

The man nodded, though he said not a word and moved toward his high desk; at the same time, a woman near the fire burst into fresh and noisy tears.

Quietly Charlotte slipped from Aslam's arms, assuring him that she now was capable of standing. "Excuse me," she said. "Could you tell us the nature of your grief?"

As the man fished through a wooden box for the proper key, he started to cry again. "It ain't just my grief, your ladyship," he said as soon as he was able to talk. "It's England's grief, the Empire's grief, the world's grief."

Aslam shook off his wet cape. "I'm afraid I don't understand."

"The old queen is dead," the man announced, and his voice seemed to provoke new waves of tears coming from the fireplace.

Slowly Charlotte sank into a near chair, shocked by the news.

"When did you hear?" Aslam asked quietly.

"Only a short while ago. Henry, it was, who brought word from Exeter, where someone else had brought it from London. It just happened, you see. The old queen was at Osborne, she was, when death paid a call."

Charlotte fought back tears, a curious combination of grief for the old queen and grief for herself, for the estrangement from her family, for the closed and locked gates of Eden.

Suddenly an idea occurred. "Aslam?" she called out.

"What is it, my darling?"

"Could this be the reason?" she asked on a surge of new hope.

"What? I don't understand."

"For the locked gates at Eden. Could the family have gone into seclusion?"

She watched his face closely for any sign that he shared her hope, but he didn't. Even as she spoke, he commenced to shake his head.

"Perhaps the guardsmen have all gone home to be with their families."

"No, my dearest, no. I'm–"

The old landlord handed Aslam the proper key. "Second floor front, it is, sir, our most comfortable. I'm sure you and your wife will find it to your liking."

Wife. Charlotte heard the word and took pleasure in it. Then she felt Aslam's arm about her. "Come, my darling, let us find a place of privacy. I'm sure this good man will prepare a warm meal for us. Nothing fancy. What you had for your dinner, sir, if you will be so good."

"Indeed, it's just boiled mutton. But I'll have my girl bring you some, with a good bottle of red wine."

"We're grateful."

Charlotte started up the narrow winding stairs with Aslam close beside her and heard the group by the fireplace lift glasses in toast.

"The queen was dead. Long live the king."

The queen is dead. Eden was dead. Her parents were dead to her, and she, to them. It was too much death to be tolerated. She clung to Aslam and took into careful account the price she had paid for loving him.

Was it too much?

No. She went eagerly into his arms, clung to him and looked forward to the act of love.

Only in such a powerful union could death be defeated, all death.

London
October 10, 1903

Alice had never felt such excitement in her life.

Mrs. Pankhurst's parlor was filled to overflowing. No one had dreamed there would be such a turnout. Every chair, every sofa, every corner was filled with women and a few enlightened, sympathetic men sprinkled about, such as Albert and his friend Colin, who stood next to him.

After Cambridge, Albert had studied law at the Inns of Court. He had done well, though he had never really opted for a legal position, preferring to spend his days in indolent inactivity, mostly backstage at Drury Lane, where Colin was performing in *Hamlet.*

"I wish Charlotte could have come," Albert whispered. "Then all the Eden outcasts would have been allied. What a grand moment it would have been."

Alice smiled and continued to look about, spotting many familiar faces, leaders of every antigovernment social and political group in London. As for an alliance of Eden outcasts, well, she wasn't certain about that. She did not feel very revolutionary. Now, as head of nursing at St. Martin's Hospital, her hours were long and difficult, her responsibilities enormous. She had been denied access to Eden Castle on the basis of her political and social philosophies. She suspected it had been her father who had done the banishing. So be it. She wrote regularly to her mother, she saw Charlotte and Aslam on a weekly basis and she had given poor Albert a home in which to entertain his homosexual friends.

In short, she was doing the best she could and would continue to do so in exchange for her complete freedom.

"Excuse me, Albert, a moment," she whispered. "I see a friend," and she moved as quickly as possible through the crowded salon.

She was less than two feet away when her old friend Christabel Pankhurst spotted her in return.

"Alice," she cried out in genuine affection, and in the midst of the rising voices and excitement, Alice and Christabel embraced, a warm reunion after a separation of too many years. When Christabel had ceased her nursing studies, she had gone back to Manchester to be with her mother. Alice had lost touch with her.

"Oh, my dearest," Christabel gasped. "You look–positively prosperous."

Alice laughed. "Anything you might have said would have been more accurate."

"Still, you do look so well. I can't believe it's you. Where did you get to?"

"Where did *I* get to?" Alice laughed. "Dear Christabel, you always got things backward. You were the one who disappeared from sight without a word."

Christabel smiled and shrugged. "It was a call I had to answer. Mother summoned me from Manchester. My father died."

"I'm so sorry."

"And we had quite a struggle. But look, here we are," and she gestured about at the very comfortable salon, tastefully though simply done out and now filled with excitedly talking women.

"And you?" Christabel went on, taking Alice by the elbow and guiding her into a relatively quiet corner of the room.

"I'm still at St. Martin's Hospital."

"Not as a student?"

"No. As head of nursing."

Christabel squealed and summoned the attention of everyone in the vicinity. "Oh, how marvelous. And you're so young, but so talented. I knew it, I always knew you'd be successful."

Alice brushed away the compliments and tried to keep her friend on track. "And you?"

"Well," Christabel said, a light of amusement in her eye. "I am now training as a barrister. Mother feels we may need a good lawyer in the family before we are done."

"A barrister. You will be perfect."

"No, I won't," Christabel added, with sly sadness.

"Why?"

"For the very simple reason that women are excluded from the bar."

For a moment the words hung on the noisy air like a recently slammed door. "I don't understand," Alice confessed. "Then why aren't you–"

"Because by the time I'm ready, we fully intend to overthrow the ruling."

Briefly the two women looked at each other, then both burst out laughing, clinging to one another, and Alice was so glad she had found her friend once more.

"We must never again become separated," Christabel whispered at the end of the embrace. "Now our time has come, dear Alice. The days of talking, dreaming and scheming are over. Mother will lead us. You shall see. Come, there are so many I want you to meet."

For the next few minutes, as still more people continued to push in through the front door, Christabel took Alice in hand and introduced her to a series of people: Mrs. Flora Drummond, whose life had been blighted by the fact that she was under regulation height to become a postmistress; Theresa Billington, a well-known socialite; Hannah Mitchell, a renegade from a Labor church, where they sang hymns such as "The Red Flag"; and, most fascinating of all, Annie Kenny, an attractive Lancashire mill hand who had suffered the loss of a finger in a mill accident and who could both speak and write eloquently on the devastating need to try to end poverty and foster equality.

All these and many others had gathered for one purpose, to form an independent women's movement, not connected with any other social or political party, with no goal other than the goal of freedom and equality for women. It was to be called the Women's Social and Political Union, or WSPU. Its ends were votes for women and chastity for men, and its most significant slogan was Deeds, Not Words.

Then, as if on cue, when not another soul could squeeze into the room, Mrs. Pankhurst appeared like a Greek goddess in flowing white robes, heliotrope in her hair and the warmest and most vibrant of smiles on her face.

All grew quiet, as though aware that what they had come for was about to commence. For a few moments she graciously greeted certain individuals. Alice watched her closely and recalled the vile criticism which had been leveled at her by the British press: "Really Mrs. Pankhurst is not seeking democratic freedom but rather self-importance . . . she paints her eyebrows grossly and is selfish and willful to a fault. She wants desperately to be a lady but lacks the humility of real heroism."

Certainly Mrs. Pankhurst was arrogant. Courage alone would scarcely have sustained her, had she not felt herself to be the messenger of a world-important cause.

"My dearest Christabel," Mrs. Pankhurst now smiled, and Alice was brought back from memories of old newspaper headlines and photos to find herself facing the great lady.

"Mama," Christabel smiled and lightly kissed her mother. "You remember Alice Eden, of course; we were friends several years ago when I was studying nursing."

"Of course," Mrs. Pankhurst smiled. "Christabel and I have spoken of you often. I'm so glad you have come."

"She is head of nursing at St. Martin's, Mama."

"Then I'm doubly glad you have come. I'm afraid that before the last woman on earth is set free, we may have need of your compassionate talents."

Alice smiled. "That is one of the reasons why I came."

"And the other?"

"Freedom for all women," Alice replied without hesitation and saw a most rewarding smile on Mrs. Pankhurst's face.

Then someone called to her from the small platform at the far end of the salon and she was gone. Alice and Christabel found themselves in the front of the meeting, the sense of excitement rising to unbearable proportions as Mrs. Pankhurst took the platform and waited until the crowded salon was totally silent.

Then, "Ladies and gentlemen, friends of freedom, welcome to the first meeting of the Women's Social and Political Union."

The room, which only moments before had fallen silent, suddenly erupted again into cheers and whistles. Alice felt goosebumps.

"Years ago," Mrs. Pankhurst went on when the cheering died down, "in Manchester I became a salaried registrar of births and deaths. I hated the job at the time, but I believe now that it was that position which opened my eyes to the vision of what the world must become."

Across the room Alice saw Albert and Colin. Albert smiled at her, and she returned his smile, realizing how fond she was of this sad younger brother.

"My duties brought me daily into close contact with the squalid wretchedness of working-class life, and it didn't take me too long to diagnose the worst ills as moral ones. Sweated labor, rape, incest, illegitimacy, prostitution, white-slave traffic, such wicked forms of social and sexual exploitation could only be eradicated by enfranchised womanhood."

As Mrs. Pankhurst spoke on, citing tragic case after tragic case, the audience seemed to become almost mesmerized by this dreadful litany of misery and death.

"It is obvious to me," she went on, "that all males, whatever their political persuasion, are locked in a vicious conspiracy against those whom they are wont to call in that revealing metonymy 'the sex.' Is it not clear that women are kept down so that men can more conveniently get up to no good?"

The audience, as one voice, answered, "Yes!"

"And these same fools," Mrs. Pankhurst thundered now, "have axioms to meet every occasion. For example, proper women do not want the vote."

"No!"

"Militant and masculine-minded suffragettes demonstrate their unworthiness to exercise it."

"No!"

"Females will not use the vote, and those that do will neglect their families."

"No!"

"Women will vote with their husbands or priests, and women will cause domestic and religious dissension by voting against their husbands or priests."

"No!"

The single shouted word echoed in Alice's head and became a battle cry against each new foolishness mentioned by Mrs. Pankhurst.

"I propose on this day, October 10, 1903, to create an organization which hereafter will be known as the Women's Social and Political Union and that our goal shall be the emancipation and education of every female, the vote for every female, the right of every female to choose her own destiny, the obligation of every female to be dependent on no man unless it is her choice to be so. Those are our purposes, those our goals, and I predict the battle will be long and painful and perhaps on occasion bloody. I also predict that we will succeed, with God as our witness."

For several moments after Mrs. Pankhurst ceased to speak, there was not a sound in the crowded salon. Then all at once, every voice broke loose in enthusiastic cheers which caused the chandelier to shake.

During the tumult Alice and Christabel warmly embraced. What a glorious moment, Alice was certain, and she was equally certain that civilization had taken a major step forward here tonight. It would be, as Mrs. Pankhurst had suggested, a long and painful battle. The world had embraced certain unfair and unjust beliefs for too long without challenge. Now they were being challenged, and some males, she was certain, would never be persuaded to any point of view, save their own.

John Murrey Eden.

Alice smiled at the thought of her father, as much a victim as those he had victimized. He would never change, he was incapable of change, she would swear to it, and there were others as well, the board of directors at St. Martin's Hospital, in fact, boards of directors everywhere, in every male bastion that would very shortly feel threatened by the movement that was designed to liberate male and female alike.

Then this was her life's goal, and with that calm and very private decision made and tucked away where all decisions go to become convictions, she looked about for Albert and found him, much to her surprise, in close and earnest conversation with Mrs. Pankhurst, who appeared to be listening to every word he was saying. Albert's friend Colin was contributing now and then, but Albert was clearly doing most of the talking.

"Isn't that your brother?" Christabel asked, raising her voice over the crowd.

"It is."

"What in the world do you suppose he is saying to Mother? She looks totally engrossed."

Alice laughed. "I haven't the faintest idea."

"Well, come, there's cold punch in the next room. I will lead; you keep your eye on the rear guard."

And in the spirit of old friendship revived, Alice followed after Christabel, admitting to a fine thirst after so much shouting and only mildly curious about what her younger brother was saying to the great lady, Mrs. Pankhurst, to so hold her attention when there were dozens of others who wanted it as well.

Because Albert wanted to do it and because he could think of no course of action that would so enrage his father, he made his offer to a very grateful Mrs. Pankhurst.

"Are you certain, Mr. Eden?" she asked.

"I've never been more certain, Mrs. Pankhurst. You roused me tonight with your words in a way I have never been roused before. And though a member of the male sex, I assure you that I feel as keenly as you on the matter of female injustice and I long, as you do, to be a part of bringing about the dawn of a better day."

"Have I heard of your family?" Mrs. Pankhurst asked, her manner now quite cautious.

"I am estranged from my family, Mrs. Pankhurst, except for my sister, Alice, who–"

"Christabel's friend," Mrs. Pankhurst exclaimed in a eureka cry.

"Yes."

"The Edens. Of North Devon. How splendid. Of course, I see the resemblance now. Is she–I mean your sister–estranged as well?"

"I am afraid that our father refuses to entertain a new idea. He considers them threatening, dangerous and treasonous."

Mrs. Pankhurst smiled. "As indeed they are."

"Then my offer, do you accept it?"

For a moment he was afraid she would not. She seemed so very cautious, so impervious to the admiring crowds pushing close around her.

Finally, when he was despairing that she would ever speak again, she smiled. "Free legal advice from a Cambridge man? I'd be a fool to turn down such an offer, now wouldn't I? Of course I accept, and I accept your presence in my home. I shall set up a small study for you and with your legal guidance we shall take on the entire British Empire."

Albert laughed, felt Colin close behind him and drew him forward for an introduction. "Allow me to introduce Colin Brand, Mrs. Pankhurst. Colin is my dear friend."

"My pleasure, sir."

"He is an actor presently at Drury Lane, performing in *Hamlet.*"

Albert looked up to see Alice and Christabel approaching, punch glasses in hand, and on Alice's face a very curious expression.

Mrs. Pankhurst called out to them. "Come, you two. I want you to meet the movement's new lawyer, Mr. Albert Eden, who has most graciously offered us the full extent of his skill and knowledge on a strictly voluntary basis. Isn't that splendid?"

Albert saw Alice blink, saw her rather awkward half smile, which generally suggested she hadn't the faintest idea of how to respond to a situation.

Then Christabel decided for her with an extended hand. "How marvelous, Mr. Eden," she said with what appeared to be genuine pleasure. "I had no idea you had gone on to study the law."

Albert smiled. "Since most of my true passions were outside of the law, it seemed the only sensible thing to do."

"I, too, am studying the law," he heard Christabel announce. "Yes, though mind you, I know beforehand that my sex is not permitted to the bar."

"It is my hope that under the leadership of Mrs. Pankhurst, all of that nonsense will be changed by the time you are ready," Albert said, and was pleased to realize that he meant every word and was doubly pleased to see the effect his words had on the three women standing close to him.

"Then tomorrow morning, my dearest Albert," Mrs. Pankhurst said. Then she was gone, swallowed up by the crowds.

"Albert, are you certain?"

This low whisper came from Alice, who took Mrs. Pankhurst's place at his side.

"Certain? No, I'm certain of nothing except dearest Colin here. Come, Colin, no need to hang back. These are sympathetic females and mean us no harm. If you ladies will excuse us," Albert now said, "I think that Colin and I need to make our way to a dank and dingy Thames-side pub, and there we need to drink heartily."

With that he was gone, taking Colin by the hand and half dragging him through the crowded salon, leaving both Alice and Christabel gaping after them in a state of surprise.

No matter. They both were good women and would forgive him. Albert generally had little to do with anybody who would not extend to him love and forgiveness. He had lived without both redeeming graces for the first eighteen years of his life. He never intended to be without them again.

"Come," he urged Colin, once they were on the darkened pavement, the noise and turmoil of Mrs. Pankhurst's salon left behind.

He started off toward the river, thinking only once of his new position. Legal adviser to the Women's Social and Political Union. Dear God, how outraged his father would be at that. Albert would have to devise a way to get word to him immediately.

Eden Castle
November 10, 1905

"Lord Nelson" stretched out on his stomach too close to the roaring Great Hall fire, slithered backward and, in the process, caused three of his own battleships to fall on their sides.

"Be careful," Chris called out, and quickly Alex righted his toy ships and bleakly wondered how many times Lord Nelson would have to defeat Villeneuve before Chris grew weary of this battle.

They had already been at it all morning. Months ago Grandpapa had ordered the toy fleets for them from a London store to coincide with that segment of history they were studying under the relentless tutelage of Mr. Neville. Earlier Grandpapa had helped them set up the Battle of Cádiz and had imposed upon Aunt Eleanor for a piece of her old blue dressing gown to serve as the harbor; now, for the third time since breakfast, Nelson was proposing to sail and fire on Villeneuve, at which point Nelson would signal his fleet, "England expects every man will do his duty," and following that, Nelson's ship, the *Victory*, would break through between Villeneuve's flagship, the *Bucentaure*, and the *Redoubtable*.

"Ready?" Alex called out.

"Ready," Chris replied, grinning. On his knees, he leaned forward over Cádiz Harbor and slowly moved his two warships forward. "Now, you—"

"I know," Alex scolded. "Here comes Lord Nelson, chug-chug-chug."

"Boats don't go 'chug-chug.' "

"Well, what do they do?"

"I don't know, but they don't go 'chug-chug.' You've never done that before. Boats have sails."

Alex grinned. "Alright then, here I come, whish, whish, whish—"

"Alex!"

"I'm sorry." Quickly he moved the *Victory* forward into position. "Alright, now it is your turn to shoot me."

"Wait. We have to have volleys first. Here comes one."

Then Chris made a strange sound like the tag end of Uncle Richard's snores, a hissing sound.

"Bang! Boom! Hit the deck!"

Still Alex pushed the *Victory* forward.

"Now your turn," Chris ordered. For several minutes, the two boys angled their ships about on Aunt Eleanor's blue dressing gown, each making bizarre sounds to represent the roar of broadsides, the crashing of masts, the rattle of musketry fired at point-blank range.

Then all at once, Alex scrambled up to his knees, turned his back and commanded, "Now shoot me."

With clear reluctance, Chris "shot" his finger, and Alex writhed gloriously and fell forward, one leg scattering Nelson's fleet as far as the edge of the fireplace.

For several moments he waited for Chris to speak. When he didn't, Alex opened one eye and saw him on his knees, holding his two battleships in his hands.

"Chris, do you want to send the message, or shall I?" Alex called out, trying to break the spell.

"You can't send it; you're dead."

"Then you send it and hurry up. I'm tired of being dead."

Still sprawled "lifeless," Alex saw Chris stand, salute and withdraw an imaginary message from his pocket.

He read, "Partial firing continued until four-thirty when a victory having been reported to the Right Honorable Lord Viscount Nelson, K.B. and Commander-in-Chief, he then died of his wounds."

Good. It was over.

Alex drew himself up, straightened Cádiz Harbor, where his knee had caused it to wrinkle, picked up one of Nelson's ships and studied it.

"Where's Rolf?" Chris asked, stretching out on his back.

"With Mr. Neville. Mr. Neville said he needed to work on his Latin grammar."

"Ugh!" Chris groaned and rolled to his stomach. "Do you like Mr. Neville?"

Alex sat cross-legged and piled all of the battleships into the cavity formed by his legs.

"He's alright. I like Mason Frye better. Mason Frye was Papa's tutor."

"I wish he were ours."

"Where is your papa?" Chris asked.

Alex thought a minute. He hadn't seen him all day. Then he remembered. "Susan told me he has gone to Exeter."

Chris nodded. For a moment both boys were silent. Then Chris said, "I'm hungry."

"Do you want to go down to the kitchen court and see Mrs. Partridge?"

"No, she'll just chase us back up the stairs. Tea soon."

"Mama and Papa are coming up for dinner tonight," Chris announced.

Alex always enjoyed it when Uncle Frederick and Aunt Marjorie came to the castle for dinner. Generally they were kept very busy from dawn until dusk at the parish church down in Mortemouth.

"Where would you rather live?" Alex asked. "Down in Mortemouth or up here in Eden Castle?"

Chris looked up at him as though he were an idiot. "Up here. I've told Mama that. That's why she lets me stay here most of the time."

"Why?"

Chris shrugged. "Because it's so big," he said, looking upward at the high ceiling of the Great Hall. "We can always have more fun here. Mama says it's alright, and Papa says Grandpapa wouldn't have it any other way."

That was good, for Alex loved Chris and wasn't quite certain what he would do if Chris had to move down to the cottage in Mortemouth on a permanent basis.

"Do you miss not having a mother?" Chris asked.

The blunt question caught Alex off guard. "Aunt Eleanor told me once that I had lots of mothers—herself, Susan, Aunt Marjorie, and Aunt Lucy—"

"But not a real one."

"No, not my real one. She died."

"I know."

"She was very beautiful, my mother."

"I know."

"Papa still misses her."

For a few minutes the only sound was the crackling of the fire. Chris said, "I'm sorry I asked about your mother."

"No need," Alex replied as he gathered up half of Lord Nelson's fleet with his hands. "Come on, let's put this stuff away and go and find Rolf."

Rolf was their unofficial leader. Both Alex and Chris looked to Rolf, two years older, at eleven, and vastly more knowledgeable about Eden Castle, for new adventure.

Now both boys drew forward the wooden boxes in which they stored the French and English fleets and folded the blue Cádiz Harbor, putting it on top of one box for the next time they wanted to play the game. They then scrambled to their feet.

"Come on, let's go find Rolf."

"What if old Neville won't let him go?"

"Then we'll explore on our own. Rolf told me last night that he had seen a ghost in the east wing."

"Nonsense," Alex scoffed. "There is no such thing."

"Is so."

"Is not."

"Is so."

"Race you to the library." And with only that scant warning, Alex shot forward, with the advantage of the one who conceives of the idea. But Chris was directly behind and gaining. As they approached the closed library doors, Alex tried to stop but his speed was too great, and Chris, coming right behind, collided noisily with him. Both boys slammed into the heavy oak doors and fell backward in a giggling turmoil of arms, legs and shrieks.

As Alex was trying to disengage himself, he saw the library door open, saw round-faced Mr. Neville. Rolf called him the pumpkin man, his spectacles perched on the very end of his round nose, his round head set on his rounded shoulders, everything about the man round, plump and pudgy.

"What have we here?" he now exclaimed. In the crook of one arm he clasped a Latin grammar, in the other a long pointer.

Quickly both boys scrambled to their feet. Alex made an attempt to straighten his shirtwaist and smooth his hair, while Chris did the same.

"When young men start colliding with library doors," Mr. Neville intoned, "I take it as a sign that they are bored and want to pursue further studies."

"No, sir," Alex said quickly, "We were just wondering if Rolf—"

"He is occupied," Mr. Neville said, rocking ever so gently back and forth on his toes. Alex glanced beyond Mr. Neville and saw Rolf standing at the blackboard, looking miserable.

"How much longer?" Chris asked, spying Rolf as well.

"How much longer until what?" Mr. Neville inquired, a new archness in his voice.

"Until Rolf is free."

"Rolf is a free man," Mr. Neville explained with suspect patience. "I am not holding him a prisoner here. He is here because he wants to be. Isn't that correct, Rolf?"

Alex found this hard to believe, peered more closely around Mr. Neville and saw Rolf nod. Alex worshipped Rolf, as did Chris. But more and more of late, Rolf seemed to be in the library with Mr. Neville.

"I had better stay, Alex," Rolf called out. "About an hour, perhaps two, and I'll meet you both on the Great Hall steps."

Alex started to point out that it would be dark by then. What in the world was the matter with Rolf? Didn't he even know what time it was?

Apparently Mr. Neville saw the disappointment on Alex's face. "Don't worry, young men, the time will come for you, as well, when you realize that in order to face the world head-on, you must have knowledge. You may come in and join us and work on your Latin grammar, which needs a great deal of work, or you can run about senselessly and accomplish nothing for the next two hours. I will leave it up to you."

Alex studied the scuffed toes of his boots and regretted ever having bumped into the doors.

"I'm sorry, Mr. Neville," Chris carefully explained, "but Grandpapa is expecting us. He wants to show us something of great importance."

Mr. Neville backed into the library, a bit of a suspicious look on his face.

"Until later then," he nodded stiffly, closing the door and leaving them alone in the darkened corridor with the weight of Chris's fib beating down around them.

"Did Grandpapa–"

"Shhh. Come on. Let's get out of here before old Neville changes his mind. Hurry, unless, of course, you want to join Rolf in his grammar lesson."

Most certainly Alex did not want to do that, so he followed Chris, allowing him to lead the way back down the corridor until they entered the Great Hall, finding it as empty as when they had left it.

There was this to be said for Eden Castle. Sometimes Alex felt like there was no one else in residence here, though he knew for a fact that his Uncle Richard and Aunt Eleanor were somewhere, as was Susan, Grandpapa and all of the servants. Many people were somewhere, but at times it was so easy to feel that you were all alone in the castle–except, of course, for Chris.

"Now what?" Chris muttered, slouching against the wall, staring down the length of the Great Hall as though its emptiness was his enemy.

Alex had no suggestion and slouched with him, wishing that Aunt Lucy and Uncle Mason were coming to visit this week. They had been here last week, and the boys had had so much fun with their cousin Anne. Though two years younger than Alex, she had been very interesting to play with, not like Chris, but very–oh, Alex did not know what. All he knew was that for the first time he had hated to see her go. She could make him laugh, could make them all laugh with her imitation of a parrot. Uncle Mason had promised to get her a real parrot for Christmas.

"Do you think Anne will get a parrot for Christmas?" Alex asked Chris as they scuffed their way around the north wall of the Great Hall.

"Probably. Uncle Mason gets Anne everything she wants. Play like if your foot moves over that crack, you will fall a million feet to your death."

Alex watched Chris closely, saw the parquet edge and followed suit, painfully putting one foot before the other. "Do you like Anne?" Alex asked, arms outstretched for balance so that he would not fall to his death.

"She's a girl," Chris replied.

"Sure, but do you like her?"

"She's alright. I like Rolf better. But he's changed."

"I know. Do you suppose what old Neville said was true, about one day we would rather be at our studies than–"

"No!" Chris said. "Not me."

As they approached the end of the wall and the first turn, the pattern in the parquet curved close to the wall. "Play like there is no ledge here and you have to jump over to that ledge or you will–"

"Fall a million feet to your death–yes, I know," Alex sighed. It was a dumb game.

Now with a great fuss of deep breathing and arms flapping, Chris stepped back, then with a huge effort jumped from one parquet tile to the other, balanced precariously on the other side, then looked back and grinned. "I'm safe. It's your turn now."

Alex drew a deep breath, flopped his arms in imitation of Chris, then with premeditation stepped directly over the edge and fell, rolling about with a howl which grew softer at the end as though he were falling a great distance.

Chris watched safe on the ledge with condemning eyes. "You did that on purpose."

"No, I didn't, really," Alex protested, grinning. "I slipped plain and simple."

"How are you going to get back up?"

"If I just fell a million feet, I'd be dead, and getting back up wouldn't be much of a problem."

Chris seemed to think on this for a moment. Then he, too, stepped over the edge and the game was over.

"Where is Grandpapa? Do you suppose he would take us for a ride?"

"I doubt it. It's raining. You know he doesn't like to get the motorcar wet."

"Well, then–"

"Come on," Chris invited now. "Let's go!"

"Where?"

"The east wing, where the ghost lives."

"There is no such thing."

"Is so. Rolf has seen him."

"When did he tell you that?" Alex demanded because he had never heard Rolf say anything about a ghost.

"Last week when Anne was here. He wanted to take us then, but he didn't think Anne would like it–you know, being a girl and all. She'd probably be scared, and he was probably right. Are you coming?" Chris demanded.

For several moments, Alex followed wordlessly behind Chris, looking carefully about him. This wing looked just like the others. The only difference was that there were fewer wall standards here, which meant that at night and on cloudy overcast days such as this one, it was a darker and gloomier place.

At the end of the first corridor, the air seemed to grow colder, as though there was a door to winter opened somewhere close by.

"Chris, where–"

Chris turned back with a scowl. "We're not supposed to be here."

"I know that."

"Then don't keep yelling at me."

"I'm not yelling."

"You were so."

Again Chris led the way down the second corridor, though this time their boots were sending back eerie echoes on the stone floors.

Then all of a sudden Chris stopped, his arms stiff at his sides, his head rigidly cocked.

"What is it?"

"Don't you hear it?" Chris whispered as Alex drew closer.

"Hear what?"

"Listen!"

At first Alex heard nothing. Then he heard a faint scraping sound as though something heavy were being dragged across the stone corridor.

Alex stared at Chris. "Come on, Chris let's get out–"

"No, wait!"

Again Chris stopped and appeared to be listening. "Come on," he whispered, "we had better get–"

But now it was Alex who wanted to stay and confront the ghost head on, if that's what it was. As his eyes adjusted to the dim light, Alex saw something, a dim white something at the far end of the corridor, a–

His eyes grew wide. He felt Chris holding onto his arm so tight that his fingers pinched into Alex's flesh, and though Alex would have loved to have run, he could not move. His muscles were paralyzed with fear as the large white specter at the far end of the corridor appeared to limp forward, leaning heavily against the wall, a white gown billowing out on all sides. Then the ghost seemed to tilt far to the other side, as though he were going to fall over, and again there was the scraping sound, which caused the flesh on the back of Alex's neck to stand out in goose bumps.

"C–come–" Chris tried to speak but couldn't, and for several moments they stared the length of the corridor, too frightened to move, not certain of what they were seeing but wishing it would go away so that they could be released from their fear and run back to the warm and inhabited part of the castle.

Then all at once the white phantom turned and faced them. Alex could see the clear outline of a human skull beneath the robe, the skin pulled tight over bone, eyes peering out at them from deeply buried sockets.

Alex took a step back and collided with Chris; as he did so, Chris screamed and the ghost turned on both of them, his terrible face growing clearer in the dim corridor.

As both boys turned to run, they collided with yet another body, this one round, fleshy and altogether too real.

"What in the hell? What are you two doing up here? You have no business here. You have been forbidden. I never–"

As the all too solid figure of Dr. Reicher continued to block their passage, Alex dared to turn around and look back toward the end of the corridor.

The ghost was gone, as though it had never existed, though Alex knew better, for he had seen it, as had Chris.

"Well?" Dr. Reicher demanded, standing back a step, his hands on his hips, his ample belly putting a strain on every button of his vest. "What have you to say for yourselves?"

When neither boy spoke, old Dr. Reicher exploded, "Impudent pups, that's what you are. Your grandfather will hear of this, I promise you. You have no business in this part of the castle. How many times have you been told that? Now, get out, both of you, and prepare yourselves for punishment, as I am certain your grandfather will–"

Both boys bolted at the same moment, Alex going around the left side of Reicher, Chris around the right, and the race to light and warmth was a dead heat, with both boys streaking down the Great Hall steps, tumbling head over heels. Nothing was bruised very seriously, though Alex could feel his heart still beating in his mouth, not because of pompous old Reicher but because of his still-sharp memory of that distant white phantom, so terrifying and mysterious, at the far end of the corridor.

"Why don't you two boys try walking down the stairs? It might not hurt you so much."

At the sound of the familiar voice, Alex looked quickly about and found a pleasant sight by the fire, his father, just returned from Exeter.

"Papa," Alex cried and was on his feet and running to his father, who bent low for a hug.

"Uncle Stephen," Chris called out, joining them by the fire.

"What have you two been up to?" his father asked now, still warming his backside by the fire.

At first Alex did not reply and glanced at Chris.

"Come on," his father insisted. "No one in their right minds, not even you two, would choose to come down those steps in that painful fashion."

Still Alex struggled to form an answer, for everyone knew that both boys had been told to stay out of that wing. A few members of the family like Aunt Eleanor had given them a reason: "That wing is cold and dusty and never used. Most unsafe as well as unpleasant." Others, like Grandpapa and Uncle Richard, had simply said, "Stay out."

Now clearly they had disobeyed, and Alex didn't quite know how to lie to his father. He never had. Should he now?

"You saw something, didn't you?" his father asked softly.

"Come on," and he led both boys to the comfortable arrangement of chairs situated around the large table at which the old people often played bridge.

"Now, tell me," his father began, settling back into his chair and loosening his jacket.

"A–ghost, Papa, or a specter, something floating in white. I'll swear to it."

"I believe you. And you, Chris, is that what you saw as well?"

"Yes, Uncle Stephen. Rolf said there was a ghost there. I don't know what it was, but it was huge, a monster–"

"And he didn't move so much as he floated."

"Rolf told us we'd find him."

"What was it, Papa?"

"Old Dr. Reicher–"

All at once his father held up both hands in an attempt to stem the flood of words. "You both have been told not to go into that wing," he reminded them.

Alex nodded solemnly, as did Chris.

"Then why did you?"

Alex studied his hands. They were still dirty from playing Nelson at Cádiz. "We finished playing with the ships and–"

"Just wanted to explore, that's all, Uncle Stephen. We certainly didn't mean any harm."

Alex saw his father stare at the flames for a minute, a new sadness on his face. Sometimes Alex thought his papa was the saddest man in the world. Seldom did he laugh like Uncle Frederick or play practical jokes like Grandpapa. His papa did none of these things except to work and love him.

"Alright, come close, both of you," his father now said. "It's time you were told. Come closer, Chris. I want to say this only once."

Alex turned about in his chair. His father seemed even more earnest than usual. "What you saw was not a ghost or a specter or anything of the other world but, I'm afraid, someone very much in this world. The ghost you saw is a man, kin to you both, Aunt Eleanor and Uncle Richard's oldest son, my first cousin."

"What is he doing–"

"I'll tell you, Chris. Just listen. Years ago, about the time you both were born, Geoffrey–that is his name–went off to fight in a place called South Africa."

"Against the Boers," Alex said.

His papa smiled. "Yes, Alex, very good. I didn't realize your history lessons had extended that far."

Alex shook his head. "Mr. Neville was explaining the difference in 'bore' and 'Boer.' It was a spelling lesson, Papa, not a history lesson."

"Well, what is he doing up there?" Chris asked, clearly excited by these revelations.

"He lives up there."

"Why? Why doesn't he live down here with the rest of us?"

"He lives there by choice," his papa said. "You see, he was seriously wounded in battle. He lost his foot, and he has suffered severely ever since, not just physical pain but an illness of the spirit."

Alex listened closely, seeing clearly the limping ghost in his memory. "Doesn't he know that we would love him whether he lost his foot or not?"

His father shook his head. "Apparently not. Your Aunt Eleanor and Uncle Richard, as well as all of the rest of us have been trying to talk to him for years. He won't let us come into his isolation. Dr. Reicher is the only one who–"

"Why him?" Chris asked, suddenly defensive.

"Dr. Reicher has cared for him since . . . it happened."

"Who won the stupid war?" Alex asked now, suddenly saddened by the thought that the ghost was in fact an unhappy man.

His papa thought for a moment. "No one really," he said at last. "In the Boer War, the Boers won a few battles and we won a few. In the end, England got what she wanted, so I suppose we won."

"Has Geoffrey never come downstairs for anything?" Alex asked.

But his father slowly shook his head, confirming the worst. "I suppose that with the exception of Dr. Reicher, you boys are the first to have seen him in years. Of course, he has some books, and Dr. Reicher once told us that he was trying to write a full account of the Jameson Raid." He hesitated. "I suppose that would be of value to . . . someone."

For several moments no one spoke, all clearly locked in private thoughts. Finally his papa stood, cleared his throat and looked about. "Perhaps I shouldn't have told you."

"I'm glad you did, Papa."

"Yes, Uncle Stephen. Now we can tell Rolf that it is not a ghost."

His father smiled. "And you must promise never to bother Geoffrey again. Will you promise?"

Both boys nodded slowly. Alex still couldn't quite comprehend that a man could live like that without a good friend such as Chris, without the feel of warm sun and cool rain on his face, without laughing at a joke or sniffing Aunt Eleanor's roses or counting the fishing packets in the channel, without Grandpapa nodding off after dinner or riding in Grandpapa's motorcar.

As the list increased inside his head, Alex stood abruptly and walked back to the fire, suddenly chilled by the prospect of such a bleak and empty life.

"Alex!" his papa called out, his manner now changed, quite playful. "We've got serious business to discuss, the two of us do."

"Not Chris?" Alex asked, suspect of anything that did not involve Chris.

"Of course he can stay and listen, but I'm afraid, this does not concern Chris."

At first puzzled, Alex started slowly back, abandoning the good warmth of the fire. "I . . . don't understand."

Then all at once he did, helped by the sight of his father reaching into his coat pocket and withdrawing a letter with a solid row of stamps on it, the parchment he recognized as coming from a place in America called Stanhope Hall in a province called Alabama.

"No, Papa," he groaned and halted in his forward progress, knowing that yet another invitation had arrived from Mr. and Mrs. Stanhope.

"Alex, we must discuss this, we really must. I don't think we can put them off much longer."

Though in the past, the same invitation had come at least a half a dozen times a year, someone always managed to think up an excuse for them not going. One year Alex had been plagued by sore throats. Susan hadn't thought it advisable for him to undergo a sea voyage. Then there was the year his father had been involved in rotating crops.

Then for several years Grandpapa had just put his foot down altogether, claiming it wasn't the right time, the condition of the seas being too hazardous.

Alex hoped that everyone in America had forgotten about him and that at last the invitations had ceased to arrive. But no, here was yet another.

"Come here, Alex," his father commanded softly. "Sit here by me."

Always a dangerous position.

"Now please listen," his father began very quietly. "These are your grandparents, as much as Grandpapa is your grandparent. They love you as much, and they want to see you; they want to introduce you to their home, to their way of life."

"Why?"

"Your mother was their daughter. You are their only link to her. Try to understand that."

He paused as though waiting to see if Alex did understand it, but all Alex really understood was that the life he loved was about to be disrupted and, worst of all, Chris left behind.

"No, Papa, I don't want to–"

Then Alex heard a step behind him and heard a third voice enter the debate. "You heard what the boy said, Stephen. Why do you continue to badger him?"

Grandpapa.

Delighted, Alex turned and ran to greet him, Chris right behind him, and Grandpapa reached down to receive both boys.

He still looked half asleep and moved slowly toward the fire. "Will they never give up?" he grumbled wearily. "How many times must we write and send our regrets?"

"They do have a right, Father."

"I'm not denying their rights. It's just a simple matter: the boy does not want to go."

"Can you blame him when you have told him only horror stories about the place as well as the people?"

Suddenly Grandpapa looked terribly shocked. "Me? I have done no such thing, have I, Alex?"

Caught between his papa and grandpapa, Alex floundered. Grandpapa *had* told him a few things. Perhaps there was no point in bringing them up right now.

The truth, the only truth that mattered, was that he did not want to go and was on the verge of saying so again when suddenly his father was at his side, taking his hand, guiding him a distance away from Chris and Grandpapa.

"Please listen to me, Alex. I am proposing that next spring we pack our bags and journey to America. First we visit New York City. I think you will enjoy that very much, and then we proceed on to Stanhope Hall for–"

"For how long?"

"For as long as you want to stay–a month, possibly two."

"Papa," Alex moaned.

"Then it is settled," his father said. "May I write to Burke and Mary and tell them that we will be coming?"

Before Alex could respond, he heard his grandfather call out, "You don't have to go if you don't want to, Alex."

"Father!"

"Then go!" Grandpapa shouted back, clearly angry. "We don't give a damn, do we, Chris? You and I can hold the fort down, can't we? No trouble, no trouble at all."

As the two of them started off hand in hand toward the library, without even inviting Alex to join them, and as his father started up the Great Hall stairs, clearly angry as well, Alex stood alone in the center of the Great Hall, fighting back tears. Only girls cried. Yet he felt so alone.

He heard the library door close in one direction, heard the diminishing echo of his father's boots in the other. Then all was silent.

America.

Then the tears came. He didn't have to hide them, for there was no one there to see them.

So heartbroken was he, so full of dread over the coming journey, so miserably unhappy and alone that at first he heard nothing. It wasn't until he felt a hand on his knee that he looked up and saw Chris opposite him.

"Don't cry, Alex," Chris whispered. "I promise you on my life that I will be right here when you come back."

London
December 24, 1906

"Holidays are hardest, particularly Christmas," Alice murmured and passed the filled wassail cup to Albert, who in turn passed it on to Colin.

Her small but comfortable flat on Tottenham Court Road, within view of the spires of St. Martin's Hospital, was decorated with all the style and appropriateness of the season. Together the three of them had placed a small Christmas tree with white candles near the window. There were garlands of holly over the fireplace and an enormous wassail bowl surrounded by at least fifty cups and a delicious arrangement of sweets, tarts, small sandwiches and a lovely Christmas plum pudding.

"More guests will come," Albert soothed and looked down into his wassail cup as though to hide the fact of his own lie.

"No, they won't," Alice said gamely. "I think I must have invited everyone on the hospital staff, but–" She shrugged. "Families, you know. They all said they would try to come, but their families were expecting them."

Suddenly she felt defeated by her own words, refilled her cup, took it to the comfortable sofa before the fire and sat close to Albert, who lovingly patted her knee.

"Chin up, old girl," he smiled. "If given a choice between the peaceful calm of your little flat and the arrogant, boasting pomposity of our shared father, I would take your simple flat any day."

"I miss Mama."

Silence again. Alice looked deep into the fire, saw shapes of dragons and damsels in distress and recalled the nursery at Christmastime,

Mason Frye always allowing them to read fairy stories in honor of the holiday.

Thinking on Mason caused Alice to think on Lucy. "Lucy was going home to Eden for Christmas."

"Good for Lucy," Albert murmured.

"Lucy writes often, did you know that? She has become a kind of clearinghouse between the revolutionaries of London and the proprietors of Eden Castle."

"A strange role for prim and proper Lucy."

"Oh, she has changed."

"So have we all."

Again the conversation died, and Alice sipped at her wassail and thought of Mrs. Partridge's kitchen court at home during the holiday season.

"Charlotte!" Albert asked. "What is our own pretty Charlotte doing this evening?"

Alice shrugged. "I sent around an invitation for both her and Aslam. No response." Albert chuckled. "For some reason, Charlotte has grown into precisely the role best suited for her, the kept mistress of a wealthy foreigner."

Alice laughed. "That is just about the way it happened too. I haven't seen her in months. She and Aslam went abroad this year. He treats her like a queen."

"And she adores it."

"Adores *him.*"

"Has any word of this crept back to Eden?"

"All of it."

"Dear God, they must be in a state of apoplexy."

Alice laughed again. "According to Lucy, they are. John will not allow Charlotte's name to be mentioned in his presence."

"Arrogant bastard," Albert muttered.

"Don't," Alice begged. "Not tonight. Tonight is–"

"Christmas, I know."

Another conversational death. Alice saw Colin stand and stretch, saw him take Albert's cup back to the wassail bowl, fill it and return it to him. All without a word. Did he ever speak?

Alice was on the verge of trying to draw him out when suddenly there was a loud rap at the front door.

She exchanged a quick look with Albert, who smiled. "There! There's a Christmas Eve guest for you. I told you we were not the only lonely ones in London tonight."

Quickly Alice handed him her cup and went to the door, a smile of greeting in place, only to find a very cold and very wet messenger on the other side, a man she had never seen before.

"I'm alookin' for Mistress Alice Eden," the man said.

"I am Alice Eden," she said.

"Message of import. I'm to wait."

Alice glanced down at the parchment in his hand and wondered who? What had happened?

"Come in, won't you?" she invited. "You might as well be warm and dry while you wait."

The man did as he was told, quickly handing her the message in passing. Alice saw Albert on his feet.

"It's warm over here, sir. You look as if you could do with a bit of wassail."

As Albert dispatched Colin toward the wassail bowl, he pushed a chair to one side and made room for the messenger before the fire.

"A cold night to be delivering messages," Albert said.

"Aye, it is," the man replied. "Though my master treats me well and pays me better, and therefore I am at his command."

"A happy relationship it is, then?"

"Oh, yes, sir, very happy."

"And a rare one, I might add, between master and servant. And who would your master be?"

"Mr. Eden, sir."

Alice looked up, shocked and saw the same shock on Albert's face.

"Mr. Eden?"

"Aye, sir, Mr. Aslam Eden."

All at once Albert breathed a noisy sigh of relief and laughed. "*That* Mr. Eden is permitted into this house. Well, go ahead, Alice, read! What does Aslam Eden want on this Christmas Eve that all of his money will not buy?"

"It is not from Aslam," Alice murmured, having read the brief message. "It's from Charlotte."

"Well then, what does Charlotte want that her fortunes will not buy?"

"Us," Alice said simply. "Listen." She read:

Dearest Alice,

Come quickly with this good man. Albert, too, if you can find him. I promise you both a Christmas Eve you will never forget.

Hurry.

With love, your cousin Charlotte.

Alice looked up from reading and saw Albert frowning at the brief message.

"What else?" he asked as though she had failed to read certain key passages.

"Nothing else. That's all."

"She sent this poor man out into this weather with five lines?"

The "poor man" was thoroughly enjoying his wassail. Still he looked up. "The lady wants you to come back with me immediately. The carriage is waiting. Will you come?"

Alice looked about at the small feast she had arranged with her friends in mind. Well then, since her friends had deserted her, she would now desert them and go to Charlotte and Aslam's party. Why not? Perhaps it was the only family circle left for Alice and Albert.

"I'm going," she said with dispatch. "Are you coming?" she called back as she lifted her heavy cloak from the door hook and swung it over her shoulders.

Albert looked down on Colin. "When are you due at the theater?"

"In two hours."

Albert turned back to Alice. "Can Colin remain here until–"

"Of course. Help yourself, Colin. Feel free to–"

She saw Albert bend low over Colin and whisper something, clearly a different sort of message. Colin looked up, and Albert kissed him. The messenger ducked his head, pulled his hat low and hurried out of the door.

Albert retrieved his heavy coat from the door, swung it over his shoulder and joined Alice in the hall.

"You look terribly displeased, Mother Alice," he teased.

"I'm afraid you shocked the messenger."

"I did? How?"

"Your kiss," she whispered.

"If love shocks the man, then he deserves to be shocked. Come, let us see what a rich table our cousin has laid for us on Christmas Eve. I daresay it will even put Eden to shame. Come, sister, the criminal element of the Eden family, the blackest of black sheep, the rebels, the traitors and renegades, the whole rotten lot of Eden offspring shall welcome Father Christmas in their own way. God, but it's cold. Hurry!"

Once inside the carriage, she looked about at the elegant interior, pale blue velvet upholstered seats, warm, soft white fur lap robes on both sides.

"Crawl beneath that," Albert invited, already snug beneath his lap robe. "Aren't you glad that our clever cousin selected a rich man to live with in sin?"

"Albert," Alice scolded. "Come," she whispered, leaning across and gently touching his hand. "This is Christmas. Charlotte has invited us to her party. You see, we will be a family after all."

And gradually Albert relaxed, though he said nothing more and seemed content to stare out of his window.

It wasn't until the carriage turned into Belgravia that he seemed to take an interest in his surroundings. "Do you suppose the king will be here tonight?"

Alice laughed. "Not likely. The royals always go to Osborne for Christmas, don't they?"

"There it is," he pointed out, leaning forward and peering out of his window at Aslam's mansion. Alice followed his line of vision and saw through the drawing room windows an enormous Christmas tree ablaze with candles and covered over with swags of red velvet.

Clearly the house was in a festive mood. Alice was glad they had come. She, too, was in the mood for excess, for too much food, too much wassail, too many people, too much laughter, singing and making very merry.

As the carriage came to a halt before the broad front steps, she slipped out into the night and noticed that the sleet had turned to snow. She looked about for the carriages of the other guests. But the pavement was deserted except for three cabs across the way that appeared empty.

Curious.

As she hurried after Albert, she tried to remember the last time she had seen Charlotte. Months ago. It was sad how involved they both had become in their own pursuits.

As the heavy door swung open, she saw a rigid old butler, his nose in the air. "And you are—" he began.

"Albert Eden," Albert announced with a faint mocking imitation. "And this is my sister, Alice, and we have both come to see our cousin."

"Yes, of course, you are expected, do come in," the old man urged and stepped back, ushering them into the Grand Foyer. "This way, please, both of you. And hurry."

To Alice's surprise, the old man hastily deposited their wraps, then led the way up the curved staircase.

"I have never been here before," Albert whispered conspiratorially. "I depend upon you for guidance. Could you answer one simple question? Why in the hell are we going to the upper floor?"

Alice shook her head. "I haven't the faintest idea.

All the way up the staircase, Alice looked ahead, thinking at any moment to get a glimpse of Charlotte or Aslam. But at the top of the stairs, the old butler directed them to the left.

"This way," he instructed, adding, ". . . and quickly."

Why quickly, Alice brooded and began to have feelings of apprehension.

Then they were standing before an ornate gilt double door. The old man knocked once, and immediately the door opened and Aslam was on the other side, his normally placid face flushed with excitement.

"Ah, Alice, thank God, thank you so much for coming. And you too, Albert. Welcome to a most unorthodox Christmas celebration."

At last he stood back to reveal a bedchamber, a very large, very grand bedchamber, and at center was a dark mahogany canopied bed and lying on the bed, beautifully gowned in a gold robe was–

"Charlotte!" Alice gasped, took one step forward, saw her protruding belly and knew why she had been summoned. As she approached the bed, she saw a lovely smile on Charlotte's face, despite the brief tension which Alice recognized immediately as being the pain of beginning labor.

Alice took her hand and realized with a wave of humor that Charlotte's fifteen-inch waist was now considerably expanded. "Why didn't you let me know?" Alice mildly scolded.

Charlotte shrugged. "There seemed no point until now." She looked beyond Alice and saw Albert. "You, too. How good to see you both. Please come closer, both of you, and give me a kiss. I had thought once I could go through this without my . . . family, but I'm afraid I need both of you."

All at once, Alice saw tears in Charlotte's pretty eyes and drew near on one side, while Albert, like a good soldier, came up on the other side, and together they embraced in an awkward tangle of arms, hugs and kisses.

"All of Eden's outcasts," Charlotte laughed.

"Eden's loss," Albert said.

Then Aslam was there. "We are now going to ask a favor of both of you. We had planned for the ceremony to take place downstairs, but nature became insistent and I was forced to send my stewards around to all our guests and cancel the festivities. Only you were told to come along."

So that explained the elegant party without guests. Still Alice was bewildered. "Ceremony? What–"

Aslam motioned toward the shadows on his left, and all at once a priest materialized, a young man, impressively robed in ceremonial Anglican robes, his Book of Common Prayer open and in his hand.

"This is my good friend, Father Crescent. He has kindly agreed to pronounce the marriage ceremony for us. We ask only for your love and your assistance as witnesses. Will you do that for us?"

"Marriage–" Alice tried to say, but could not finish.

Charlotte nodded. "It's about time. Don't you think?"

Albert laughed. "If we hurry–"

Aslam stepped closer and took Charlotte's hand. "I have proposed marriage every morning at breakfast for the last eight years at approximately the same time–between eight-thirty and a quarter to nine–and every morning she has said no, except *this* morning."

Charlotte smiled. "It is for the baby, of course. What I choose to do with my life is my business, but it is not my right to make this judgment for my child."

Alice listened carefully, impressed at this new maturity.

Suddenly Charlotte gasped. Her head pushed back against the pillow. Alice stepped forward and gently felt the infant turning slowly inside Charlotte's womb.

"Come, Father Crescent, I think you had better perform a shortened version of the marriage ritual. And even at that, please speak lively."

At the same time, she motioned for Aslam to come forward and he took a position close beside Charlotte. Alice joined Albert on the opposite side of the bed, and Father Crescent took his position at the foot of the bed.

With the wedding party thus arranged, Alice tried to relax and hoped the birth would postpone itself for a few minutes and prayed further that it would be an uncomplicated one, for it had never occurred to her to bring her bag to a Christmas Eve party.

"Dearly beloved, . . ."

As the priest moved instantly into the ritual of marriage, Alice shut her eyes and prayed briefly for the strength and skill to safely deliver Charlotte of her child. It was with her eyes closed that she marveled at the deep and abiding love that had grown and developed between Charlotte and

Aslam, and she wondered bleakly, as she often had of late, if she would ever be fortunate enough to find her true love. She feared that time was running out. Over thirty she was, clearly headed for the life of a spinster.

Now as she listened to the vows to love, comfort and honor "so long as ye both shall live," she brooded on her own old age. Cut off from her family, isolated from her home, she envisioned a life lived to its end in second-floor flats, depending always on the loyalty of friends and the generosity of colleagues. Of course, Albert would always be with her, a good and loyal brother, even though she suspected in the process he would go through a long line of Colins.

So be it.

"Those whom God hath joined together let no man put asunder . . . I pronounce that they are man and wife."

As the priest reached the end of the ceremony, Alice saw Aslam reach into his vest pocket and withdraw a square black velvet case. Carefully he opened it and withdrew a dazzling diamond, like an eye of fire. He took Charlotte's left hand, placed the diamond on her finger, then kissed her hand and effortlessly found his way to her lips. As the two newlyweds indulged in a moment of passion, she saw the young priest turn away, saw Albert walk a few steps toward the door and decided to follow suit, at least until–

"Alice, come quick, please."

Clearly the kiss was over, and Alice looked back at the bed to see Charlotte flattened against the pillow, both hands gathering up large amounts of the bedclothes as clearly the baby was getting down to the serious business of being born.

"We need privacy," Alice requested with a smile and indicated the room must be cleared. She made simple requests of Aslam–hot water, clean linens and a pair of sharp sterilized scissors. Pray to God that that was all she would need.

"Wait outside," she smiled as she escorted the men to the door. Seeing Aslam's concerned expression, she added, "I anticipate no trouble."

Then she closed the door behind her and saw Charlotte clutch again at the bedclothes. "Alice, where are you?"

"I'm here, Charlotte, right here."

As Aslam paced off the long corridor outside Charlotte's bedchamber, he kept one eye on the door in the event Alice needed something else.

A few minutes earlier, she had sent a message down to his kitchen staff, enlisting the assistance of any woman who had had experience with delivering a baby. One of the upper-house parlormaids had volunteered. Now those two had been in Charlotte's bedchamber for over three hours.

"Dear God, don't let anything go wrong," Aslam prayed and tried to ease his mind with thoughts of the hasty marriage ceremony. Now, at least in the eyes of society, they were legally man and wife. Strange, but he had considered her his wife for years, had come wholly to rely upon her nearness, her sweet nature, her beauty to sustain him every day as well as every night. The rich mosaic that was her personality became deeper, broader and more complex with every passing minute, and his only regret was for the years he had already used up before he met her.

Abruptly he looked up from his thoughts, thinking he had heard something. He had sent Father Crescent and Albert down to the drawing room over an hour ago for something to eat and drink. They had kindly offered to send food up to him. But he had declined.

How long would it take? Why didn't Alice–

Then he heard something.

He froze directly in front of the door that led to her bedchamber. Listen! He heard it again, heard it clearly this time, a baby's angry cry, a wail of protest at being pulled from the warm womb.

When he heard it yet a third time, his eyes filled with tears, and at that moment the doors opened and there stood Alice, a small bundle in her arms. "Your daughter, Aslam, hale and hearty, a beauty, I predict, with the blackest hair and the darkest eyes I have ever seen."

All the time she talked, he could not take his eyes off the child. A daughter. Never in his wildest imagination had he ever thought that he would possess a daughter.

"Charlotte–" he whispered, still aware of the tears brimming in his eyes.

"She is fine. Come and see for yourself. And here, you take your daughter."

As he walked toward the bed, he drew back the baby's blanket. He peered in and saw that Alice was right, saw two deep blue eyes peering up at him, saw smooth olive skin, and a crown of black hair. She *was* beautiful.

"Oh, my darling," Aslam murmured upon seeing Charlotte. He bent over, placed the baby in her arms, then gently gathered all to him and offered up thanksgiving to the generous God who had so blessed him and vowed to try to live the rest of his life so that he might be worthy of these gifts.

Eden Castle
January 15, 1907

As luck would have it, Susan was outside the gate, awaiting the return of John, Chris and Alex. Earlier this morning he had driven them down the coast road to Clovelly—"a short day's outing," as John had put it, before Alex is "taken against his will to visit the cotton farmer in America."

Now, as Susan pulled the hood of her jacket over her head as protection against the January wind, she saw the Royal Post dispatcher approaching from the moors in his smart new motorized vehicle. Motorcars everywhere now, or so it seemed.

One of the guardsmen came up alongside her. "You better get inside, ma'am. I'll fetch the dispatch bag."

She nodded her thanks and glanced again in the direction of the coast road. No sign of the motorcar, though they should have been back hours ago.

"I'll wait in the Great Hall," she called back to the guardsman. "Bring the mail pouch directly in."

Inside the Great Hall door the temperature was not very different from outside. At the end of the hall she saw the beckoning fire and instructed the young guardsman to place the mail pouch on the table, then go directly down to the kitchen court for some of Mrs. Wollcot's hot mulled wine.

Susan's beloved old Mrs. Partridge had died only last year, and Eleanor had hired Mrs. Wollcot from Lady Stratford, who claimed that the woman was a good, solid English cook with at least twenty years left in her. Thus far, she had worked out splendidly.

As she approached the fire, she drew off her heavy coat and examined the post, the usual glut of London papers and journals that John and Richard devoured, and–

All at once her eye fell on familiar handwriting, a letter from Albert. How she missed him, missed them all, Alice, even Charlotte, though Charlotte had so thoroughly disgraced the entire family that no one at Eden spoke her name.

Now she glanced about, praying that her privacy would last for a few minutes longer. Quickly she split the seal on the envelope and withdrew Albert's letter.

> Dearest Mother,
>
> Happy news, at least I hope so for you and everyone at Eden, an accounting of how Alice and I spent last Christmas Eve. It was a unique celebration to say the least, with cousin Charlotte as hostess, who took advantage of the Christmas spirit to wed her Aslam, then only a few hours later, to produce a lovely baby daughter which she named Dhari after Aslam's mother.

Slowly Susan lowered the letter and closed her eyes. Charlotte married . . . a mother . . . Aslam . . . a daughter, Dhari . . .

All at once a smile erupted, a glorious smile as her mind raced ahead to reunions, to all the prodigals coming home now.

Charlotte was married. Why would John object now? Why would any of them object, for in truth John's condemnation of Charlotte had spread to Richard and it was Richard who never wanted to hear her name spoken in his presence. As for Eleanor, she had simply taken all of her grief into herself. She kept more and more to her private apartments, to her garden in particular. The only company that would draw her out was Lucy, Mason Frye and little Anne, now nine and growing prettier by the day.

Susan stood with dispatch and hastily read the rest of Albert's letter, which contained little news except to say that Alice was now running St. Martin's virtually single-handedly and that he was doing quite well with the Pankhurst organization. They had even managed to pay him a few coins now and then, though, make no mistake, he was coping very well on his yearly allotment from the Eden coffers. All in all, he had no major complaints except that he missed his dear mother.

For a moment Susan stared down at his penmanship and dared to hope that now he and Alice would come home. They had been gone far too long. It was time that all the Edens were reunited. On that note of hope and excitement, she started toward Eleanor's apartments, eager to convey to her the happy news that she was a grandmother again, that the long exile was over, that her daughter was now respectably married.

Then she heard it, that damnable motorcar being driven too fast over the grate. Dear God, how she hated it. It seemed to represent all that was despicable about a future that had yet to arrive. Apparently any fool could crawl behind the wheel and exercise the power of life and death, like a bogus god.

Then she heard a scream of brakes, heard laughs and shouts of the culprits themselves.

"Rolf beat you, Grandpapa. We timed it. Rolf won by at least three minutes."

"Nonsense. Your watches are broken."

"They are not. You gave them to us. You said they were the best in the world."

"Well, something was wrong. We'll do it again tomorrow, and then we'll see."

"You're on, Grandpapa."

Susan stood perfectly still, with her head down, listening to the voices in the inner courtyard. Then they burst in through the Great Hall doors, ruddy-cheeked, laughing, all hurrying toward the warmth of the fire.

"Susan! Is that you?"

As he spoke, he came directly over to where she was standing and delivered a kiss to her cheek. Alex and Chris giggled and blushed, while Rolf turned away and looked into the fire.

"What's that in your hand?" John asked.

Too late, Susan looked down on Albert's letter. She had hoped to share the good news with Eleanor and Richard first. They were the ones who deserved to hear it. But now–

"Ah, the post," John exclaimed, seeing the rest of the letters and papers on the table. "Why didn't you say so? Come, boys, let's find out what is going on in the rest of the world. Rolf, you take the *Times.* Chris and Alex, grab one of those, and we'll settle in here by the fire and pass judgment on the antics of other men."

Susan held perfectly still, hoping that John had forgotten about the letter in her hand in his need to arrange the boys in a close circle about him.

When they had settled, toes to the fire, back to her, she turned quietly and started toward the staircase.

"What does Albert have to say for himself?" John called out, not bothering to lower his paper.

"It's about Charlotte and Aslam."

She saw him visibly stiffen, saw the newspaper start to lower ever so slightly.

"I don't know those names," he said in a leveled voice.

"Yes, you do. They are married now, and parents. Apparently the events happened in a close sequence. Albert and Alice spent Christmas Eve with them and served as witnesses for their–"

Abruptly John stood and crushed the newspaper at his side. He turned on Susan with a fierceness that alarmed her. "How dare you speak of those obscenities in front of the boys."

Susan stood her ground. "We are speaking of Charlotte, your niece, as well as Alice and Albert, your children."

"I have no children save these three. These are my children."

She looked toward Chris and Alex, who were wide-eyed at this new tone of voice. "John, please you are not–"

"Will you leave, or shall we?"

Dear God, how she loathed that tone of voice, that imperious stance.

Slowly she turned away from his angry glare and started walking toward the staircase. Behind her she heard nothing, though apparently the four of them were watching her closely.

She was tired, a sign of age no doubt, too tired even to turn and confront him. First she would talk with Eleanor and Richard; then she would make a decision, one that very well could affect her for the rest of her life.

At some point in the past, it had been completely impossible for her to conceive of life without John. Now it was becoming increasingly impossible to conceive of spending the rest of her life with him.

Eden Castle
April 10, 1907

Chris had never believed that this awful day would come. And yet here it was, the stewards busily carrying heavy steamer trunks down to his father's motorcar, the entire castle in an uproar. Even Mr. Neville had suspended all classes for the day, something he never did unless it was a major holiday. And this certainly was no holiday. In fact, it quite probably was the worst day of Chris's life.

Now, as he walked the headlands for the last time, ahead of Alex and Rolf, he looked back to confirm their presence. Yes, Alex was still there, though within the hour he would be gone, on his way to far-off America.

"What do you want, Chris?" Alex called out. "Rolf has already given me a list of everything he wants me to bring back from America. What do you want?"

"I don't want anything," Chris muttered and walked faster, as though all he really wanted was to put distance between himself and the other two boys.

"Come on, Chris," Rolf called out. "You told me you wanted Alex to bring you a cowboy's hat."

"I did not," Chris yelled back. "Why would I want him to bring me something as stupid as that?"

There was a stone bench straight ahead, and Chris made for it, sat down and stared out across the channel, hoping the other two would just pass him by and go on down to the end of the headlands, discussing such foolish things as gifts from America.

But they didn't. In fact, Alex sat on one side and Rolf sat on the other. For several long moments no one spoke, all three boys staring out across the channel.

"Do you know what I thought about last night?" Alex asked quietly. When no one answered, he went on. "I thought about running away."

"Where would you have gone?" Rolf asked.

"Anywhere. I could have gone to Exeter. Lucy and Mason would let me stay with them for a while."

"Would not," Chris argued. "Old Mason would have thrown you in the back of his wagon and dragged you home."

"Then I would have run away someplace else."

"Where?" Rolf persisted.

At last Alex lost patience. "I don't know. Anywhere but here."

"Would you have told me?" Chris asked with his head down.

"Of course. You were coming with me. And you too, Rolf. We could have gone someplace. Even across the channel to Wales."

"What would we have done in Wales?" Rolf asked.

"Anything. We could have gotten jobs on a farm. Look! They have barns and silos just like we have. We could have worked as tenant farmers and sat on that headland and looked back over here."

Chris smiled. The idea held great appeal—out on their own, without parents to pry and nag, scold and correct. Perhaps it was not too late.

"I know where there is a boat," he offered softly.

"So do I," Alex added. "Right below. All we have to do is slide down the headland to reach the rowboat and—"

"It has a hole in it, remember?" Rolf reminded them. "How far do you think you would get in a rowboat like that?"

"We could fix it," Chris offered.

"With what?" Rolf asked.

And lacking an answer, Chris fell silent, as did Rolf, and again the three of them sat without speaking.

Then Chris heard a voice, quite distant, calling to them. The others heard it as well, and they all looked back toward the castle and saw Grandpapa hurrying toward them. At least, he was hurrying as fast as he could. He now walked with a cane and sometimes walked very slowly. Chris had heard him complain of aching joints.

"Grandpapa," he called out and waved his hand, knowing that an ally was on his way, someone who was as opposed to this foolish trip as he was.

"Before he gets here," Alex suddenly whispered, drawing the boys close on either side, "I want us to take an oath. Will you?"

Chris caught the new solemnity in Alex's voice and saw Rolf move closer and whisper, "Hurry."

"All right," Alex began, his face very determined. "I have a needle, see? I found it in Susan's sewing basket. I want us to prick the tips of our fingers and touch each other and let our blood mingle and then take a solemn blood vow that nothing will ever separate us. Will you both do that with me?"

Though impressed, Chris had one question. "Will it hurt?"

"No," scolded Rolf. "Haven't you ever pricked your finger before? Go on, Alex, hurry. I think it's a great idea."

As Chris watched, Alex withdrew a needle from behind the lapel of his jacket and barely stabbed Rolf's finger, and within the instant a red dot of blood darted up and just sat there.

"Now, you, Chris," Alex said, and with his eyes pinched closed, Chris gave Alex his hand and felt only a tiny prick.

Then Alex did it to himself and quickly looked over his shoulder to check on Grandpapa's progress. Approaching rapidly, but still a safe distance away.

"All right, let me have your finger. Don't spill it," Alex warned. Quickly Alex pressed his blood into Chris, and Chris in turn pressed his into Rolf, and Rolf completed the circle by pressing his finger against Alex's.

Alex smiled, a look of relief in his eyes. "There. Now at least I know that both of you will be waiting for me when I return."

"Where did you think we'd be?" Chris asked.

Then Grandpapa's voice cut across the distance.

"I've been looking all over," he called ahead, "I might have known I'd find you three out here."

As John drew nearer, Chris could hear him huffing and puffing. Now the old man was pounding his chest as though to get more air.

"Did you know they're searching all over the castle for you?" he said to Alex, smiling. "I offered to go and collect you. It's time. Your father doesn't want to drive too late at night."

John glanced down, apparently seeing the smudge of blood on each finger. His face grew suddenly sober. "A blood oath, or I have missed my guess."

Alex nodded. "Yes, Grandpapa. I wanted to be certain that Chris and Rolf would be waiting for me."

He stopped talking and looked across the channel as though someone had called to him from the other side. Crying? Not Alex. Alex never cried.

Chris watched his grandpapa move directly to where Alex stood and place his arm gently on his shoulder. "Do you still have the needle?"

Alex nodded.

"May I borrow it?"

He reached behind his lapel, and to Chris's shock, he did see tears in Alex's eyes.

But then all of their attention was summoned back to Grandpapa, who had pricked his finger and now shook it once and held it up, the blood dripping down his hand.

"Well, come on," he ordered, "before I bleed to death, all of you, and I want it to be clearly understood that this is a sacred bond, uniting the four of us for all time, even unto eternity. Is that clearly understood?"

He pressed his finger to Alex, then to Chris, then to Rolf and at last held his hand up to the wind and made it into a dramatic fist, as though threatening heaven. "You powers that be up there, I command you to return this young man to us safe and sound and within a reasonable length of time. He belongs here at Eden, with Eden kin. So return him to us or else answer to this, our sacred blood bond."

The combination of Grandpapa's voice, the blowing wind and the imminent separation caused goose bumps to climb up Chris's arm.

"Now," Grandpapa said with dispatch, sucking the tip of his finger. "All of you do the same. Your own spittle will cleanse the wound and help it to close. But remember what took place here today, not a mere boy's game but a solemn ritual recorded in the book of time. And more important, a heavenly guarantee that we shall be reunited, despite this stupid journey."

Chris couldn't have agreed more and was on the verge of saying so. Then Grandpapa reached into his vest pocket and drew Alex close.

"This is for you," he said, his voice suddenly low and quite sad. "Look, a white rabbit's foot with a key to the motorcar attached. As soon as you return, I promise I will teach you how to drive the motorcar. But that is a secret, just between us, on the very honor of our blood oath."

Alex couldn't speak. Chris could see the amazement in his face, shared it and, worse, was envious of it. "Me too, Grandpapa," he asked quickly, wanting to establish that going away gifts were one thing, but such a glorious promise had to be extended to all.

"Of course, you too. But this is especially for Alex, since he's the one who must leave us."

That was all right with Chris. It would be good to think of Alex with that white rabbit's foot and his own special key to Grandpapa's motorcar way across the ocean. If anything could draw him back, it would be that combination.

"Come on now, you boys. The sooner we get this damnable journey under way, the sooner it will be over."

And they started off, Alex holding the rabbit's foot in one hand as though he intended never to put it down and Grandpapa's hand in the other. Rolf walked on one side of Grandpapa, and Chris brought up the rear.

He still couldn't believe it, that within minutes Alex would be gone from here.

What was he going to do? Especially after lessons? Who would he play with? Explore with? Rolf always worked late with Mr. Neville. What would Chris do with Alex gone and Rolf working late, when Grandpapa was sleeping and Mama and Papa were busy with the church in Mortemouth.

Suddenly, premature loneliness swept over him as raw and as painful as anything he had ever felt. He was glad now that he was bringing up the rear of this sad parade because that way no one could see him cry, no one could see that no matter how hard he tried to brush the tears away, more came to take their place.

Patiently Alex worked his way through the confusion on the Great Hall steps, clutching his rabbit's foot in one hand and feeling a slight ache in the tip of his finger. Both sensations were good. They served to remind him of the very important ritual that had just taken place on the headlands. The blood of his three favorite people in the whole world now mingled with his. That thought alone, combined with Grandpapa's promise that he would teach him to drive the motorcar upon his return, would surely see him safely to America and back again.

He renewed his grip on his rabbit's foot, closed his eyes and braced himself for a series of goodbye kisses. Why all the women insisted upon kissing him, he would never know.

Now he waved goodbye to all the others, to Mr. Neville, to Maxwell, the new butler hired to take the place of old Ghostly, who had died a few months ago, and to a large contingent of servants, and his father quickly pointed his attention to the top of the steps, where he saw Dr. Reicher and his wife joined now by Rolf.

Everyone, just everyone, had come out to the inner courtyard to see them off. Alex stepped into the motorcar and was just settling into the seat when suddenly he remembered.

"Wait!" And he was out again, shouting, "Chris, where are you?"

Then all of a sudden he saw him way down the walkway, standing alone and apart. Alex ran to him and promised quickly, "I will think of you every day at exactly twelve o'clock. You think of me at the same time and that way we will be together."

Chris nodded and Alex promised, "I'll come home as fast as I can."

Again Chris nodded, and though it wasn't the manly thing to do and although Alex knew full well that everybody was watching them, nonetheless he reached out for Chris and hugged him awkwardly, just a quick hug. Then he ran back to the motorcar, pushing inside past his father and sinking down in the far seat so he wouldn't have to see anyone else, wave to anyone else, call goodbye to anyone else.

Slowly he raised up as he heard the tires fight with the grate at the gatehouse. He looked back out of the rear window and saw everyone on the Great Hall steps slowly disbanding, turning to go back up the stairs, the servants disappearing down into the kitchen court. Everyone gone.

Everyone save one.

Chris was there, for as long as Alex could see him.

Stanhope Hall
June 1, 1907

All Mary could think of as she looked about her crowded veranda was Sis Liz's favorite saying—"Be careful what you wish for. You may get it."

Now look what had happened. For years Mary had begged, pleaded, cajoled and threatened in order to get Stephen to bring young Alexander to America. But every year there had been something to prevent the journey.

Now, here they were, and they couldn't have come at a worse time. David was here as well, along with his wife, Sharon, and the greatest of all joys, her two new grandbabies, twins, a boy and a girl, born only three months ago at Sharon's family home, the Meriweather Mansion in Natchez.

David was now working as a journalist on the Mobile *Register* and as their home in that city was undergoing much needed expansion, David, Sharon and the babies had moved out for an unlimited stay at Stanhope Hall.

Then, two days ago, to add to the confusion, Stephen and Alexander had arrived from England.

Well, nothing to do but the best she could, Mary decided and tried to determine where she was needed most.

At the far end of the veranda in one direction she saw Burke, David and Stephen in a heated discussion that had begun over luncheon, a foolish discussion really on the possibility of war. Stephen seemed to feel, and David had agreed with him, that certain thunderclouds were gathering. King Edward was weak and more interested in his drink, food and women than he was in pacifying the German and Austrian diplomats who had come to see him in London.

But Burke, with the wisdom of an elder, had merely laughed at these two young men and had advised Stephen to take a close look at his own history, had gently reminded him that it was Victoria's grandson at the head of the German Empire now, that in essence Germany was merely an extension of the British Empire, that war was about as remote as the moon.

Mary heard them laughing, a good sound, and held her position in the doorway.

She saw Sharon and her nurse-maid, Hester gathering up the twins, preparing to take them to the upstairs nursery for their afternoon nap. At three months they were wholly irresistible.

"Sleep tight, my sweets," Mary whispered and kissed each infant before they started up the stairs.

At last Mary turned back to the veranda, finding now the one who perhaps needed her the most, young Alexander, sitting on the railing at the far end of the gallery. He looked so lonely.

For the last three days he had kept to himself and seemed to be happiest when he was fondling a large white rabbit's foot with some sort of a key attached.

Yes, that was where she was needed. As yet, she had had little more than perfunctory conversations with him, questions which he had managed to answer with a very shy yes or no.

Of course, she had to confess that she was a bit disappointed. There was so little of Eve in this eleven-year-old boy. He was his father's son in all respects.

Enough, she scolded herself. See to the needs of the three men and then devote the rest of the afternoon to young Alexander, perhaps invite him to go for a walk with her. She wanted desperately to get to know him, to make him feel comfortable and at home here at Stanhope Hall. Perhaps then he would not wait another eleven years before he came back.

She heard Burke laugh aloud, heard him exclaim, "We all enjoy a degree of nationalism, Stephen. Why is that wrong?"

Slowly Mary started down the long veranda, drawn by the sight of the three uniquely handsome men seated in white wicker chairs, the rays of a midafternoon June sun highlighting the strong features of their good faces.

"Nothing is wrong with nationalism, Burke. I didn't mean to imply that there was. But when it takes the form of distrust and hostility toward other nations, then I am merely suggesting that you may have a national problem."

David sat up on the edge of his chair, clearly delighted to be able to contribute. "I think what Stephen means, Papa, is that national consciousness is more specific and more demanding than patriotism, an attitude common to all ages which holds that one's own society is good because it *is* one's own."

Stephen smiled with pleasure. "Exactly. And you would be horrified to hear that this patriotism or nationalism, call it what you will, is now running rampant in England."

Mary approached cautiously, not wanting to interrupt, not as interested in what they were saying as in their very unique and beautiful tableau.

But Burke saw her and stood immediately. Stephen and David followed suit, and to her dismay, she realized that she had interrupted them. "I'm sorry," she murmured. "Please go on. I'm interested. May I fetch you something? Anyone? Tea, Stephen, would you like–"

"Nothing, Mary, please I assure you. Luncheon was delicious and ample. It was far more than I am accustomed to eating at home."

"And what do you eat at home?" she asked, settling on the arm of Burke's chair, insisting that everyone take their seats as usual.

Stephen laughed. "At home for luncheon, I'm generally out in the fields with the tenants. Cook fills my knapsack with hard rolls and good English cheddar and an apple or two in season."

"You work alongside the tenants?" Burke asked, the subject of nationalism momentarily abandoned.

"Of course; it helps them to work better. They're good men. And I enjoy it. And apparently it's paid off because we have tripled our productivity. Of course, the hard part is keeping them on the land. More and more they tend to believe that Utopia lies directly alongside the Thames."

David nodded. "It's the same here. The urban centers are filled to overflowing, while private plantations suffer."

"Then why didn't *you* stay at home?" Burke asked with a smile.

David held up his hands in a gesture of surrender. "I'm home now."

"To stay?"

"Who knows?" David grinned. "I do like my work as a journalist. I like reporting on people."

"And he's good," Mary bragged. "I'll have to show you some of his stories, Stephen. Of course, I've kept them all."

"I'd like very much to see them. I still have trouble thinking of you as grown, David. I remember when Eve and I–"

His voice ceased. Mary saw the shadow that passed over Stephen's face. It was the first mention of Eve since he had arrived.

Now, as the gloom of memory threatened to undo everyone, Mary felt it was her responsibility to restore this lovely party to the high, safe, objective plateau on which she had found it.

"Yes, Stephen, I have saved every story David has ever written. Only last month he did a fascinating piece on a new family of German immigrants who recently settled in Mobile. You were writing about nationalism then, weren't you, David?"

"I was, Mama, very much so. I was astounded to hear them speak of 'the Fatherland.' So much love, so much reverence. The man said that German teachers always stressed national consciousness in all elementary school systems. The homeland was presented as everything that gave a child his identity; birthplace, mother tongue, family, friends, religion, all customs, and history."

Stephen laughed. "I would say that you might have difficulty Americanizing that family."

Burke agreed. "But I assure you, we will. In time we will replace German nationalism with good old reliable red-white-and-blue nationalism."

As Burke spoke on and David and Stephen listened intently, Mary stood quietly. They did not need her. It was her opinion that they might sit and talk like this for the rest of the afternoon.

What a perfect opportunity to get Alex alone and get to know him, find out what his dreams were, his secret wishes.

But she noticed the far end of the veranda deserted now, the railing on which Alex had perched empty, not a sign of him.

For several moments she stood looking all about, searching each and every shadow. But nothing.

Undoubtedly Alexander had gone off on his own in search of an adventure, something more exciting than squalling babies and earnest adults.

Let him go. She would see him at dinner and warmly invite him to share his adventures of the afternoon with everyone, as she always had with David and Eve.

Never in Alex's life had he been so miserable, an awful combination of homesickness and loneliness for Chris and Rolf. Added to that, he felt mildly sick at his stomach. The food here was too heavy and thick, everything drowned under sauces and gravies. The heat was terrible, and he couldn't find any cool, clean air like he used to find on the headlands of Eden.

It was in this state of boredom and loneliness that he had hopped down from the porch banister, landed on his feet and started off on his own. Why not? Nobody seemed very interested in him. Everyone was acting silly over the babies, even his father, and Alex couldn't understand why they had come all this way if nobody really wanted to see him.

Now, as he cut through a dense woods, he looked about, amazed at how quickly he had left Stanhope Hall. He only wanted to be by himself, to think on what Chris, Rolf and Grandpapa might be doing.

Growing angrier by the minute that they were there and he was here, he increased his speed, tripping once over huge exposed tree roots. The air was even heavier in this thick foliage, no breeze, not a trace of a wind. As his jacket began to stick to his back, he stopped long enough to pull it off, retrieving his white rabbit's foot.

He started walking again, moving slowly this time, picking his way carefully across the rough terrain. When could they go home?

He bent over, picked up a long, straight stick, examined it for imperfections, found none, brushed it off and converted it into a walking stick.

A few yards ahead he saw a clearing, approached it carefully, and saw what once had been a path, saw now that the path led up to steps and a stone foundation.

A house. There once had been a small cottage here. Curious, Alex picked his way through the underbrush, hopped up on the foundation, walked around it and saw that it formed a perfect square.

There was a small raised stoop where clearly a back door had been. For several minutes he explored and tried to piece the mystery of the puzzle together. A fire was his guess. The small cottage had burned. A long time ago.

Listen! Voices, clearly voices, not too far away, coming from—

He stood still and tried to determine the direction of the voices and decided—there, that way.

Quickly he stepped out of the ruins and started off on a barely discernible path.

A few minutes later, he broke speed and kept to the shadows of the woods. He peered out and saw a large sunny clearing, saw several boys, barefoot, dressed in faded blue overalls, bare-chested, encircling another boy, this one black, dressed quite differently, wearing shoes, a white shirt and dark trousers. The black boy was simply standing at the center of this clearing while the white boys encircled him, calling him the most awful names, calling him "nigger," going around and around him, poking him now and then with the end of a stick, while he held perfectly still, his head bowed.

"Where'd you get those shoes?" one boy demanded, moved closer to the black boy and shoved him.

The black boy struggled to maintain his balance. "My papa gave them to me."

"And where'd he get them? Did he steal 'em?"

"No, he did not steal–"

"And where'd you get that fancy shirt?"

"My mama made it for me."

"His mama made it," one of the boys jeered. "Black boys aren't supposed to wear clean shirts like that. Let's dirty it up for him, boys, what do you say?"

And laughing, all of the boys scooped handfuls of dirt and threw it at the boy, rubbed it into his hair and across the back of the clean white shirt.

Still the boy stood perfectly still at the center of his tormentors, not speaking unless spoken to, and then answering with extreme politeness.

Both fascinated and horrified, Alex pushed closer, taking care not to be seen or heard. All of the boys appeared to be about his age, though two of the white boys were larger, with red hair, their shoulders covered with freckles. It was these two who were leading the others, suggesting new humiliation for the black boy.

Why doesn't he fight back? Why doesn't he run?

But he did neither and continued to stand, head bowed, accepting their jeers, taunts and insults. Alex found himself wishing that Rolf and Chris were with him. The three of them could easily take care of the four bullies.

Then all at once, the large boy withdrew something from his back pocket. The others saw him, grinned, reached into their pockets and withdrew a similar contraption, a forked piece of sanded wood with what appeared to be a heavy piece of rubber tied on each fork.

"Yeah, Junior," one of the boys grinned. "Let's hunt us some blackbirds."

"Hunt?" Junior grinned. "I think we found ourselves one."

All the time they talked, they slowly encircled the black boy, bending over now and then to pick something up and pocket it.

A few minutes later, Junior called out, "You ready?"

The other boys loaded something into the wooden fork, held it suspended and aimed it directly at the black youth.

"I get first shot," Junior proclaimed. He lifted the wooden fork, took aim on the black boy, drew back hard on the piece of rubber until it was stretched taut and let go.

The boy yelped and reached for his shoulder. When he took his hand away, Alex saw a dot of red on the white shirt.

"My turn," one of the boys shouted, and he did the same thing, striking the black boy in the back this time.

Another outcry and again he tried to reach the injured area, but while he was in the process of doing that, a third shot struck him on the cheek, and he fell to his knees. Alex closed his eyes against the horrible scene, fiercely debating what he should do about it. It was too far to run back to Stanhope Hall for help. He wondered why the boy didn't fight back? Or why didn't he run? But he continued to kneel, head bowed, and take shot after shot, a curious expression on his face as though he felt sorrier for his persecutors than he did for himself.

Then Alex had seen enough. He had to do something. He wasn't as large as the boy called Junior, but he was larger than the other three and he did have the walking stick he had recently picked up in the woods.

Well, then–

As he stepped out of the woods, the black boy saw him first. As he looked toward Alex, he seemed to be saying go back.

Then the others saw him, Junior first. "What in the– Where in the hell did you come from?"

"Stanhope Hall," Alex answered as forcefully as he could, and he was about to say more when one of the other boys muttered, "Come on, we better get outta here."

Junior held his ground for a moment, aiming his curious weapon at Alex now. For a moment Alex was certain that he would fire it at him. But he didn't. All he did was curse the black boy again, then hurry after his rapidly departing companions, all of them disappearing back into the woods now.

Quickly Alex approached the kneeling boy and saw red dots on his shirt, a particularly bad cut on his forehead.

"Are you–"

"I'm alright. I was worried about you."

"Why didn't you run away?"

"They would have run after me."

As blood from the cut on his forehead dripped down his face, Alex withdrew his handkerchief and handed it to him. "Here, hold this tight against it. I'll take you back to Stanhope Hall. They will–"

But the boy shook his head. "I live not far. What's your name?"

"Alex Eden."

"You visiting Stanhopes?"

Alex nodded. "They are my grandparents."

"You talk funny."

"You talk pretty funny yourself."

The boys grinned at each other. Alex extended his hand to help him to his feet. "Come on, I'll walk home with you."

The boy accepted his hand, and Alex pulled him to his feet and saw him grimace. "Does it hurt?"

"Stings a little."

"What's your name?"

"Henderson," the boy replied, still dabbing at the cuts on his face. "Henderson Jones. My father is the minister over there at the Baptist church."

"Why were those boys picking on you?"

Henderson shrugged. "They always pick on someone. It was me today."

"Why doesn't someone pick on them?"

Henderson laughed. "Why?"

"Maybe they'd stop then."

For a moment the two boys exchanged a curious glance, as though neither understood a thing about the other. Henderson smiled. "Yes, you'd better come home with me and meet my father. He will explain."

Alex went along, rather pleased with his discovery of Henderson Jones.

"How old are you?" Alex asked.

"Twelve. And you?"

"Eleven going on twelve."

"You are not from Alabama," Henderson announced, still holding the handkerchief tight on the cut.

"No, I'm from England."

"That's a long way away. Are you homesick?"

"Yes."

"Why did you come?"

"My grandparents wanted to see me."

"We turn here. Don't worry. Junior won't bother us anymore today."

"Where does Junior live?"

"His father is a tenant farmer. All of them are. They work for Mr. Stanhope."

Alex smiled. "No wonder they backed off." He couldn't keep his eyes off of Henderson Jones. He was taller than Alex and seemed so confident, striding through the hot sun with his bloodied shirt. "Why are you all dressed up like that?" Alex asked.

"I was on my way to teach school."

Alex gaped. "You are a schoolteacher?"

Henderson nodded. "I can read and write. My father taught me. He is a graduate of Tuskegee. Do you know where that is?"

"No."

"My father says anyone who can read and write has a duty to help those who can't."

"Where do you teach school?"

"Mostly on the steps in the ruins. There was an old slave cabin there, but it burned a long time ago. But the steps are good. The tenant children come, a few of them, though not every day, mind you. Then there are those who don't like being taught by a black boy."

Alex listened closely. It was very confusing, this southern world.

"There it is," Henderson called out and pointed ahead to a small, white frame house at the end of the dirt road.

Alex looked ahead. The cabin was quite neat, and now he could see that a plump black woman was sweeping the small front porch.

"Are you alright?" she cried out, while they were still a distance away.

Henderson assured her that he was and stood still as she came up to them and carefully examined all of his cuts.

"A slingshot," she murmured. "Who?"

"Junior and his pals. No matter. I'm not hurt. I want you to meet a new friend. His name is Alex Eden, and he is kin to the Stanhopes."

The woman smiled. "Alex," she said.

"I'm sorry about what those boys did," Alex said.

"No matter," Mrs. Jones smiled. "Henderson has something they'll want. Sooner or later they'll come around. You'll see."

Bewildered, Alex wanted to ask just what it was that Henderson had, but now Mrs. Jones was urging them both to the front porch. "Hurry up," Mrs. Jones called out, "your pa is waiting for you. He wants to know everything that happened. He always wants to know, you understand."

As they started up the stairs, Henderson said, "I want you to meet my father."

Mrs. Jones held the front door for them. Henderson led the way in, Alex right behind him. For a moment the sudden darkness after the blinding sun impeded Alex's vision and he could see nothing at all. Then the spiraling dots began to clear and he stood just inside the front door looking at a scene as remarkable as Henderson himself.

The small room had only a few pieces of furniture and was lined with books, books everywhere, books stacked on top of each other, books lining the wall in makeshift bookcases, books in packing crates, books on top of the tables, books beneath them, books to the right of chairs, books to the left. Beyond the front door he saw a man in a wheelchair, but not an old man; his hair was curly and dark, his eyes alert. One hand lifted as Henderson drew near. Only one hand.

"Papa," Henderson said with obvious affection and kissed the man on the forehead. "I have found a new friend. You'll like him. He came striding out of the bushes to my rescue. He was carrying a very large stick and my enemies ran away."

Alex stood erect as Susan had taught him to do, head back, shoulders straight, and he stepped forward the moment Henderson summoned him.

"This is my father, Preacher Jones. And Papa, this is Alex Eden. He is kin to the Stanhopes."

The man seemed to become agitated. His mouth moved, but nothing came out.

"I know, Papa," Henderson nodded. "I will tell him." He turned back to Alex. "My father worked for Burke Stanhope once. Mr. Stanhope paid for his tuition at Tuskegee, enabled him to study under Booker T. Washington. He says that any kin to Mr. Stanhope is more than welcome in this house."

Alex smiled and wondered how Henderson knew what the man had said. But it was obvious from the relief on his father's face that Henderson had said exactly what he had wanted him to say.

Now the man was struggling again, the mouth contorting, the tongue moving in and out, a thin stream of saliva slipping out of the corner of his mouth.

Henderson watched him closely. "Papa wants to know where you come from."

"England," Alex replied, feeling very self-conscious, but fascinated all the same. "North Devon, a place called Eden."

Alex heard Mrs. Jones coming back from the kitchen, a tray in her hand, four tall glasses of something yellow in them.

"Here, Alex," she offered. "This will cool you."

He took the glass, saw Henderson take one and place it on a small table beside his father's wheelchair, then take another for himself.

"Thank you, Mama," Henderson said and drew up two straight-backed chairs.

"Please sit down," he invited Alex, then took the chair nearest to his father, holding the glass of lemonade close to his lips.

The man drank noisily, and most of the drink ran down the sides of his mouth. Gently Henderson dabbed at the excess with a napkin. As he worked, he spoke.

"My father suffered a stroke two years ago. He was our preacher. Since the stroke, God has let him speak through me. I do all the preaching now as well as the teaching."

"And he does it very well," Mrs. Jones bragged, "so well that our membership is on the increase, isn't it, Henderson?"

"Mama, members are not that important, you know it."

All at once his father was trying to speak again.

"I know, Papa, and she knows it as well: 'Wherever two or more are gathered in My name, there will I be also.' "

His father spoke again. Henderson interpreted.

"He wants to hear all about you. What you are doing so far from home. Talk to him. He wants to hear, and he will understand."

Alex took a sip of his lemonade, found it tart and sweet all at the same time, as well as cold and very good. He took another swallow, then angled his chair about until he was facing the black man in the wheelchair. Then he began to speak of scenes and climates remote from this hot southern American world.

They seemed so interested, both Henderson and his father. They leaned close, Henderson asked questions, and his mother stayed for a while, then excused herself and went back into the kitchen. A short time later Alex smelled the most delicious smells.

"Alex, will you stay for dinner?" Mrs. Jones called out from the kitchen. "Just fried chicken and greens."

Alex didn't know what either of those things were, but said, "Yes, thank you," without hesitation, and then Henderson asked, "Do you go to school in this place called Eden?"

"Oh, yes, we have a tutor, Chris, Rolf and I do. His name is Jeremy Neville, and he is short and round and bears a resemblance to a friendly frog."

Henderson laughed and his father smiled. Again Alex noticed the man's right hand move ever so slightly.

"What, Papa?" Henderson asked.

Again the mouth and face contorted.

"He wants to know who instructs you in the word of God?"

Alex blinked, stymied. "The word of–the Bible?" he asked.

Henderson nodded.

"Well, no one, actually, I'm afraid," Alex confessed. "My uncle is a priest in Mortemouth, and he comes up when he has time and helps us to read the Book of Common Prayer. And on occasion my Aunt Marjorie reads the Parables to us–"

"And that's all?" Henderson asked.

Alex felt very inadequate all of a sudden.

"Have you ever read the Bible?"

"No."

Henderson looked back at his father and smiled.

His father spoke again or tried to.

Henderson laughed. "Papa says you are too young and innocent to have any sin on your soul. But you will need the Bible one day, its teachings and its strengths, and when you need it, you will find it or it will find you."

"Supper," Mrs. Jones called from the kitchen door. "Come along, all of you. You better move along, Henderson; you preach tonight."

"How could I forget, Mama?"

Alex stood back as Henderson pushed his father's wheelchair through the cluttered stacks of books and into the narrow kitchen. Then he followed.

Mrs. Jones had opened the back door of the small cottage in search of a summer breeze. Now Alex saw a blue oilcloth which covered a simple white frame table and in the center one gigantic sunflower, white pottery plates spread about and an enormous platter of something brown, crispy and delicious smelling.

"Come, sit down, Alex, sit all of you. Henderson, please say the blessing."

After Henderson had wheeled his father up to the table, he sat down next to him, closed his eyes and turned his face toward the door and the fields beyond.

For several minutes he said nothing, and Alex held perfectly still, then opened both eyes to Henderson's face.

"Our Dearest Father," Henderson said, and Alex noticed that his father's lips were moving along with his. "We thank You for Your many and generous blessings, and we thank You for this gift of Alex Eden, for allowing him to enter our world as well as our hearts. We ask Your mercy on Junior and his friends. Give us the strength to love them, and one day grant us the opportunity to nurture them. We thank You for all Your gentle mercy, and we ask that You make us truly worthy. In His name, amen."

Mrs. Jones said amen as well. His father tried to speak the word. Henderson repeated it for him, and then Alex spoke the benediction.

"Now," Henderson exclaimed and shook out his napkin and instructed Alex to "dive in" to the best fried chicken this side of the Mississippi River.

While Alex was not quite certain what he was supposed to do, Mrs. Jones handed him the platter, and he lifted a piece of chicken and tasted it, then tasted it again and ate as he hadn't eaten since he'd left England, and listened, enthralled, as Henderson spoke on a number of subjects–precisely how he listened to what his father said with his heart, not with his ears; how he had come to enjoy teaching and preaching, looking into the faces of both the young and the old who needed his father's wisdom and his own love; how violence of any sort sickened him to the point that he could not respond to it; and how important it was that the world come to understand the importance of peace in all matters.

Alex could have listened to him talk forever. He had never known words like the ones Henderson was using.

"Will they be expecting you back at Stanhope Hall?" Mrs. Jones asked at the end of the meal.

"No, ma'am, I don't think so."

"Then would you like to come and listen to me preach?" Henderson invited with a smile.

Alex grinned. He was beginning to suspect that he might willingly follow Henderson anywhere, just so long as he could be near that mysterious face, that glorious peace, that never-before-experienced sense of alrightness.

"I'd like that very much," Alex said. "May I have another piece of chicken?"

Mrs. Jones smiled and pushed the platter toward him. Henderson sat back and held a "talk" with his father.

Alex ate, contented for the first time since he had left Eden.

Eden Castle
June 1, 1907

With a degree of reluctance, Chris completed his Latin grammar and waited for Mr. Neville to dismiss him from the classroom. As always, the late-afternoon study hours were reserved for Rolf alone, to "prepare him for advanced standings."

Chris didn't give a damn about Rolf's advanced standings. What he did care about was being expelled from the classroom into the empty castle with no one to talk to and no one to play with.

Yesterday he had tried to play the Battle of Cádiz all by himself. But it just didn't work. One couldn't fire a broadside at oneself and fall dead all at the same time.

"Alright, Christopher, very good. You've done well. You're dismissed now," Mr. Neville called out.

There it was. Dismissed to do what? Slowly, reluctantly, Chris left the room and closed the door behind him. He stood for a moment looking up and down the empty corridor.

What to do?

Grandpapa was napping, as he always did in the afternoon. Uncle Richard was in his library attending to correspondence. Aunt Eleanor was working in her garden. His mother was helping Susan at the clinic. He had no idea where his father was, but it didn't really matter. His father never had time to play with him.

Then what?

Slowly, head bowed, he started down the stairs that led to the Great Hall. He heard footsteps and saw Trudy carrying a stack of fresh linen.

"Master Chris," she smiled as she passed him. "You look dreadful," she called back over her shoulder. "Go out and sit in the sun."

He didn't want to go out and sit in the sun. He wanted Alex. In his room behind the door he had drawn a large square calendar with the days marked as well as the dates. Every morning he made a ritual of marking off another day of Alex's absence. His very worst thought was that Alex was having such a good time that he would not want to come home.

All at once, he heard the sound of footsteps and saw his father walking with purposeful strides across the Great Hall.

Where was his father going? Then he remembered. Almost every afternoon his father would go up into the east wing to pray outside the sick man's door.

What exactly went on up in that remote part of Eden Castle? Once, a long time ago, he and Alex had crept up there in search of the ghost. They had seen something, but their investigation had been cut short by the appearance of meddlesome old Dr. Reicher, who had scared them to death by creeping up behind them, then scolding them soundly.

Well, what harm would there be in following his papa up to the east wing? He might have a great adventure to report to Alex when he returned home.

Thus convinced that he was doing nothing wrong, Chris eased down the stairs and kept a close eye on his father, just starting up on the other side.

Once his father was out of sight, Chris quickly checked the Great Hall for further traffic and found it empty. Then he ran as fast as he could across the Great Hall, and at last he reached the safety of the other side. Moving more cautiously, he started up the second flight of steps, walking on his toes, not wanting his father to hear the echo of his footsteps.

Just as he reached the top he saw his father's jacket disappearing around the far corner at the end of the long corridor. It was at that exact corner that he and Alex had seen the ghost.

Now Chris hurried down the corridor, keeping well to the side, spying a large linen closet at the end of the corridor and praying with all his heart that it was unlocked. It would afford him a perfect place from which he could see everything and yet not be seen.

He slipped to the opposite end of the corridor, peered cautiously around and saw a bizarre sight. It was his father, on his knees before the closed door. He held his open Book of Common Prayer in his hand, and though Chris couldn't hear anything, it sounded as though he was reading from the Eucharist, his voice low and steady, his head bowed.

Quickly Chris hurried across the corridor, gave the door on the linen closet one good jerk, found it open and slipped quickly inside, pulled the door almost shut but leaving a hairline crack between the hinges from which he could peer out at everything that was going on.

Then all at once he heard his father's praying voice cease, heard him call out clearly, "Geoffrey?"

Chris shut one eye, the better to see, and peered out.

"Geoffrey? I know you can hear me, as I know you have heard me every day that I have come to visit you. We all still love you, and I have confidence that one day the knowledge of that love will allow you to open this door and come out into the welcoming embrace of your family, a true prodigal."

His father slowly closed his Book of Common Prayer, though he remained on his knees as though it were a position that suited him the most.

"Now for news of your family, Geoffrey," he began, his tone of voice changed, more conversational, less prayerful. "As you know, Stephen and young Alex are in America now. We miss them. Chris and Rolf are hard at their studies. They are very bright and will do well in the world, I'm certain. My work and Marjorie's knows no end down in Mortemouth. I tell you, the community has changed from the days of our growing up. Once God-fearing, I meet men daily who seem to fear nothing, least of all God."

Chris's father talked to the doorknob, as though he fully expected the doorknob to respond at any moment.

But it didn't, and Chris saw his father, having talked himself out, rise slowly to his feet. "God bless you, Geoffrey. I'll try to return tomorrow. Remember to open your windows. The roses are in full bloom, their fragrance intoxicating."

Slowly he reached out and touched the closed door, as though it were a man in need. Then he turned about and started down the corridor, coming straight toward Chris and the linen closet.

Chris held perfectly still and listened as his father's footsteps approached, grew louder and then passed him by.

Now he ventured out of the linen closet and walked quietly all the way down the corridor until he was standing directly before the closed door. He wanted to see it for himself up close.

Then suddenly, without warning, the door swung open. Chris jumped back, scared out of his wits. In the process, he lost his balance, fell flat on his behind, tried to scramble up, couldn't, and found himself staring straight up at the ghost himself, a wild-eyed man, fully bearded, his hair long, gray and matted together. The man was supporting himself on a single crutch, which gave his body a distorted appearance, one shoulder raised beneath his dark gray dressing gown, his torso leaning to one side as Chris gaped at the hem of the robe and saw only one slippered foot.

"I–"

Chris tried to form words, but he could not. His tongue felt like butter and stuck to the roof of his mouth. The man was glaring down at him with feverish, angry eyes. Chris felt certain that he was about to be murdered.

The man dragged himself closer to the door and peered out in both directions. "Is the meddlesome priest gone?"

Chris assumed he meant his father and tried again to form words but couldn't.

"Bastard," the man cursed. Chris saw him grimace, as though to walk with the crutch caused him pain, yet he could not walk without it.

"Who in the hell are you?" he demanded.

"C–Chris."

"You live here?"

"Y–yes, sir."

"What are you doing outside my door?"

"I don't have anyone to play with," Chris replied, still on his backside.

The man continued to stare down on him, as though he were making a decision. At last he muttered, "Come on in if you want. Makes no difference to me."

Then the man disappeared, leaving the door ajar.

Had Chris heard correctly? Had the man invited him to come inside?

Torn by a combination of fear and indecision, Chris pushed up from the floor.

"Are you coming or not? Make up your mind if you have one."

Chris took a final look down the corridor, drew a deep breath, wiped the perspiration off the palms of his hands and wished with all his heart that Alex was with him.

Then he went in.

Stanhope Hall
June 1, 1907

"He's not there," David announced, coming down the stairs after checking on Alex's room.

He saw the expression on Stephen's face turn to worry. "Then where in the–"

"Don't worry, Stephen," Mary soothed. "I'm sure he hasn't gone far. David was forever disappearing for hours at a time."

"What do you suggest?"

David came all the way down the stairs. "A search. Papa, you and Stephen take the back road that leads to the fields. I'll go out the front way."

As his father and Stephen started down the corridor that led to the back veranda, David called after them, "Pick up whatever help you can find on the way. Tell the men who you're looking for. Maybe, if we're lucky, someone has seen him."

Burke gave him a backward wave, before they disappeared into the rapidly falling dusk.

David looked back at his mother and saw the worry in her eyes increase. "Where could he have gotten to?" she murmured.

David shook his head. "He's a quiet boy. I suspect that he's homesick."

"I know," Mary agreed, a touch of sadness in her voice. "And I don't know how to approach him. He seems so distant."

"Well, let's hope he's not too distant. I'll hurry back as fast as I can. If he should by chance come in on his own, have Clarence ring the yard bell. We can hear it at least this side of the river."

He took the stairs down in a couple of giant steps and increased his stride as he approached the avenue of live oaks and tried to remember where he used to go when he was eleven. But it wasn't quite the same. Alex was thousands of miles away from home and feeling quite lonely.

At the end of the live oaks, he moved toward the tenant houses and the river, his logic being that the tenant houses meant company, and the river meant fun. He increased his step in the dusk and prayed that his choice had been the right one.

About twenty minutes later he saw the end of the road and the dirt path that cut to the left and ran parallel to the river. The opposite path led to the tenant cabins.

Which way now? He stood for a moment, looked in both directions and realized he hadn't passed a living soul. Then he remembered it was Wednesday night, church night.

He glanced toward the right, toward the little whitewashed frame church that sat apart from the cabins and yet was the heart of all tenant life, particularly black tenant life.

Would there be a congregation tonight? He had heard that Preacher Jones had fallen ill and wondered who was filling the pulpit.

As he started to the right, he heard the distant singing of a gospel hymn. He approached the church and walked directly to one of the low windows, opened for the night breeze. He moved back a few yards so that he would be less visible, then peered in.

The pews were filled. Clearly someone quite effective had come to take Preacher Jones's place.

As David looked into the crowded church, he found the one face he had been looking for: Alex!

He was sitting between a plump, middle-aged black woman and a man in a wheelchair who sat rigidly still.

David looked more closely. The man in the wheelchair was Preacher Jones, whose attention was focused on the pulpit, on a young black dressed in a white shirt and wearing a tie. He was holding a well-used Bible in his hand and preaching his heart out.

Relieved that Alex had been found, David discovered himself listening carefully to the remarkable young man, who clearly was holding the entire congregation in the palm of his hand.

The most attentive person of all appeared to be Alex Eden, who sat on the front row, his face lifted toward the young preacher. At some point David found a convenient tree to lean against, and began to listen more carefully. The young man's voice was deep, with little trace of either a southern accent or a black one. It was a voice that captured and held attention, that spoke of promises and dreams, spoke of a wisdom far beyond the capacity of his years.

No wonder Alex had fallen in with such mesmerizing company. It would be an impossible voice to resist, a voice that promised peace, love, generosity of spirit and the most difficult lesson of all, the necessity to forgive those who wrong you, to love your enemies and to have faith in their redemption.

David listened to it all, first with a degree of objective interest. But at some point the young black man captured even his objectivity and left only a willing heart and an open mind. He found himself whispering amen along with everyone else.

Then he heard an out-of-tune piano commence to play a hymn, "The Old Rugged Cross," and as the churchgoers commenced to sing, David stepped forward and saw Alex sharing a hymnal with the woman who sat next to him, saw now that the young preacher had descended from the pulpit and was kneeling before the man in the wheelchair.

Bewildered, David found himself humming along with the music, the same music he had grown up with and had heard coming from the tenant cabins all his life.

At the end of the hymn the young preacher stood up from his kneeling position and pronounced the benediction.

Then it was over and as the congregation started down to shake the young man's hand, David saw Alex step forward first and say something, saw the young boy laugh, draw Alex to one side and insist that he stay close beside him.

All at once he saw the young preacher look directly toward the window. "Mr. Stanhope, are you out there?"

David felt his heart beating too rapidly. How did–

"Won't you come in?" the young man called. "You are most welcome. Alex is safe with me."

"Yes," David stammered, pushed away from the tree and started slowly toward the front of the church, where the congregation was beginning to file out.

A few of the men swept off their hats at David's approach, and the women smiled. All seemed so at peace. As David made his way through the crowds into the small church, he saw the young black man coming forward to greet him.

"Good evening, Mr. Stanhope. My name is Henderson Jones. Alex has been with me most of the day."

"I hope I didn't worry you," Alex said. "Everyone at Stanhope Hall had something else to do. I had nothing to do, so I–"

"Went on your own adventure," David smiled. "I used to do exactly the same thing."

As he spoke, he noticed the black woman pushing the wheelchair forward and recognized Preacher Jones.

"This is my father," Henderson said, "and my mother. I believe you know them."

"I do," David smiled and extended his hand to Mrs. Jones. He was at a loss as to how to greet the man in the chair.

"Speak directly to him, Mr. Stanhope. He understands everything," Henderson advised.

David cleared his throat and tried to look at the distortion that was now Preacher Jones's face. "Good evening to you," David began. "I heard that you had suffered–"

"A stroke," Mrs. Jones said, without a trace of grief or regret in her voice. "He's quite well now, only limited."

"New limitations, new challenges," Henderson said.

"Uncle David," Alex said, quite excited, "Henderson talks for his father, don't you, Henderson?"

"Not for him," Henderson corrected. "Through him."

Then Mrs. Jones was pushing the wheelchair down the center aisle, with Henderson following close behind. "I'm glad you came tonight, Alex."

"So am I," Alex replied, keeping up. "May I visit you tomorrow?"

"I'll be teaching in the morning."

"Where?"

"At the ruins at the end of the woods. The place I mentioned to you earlier. Meet me there. I may force you into service."

"I don't understand."

"Do you know your multiplication tables?"

"Of course."

"There are children here who don't. While I do the reading classes, I may let you handle the multiplication."

"Oh, may I, Uncle David?" Alex begged, as excited as David had ever seen him.

"I don't know why not. We will ask your father."

"He'll say yes," Alex cut in.

On the darkened porch, Mrs. Jones and Henderson lifted the wheelchair down the steps.

Henderson pushed the chair over the rough terrain and stopped where the paths divided.

"Thank you for rescuing me, Alex. It took courage to step forward as you did. Good night then. I will see you tomorrow."

"Good night, Henderson. Thank you for dinner, Mrs. Jones. Good night, Preacher."

Alex followed longingly after the three for a few steps.

"What is that about you rescuing him?" David asked as he guided Alex back toward the road which led to Stanhope Hall.

"Uncle David, you should have been there. There were these boys, white boys they were, and they had these weapons called slingshots. Do you know what that is?"

David laughed and walked easily beside Alex, who literally moved all over the road in his excitement as he told the story of how Henderson knelt at the center of his tormentors and how it was Alex himself who had stepped out of the woods and had single-handedly driven them all away.

As Alex talked on, David suspected that at last the boy had found something to engage his attention during his visit to Stanhope Hall. The remarkable young Henderson Jones.

For that matter, David had been rather engaged by the young man himself.

There was something about him.

Eden Castle
June 1, 1907

"Well, are you coming or not?"

As the angry voice carried from the next room to the door, Chris closed his eyes and wished again with all his heart that Alex was with him. Or Rolf.

"Well?"

"Y–yes sir, I'm–coming."

"Then hurry! And close the door quickly. Do you hear me?"

Chris heard. How could he not have heard? The man shouted every word as though Chris were deaf.

Once inside the small dim reception hall, Chris closed the door, turned the bolt, kept one hand on the doorknob and looked carefully about.

It was a small room no larger than the linen closet in which Chris had recently taken refuge. To one side on a table he saw a half-eaten breakfast. The cold, congealed eggs smelled awful. In fact, the whole room smelled awful, like soiled linen and unwashed bodies. There was no direct light, save that which was coming from the large sitting room windows straight ahead.

At the doorway Chris stopped, brought to a halt by the incredible sight before him. The sitting room, quite large, had been stripped of all furniture except for a small daybed which Chris saw pushed against the far wall. In the center of the room on a large table was a miniature battlefield quite skillfully done, a vast panorama of hills and roads and in the distance the cutout skyline of a small city with square whitewashed block towers and here and there a church spire. To the right of where Chris stood, he saw a tiny regiment of soldiers, approximately five hundred in all, maybe more. They had been skillfully carved out of soft wood and carefully painted with red jackets and low-slung gray slouch hats. At this moment they were in marching formation approaching a small native whitewashed settlement of no more than three houses and one small church.

Everywhere Chris looked he saw a miraculously accurate reproduction of an actual object. He saw a line of tiny wagons, a Red Cross cart, a barnyard full of animals and, tending the animals, a tiny girl. He knew it was a girl because she was wearing a long black skirt and a white apron.

Chris looked in all directions at once, unable to take it all in. It was a wonderful reproduction, and it literally filled the large room. There to the left he saw a line of artillery he had not seen before, and behind it hundreds of soldiers all on horseback, and this attack force far outnumbered the small regiment on the hill.

"Do you know what this is?" the man demanded now, standing on the opposite side, apparently willing to give Chris all the time he needed to look his fill.

"It's a battlefield. Alex and I play the Battle of Cádiz often."

"This is not a game. This is Jameson's Raid," the man interrupted, and Chris noticed that the man was using his single crutch, tucked out of sight beneath his robe, and that crutch was now serving as his missing foot.

"Do you know of Jameson's Raid, boy?" he asked now, moving rapidly up and down the far side of the battlefield, his eyes darting in every direction.

"N–no," Chris stammered.

"Then I'll tell you," the man offered, quite calm now, as though he had received the answer he wanted.

"Come, come further in. I won't bite you. Who is Alex?"

"My cousin."

At some point, the man's anger had faded and was now replaced by an attitude that Chris knew well. All Geoffrey had wanted was a playmate.

"Do you like battles, boy?" Geoffrey asked as he balanced himself on one leg and, using his crutch as a hand, carefully guided the long line of horsemen back into the perimeters of the cutout city. He hopped down to the opposite end of the table and, in like manner, pushed the marching regiment up the hill and down the other side. A few fell in the process. He cursed.

"You know, it has recently occurred to me that if we could attach these soldiers to flat boards in groups of twenty-five, we could move them faster. What do you think, Chris?"

Bewildered, Chris struggled for an answer. The man was acting as though Chris had had a hand in this.

"Yes," he agreed.

"You see, this is exactly as it was on that last morning before the battle commenced. We were–there," he explained, indicating the regiments of marchers frozen in time who yet somehow gave the appearance of coming up the hill. "Our destination was–there," and he pointed toward the little whitewashed settlement. "Doornkop–have you heard of it? No, probably not, though you should have by now. By now, every English schoolboy should have the name burned into his consciousness as the site of infamy, betrayal and treason."

"Was this battle where you . . . fought?" Chris asked.

"Yes, I fought there, but more to the point, I was betrayed there, along with every Englishman, betrayed by our so-called allies and friends."

Suddenly he wagged his head back and forth in a violent rejection. "Trust–no one," he advised simply. "Did you hear me? I said trust–no–man, not even those who claim to love you for they may be the most vicious traitors of all."

Chris started to disagree, then decided that Geoffrey probably did not want an argument.

"Now, come closer," Geoffrey commenced, "and let me speak to you of a morning eleven years ago, January 2, to be exact, and here we are, the South African Company." Using his crutch as a pointer he indicated the smartly dressed regiment marching up the hill toward the town with the funny name of Doornkop.

"Pay close attention," Geoffrey commanded now. "You must understand everything, the glory of battle as well as the pain of betrayal. Both are the same coin, do you understand? Different sides, that is all."

Chris listened carefully, not always understanding but becoming increasingly fascinated by the man himself.

"We had traveled all night, don't you see?" he began, his manner conspiratorial. "We were to wait–here," and he leaned over to indicate the little whitewashed country village. "That night, after having cut all wires of communication leading into Johannesburg, our friends were to meet us here," and the crutch stabbed forward to a halfway point between Doornkop and Johannesburg.

"From there," Geoffrey raised up on a note of triumph, "we were to ride into Johannesburg under cover of night and join other allies and take the city in a bloodless maneuver."

All at once his eyes glazed over. "I can't tell you," he went on, his voice low, "how many times I have gone over that night, both in my mind and on this field. Every day, every morning, every night–"

He shook his head as though astonished by his own actions. "That's why I built this years ago. I thought that perhaps I was missing something. For example, we had guards posted all about Doornkop. Then why weren't the Dutch bastards seen approaching? Why was there no battle cry raised while there still was time to do something about it? Why–oh dear God, so many whys. I have drowned in whys over the years, and still no answer."

Chris made a simple suggestion. "The guards, if they had seen them coming and did not report them, then they, too, were traitors."

Geoffrey turned slowly. "That has occurred to me, though I find it an intolerable thought."

"Were there no troops of support?"

"None, none whatsoever."

"What made you think that there would be?"

"Jameson," Geoffrey said, obviously eager to talk about all aspects of that day. "Jameson himself had been in touch with Kruger. He was the one who made certain claims and promises. He was the one who–"

All at once he shook his head. "Still, in a way it was a glorious day," he went on, moving slowly around the battlefield now, leaning heavily on his crutch, bending over to straighten a building in Johannesburg as he passed, righting several of the horsemen who had toppled over on their mounts.

"There is a feeling in the pit of a man's stomach, Chris, when a battle is ahead. A good warrior can sense it and knows what it means. It means that a very generous Divinity is about to provide you with an opportunity to prove yourself worthy of the name 'soldier.' "

He was on the far side of the miniature battlefield now. A ray of sun coming through the high smudged windows struck him directly in the face and caused his eyes to glitter.

Chris stood perfectly still, almost afraid to move for fear of breaking the spell that the man had woven.

"Nightfall now," Geoffrey said, his voice low and taut. "Here we had made camp on Jameson's orders. We had ridden hard for several days. A night's rest seemed in order. Then they came out of the darkness, like apparitions. Men were still eating, drinking their coffee, and suddenly the enemy was upon them, hundreds of them."

He was ranging freely about the battlefield now, pushing the horsemen directly into the center of the troops and, with the tip of his crutch, sending men and horses sprawling in all directions.

Chris saw small muscles in Geoffrey's face jump beneath his skin, saw his mouth open, eyes distended as clearly the battle going on in his head was now much more real than the miniature battlefield before them.

About fifteen minutes later, not one soldier in red was left standing and many of the horsemen had been toppled as well.

Geoffrey limped around the battlefield, surveying his destruction with almost a sense of pride. "A few of us played dead," he boasted, "at least until we could be certain the Dutch bastards had satisfied their blood lust. No honor there, just plain-faced, blunt-nosed farmers who probably were more expert at wielding a shovel than they were a—"

His voice broke. "There was no excuse for that defeat," he grieved. "We were superior men in all ways. But no soldier, no matter how superior, can triumph over lies, cunning and deceit."

At last his hate deposited him on the edge of a couch, where he sat wearily and stared out over the length of his battlefield. "There was no communal glory on that day. Our wounded were put unceremoniously in the back of carts in disgrace and carried away. Jameson was hauled to prison in the back of a hay wagon. Still the glory was there, the one common knowledge that it took traitors to defeat us, that it took deceit and betrayal to defeat us. In those circumstances, do you think that we could still stand erect and hold our heads high? Do you agree?"

It was such an urgent question. Chris was startled out of his silence by a sudden involvement. But the answer Geoffrey wanted to hear was clear upon his face.

"Yes," Chris replied.

Slowly Geoffrey smiled as though the battle had been put to rest for another day and lay back on his couch. "The sights and sounds of mortal conflict," he mused, eyes closed. "There is nothing like it, Chris. The call of one's country. It is the highest honor that God can bestow upon a man. To be a soldier is to be a God, in charge of not only one's fate but the fate of others."

His voice was fading with fatigue.

"Chris?"

"Yes, sir."

"Before I pass into dreams, would you do me a favor?"

"Yes, sir, anything."

"Yesterday, from my high window, I saw a wagonload of virgin timber being hauled into the farmyard. Go to the yard master and ask if you might have the end pieces, the thin and smoothly planed ones. Tell him Lord Geoffrey desires them. Bring those end pieces to this room tomorrow at this same time, and the two of us will make fast work of attaching our soldiers and then we'll be able to fight the battle several times in one day. Would you do that for me, Chris?"

"Yes, sir."

"Good boy. Tell no one. Our secret–"

Then he was asleep.

For some minutes, Chris stood and stared, fascinated by all he had seen and heard. Geoffrey was as lonely as Chris was, wanted someone to play with. Out of all the inhabitants of Eden Castle, he had chosen Chris. How much he would have to tell Alex.

Taking care not to awaken Geoffrey, Chris backed out of the room, stealing a final glance at the immense and magnificent battlefield. He had never seen anything like it, and neither had Alex.

Then he slipped into the reception room and out of the door, closing it ever so quietly behind him.

His first impulse when confronting the empty corridor was to run, to bolt for safety before anyone discovered him.

Now there was no need to run. Instead, he straightened his shirtwaist, pulled up his trousers, walked very sedately down the center of the corridor and almost prayed that he would encounter someone.

No need for deception or concealment now. He was an invited guest of Geoffrey Eden's and, as such, no longer had need to run and hide.

Stanhope Hall
July 15, 1907

Stephen took his morning coffee to the veranda and looked out over the beauty of Stanhope Hall, dark, emerald green lawns, the ancient live oaks forming a perfect avenue of grace and beauty, the heavy fragrance-laden southern air all so evocative of–Eve.

How greatly she had enriched his life. How much they had shared together in a few short years, and it all had started here, almost in the exact place where he was standing now.

"My dearest," he whispered and paid homage to her, then tried to address the more urgent problem, should they leave and go back to England?

Mary was busy with the babies, David had gone to his office in Mobile and Burke was sequestered in his study.

And Alex–

No need to ask where Alex was–always with Henderson, generally coming home so late at night that he only had the energy to eat a quick meal and then fall into bed.

"There you are."

He looked up at the sound of Mary's voice and saw her just coming through the door. She still wore her apron, having been up to help Sharon feed the twins.

"I'm not sure who needs a bath the most after those feedings," she laughed and held up her apron splotched with food. She slipped it over her head, dropped it onto a near chair and walked to his side.

"Such a lovely morning," she mused, looking out at the same scene which Stephen had admired.

For several moments neither spoke, and Stephen listened to the music of the morning–blue jays screeching noisily in the live oaks, cicadas warming up with the heat of the day, the servants calling out to each other from the kitchen gallery.

"I'm so glad you came, Stephen," Mary said and covered his hand on the railing with her own.

"I am too. But I'm afraid I must apologize for Alexander."

"Oh, no need. He's a good boy. I know he is lonely for his cousin."

Stephen laughed. "Henderson just may have replaced poor Chris in Alex's affection."

"He does spend a lot of time with the boy."

"Mary, . . . I think that we should return to England."

He watched carefully for her reaction, anxious to interpret it accurately, not wanting to hurt her in any way.

But as carefully as he watched her, he saw nothing. She lifted her head to the sky, held it there for a moment, then said, "I suspected as much."

"Now, of course, if you–"

"No, no, I fully understand. In a way it was very selfish of me to insist for all these years that you come. I'm sure I've worked a hardship. I've lived with a farmer long enough to know that spring and summer are the months reserved for the land."

Stephen smiled. "And January is not the time to be on the North Atlantic."

"No, of course not."

There was a pause.

He heard Hester behind him at the front door. "Mrs. Stanhope, Miss Sharon asked if you'd come and look at Elizabeth. It's that rash."

"Of course, Hester, tell her I'll be along in just a minute."

Then she turned back to Stephen with a smile of apology. "I really must go before the babies take their naps."

"Of course." Then, "Mary."

His voice stopped her. She looked back from the door.

"If you want us to stay, we will. But if you are–"

"I am fine, Stephen," she smiled reassuringly and came back and took his hands in hers. "I really am. The human animal is amazingly resilient. I doubt if a day goes by that I don't think of Eve. But the pain is greatly diminished. All I feel now is gratitude to God for having known and loved her, and only mild sadness that her life was so short."

Stephen listened with a degree of amazement. She had just described *his* feelings. She stood on tiptoe and kissed his cheek. "Go home, Stephen, and take Alexander home please. All I ask of both of you is that you always reserve a portion of your heart for Stanhope Hall and for the people who live here."

Then she was gone. Stephen watched the door close, saw her through the screen as she hurried up the stairs.

Well then, homeward bound they were, after less than six weeks. Quite a distance to come for a mere six weeks. Had it been worth it? In a way, yes.

He started down the veranda steps, intent on finding Alex and giving him the good news.

At the bottom of the steps, he stopped.

Where?

Three men crossed around from the back of the house, heading toward the cotton fields below the road. "I beg your pardon," Stephen called out, "but I was wondering if you could tell me where I might find the young man named Henderson?"

The tall man in the middle stepped forward. "Henderson is where he generally is at this time of day," the man said.

"And where would that be?" Stephen asked.

"In the old ruins is where they usually meet the young'uns."

Then they were gone.

The ruins.

Stephen knew of only one, a disastrous one, Sis Liz's cottage, the one that burned the night that Eve had been kidnapped.

It was as though the past was sorely testing him. Now his son and Eve's was with a black boy in that same spot, teaching the children of white tenant farmers to read and write.

He shook his head, amazed at the ways of this world and the people who inhabited it.

Eden. Home. That thought alone urged him forward, that and how eager he was to see the reaction on Alex's face when he shared the good news with him.

Alex had discovered that the best tool for teaching arithmetic was a bushel basket of green apples. Every morning the old cook had kindly provided him with one. He had picked it up on the back porch of the kitchen annex and had hurried to meet Henderson with the most incredible sense of excitement, through the woods which he knew now by heart to these ruins where Henderson would be waiting with the tenant children.

Now, as Alex confronted his nine students, boys and girls, ranging from six to ten, all perched on the steps of the burned-down cottage, he realized he had seldom been so happy in his life as he had been these last few weeks. It was such fun watching their progress. Leah could now do her multiplication tables up to fives and six-year-old Jason could both add and subtract. They were dirty, to be sure, mud-encrusted, barefooted and wearing soiled garments, but they all possessed eager minds. Alex sorted out twenty-four green apples, then asked the three youngest students to count along with him as he laid them carefully on the ground.

Above their piping voices, he saw Henderson with his students lined up on the foundation like birds on a fence. They had only three well-worn primers between fifteen students, so they had divided themselves into three huddled groups, each trying to follow the simple story as Henderson read it to them.

"Alright, students," Alex began as he straightened his shoulders and was stunned to hear how much he sounded like old Mr. Neville.

"Now pay close attention. We will start with addition, then do a few subtraction problems and then I'll take the apples away and let you see how you do on your own."

As he knelt down to separate ten apples from the twenty-four, he caught Henderson's eye. The two exchanged a smile. Alex thought him to be the most remarkable person he'd ever met. His only real regret was that Chris wasn't here with him to know Henderson. How in the world would Alex ever be able to describe him?

"Alright," Alex began, "I have ten apples here and I'm going to take four away. How many do I have left? Scott?"

But before Scott could answer, Alex heard movement in the woods to his right, and just as he turned, he felt something sharp strike him on the side of his face, a sudden stinging pain that caused his hand to shoot reflexively up, and within the instant he felt moisture on his fingers and saw blood.

He looked toward the woods and saw Junior just emerging, slingshot in hand. Behind him came his three shadows, the boys who were always with him.

Alex started forward in anger and pain. What right had the boy to strike him, to interrupt? What had Alex done to him to warrant such behavior? But he had taken less than half a dozen steps toward him when he remembered how Henderson had reacted on that morning weeks ago.

Now Alex stopped, still dabbing at the cut with his hand. He heard a new silence behind him as the classes all came to a halt. He expected to hear Henderson say something, but Henderson was silent.

He stood less than four feet from Junior, who continued to grin at him as though the sight of pain and blood brought him pleasure.

"You're bleedin', white boy," he sneered, "and it's drippin' all over your pretty white shirt."

"I can see that," Alex replied.

"You workin' for the nigger man?"

"No, I'm working with him."

"What's you doin' with those apples?"

"We're learning how to add and subtract," Alex replied.

For several moments, Junior seemed content to look about the ruins and study all the children.

"Alright," Junior declared at last, as though angry. "If you're so smart, how much money is that?" Suddenly he withdrew his hand from his pocket, and Alex saw several coins and a single bill land in the dirt at his feet.

Baffled, Alex looked first at the money, then at Junior. "I–don't–"

"If you're so smart, how much money is that?"

Alex dabbed a final time at the cut on his face, then slowly approached the hurled coins.

"Is this your money?"

"Sure it's mine. You saying I stole it?"

"No."

"It's my share of the egg money. If I clean up after those damn chickens, my mama says she'll start giving me half of what she gits. That's what she give me today."

All at once Alex looked up at Junior and saw not a bully but someone who looked scared. What good was money if one did not know the amount and value?

Quickly Alex assessed the coins and added the dollar bill. "Junior, you have exactly two dollars and seventy-seven cents, unless I've missed something."

The boy blinked at him. "How do you know that?"

"I counted."

"How . . ."

". . . do you count?"

A look crossed Junior's face as though he were in pain, as though someone had just shot him with a slingshot. "Yeah," he muttered.

"It's really simple," Alex smiled. "Look, Leah there is only six, and she's quite good at it."

Junior looked around Alex to where the students were seated upon the steps. "I don't want to sit on them steps," grumbled Junior.

"Sit where you like," Alex invited cordially, "and your friends as well. Come along, pick up your money, and I'll show you how to count it next time."

"This is gonna be as close as I come," Junior called out, and Alex looked back to see the boys sitting cross-legged at the very edge of the woods.

"Alright, pay attention," Alex said. "There are one hundred pennies in every dollar bill and we will let one apple represent one penny. Do you understand?"

With his mouth open and his brow knit, Junior nodded, and Alex saw the slingshot fall uselessly into the dirt as Junior carefully examined his one-dollar bill and tried to find one hundred green apples in it.

Carefully Stephen made his way through the woods, dreading his first glimpse of Sis Liz's burned-out cottage, fearing that this could well be the most difficult test of all.

He heard voices then, still distant, though growing clearer. Alex.

He increased his step, pushing his way through the dense foliage, thinking ahead to how he would tell Alex the good news. There were still the logistics to be worked out. How soon could he make arrangements? Passage would have to be booked on the first possible ship heading out. And, of course, a message should be sent ahead to Eden to let them know. Then a thought occurred. No. Let it be a surprise.

At the edge of the woods, he stopped and looked ahead to a most interesting sight. Where Sis Liz's cottage had been, the rough gray stone foundation was lined on one side with a dozen or so children, their bare feet swinging back and forth. Standing before them was Henderson, immaculately dressed in his daily uniform of white shirtwaist, neatly pressed trousers and a dark necktie.

Henderson was reading a book to his students, his voice deep and mysteriously full of musical inflection. The story was *Huckleberry Finn.*

Then Stephen saw Alex. He was involved with a smaller group of children seated on the steps. To one side, Stephen saw a group of four larger boys, and Alex was addressing both groups, hurrying back and forth between them, making points, arranging and rearranging green apples.

After a few minutes, Stephen understood. Alex was teaching them arithmetic.

He watched and shook his head, softly smiling and thinking, Oh, Eve, if only you were here. What fun it would be to hide with you and watch our son grow up.

So fascinated was he by this school in the woods that he found a convenient stump and perched on it, unable to bring himself to disrupt the classes, even though he did have vitally important news. It would keep. Let the mathematics instructor teach to his heart's desire. Stephen would watch and burst with pride. They both would have so much to tell the family back at Eden Castle. They would have to take turns talking.

About two hours later, as the hot southern sun climbed to a noon position and the trees overhead did little to filter out the heat of the day, Stephen wiped his forehead with his damp handkerchief and at last saw Henderson slip a bookmark into a section of *Huckleberry Finn* and amidst groans and protests promise, "More tomorrow."

Reluctantly the children hopped off the foundation, a few with glazed eyes, clearly still in Huck's world.

In similar fashion, Alex was now restoring his green apples to a bushel basket, all the time talking to the large boy in faded overalls and no shirt.

"You've done very well, Junior. I suspect that you will master it all in a short time."

The large boy seemed to duck his head in modest embarrassment. As he hurried forward and helped Alex put the rest of the apples in the basket, he paused and looked longingly at one.

"Help yourself," Alex smiled. "All of you, have an apple. I can get more."

Without requiring a second invitation, the children came forward and picked out an apple for themselves and began to eat hungrily.

The big boy polished his on the seat of his pants and pocketed it. As he did so, something fell to the ground. He bent over and picked it up and studied it. Then he approached Alex almost shyly. "Here. You take it. I'm sorry I hit you."

The two boys exchanged a curious glance, as though aware that something had been shared between them, something more important than a slingshot and a green apple.

"Papa!"

Alex caught sight of Stephen standing just at the edge of the woods. The other children saw him as well and apparently interpreted the presence of an adult as a sign that they should run away.

Stephen was sorry for that. A few moments later he found himself in the clearing alone with Henderson and Alex, who was still gathering up primers and green apples.

"You are a good teacher," Henderson said. "The children listen to you."

Stephen saw his son swell with pride under the influence of Henderson's compliments.

Then Alex asked a blunt question. "What are you doing here, Papa?"

"Can't I come and visit my son?"

"For the last few weeks you've been visiting with Mr. Stanhope and David."

"And now I'm visiting with you," Stephen smiled. "Actually I've come to deliver a special message."

"What is it?"

"It's about us. We're going home."

For a moment there was neither light nor movement on Alex's face. "I . . . don't understand."

Stephen laughed. "You've never been dense before Alex. We–are–going–home," he repeated. "Back to England, back to Eden, back to–Chris."

Alex stood absolutely still at the center of the ruins, the slingshot in one hand, a green apple in the other.

The only move he made was to turn slowly, sadly and look straight at Henderson, who returned his glance with matching sorrow.

Stanhope Hall
July 27, 1907

Throughout the entire week of preparation for departure, Alex had tried to keep his feelings under tight control. Already his father had scolded him for being sullen and unhappy. He didn't mean to appear sullen. But he *was* unhappy, and though he tried to hide it, the closer he came to the moment of departure, the more he realized it couldn't be hidden.

Once his father had lost his temper at him and shouted, "What do you want?"

It was an impossible question because what Alex truly wanted was to stay here at Stanhope Hall with Henderson and to go home to England and Chris.

Never had he felt so torn in his life.

Now he sat well out of the way on the steps of the veranda as the servants made countless trips back and forth into the house. He and his father had tickets on the late-afternoon train to New York. Four days from now, they would be sailing home to England and Chris.

Abruptly Alex walked to the far side of the veranda. Upstairs in the nursery he heard one of the twins crying. His grandmother had promised him that she would be down shortly to tell him goodbye.

If the truth were known he had no regrets about leaving any of them at Stanhope Hall. Except one–Henderson.

They had said goodbye last night, Mrs. Jones had invited him to a special dinner of fried chicken, grits and cornbread. Henderson had walked back with him to Stanhope Hall. He had said that maybe he would see him in the morning before he left.

"Are you ready?"

The voice came from his father who stood at the top of the steps. Grandfather Burke was with him, as was Uncle David. He saw his grandmother Mary just coming out of the door, and his aunt Sharon.

Here we go again, he sighed. And he was right. There were kisses, lectures, warnings and blessings. He drew a deep breath and took a final look around the side of Stanhope Hall in the direction of the ruins, the place where Henderson would appear if he were coming.

Perhaps it was just as well.

Then he climbed into the backseat of the motorcar while his father crawled into the front seat next to Uncle David.

Amidst waving and shouting, the motorcar pulled away from Stanhope Hall, and Alex was left with the sad realization that in less than a month he wouldn't even be able to remember what any of them looked like—except one.

"Wait up!" Uncle David said as he approached the road. "I think someone has come to say goodbye to you, Alex."

Alex leaned up, peered out of the front window and saw him.

"Why don't you hop out?" Uncle David suggested. "We'll drive slowly up ahead and wait for you."

Alex did not need a second invitation. As he scrambled out, he saw Henderson smile, saw his arms filled with a wicker basket of some sort.

Alex had been wrong. He was so glad Henderson had waited for him here at the end of the road for a private farewell.

"Here," Henderson said and thrust the basket at him. "Mama says train food isn't fit for the hounds. She says that this will get you and your papa to New York City."

From the weight of the basket, Alex suspected it might just get them across the ocean as well.

"Thank you," he said, shifted the basket to his other hand and walked beside Henderson, studying the sandy road, watching his polished shoes get covered with red dust.

"Will you write?" Alex asked.

"Of course. And I want you to write back."

"I will. I promise."

Silence. Ahead he heard the engine of Uncle David's Ford motorcar grumble under the duress of the slow speed. He could think of a thousand things he wanted to say to Henderson, yet in the next instant he could think of nothing to say.

"I'll miss you," he blurted out and was appalled at how much he sounded like a child.

"And I'll miss you, but never mind. We've shared enough of our hearts to last us for a while."

Alex wished that he could think of something fine to say like that.

Up ahead he heard his Uncle David honk the horn. Time to go.

All at once he reached into his jacket and withdrew his white rabbit's foot. "Here," he said and placed it in Henderson's hand. "You keep this. It's very important to me, and I will like thinking that you have it."

Then Alex ran toward the motorcar, slid into the backseat, looked quickly out of the rear window and saw Henderson standing in the middle of the dusty road studying the rabbit's foot. At last he slipped it lovingly into his pocket.

The simple gesture pleased Alex. How good it was to think that a part of him would always be with Henderson.

Eden Castle
August 1, 1907

As Dr. Reicher stood outside Geoffrey's locked door, knocking and receiving no answer, he reached a hard decision. They were going home. Back to Germany. His wife would be pleased; Rolf was a different matter.

"Geoffrey? I have brought your tea."

Still no answer, though Dr. Reicher knew very well that Geoffrey was waiting for Chris. The child was now doing everything for Geoffrey that Dr. Reicher once had done, and it truly was a bizarre relationship, one that was being gossiped about among the servants, yet one that was being encouraged by everyone else in the castle, a relationship that seemed to have aroused a deep reservoir of hate and prejudice. Twice in the last week, Geoffrey had called Dr. Reicher a Hun.

"Geoffrey, let me come in."

"Go tend your sausages, German," came an angry muffled voice.

"What have I done?"

"You betrayed me."

"When?"

"At Doornkop. You were supposed to . . ."

The voice faded and grew muffled, the logic more so. Many times Dr. Reicher had told him that he was not at Doornkop. He had been in Munich. He had had nothing to do with Kruger and his broken promises.

Munich. Pleasant memories. With a sigh of resignation he placed the tea tray on the floor and looked nervously about. He had had the feeling lately of hostile eyes everywhere. Sonia had understood. Only Rolf had laughed.

Rolf. There was the problem. Rolf loved this English world, felt at home in it. Sonia said that at times their son struck her as being more

English than German. Poor Sonia. She had never really been happy here, except for her brief friendship with poor Eve Stanhope. Dr. Reicher knew he would have no trouble persuading her to return to the Fatherland. It was Rolf; there was the problem.

Now Dr. Reicher leaned against the opposite wall of the corridor and stared straight into the face of hard fact. The truth was, he had wasted his life here. In an effort to keep his family safe, he had sold his talents to the highest bidder in return for–safety.

Well, perhaps it was not too late. If he returned home right away, perhaps with study and effort he could qualify for the Sitting Board at Munich University. It was a prestigious post usually given to a German who had practiced and studied abroad.

Listen–

He held his position before the closed doors and heard voices coming from the Great Hall, "Do you have it? That's a good boy. Here, now be sure he gets these."

"Yes, Grandpapa."

"And give him these from his mother. She was most particular that she wanted him to have these."

"Yes, Papa."

"And remember to be polite and listen to everything that he says to you and don't argue."

"No need for lectures, Frederick. Clearly the boy has done better than any of us, has accomplished what none of us could have accomplished."

"Well then, be off with you. Can you handle the wagon alone?"

"Yes, Grandpapa."

Dr. Reicher held still and knew what was happening. John Murrey Eden and Frederick had sent Chris for his daily visit with Geoffrey.

The boy caught sight of Dr. Reicher at the far end of the corridor. "What are you doing there?" he called out.

"What am *I* doing here," Dr. Reicher brooded with contempt. "I might ask the same of you."

The boy didn't answer but continued to drag a small wagon down the corridor, leaning away from its weight.

"Geoffrey is expecting me," he announced. "And I believe he told you to–"

"I know what he told me," Dr. Reicher muttered. "Believe me I do not need any advice from you."

"What is all that junk?" Dr. Reicher demanded now.

"They are things for Geoffrey," came the blithe reply.

"What sort of things?"

"Food," he said, pointing to a large wicker hamper.

"What kind of food?"

"Food Geoffrey said he wanted. And the London papers. Grandpapa thought he might enjoy them."

"He has never asked for London papers before."

"And these are books that Aunt Eleanor sent."

With clear disdain, Dr. Reicher lifted one and read the spine—*King Lear*, by Shakespeare.

"And these are shingles from the barnyard," Chris explained, pointing to the bulk of what was in the wagon.

"And what are they for?" Dr. Reicher asked.

Chris was on the verge of answering when suddenly the door was jerked open and there stood Geoffrey, leaning heavily on his single crutch, his hair unkempt, his beard ragged, his robe food-stained. Obviously no one had thought to keep him clean during the last few days.

But it was his face that held Dr. Reicher, a madman's face if he had ever seen one, a glint in his eye that spoke of self-indulgence and shattered reason.

"Hun," Geoffrey began, his voice low. "I had hoped to make myself clear through the closed doors and thus avoid a direct confrontation. But apparently that was not to be. Very well, listen closely to me. You are dismissed from these services. Is that clear?"

The voice was beginning to rise. Instinctively Dr. Reicher moved back. At the same time, Chris moved forward, dragging the wagon after him and slipped through the door.

The sight of such preferential treatment accorded to an eleven-year-old boy infuriated Dr. Reicher. "You are insane," he murmured, backed away and saw Geoffrey lift the crutch as though to attack him.

"Uncle Geoffrey, I need your help in here."

As Chris's voice was heard from the inner room, Reicher saw Geoffrey glare a final time. "You goddamn Hun," he cursed, "you are not worth the energy it takes for me to hate you. Get out of my sight, get out of my life, get out, get out!"

Dr. Reicher turned about, alarm increasing, but the angry voice followed him all the way down the corridor.

Then enough. Dr. Reicher had seen and heard enough. Clearly he had been betrayed by the man he had served loyally and well for almost ten years.

Then what did that leave? That left only the Fatherland. That meant a delighted Sonia and a heartbroken Rolf.

Well, he would get over his sadness soon enough. According to Mr. Neville, the boy was ready for university. The German environment and discipline would be good for him.

They had certainly spent enough time in this spoiled, arrogant and decadent English society. Reicher himself was hungry for the good clean lines of purpose and self-denial and patriotism. He was ready for–home.

Greenfield Academy
August 10, 1907

Anne stole a final glance in her looking glass and hoped to see someone who looked at least twelve years old. Unhappily it was only a little girl's face that stared back at her.

At last she decided that it was the braids that made her look nine years old. If she could only undo her braids and let her hair fall about her shoulders, that might make her look older.

Of course, she didn't want to look a lot older, just as old as Alex Eden so that he would no longer ignore her as the bothersome tagalong that she sometimes was.

Alright then, undo the braids and fluff out her hair to make her face look fuller; then she would pinch her cheeks as she had seen her Mama do.

"Anne, I could use some help down here. They'll be here any minute."

"Be right down, Mama."

Now she smelled the good odors of a company meal, the entire house in a turmoil since the telegraph yesterday from London announcing the surprise arrival of Uncle Stephen and Alex back in England from America.

Alex.

She had missed him. They had made several trips to Eden since Uncle Stephen and Alex had gone to America, and it had been dull, nothing to do but sit on the headlands in the sun and try to think what Alex was doing at that same moment in far-off America.

Second braid undone. She combed her hair back and tried to smooth it down and remembered her new pink hair ribbon, which Mama had made from a scrap of blouse material. The first time she had worn it Papa had said how pretty it looked in her dark hair.

"Anne, please, there is the table to set. I want everything ready when they arrive."

"I'm on my way down, Mama." She stole a last moment to pinch her cheeks, took a final look in the mirror and decided that she did not look nine anymore. She looked at least ten now, definitely ten.

Then she hurried out of her room at the top of the stairs and hoped that her Mama would be so busy that she wouldn't notice her loosened hair.

"Do you think that Alex will like our new motorcar?" she called out to her mother in the kitchen, as she reached up to the sideboard for the best china.

"How many times must I tell you, Anne, the motorcar is not ours. The Board of Governors purchased it for the use of the school."

"But Papa drives it all the time."

"Yes, but still it is not ours. Be sure and use the best china," Mama called out. "I want this to be a proper homecoming, though for the life of me I don't know why they have returned so soon. It seems as though we just saw them off."

"Maybe they got homesick."

"Perhaps. I hope nothing has gone wrong."

Her mama appeared in the doorway. "Whatever did you do to your hair?"

Anne shrugged. "I just took it down."

"You just asked me to put it up."

"I know. I'm sorry. I've changed my mind." She continued around the table setting plates, napkins and silver.

"Oh, well," her mama sighed. "It looks lovely that way too, makes you look–older."

Anne closed her eyes and gave a little prayer of thanksgiving.

Then suddenly, "Do you hear that?" her mama gasped. "It's the car. They're back. And they're early. Oh dear, do hurry, Anne. I'll only have time to greet them; then I must go and finish the roast beef. And the vegetables are yet to be done–"

"It will be alright, Mama. "I'll finish the table and you go and greet them."

"Good girl, Anne, you are a good girl."

Then her mother was hurrying down the hall toward the front door. Anne stayed for a moment and heard her Papa's motorcar rattle to a halt, heard a call of greeting; then a moment later, through the crack in the door, she saw Uncle Stephen first, tieless, his shirtwaist undone at the neck, looking quite tired, though smiling and kissing her mama.

A moment later, she saw–him. Alex. Good heavens, he had grown a foot since she had last seen him. She would never catch up now. He appeared to be almost as tall as her father. And he was so good-looking. Anne was certain she had never seen anyone as handsome as Alex Eden. And it wasn't as if she had no standard of comparison. She had plenty of boys against which to judge him. She lived in a place surrounded by boys, attended classes with boys, ate with boys, studied with boys, and not one had Alex Eden's eyes, Alex Eden's nose, the line of his jaw or his beautiful wavy hair.

At last she drew a deep breath, straightened her shoulders as Mama had taught her to do and hoped that Alex hadn't fallen in love with some American girl.

She found them all in the front parlor. Her father was pouring sherry around for everyone. "Anne, there you are. Come, and greet your uncle and your cousin."

She stood on tiptoe and kissed Uncle Stephen on the cheek.

"Anne," he smiled and held her at arm's length. "How pretty you are and so grown up. Look, Alex, look at her."

As Anne felt a blush scorch her face, she found that she could not look at Alex. "Hello, Alex," she said to the tips of her shoes. "I'm glad you're back." Then she practically ran to the chair in the far corner, felt her heart pounding and was grateful when she heard the conversation resume.

"If you'll excuse me," her mama said. "I'll finish the roast, and we'll eat as soon as possible. Come, Anne, you be the hostess while I'm gone. Don't hide in the corner."

Then Mama was gone, and blessedly her papa and Uncle Stephen were talking again. Alex was sitting on the arm of the sofa looking very grown up.

Slowly she came up on his left. "Did you have a good time in America?" she asked politely.

"Yes, I did, thank you."

"What did you do?"

"I met a very interesting boy."

"What was his name?"

"Henderson."

"Tell all of us, Alex," his father invited. Apparently he had heard their conversation and had interrupted his own.

Alex smiled, and his eyes took on a different light. "I have never known anyone quite like him. When I first met him, he was being tormented by some white boys. Henderson is black. They had surrounded him and were beginning to hit him with stones shot from a slingshot. He stood at the center of the clearing and did not move, did not fight back in any way. Rather, he seemed to exhibit the greatest patience and tolerance."

"What happened?" Anne asked, horrified by the story of such cruelty.

"Nothing happened," Alex smiled. "He simply held his ground. They struck him and they drew blood, but ultimately they lost interest."

Uncle Stephen interrupted. "You came to his rescue, isn't that correct?"

"No, I stepped forward, but Henderson was the one who defeated them without lifting a finger. He did not need my help."

Anne saw her father listening carefully. "A remarkable young man. It has always been my belief that mankind could profit from nonviolence. It is a hundred times more effective than battle. The latter accomplishes nothing, while the former holds true moral victory."

"Dinner is served," Mama called from the doorway, and Papa looked up, mildly irritated by the interruption, then smiled. "Later. We'll hold everything for later, Alex. But I promise you I want to hear it all."

"Of course, Mason, and I have much to tell you."

As Papa led Alex into the dining room, Anne and Uncle Stephen brought up the rear.

Mama was already seated, and the rest of them took their places. Papa folded his hands on the table, closed his eyes and spoke the blessing.

"Dearest Heavenly Father, we thank you for the safe return of our family from America and we thank you for this reunion of hearts, minds and soul. We pray that Your peace and love will flourish in all men's hearts and lead us away from the paths of violence, in His name, amen."

As the plates were passed around, Anne listened closely to everything that Alex said, and wished with all her heart that he would never cease talking. He was so beautiful when he spoke, his face so animated. He seemed so grown-up, using words she had never heard before, the adults at the table listening as closely and as intently as she was.

Her heart sank. She felt very much like a little girl in his presence. He had paid no attention to her beyond the requirements of politeness. He would never see her as anything but a tagalong.

Would she ever grow up? Would he ever look directly at her and see *her?*

Unhappily, she knew the answers to all those questions.

Eden Castle
August 12, 1907

Chris perched on the foot of the daybed and watched carefully as Geoffrey dragged out a large black trunk from beneath the bed.

"My prize," Geoffrey smiled mysteriously and hoisted it onto the daybed.

Chris knew better than to offer his help. Nothing outraged Geoffrey more than an unsolicited offer of help.

At last the heavy trunk was up on the daybed, and Geoffrey sat at one end, Chris at the other.

"I have never shown this to anyone," Geoffrey said and he looked almost shy as he fidgeted with the lock. "Oh, I open the trunk many times myself, but only when I'm certain that Reicher is no place about."

"My mother said that Dr. Reicher may be leaving Eden Castle soon," Chris said, excitement mounting over the mysterious black trunk.

"Good riddance," Geoffrey snapped. "Tell them they must fumigate when he leaves. Will the German bitch be going with him? And the German child as well?"

"I don't know." When Chris had heard his mother speak of Dr. Reicher's desire to return home to Germany, it had become Chris's worst fear that Rolf would leave before Alex returned.

"Look, Chris!" At this command, Chris put his fears behind him for now and looked up to see the trunk open, Geoffrey lifting out a gray slouch hat, a large version of the ones that Chris had seen on the toy soldiers.

Geoffrey's mood had become quiet, his manner almost reverent as with deep feeling he caressed the brim of the hat. "Look," he murmured and held it closer so Chris could see a pattern of irregular brown spots on the gray felt.

"Blood," Geoffrey smiled. "My blood and partly that of the Boer bastard who hacked off my foot, for I left him with a scar on the side of his face that, I warrant, he carries with him to this day if he still lives."

Carefully Chris took the hat and examined it, amazed that this small piece of fabric had seen the heat of battle, had heard the cries of the dying, had borne witness to the white flag of surrender.

"Put it on," Geoffrey invited. "Go ahead. Put it on. Then close your eyes. If you are a true warrior, you will hear the song of battle. Listen closely."

Chris took the hat and placed it carefully on his head. He closed his eyes and felt the magic that he always felt in this special room with this special man.

"What do you hear?" Geoffrey whispered.

"I hear a wind."

"There was a wind that day."

"I hear . . . horses."

"Yes."

"They're coming fast."

"Yes."

"I hear . . . men shouting, I hear screams, injured horses, I hear—"

Suddenly he opened his eyes and scooped off the hat, his hands trembling. The mood was too real, too close. He looked at Geoffrey, still frightened. "I . . . heard it."

"I know you did," Geoffrey smiled. "I could tell by the expression on your face. You are a natural warrior."

There was such a look of pride on Geoffrey's face. Chris fed on it and fondled the hat as Geoffrey dug deeper into the black trunk.

"Now this, too, must be our secret," he warned, plunged his hands down to the bottom of the trunk and came up with—

"A rifle," Chris marveled.

"Not my rifle," informed Geoffrey. "It's a Mauser, the weapon used by the German traitors. It was lying right outside the field hospital, half covered by a bloody tunic. I told my aides to stash it in my trunk, and here it is."

"Has it killed a man?" Chris asked, aching to get his hands on it.

"Several, I warrant," Geoffrey said. "They were expert shots with the

Mauser as well as with the Mannlicher, though still we could have defeated them handily, had they but fought with honor."

It was Geoffrey's ancient theme, one of deceit, betrayal and lost honor.

"Here," Geoffrey at last invited and handed over the Mauser. Chris eagerly took it and was instantly amazed by its weight.

As he admired it, Geoffrey asked a strange question. "Tell me, Chris, what are they saying in the rest of the castle?"

"About what?"

"About us."

Still examining the gun, Chris smiled. "They like it," he said. "My mother and father feel that it is for the best."

"They would," Geoffrey laughed. "And what does your grandfather say about our visits?"

Chris shrugged. "Not much. He doesn't object. He's very proud of you. He says you served your country well, and your wishes, whatever they may be, deserve to be honored."

All the time Chris talked, he fondled the rifle, turned it over and over in his hand, rested its weight against his leg. "Geoffrey, show me how to hold it, please?"

Geoffrey shook his head soberly. "A true warrior knows instinctively how to handle a gun. Stand up. Lift it. It will go where it is supposed to go."

Slowly Chris stood and lifted the rifle to his shoulder.

"Bravo," Geoffrey laughed, applauding. "See I told you and this hand goes–there. And that one–here. Now, how does it feel?"

Suddenly from below the open window came the sound of a motorcar approaching in the distance with horn blaring.

"What in the–"

From Geoffrey's window, the east side of the castle obscured the view of the gatehouse and the inner courtyard. Across the corridor was a room from which Chris could see down into the courtyard. "Just a moment, Geoffrey, let me go see–"

"I'll come with you."

The chamber across the corridor was dusty, a never-used suite, except in the case of grand parties. Now Chris pushed open the door and moved straight toward the windows on the far side of the room.

The commotion down in the inner courtyard sounded even louder here, several men shouting at once and the alarm bell clanging outside the gate. What was happening?

With one hard tug, Chris drew aside the heavy window coverings. Stewards were running every which way, and the guardsmen were standing back to make way for a motorcar as it moved slowly across the grate.

"Who is it?" Geoffrey asked, holding well back at the door.

"I have no idea," Chris said. "No one was expected."

Chris peered down on the top of the motorcar that now was making a wide swing in preparation for its approach to the Great Hall steps. He was certain that he had never seen that motorcar before in his life.

"Is it worth staying for or not?" Geoffrey snapped, growing impatient. "If not, then come on back. I have something for you, something I prize greatly."

Chris looked back. It sounded very much like a lure. Geoffrey was leaning against the doorframe. He looked very tired. He had told Chris once that his arm hurt him perpetually from where the crutch cut into his flesh.

"Come, little Chris," he said now, his tone more inviting, "what need have we of the goings and comings in the courtyard?"

There was something almost hypnotic about his voice and manner. He inhabited such a different world from the rest of the castle.

Just as Chris was turning away from the window, the door on the driver's side swung open. He looked down, saw Mason Frye step out and greet the stewards.

Then he saw the passenger door open, saw Uncle Stephen!

Now, frantically, he used both sleeves to clean an even wider circle on the window and pressed his forehead against the glass and saw–

"Alex!"

He shouted the name, then shouted it again and tried to raise the window, but it was stuck.

"It's Alex, Geoffrey," he shouted, almost unable to contain his excitement. "I must go and–"

"No!"

The single word stopped him before he reached the door.

"But it's Alex. I've told you about Alex. He has been to–"

"No."

There it was again, that single word spoken without inflection.

"Now you listen to me," Geoffrey said, and angled his crutch about and started walking slowly across the corridor toward his chambers. At his door, he stopped. "If you leave me now, do not bother ever to come back."

Shocked, Chris gaped. "But all I want to do is go and fetch Alex. I'll bring him back. You'll like him. I'm sure you will."

"If you go to him now, do not ever come back to me, because this door will be locked and bolted to you. Is that clear?"

No, it wasn't clear. Why couldn't Chris be friends with Geoffrey and still love Alex? He started to ask this very specific question, but Geoffrey stepped back and placed the door between them.

"Make up your mind," he warned. "If you bring anyone else up to this door, our friendship is over."

"But Geoffrey–"

"No argument. No debate."

Chris heard rising voices coming from the Great Hall steps. What was he to do?

"Come, my little Chris," Geoffrey invited in a most pleasing tone. "We belong together. I need you and you need me. This Alex–does he need you as much as I do?"

The question was unanswerable. Perhaps it was Chris who needed Alex.

"Come," Geoffrey beckoned. "I have a rare gift for you. Will you accept it?"

Chris closed his eyes. He would see Alex later. Geoffrey always tired in the afternoon and took a long nap.

When he went to sleep, then Chris would slip out, go down and greet Alex.

"Coming, Chris?"

Reluctantly, Chris crossed the corridor and went into the entrance hall.

"Close the door, Chris. And bolt it."

"Yes, sir."

He did as he was told, though in his heart he was still aching to disobey. But as Geoffrey had told him a hundred times, good soldiers do not disobey orders.

As he entered the large sitting room, he saw Geoffrey seated on the edge of his daybed, a small blue volume in his hand.

"Come, Chris, this is for you."

As Chris sat on the edge of the bed, he saw Geoffrey lift the volume for his inspection.

"Look," Geoffrey instructed and opened the book to the flyleaf, where Chris saw smudges of dried brown stain.

"My blood," Geoffrey claimed proudly. "I carried this all through the South African campaign. It contains the writings of one of the greatest warriors the world has ever known."

Chris sat up on the edge of the bed, one ear listening to what Geoffrey was saying, the other attuned to the gradually diminishing sounds coming from the inner courtyard.

"His name was Jean de Bevil. He was a knight in the fourteenth century. He possessed the true voice and the truer spirit of a genuine warrior, a man who lived for battle. Do you understand?"

Chris nodded, captivated by Geoffrey's strong conviction.

"Here," Geoffrey said and handed the volume to him. "I'm going to lie back and rest. I want you to read to me. Will you do that?"

Chris took the volume and handled it carefully. It appeared to be quite old.

"Begin Chris. Listen to the words carefully as you read them."

Carefully Chris opened the volume and commenced reading.

" 'It is a joyous thing, a war. You love your comrades so much in war. When you see that your quarrel is just and your blood is fighting well, tears rise to your eyes.' "

"Yes," sighed Geoffrey, his head resting easily against the pillows, eyes closed. "Go on, Chris. You read well."

Buoyed by the compliment, honored by the gift, pleased with the company, Chris resumed his reading. He would see Alex later. For now this was more important.

He angled the book around and commenced reading. " 'A great sweet feeling of loyalty and of pity fills your heart on seeing your friend so valiantly exposing his body. And then you are prepared to go and die or live with him, and for love not to abandon him.' "

Geoffrey was asleep now. Chris could hear his regular breathing.

But he was so fascinated by the book that he went on reading all the same, quietly now, to himself.

Alex was the first one up the steps, racing through the Great Hall door, shouting, "Chris!"

But the Great Hall was empty, not even a steward in sight. For a moment Alex stopped and looked in all directions. Just behind him and keeping pace with him, he heard Anne, who had done little since they had returned but shadow his every step.

"Where is everyone?" she asked and came up alongside him.

"How should I know?" Alex snapped, hurt by the lack of a reception. For days he had imagined it all so differently.

"No need to feel bad," Anne soothed. "After all, no one even knew you were coming home."

Through the Great Hall doors he saw his father and Mason Frye, followed by Aunt Lucy. Now all of them stood just inside the door, glancing about at the empty Great Hall.

"Where is everyone?" Aunt Lucy murmured.

"Midafternoon. I would say they were all hard at their naps," Mason replied.

"I thought we made enough noise coming in to wake the dead," Alex's father said.

"Well, I'll go and see what I can find out," Aunt Lucy offered. "You, Anne, come with me–"

"Please, Mama, I want to stay here."

Mason spoke up. "It's all right. She can stay."

Alex's eyes lifted heavenward, as he knew full well who would be saddled with Anne. In an attempt to avoid that fate, he started off on his own toward the corridor to the left that led to the small library.

"Wait, Alex, can I come with you?"

Damn. It was blasted Anne again.

As he turned back, he saw his father and Uncle Mason directing the stewards on where to put the mountains of luggage. Then out of the corner of his eye, he saw someone on the Great Hall steps.

"Rolf," Alex called out and saw the boy peer quizzically in his direction.

"Alex! I cannot believe it. When did you return? We weren't expecting you. No one was. Why didn't you– Hello, Anne." As Rolf drew nearer, Alex's father and Uncle Mason joined them.

Still puzzled, Rolf looked from one to the other. "Did anyone know you were coming home?"

Alex's father laughed. "I'm afraid it's my fault, Rolf. We wanted to surprise everyone."

"Well, you did," laughed Rolf. "I am afraid everyone is napping. They generally do about this time of day."

Alex spoke up. "Where is Chris?"

"You want me to get everyone?" Rolf offered, ignoring Alex's question.

"No," his father insisted. "I'm sure they'll all be down for tea shortly."

"Yes, sir, tea around five."

"We'll see them then. For now, we must unpack. Alex–"

"In a minute, Papa."

As his father and Uncle Mason went back to directing the stewards with the luggage, Alex followed Rolf a few steps into the Great Hall. "Rolf, where is Chris? I called for him, but–"

Abruptly Rolf turned on him. "You won't find him here," he said. His attitude seemed to change from one of joy to one of sadness.

"I don't understand."

"I can't say it any clearer, Alex. You will not find him here," Rolf repeated. "Now if you'll excuse me, Mr. Neville is waiting for me in the upstairs sitting room. He sent me to the library to exchange this volume."

Then he was gone, walking away from Alex, as though nothing unusual had occurred, as though Alex had just returned from a trip to Exeter instead of a trip clear across the ocean to America.

"Rolf–"

He saw Rolf retrace his steps to the point where Alex and Anne stood. He issued a soft apology. "I'm sorry, Alex, but– I'm afraid that things have changed here."

"Rolf, tell me, is Chris alright?"

"Oh, he's fine. Just not here anymore."

"I don't understand. Where is he, then?"

Then Rolf indicated that Alex was to follow him as he led the way directly across the Great Hall, heading toward the stairs that led up into the seldom-used east wing.

"Wait right here," he instructed, with a growing air of mystery. "If you are lucky, Chris will be down in time for tea. Though on occasion, he stays up there through dinner, and on other occasions he has spent the night."

"Stays where?" Alex asked.

Rolf sat slowly on the bottom step. "Chris has started visiting with Geoffrey."

Alex blinked. "Geoffrey? The one who lives–"

"I'm afraid they have become good friends. As a result, my father has been dismissed and my parents are returning to Germany."

Alex couldn't believe what he was hearing and sat slowly on the step above Rolf. Directly behind him he heard the tagalong Anne settle on the step above him.

"He . . . visits with Geoffrey?" Alex asked again, trying to sort through everything he had heard.

"He does more than that. He takes up his trays. He sits with him. A few days ago he asked for a shaving razor."

"But your father used to–"

"Apparently my father is not needed anymore for any of those things. Geoffrey has become quite abusive toward him."

"I'm sorry, Rolf."

Rolf shook his head. "Your grandfather is going to talk to my parents and see if he can persuade them to let me stay and complete my studies with Mr. Neville."

"That would be wonderful."

Rolf stood with dispatch. "For now, I must be getting back. You wait here. Chris will be down–sooner or later." He took a few steps across the Great Hall, then looked back.

"I'm glad you're home, Alex. I want to hear everything as soon as I finish my studies with Mr. Neville."

Then he was gone, walking back across the Great Hall.

Alex straightened around on the step and rested his chin on his hands. He felt such a sadness, such a sorrowful longing–for what? He had wanted to come home. Well, he was home. Then what was the matter with him? What exactly did he want?

"Alex?"

He looked behind and saw Anne perched on the step above him, looking like a frightened bird. Why hadn't she gone with her mother?

"What is it?" he said.

"I'm glad you're home."

This was so sweetly spoken that Alex relented a bit in his judgment of her. She *was* a tagalong, but she was loyal, and apparently that was more than he could say about someone else.

"Thanks," he muttered.

"Don't be sad."

"I'm not sad. I just–"

Anne slid a step closer to where he was sitting. "Sometimes I get so mixed up," she began, "I get mixed up inside, and I don't know what I want. First I want Mama to braid my hair, then I want her to undo the braids. I want to go and play with Penny, then I want to come home. Do you ever feel like that?"

Alex listened closely and smiled, though he took care to hide his face from her. "You're a girl," he said flatly. "Girls have problems like that."

"Don't boys?"

"Boys don't have braids."

"No, but–"

"Listen!"

He shushed her just in time to hear footsteps coming along the third-floor corridor. Slowly he stood and turned in that direction.

Please God, let it be Chris.

And it was, though it was a slow-moving Chris, not at all like the one who used to dash everywhere. This Chris was walking with his head buried in a book, and on his head he was wearing some sort of a strange hat, dark gray like an old army hat.

Well, no matter. It was Chris, and Alex started up the stairs, calling his name. He saw Chris look up at the sound of his voice and his face break into a smile of recognition. "Alex? Is it you?"

"It's me. I promise–"

Then Chris was running toward the stairs at such speed that his feet got tangled and he did a slow circus roll to the bottom of the steps. Alex burst out laughing and was upon him within the minute, wrestling him this way and then the other. Above the sound of their laughter, Chris shouted, "Be careful of the book. Geoffrey gave it to me."

Quickly he extended both the book and the hat to Anne's waiting hands. Then, "Alex, now you are in for it."

And with a shriek of delight, he pounced on Alex's back, and together they rolled about at the foot of the steps, to Anne's amusement. A moment later, Alex allowed Chris to pin him to the floor, and out of breath, he looked up into Chris's face and was so glad he was home.

John Murrey Eden heard the caterwauling from his second-floor apartment and suspected what had happened, that Stephen and Alex had come home early.

Now he walked as fast as the pain in his left knee would permit, eager beyond words to see them, to hear the stories of life with the cotton farmer in America. Obviously it had been far less than idyllic. Otherwise why were they home in less than two months?

At the top of the Great Hall steps he stopped and looked down on the bustling scene below. The rest of the family had already gathered. Quite a crowd it was. It would be a good tea.

There was Frederick and Marjorie up from Mortemouth. There was Eleanor deep in conversation with Stephen, who looked quite well, considering the rigors of ocean travel. John sincerely hoped that his son had now gotten everything American out of his system.

There, too, was Mason Frye and Lucy over from Exeter, the whole clan gathered for the homecoming. Well, not the whole clan, but at least the members worthy of bearing the noble Eden name.

Then he saw them, Chris and Alex reunited in their perennial wrestling match. John had never seen two boys more given to loving combat. Two true sons of England, of that he was certain.

"You two!" he bellowed in a voice that not only carried across the Great Hall but which topped all those lesser voices engaged in conversation.

Everyone looked up. Alex spoke first, a shriek more accurately. "Grandpapa!"

Then he was running, dragging Chris behind him for a step or two until at last the boys became disengaged, then both were hurtling toward John at full speed, with the hot energy of youth.

Alex hugged him with such force that for a moment John tottered about at the top of the steps.

"Well, come, let me look at you," he ordered now, waving Alex to step back.

Blushing with self-consciousness, Alex obeyed, and John was aware of the rest of the Great Hall quiet now, all apparently watching their antics on the steps.

"Well!" John exclaimed and drew Chris close as an ally. "What do you think? Do you think he looks . . . American?"

The word came out a sneer, which was precisely the way John intended it. "Look closely," John commanded now, "do you see a sign or signature of the cotton farmer?"

Alex withstood the comic examination with grace. John dropped the comic pose, sensing that there was a new seriousness to the lad, a new sadness as well.

"Did they treat you as you deserve to be treated?" he demanded, the comedy over.

"Yes, Grandpapa. They treated me very well."

"And how did you enjoy it?"

"At first, not at all."

"I thought as much."

"But later, I met a–"

"And you," John interrupted, tousling Chris's hair. "Has this one told you what he has been up to while you were away?"

Alex shook his head.

"Well, come on, speak up," John urged Chris. "Tell him how you have passed your afternoons."

Chris grinned, clearly very pleased with himself. "I visit Geoffrey," he said.

"Is that all you're going to say?" He turned toward Alex. "This young man here, your cousin, has succeeded in breaking down the doors of silence and isolation, that's what he has done. He has done what nobody else has been able to do. He has persuaded Geoffrey to open up to someone other than Dr. Reicher."

John bent low for a secret. "In fact, if the truth were known, Geoffrey has sent Dr. Reicher packing."

He saw the concerned look on Alex's face. "Rolf is not–"

"No, not Rolf. I have just received permission from Sonia Reicher for Rolf to remain here at Eden Castle and continue his studies with Mr. Neville."

He saw Chris and Alex exchange a grin, saw them both glance down to the Great Hall in search of their friend.

"Now wait a minute, both of you. I'm not finished with you. You, Alex, alright, now where is it?" John demanded now with mock fierceness.

"Where is what, Grandpapa?"

"Where is what?" John said in imitation of Alex's wide-eyed innocence. "You know very well what I'm talking about."

"No, I don't."

"The rabbit's foot. The white rabbit's foot with the key attached, the one I gave–"

It was the stricken look on Alex's face that cut John short. "Don't tell me. You lost it."

"Oh no, Grandpapa. I'd never lose it."

"Well, then, if it isn't lost, may I have it?"

"I . . . gave it away."

John frowned. "You gave it away? I told you to keep that with you always."

"And I did, Grandpapa, until it was time to say goodbye to Henderson."

"And who is Henderson?"

"Oh, Grandpapa, you'd like him so much. He's older than me and Chris by only a year, but he is so–"

"What?"

"When I first saw him, he was being tormented by some white boys."

"Henderson is–"

"Black, Grandpapa."

"Oh."

As Alex spoke on about Henderson Jones, John listened closely and tried to make sense out of the boy's gibberish.

"And then Henderson took me to the small church where his father once had been the minister, but his father had suffered a terrible illness and couldn't talk or walk or preach. So Henderson had taken over for him and he–"

The boy was rambling on in an incoherent fashion, and John could tell from the expression on Chris's face that he couldn't understand what was being said either.

What in the world had gotten into Stephen to allow Alex to run wild over the southern countryside, falling in with black boys and nigger preachers.

Then he saw Susan at the bottom of the steps. "You had better come and get your tea, the three of you."

"In a minute," he called down and waited until she had walked back to the chattering company.

"Then, go on, Chris, tell Alex everything."

Chris waited for Alex to sit down on the steps, then quietly reached behind him and withdrew the hat.

"Where did you get that?" John asked and took it from Chris, recognizing it as the gray slouch hat of the South African campaign.

"Geoffrey said I could wear it. Look, there's blood still on it," and quickly Chris pointed to the brown smudges along the brim and over the crown. "That's Geoffrey's blood," he went on, his voice filled with awe.

"And look, Geoffrey claims that if you are a true warrior, when you put it on and close your eyes, you will hear the sound of battle."

He adjusted the hat, then sat erect and closed his eyes.

A moment later he commenced to nod slowly. "Yes, I can hear it. A bugle cry, a horse, more are coming, a shout–"

All of a sudden he pulled the hat off and opened his eyes, and John saw an incredible expression on his face. "I heard it, Grandpapa. I really did."

Now Alex scooted closer in curiosity. "Let me try it. How did you get Geoffrey to open his door? Is he nice? Rolf used to call him a ghost, do you remember?"

Chris laughed. "He's no ghost. He's very real."

As he spoke, Chris handed the bloodstained hat to Alex, who took it, gingerly at first, and turned it over and over in his hands.

"Put it on," Chris urged, "and close your eyes. See what you hear."

For a moment Alex hesitated. Slowly he lifted it carefully above his head.

John watched carefully, sensing Alex's distaste.

"Well?" Chris asked.

"I . . . hear–"

"What?"

"Mason Frye laughing," Alex said in all seriousness. "And now I hear Aunt Eleanor blowing her nose." Then he burst out laughing.

Chris scolded. "You aren't taking it seriously at all."

"Well, it smells bad," Alex complained and quickly removed the hat and thrust it back at Chris. "Come on, I'll race you to the tea table. I'm starved. Chris, will you take me to see Geoffrey tomorrow? Have you told him about me? I'm sure you have. What did he say? Can I come with you?"

All the time Alex spoke, John watched the clouds gathering on Chris's face and knew the nature of the problem but could not even imagine a solution.

It wasn't until Alex started down the Great Hall steps that Chris spoke the dreaded words. "Alex, I can't take you to see Geoffrey. He doesn't want to see anybody."

Alex stopped. "He sees you."

"But no one else. In fact, he has said if I bring you, he will never open his door to me again."

It broke John's heart to see the look on both their faces. Damn this summer of separation. Damn the cotton farmer in America. It was all his fault. If Alex hadn't gone to America, Chris wouldn't have been exploring on his own. If Geoffrey had seen both boys together, he would have accepted both of them. Now–

"Very well," Alex murmured with stiff politeness and walked on down the stairs, the challenge of the race forgotten in his hurt.

"Alex, wait. I want to–"

But Alex didn't wait. Instead, he spied Rolf talking with Mason Frye and hurried toward them, leaving John and Chris alone on the stairs.

"Oh, Grandpapa, what am I going to do?"

"Well, it appears to me that you have two courses of action before you. One, you can stop seeing Geoffrey, which in my opinion would be the wrong thing to do. You are now performing a service for this family, helping to lure Geoffrey back to our society, where he belongs."

"Well, what then?"

"Keep telling Geoffrey what a splendid fellow Alex is, see if you can't persuade him to take both of you into his confidence."

Chris listened closely and finally nodded, though it was a bleak nod. "He gets so angry when I–"

"Then you'll just have to keep trying, won't you?"

"Yes, Grandpapa."

"Run along now. Be with Alex. Welcome him home in a proper fashion. He needs us now. We must help him get rid of all those foolish American stories and memories. They will not serve him well in the long run."

Chris gave John a half smile and started slowly down the stairs, walking like a man of fifty instead of a boy of eleven.

Life and loyalty were very hard on an eleven-year-old boy. It all seemed so complicated. John could remember his own pain. But he knew that Chris would recover. He knew as well that Alex would cleanse himself of all things American, and John felt absolutely certain that by Christmas they would all be back on track.

Eden Castle
April 12, 1910

Rolf heard clearly because he was seated next to Chris.

"What did Geoffrey say?" Frederick asked, staring at Chris, who had had the misfortune to be the messenger.

Rolf felt sorry for him. He loved Chris and hated to see him caught in this conflict between his father and his uncle.

"Chris, repeat what Geoffrey said to you."

Chris cleared his throat and placed his napkin on the edge of the table. "He said he would not come out of his room until the castle was cleansed of all German blood."

Now it was Rolf's turn to bow his head and study the hem of his napkin. He had known for some time that England was no longer his home, Eden no longer his sanctuary. He had stayed well beyond his mother's promise of one year. In fact, one year had stretched into three, and now letters from his parents spoke glowingly of the German state, the superior Fatherland that required the services and loyalties of its most gifted sons, like Rolf.

"Rolf, would you please accept our deepest apologies," Frederick was saying now.

"I understand," Rolf murmured and wished that he really did understand, wished with all his heart that someone would explain to him why he suddenly felt ill at ease among these people who had been his family for almost fourteen years.

"He is still quite irrational at times, my poor Geoffrey is, you know," Eleanor said, always a tone of sorrow in her voice when she spoke of Geoffrey.

Rolf wished that they would drop the subject. He glanced up and saw

Alex staring straight at him from across the table, a hundred messages in his eyes, all of them sympathetic.

Now it was Susan's turn to apologize, and Rolf's embarrassment grew by leaps and bounds. "He is, of course living with an ancient hatred," Susan said quietly by way of explanation.

"Well founded, I would say," contributed John Murrey Eden, who scarcely looked up from cutting his luncheon chop.

"Well founded but ancient," countered Susan.

Slowly Rolf stole a glance all around at his beloved adopted family. How greatly they all had changed since his childhood. Lord Eden scarcely spoke at all now, simply moved through and around the family rituals with a sense of obligation, then quickly disappeared back up to his sitting room. Lady Eleanor kept to her gardens and was always appearing now in muddied slippers. Susan was kept busy with her clinic, and John Murrey Eden slept a lot when the boys weren't around, a morning nap and an afternoon nap and sometimes he'd doze off in the evening before the Great Hall fire.

Rolf loved them all and, because of this love, knew full well that the time had now come for him to leave.

"Then, let's consider it settled," Frederick pronounced. "And Chris, we will appreciate it if you would confine what Geoffrey says to Geoffrey's chambers."

It was a sharp reprimand and one that did not sit well with Chris. Rolf could sense his embarrassment and rising anger.

A few moments later, John Murrey Eden stood and left the table without a word. Chris followed suit, and the very brief mood of reconciliation was shattered. Frederick, the peacemaker, was left gaping at two empty chairs.

Rolf took a deep breath, folded his linen napkin neatly, placed it on the table and slowly stood.

"Please," he began, "try to understand. I do think the time has come for me to leave."

"No," Alex protested and stood opposite him.

"Yes," Rolf smiled. "Oh, not because of what happened today. My parents have been writing to me for months, begging that our family be reunited."

"But your studies," Alex protested.

"They can be completed in Germany. There are good tutors there, I promise," he smiled.

There was a pause. Curious, but he had expected protest to come from more than one quarter. Frederick perhaps or Susan, always his champion.

But both of these pillars of support were strangely nonsupportive, as though with his decision and his announcement a great load had been lifted from both their hearts.

"Part of me will always belong here," Rolf said, "but I do think the time has come to go home."

He stepped away from the table and was amazed at the quick sense of distance that had already sprung up between them. Everyone sat with head bowed, as though at prayer. Only Alex gazed up at him with what appeared to be true anguish in his eyes.

Frederick stood at last and made a futile attempt to dissuade him. "This really isn't necessary, Rolf."

"I think that it is."

Marjorie said, "I don't know why any of us should pay serious attention to Geoffrey. But we do. I'm afraid it really angers me sometimes."

Eleanor sniffed into her handkerchief. "He is my son, dear Marjorie," she murmured.

"I'm sorry," Marjorie apologized, newly embarrassed.

As the muddle increased, Rolf stepped quickly out into the corridor, followed by Alex.

Rolf held up a restraining hand. "You know this is what I must do, Alex."

"No, I don't know that. Please explain it to me."

"You're not dense, Alex."

"You're letting a madman drive you out of your home. You heard Aunt Marjorie. And she's right."

"I'm not certain anymore if it is my home. Perhaps it was never my true home."

"You know better than that."

"Do I? Oh, come, Alex. It's not the end of the world. I'll go home. See what a true sausage-maker looks like. Who knows? I may be more German than even I realized."

Purposefully he walked ahead of Alex, wanting very much an interval of privacy. Leaving Alex and Chris would be the hardest of all, though even they had changed along with the old people. The worst was that they were drifting apart, Chris spending all his free time now locked in Geoffrey's chambers, Alex spending sometimes two weeks in a row at Greenfield in Exeter. He seemed to enjoy the academic life, seemed to enjoy

Mason Frye on a different level. Mason had once said that he saw a gifted teacher in Alex and was working to that end.

Now Rolf walked faster and at the end of the corridor looked back to see Alex a distance away watching him as though he knew he was to be left behind.

It was impossible to say how much Rolf would miss him.

Better to leave quickly then and get it over with.

He waved a cheery salute, turned the corner of the corridor and ran all the way to his rooms on the third floor. He closed the door quickly behind him and gave in to only a few tears. Then hurriedly he wiped them away and began to plot a future which might not be so bleak after all.

Germany *was* growing, according to his father, productivity was up, and the Fatherland was in the process of preparing itself to be strong in the face of any enemy.

What enemy? Rolf wondered. Well, he would find that out in time as well. For now, write letters, make plans and start to pack up his life. It would be a sorrowful task at best.

One week later Rolf stood at the bottom of the Great Hall steps in a blaze of warm English sun and watched Frederick carefully drive his motorcar around the inner courtyard toward the steps.

All around him was the family. "Now please remember to give your parents our love," Susan instructed. "And when you get to London, call this number. It's Alice's number at the hospital. She'll come and fetch you for a cup of tea. Albert, too, if he's in town."

Rolf noticed that she lowered her voice on this last instruction so that John Murrey Eden wouldn't hear. He still forbade anyone mentioning the name of the three in London, the Eden outcasts, Charlotte, Albert and Alice, but Rolf knew, as did every member of the Eden family, that Susan wrote regularly to all three and had journeyed to London on several occasions to see her children.

Stephen was there, hand extended. "Let us know where you settle, Rolf, your address, if you please."

"I will, sir, I promise."

At the top of the steps he saw John Murrey Eden, looking skeptically down.

"Goodbye to you, sir," Rolf called cheerily up. "I'm truly sorry for having beaten you so often in the motorcar races."

John laughed and came down the steps. "You didn't beat me, you scoundrel," he scoffed. "I let you win."

Then to Rolf's complete amazement, John came all the way forward and embraced him, a seemingly warm and sincere embrace.

"I am so sorry, Rolf," he said, his voice quite husky. "It's difficult sometimes to know precisely what to do."

"I know, sir," Rolf said.

Then he turned away and confronted the most difficult two of all. Alex and Chris.

"All right," he said with stern dispatch. "Come, both of you. I want to tell you that I–"

He saw a tear in the corner of Alex's left eye, saw Alex reach up angrily and brush it away. Then the floodgates broke for all of them, and their embrace was jumbled, awkward, terribly embarrassing and terribly necessary.

He could feel Alex's face wet against his. "I'm so sorry–"

"No need," Rolf whispered. "Don't think for a minute that this is goodbye," he added. "After all we share a blood bond, remember?"

Then he pushed away, climbed into Frederick's motorcar and kept his eyes focused straight ahead. He did not alter his position or his vision until Frederick was miles away from Eden Castle, pulling up onto the turnpike for Exeter and the London train.

London
April 20, 1910

Alice was just leaving St. Martin's at the end of a long day, anxious to get home to her flat before the rain increased, when the telephone operator sent word that she had a message.

Damn! What now?

"She said it was urgent, Miss Eden," the orderly answered, "and that you were to come right away and fetch it."

"Very well," Alice sighed and closed her umbrella.

Urgent? What could be urgent? Albert was dining with Colin this evening. Aslam and Charlotte and little Dhari were at their home in Switzerland. Emmeline and Christabel Pankhurst were out of Holloway Prison for the first time in months. What in Alice's world could be urgent except her aching feet and her grumbling belly? She hadn't had the time to eat all day.

"There you are," the telephone operator called out cheerily as Alice approached the great bank of wires, cords and funny little boxes at the end.

"I was told–"

"Yes, indeed," and with a great show of efficiency the woman riffled through a stack of messages.

"Ah, here we are," and with a maddening smile she handed Alice a slip of paper on which was penned a curious message.

> I will be at the tea shop in Victoria Station for one hour. Your dear mother, Susan Eden, instructed me to ring you. If it is convenient and if you so desire, perhaps you will take tea with me.
>
> Your friend, Rolf Reicher

Rolf Reicher?

Alice looked up from reading the message. The only Rolf Reicher she knew was the little German boy who lived at Eden Castle with his parents, the son of the German doctor with whom she had tangled years ago during Eve's difficult labor.

"Is this all?" she inquired of the switchboard operator.

"I'm afraid so, ma'am. He sounded quite nice. Very polite if you know what I mean."

Rolf Reicher? Was it the same? And what was the child doing in London? And where were his parents? And why had Alice's mother instructed him to contact her?

Well, nothing to do but go and find out. She hoisted her umbrella aloft, stepped out into a driving rain and called out, "Taxi!"

About twenty minutes later, she paid off the driver and ran into ornate Victoria Station.

She stood for a moment just inside the door but well out of the flow of late-evening foot traffic, shook her umbrella free of rain and made a foolish attempt to wipe off the moisture from her face and cloak.

She turned about and walked further into the cavernous old station and scanned the various shop fronts until she saw the tea shop sign on the far side of the terminal.

"Miss Eden–"

At her name she turned about and saw a very handsome young man, quite tall, slim and fair standing before her.

She did not recognize him. "I'm . . . sorry . . ."

"I'm Rolf Reicher," he smiled. "The last time we were together, I was about four, perhaps five."

Alice took a step backward as though distance might help and looked up into the clearest blue eyes she'd ever seen, the smoothest complexion, the kindest smile.

"I don't believe it," she said.

"Time has a way," he shrugged and looked mildly self-conscious.

For several moments they stood in the middle of crowded old Victoria Station grinning foolishly at each other, resurrecting in private memories whole sections of their childhood and youth.

"I remember hearing about the New Year's Eve theatrical when the century turned," Alice laughed. "My father was Father Time and you were–"

"I was master of ceremonies, yes."

"And nothing, absolutely nothing, went according to schedule–or so I was told."

"It so seldom does," he smiled.

"Yes."

There was a strained silence now as she studied him closely. She remembered him in the constant company of Alexander and Christopher, "Eden's three musketeers" as her father had lovingly called them.

"Come," he invited as the crowds continued to jostle against them. "Let me buy you a cup of tea. I have a few minutes before the boat train leaves. I believe we could do with a quiet corner for all this remembering."

With a gallant gesture, he tenderly took her arm, led her toward the tea shop and straight into the back room, where there were only a few customers.

Once settled, Alice shook off her wet cloak, propped her umbrella in the corner and draped her gloves over the handle. She turned back just as Rolf completed ordering a pot of tea and two scones.

"Would you like a platter of sandwiches?" he asked.

"No, no thank you."

Alice couldn't quite get over how grown up he was and said as much. "I can't– You've grown up very well. You're very handsome."

Again she saw that subtle blush and vowed privately to stop embarrassing him. She tried to move on to a safer conversational ground. "The message said my mother sent you."

"She gave me your number at the hospital and invited me to call you. I hope that was all with your permission."

"Of course, it was just that I didn't know who you were."

"It's quite understandable."

"Well, what are you doing here?" she asked and settled back in her chair.

"I'm on my way home, back to Germany."

Alice laughed, certain that he was joking. "Germany is no more your home than it is mine, Rolf. Eden is your home."

"My adopted home, yes. But my parents have already returned to Germany and–"

This surprised her. She had envisioned old Dr. Reicher hanging on to a good thing to the very end. "Why?"

"They were dismissed."

Shocked, she sat up. "I didn't–"

"By Geoffrey. He no longer requires my father's services."

"Has he come out of his seclusion?"

"No, but he will, or so he has promised, as soon as Eden is cleansed of all things German."

He said this with no bitterness or rancor. In fact, he was smiling, a curious counterpoint to the ugliness of what he was saying.

"I'm afraid I– Were you sent away?" she asked, bewildered by what she was hearing.

"Oh no, I left of my own volition. But I think the time had come."

"Who tends to Geoffrey now?"

"Chris."

Again she started forward. "Little Chris?"

Rolf smiled. "He is fourteen now, as is Alexander."

Slowly Alice leaned back, shook her head and closed her eyes. "Where in the world has time gone? Haven't we all stood still? I know I have."

He was looking at her very intently, and again she was certain that she had never seen such clear blue eyes.

The girl arrived with their tea and scones. Alice poured for both of them.

Settled at last, they lifted their cups together, made a gentle clink and sipped at the same time.

"Eden," she said quietly. "Tell me of Eden."

"It's beautiful and peaceful, and will always occupy the largest part of my heart."

"What are your plans now?" she asked.

"To return to Germany, to the home of my parents. Thanks to Mr. Neville I'm prepared for advanced levels at the university."

"Mr. Neville?"

"He took Mason Frye's place."

"Yes, of course. And my mother? Tell me of my mother."

"She's well. She works hard in her clinic from early morning until late at night frequently."

"Tell me about Aunt Eleanor and Uncle Richard."

Rolf smiled. "They're growing old together. They keep to themselves and they seem quite content."

"And the two little boys?"

"They are my brothers, as much as if I had true brothers."

Again she heard a sadness in his voice and suspected that his hasty exit from Eden had been a particularly wrenching one.

She refilled their cups and saw him check his pocket watch.

"What time?"

"Soon."

"Your train leaves–"

"In about twenty minutes."

"Time. So little time for anything."

"Do you know John Milton's 'On Time'?" He asked this with joyful eagerness, as though he longed to take refuge in the mind and heart of someone else.

"No, I'm afraid I don't. I was not a very good student."

"May I recite part of it for you?"

"Oh, please do, yes."

He straightened in his chair and pushed his tea cup aside.

" 'Fly, envious Time,' " he began, " 'till thou run out thy race . . . and joy shall overtake us as a flood, when every thing that is sincerely good and perfectly divine, when Truth, and Peace, and Love shall ever shine about the supreme Throne . . . then all this Earthy grossness quit, attir'd with Stars, we shall for ever sit, triumphing over Death, and Chance, and thee O Time.' "

At some point in his beautiful reading, noisy and smelly old Victoria Station fell away and left Alice on a pinnacle of pure enjoyment, in a black silence filled only with Rolf's voice and Milton's soul.

She found that for several minutes she was unable to move.

Rolf bowed his head at the conclusion of his verse, and there was a moment between them of something quite rare, she couldn't say what, for this young man was a mere fragment from her past, but for now, for this moment, he had shared with her in a most intimate fashion a portion of his heart.

It was the sudden blaring of the station master's voice that broke the spell and deposited her back in Victoria Station.

Rolf stood immediately. "I'm afraid it's time for me to go." He withdrew a shilling from his pocket, placed it on the table and apparently saw the protest forming on her face.

"Dear Alice, please stay here. Stay warm by the fire and finish your tea. You were so kind to have come to meet me. I'll remember you always."

Then without warning, without any indication that he was about to do so, he bent over and kissed her lightly on the forehead as though she were a little girl whom he worshipped very much.

"Rolf–"

But as she turned to call to him, she saw that he was already out of the door and was in the process of being devoured by the throngs of passengers in their frantic comings and goings.

Alice held her position and could still feel the moisture from his kiss on her forehead, could still see his beautiful young face across the table from her, could hear his voice–" 'attired with stars, we shall forever sit, triumphant over death and chance and thee, oh, time.' "

She looked again out into the busy station in the hope that she could still see him, but he was gone.

"More tea, miss?"

"No, no thank you. If I might sit here for just a while–"

"Of course, you take your time."

"Thank you."

She sat for ever so long, hearing all the discordant voices of a busy station, remembering one melodious voice, seeing one sweet and solemn child, recalling the brooding darkness of the corridors of Eden Castle, and praying that the young man from now on would know only the breath of spring and the heart-easing mirth of true love, for if ever anyone was worthy of all of God's goodness, it was Rolf Reicher.

Eden Castle
May 7, 1910

Susan was suffering from a severe case of nerves and suspected that everyone in the castle was suffering in similar fashion.

Geoffrey was coming downstairs.

For the first time in fourteen years.

Chris had conveyed word to him that at last "Eden Castle had been cleansed of all German blood," and Geoffrey had agreed to end his long seclusion. For some reason the image of a pouting child continually plagued Susan as she brushed her hair up into a French knot and fixed it with a clip.

Her eyes in the mirror caught a reflected image of her last letter from London, a poignant account from Alice of her hurried meeting with young Rolf Reicher. Apparently she had been very impressed with him and spoke eloquently of his sadness at having to leave Eden and his "brothers," Chris and Alex.

For a moment Susan sat at her dressing table and tried to clear her mind of the various worries that were plaguing her, the least of which was Geoffrey Eden, though shortly she would have to go downstairs and join in the royal welcome for the tardy and spoiled prince.

What *were* her primary worries? Well, for one thing the old king was ailing, quite ill at Osborne, or so her London agent had informed her only yesterday morning. Then there was the matter of young Chris and Alex. It was clear to everyone that they were drifting apart because of Geoffrey's hold on Chris. Alex was spending more and more time in Exeter with Lucy, Mason Frye and little Anne. Chris missed him and that absence seemed to send him deeper into bondage to Geoffrey. At times it did seem more like servitude than friendship.

Briefly Susan closed her eyes. Perhaps she was being too judgmental on poor Geoffrey. He had undergone a terrible ordeal, though his seclusion was one of his own making.

"Susan? Are you ready?"

She looked up at the sound of the voice. It was John, who had promised to come for her before he started down to the Great Hall.

She hurried to the mantel and retrieved Alice's last letter and slipped it into the top drawer of her bureau, deeply resenting the fact that she was forced to hide her children's correspondence from her own husband, their father.

"Susan?"

"I'm ready," she said as she opened the door.

"You look lovely." He leaned forward and kissed her almost shyly on the cheek, like a bashful schoolboy.

The gesture pleased her. She took his arm and wondered whether she would ever fully understand this complex man if she lived to be a hundred.

"Important day," John said quietly, walking easily beside her.

"I would say so, yes."

"Fraught with the potential for disaster, however."

"How do you mean?"

"Oh, come now, Susan. Try to imagine your own feelings after a fourteen-year imprisonment of isolation."

"One of his own making, need I remind you?"

"Worse, then."

John shook his head. "Chris says at times he is quite normal. And yet at other times–"

"What?"

"Chris won't say precisely. All he says is that sometimes Geoffrey scares him. Do you know what he has been doing all of these years?"

"No, what?"

"He's been fighting that battle over and over again, Jameson's Raid. Chris says that he has constructed a complete landscape, a recreation of the veld between Doornkop and Johannesburg, and that he has filled it with hundreds of toy soldiers that he has carved. Chris says they 'play the game' at least once a day."

Susan listened with her head bowed, suffering a growing sense of anxiety.

"Well, it will be interesting, won't it? Sometimes I think that's all we have a right to ask of life–be interesting."

He patted her hand. "We've had our ups and downs, haven't we? But it has been interesting."

She nodded, not trusting herself to speak.

"And through it all, I have never loved you less. In fact, I love you more at this moment than I have ever loved anything or anybody in my life."

His voice, his manner, his hand on hers had become suddenly urgent. She knew that his kiss and his embrace were coming, and she was eager to receive them. As she felt the pressure of his arms about her, the moist pressure of his lips, she closed her eyes and realized that she still loved him.

Now they were walking again toward the top of the Great Hall steps and beyond which she could hear a hum of voices, everyone already gathered for the big event.

At the top of the stairs, she looked out and down, and saw Eleanor first, overdressed and overrouged, standing near the opposite stairs as though wanting to be the first to greet her son.

Richard was lounging before the roaring fire. It had been a chilly spring, and now, despite it being May, a cold rain reminiscent of February was falling outside in the sunless late afternoon.

Near the large sofa she saw Marjorie and Lucy in close conversation. Behind the sofa was Alex and Mason Frye. There was a new closeness there, despite their ages. They seemed most compatible, and Mason was tutoring Alex again in upper levels, hoping to gain a new teacher for his school.

Stephen and Frederick were near the tea table. She saw them eating heartily from a pretty arrangement of scones and sandwiches. Last of all she saw little Anne, seated on the bottom step of the far staircase, watching all of the others with the singular sense of lostness that only a twelve-year-old girl can feel.

Susan felt sorry for her and chose her as a fitting destination. At the same time, as though on cue, Susan heard all of the conversation going on around her drift into silence, saw everyone turn slowly toward the stairs and the distant noise.

Eleanor pressed her handkerchief against her lips. Richard struggled slowly up out of his easy chair. Stephen and Frederick stopped stealing candied apricots from the silver epergne.

Still it came, that peculiar noise, something scraping against the stone floor of the corridor.

Then all at once Chris was at the top of the stairs, his face flushed with excitement. He looked down to the Great Hall.

"Ladies and gentlemen," he said in a voice that cracked, a comic reminder to all that he was passing out of childhood and into adulthood. "It gives me pleasure to present to you Captain Geoffrey Eden of the South African Company."

Susan hid a smile and noticed Lucy doing the same. Obviously Chris and Geoffrey had worked out the last details of his formal introduction, and in a way it did seem to ease the tension, young Chris presiding at the top of the stairs in the manner of a theatrical manager.

Then Geoffrey appeared, and Susan found it a difficult sight to witness.

He resembled an old man. His hair was gray, and he had tried to fit himself into his uniform, though clearly the years of inactivity had taken a toll in the addition of extra flesh.

He stood at the top of the stairs, his body distorted by the sharp angle of his crutches, and he looked down on the gathered company with suspicious eyes. He wore a single army boot and the footless leg was drawn slightly up as though in an attempt to conceal the lack.

Please, someone go and greet him, Susan begged silently, and as if in answer to a prayer, Eleanor started up the stairs, a handkerchief pressed to her lips. Geoffrey started painfully, carefully down, swinging the crutches, then grotesquely lowering his body after them.

Before such a spectacle of human effort, Eleanor backed down the stairs and held her position until Geoffrey was on the next to the bottom step. Then awkwardly she embraced him. Geoffrey seemed merely to endure her kisses and made no effort to return her affection, save for a curt and murmured "Mother–"

Next came Richard, who approached his son as though he were a marauding enemy, extended his hand, quickly realized that Geoffrey could not take it, then patted him lightly on the shoulder as though he were a schoolboy and fled back to his chair before the warm fire.

As Geoffrey swung down to the floor of the Great Hall, Stephen and Frederick drew near to him from the side of the tea table. "We are so glad to see you, Geoffrey," Frederick said in his deep, rich priest's voice. "You have no idea how greatly you have been missed."

Stephen said something too low to be heard. Then all the others were drawing near, some almost timidly like Lucy, Anne and Marjorie, the three of them kissing him on the cheek.

Then came John, his hand shoved in his pocket.

"We want you to know, Geoffrey, that every member of this family is proud of you and indebted to you for performing with honor on the field of battle. You have brought new nobility to the Eden name, and for that we all are eternally grateful."

Then Susan started forward, and out of the corner of her eye she saw Mason and Alex make the same motion, as though in a race to get there first. Susan increased her step and won the race. She was appalled at how ill Geoffrey looked up close, his skin a yellow tint, his eyes bloodshot, his fingernails unkempt, his white hair quite long, scraggly and matted.

"Geoffrey," she said and tried not to see his physical condition but to see through to the man inside. "We are very grateful that you have ended your long imprisonment. I'm not certain that any man was meant for solitude."

"It suited me," he said, somewhat snappish, and looked beyond her to where Alex and Mason were waiting.

Thus dismissed, Susan moved back toward the others and saw an apology on Eleanor's face.

"Do you remember me, Geoffrey? I'm Mason Frye. I taught you–"

"Of course I remember you," Geoffrey said, without a trace of warmth or light on his face.

"And this is Alex," Mason went on, "Stephen's son."

"You are Chris's friend," Geoffrey said, shifting slightly as though something were beginning to cause him discomfort.

"Yes," Alex smiled. "Chris has told me–"

"I need him now, you know." Geoffrey said, interrupting. "I'm sure you will understand. Now where is he?"

Awkwardly Geoffrey twisted about until he found Chris on the steps directly above him. "Come, stand here beside me," he commanded and instantly Chris obeyed.

In the meantime, Mason backed away, taking Alex with him. No one was speaking. All were being slowly enveloped in an ominous silence.

Suddenly, Susan heard the distant ringing of the alarm bell outside the castle gate. She looked up sharply, as did everyone. The bell meant someone was coming, someone unannounced. They were expecting no one.

"Who in the hell–" John muttered and started toward the Great Hall doors, followed by Stephen.

The ringing persisted, growing louder. Everyone shifted their focus from Geoffrey to the Great Hall doors. Even the servants hovering about the tea table looked up like startled animals.

Susan heard shouting outside in the late afternoon dusk and rain, guardsmen's voices calling out something.

John reached the door first. He pulled it open and stepped back out of the driving rain, and at the same time, he motioned to a single guardsman who was just hurrying up the Great Hall stairs.

Once inside John quickly closed the door, stood back from the rain-drenched man and received an urgent message of some sort.

Stephen must have heard too, clearly a grim message, for he bowed his head, and Susan could sense a new sorrow.

With all eyes still upon them, they started back across the Great Hall, their faces reflecting new sadness, while all members of the family were on their feet, Geoffrey momentarily forgotten in this unscheduled and grim interruption.

Soberly John announced, "The king is dead," and Susan heard gasps all about, heard instant weeping coming from the servants.

"Poor Edward. Such a brief reign." That was all that Susan could manage. He had waited so long for the throne to be his and had really done very well, despite the random criticism of his personal habits.

Poor England, she thought further. What kind of king little George would make was anybody's guess. He seemed at times to be a reluctant prince. Would he be as reluctant a monarch?

Now she looked up to see teacups being passed around, saw John holding his aloft, ready to propose an initial and brief toast. Doubtless there would be countless others with champagne throughout the course of the evening.

When everyone had been served, John lifted his cup higher. "The king is dead. Long live the king."

The company repeated this in a muddled choral reading. Eleanor's sniffling topped everything. And at the conclusion of the salute, they all were left with their grief, their private fears for themselves and for England.

Then, "I'm cold," was heard throughout the Great Hall, a loud, slightly angry, mildly petulant announcement that summoned everyone's attention back to the east-wing stairs and Captain Geoffrey Eden. "I'm cold," he repeated. "I had completely forgotten how drafty this damn hall could be."

"Oh, of course, come, my darling," Eleanor invited, dabbing at her eyes and clearing a way for him at the fire. Hurriedly she gestured for Richard to vacate his chair, which he did, and now she continued to wave Geoffrey forward in his limping gait.

"Come, this way."

"I know the way, Mother. I have lost a foot, not my eyes," and slowly, laboriously he dragged himself forward, bumping into furniture, cursing aloud with each collision.

Once seated in the chair before the fire, he then announced, "I'm hungry. Would anyone have the decency to serve my tea?"

It was Marjorie who moved forward toward the tea table and within a matter of moments presented him with a platter filled with sweets and sandwiches, and a cup of tea.

"I take sugar," he muttered.

She returned to the tea table, corrected her error and returned his cup.

Then Geoffrey ate with perfect deliberation and calm egocentricity, apparently unmoved by the message of the king's death, unmoved by anything save his own wants, his own needs.

A new and worried silence settled over the family. It was as though a highly infectious disease had just entered their ranks, and all were wondering how many would succumb, how many would survive.

Eden Castle
Christmas Eve, 1912

Marjorie was positive she had never seen this old dining hall look so festive since her first Christmas at Eden Castle sixteen years before, the year she had arrived there as a very nervous young bride. In fact, the entire castle was lavishly adorned in holiday finery, swags of evergreen intermingled with bright red holly berries, spice and mistletoe balls hanging everywhere and lovely red velvet bows affixed to "anything that stood still for five seconds," according to John Murrey Eden, who clearly relished it even as he grumbled about it.

There was an enormous decorated Christmas tree in the Great Hall and yet another in the dining hall. The entire family had set to, with considerable help from the servants, to decorate both trees, and now both glistened and sparkled as though with lights from within. All day long, members of the family had been sneaking down and depositing gifts beneath the evergreen boughs. A cup of hot tea and a plate of ginger cookies had been left for Father Christmas, a custom dating back to when Chris and Alex were babies.

As Marjorie took in the beauty around her, she tried to blot out the male voices rising in anger to her right, tried hard to concentrate only on the good memories of her life here at Eden.

Babies. She missed having babies around. Everyone was grown-up now. Look at her Christopher, so like his father in many ways save one. And Alexander. How proud Eve would have been of him. At sixteen, both boys were ramrod straight, with the Eden jaw and clear, steady blue eyes.

Marjorie adored them both, but she really believed she had loved them more as babies. Now they alarmed her sometimes with their unique convictions and incredible energy.

Still, she missed having a baby around. She had lost three after Christopher, unexplained miscarriages. Frederick had mourned and then had claimed, "God's will." Marjorie made no claim. She couldn't. It would not be possible for her to love a God who created life and then killed it.

Now she looked down the table in the opposite direction toward Anne. Even little Anne was grown-up. At fourteen, she appeared much older, a shy, introspective young girl who seemed deadly serious most of the time; but when she laughed, it sounded like music, and when she smiled, it was impossible for anyone to stay grumpy for long. She was very pretty and, Marjorie suspected, very much in love. She had wished on more than one occasion that little Anne had fallen in love with Chris instead of Alex, but one could not dictate to the human heart. Sometimes she worried if her Chris would ever settle down completely. Frederick had said that he hated to take him into Exeter with him anymore. Every pretty face and soft bosom caught his eye and turned his head.

Then Geoffrey's voice interrupted her thoughts. "You call it international anarchy," he suddenly shouted at Mason Frye. "I call it strength, national strength."

As Mason prepared his reply, Marjorie closed her eyes and bowed her head. Why this evening? This stupid debate on war versus peace had raged for days throughout Eden Castle. Everyone, including her, was sick to death of it.

Battle lines had already been clearly drawn. Chris, John Murrey Eden and Geoffrey on the side of war and honor, and Mason Frye, Frederick and Alexander opposed to it on the grounds of morality and humanity. Several times in the past they had tried to involve Richard, but they hadn't been able to keep him awake long enough to participate.

"But why the need for strength, Geoffrey?" Mason asked in his well-modulated voice of reason.

"You prefer weakness?" Geoffrey snapped.

"I don't call it weakness," Mason replied, "when I am not certain who it is I must be strong against."

Marjorie glanced up and caught a glimpse of Geoffrey, glowering at Mason, who sat across from him at table. This was always the pattern, the argument starting between Geoffrey and Mason, and ultimately spreading out and involving everyone else foolish enough to become involved.

Yet in a curious way Geoffrey held her fascinated. He had long since recovered from his actual wounds. But there was another, more serious sickness running rampant in him, a lingering resentment of "his defeat on that far-off battlefield." What angered Marjorie most was the way he had taken over Eden Castle and everyone in it: "Are you comfortable, Geoffrey?" "Would you like more tea, Geoffrey?" "Are you warm enough, Geoffrey?" "Of course it's all right to move your toy battlefield down to the Great Hall, Geoffrey." "Let us help . . ."

They had. It had taken eight servants the better part of the day to move that enormous "game" down to the center of the Great Hall, where they set it up under Geoffrey and Chris's supervision. Since then, at least once a day the family had been treated to a recreation of Jameson's Raid.

"Your ignorance is not an excuse for lack of preparation," Geoffrey countered now, pushing back from the table and with effort lifting his stump on to the empty chair next to him. Geoffrey always required an empty chair next to him on which to rest his leg.

"Preparation against what? Whom?" Mason begged. "All I ask is please tell me who my enemy is."

A look of incredulity crossed Geoffrey's face. "Germany is arming herself to the teeth, complete mobilization and conscription is the law. You know that."

"How has Germany offended England?"

Now John Murrey Eden placed his napkin on the table and entered the fray. "Fortunately for all of us, England is not listening to Mason Frye and is already in the process of mobilizing her . . . various strengths."

Then along came Alex as though he felt a need to keep the sides even. "If Germany does prove a threat, there is the matter of international law."

Geoffrey laughed. "And what is that? What is this European solidarity?" he sneered. "I wouldn't trust European solidarity any more than a mongrel dog."

Now it was Frederick's turn. "And yet, I cannot believe that the people of Europe will provoke war at a favorable moment."

"War will come," Geoffrey pronounced now, and the table fell silent, the lovely warm mood of Christmas Eve slowly being destroyed.

Marjorie was on the verge of suggesting a different turn to the conversation when suddenly Chris spoke up.

"I cannot believe what I'm hearing," he exclaimed with youthful indignation. "Are there those seated here at this table who would not consider it a sacred honor to defend not merely the national pride but the national existence?"

"It appears that way," Geoffrey smiled, wincing slightly as he shifted his stump upon the chair.

Then Alex spoke. "To greet with enthusiasm the possibility of global warfare is its own condemnation," he said succinctly. "Only madmen prepare for nonexistent battles."

"Now, wait a minute," John Murrey Eden scolded, wagging a finger at Alex. "If war comes," he went on, "I hope that every Eden male would acquit himself as nobly and with the same degree of honor as Geoffrey has done. We want no white feathers under this roof. Is that clear?"

"Even if the war is wrong?" Alex asked.

"If the king calls, then the war is just. Who is to defend a country but its young men?"

Marjorie felt new tension. She had never heard Alex so vocal. She had never seen Geoffrey so angry or John Murrey Eden or Chris, who gazed across at Alex as though he were a mere stranger on a train.

Now Geoffrey struggled up out of his chair, his eyes glittering in an unnatural way. "There are no soldiers here," he said sadly and looked up and down the table as though the lack were more than he could bear. "Yet if war comes, the problem will be to dispose of the armed and trained manhood, to strike with the utmost speed a blow strong enough to destroy the opponent's will to resist."

With great patience, Frederick joined the battle. "What if no one resists, Geoffrey? What if there is no need to dispose of an armed and trained manhood?"

"Someone always has a capacity for mischief," Geoffrey snapped.

"Then it is simply a matter of appointing enemies," Frederick concluded with a smile. "Like a child's game. You be it, and I'll go and hide."

"No," Chris objected. "Father, you are being terribly unfair to Geoffrey. You have never known war. What gives you the right to speak with such authority?"

Shocked by her son's insolence, Marjorie was on her feet. "Chris! You must apologize."

"It's perfectly all right, Marjorie," Frederick soothed. "I don't believe that it was our intention to raise a parrot for a son. I'm very pleased that he speaks his own mind."

Marjorie was on the verge of leading the ladies out of this embarrassing battle and into the warmth of the Great Hall when suddenly Alex was on his feet, a calm expression on his face.

"It's not too late," he said. "Nothing is set, no die has been cast, no boot fitted, no bugle sounded. We must never think of war as being inevitable. Nothing is inevitable so long as—"

"What if Geoffrey had refused to fight?" Chris demanded.

"I daresay he would have been a very different man."

"I would have been a coward," Geoffrey shouted. "I would have been a coward and not fit to bear the name of Eden."

"You might have been more fit."

"To hell with you. Let's get out of here," Geoffrey muttered. "I don't like the smell."

"Please stay," Alex begged and looked suddenly stricken.

John Murrey Eden stood to give Geoffrey a willing arm. As he passed Alex by, he said, "You have filled your head with the wrong concepts. I sincerely hope that you are capable of correcting your errors."

Mason Frye was on his feet. "There were wrong ideas expressed here this evening, but they weren't coming from Alex."

John turned back, his face flushed with anger. "What has happened to you, Mason?" he demanded. "You once possessed the keenest mind I've ever met."

"My mind is still intact."

"No, it's different. You're different. And the time may come when–"

He broke off speaking.

Again Marjorie bowed her head and closed her eyes. Shambles. Everything was in a shambles. Christmas Eve was over before it had even begun. The lovely feeling of peace, the warm fellowship, all gone, destroyed as surely as though there had been an actual battle in the dining hall.

And yet there was one more volley, coming from Geoffrey. "Tell me, all of you weak sisters, do you sleep secure in your beds at night?"

The three "weak sisters," Alex, Mason and Frederick, looked at each other. But before they could reply, Stephen stepped forward and placed a loving arm about Alex's shoulder.

"It is true, Geoffrey, that the growth of insecurity corresponds with the growth of armaments. But I'm afraid you have picked your quarrel with the wrong three. You see, a really good war can only be waged by those who love it, who love the smell, the feel and the sound of battle, love with a kind of perversity even the screams of the dying. It's my guess that these three here prefer Mozart and a daffodil. I'm afraid you'll never get them into your war. Sorry. You'd best look elsewhere."

Blessedly everyone at the table laughed. Everyone except the three at the door, who glanced back at Stephen with expressions of varying degrees of condescension.

Then with Chris on one side and John on the other, Geoffrey disappeared into the corridor, the silence of the room now filled with the peculiar rhythm of his crutches.

Quickly Alex left the dining hall by the opposite door, a hurried departure, a look of sadness on his face. Following immediately after him was his adoring Anne.

For the rest of them, they sat slowly back down in a scattered arrangement of chairs and exchanged worried looks. Somehow Marjorie knew that though there were presents yet to be opened beneath the tree, a glorious plum pudding to be consumed, Christmas carols to be sung, gifts to be passed out to the servants, despite all this, she knew perfectly well that Christmas Eve of 1912 was over.

Perhaps next year all this talk of war would be concluded, and they would have a better Christmas Eve.

Alex had no specific destination. He simply wanted to leave the dining hall, where he knew he had said too much to the wrong people, briefly forgetting one of Henderson's main lessons—how foolish it was to antagonize the very people you want to influence.

Now he hurried down the corridor that led to the kitchen court steps and knew full well that he couldn't go down there for refuge. The servants were preparing for their own celebration. Then where? He needed to clear his head and see if he—

"Alex."

He looked back and saw Anne following after him. She looked very pretty tonight in a red velvet gown with white lace collar.

"Alex, wait. Where are you going?"

"I'll just be gone a—"

"Come on, I know a place."

Quickly she caught up with him, took his hand and led him to the end of the long first-floor corridor.

"In here," she invited. She pushed open a door and stood back.

For a moment after she closed the door it was pitch-black. He heard her strike a match and saw the flickering light of a single candle.

"What is this place?"

Anne smiled. "It's called the mending room," she said. "All the torn linens are sent here to await their resurrection." She paused, then laughed. "The only trouble is, nothing ever gets mended. Poor Aunt Eleanor forgets about them and simply buys more linens at Fortnum and Mason's in London. I would imagine that there are fifty years of torn linens in this small room. Look."

Quickly she lifted a white sheet from a nearby shelf, shook it open and peered comically through a jagged hole in one end. "Grandpapa's big toe caused this, I imagine."

Alex watched her closely. She looked very pretty tonight.

"I'm sorry for what happened in the dining hall," she said softly and sat on a nearby footstool.

"Not half as sorry as I am," Alex muttered and sat on another footstool. "I don't really know why we persist in that foolish debate."

"It isn't foolish. One of my father's strongest convictions is his philosophy of pacifism."

"I know. He's a remarkable man."

"And he thinks the world of you."

"It's reciprocal."

There was a pause. Again Alex looked about at the countless shelves laden with torn fabric. Now he was afraid that because of him the fabric of his deep love and friendship with Chris had been torn as well.

"Do you think war will come, Alex?" Anne asked, the candlelight bobbing gently under the caress of her breath.

"I don't know. When a nation mobilizes, it must find an excuse to use its new strength. But as Geoffrey says, not to mobilize is to be weak."

"Geoffrey," Anne scoffed and turned slightly on her stool as though she had no desire to even think of the man.

"You don't care for him?"

"No, do you?"

"He's a member of our family."

"He is a spoiled brat, according to my father."

Anne's severe condemnation interested Alex.

"Mama says when they were growing up, Geoffrey could do exactly as he pleased, at all times, in all matters. Mama says that she and Aunt Charlotte quickly learned it was easier to let him win all games, all arguments. Mama says—"

Abruptly she broke off and appeared to be closely studying her hands. "Oh well, what he once was is unimportant. Sometimes he frightens me. He looks so unhappy."

"He is. Still, Chris worships him. And Grandpapa listens to his endless stories."

"You mustn't let any of them dissuade you from your own convictions."

Alex looked up, moved by her sweetness, her loving consideration. "Even if it means constant warfare like tonight?"

"It won't. It simply means that there are certain subjects that this family should not discuss, since we all know full well that such a discussion will lead to . . . trouble."

"Trouble!" Alex repeated, effortlessly recalling the hurt expression on Chris's face and the disappointed expression on his grandfather's face.

"No, I mean it, Alex," she said with new intensity, leaving her footstool and kneeling directly before him. "My father has taught me that all a man is—and a woman, too, for that matter—is his convictions, what he believes within his heart, what his conscience tells him is right and what is wrong, and that inner voice is not always compatible with society's or even the world's."

He was fascinated by her closeness as well as the calm and mature way in which she was speaking. What had happened to that quiet little tagalong who once had shadowed his every step?

"I have a good friend at Greenfield," she went on. "Her name is Penelope Price. I call her Penny. Her father teaches the Italian Renaissance. We've known each other since we were children, have grown up the only two girls in a boys' school." She paused. "It has been awful."

"How do you mean?"

"Well, nothing we ever do for any of our tutors is quite as good as the young men who do the same work. We can't play in any sporting event except archery, and that we have to do behind the stables, where we can't be seen."

Alex laughed. "Why? I don't understand?"

"Neither do we," she protested. "Sometimes it's like being in prison. We can't go out alone. We can't walk the common after five in the afternoon. We must always stay in each afternoon after tea." She broke off and shook her head. "Penny and I have plotted frequently to run away."

Surprised, Alex listened, as fascinated by what she was saying as he was by the absolutely mesmerizing beauty of her face.

"Where would you go?" he asked.

"London, I suppose."

"What would you do in London?"

"We had planned to go into service. We often thought what fun it would be to go to Aunt Charlotte's big house in Belgravia and apply for the positions of upper-house parlormaids."

"But you're not a servant."

"No, but I could be. I'm well trained. Mama saw to that. I could even mend all the torn fabric in this room if I wanted to."

"I'm afraid you'd be here for the rest of your life."

"Possibly, but at least it would be better than going back to Greenfield."

She seemed sad. She toyed with the edge of her lace collar, her hand so small and white in the semidarkness.

Alex watched her as he had never watched her before, saw her as he had never seen her before. Yet he had known her always, could not remember a time when "little Anne" wasn't present, sitting shyly in the background or following him everywhere.

When had she so changed? Where had this lovely young woman come from, the one glancing up at him now with such appealing and yet timid eyes?

"I like very much being here with you," she smiled shyly. "All my life I have liked being near you."

He nodded because it seemed safer than trying to speak, for his mouth felt strangely dry. He wanted more than anything in the world to touch her, just to touch her skin, to see how it felt.

"Alex?"

"Anne–"

"Please never change. Please don't let them change you. Not like they have changed Chris. Please, will you promise me?"

Now in the urgency of what she was saying, she rested her hand on his knee, and the place where she had touched him suddenly ignited with the most pleasing sensation of warmth.

Alex continued to feel a curious tension cresting deep within him. He had never felt anything like it in his life. At first it frightened him, but now the sensation was becoming so pleasurable, his needs so exquisitely painful that before he realized what he was doing, he leaned forward and took her by the shoulders and drew her close between his legs. The merest pressure of her body touched his groin, and he felt desire as sharp as any he had ever felt, a desire that could only be satisfied by her closeness. He drew her yet closer until she was in his arms, a most willing captive, her arms entwined about his neck as though she, too, were suffering in a similar fashion, and as their lips met for the first time, Alex closed his eyes in utter awe of this wonderful thing that was happening, this sweetest of unions.

The kiss ended only when both felt the need for breath. They continued to cling to each other, foreheads touching, like exhausted children at the end of a day of play, saying nothing, for what words would be equal to this miraculous moment.

Eden Castle
June 4, 1913

It had happened far too fast, of that Lucy was certain, her little Anne all grown-up and quite beautiful beyond description in her white wedding gown, shortly to walk down the Great Hall steps on Mason's arm to greet Alex, her bridegroom.

Now, as Lucy took a brief tea break from overseeing the decorating of the Great Hall, she looked about and was very pleased with what she saw. There were roses everywhere, literally hundreds of June roses, some from Eleanor's private garden, the rest generously donated from gardens all up and down the North Devon coast. Pink roses, white roses, yellow, red, orange and all shades in between.

A large carved-ivory screen had been brought down from the chapel and had been set up to obscure the enormous and now-useless fireplace. In front of the screen, the stewards had set up a delicate white trellis, and now the parlormaids were busy weaving pink roses in and out of the filigree.

The Great Hall doors had been swung open and the kindest June breeze wafted in through the opened doors.

Despite Lucy's fatigue, she was forced to admit that it all looked lovely. Now she sat on the arm of the sofa, finished the tea which Maxwell had thoughtfully brought to her and worried as she had worried for the past three months that perhaps she and Mason had been too quick to give the young people their blessing. Both Anne and Alex were little more than children, Alex scarcely seventeen, Anne scarcely fifteen. It was true, as Mason had said, that they both seemed older, and it was also true that they had known each other all their lives. Still–

"There you are!"

At the sound of the voice, Lucy looked up and saw Susan just coming down the Great Hall steps. She looked quite lovely in a dark navy blue silk frock, but Lucy looked closer and discovered with a pang of sadness that she also looked tired and somehow old. It had become difficult for Lucy to accept the fact that her family was growing older, that once energetic Susan now leaned heavily on the banister. By the time she had reached the bottom, her smile was back in place, as warm and as youthful as ever.

"How lovely everything looks," she beamed and joined Lucy by the sofa.

"I'm afraid it still looks like the Great Hall," Lucy sighed, lifting her eyes to the cavernous old ceiling. "No way to disguise it, I'm afraid."

"Nor would we want to. I'm so glad the children decided against the chapel. This," and she looked about, "is the true heart of Eden."

She sat on the sofa near Lucy and reached for her hand. "And you look lovely as well," she said, "far too young, of course, to be the mother of the bride."

"If I'm too young to be the mother of the bride, what of the bride herself?" Lucy brooded. "Do you think they are too young?"

Susan shook her head. "No. They have known each other forever."

"That's what Mason says, but–"

"And I believe that they are deeply in love. I'm fairly good about recognizing such things." Susan laughed.

Lucy listened closely, respectful of Susan's opinion. If Susan thought it would all be alright, then Lucy would try to dismiss her own worries.

"Well, perhaps I should go check on the bride then."

"I did that coming down. She is beautiful. She and Penny are upstairs in the sitting room giggling like schoolgirls."

"They *are* schoolgirls," Lucy frowned.

"Dearest Lucy," Susan soothed in a new and compelling tone, "the human heart sets its own timetable, and no two are alike. When did you know that you were absolutely in love with Mason Frye?"

Lucy laughed. "The first time he lectured on the Lake poets."

Susan nodded. "Then there you are. Don't worry. Don't spoil this day made in heaven on one wisp of doubt or fear. This family, this world is always due an interval of soft breezes and high mild suns. I think our season for happiness has come. Let us enjoy it to the fullest against the day when winter returns, as it surely will."

Lucy watched the way the light from the open door played across her face. Curious, but she seemed to be in a state of great happiness and great sorrow simultaneously. Lucy felt sorry for her, exiled from her children just as Lucy's own parents were cut off from Charlotte by the arrogance of one man.

Then she heard a voice, "I thought you were going to wait for me."

At the sound of this bellowing voice, which shattered the midday peace, Lucy looked toward the top of the stairs and saw John Murrey Eden, looking dapper in gray morning clothes with a bloodred cravat at his neck.

As he started slowly down the stairs, Lucy bent quickly down and kissed Susan on the forehead. "I'll go check on the schoolgirl bride," she whispered.

"Coward," Susan smiled and winked at Lucy.

"Good morning, Uncle John," Lucy said pleasantly as she passed the old man on the steps.

"Could you tell me whose blasted idea this was to hold a wedding so early in the morning?" he grumbled.

"It's midday," Lucy said, "and the decision was made by the bride and the groom."

Then she lifted her skirts and hurried up the stairs, wondering how any of them had managed to put up with the irascible old man for this long.

At the top of the stairs, she glanced down the corridor and saw Frederick resplendent in his vestments chatting with Stephen. She waved at both of them, then started down the opposite corridor. Even from this point she could hear Penny and Anne giggling, two young girls who should be memorizing their Latin grammar instead of gossiping about wedding nights.

John sat at the back of the company, his foot propped up on a low footstool, suffering the excruciating pain of gout, while Frederick recited the wedding ceremony to Anne and Alex.

Perhaps when one's grandchildren commenced to marry, one had lived far too long.

Damn! The pain felt exactly like a red-hot poker being dropped on his big toe. Good drink helped, as did good companionship, and now with this blasted wedding, he was losing one of his best companions, Alex gone to his wedding bed, to wedding slavery, gone from John's life.

Still, he had Chris, though as he watched the way Chris now was ogling little blond Penny Price, John had new cause to worry. Both boys were at the age when the blood ran hot and the groin ached almost constantly. Yet what were they to do? What was any decent man to do about this curse of nature but wed and bed a decent woman who would do his bidding and then get on with his life.

". . . I pronounce that they are man and wife."

Then it was over. The two kissed, a rather sweet and chaste kiss. John hoped that Alex could muster more fire than that tonight in his wedding bed.

The newlyweds were only going down the coast to Tintagel. It was their plan to return then to Eden while their cottage at Greenfield was being done over. Thereafter Alex would join the faculty at Greenfield, teaching the younger students mathematics, and so, at last, Mason Frye would have had his way. He had been trying to make a teacher out of Alex from the beginning.

Marjorie was playing the recessional on that blasted out-of-tune pianoforte, and blessedly it was all over except for the weeping and the females' giggling.

Annoyed, John struggled to his feet. As the blood from his leg rushed down to his foot, it felt as though someone were holding a lit torch to his bare flesh, and even as he winced, he caught sight of Geoffrey fighting his way up out of his chair with the aid of his crutches. John decided that he had best not complain, lest God hear him and send him more grief.

Well, nothing to do now but to join the line of well-wishers and give the bride a kiss, the groom a handshake, then see if he could not find a corner somewhere in this flower-bedecked hall that did not smell of roses, and there, armed with a good bottle of whisky, wait out this female ritual.

Eden Castle
July 18, 1913

If Eleanor lived to be one hundred and fifty years old, she knew she would never see a more beautiful sight, the headlands of Eden resembling rich green velvet, the channel water a cobalt blue, the high sky filled with fleecy white cotton clouds, and cavorting ahead were the four young people, Alex and Anne, still drunk with the happiness of newly wedded bliss, and Penny Price and Chris, a budding romance if Eleanor had ever seen one. All four young people were dressed in white, the girls in billowing white silks, the young men in white tennis shirts and trousers, all walking arm in arm ahead of the four old grumblers who were bringing up the rear.

"Were we ever that young?" Susan murmured, apparently focused on the same beauty as Eleanor. She leaned heavily on John's arm, while he in turn leaned heavily on his walking stick.

John answered for them all. "Speak for yourself. I still feel incredibly young."

"Nonsense," Susan scoffed. "It takes you an hour every morning to persuade your bones that they must now get moving."

Richard snickered and squinted ahead at the four who were playing an impromptu game of tag, Anne and Penny touching Chris and Alex, then running from their pursuit in graceful patterns of joy and laughter like white birds.

"Here," pointed Eleanor, indicating the stone bench. "Let's sit here and watch 'tomorrow' at play and be content with who and what we are."

She sat heavily on the end of the stone bench. John sat next to her, Susan next to John and Richard on the end. "Four old crows," she muttered and waited for the rhythm of her heart to grow steady and for the wheezing of the others to grow silent.

"This was your idea–a walk," Alex called out, laughing, seeing the four of them seated on the bench.

"Even a king fallen on the field of battle is free to call out king's ex," John retorted.

"You entertain us," Eleanor suggested. "We would like that."

Chris laughed and bowed low. "The court jesters at your service." He reached out and grabbed Penny and spun her about. The young girl laughed and lifted her arms to the sun as though to embrace it.

Then Alex and Ann linked arms for an impromptu cancan. Chris and Penny joined the line, and at some point, someone shifted the balance and threw the lot of them off course and they collapsed into a charming pile of pale white arms, golden hair, sparkling eyes and laughter that would soothe the most irascible spirit.

Eleanor was aware of the others watching along with her, only a touch of the classic envy that always accompanies the relationship between youth and age. But envy was not the predominant emotion on this perfect day.

Rather, they all seemed to be deriving a sense of great pleasure from the beauty before them and the peace of their surroundings.

Eleanor relaxed against the bench, closed her eyes and gave a quick prayer, thanking God for His many blessings, promising to try to understand when things did not go her way, but in the end leaving it all to Him in faith and love.

"Is anyone hungry?"

At the sound of the voice, she looked up to see Lucy and Mason, and Stephen and Frederick carrying large wicker picnic hampers between them. Behind came Marjorie, carrying a white linen cloth.

Lucy called ahead in explanation. "It was Mason's idea. He has always loved picnics on the headlands–a child at heart, Mason is."

"A splendid idea," John agreed. "I only hope that one of you had the good sense to bring a bottle of wine."

"Three, Papa," Stephen laughed.

The young people called a halt to their antics and rushed forward to help in any way that they could, and in a matter of moments the large white linen cloth had been spread before them, a veritable feast laid upon it of several rounds of good English cheddar, roast chicken, freshly baked breads still warm from the oven, fresh fruit, tea cakes and tiny cucumber sandwiches.

"We tried to talk Geoffrey into coming with us," Lucy explained. "But he declined, said the rough terrain was very difficult for him to walk on with crutches."

The mention of Geoffrey seemed to dash a bit of cold water on the impromptu festivities. But as Stephen and Frederick uncorked the wine and passed the glasses about, the spirit revived. Eleanor took her glass, looked out over the blue water and issued one more brief prayer just in the event that God was still listening.

"This is how Your world was meant to be. Thank you. Amen."

Eden Castle
March 13, 1914

"War will come," Geoffrey pronounced to the steady background of a driving rainstorm. He peered over the top of the London *Times* to see how his announcement had been received by everyone huddled about the Great Hall fire for warmth.

"Listen to this," and he straightened the *Times* in order to read the proof of his claim. " 'The threat of war has created on the Continent a profound transformation of life. Not only have all men of military age been called to the Colors, but districts under the threat of invasion have been withdrawn from the safeguards of ordinary law.' "

He paused in his reading and again peered over the top of the newspaper. From where he sat nearest to the fire, they looked to be a somnambulent group. In fact, he began to wonder if anyone had even heard what he had read.

To his right sat Chris, dear loyal Chris. Chris had heard, for he was looking at Geoffrey now with a most eager and concerned expression. It had long been Geoffrey's opinion that Chris was the best of the lot.

And the worst of the lot? Without a doubt, Alex there, his bride leaning back in his arms before the fire, their faces bland and unconcerned. Weak to the marrow, that one was, and heaven help the country who counted on him for protection.

Across from him were the predictable snorers, his father and John Murrey Eden. At times it seemed as though they were holding a snoring contest. Was this the reward for a long life? A constant round-the-clock nap? Only a short time ago Stephen, Frederick, Marjorie and Susan had been there. But cold rain outside and constant drafts in the Great Hall had driven them to the upstairs sitting room.

"Did anyone hear?" Geoffrey demanded. "You, Alex, did you hear?"

Rather sleepily Alex nuzzled the side of Anne's face. Did they do nothing but cling to one another? Now they were waiting for the rain to subside before returning to Exeter after spending the day here visiting Stephen.

"I heard, Geoffrey," Alex said, "but I recall the Danish socialist Brandes, who once made the terrible but true comment that 'war always means the assassination of truth.' "

"Are you doubting the London *Times?*"

Alex laughed outright. Anne smiled. "The London *Times* is not writ by God, Geoffrey, but rather by men with as many vested interests as yourself."

Shocked, Geoffrey drew a deep breath in order to make an effort at control. "What precisely is it that you doubt, Alex?"

"Everything. How do we know what is happening on the Continent or in any given country?"

"We know what's going on here in England, which is exactly nothing," Geoffrey snapped. "According to this same article, the main British contribution to the cause will be only in money and labor. It will be business as usual here."

"Not a bad idea. Far better than killing each other."

"But don't you see? Such a position leaves us vulnerable. You yourself have said in the past that ultimately a war machine must be used."

"Exactly!"

"And who will the war machine be used against? It will be used against the weak, the unprepared, the unwitting."

For a moment Alex did not reply. Anne shifted in his arms and sat up sleepily. Only Chris stirred with any degree of strength and purpose.

"Sometimes, Alex, I don't think I know you at all."

Alex smiled tolerantly, "I know you, Chris. And I know the influences that have come between us."

Geoffrey smoothed the London *Times* in his lap and warmed to the conversation, which was growing personal and ugly. "You mean me, of course, don't you, Alex?"

Chris objected strenuously. "No, he doesn't mean you, Geoffrey. Frankly, I don't think Alex knows what he means these days."

Anne stood and straightened the waistband on her skirt, a slight look of apprehension in her eye. "Come on, Alex," she whispered. "I think we can make it now. Let's go and tell your father goodbye. Papa expects us home for–"

"Speaking of influences," Geoffrey said, suddenly aware of how hungry he was for a battle, even a verbal one with this mere boy, "I would say that your new father-in-law has had a terribly damaging influence on you."

Ah, he had struck a raw nerve there, had, in a sense, criticized his vapid little wife and Mason Frye in one blow. Good clean strike.

Slowly Alex stood. Geoffrey tried to read the expression on his face, tried to see when and how the next volley would be delivered.

But to his surprise there was no volley at all, just a look of sadness on that coward's face as he put his arm around Anne and led her toward the Great Hall stairs.

Enraged by this snub and unable to contain it, Geoffrey shouted, "You're a coward, Alex. You possess nothing that is worthy of the Eden name. In fact, you leave a foul odor wherever you go. Why don't you take your female baggage, do us a favor and spare us of ever looking upon your cowardice again."

For a moment he heard only the echo of his own diatribe and the reliable sound of his father's snoring. He was equally aware of the shocked look on Chris's face and saw John Murrey Eden just stirring himself out of his brief nap.

"What's the shouting about?" he muttered sleepily and sat up.

"I don't like to sit in the presence of cowardice," Geoffrey pronounced and saw John newly alert, his eyes blinking rapidly as he looked about.

Now it was Chris who came to Geoffrey's aid. "Alex called Geoffrey a liar," he said, "called the London *Times* a liar as well."

John blinked at these strong accusations and now walked slowly toward Alex and Anne.

"Is this true?" he asked, not really angry. Geoffrey would have preferred a much greater indignation.

Alex smiled and shrugged. "It was not my intention to–"

"But is it true?"

"I did not call him a liar, and all I said concerning the *Times* was that their editorial staff had as many vested interests in perpetuating and advancing war as did Geoffrey."

There was a pause, a good one in that Geoffrey sensed John's bewilderment. "Do you think that Germany gives a damn about the vested interests of the editorial staff of the London *Times*?"

"No, but I doubt seriously if the German people want to kill us anymore than we want to kill the German people."

Slowly John shook his head. Geoffrey was so eager to join in the fight, but for now he held his tongue. Let John realize for himself the full extent of this weak grandson.

"Then what do we do?" John asked, with an air of forced patience. "When the Hun comes marching down Pall Mall, do we invite him to put his bayonet away and come in for a cup of tea?"

Alex laughed. "Not a bad idea, Grandpapa. Sometimes I suspect that modern war is too serious a business to be entrusted to soldiers. Let the shopkeepers, the greengrocers, the flower vendors, the corner butchers handle all hostile aliens. They would know precisely what to do."

Now Geoffrey saw John step up to the bottom stair. "You seem to be unable to grasp the seriousness of the situation, Alex," he said with continued and admirable patience. "The world, I'm afraid, is on the brink."

"Then the world can back away," Alex replied. "The world has a free spirit. It is not obligated by law or duty to perform in any set manner."

"And what of honor?"

Alex looked truly puzzled. "And what of it?"

"How do you propose that we acquit ourselves as men? Do we turn and run with our tails between our legs?"

"No, we shake hands with our so-called foe and ask him with great patience and civility to articulate our differences so that we might sit down like civilized men and try to work our way through them without the unnecessary slaughter of hundreds of thousands of human beings."

Then Geoffrey could stand it no longer. "And what of the soldier? Where does that leave the professional soldier? If diplomacy is to be the order of the day, what will happen to the nobility and the honor of the professional soldier?"

"I see nothing noble or honorable in being a soldier, Geoffrey," Alex replied with perfect calm, as though he hadn't the slightest idea how treasonous his words were.

"In fact," he went on, "it is my suspicion that soldiers, particularly officers schooled for many years in hierarchical obedience are lacking in alertness, are quite probably very unimaginative and very conservative."

In the process of struggling up out of his chair, Geoffrey struck his stump and out of habit groaned. Chris was at his side within the instant, a look of concern on his face. The pity there was so appealing that Geoffrey played off of it and fell back into his chair, as though freshly wounded. He had never in his life heard such irresponsible and dangerous talk, and coming from a mere child who had no concept, no idea of the seriousness of what he was saying.

Apparently neither had John, for now he saw John gaze up at the two on the steps as though he had caught two strangers wandering about Eden Castle.

"I no longer know you, Alex," he said almost pitiably.

"I'm the same as I've always been, Grandpapa."

"No, oh no, you're wrong. You have changed. I'm afraid I'm not able to say when or how it happened, but it's unimportant and the change is complete. What is important is that you cannot make statements as you have just made, statements amounting to insults really, and remain in this household. The Eden name is an honorable one. Oh, we've had our share of rascals through the centuries, but to the best of my knowledge we have never suffered a coward."

"I'm not a coward, Grandpapa. I simply do not believe in man killing his fellow man. I feel that–"

But even as Alex was in the process of speaking, John turned, walked away from him and interrupted him further by issuing a clear and unmistakable command.

"I think you had better leave Eden Castle, Alex. I don't simply mean at the conclusion of this visit or this evening. I think it best if you . . . not return for a while."

"Grandpapa–"

This shocked protest came from Chris, who clearly was willing to love and accept Alex on any terms.

Well, Geoffrey wasn't, and now, delighted with the banishment, he took steps to see that it would be fully carried out.

"Alex," he called out in a voice that penetrated through the hurt looks that were being exchanged between Chris and Alex. "If your country called you, which it will surely do–within the year would be my estimate–what will be your course of action?"

For several minutes there was no response from the stairs. John had turned back, apparently interested in this all-important response.

"Well?" Geoffrey demanded.

At last Alex lifted his head, tightened his grip on Anne and said without hesitation, without apology, "I would not respond. I would work with all my energy and spirit to persuade others not to respond either. Because if countries fail to produce armies, there will be no war and the munitions makers and the arms dealers and the professional soldiers will have to look elsewhere for their sport and profit."

Ah, good. Geoffrey could not have hoped for a more appropriate response. Now he tried to conceal his pleasure as John Murrey Eden issued a final and angry order.

"Get out!" he commanded. "Both of you. Geoffrey was right. There is the clear stench of cowardice in this honorable Great Hall."

"Grandpapa, please let me–"

"No, nothing more from you. Just take your wife and get out."

"Might I stay long enough to say goodbye to my father?"

"I'll say it for you.

At last Geoffrey saw the two on the stairs start slowly back down, hand in hand.

They stopped at the cloakroom to retrieve their coats.

"Alex–"

It was Chris, suffering one last pang of separation. As he started forward to exchange a few final words with Alex, John physically intercepted him and forcibly turned him back.

Then Alex and Anne were gone, the doors closing heavily behind them.

Geoffrey felt no need for words. His vindication was sweet. He had finally driven old John Murrey Eden into exiling one of his beloved grandsons. He could not describe how extremely pleasant it was to look up at someone else who also was in pain.

Exeter
May 5, 1914

Alex arrived at his father-in-law's house at precisely eight-thirty, not knowing what to expect. The message had been sent through Anne of a special meeting that was to take place tonight in Mason's front parlor.

"Alex," Lucy smiled as she opened the door and stood back. "Please come in. Mason and the others are in the parlor."

Alex handed her his cap and jacket. The short walk from the cottage that he and Anne shared at the far end of Greenfield Common had felt good.

Alex was enjoying immensely his life at Greenfield. In fact, he could not conceive of himself wanting anything more out of life, except perhaps to be welcomed back into the good graces of his grandfather and Eden Castle. But even his father had advised him not to take it all so seriously. John Murrey Eden would realize the error of his ways and come around.

"Are you feeling alright?" Lucy chided, apparently seeing the faraway look on his face.

"I'm sorry, yes, of course."

"Then come, and I'll show you where they are."

As he followed Lucy down the hall, it made him smile to think of her as his mother-in-law. She seemed more like a sister. Countless times a day she could be seen hurrying to visit Anne. The two women had grown closer, adding to this harmonious world in which Alex was fortunate enough to find himself.

As Lucy pushed open the parlor door, Alex saw Mason standing before the fireplace. There were about half a dozen men seated about the room, and all looked up as Alex entered.

"Ah, here he is. Come, Alex. Come on in. I want you to meet these gentlemen."

As Lucy closed the door behind him, Alex found himself facing six men, all of whom were strangers, except for Dr. Maclean, who taught Greek and Latin to the upper forms at Greenfield.

To the gentlemen Mason smiled, "I'm very happy and proud to present to you my son-in-law, Alexander Eden, a young man for whom I can vouch as though he were my own son, for I have had a small hand in the molding of his mind."

Alex took his place beside Mason before the fire.

"Alex, first I would like you to meet Reverend Varney, Reverend Robinson Varney, who is pastor of the Baptist church in Exeter."

Alex extended his hand to the tall, distinguished-looking gentleman soberly dressed in a black suit. He was quite thin, middle-aged, a beginning of gray in his hair–midforties was Alex's guess.

"And this is Alfred Weeks," Mason went on. "Mr Weeks is the librarian at Exeter Hall."

Again Alex acknowledged the gentleman, a grandfatherly appearing man with receding hair and great horn-rimmed spectacles which caused his eyes to appear quite large.

"And this is Tobias Rutland of Rutland House."

Alex recognized the name as being that of the local landed gentry, a young aristocrat if he had ever seen one, pale face, quite pale blue eyes, the fairest of skin, the helplessness of the youngest son etched on his face. Apparently there was no part at all in this world for the youngest son of the aristocracy. Nothing to do but ride to hounds, dance away the evenings and try for the sake of the family to stay out of serious mischief.

On the opposite side of the parlor sat three more gentlemen and quickly Mason called the roll. "This is Mr. Oliver Crowne, proprietor of The Crown and Horn just outside Exeter. And may I introduce his son-in-law, Mr. Clive Collier, and last of all Father Joseph Butler, a Jesuit priest who has kindly agreed to join our ranks and lead us forward. Please, Father Joseph, the floor is all yours."

At the invitation, Mason yielded the focal point of the room to the priest, who stood up immediately and took a position before the fireplace.

"Gentlemen," he began, "Mr. Frye has kindly invited me here tonight for one purpose, and that is to form, with your help, the Exeter chapter of the War Resisters League."

Alex heard the words for the first time. Remarkable words. An organization bearing the name of his most deeply felt conviction. The War Resisters League.

"We are a small minority, as you can well imagine, in this beloved country of ours, which now is suffering from the most dreadful illness imaginable, an illness of spirit, purpose and intent. And yet, as long as one of us has a voice with which to raise a protest to this madness, I swear to God that it is our sacred duty to do so."

Alex noticed each man listening intently to Father Butler.

"Now, our calling," Father Butler went on, "is a difficult one. I must stress to all of you that we cannot represent any singular religion. I deeply regret my garb for this is not merely a Catholic cause. This is a humanitarian cause, a universal cause, a plea for all men to come to their senses, to reject the chaos and destruction that is beginning to surround us and to return to that God-given state of peace and harmony and unity in which the Divinity clearly intended His children to live."

Now as the group started to speak together, Alex felt his own spirit soar. It was a miracle. He was no longer alone in his hatred of war, no longer alone in his apprehension of what a massive armed conflict could do to the world, no longer alone in his deep desire to practice those terribly important lessons first taught to him in the heat and red dust of Alabama by Henderson Jones.

"And the most important aspect of our ministry," Father Butler was saying now, "and make no mistake, we all from this moment on are ministers of peace, and our goal is to instruct anyone who cares to listen in the strategies of nonviolence, in the challenges and benefits of working with those who disagree with us. You must be warned, and you must all fully understand, that frequently this will mean that we are the recipients of abuse–physical, mental and emotional. And I want you to know this so that before you accept this challenge, you will also accept the hazards and the liabilities of loving peace in a world primed for war."

Alex saw a brief moment of self-examination on each face. Then they were talking again, each wanting to know what their specific roles would be and when they could get started and what precisely they were to do.

As Father Butler began to answer each of their questions, Alex saw Mason come up alongside him. "What do you think?" he asked softly.

"I think it's a marvelous idea," Alex smiled. "Why didn't you tell me earlier?"

"I wasn't certain anyone would come," Mason confessed. "And yet, just look. Six. I predict that at the next meeting we will double our numbers."

"Then we aren't wrong after all."

"No," Mason said, "but being right does not guarantee us an easy campaign. I have never in my life seen such widespread war fever."

"Eden," Alex said and let the word stand by itself.

"Yes," Mason said and moved closer. "If word of this organization reaches John and Geoffrey, I'm quite certain that neither of us will be able to go back again. I want you to think on that. It's your home."

Alex did think for a moment, saw the men before him eagerly talking, preparations being planned, public meetings in the market square, street corner ministries, an evangelistic tone reminiscent of Henderson and his family.

"*This* is my home," Alex said.

"You there, Alex," Father Butler called out. "What can we put you down for?"

"Anything you need, Father," Alex replied with eager enthusiasm.

With that, he left Mason's side and joined the others all talking excitedly, men whom he had not met before but with whom he shared the same philosophy embraced centuries ago by the carpenter of Nazareth, that love was always better than hate, that peace was better than war.

London
August 15, 1914

Three days after the declaration of war, Albert was walking home from the Drury Lane Theater and saw a man posting a recruiting notice:

YOUR KING AND COUNTRY NEED YOU

A CALL TO ARMS

For some reason it appealed greatly to his macabre sense of humor, and so after the man had moved on to the next lamppost and before a crowd of curious onlookers had gathered, Albert quickly reached up and removed the poster, hurriedly rolled it up, tucked it inside his vest and walked rapidly away.

Safe inside the flat he shared with Alice, Albert unfolded the poster, propped it up in front of the tea table and sat back on the sofa and studied it with Alice at his side.

"Mad," Albert brooded. "Sheer madness."

"Perhaps, but–"

"No buts about it, Alice. Young men are swarming to the recruiting offices like lemmings to the sea."

"Still–"

She broke off to sip her tea. Albert looked sideways at her and wondered what in the hell was the matter with her. She seemed so nervous, so fidgety, both qualities so unlike Alice.

"My dearest," he murmured, "what *is* the matter? You look as if–"

"Nothing is the matter. I'm just not certain we should be making fun of such a tragic–"

"For God's sake, I'm not making fun," Albert protested heatedly.

"Quite the contrary. I think it is terribly regretful, and doubly so because I'm not convinced that war is truly necessary."

Still Alice brooded next to him on the sofa. Something was bothering her. He knew her too well, loved her too well, cared for her too deeply, the sweetest of sisters who had rescued him from himself and the condemnation of his family and who loved him unreservedly.

"My darling," he said now, trying to make his tone thoughtful. "Did things not go well at the hospital today?"

"Things went very well," she snapped as if by rote.

"Did Charlotte ever come around?" He knew that she had been trying to reach Charlotte for days. The two cousins had grown very close.

Now Alice left the sofa and moved closer to the hideous poster as though wanting to see it close at hand. "Charlotte sent her maid around for me in the carriage. I was at Belgravia earlier for tea."

"Lucky you," Albert smiled. "And I take it that all goes well in paradise?"

"Oh, very well. Dhari is the most beautiful child I think I have ever seen. And Aslam simply dotes on her."

"Are they going to stay put for a while in London? Or is it back to Switzerland or off to France for them?"

Alice shrugged. "Aslam says that Charlotte and Dhari would be safer in Switzerland. But he says he must be here, at least for a while to look after some business concerns and–"

" 'Whither thou goest,' " Albert quoted with a knowing smile.

"Yes," Alice nodded. Then she said the most peculiar thing. "I envy them sometimes."

"How do you mean, you envy them?"

"Oh, it's obvious, isn't it? I don't think I've ever seen two people so deeply, so hopelessly in love with each other. It has been years now, hasn't it, and nothing for them ever seems to pale, nothing goes flat, nothing in their love loses its luster, everything only grows stronger, clearer and brighter."

"Do I sense loneliness?"

"Perhaps. Aren't you lonely sometimes? More accurately, however, I sense no purpose, no meaning in my life."

Indignantly Albert sat up on the edge of the sofa. "How in the hell can you say that? You practically run one of the largest, most efficient hospitals in London."

"A job I've held since I was twenty-five. Where is the challenge in that?

And I'm at the top of my field. I can go no further. Yet I'm not middle-aged. I have the bulk of my life yet ahead of me, and I can look forward to doing the same thing day in and day out.

Albert listened closely, trying to hear what she was not saying as well as what she was saying. She paced restlessly now before the recruiting poster and bent over to read the fine print below the bold call to arms:

> An addition of 10,000 men to his Majesty's Regular Army is immediately necessary in the present grave National Emergency.
>
> Lord Kitchener is confident that this appeal will be at once responded to by all who have the safety of our beloved Empire at heart.

She ceased reading, though she continued to stare at the words. "I take it you doubt the gravity of the national emergency?" she asked quietly.

"I don't know. I just somehow think that it is in bad taste for men to start blowing each others' heads off because of something that Lord Kitchener says."

"He's secretary of war."

"He's a jackass."

Still Albert watched her closely. Something *was* wrong, of that he was certain. "Alice, what–"

"It's going crazy out there, you know," she said softly and moved past the recruiting poster to a position in front of the big bay that gave a view of the street below.

"Men are rushing to join," she said as though that was a point in her favor.

"Of course they are. The Propaganda Bureau has made it sound as appealing as an afternoon at Wimbledon.

"I heard someone in the hospital say they probably wouldn't even have to conscript."

"I doubt it. Any voice raised in protest will soon be drowned by the general enthusiasm."

"Charlotte has received a letter from Lucy," Alice said. "She wrote that young Alex had certain strong pacifist views and that Geoffrey and Papa in a rage had asked him to leave Eden Castle."

Albert swallowed the last of his tea, cold and bitter now, like this latest news. "What in the hell right have they to–"

"Oh, come on, Albert. Papa got rid of us. You should know by now that our father is constitutionally incapable of coexisting with anyone who disagrees with him."

"But Alex is far too young to be–"

"He's almost eighteen."

"I thought he was about six," Albert said weakly.

"He was. Twelve years ago."

"Has Christopher been exiled as well?"

"Oh no. Apparently he and Geoffrey have become the greatest of friends."

"And poor Alex?"

"Lives at Greenfield with his new bride, Anne."

Yes, that was old news. Albert could well remember the glowing reports of the "sweetest wedding," and he really didn't want to hear about it all over again.

"Albert–"

He looked up as Alice spoke his name and saw her staring at him with alarming intensity. "I have something I must tell you."

"I thought as much. Come, sit, let Father Albert hear your confession."

She smiled, the first time all evening, and sat comfortably close beside him.

"Here, let me warm you," he offered and put his arm around her, and for several delicious moments only peace reigned in their comfortable flat, a good sense of harmony, compatible black sheep perhaps meant by nature to look after each other. In fact, at times Albert was convinced that the only anchor he ever needed in his life was Alice.

"I have heard such awful things at the hospital, Albert," she murmured now.

"Such as–"

"Stories of German atrocities in Belgium, enemy soldiers who had cut off the breasts of nurses, corpses of slain French soldiers being rendered down in the Kaiser's laboratory for fat and tallow–"

She shuddered, and he tightened his grip on her, wishing that she wouldn't focus on such horror.

"Outside the hospital tonight there were three women with boxes of white feathers. I watched them from inside the hospital door for ever so long. They would stop any young men who passed by, and they would ask them if they were on their way to the recruitment office. If they were not, they pinned a white feather on their jacket."

In a curious way, Albert was very pleased that she was aware of the madness, the increasing war fever, which threatened to infect all of this normally placid and courteous little island.

He, too, was more than aware of it, hence his bringing home the recruiting poster. "Listen to this," he invited and reached for the *Times* on the far end of the sofa.

He opened the second page, found immediately what he was looking for and read, "And further we advise all our readers to refuse to be served by an Austrian or German waiter. If your waiter says he is Swiss, ask to see his passport."

Albert hurled the paper back toward the end of the sofa, newly outraged at the stupid suggestion, terribly afraid that most of the readers would do exactly as the newspaper had suggested.

"Property owned by foreigners will not be safe, you know," he brooded. "And the madness will not be aimed just at Germans. Mark my word. Russians, Jews, particularly Jews, Swiss and even Chinese will rue the day this bloody conflict was born."

"But what if they all are right?" Alice asked and sat up on the edge of the sofa, moving away from the warmth of his arm.

"What if who is right?"

"That," she said and pointed toward the recruiting poster. "What if Lord Kitchener–"

"Alice, are you out of your mind? That's what we have been talking about, isn't it? War propaganda? The dangers involved in–"

Abruptly she stood up, her agitation almost too much to bear. He stood beside her now, concerned and still quite baffled by her behavior. "You were about to tell me something," he reminded her, "a confession I believe."

"Wait here," she smiled. "I will be right back."

With that she disappeared into her sitting room and closed the door behind her.

He paced back and forth before the sofa and mulled over all that she had told him. Another Eden exiled. Young Alex age eighteen? It wasn't possible. Apparently old Eden Castle was in as much a turmoil as ever. What else could one expect with mad Geoffrey and John Murrey Eden running the show now.

The thought of his father was a sobering one. Albert tried not to think of him very often, but when he did, it always gave him pause. He stopped pacing now, as though halted by a blow, and looked down onto the street. The traffic was already clearing in the early evening dusk, shopkeepers in shirtsleeves were sweeping the debris from the day out of their walkways, women were lovingly watering red geraniums and white daisies in flower boxes.

This was the world on the brink of a grave national emergency? Albert smiled, reassured by the life below him. Let madmen like his father go and fight their battles elsewhere, preferably far away from all English soil. This island kingdom was not a world designed for blood, pain and conflict.

"Albert?"

At first Albert wasn't certain he had even heard her voice, so shy and apologetic it was.

Then he turned. And gaped. The protest started deep in the pit of his stomach, and all he was capable of saying was "No!" shouting it, more accurately, at this woman standing before him, dressed now in the dark blue woolen uniform of an army nurse.

"No!" he repeated and within the instant saw her, his beloved Alice, so necessary to the order of his life, dead on some ridiculous battlefield.

"Albert, don't, please," Alice begged.

"Why did you–" He tried to pose the question but was cut short by the amazement and embarrassment of the sensation of tears. He had not cried openly since the death of old Yorrick Harp.

She took out her handkerchief and wiped at his eyes as though he were a child. "I felt it was right," was all she could say in her own defense.

"Well, it wasn't right. I need you. What am I supposed to do?"

"I will be back."

"And how will I–"

"You will do very well, Albert. You are a grown man."

"I will miss you so much. And I will worry myself to death."

"And I will miss you. But if I can be of help to even one soldier, then I must go."

And at last he drew her close into his embrace, felt the rough woolen texture of her heavy cloak and could already smell blood and death on it.

Eden Castle
September 21, 1914

"But why can't I go?" Chris demanded angrily of his family, which now appeared to be sitting around the Great Hall like judges, intent only on blocking him from his heart's desire.

"Please sit down, Chris," his father requested. "I'm not absolutely certain that shouting is required or desirable."

Chris started to debate that point, but he glanced toward Geoffrey and changed his mind. Without words, a communication had been sent. Geoffrey seemed to be suggesting patience and courtesy.

Now slowly, still somewhat stunned by the opposition from this unexpected quarter, Chris took a seat near Geoffrey and his grandfather, clearly aligning himself with the two who shared his enthusiasm as well as his point of view.

In doing so, he realized that he had divided the company straight down the middle, for opposite him sat his mother, a terribly worried look on her face, and behind her stood his father, Susan and old Aunt Eleanor. Uncle Stephen was busy overseeing the tenants' harvest or he would have been there as well. Since Alex had been sent away, Uncle Stephen had kept strangely quiet on all matters relating to the war.

There were those who said that the war would be over in a matter of months. If that was to be the case, then Chris would have to hurry if he wanted to be a part of it. No one in this whole company except Geoffrey understood his hunger to wear the British uniform, to train under the Union Jack, to experience the camaraderie of British troop life, to be given the chance to honorably acquit himself and his family on the field of battle in defense of his country. Was there any greater goal or desire in the heart of a man? Why, then, were his parents denying him the very opportunity he had spent his life waiting for.

He sat impatiently in the grim silence with his head down, trying to contain both his anger and his disappointment. Just when he thought that no one would ever speak on his behalf, Grandpapa did.

"What the young boy desires is only natural, I'm sure you understand that," he began in his most subdued yet authoritative voice.

Predictably Chris's mother spoke up. "No, we don't understand it, John. You were never faced with the horror of sending your sons into battle."

"I assure you, dear Marjorie, that had the opportunity presented itself, I would have done so with eagerness and honor."

"Easily said," Marjorie countered.

"No, I *mean* it," John snapped, the subdued quality of his voice replaced with anger. "Believe me, nothing in this world is more important to a man than his sense of honor, of measuring up when the call comes, of being accountable in all ways and fulfilling the destiny of his manhood as well as the honor of a family name."

Suddenly Aunt Susan was on her feet in direct confrontation with Grandpapa. "Honor!" she said and her tone was one of clear contempt. "Honor!" she repeated. "I cannot tell you how sick to death I am of that empty word."

Everyone in the Great Hall seemed to suffer the shock of what she had said.

"Please," she said in a softer tone, "let's have no more talk of what is and what isn't the honorable thing to do. In the past it has led this family into deep grief and deeper loss. Let us–"

"Spoken like a true woman," Grandpapa said.

"And what is that supposed to mean?" Aunt Susan persisted.

Grandpapa smiled warmly. "It simply means that the word 'honor' holds little or no meaning to a woman. Why should it? Women are not required to confront the enemy. Women are not required to go that final step beyond the end of courage. Women are not required to acquit themselves under fire. Women are not required by nature to fully understand or comprehend the meaning of the word 'honor.' "

At the end of Grandpapa's good speech, no one moved in the Great Hall. At last, Aunt Susan looked at Grandpapa with a curious expression, as though she partly pitied him and partly despised him.

"Sometimes you do amaze me, John. I did not think it possible for such a bright man to display such depths of denseness and insensitivity. A woman knows fields of battle that are well beyond the scope of your comprehension. This is not a battle of the sexes."

"Then what is it if not a–"

"It is about the lives of these boys. It is about the future of this family. It is about the stupidity of the wanton killing that is taking place now all in the name of nationalistic fervor and adolescent patriotism."

Chris was certain he had never seen his aunt so angry. He was equally certain she had never been so wrong.

"No, Aunt Susan," he said at last, no longer able to sit still and let Grandpapa do his fighting for him. "I'm afraid you have no conception of what I'm feeling. I want in the worst way to serve my country. Is that so wrong? I want to see everything that Geoffrey has told me about."

"But don't you see, Chris?" she now pleaded, coming up beside him as though her words were meant for him alone. "That is just my point. You are making this most serious decision based on the romantic tales of someone else."

Geoffrey was stunned. "There is nothing romantic on a field of battle."

"I'm quite certain," she agreed. "The romance clings to it in the telling, when one conveniently overlooks the pain, the violent deaths, the stench, the waste–"

"Oh, for God's sake, enough!" shouted John. "Women's drivel again. Leave the boy alone. Do you want to turn him into an effeminate sodomite as you did your own son?"

Then Chris was lost. He had no idea what they were arguing about now, no idea why Aunt Susan looked as if someone had struck her in the face.

Chris thought she would speak again, but she did not. At last she turned away, and Chris was certain he had seen tears in her eyes, saw his mother go to Susan's side, saw Aunt Susan wave her away as she went slowly up the Great Hall stairs.

Then his mother took the floor, her voice as cold and unbending as Chris had ever heard it. "I will not engage in verbal warfare with my son present. All that needs to be fully understood by everyone here is that Chris cannot sign any paper of commitment without my signature and that of his father. And I want it clearly understood by everyone present that neither myself nor Frederick will give either our signature or permission."

"Mother, you have no right."

"Oh, but you're wrong. I have every right, as does your father. And I want no more talk. This subject is closed. You have your studies to attend to, and Mr. Neville tells me you have been distracted of late. I want you to concentrate on preparing for your upper levels, and I want all other influences inside the castle to recede. Is that clear?"

Never had Chris been so humiliated.

"Mother, I am eighteen years old. I have a right to–"

Then his father took over. "You have only one obligation," he said, in his Old Testament voice, which seemed to thunder endlessly about the cavernous Great Hall, "and that is to obey and respect your mother and her wishes. Do you understand?"

Chris was no match for his father when he was angry. He had seen him angry so seldom in his life that the sight of it now was startling.

At last he turned away and went back to the fire to await further orders.

There were none forthcoming, only an angry silence that filled the Great Hall, followed by the sound of rapidly departing footsteps. When he looked back a few moments later, only two remained, his favorite two in the whole world.

"It will be alright, Chris, my boy," Grandpapa soothed.

"They don't know, they can't understand," Geoffrey commiserated.

Then the three of them came effortlessly together before the fire, Grandpapa on one side, Geoffrey on the other.

"Calm down, Chris," Grandpapa urged. "You must believe me when I tell you that your day will come."

"But the war will be over," Chris complained. "A matter of months is what everyone is saying."

"Well, between you and me, I think everyone is wrong. Learn to be patient. All things come to the man who is patient."

"He is right, Chris, listen to your grandfather. He is a most remarkable man."

"Thank you, Geoffrey. Come," he motioned to Chris now. "Come, sit with us. To hell with Mr. Neville. Geoffrey and I will be your tutors. Let us teach you all you will need to know of manhood and honor. Pay no attention to what anyone else might say. That word, that single small word, is perhaps the most important one in the entire English language. It is precisely what enables a man to live comfortably inside his own skin, to confront himself every morning in the looking glass, to close his eyes and be at peace with his soul and his Maker each night. Honor, Chris, honor. Never forget it, never forget what it means and what it demands of you."

"I won't, Grandpapa."

He took a chair close to Geoffrey's right side, settled back and crossed his legs just as Grandpapa had done and stared into the flames, seeing a magnificent field of battle, seeing himself on a snow-white charger, saber raised, leading a regiment of valiant and noble men into the sunrise of victory.

Neuve-Chapelle, France
March 17, 1915

Alice took pride in the fact that in all these many months she had not yet shed a tear, though many of her nurses had suffered complete breakdowns when confronted with the carnage of continuous battle. Still she had been strong, though she was certain that she had never been so cold in her life.

Now she stood just inside the tent opening of the hospital unit and looked out on a scene reminiscent of Dante's Hell. For one thing there was mud as far as she could see, and the mud nearby was stained with the blood of newly arriving casualties.

Behind her, inside the makeshift surgery, she heard mass confusion. The trouble was not enough beds, not enough medical personnel and, worst of all, not enough medicines.

"Lieutenant Eden," someone shouted far behind. "We need–"

"Leave her alone," someone countered. "She's been on forty-eight hours. I sent her out for a breath and a cup of tea."

Alice closed her eyes and shivered. Strange, but why should Colonel Chance's kindness weaken her so? But it did, and she clung for a moment to the rough-hewn pine standard that supported the front of the hospital unit, and considered returning immediately to the ward. She was desperately needed there, no doubt. That she was capable of functioning efficiently in her present state of fatigue, hunger and cold there was considerable doubt.

"Alice, over there. Go to the mess tent and at least have some food and a hot cup of tea. We'll need you back here as soon as possible."

She felt hands on her shoulders, looked into Colonel Chance's good strong face and saw fatigue there as well.

"Here, take my muffler and go."

Gently he wrapped his wool muffler about her neck and pointed her toward the mess tent about fifty yards down the muddy road. "Take your time quickly," he called after her.

She waved without looking and concentrated on the treacherous terrain underfoot, the mudholes and the gullies in which only yesterday one of her young orderlies had found a human leg, still clad in the uniform of a British soldier. Now she walked very carefully, not wanting to repeat the grisly discovery of yesterday.

Ahead through the early dusk of late afternoon she saw what was left of the tiny village of Neuve-Chapelle.

Not much. They had been here over a week, and all the ground won in the three-day battle had been won in the first three hours.

The enemy's artillery, none of which had been captured, knew every inch of the ground which they had momentarily lost. Consequently every hour's delay lessened the difference between the opposing forces.

As far as Alice could tell, the French and British were in possession of the small village, populated mainly by about twelve hundred German prisoners. Where the French natives had gone, she had no idea.

As she trudged carefully down the muddy road toward the mess, she heard the sudden blaring horn of an army ambulance.

"Would you like to move over, your highness?" the driver shouted down.

Quickly she stepped to one side and let the vehicle pass her by. She continued to stand in what had now become a steady downpour to see where the ambulance was headed. Pray God not to the hospital. There was no room.

On the other hand, if it turned into the road which led to the morgue, that meant more dead, more letters to be written to families with unpronounceable names, more grief.

At the muddy intersection the truck paused as though not certain itself which way it was to go. Then Alice heard the engine cough twice and die, heard the unproductive rattle as the driver tried to get it going again. But no luck. The ambulance was stalled, the rear tires sinking fast into bottomless mudholes, the entire vehicle resting at a dangerous angle now.

Alice had just started back toward the mess tent, convinced that it was none of her concern, when suddenly she saw the driver jump down, heard him cursing and saw him wave toward a group of soldiers.

"Over here," the driver shouted. "I need your backs for some dead Huns. Hurry along. Then I will happily send you off to kill some more."

At first the soldiers, about a dozen in all, looked baffled, as though not absolutely certain they should obey the ambulance driver.

But then she saw Colonel Chance step out from the surgery with a shout at the men that left no room for debate.

One soldier was chosen to hold their weapons and the remaining men hurried toward the back of the tilting truck. As they arrived, the ambulance driver threw back the heavy canvas flaps and revealed the grim and grisly cargo.

Bodies were stacked as high as the roof of the truck, a hideous tangle of arms, legs, blood and torn white flesh.

Alice turned quickly away. It was her job to look upon British suffering. She doubted seriously if she had the capacity to look upon German as well.

Then she heard, "Lieutenant Eden, over here. There's life–"

At the sound of Colonel Chance's voice, she looked back toward the ambulance and saw that two separate arrangements of bodies were being made, the larger line clearly that of the dead, the smaller line apparently that of the half-dead.

"Come on, take a quick look," he ordered further. "See if there is anything we can do."

"Coming, sir," she called back. As she drew near, Colonel Chance went into the surgery tent as though certain he had left affairs in capable hands.

Now, as she approached the back of the truck, the ambulance driver, who was helping the soldiers remove the bodies, scowled at her. "If you lift so much as a finger to help them bloody Huns, you deserve to be shot as a traitor."

For a moment she was impressed with the depth of hate in his voice. "Stand back, Sergeant," she ordered, summoning all the authority at her command to counteract the feisty little bantam rooster who appeared to be daring her to perform her task.

When he did not move, she repeated, "Stand back, I said," and this time she shouted it at him, suddenly loathing his red hair and his arrogant freckled face. How he must have hungered for this war, any war in which he could strut about like the rooster that he was.

At last he backed away, showering her with obscenities as he went. But she had heard them all before, and for now her attention was focused on the six German soldiers who had been placed in the mud to the right of the ambulance truck, the driving rain pelting their poor bloodied faces.

"Are you really gonna doctor them bastards?" one of the soldiers called out.

"I'm going to try."

"What's the point? We'll just kill 'em next time around."

As Alice approached the first soldier, she bent over and saw torn and jagged flesh in the area of his left shoulder and neck. He looked straight at her, his eyes pleading, his lips moving uselessly, no words being formed.

Too late. Of that she was certain. He'd lost too much blood. The pallor on his face spoke for that, the chalky whiteness that immediately precedes death. Only a matter of minutes until–

Now she hurried to the next soldier, refusing to look upon death at the moment it descended. For the second soldier, death had already blessedly arrived, and the jagged stumps that now were his right and left arms protruded crazily upward at a distorted angle, as though he were pleading with someone to lift him up like an infant.

Blessedly the third suffered only superficial wounds. He would survive to fight and die again. She looked toward the surgery hoping to catch sight of some orderlies who might come and carry him into the safety of the hospital itself.

But there was no one in sight.

"Easy, soldier," she whispered to the German. "You will be alright." She was certain that he could not understand English, but she could not speak German. Somehow the half smile on his face suggested that perhaps he had understood, if not her words, at least her tone of voice.

Then she moved on to number four. Dead. And number five. Dead. And number six–

She paused, stepped over his lifeless legs, and looked down on him and thought, Number six–dead. A good half of his skull was missing, the gray matter of his brain spilling out onto the mud.

Then miraculously he moved, one hand lifted. Astonished, Alice stepped back, the better to see him–but she saw too much, saw his face, saw very familiar blue eyes, saw the blond hair now blood-matted.

Within the instant she fell on her knees beside him, still not certain, praying, "No, please God," praying, "Let him be dead," praying constantly, trembling, and saw his lips moving and heard him speak her name, merely a whisper, a last-breath whisper.

"Alice . . ."

It was Rolf. She had known it when she had first seen him, some element of recognition dawning, despite the dreadful damage done to his head.

"Rolf," she murmured and bent closer in examination of his wounds and wondered why in the name of God he was still alive.

"Orderly!" she screamed. "Orderly! Where are you?" she screamed again and felt Rolf's hand tighten on hers as though to summon her attention, and she looked down on him and saw the handsome young man who had flawlessly quoted John Milton to her in the smoky tea shop of drafty old Victoria Station.

"Rolf, please," she begged, "stay with me until–"

"A–Ali–"

He tried to speak her name a final time and couldn't. His head rolled to one side in the mud, his eyes became fixed in their sockets and his grip seemed to tighten on her hand as though he wanted her to come with him.

"Well, look at that! Ain't that the sweetest? Sweethearts! Would you believe it?"

Someplace behind her she heard the cackling giggle of the preening little bantam rooster.

"You want to kiss him goodbye, sweetie? You want to crawl in his pants with him? You have a preference for bloody Huns?"

As the filth spilled down on her, she felt the beginning of tears, the first she had shed in this hideous war, felt them hot and burning. She lifted Rolf's hand to her face, pressed it against her cheek and wept.

"What's going on?"

She heard the voice, recognized it as Colonel Chance's and could not respond.

"Lieutenant Eden! Look at me. What has–"

At last she looked up, sobbing. This man, this soldier," she wept. "He is not German. He is English."

Colonel Chance looked about, bewildered. "I don't understand. If he is English, what is he doing in a German uniform?"

"I don't know," Alice sobbed and placed her head on Rolf's chest, lifted him to her and held him close. "I don't know, I don't know," she wept and repeated the words over and over again, vaguely aware of all of the soldiers staring down on her, aware of the spectacle she was making of herself, though she could do nothing to alter it in any way.

All she could do was cling to Rolf Reicher's hand and weep as she had never wept before, sobbing over and over and over again, "I–don't know, I don't know, I–don't–know . . ."

Eden Castle
June 16, 1915

Susan could not get over how quiet breakfasts were now. This Grand Dining Hall that had seen lavish banquets for hundreds of guests was now set daily for two. Herself and Eleanor.

On occasion when Frederick and Marjorie were up from the parsonage in Mortemouth, they would take breakfast in here with Susan and Eleanor; and Stephen, on occasion, ate with them, but generally he preferred to eat early down in the kitchen hall so that he could be out in the fields with the tenants by daybreak.

For the rest of them—John, Geoffrey and young Chris—they had given the servants strict orders that all of their meals were to be served in the small library.

Poor old Richard was the only one welcomed in both camps, and now he spent most of his time shuffling back and forth across the Great Hall in his bed slippers, dependent upon two canes because of his worsening gout, reporting to one enemy camp on the other, and vice versa.

Now, as Susan poured her breakfast tea, she felt that Eden Castle resembled a battlefield, a war raging within the Great Hall as it was raging in France and Belgium. Still, peculiarly, she missed the others, missed youth, the babbling affairs that breakfast used to be when all the children were young and when she was young.

"Did you sleep well?" Eleanor asked Susan as she had asked her every morning of every day of every week for as long as Susan could remember.

"So-so," Susan replied as she had replied every morning of every day of every week for as long as Susan could remember.

"Those others were up early. Did you hear them?" Eleanor asked.

"Those others" was the label she had assigned to John, Chris and

Geoffrey. She always spoke the words with a faint air of disdain, as though they were strangers in her midst instead of quarreling family members.

"No, I'm pleased to say I did not hear them. What were they up to?"

"God alone knows. I was only half asleep, but I swear to God I heard sounds of marching."

Susan looked up. "Dearest Eleanor, I'm sure you were dreaming."

"No, I wasn't," she replied indignantly.

"Why in the world would they be marching?"

"You know as well as I. 'Those others' are preparing young Chris for the military."

"It will break poor Marjorie's heart."

"I don't think they care a whit."

Susan heard a step at the door and looked over her shoulder to see Richard shuffling into the room.

"Good morning," she called out in her cheeriest voice. Poor dear Richard. He was looking very old, and his color wasn't good, the ominous yellow tinge of a failing liver. Susan felt sorry for him and always had. He reminded her of a man in search of his proper place in this confusing world. To the best of her knowledge, he had yet to find it.

"Tea, Richard?" Eleanor called out, lifting her voice to accommodate his hearing loss.

"Yes, my dear. I have just traveled a very long way."

"Of course you have. Come and sit," Susan smiled and motioned him down into the chair next to her.

"Not a bad morning, is it, Richard?" Susan asked in an attempt to make light conversation.

"Cold. But then January always is cold."

"It's June, my dear."

Eleanor placed his tea before him, along with a slice of toast. "Now drink it while it's hot. It will warm those old bones."

For several minutes the three of them sipped and dipped, and Susan looked about, resenting the fact that she was a part of this sad tableau, and yet–

"The morning post, madame."

At the sound of Maxwell's voice, Susan looked up to see the old butler place a stack of letters and papers on the long buffet.

"Thank you, Maxwell."

As she hurried toward the buffet, she heard Richard softly chant, "No news is good news. Remember that, Susan, my girl."

"I will, Richard," she called back in a humoring tone.

At the buffet, she shuffled rapidly through the envelopes, some bills from tradesmen, a few for the servants downstairs, one for Eleanor from sweet Lucy at Greenfield, and one from–

Carefully she picked it up and lifted it free of the others, this special-looking letter, dark brown official army stationery, the postmark blurred, though the handwriting was achingly familiar–Alice.

Unless Susan missed her guess, Alice had written this from some army post in France. It had been months since Susan had heard from her, and while she had not truly been worried, it was now good to see her handwriting. Alice was so competent, so capable of looking after herself as well as a large portion of the world. The one Susan worried about constantly was her poor, helpless Albert, left on his own in London.

"From Alice," Susan smiled. "Now we all will have a good read." Quickly she broke the seal and withdrew a single sheet of stationery. This was different, most unlike Alice, who generally wrote small volumes that passed for letters.

Curious, Susan commenced reading, though with the salutation "Dearest Mama," she saw that something was wrong. This was not Alice's good firm handwriting. These squiggles and wiggles looked as if they had been printed by a frightened and exhausted child.

At first she started to read aloud then changed her mind. Something warned her against it, and her eyes scanned the first paragraph, she found the reason, the blunt, heart-wrenching announcement:

> . . . and Mama, I was attending to German wounded last week at the hospital outside Neuve-Chapelle and I knelt down beside one who was suffering from severe wounds. I was almost ready to pronounce him dead when he took my hand. I looked closer, Mama, and it was Rolf Reicher.

Reflexively Susan crushed the letter in her hands and closed her eyes. She saw the little fair-haired boy with brilliant blue eyes who had grown up at Eden Castle and enchanted everyone with his manners and sweetness.

"Susan, what is–"

Quickly she shook her head, felt anger rising and snapped at Eleanor, "In a minute, please." She felt compelled to read the hideous message to its end before punishing others with it.

Now she brushed at her eyes and read the last few paragraphs, detecting a seriously wounded Alice as well:

. . . and Mama, something is wrong with me. I cannot stop crying. I feel so silly. They have given me time off. I probably will take it, though I know I shouldn't. They are in such desperate need for all the help they can get in this place of death. But I'm no good to anyone like this. I don't know what's the matter with me. I cry when I don't want to cry. I can't stop crying even though I embarrass myself hourly, daily. I have even prayed to God for help. But He does not seem to be listening. Small wonder. There are so many others who need Him more. Still I don't know what I shall do.

I can't tell you, to see men like this. I couldn't– I must go now–
Alice

For several moments Susan stared down on the letter, as fearful as she had ever been in her life. Then Eleanor was at her side, leaning close in an attempt to offer comfort.

"My darling, what is it? Please let me help."

Susan thrust the letter at her, left her chair and walked to the far end of the Grand Dining Hall, hearing Eleanor's voice as she commenced to read the letter aloud to Richard, hearing her tears commence, then hearing nothing beyond "Rolf Reicher is dead."

In the silence, Susan sat heavily in a near chair. She closed her eyes and tried to clear her head so that she could offer up a prayer for young Rolf, for poor Sonia Reicher, for Dr. Reicher, for everyone in the castle who had loved the little boy as their own, for Alice and for herself, for this first unnecessary loss that had struck so close to the Eden family.

It was while she was at prayer that she heard Richard shuffling out of the room, leaning heavily on his canes, groaning with each step.

Pain seemed to be the order of the day, pain and grief, waste that accomplished nothing, that proved nothing.

And what of Alice? When would she come home? Should Susan go to her?

The questions, all unanswerable, drove her back into the chair, where she sat, hollow-eyed and drained, watching Eleanor weep at the far end of the table.

Chris couldn't believe it. It was the good news that he had been waiting for his entire life, now just delivered by old Maxwell, who so calmly had placed the envelope on the library table with the bland announcement "It is for you, Master Christopher, from the army, I believe."

Chris was aware of Geoffrey beaming while he ripped open the envelope and almost tore the parchment in half in his eagerness to get to its contents, his acceptance into the Royal Devon Regiment, with the rank of second lieutenant. He was to report to the recruiting office in London for his training assignment no later than August 15, 1915.

"Do I have to wait that long?" he asked his grandfather, who was lounging in one of the big bay windows, grinning his head off.

"It said no later than the fifteenth, which of course implies you can come anytime before then."

"Then I intend to leave now," Chris announced.

Grandpapa laughed. "Your parents may have something to say about that," he counseled.

Chris read the letter again and couldn't believe his good fortune. "I wish that Alex–"

Geoffrey interrupted. "I would say nothing to Alex about this if I were you. As you well know, you have chosen a different path."

Chris nodded, though a portion of his heart still ached for Alex. Of course, he wouldn't let either Geoffrey or his grandfather know that, but sometimes in his bed, he recalled the nights he had spent talking with Alex, making plans, dreaming. If only Grandpapa hadn't sent him away.

Then he heard Uncle Richard at the door. He was leaning heavily on his two canes and something was wrong. There were tears in his eyes. Grandpapa saw them as well.

"Richard? What is it? You haven't been peeling your onions again, have you?"

The old man sat heavily on a chair near the table. He withdrew a handkerchief and wiped at his face.

"Letter–" he began.

"What letter?" Grandpapa asked.

"From Alice."

Immediately Grandpapa moved away as though not wanting to hear the name. But as he reached the bay window, his curiosity got the best of him. "What about Alice?" he asked of poor Uncle Richard, who seemed scarcely able to talk.

"She wrote to Susan and informed her that the boy was dead."

Slowly Grandpapa stood and came back from the window. "What boy?" he demanded.

"The German boy. Rolf Reicher. Alice found him dead in a trench filled with mud."

Uncle Richard buried his face in his handkerchief. Chris walked slowly to the far end of the library. He wondered whether he should believe this awful news.

Rolf Reicher, dead.

"I tell you there is a ghost in the east wing—"

"There is not."

"There is so. He wears a white robe and floats through the air down the corridor."

"Rolf, are you trying to scare me?"

Chris closed his eyes and pressed his forehead against the window glass. He looked down over the headlands and tried not to see the tall, slim German dressed in white, pointing out certain fishing packets, judging their catch for the day.

"What in the hell is all this about?" came Geoffrey's voice from behind. "He *was* a German."

"He grew up here at Eden."

"Listen to me, Chris, lad," Geoffrey began, wheeling his new chair close to where Chris stood. "I want you to put all of this out of your mind. Do you hear? Rolf Reicher had been in the Fatherland for three years. I think I can assure you that his indoctrination had been complete. He would have killed you before you could have killed him. He was wearing a German uniform and he was fighting with the German forces for the German cause. I find it appalling that anyone here is wasting a moment's grief on him. Come, I say we have need of a celebration. Ring for some bottles of champagne, John. Our young warrior here is going off to battle, to bring honor to the Eden name. Don't you think this is worthy of a celebration?"

"I do," Grandpapa said at last, though Chris could tell his enthusiasm was less than Geoffrey's.

Perhaps what Geoffrey had said was true. Rolf *was* different, *was* German, and perhaps in the three years since he had been gone from Eden he had become the enemy. In which case his death meant that he could no longer slaughter British soldiers.

"Come, it's time for a toast," Geoffrey announced and wheeled himself over to the bell cord, gave it three good tugs and looked back at Uncle Richard, who still seemed incapable of stopping his tears.

"For God's sake, Father, if you want to weep, go and join the women. This is a man's gathering, a party in honor of a young Eden warrior. Either join us in the proper spirit or leave."

Uncle Richard blew his nose and put his handkerchief away.

"I'm so proud of you," Geoffrey now said to Chris.

This was all Chris needed to hear. Grandpapa was on one side, Geoffrey on the other, giving him advice on all subjects, how to behave, what to expect, who to follow, how to judge.

Chris listened politely, courteously, though all the while his mind was whirling on his dream come true.

He was going to war! At last he was going to war!

Exeter
July 18, 1915

As no one was able to drive him to the war, Chris had kissed his weeping mother goodbye and had shaken his father's unenthusiastic hand. He had waved goodbye to his beaming grandfather and wildly excited Uncle Geoffrey and had accepted a ride in the back of a farmer's wagon taking hay from Eden to Exeter.

The farmer had dropped him off at the train station an hour and a half before the six-fifteen to London. For the first few minutes he had picked hay out of his clothes and hair. Then he had a cup of tea and a sandwich at the station shop, and now he paced the waiting platform, still unable to believe his good fortune.

Only one thing was missing. Alex. Chris wanted with all his heart to see Alex again. How would it hurt? No one at Eden would ever have to know, even though Geoffrey had warned him against it. If Chris missed the six-fifteen to London, there was an eight o'clock after that. He could easily walk the three miles out to Greenfield and be back in time for one train or the other.

He stood a moment longer, then all at once scooped up his satchel and deposited it inside the stationmaster's door with the promise that he would be back in time for the six-fifteen.

A little over half an hour later he saw the black iron gates of Greenfield, saw the old red-brick school bathed in the rosy hue of dusk. It looked very beautiful, something worth dying for.

As he approached the gate, he saw a group of boys, no more than ten years old, perhaps eleven, all looking very dapper in their school blazers and matching ties.

"I say there," Chris called out cheerily. "Could any one of you tell me where I might find Alex Eden?"

"Yes, sir, just down there, at the very end. He's probably just having his tea."

"Thank you very much," he called out.

"You're welcome, sir."

Chris passed on a few steps only to hear, "Sir? A minute, if you please?"

"What is it?" Chris inquired, coming back.

"Well, sir, we were wondering, have you been in the war?"

Slowly Chris smiled and came all the way back, his hands shoved easily into his pockets, so very pleased with the response that he was about to deliver.

"I'm just on my way," he said proudly, "this very evening. Tomorrow first thing I will report to the recruitment offices in London."

Even as he spoke he saw the looks of admiration and envy on the young faces before him.

"Will you get to kill a German?" one boy asked near the rear of the group.

"I rather imagine," Chris laughed. "I certainly don't want him to kill me, do I?"

The boys laughed at his joke and seemed to be jockeying for a position nearer to the front, as though all had additional questions to ask of Chris.

"Where will you go first, sir?" one asked.

"I have no idea. I will, of course, follow all orders to the best of my ability, as you should at all times."

"Yes, sir, of course, sir, but it's all going to be over by the time we are old enough."

"I know," he nodded sympathetically. "Still, there are many ways in which all of you can be good soldiers. You can do your bit here on the home front, can't you? Ask your headmaster. I'm quite certain that he will give you more than enough ideas."

All at once the little boys seemed to turn away.

"What's the matter?" Chris asked, puzzled by their rapid change of mood from one of exuberant enthusiasm to glum dejection.

"Our headmaster is not . . . a soldier," one little boy said, and he seemed to be straining after a degree of diplomacy.

"No," Chris admitted, "I know that. But Mason Frye is–"

"A coward!"

This blunt epithet came from the rear of their ranks.

"I beg your pardon?"

"He's right," the spokesman said. "Master Frye is a coward. He has organized a chapter of the War Resisters League right here at Greenfield and–"

"I don't believe you," Chris said bluntly, truly shocked by their adolescent accusations.

"It's true, sir. If you are going to see Mr. Eden, ask him. He is a member as well."

Suddenly, off in the distance a bell was heard. The boys glanced in that direction and began to straighten their ties and jackets.

"We must go now, sir. Study hall. Good luck with killing Huns. Kill one for us."

Then they were running back across the emerald green common, their accusations rattling around inside Chris's head.

Surely they were mistaken. Little boys had been exaggerating since the beginning of time. He had certainly done plenty of it in his day, as had old Alex. Oh, the tall tales they used to tell.

Suddenly he felt a hunger to see Alex, to talk with him as they used to talk as boys. He started off across the lawn and made a diligent attempt to put everything out of his mind except how much he loved Alex and how much he was going to miss him.

Anne had just served their tea in the small front parlor when she looked out of the window and saw–

"Chris! It's Chris!" she exclaimed to a startled though very pleased Alex.

In three steps he was at the door and had flung it open while Chris was still several yards away.

Without hesitation or embarrassment, Alex opened his arms to this man he viewed as a brother. "Chris," he murmured, "what in hell are you doing here?"

At the end of the embrace, Chris stepped quickly around Alex and went straight to Anne, who was smiling at him from the stoop.

"I still can't believe that you are Alex's wife," he smiled and took her in his arms. "Why aren't you mine?"

"You never asked me," she grinned and kissed him on both cheeks.

"Come, you're just in time for tea. Hurry before we let all the fireflies in for tea as well."

Just then, Chris observed that most of the light of day had passed and the early evening was dotted with the darting light of thousands of fireflies.

"Remember how we used to catch them at Eden and put them in bottles?" Alex said and took Chris by the arm and led him into the parlor.

Anne returned with an extra teacup. Alex and Chris sat opposite each other while she poured. Alex still couldn't believe it. Then a thought occurred. "Is anything wrong at home? Is everyone–"

Hurriedly Chris nodded. "Well, quite well, though everyone is getting older. I seem to notice it in so many little ways now. Grandpapa is afraid to drive. His eyesight, you know. And Papa has something wrong with his stomach. He has to be very careful of what he eats. And, of course, poor Eleanor is perpetually complaining about something."

Abruptly he broke off and sipped his tea, and then he laughed. "This is my second cup. I had tea at the station."

Alex watched and listened closely. Chris seemed changed. He seemed unduly nervous. What was he doing at the train station in Exeter?

"More tea?" Anne offered, and Alex suspected that she had as many questions as he did.

"No, thank you," Chris said and seemed to be growing more uncomfortable by the minute.

"Chris? What is it?" Alex asked at last.

"Nothing, nothing at all. I was wondering if I might ask a favor of both of you."

"Of course, anything."

"You, Anne, please say nothing to your parents of my visit here this evening."

"Of course, Chris."

Chris's look of relief was massive. "Thank you."

"Did someone tell you not to come here?" Alex asked bluntly.

For a moment Chris looked embarrassed. Then, "Yes."

"Was it Geoffrey?"

"Yes."

Then Chris seemed to revive. He stood up from the tea table and walked the short distance to the door. "You see, I'm on my way to London."

"Whatever for?" Anne asked.

"I've joined up. I'm due at the recruitment office tomorrow morning. North Devon Regiment."

"Why?" Alex asked softly.

"Why not?" Chris countered with a force and defiance that sounded exactly like Geoffrey and Grandpapa. "I'm needed. You're needed. The Empire needs us both."

Slowly Alex stood as though to move away from a dangerous subject. "Chris, I–"

"No, say nothing else, Alex. I did not come here tonight to fight with you or to argue with you. I think you know that I love you too much for that."

"Why did you come here?"

"To say goodbye, to say . . . I am sorry, to say–"

Then suddenly Chris seemed undone by his own words or perhaps by the moment. He turned away and went straight for the door.

"Wait," Alex called out. "I'll walk with you."

Anne caught up with Chris at the door. "Please, be careful," she whispered, stood on tiptoe, kissed him and held his face for a moment between her hands. "We may disagree, Chris, but we have never ceased to love you, nor will we."

"Sweetest Anne," Chris murmured, then hurried out into the evening.

As Alex passed her by, he bent over and kissed her. "I'll be right back," he whispered.

"Don't fight with him," she begged.

It had never been his intention to fight with Chris.

A few steps across the common and he caught up with Chris, who seemed newly dejected for some reason.

"I shouldn't have come here," he said to the tips of his shoes as he walked across the common.

"Why?" Alex asked. "I can't tell you how glad I am that you did come."

"I wanted to see you."

"And I have missed you."

"What happened between us?" Chris suddenly demanded, confronting Alex.

What happened?

How in God's name could Alex ever successfully answer that? "We chose different paths, Chris, or had them chosen for us, and the miracle is that it hasn't affected our love for each other. I wish I could dissuade you from catching that train to London."

"Even you could not do that," Chris smiled. "And I, for one, think that you are wrong, terribly wrong. We should be catching that train together."

"No."

For several moments they stared at each other as though trying to focus on what was familiar in each face and ignore what was foreign.

"I must go."

"Yes."

"Take care."

"You too."

"I will."

"Goodbye."

Slowly Chris started away. He had taken no more than three steps when he stopped again, head down and whispered, "I will always love you, Alex."

"And I you."

Then he was walking again, picking up speed now, at last breaking into a run and finally disappearing into the night altogether.

For several minutes Alex stood alone in the dark, suffering the most painful feelings of loss and separation. It wasn't too late. Not yet. He could still run after him and try forcibly to bring him back.

But no, he couldn't do that any more than he would want someone to turn him away from *his* purpose, *his* conviction.

Who was right?

Who was wrong?

No answer, and in the wave of new grief that now was washing over him, right and wrong seemed so unimportant.

What truly mattered was that a large portion of his soul and heart had just walked off into the night.

London September 15, 1915

Albert had received the telegram only that morning. At first when he had seen that it was from the army, his heart had stopped. *Alice—dear God, no—*

But then he had managed to conquer his shaking hands enough to open the letter, had discovered that it was from a Colonel Chance, who was simply informing him that his sister was coming home on leave, to arrive at Victoria on the seven o'clock and that it might be advisable if a member of the family could meet her.

His pocket watch said ten till seven and Albert stood to one side of the crowded loading platform, and that one ominous line was still causing him trouble–

It might be advisable if a member of the family could meet her.

What in the hell was that supposed to mean?

No matter. From the size of the gathering crowd, one could tell that the train was due soon, and he planned to hug and kiss her warmly and then whisk her home to their flat. He had had a lovely roast chicken–not easy to come by now–plus a bottle of wine.

How he was looking forward to it, though he did have one slight dread: he sincerely hoped that she did not insist upon spending the evening telling him all about her war experiences. He had had enough of this foolish war. He could scarcely bear to walk down any street of London. He had had so many white feathers thrust at him that he could stuff his own pillow. It used to bother him, but it didn't anymore.

Now he leaned further out into the crowds and checked the clock across the way. Only a few minutes until seven. Colonel Chance had said she was home on leave, but it was Albert's full intention to spend the next few days trying, to the best of his ability, to talk her out of returning to France. She didn't belong there. She had done her bit for king and country. All Albert wanted now was to see her home.

Then he heard the distant steam whistle and saw the crowd surge forward.

Albert held his position as the enormous black steam engine rattled into view. High up, he saw the engineer looking placidly down on all lesser humanity.

Then the train rattled to a stop. All was chaos now, people running every which way, searching for specific car numbers, for a familiar face.

Walking quickly down the length of the train, Albert observed able-bodied and eager soldiers spilling out of the open doors and into the arms of loved ones.

It was a good scene. Albert had no quarrel with love, harmony and happiness, only death and sorrow.

Then he saw the last three coaches marked on the sides with enormous red crosses. Orderlies from the long line of ambulances waiting outside were now running into the station and hurrying forward, a litter between each two, a veritable parade of empty litters, though Albert knew that within moments the parade would be heading in the other direction, toward the line of ambulances, bearing a grisly cargo of wounded to various London hospitals.

Now, as Albert made his way through the crowds to a position near the Red Cross coaches, he saw the awful parade just beginning. Some of the wounded were capable of walking by themselves, their hollow eyes staring out at the crowded station.

Then came the litter cases, men lying beneath white sheets, the contours of their bodies lacking in some quarter, a leg gone, an arm, a face entirely concealed behind bandages, large red coins showing on white gauze, the smell of chloroform, and the terrible unspoken sense of unendurable pain somehow being endured.

Poor Alice. What in the world had ever possessed her to enter into this stupid war?

Still it came, the unending parade, and now what struck Albert as too macabre was how quiet it was at this end of the train. He still could hear shrieks of recognition at the front end, cries of joy and reunion, the laughter of children as long-absent fathers scooped them up into the air, the lovely din of human voices raised in happiness and thanksgiving.

But Albert was at the rear of the train, and here no one spoke, no one smiled, certainly no one laughed, no one even cried, as though they all were well beyond the comfort of tears.

Then he saw four nurses step down from the train and walk smartly after the caravan of the wounded, their heavy woolen cloaks billowing out with a certain dramatic flair in the drafty old train station.

He looked back at the doors of the train and saw them empty. Alice? Where was–

Then all at once, another nurse appeared, quite tall she was and clearly interested in finding someone. Albert watched her for a moment until at last her searching eyes fell on him.

"Would you by any chance be Mr. Albert Eden?"

"Guilty," Albert joked and stepped forward to the door of the train. "I have come to meet my sister, Alice. Please don't tell me she missed the train. If so, I'll never forgive her."

All the time he talked, he thought he noticed a changing expression on the nurse's face.

"My name is Beth," she said and extended a businesslike hand to him. "Alice and I went to France together from St. Martin's, and yes, she is on the train. I think . . . she needs you. Please follow me."

Suddenly Albert shivered. Damn cold, this old station, and there was something about the nurse's tone of voice. Still, he followed after, ducking his head as he stepped up through the low door that led into the train.

The first thing he saw in the vestibule was a pile of bloodied and discarded bandages, some more red than white, fresh red, red that still glistened. And the stench! Quickly he put his hand over his nose and peered the length of the coach to see where the nurse named Beth was leading him.

At last he saw his beloved Alice, sitting at the far end of the coach, just sitting there, looking quite prim and quite lost.

"Here, sir," Beth signaled to him. "Here she is. I think–"

But Albert didn't hear what the nurse thought, concentrating as he was on Alice, on her face, on the hideous vacancy there, the eyes lost in dark hollows, the hands, once so capable, now folded uselessly in her lap.

"Alice?" he whispered, knelt down beside her, touched those folded hands and found them to be as cold as winter.

"Alice, it's me, Albert. I have come to–"

Abruptly he stopped speaking. Something in her eyes, in her unresponsive eyes, informed him she wasn't hearing anything he was saying.

"What happened?" he asked of Beth, who still stood over him.

"She . . . was nursing German wounded and found someone she knew."

"Who?"

Beth closed her eyes as though searching her memory. "Reicher I believe was his name–Rolf Reicher, yes, that was it. For several weeks all she did was cry. And a few weeks ago, she stopped weeping, but–"

Beth broke off speaking. There was no need to finish. Albert could see for himself.

Oh dear God. Gently he leaned forward and kissed Alice's cold hands, enclosed them in his own and tried to warm them.

"Colonel Chance says he thinks she will be alright, but she needs . . . attending to, needs to feel secure again, loved–you know, cared for."

Albert knew. He brushed quickly at his eyes. Alright then, for once in his life, here was someone who needed him, someone to take care of.

"Come along, old girl," he whispered, stood beside her, put her arm around his shoulder and gently helped her to stand.

She went without protest, susceptible to any suggestion.

"Come along," Albert urged gently and guided her along the narrow passageway, past the mountain of bloodred bandages, down the narrow steps and out into the cavernous Victoria Station.

"Good luck, sir," Beth called after him from the door. "I will be at St. Martin's for the rest of my leave if you need me. I . . . love Alice. Please help her if you can."

You love her, Albert thought as he turned.

Then he tightened his grip on Alice, led her steadily forward and tried not to focus on the vacancy in her eyes or the way, on occasion, she would give a deep sigh, as though somewhere within her private imprisonment there was recurring sorrow.

"Home, old girl, we're going home now," Albert whispered. "I have tea ready. Hang onto Albert. Hang on tight. He will take care of you and never leave you."

London
December 18, 1915

Once inside the safety of her motorcar, Charlotte asked Jenkins to take her home. Quickly she closed her eyes and tried not to see Alice as she had just seen her, seated in that big green plaid chair before the window, Albert tenderly feeding her. Dearest Albert was attentive to all her needs, truly a loving brother. Still–

Quickly Charlotte shook her head. Although Albert had claimed that he could notice significant change, Charlotte now was forced to admit to herself that she had seen none. Alice was as passive and silent now as she had been three months ago, when she had first returned from the battlefields of France.

Well, there was nothing to do but keep after it, as Albert had said. He read to her and took her for walks almost every day, despite the weather. He had told Charlotte that on a recent walk, Alice had seemed to respond to a small homeless kitten. Now that kitten lived luxuriously in a warm box beneath the stove in the kitchen.

Charlotte rested her head against the back of the seat and thought of her daughter, Dhari, her beloved Dhari, safe at boarding school in Switzerland. She missed her so much, particularly now in the Christmas season. Aslam had promised her that if conditions permitted, they, too, could go to Switzerland after the holidays. Somehow Charlotte knew that conditions would not permit. Well, this dreadful war couldn't go on forever, and she only wished that she could do more to help end it sooner. Twice a week she now turned over all of the public rooms in their Belgravia mansion to the Red Cross, and ladies came and went all day, making bandages and chattering over tea.

Now she looked out of the car window. Marble Arch to her left. Almost home.

Home. Aslam. The two words echoed pleasantly about her head. Of course, he would be there waiting for her. He had wanted to come with her to visit Alice, but a business call at the last minute had altered his plans.

They were going to hang holly tonight. Just a few bowers, some greenery to make the enormous old rooms look festive and smell nice. Then they were planning to write to Dhari, one of their famous joint letters that seemed to bring their daughter closer to them.

"Trouble, madame, I'm afraid–"

At the sound of Jenkins's voice, Charlotte stopped her daydreaming and leaned up to see that they were just approaching Knightsbridge, Belgravia straight ahead and–

"What is that?" she asked leaning further forward, seeing an ominous red glare in the pale gray night sky.

Jenkins drove the car straight into Belgravia despite the glut of emergency vehicles, drove toward the end of the crescent where the glow was growing brighter, clearly a fire, a large and uncontrollable–

"Oh my God," Charlotte gasped, and through the front windshield she saw the Belgravia house in flames.

"Madame, wait–"

But she had no intention of waiting and now flung open her door and ran, ignoring the shouts of policemen and fire officials who tried in vain to draw her back.

As she approached the conflagration, she shielded her face with her hands and could only think of one thing. What if Dhari had been home? What if–

Aslam—

"Aslam!" she screamed and started to move closer to the house, but suddenly two strong arms caught her from behind and restrained her.

"No, Mrs. Eden, you mustn't get any closer. It's not safe. Come, come along. We'll wait back here where–"

"Aslam!" she screamed again, struggling against the hands that restrained her.

"It's her husband she's calling for," a voice said close by.

"Where is he?"

"I don't know."

"Did all the servants get out?"

"Not all. A few. There are some missing, according to the housekeeper."

Charlotte heard the voices as though from underwater. Still she struggled against the arms that restrained her. Still she cried out, "Aslam . . . Aslam . . ."

"Where was he?" someone asked behind her.

"The last I saw, he was in his office on the third floor."

"The bomb was thrown through the lower library window."

"Then he is–"

"Shhh–"

"Come, madame, let us–"

But she wasn't interested in any suggestion, any voice, any action except to break free and run into the burning house to either find Aslam or die with him.

"Aslam–" she screamed again and again until her throat felt raw and bleeding.

"Mrs. Eden, I beg you, you must move away. The firemen fear the walls will collapse."

She looked up at this voice of authority and saw a tall man in an inspector's coat, saw two police matrons behind him, their eyes curiously circumflex with pity, as though they knew something that she did not know.

"Come with us," one smiled. "I promise you, we will wait right over here. We will stay here until–"

But all Charlotte could do was shake her head and try not to cry, for tears solved nothing. Surely Aslam had gone out. Hadn't he said he had to go out? On business?

Yes, of course. Then he would return. Dhari would come home from Switzerland. This awful war would end, and life would be beautiful and peaceful again.

"Come, madame," one of the matrons urged and put her arm around Charlotte's trembling shoulders.

To one side she saw three fire inspectors shining a torch down on the drive that once had led to the front of the mansion.

"Look," one invited and Charlotte looked down in passing and saw three words crudely painted on the pavement: "Foreigner, go home."

Foreigner? There were no foreigners here. Aslam had been an Englishman since he was seven, had been raised by an Englishman, educated in English schools. There were no foreigners here.

"I–don't–understand," Charlotte sobbed.

"No, neither do we, madame," one of the matrons said in a patronizing voice. "Come on. We'll sit over here like good girls and wait for everything to settle down. Then we will see what we will see."

It was perhaps the most stupid statement Charlotte had ever heard another human being make. But she did as she was told, because she had no more energy for resistance. Of course, Aslam wasn't in the house. She was certain of that now, equally certain that at any moment he would come striding up the pavement in that good strong manner of his, head erect, walking precisely as the great-grandson of the last emperor of India should walk. Then he would take her in his arms and hold her close and make the world right again.

Greenfield
June 24, 1916

Eight months pregnant, Anne rocked back and forth while her mother read the terrible letter from Albert. According to the letter, the remains of Aslam Eden's body had been found in the tragic fire in Belgravia. Albert wrote further that Charlotte had left immediately for Switzerland to be with Dhari, to try to help her to understand the death of her father. He wrote further that Alice was still making slight but steady progress. She had named her cat Wee Willie, though Albert hadn't the faintest idea why. But the cat was the only thing to which Alice would respond. She cuddled it, buried her face in its soft fur and always insisted that it sleep with her to keep her safe.

"Oh, Mama," Anne grieved and looked out of the near window at the rainy June afternoon. She had planned to go home after lunch and do some last-minute sewing in preparation for the arrival of the baby. Then the rain had started, the post had come, her mother had read Albert's letter and now Anne did not want to walk home in this downpour. She most definitely did not want to be alone.

"Poor Charlotte," her mother murmured. "I really should go to her, you know."

Anne held her breath, hoping that her mother would change her mind. Selfishly Anne needed her here. Alex was gone so much of the time now, working in Exeter with the War Resisters League. And thank God he was, for at least she knew he was safe, would still be safe after all this war madness was over.

"I don't know who to feel sorrier for," Anne said quietly, "Charlotte or Alice."

"My heart goes out to Charlotte," her mother said without hesitation. "To lose someone you love–I can't imagine that pain."

Anne resumed her rocking, a motion that soothed her unborn baby as much as it soothed herself. The rain seemed to be increasing. She watched her mother dab a final time at her eyes.

"Will you go?" Anne asked almost fearfully.

"Where, my dear?"

"To Switzerland. To see Aunt Charlotte."

"No. I would like to go very much. But my place is here with my family, with you. I wouldn't miss the birth of my grandchild for anything."

Anne was grateful for her mother's words. "Thank you, Mama," she whispered.

Anne kissed her mother, then walked to the front windows and looked out at the rainstorm which seemed to be growing worse.

"I wish Alex–"

"Is he with Mason?"

"As far as I know. They were going to try to attend the city council this afternoon, see if they could get permission to speak at the Guild Hall on a regular basis."

"I'm afraid they're pushing their luck," her mother said. "From the street gossip I hear at market, the League is simply being tolerated because it is composed of respectable, though misguided, citizens. No one is paying the slightest attention to what they are trying to say."

"They don't want to hear."

"No, of course not."

Then she heard a motorcar just turning into the gates of Greenfield.

"Mama, I think they're coming."

Lucy joined her by the window. "They're back. Good. After tea I will have your father drive you and Alex home. I don't want you–"

Then something else caught her attention, the speed with which the motorcar was being driven, so unlike her husband.

With sudden dispatch Lucy ordered, "You wait here."

Anne obeyed and saw her mother hurry out of the parlor, heading toward the front door. She pushed it open just as the motorcar came to a halt before the stairs.

Because the rain obscured her vision, Anne couldn't see clearly, but through the downpour she managed to glimpse the passenger in the front seat get hurriedly out and reach back into the rear seat for someone who seemed to move with a little less haste.

She saw her father join them on the passenger side and assist with the other man, who appeared to be having difficulty walking.

Quickly they all moved toward the front hall and then they were crowded into the parlor, and–

It was Tobias Rutland, the youngest son of the local gentry, Lord Rutland. He had been a tireless worker in the League, according to Alex, and now he appeared to be bleeding profusely from a head wound.

"Sit down, please, Mr. Rutland," her mother ordered. Anne saw her father leave the room and quickly return with a stack of towels. Her mother folded one and placed it gently against Mr. Rutland's wound, which appeared to be a large cut directly above his left eye.

During these ministrations, Alex came to her side and put his arms around her.

"What happened?" she whispered.

"We were coming out of the Guild Hall," Alex began, "where the council had just turned down our request to speak, and as we stepped out of the door, ruffians set upon us, at least a dozen or so. Quite a cowardly attack. They carried large sticks, all of them, and began to beat us. I'm afraid that poor Tobias got it in the head."

"Are *you* all right?" Anne asked, worried.

"I'm fine. There will be bruises tomorrow, but that's all."

"Did you recognize any of them?" her mother asked.

"I recognized all of them," her father said. "Though what good is recognition? I had the distinct feeling that the constabulary knew precisely what was going on and they made not one move to stop it."

"I have never heard such ugly threats," Alex said, shaking his head.

"What threats?" Anne asked, beginning to feel uneasy.

"They said we must not come back and pollute their town of Exeter with our cowardice. They said they would be waiting next time with more than sticks."

For a moment the ugly threat hung heavy upon the air, silent except for the mild punctuation now and then of Mr. Rutland's groans.

"Then of course you must not go again," her mother said.

"No, Mrs. Frye, you're wrong," Mr. Rutland contributed. "If we back down now, we will simply be proving their accusation of cowardice."

"Mr. Rutland, you're badly hurt."

"No, I'm fine," he countered. "Just a passing blow. And I'm ever so grateful for your help."

He stood and patted at the bandage. He wobbled a bit on his feet and then seemed to grow steady. "Well, I'd better be starting back."

"Wait," Anne's father called out. "You can't walk home in this–"

"I'm not walking home," Mr. Rutland smiled, the side of his face already beginning to swell. "I'm staying at The Crown. My father told me several months ago that I was not welcome at home."

A look of pained sympathy crossed her father's face. "Why didn't you tell me?"

"Nothing to tell. I'm comfortable there, free to speak my mind, to act upon my convictions. Sometimes it seems that nothing angers a father more than to have a son who acts upon his own convictions."

Anne's father smiled. "I'm afraid we all know that very well Mr. Rutland. But you can't go out in this rain. You'll stay here tonight, and then we will see what tomorrow brings."

France
The Somme
July 1, 1916

The extent to which a human body could be mangled by the splinters of a bomb or shell without being deprived of consciousness had to be seen to be believed, and Chris had seen enough.

For weeks his regiment had been fighting around the chalk slopes of Bapaume, trying to angle into a viable position for the Big Push.

Now, as he watched dawn from beneath the eaves of a shell-wracked barn, he realized that it was the first time in several days that he had not been awakened by the sound of men screaming or crying for death.

He thought he heard, astoundingly, the distant chirp of a lark echoing around the clear sky, far beyond the reach of shot or shrapnel.

Lucky lark–

On occasion, as on the day before when the guns had fallen briefly silent, he was certain he had heard the song of a nightingale and persistent cawing of rooks in the tall shade trees overhead.

Now, he slowly stretched and got a whiff of his own stench. It had been days since he'd had the luxury of even a pond bath. All around him were sleeping men, a large majority of Kitchener's army, who had met in this place with one simple resolve–to put the Germans in their place once and for all.

Most of the soldiers had been at the front for many weeks. Like Chris, they had held the trenches, had in a way become hardened to the discomfort and generally immune to the shell fire. Until now, the majority of Kitchener's army had run a greater risk of dying from boredom in the trenches. The common wisdom was, "If you can't take a joke, you shouldn't have joined."

But now all this was coming to an end, or so they had been told, and quite possibly the war was coming to an end as well.

The Germans occupied the village of Thiepval and had now spread purposefully across the hills on either side. At night their troops could be heard digging trenches on the crest of Thiepval Ridge.

Chris knew, as did every soldier, that the Germans had to prove something here at the Somme. They had backed off to build a line that hugged the spurs and contours of the downline so that every slope, every natural ravine could be turned to advantage for observation, concealment and defense.

What struck Chris as strange was how much the Germans sang at night. He couldn't get over that. Of course, their musical taste tended toward the sentimental, but in the damp darkness of quiet nights the soulful strains of "Die Wacht am Rhein" could be heard drifting across from the German side of no-man's-land.

Slowly Chris stirred, sat up, rubbed the stiffness out of his back from sleeping on the ground and peered up at the dazzling blue summer sky through the jagged roof of the old French barn. In the early dusk of the previous evening, Major General Allison had gone forward to have a look for himself at the Thiepval Ridge, where his division was going to attack come morning. Chris had been invited to go with him as aide, and both of them had stood on the edge of Aveluy Wood and found that they had no need of binoculars. The ground under their feet had quivered with the vibration of German guns. Like the tall church and every other building in the village, the château had all but disappeared. All that remained were a few outlying and isolated farms like this one in which Chris and over five hundred men had taken cover for the night.

The general had shouted to Chris over the pounding of the guns. "It appears that all we will find in Thiepval when we go across in the morning will be the caretaker and his dog!"

Somehow this summing up had made it back to camp and had been passed on to the infantry and now everyone sincerely believed that what the general had said would come true.

Chris stood and looked to the right, down the road toward the intersection where soldiers from other regiments were beginning to assemble, troops on the move, each man wearing on his shoulder a flash of the identifying color of his division. This brilliant rainbow spanned more than two hundred thousand soldiers.

Now, all around him, men were stirring, and the birdsongs he had heard earlier had gone sadly quiet or were lost among the shouted obscenities and various grunts and groans of men awakening to battle.

The order of the day was Battle Order, which meant that each man would be weighted down with more than sixty pounds of equipment. At the divisional dump just beyond the farmhouse, Chris saw that they still were handing out spades, pickaxes and rolls of barbed wire.

"Move in ten," the major called out now, and Chris speeded up his packing, as did all those about him.

"Nervous?" the man named Dodd asked, the lad who had slept next to him for the past two nights. Chris didn't know his last name.

"At least we're moving," Chris replied and drew the buckle on his pack tight across his chest.

"A proper go at the Hun," Dodd smiled. "After all, it's what we come for."

At last came the call for formation, and Chris hurried out of the shelled old barn, looked up at the sky and thought how very much it resembled the blue of the sky over the North Devon headlands.

"Hurry, soldier," shouted someone behind him, "hurry up or we'll be late for the war."

Chris stopped daydreaming and took his marching place. He felt a thrill as the line moved steadily forward toward the intersection where morning light was creeping over the Somme in a fair golden haze.

By half past seven, they were in position at the edge of the battlefield. All along the straggling miles of the front the mist was beginning to burn off. The trenches were straight ahead. Chris could see them. Just as the first hundred thousand men went over the top, the sun was already shining brightly.

Chris was scheduled for the second wave and now crept up through the dust and fumes of battle to take his place.

"Head down," someone whispered next to him.

"Eyes down," came another whisper close by. "Don't look up. You won't like what you see."

"And wait for the signal–"

But Chris disobeyed, looked up and saw that Thiepval Ridge resembled a furnace. There appeared to be fires everywhere, and less than twenty feet in front of him he saw dead men lying amidst churned earth and broken artillery. One soldier was quite close. His face and body were terribly gashed, as though some terrific force had pressed him down.

Blood flowed from a dozen wounds. The smell of blood, mixed with the fumes of the shell, filled Chris with nausea.

"When will it come, the signal, damn it," cursed the man next to him. "Have they forgotten us? Do we get to go over or not?"

Chris tried not to look at the dead so close in front of him and tried to remember whether Geoffrey had ever told him about the dead, but he couldn't.

As he waited, he continued to study the fallen. The dead were so quiet. There was movement all about, the artillery being shifted forward, then drawn back, the restless impatience of the men around him. But there was no movement at all from the dead men. How odd to see men living and then suddenly empty of life.

Then came the command. Chris heard it echoing down the line and held his breath waiting for it to reach him. As he waited, he thought of his grandfather and of Geoffrey, and gave one quick prayer that he would acquit himself honorably on the field of battle.

As he started out along with the rest of the men, he approached the corpses he had watched from the safety of the trench. It seemed a sacrilege to step over them, worse to step on them. One was still alive. Chris could see his hand moving.

He hesitated, and in that moment of hesitation someone shouted angrily behind him, "Move it out, we are fully exposed!"

Chris did as he was told, like a good soldier, and forced himself to step directly onto the bodies. As he lifted a foot, he heard the shell back to his right and ducked to protect himself against flying shrapnel. Suddenly he felt a curious burning in the center of his chest, not bad at first but quickly growing worse, and even as he tried to put his foot down and move forward to cover, he fell directly on top of the corpses he had pitied only a few moments earlier. Briefly, only for a minute, he lost consciousness, and when he came to, others were lying all about him, some dead, some half-alive, trembling, white-faced in dull endurance.

Chris tried to move, but the burning in his chest was now exploding into unbearable pain. He looked down from where he lay upon the lumpy mattress of corpses and saw that his chest was a pool of blood, blood pouring out in a steady river.

He closed his eyes against the sight and heard a young boy weeping for his mother. All around him there were the sounds of weeping and cursing.

"How long?" someone begged.

Chris tried to lift himself off of the dead man beneath him, but the pain would not permit movement. He closed his eyes, lay back against the dead soldier, thanking the lad for providing him with such a comfortable pallet, and wondered if the medic would get there in time.

Then he heard them. He saw two medics bent over a lad three feet forward from where he lay.

The soldier's feet were gone, and under the bright sun his face looked ashen. The medics wiped at his mouth.

"Shall I live, sir?" he asked.

"Live? Good Lord, yes."

"Thank you, sir."

The medics turned away. The boy died. Chris watched him die.

Then they were bending over him. But he did not ask the question. He looked up into a near face and asked, "Where are the birds?"

"Birds?"

"The singing birds."

"No singing birds, lad; there's nothing to sing about here."

How sad, Chris thought and closed his eyes against the pain.

"My God," someone muttered close by. "They look like run-over dogs in a ditch."

Chris closed his eyes, tired of waiting, sorry that the battle hadn't gone as he might have wanted it to go.

Why was he here? He couldn't remember.

Where was he going?

Oh yes, he was going to find the singing birds.

Eden Castle
July 9, 1916

Susan would always remember two bizarre aspects of this tragic and dreadful day—how terribly hot it was and that the message of Chris's death had come by bicycle.

The sergeant's army vehicle had run out of petrol four miles from Eden Castle, and as he had his bicycle stashed in the boot, he had simply wheeled it out and had pedaled his way into the inner courtyard of Eden Castle.

They had just finished having lunch when she had read the message and then had painfully handed it over to Marjorie, whose expression suggested that she knew the nature of the words even before she read them. She had addressed God once, and then carefully she had handed the message back to Susan and had walked slowly to a far corner of the Great Hall and there she sat now, head bowed.

Susan had sent a steward down to Mortemouth in search of Frederick and then she had handed the message to Eleanor, who weeping, had fled up to her private apartments on the second floor. A group of servants who somehow had gleaned that it was a death message now wept indiscriminately along the far wall.

Now Susan held her position before the miniature battlefield of the Transvaal, the message in her hand exactly as Marjorie had returned it to her. She was baffled by her one predominant emotion, which was not grief but anger, hot, uncontrollable anger that she knew she would have to release soon for her own good. Oh, grief would come later, of that she was certain. But for now it didn't stand a chance before the force of the fury which was building deep inside her.

She looked back over her shoulder. Marjorie had not moved. She should go to her. She knew that. But she was waiting for the two who were primarily responsible for this tragic news, for John and Geoffrey, who had excused themselves early from luncheon, claiming that the yardmaster was expecting a shipment of virgin pine, perfect for carving. It was their intention to carve an entire new set of soldiers for Jameson's Raid, the point of which would be to "surprise old Chris."

Suddenly Susan felt sick at her stomach. Her undigested luncheon was churning. She moved away from the miniature battlefield and walked aimlessly toward the light of day at the door, the message still clutched in her hand.

Chris dead. She couldn't believe it, and yet in a way–

Then she heard them, that dreadful rhythmical clop of Geoffrey's crutches as he negotiated the narrow hall coming from the yard at the back of the castle. And with him, talking all the way, was John, who now laughed heartily at something exchanged between them.

She thought, Let him enjoy his laugh; it will be a while before he feels the impulse again.

"Here we are," she heard him exclaim, and she looked back to see the two men approaching the miniature battlefield. Geoffrey's cheeks were flushed with excitement, and John was carrying an armload of freshly cut pine pieces. He placed them carefully on the very edge of the battlefield, then looked quickly about as though sensing a hostile presence.

"Oh, it's only you, Susan," he said, a blank expression on his face.

She held her ground, feeling a peculiar conflict. Should she tell him or let him read it for himself?

"Is that old Marjorie I see over there in the corner?" he asked, squinting into the far corner, frustrated by his failing eyesight.

"Yes, it's Marjorie," he said, answering his own question. "Has she been a naughty girl? Is that why you have placed her in the corner? To punish her?"

Geoffrey laughed at this and began to examine the new wood, clearly seeing soldiers in it.

"This will work fine, John," he boasted. "Chris will be so pleased."

John still appeared to be listening to Geoffrey, while keeping his eye on Susan.

"What in the hell are you doing there?" he called out, losing patience with what he failed to understand.

Then all at once she started forward, still clutching the message in her hand, such a simply worded message, no frills, no explanations, no apologies: "Lieutenant Christopher Edward Eden killed–1 July 1916 near Thiepval in the Somme."

"Susan? What are you–"

As she approached him, she saw a flicker of dread in his face, as though he knew something momentous was about to happen to him.

"Susan–"

Despite his soft pleading, she approached him directly and handed him the message.

"Read it, John," she ordered.

Slowly he lifted it toward the light coming from the Great Hall doors, squinting in an attempt to see the words.

She saw the breaking pain within the first second, heard his violent protest of "No!" within the second, saw him turn about and thrust the message at Geoffrey, then saw him crumple forward, resting both arms on the edge of the miniature battlefield, his head hanging so low that it looked as if he had been decapitated.

For several minutes there was no sound in the Great Hall. Susan held her ground, still wondering when her own grief would descend. She hungered for it, ached for the solace of tears. But mere tears did not stand a chance against the fury that still was building within her.

Then all at once she heard a terrible sound, the choking sound of tears, saw John's shoulders heaving under the duress of his grief. At the same time, she saw Geoffrey let the message flutter to the floor.

Quite suddenly she heard John shout, "No! Oh God, no!" and saw him turn angrily away from the battlefield and stand like a madman, glaring in all directions about the Great Hall, as though there were someone here who could erase the message.

"John, come with me, it–"

But as she tried to assist him, he backed away from her, and she saw his head shaking as though he were palsied, still denying everything.

"John, please," she tried again. "It will help if–"

"Nothing will help," he shouted and started off in one direction as though he had a destination, only to stop abruptly and turn back in the direction from which he had just come. He reminded Susan of a caged animal, looking feverishly for a way out of his pain.

There was no way out, and at last he stood less than ten feet from her and lifted his face upward and cried aloud, "No, not Chris, please God, don't do this to me. Please–"

All at once he looked directly at her, his expression altered yet again.

"Where is Alex?" he demanded and wiped angrily at the moisture on his face. When she didn't answer right away, he shouted, "Where is Alex?"

Still fearful for his state of mind, Susan replied as calmly as possible, "He is not here."

"Where is he?"

"He is in Exeter, with his wife."

"Go and fetch him. I want him back. I want him safe here with me at Eden."

There was the anger again, the fury still close to the surface. "You go and fetch him. You sent him away. You go and bring him back."

Out of the corner of her eye, Susan saw Geoffrey returning to the battlefield, examining the new wood, as though the nature of the message had been forgotten and it was business as usual.

"No," she said, more to herself than to anyone else, at last finding an outlet worthy of her grief as well as her fury.

Ignoring John, she moved to the edge of the miniature battlefield and studied it carefully, this obscenity that had been placed at the core of all the activities of Eden Castle.

"You," she called out, as she saw two young stewards hurrying toward the kitchen court steps.

A few moments later they stood before her, looking baffled and alarmed.

"I want a fire," she said simply.

One drew as close as he dared. "But, madame, it is July. It is warm."

"Go down to the kitchen court and fetch me an ax," Susan instructed further. I want a fire built of—*that!*"

She pointed toward the miniature battlefield, saw protest forming on Geoffrey's face and dared him to give voice to it.

He didn't, though once he looked to John for help. But he quickly saw that John was well beyond giving help to anyone, and at last Geoffrey retreated to the far side of the Great Hall, where he sat heavily on a chair, his stump extended before him, as though he wanted all to see and take pity on him.

As for Susan, she was sick to death of him, of his stump, of his war games, of his influence on everyone in Eden Castle. Enough. It had to be stopped now.

A few minutes later the two stewards, armed with axes, made one tentative assault on the battlefield, and seeing their hesitancy, Susan lifted an ax from one and with a clear, hard blow splintered the battlefield down the middle and watched with incredible satisfaction as all the toy soldiers, toy cannons, toy wagons and toy artilleries slid in a useless cascade toward the collapsed center.

She lost count of time, in the extreme pleasure of lifting the ax and letting it fall, of seeing the carefully painted wood splinter, of watching the stewards collect it and feed it into the fire which now roared in the fireplace.

Only once did she look up, and that was to see Marjorie watching her. She started to invite her to come forward and join her, but at that moment Frederick rushed in and went directly to her. As Susan watched, Marjorie relayed the sad message. Frederick was on his knees before Marjorie, his face buried in her lap.

"Don't miss those pieces over there," Susan instructed now, seeing the new timber scattered under the force of her blows. "Don't miss a single scrap of wood. I want it all to burn every last bit, and then I want this part of the Great Hall swept and scrubbed, not a trace left, not a trace, do you understand?"

She still saw fear on the young faces of the stewards. She was sorry for that and knew that probably within the year both boys would be old enough to join the army. They would be gone from Eden, and in a matter of months, their parents would receive death messages.

All at once she looked about for the crumpled piece of paper which had been delivered to Eden Castle by bicycle. There it was, and as she walked to pick it up, she heard John still demanding to know where Alex was.

"I want to see him," he announced. "Please, someone, anyone, help me find Alex."

Susan watched the disintegration as long as she could; then, slowly, she stepped back from the heat of the blaze and saw the stewards now sweeping the floor where the battlefield had been positioned.

She saw Marjorie and Frederick, leaning heavily on each other, start slowly up the stairs. She suspected that their destination was the chapel. She hoped they didn't mind if she joined them, for that was her destination as well.

She felt an acute need for God's presence, a need to feel His strength and, most important, the need of His peace, for everywhere she looked she suffered a memory of Chris Eden; Chris being held by John during the Midsummer fete so many years ago, Chris racing with Alex and Rolf, Chris tumbling across the Great Hall in an endless wrestling match.

Gone. All over. Why?

She closed her eyes and walked like a blind woman up the Great Hall steps.

Someone must go to Exeter and tell Alex, Anne, Lucy and Mason. Not an easy job, that. Perhaps she would ask Stephen. Tomorrow morning. Perhaps Stephen could persuade Alex to return to Eden only for a while, to enable them to see him, to embrace him, to thank God for sparing him.

At the top of the stairs she heard Frederick praying aloud a few yards ahead of her.

Behind she heard John weeping.

Caught between the praying and the weeping, she wondered which, if either, would do any good.

Exeter
July 10, 1916

Still grieving for Chris, certain that Frederick needed him more, Stephen felt a certain resentment that Susan had persuaded him to make this tedious Sunday-morning journey to Exeter.

But one look at his father, sitting silently beside him in the passenger seat altered that resentment.

Now, as Stephen herded the old motorcar over the rough road leading into Exeter, he realized that he, too, was most eager to see his son. Thank God that Alex had not shared Chris's war fever. Perhaps the sparing of his son was a gift from a benevolent God, a kind of apology for taking Eve from him almost twenty years ago.

"Are you alright, Papa?" he asked now, disturbed by how quietly his father was sitting in the seat beside him.

No answer, only the bent old head fixed rigidly, his gray hair wild and mussed about his face, his eyes focused on the road ahead. He looked like a ghost.

"Papa, I am so sorry," Stephen murmured. "You must not blame yourself."

"Chris is gone," came the raspy voice.

It was a quiet and warm summer morning. The road for the last few miles had been largely deserted, all the good citizens tucked safely into their family pews in one church or another. Earlier Stephen had heard church bells coming from the large Anglican church at the center of town.

Then he saw it straight ahead, the lovely pastoral setting of Greenfield. He saw that the gate was open and drove straight through, though at a reduced speed. Perhaps everyone was still at chapel.

"Over there," his father ordered, pointing toward Mason and Lucy Frye's home, as if Stephen didn't know.

"I know, Papa."

"My God, but I dread this," his father muttered beneath his breath.

Surprised, Stephen glanced his way. "I thought this was what you wanted."

"It is, but someone must tell Alex about Chris. Who will do that?"

"I will try," Stephen volunteered and broke speed even more.

Chris was dead.

There still was such a dreadful air of unreality to it. Stephen remembered last night hearing Eleanor foolishly suggest that perhaps there had been a mistake and the officials had identified someone else's body as being that of Christopher Eden. No one had even tried to dissuade her from the hopeless theory, as though all were willing to let her cling to whatever comfort she could find.

"Look."

As his father pointed ahead, Stephen saw Mason Frye just stepping out of his front door, peering curiously at the car, as though he had recognized it but was still baffled by it.

Stephen took his time guiding the motorcar around the wide circular driveway.

How would he tell any of them that Chris was dead?

"Will you do it, Stephen?" his father whispered in a soft, fear-ridden voice.

"I said I would, Papa. I will do my best."

Lucy had spotted the car first. Then Anne had seen it through the curtained windows as well, and at last Mason had gone out to greet these unexpected visitors from Eden.

He had told Anne to stay inside. The baby was due momentarily, and it made him very nervous to see her moving about so vigorously.

"Is it you, Stephen?" he now called out cheerily and bent low to peer at the familiar face behind the driver's wheel.

But as Mason bent lower, he saw that Stephen had a passenger.

"John! John Murrey Eden. How good to see you. What a very pleasant surprise. Come, both of you."

The longer he talked, the easier it was for him to mask his shock. The very last person he expected to see on this fine July morning was John Murrey Eden.

Stephen was out of the car first and from one glance at that honest face, Mason knew that something was wrong.

If he had failed to see it in Stephen's face, he had only to glance down at that old man sitting rigidly in the passenger seat, eyes fixed front.

"John, won't you please get out and come in? Lucy would be so–"

"Where is Alex?" the old man demanded.

"Alex? Alex is not here."

"Then where is he?"

Quickly Mason looked to Stephen for an explanation. Something *was* wrong, terribly wrong.

Lucy appeared at the top of the stairs, followed by Anne.

"Stephen, what has happened?" Anne asked and came all the way down the stairs with great difficulty.

Gently Stephen took her by the elbow and without a word led her back up the stairs and into the parlor. Mason and Lucy followed, and as Mason looked back, he saw John just getting out of the motorcar.

"Tell Stephen I'll wait out here," John said in a gruff voice. "I know what he's going to say. Tell him to hurry. Do you hear me?"

Stunned, Mason searched that grim old face for one spark of recognition and could not find it. It was as if the John Murrey Eden he had known had crawled out of that skin and left this brooding, jowly old man.

When Mason arrived at the parlor door, he saw all eyes on him, as though everyone had been waiting. "What has happened, Stephen?" Mason asked and silently braced himself for the reply.

"We received word yesterday," Stephen began with great difficulty, "that Chris has been killed."

There was one brief outcry. Lucy or Anne, Mason didn't know.

"In France," Stephen went on, "the first of July near the Somme."

Chris dead—

"Dear God, be with us," Mason prayed privately. He looked quickly over his shoulder now and saw Anne weeping, Lucy close by, trying to offer comfort, though she, too, looked in need of attending.

Stephen went on. "Papa feels– He wants very much to see Alex, to ask his forgiveness, to– Oh, I don't know, to reassure himself that at least one of them is still–"

"I know," Mason nodded. And for a few moments the only sound in the small parlor was the sound of Anne crying.

"Come, Anne," Lucy was coaxing, trying to get Anne to her feet in an attempt to lead her to a place of privacy.

"Papa," Anne wept, "please go and bring Alex to me. I want Alex."

"I will, my dearest," he promised. "You go with your mother."

Stephen and Mason waited until the two women had left the room. When they had gone, Stephen asked with increased urgency, "Do you know where he is?"

"Of course. He was to pick up some new pamphlets from The Crown and Horn, from Tobias Rutland, and then he was going to the market square, a place of congregation after Sunday services. He thought that people fresh from prayer would be receptive to words against the war."

"Can you show me where this place is?"

"Of course. I'll take you there myself."

Mason led the way back out into the bright sunshine of high noon. In the distance he heard church bells pealing, signaling the end of chapel all over Exeter.

Yes, the market square. That was where they would find Alex, trying his best to persuade anyone who would listen to him that peace was better than war and that love was better than hate.

"Dirty socialists!"

Alex ignored the taunt and walked straight down Highcastle Street, heading toward the market square.

His tormentors were hovering close behind him. He could sense them.

Tobias Rutland was to have come with him today, but poor Tobias still suffered excruciating headaches from his recent blow on the head. Alex had urged him to stay in his bed and had volunteered to distribute pamphlets by himself. He could still be home in time for Lucy's good Sunday lunch.

"You're a Hun-loving socialist," came another taunt, and Alex heard footsteps scuffling not too far behind him and increased his speed, confident that the ruffians would not pursue him in the broad daylight of Sunday noon.

He was right. About half a block later, he looked back and they were gone.

Good. Then it was Alex's plan to make quick work of this and hurry home to Anne. She was so beautiful now and so pregnant. A child at any moment– Alex smiled and shook his head, still unable to believe it. Chris would be an uncle. Suddenly he laughed outright. What a marvelous uncle Chris would be.

A girl? A boy? Did anyone really care so long as both baby and Anne survived the birthing process?

As he strode down Highcastle Street, he lifted his face to the warm sun and gave a prayer of thanksgiving for all that was beautiful in this world.

As he reached the bottom of the hill, he looked ahead the distance of one short block and saw a large crowd gathered about the market square.

Was somebody else already there and holding forth? Father Butler perhaps? Oh well, Alex would take one side and the good Father could take the other. Two voices were always more effective than one.

Now he increased his step, eager to see what was holding such a large gathering so enthralled.

As he grew near to the gathering, he saw a little girl about eight years old turn away weeping and run to the far side of the street, both hands covering her face, as though she didn't want to see what was going on.

Newly alarmed, Alex considered running after her. Then he heard something amidst the laughs and shouts of the crowd, heard a sharp yelp, then another and noticed that near the front of the crowd, men were throwing something.

Alarm increasing, he made his way down the side of the crowd to the front and saw the horrible sight. Someone had tied a handsome German shepherd dog to the market cross, and now the mob was hurling jagged stones at her. With each blow, the poor animal yelped and howled. Blood was already showing.

Carefully Alex placed his stack of pamphlets to one side and, as he bent over, quickly asked God directly, simply, to walk with him to where the injured animal was tied, asked Him further to guide his steps and his actions in all matters.

"Please, don't do this," he shouted, walking straight toward the cross and saw the surprised faces near the front, saw the men with stones still grasped in their upraised hands, ready to be hurled.

"Please, listen," he implored and continued to walk toward the dog who now looked up at him with dark brown and pain-ridden eyes.

"Good girl," he soothed in an attempt to convince her that he meant her no harm. Quickly he bent over and loosened the leather cord that held her in tight suspense against the old stone cross.

"Run," he murmured, "go along home. You'll be alright." He gave her a friendly pat on the rump and was delighted to see her dart to the left behind the Guild Hall and disappear down the shadows of an alley.

Good! She would be alright.

Now, slowly, still holding the leather cord that had bound the dog, Alex turned to face the mob.

They were stirring sullenly about, a few calling obscenities to him, a few others muttering among themselves.

"Please," Alex begged, "listen to me. It would have done you no good to harm that poor animal. Is your quarrel with a dog?"

"She was a German dog," someone shouted from the crowd.

Alex smiled. "I doubt very seriously if she knew that. Furthermore, I suspect that she is the loyal companion of a good Englishman. How would you have explained your actions to him, your fellow English?

"Who in the hell are you to question what we do?" someone shouted from the back.

"I'm not questioning. I'm simply suggesting a better–"

"It's the bloody socialist, that's who it is, the Hun-loving socialist!"

There was a rustle of recognition among the crowd. "It's the white-feather man."

"He's been given enough feathers to be a goose."

"He's a Christmas goose then."

The crowd laughed as the banter grew uglier.

"And what do we do here in Exeter with a Christmas goose?"

"We eat it, of course. But first–"

As Alex was trying to form another reply, he saw movements on both sides of his peripheral vision, someone approaching him stealthily on his right and on his left. As he turned to the right, he felt strong arms drop a rope over his chest.

Before he could protest, he felt himself being dragged backward to the old market cross, felt his back come into rude and scraping contact with the old Celtic stone, felt the rope around his chest being drawn tighter and tighter and at last anchored, another rope about his ankles bound him in similar fashion.

In the very instant that he realized the helplessness of his position, he still was so grateful that he had spared the dog.

"Now, look at you, socialist," someone shouted and the crowd seemed to be drawing closer, their ranks forming a tight half-moon around the market cross. In the front row he saw the ruffians from The Crown and Horn.

"May I say something?" Alex asked with bizarre politeness.

"Speak your head off," one man said ominously, "before we knock it off for you."

"Will you tell me how I have offended you?"

"You're a bloody coward. Daily you preach against our good brave lads."

"No, I simply want you to see–"

"Oh, we see very well. It's you who has the problem. Look at you, all bound and tied like a Christmas goose in July."

Alex was on the verge of speaking again when he saw a man to the far right take one step backward, lift his arm and hurl the first stone. It was large and rough-edged, and it struck him on the forehead. He felt only a brief cutting pain and saw a trickle of blood fall onto his jacket. He made a mental note to try to remove the blood before he went home. He did not want to alarm Anne.

The second stone was hurled and fell wide of its mark. As though to compensate for the stone that had fallen short, additional stones were hurled, and these struck him about the lower part of his body, his legs, his ankles.

Then he understood. He had released the dog. Now he would have to take the dog's place.

"Please," he begged softly, growing frightened, "there is no need. Let us–"

There was another stone, this one hurled with murderous accuracy against the side of his face, then still more, one striking his neck, the other the area of his hip.

As he shook off the blood and the pain, he observed that the crowd had gone strangely silent now. No more talk. No more taunts.

As he saw several men pick up stones to hurl them, he lifted his head to the high blue sky and saw a perfectly clear image of Henderson Jones kneeling in the hot red Alabama dust.

He spoke the name, deriving strength from it. The next volley of stones came with great accuracy, and as he felt the flesh on his face tear, he closed his eyes and focused with all the powers of his concentration on what he believed to be right, on what he had learned from so many people about how men should conduct themselves for their brief time on this earth.

Still more stones, in groups of five and six now, a hailstorm of stones, and one struck Alex against the side of his head. He began to lose consciousness, began to slip against his bondage. The pain was curiously diminishing, as though someone was giving him strength to endure.

"Anne," he whispered as he began to pass out of consciousness and felt one crushing blow to the back of his skull. His head fell forward; he saw the ground at his feet moist with blood, his blood mingling with the blood of the dog.

The dog was safe. That was good. Anne was safe. That was good. Chris was safe.

How he longed to see Chris.

In his last moments of consciousness he prayed to God that all the horror would be over soon and that he and Chris would race the headlands on a high blue summer day much like this one and live out the rest of their lives in perfect peace.

"Please, God, let it be so."

Mason knew something was wrong when he saw the crowds running. People did not run in Exeter on a warm, clear summer Sunday morning.

They were yet two blocks from the market square, though they were driving past groups of people, running as though from a mortal enemy, women lifting their Sunday finery to avoid tripping, men quickly herding their children ahead of them as though fearful they would fall back and be devoured by something.

"What's happening?" Stephen asked, trying to keep a tight grip on the wheel and at the same time watching out for the rapidly darting crowds.

"I don't know," Mason said, straining forward in his seat in an attempt to see what had caused this panic.

John was sitting in the backseat, his left hand resting uselessly in his lap and shaking out of control.

"Pull over there," Mason instructed Stephen and pointed toward the pavement that bordered the market square. For the first time Mason noticed blowing pamphlets, a scattering of white papers lifting and dancing in the wind.

Had Alex already distributed them and had they been discarded? Most unlike him to be so careless and let them–

Mason saw it first from the blessing of a safe distance, the market cross yet a good sixty yards away, something attached to it, something crumpled forward, as though someone had draped an old suit of clothes over it, or perhaps–

"Wait here," he said to Stephen. As Mason got out of the motorcar, he saw his own hand trembling.

As he started walking toward the market square, now deserted except for the blowing pamphlets, he kept his eye on the market cross. Generally the sculpted lines of ancient stone were clear and well defined, and yet now they seemed to have a new dimension as though–

He was less than twenty yards now.

And he saw. Too clearly. All at once he felt a thickness in his throat that briefly choked him, an obstruction to his breathing, as though his body were trying to warn him that consciousness would be painful from now on.

Still he proceeded, denying what he saw even as he saw it, the red and bloody pulp that once had been a human face, the garments so painfully recognizable, torn repeatedly to reveal white and bleeding flesh on his shoulder, his abdomen, his legs, his arms.

For a moment Mason could not go closer. The ground around him seemed to be wavering. He tried to swallow and couldn't. He tried to draw a deep breath and couldn't. Briefly he closed his eyes and heard himself breathing as though he had just run a great distance.

"Mason?"

No! It was Stephen calling to him.

"Go back. Go back, I beg you."

But clearly there was something in Mason's tone that caused Stephen to increase his step until at last he was running straight toward the atrocity that once had been his son.

Mason stepped out of the direct line. He needed time before he could bring aid to anyone else. Alex was dead. There was no doubt. That the rest of them would survive, there was considerable doubt.

Abruptly he did a foolish thing. He took off his jacket and spread it on the ground. Why he did it or what he was going to do with it, he had no idea.

But at least it gave him something to do while Stephen was approaching the remains of his son.

Mason saw a hand go out, then saw it quickly withdrawn, heard a moan, one curse, an outcry and saw Stephen now move behind the cross and undo the ropes. He saw Alex slump to the ground.

Mason knew he would never forget the expression on Stephen's face, as he knelt to lift Alex in his arms. Mason saw John Murrey Eden hobbling toward them and thought, Dear God, no more.

But God apparently wasn't listening or didn't care, for John approached slowly, stopped and with one trembling hand indicated to Stephen that he was to place Alex back on the ground.

As Stephen did so, John fell to his knees, leaned forward and cradled Alex's head in his lap. He kissed his lips and tried to wipe the blood away with the back of his hand and wept as Mason had never heard anyone weep, without shame, without apology, without hope of solace.

Mason lost all track of time. The crucible was just beginning. There was Anne yet to be told and–

He lost control and grasped for the jacket he had just spread on the ground and knew there would be no justice, knew that this barbaric stoning had been the work of at least a dozen men and those dozen men all would be eager to protect each other, knew as well that with Alex's death, he had been stripped of all spirit of perseverance.

There was nothing to persevere for now. Let the flames of war rage on. Let this world burn itself out for the aberrant and diseased thing that it was. Perhaps the next world would be a wiser and a better one.

Eden Castle
July 11, 1916

Eleanor, Lady Eden went up to the parapet alone in the early morning to escape from Anne's cries of grief and labor. She wanted to watch the dawn and try to understand everything that had happened.

To the best of her knowledge, no one had slept at Eden Castle for over two days. They had brought Alex's body home yesterday afternoon wrapped in a white sheet, blood showing through the length of the body. John had ordered the gravediggers to work immediately, had supervised the digging of two graves, one to remain empty in honor of Chris.

Everyone had moved throughout the long day as though they too were dead, a house of the dead, in a world of the dead. As they had buried Alex, Frederick had tried twice to speak words but couldn't. John had tried but couldn't. Marjorie had tried but couldn't. Even Susan had tried but couldn't.

John had sat in the graveyard until well after dark. At last he had come back into the Great Hall and had started to pace. He had been joined by Geoffrey, neither man speaking. They had simply started an endless pacing, and thus they had passed the night. They were still down there, walking back and forth, up and down the length of the Great Hall with bowed heads and uneven gaits.

Now Eleanor lifted her head in search of fresh morning air and a new line of thought. Late last night Anne had gone into labor. Susan, along with Lucy, was now attending her, and all during this long and dreadful night it had been difficult to tell if Anne's cries were those of pain or grief.

As for Eleanor, she was almost blessedly beyond feeling anything else. Long ago she had washed her hands of this dreadful world where young men were taken from their families and sent to perform murderous acts in some remote corner of the globe, all in the name of honor.

She shuddered, despite the rising heat, and looked out across the moors. It was so beautiful, distant mauves blending with darker purples. The physical beauty of this world was the one foundation of her belief in any God, and even that wavered from time to time. A beautiful field of lavender was a poor substitute for two young men, three counting Rolf Reicher. All gone, all wasted, as though they had never existed.

Why?

"There you are–"

The unexpected voice gave her a start, and she looked up to see Susan just coming through the low parapet door. Only then did Eleanor realize that Anne's cries had ceased. Was it over? Another death to join the long line of deaths? How easily the mind moved toward death.

"Is Anne–"

"Fine," Susan smiled and lifted her face in search of a cool breeze. "You are a great-grandmother, are you ready for that? A little girl. Perfect in all ways. Anne has named her Alexandra."

For some reason the joyous news provoked more tears, stupid as they were, and Eleanor and Susan clung together for a few moments.

At last Eleanor broke free and, using the old stones of Eden Castle for support, made her way slowly down to the end of the parapet. "A baby," she murmured. "It's sad but I can't think of anything worse than to be young again."

"You don't mean that."

"I do. Oh, I *do.*" She looked puzzled at Susan. "Would you go through this world again?"

Susan hesitated before answering. "I probably would but only on the condition that I would try harder to improve upon certain conditions."

"You are insane," Eleanor muttered flatly. "No one could do more than you have done."

"That's not true. Everyone can always do more, do better," Susan replied. "But come and see your great-granddaughter. I think Lucy needs you, as does Anne. We have reached the age, Eleanor, where the mere fact of our longevity proves something."

Eleanor wasn't sure what and took a long skeptical look at this remarkably strong woman. To the best of Eleanor's knowledge, Susan had attended to everyone last night, had held Marjorie and prayed with Frederick, had walked with John and said nothing, merely kept him company on his endless pacing as he tried to work his way through his grief. She had sat with Stephen and Mason, comforted Lucy and at last had seen young Anne through her labor.

"What would we do without you?" Eleanor murmured.

"Come," Susan smiled. "Hold your great-granddaughter in your arms and set your vision on the future. It's the only direction that has ever made any sense."

"Thank God she is a girl," Eleanor sighed, "and will never have to go to war."

As Eleanor followed Susan back to the parapet door, she asked, "There will be no more wars after this one, will there, Susan?"

"No, I'm certain of it," Susan said with her quiet wisdom. "This will be the last. The very last. Men will not be so stupid again."

About the Author

Marilyn Harris is the popular and award-winning author of many novels in a wide variety of genres, including the occult, historical romance, contemporary realism, literary works, and books for young readers. Among her bestsellers are *Hatter Fox, Bledding Sorrow, The Last Great Love,* and the immensely successful Eden series. Marilyn Harris lives in Norman, Oklahoma.